AMBUSH IN ATTICA

As Jes and Wona approached Athens they encountered five armed men marching down the road toward them. Jes had rearranged her homespun cloak, tying it in the masculine way, playing the part of a man. But they would soon see Wona was a woman.

"Spartans!" Wona exclaimed.

"No. Persian mercenaries," Jes said tersely, bringing her bow down from her shoulders. "Too many to fight, too late to escape." Her heart was pounding, but she had already appraised the opposition.

"We'll have to take desperate measures," Jes continued. "I'll flee; you open your robe and scream helplessly."

"But your oath—" cried Wona.

"I'm not deserting you!" Jes snapped. "I can take out two with arrows; you can take out one with your knife. It's the other two we have to finesse. You must distract them, just long enough. Do you understand?"

Cunning showed through Wona's fear. She nodded. The knife was in her hand, hidden behind a fold of her robe . . .

HOPE OF EARTH

Geodyssey: Volume 3

PIERS ANTHONY

A TOM DOHERTY ASSOCIATES BOOK
NEW YORK

This is a work of fiction. All the characters and events portrayed in this book are either products of the author's imagination or are used fictitiously.

HOPE OF EARTH

Copyright © 1997 by Piers Anthony Jacob

A Tor Book
Published by Tom Doherty Associates, Inc.
175 Fifth Avenue
New York, NY 10010

Tor Books on the World Wide Web:
http://www.tor.com

Tor® is a registered trademark of Tom Doherty Associates, Inc.

ISBN: 0-812-57111-8
Library of Congress Card Catalog Number: 96-53954

First edition: May 1997
First mass market edition: March 1998

Printed in the United States of America

0 9 8 7 6 5 4 3 2 1

CONTENTS

INTRODUCTION

THIS IS THE THIRD VOLUME of the *Geodyssey* series, following *Isle of Woman* and *Shame of Man*, concerning evolution, history, the nature of mankind, and the possible fate of the world. Each novel stands independently, so readers need not fear to try this one if they haven't read the prior two, and they don't have to read the volumes in order. Each book tells the story of a seeming family as it follows its course in both the personal and historical senses. The first novel traced three generations, or about seventy years; the second followed one generation, or about twenty years. This third novel follows six orphaned siblings—three brothers, three sisters, of varying ages—as they grow up and love and marry in the course of about ten years of their lives. The history they experience covers five million years. Thus they are *Australopithecine*—ape-man, if you will—when they start, and modern human beings when they finish. They are usually together, and their family relationships are always the same. So for convenience in reading, they may be considered to be the same folk, though that is not possible in reality. They always speak the language of their local setting, so nothing is made of that in the novel; for this purpose we don't care much whether it is ape-primitive or contemporary English or future Spanish. Language itself is a defining characteristic of mankind, as we shall see, but in this sense, one language is about as good as another.

What is true in reality is that all human beings are related, all descending from common ancestors and capable of interbreeding. The passions, fears, desires, and joys of all are similar, though there is much variation. So the family presented here is consistent in the human sense, and the transient details of appearance, such as skin color, hardly matter. Just think of the people herein as similar to those you know. They are, really. Yes, even in their differences. Some are healthy and handsome, but most are imperfect. So in this novel each major character has a difference or a problem. Sam is convinced he must marry an ugly woman, and he does, though not the way he expects. Flo gets really fat, and thus is considered quite attractive in one culture, and ugly in another. Ned is brilliant, but gets seduced by a wrong woman and suffers. Jes is lanky and plain, so prefers to play at being a man, yet underneath wishes she could be a woman. Bry feels inadequate, yet is not. And Lin is lovely—and has a six-fingered hand. No, this is based on reality; some children are born with extra fingers or toes, which are often surgically removed early in their lives. One famous woman with this affliction was Anne Boleyn, second wife of England's Henry VIII, mother of Elizabeth I. It seems to be a shame to cut off a working finger, so Lin kept hers, but always had to hide it, because people can be truly cruel to anyone who is different. So these people have curses that are echoed by many of us, which are really more shameful in our self-images than in reality.

This is a "message" series, and the message is that the qualities that enabled our species first to survive in a difficult and dangerous world, and then to prosper, are now in danger of destroying that world. There is for example no automatic check on population growth. Originally the panthers and other predators did it, feeding on human babies as well as on other creatures. There were also limits of food, so that when a species outgrew its resources it starved. There was disease, at times devastating. Mankind has been as successful as any species in overcoming such limitations, and now dominates the planet, driving other species toward extinction. If this is not curtailed sensibly, it will lead to a truly ugly finish, because the world is not limitless.

However, those who prefer straight entertainment can skip the italicized chapter introductions and endnotes and just read the ongoing story. The permutations of history are endlessly fascinating, and challenge and love are always in style.

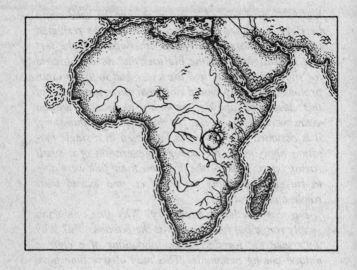

Chapter 1

COMMUTER

Five million years ago, in the western arm of the Great Rift Valley in Africa, the chimp that walked like a man was perfecting his stride. Australopithecus afarensis *was forced to forage on the dangerous open ground because the forest had diminished and there was too much competition for the resources of the trees. To do this, he had to lift his upper body up and balance on his hind legs. The supposedly simple act of walking habitually on two feet—bipedalism—entailed a complicated series of bodily adjustments. The spine had to reverse part of its curve so that the head could be right above the feet, the pelvis had to be reshaped to support a torso that would otherwise sag, the feet had to straighten out the big toes and develop arches for shock absorption, and the knees had to lock so that prolonged walking would not wear them out. None of this developed quickly; probably at least a million years were required. But for the purpose of this story, it is assumed that the knees happened in a single mutation applying to the younger generation of a small roving band. Thus for the first time these folk were able to travel comfortably on two feet, and extend their range considerably.*

But was bipedalism necessary? Why didn't mankind simply range out four-footed, as the baboons did? Why undertake the formidable complications of a change unique among mammals? This may at one time have been a close call. But Australopithecus, *having descended from the trees with his head set vertically, had the ability to go either way, and there was one compelling reason that two feet were better than four. It would have been better for the baboons, too, had they been able to do it.*

At this stage speech would have been extremely limited, with an assortment of sounds perhaps emulating the animals they represented, and a few key connecting words. But the expressions of chimpanzees in the wild are more varied and useful than some may credit, and the brain of Australopithecus *was slightly larger than that of the chimp. So probably his vocabulary was larger and more effective than the chimp's, though not by much.*

SAM RANGED OUT ACROSS THE eerie barrens. He was the eldest juvenile male of the band; soon he would be adult. But the adult members would not take him seriously until he proved himself. So he had to survive alone for long enough to prove his capability, and locate a good source of food; then he would be allowed to help protect the band and to mate with all its grown females except his mother. Mothers were funny about that; they would accept attention from any male of any age except the one they knew best. So now he braved the unfamiliar region, hoping there was something there. Part of the challenge was nerve; it took courage to go out alone, and courage was one of the differences between adults and juveniles, among the males, at least. He was nervous, but refused to turn back until he found something.

The sun was hot, very hot. Normally the band folk found shelter in the middle of the day, grooming each other's pelts, copulating, or merely snoozing. But Sam didn't dare relax while alone, because there was no one to watch out for him. A leopard could attack. Of course a predator could attack anyway, especially since Sam was alone, but was less likely to bother an alert person. So he forged on despite the discomfort. The heat made him tired, and he staggered, but wouldn't quit. He had to prove he was adult. Had to keep going, no matter what.

He followed the known path to its end, then cast about for some animal trail. Sam was not the band's smartest member, but he had a good eye for paths, and that had always helped him get around. People paths were easy to follow, and not just because they were close and familiar; the smell of people feet was on them. Animal paths varied; they could be discontinuous, or pass under brambles, or enter dangerous caves. But they were better than nothing, because any path led somewhere, and it was more useful to go somewhere than nowhere. Sometimes they led to water that wasn't otherwise easy to find. So he continued along the animal paths, going wherever the animals went. Until at last the ground became too dry and hard to show any path clearly, leaving him uncertain. The only path was now the trail of scuff marks his feet left in the dirt behind him. But of course that path led in the wrong direction.

The sun beat down on his fur, making it burningly hot.

It was midday, and the heat blurred his vision. He thought he saw pools ahead, but knew from experience that it wasn't so. There was no water out here on a dry day like this. The thought made him thirsty, but still he refused to turn back in defeat. He was determined to find something, anything, and be an adult. So he plowed on through the blur, trying to ignore the heat and his thirst.

He felt tired, then oddly light. His feet moved slowly, but hardly seemed to touch the ground. It was as if they were detached from him, moving of their own accord, carrying him along like some separate burden. His head seemed to want to float from his shoulders. How long had he been walking? He didn't know, but it felt like days. Everything was somehow different. But he just kept going.

Something strange happened. The sun seemed to expand, becoming enormous. It bathed him in its fierce light, making him dizzy. A dreadful foreboding came, and then a horrible fear. Something terrible was happening:

The fiery fringe of the sun passed beyond him, enclosing him within its territory. Great vague shapes loomed within it, threatening him, glaring with eyes of flame and licking with tongues of smoke. *Doom! Doom!* they cried, saying the sound of warning, of terror, of grief. Sam wanted to turn about, to flee, but would not, though he knew it meant destruction. Anyway, he had no path to follow, so would only get lost if he fled.

Then he was falling, falling, for a long time, the barren plain tilting around him. He felt the shock of landing, but it was far away. He was down, and had to get up, but somehow he could not. Something awful was going to happen if he didn't flee, but his body would not move.

Why hadn't he fled back along his own path, while still on his feet? Because he had been unable to admit defeat. Now he had suffered that defeat anyway.

A long time passed. Then he discovered that the sun was down, and the cool of evening was coming. He had to return home—and he had failed to find anything.

Sam got up. He was logy, and his head hurt, but he seemed merely bruised, not injured. He brushed off his fur and started back, dejected, following his own spoor until he could pick up a suitable animal trail. He had failed to find food. He was not yet an adult.

He moved slowly back the way he had come, quiet because he lacked the vigor to be noisy. The land darkened around him. Then he heard something, and paused, looking.

Two warthogs were stirring in the bush. One grunted and snuffled at the other, its projecting teeth-tusks gleaming in the twilight. Sam looked warily around for a rock or stick he could use to try to beat the boar off, as there was no nearby tree to climb. But the hog ignored him. It scrambled up, putting its forelegs on the back of the other, who was squealing in seeming protest, and pulled in close. Oh——they were mating. No threat there, as long as he didn't try to interfere.

Mating. Which was what Sam wouldn't get to do, having been unsuccessful on his mission. Dispirited, he walked on. He found increasingly clear paths, which he could follow even in the darkness. So he would make it safely back, for what little that was worth.

When he reached the camp, his sister Flo was the first to spy him. She was almost as old as he, and would soon have to leave the band and find another band, so she could mate and have a baby of her own. It would be sad to see her go, for she was his closest companion and friend, but it was the way it was.

Flo ran to him, and hugged him. Her fur was sleek and fine. "Find?" she asked, making the general purpose query sound.

"Doom," he said, repeating the horror of the sun, and shivering, though it was not yet cool.

Now the other young folk clustered around, eager to know how he had done. They did not understand doom, because he had returned safely. "Find! Find!" they chorused.

So he tried to tell them what else he had seen, making the grunt and squeal of the mating warthogs. They laughed. "Sam grunt ugh!" The implication was that Sam wanted to mate with an ugly warthog.

But Flo did not laugh. Her face showed concern. She knew that he had sought experience and status. She knew he had failed. She hugged him again, trying to cheer him, but it was no good. Maybe the children were right. Maybe it was a curse on him, to suffer disaster and humiliation.

Flo tried once more. She brought him a fruit to eat. This was unusual, because normally sharing occurred only when a female mated with a male and took food from him, or when a female gave her young child food. The two of them would never mate, because they were band siblings, though neither was really a child. Oh, they *could* mate, as some other siblings did, but were not inclined; they were too close. He accepted the fruit, because he was hungry after his day without eating. Then he went to his favored tree and climbed into it to sleep. Maybe in the morning his shame of failure would hurt less fiercely, in the manner a cut toe eased as it healed.

Two days later the group of elder children was foraging in a deep valley when a storm threatened. They tended to forage together, because all of them were in that awkward stage between weaning and maturity, too old to be cared for by the adults, and too young to be adults themselves. Sam hated still being a child, but until he went out alone again and found significant good food for the band, he would not be accepted as adult. He couldn't do that yet, because of the overwhelming feeling of doom his first attempt had left him with. He seemed to be cursed, but he couldn't understand how or why.

They started to return to the safety of their camp, but the storm rushed in too swiftly. The clouds swelled and hurled down their rain in a sudden deluge. The drops were cold despite the heat of the air. They blasted the children and the rocks, thickening into a torrent. The water sluiced through the narrow cleft leading from the safe upper valley to the richer lower valley, making it into a turbulent river. The group had to retreat from it, bowing their heads before the onslaught; they could not pass that water.

Sam, staring at it, felt again the horror of his vision. "Doom," he said. The sky itself was chasing him, trying to hurt him. Now he was with the others, and it was attacking them all.

Flo heard him, despite the angry roar of the wind. She understood his sentiment. "Flee," she said, saying the word for running away from danger.

Sam hesitated, because that meant leaving the known path. It was always dangerous to leave the path when distant from the most familiar grounds, for only the path knew the way home. Yet that path was clearly impassable; no hope there. So, reluctantly, he nodded.

Soon the group was walking away from the cleft, deeper into the valley, though this was not a comfortable direction. There were animal paths that all of them could trace, but they led in the wrong direction. The great wide plain beyond was dangerous, especially at night, and they all feared it. Sam himself had been lucky to return from his venture onto it; there had been others who never came back. But it was not yet night, though the storm made it seem as dark; they would be able to return once it passed and the water drained.

There was a loud cracking noise and a great flash of light behind them. They all paused and turned to look. The storm was smiting the cleft!

Dirty water surged around their feet, as if it, too, was trying to escape. Then it thinned, spreading out. The storm passed, leaving bands of vapor rising into the sky.

They reversed course, walking back up the valley. But as they approached the cleft, they paused, staring with confusion and consternation. The cleft was gone! It had become a tumble of stone below a steep cliff. There was no way they could climb up that sheer ridge.

"Doom," Sam muttered. His vision had been true.

Flo was more practical. "Around," she said, speaking a more difficult concept. When there was something in the way, people went around it. They would go around the mountain, and get home another way. Sam agreed, because he had no alternative to offer.

They started out, walking swiftly, the two of them in the lead, the lesser children following. First they had to get all the way out of the valley, because its rocky ledges were impassable throughout. That turned out to be a longer distance than it looked, because as the valley widened and the sides curved away, more came into view. Fortunately there were good animal paths here, making rapid walking feasible.

Three of the children were trailing. Sam saw that they were the bent-knee ones. Most of them walked with straight knees, but some didn't. They never had. It didn't make much difference around the home camp, where there were always things to hold on to and places to rest, but now it did. The three were tiring, and couldn't keep up.

Flo saw him looking, and glanced back herself. Then she looked forward. He knew what she was thinking: they had a long way to go, to get around the mountain, and if they didn't go fast enough, they could be caught out here by night. Then the leopards would come, and the big snakes, and other things they feared without knowing.

So they didn't dare go slow. The bent-knees would simply have to follow at whatever pace they could, tracking the spoor of the others. Maybe they wouldn't be too far behind when the way home was found. When night came.

When Sam next looked back, he didn't see the three laggards. That made him feel uneasy, but he didn't know what else to do but keep moving on. He could tell that Flo was similarly disturbed.

At last the valley opened out into the frighteningly broad plain of the unknown. No one foraged alone this far out, because it was too far from their safe retreat. Now they had to.

It was hot out here, with no shade. The sun was near the

top of the sky, with no clouds. Sam was wet with sweat, and he saw it matting the fur of the others. His sense of doom returned; the sun was dangerous. But so was the night, in the open.

There were bushes here, rich with ripe berries, and Sam recognized several good tuber plants. Excellent foraging! But could they pause to eat? He looked at Flo, and she looked at the sky, then shrugged. She glanced back again: maybe if they remained here a while, the three lost children would catch up.

They ate the berries, which were rich and juicy. Not only did this feed them, it allowed them to rest, and to cool. Had they known how good the foraging was out here, they might have braved it before.

Flo kept looking back the way they had come. She was hoping the bent-knee children would catch up. But there was no sign of them. They had probably returned to the head of the valley. Maybe they would find a way past the new rubble and cliff. It was better to think that, than to think of what else might happen to them.

Soon, somewhat restored, they resumed walking, this time not quite as fast, because of the awful heat. The animal paths were good, and this helped. The mountain curved on around, allowing them to head toward another great valley. There were trees at its end, and it looked passable. In fact, they discovered a people path leading there. Encouraged, they walked along it. Only to encounter hostile folk.

As they approached the trees, several bent-legged people came out led by a scowling man and a rather interesting woman. At first Sam thought the others were coming out to welcome them, but when they got close the man made gestures of striking with his fist and biting. Perplexed, Sam halted, and so did the others with him. What was the matter?

"Who?" he called, saying the recognition word.

"Bub," the man said, frowning. He gestured to the woman. "Sis." She smiled, but not nicely. Had she been a new member of the home band, it would have been nice to

breed with her, but she evidently had no interest in doing it
with strangers. Despite his fatigue, Sam regretted that.

"Sam," Sam said. He indicated Flo. "Flo." He indicated
the four smaller children. "Us." It was a formidable introduction, but he managed it.

Bub pointed toward the plain. "Go!"

Sam tried to explain. "Far," he said, indicating the valley
beyond them. That meant that they intended to go beyond
the territory of this band, to reach their own band.

"Go!" Bub repeated. He bent down to pick up a rock.

Sam recognized the challenge. He would have fought, had
he been grown. Had he not been hot and tired. Had there
not been too many adults before him, and only children
behind him. But as it was, he had to retreat.

He turned, and the children turned with him, weary but
knowing they had no choice. Outsiders could not enter the
territory of a hostile band without getting beaten or killed.
So they started to walk away.

All except Flo. "Bad," she said, for a moment standing
up to Bub, letting him know her sentiment.

Then something unexpected happened. Bub looked
closely at Flo, sniffing, then grabbed her. She screeched in
protest, thinking he was attacking her. He was, but not in
the way she supposed. He wrapped his arms around her
body, hauled her up, and threw her down on the ground.
This was easy for him to do, because he was twice her size,
being a grown male.

Sam leaped to Flo's defense, but another bent-knee male
caught him and held him, pinning his arms to his sides. The
male might not be able to stride as well as Sam on the plain,
but he had more strength in his body than Sam did, and Sam
was helpless. The children didn't dare even voice a protest.
They could only watch what Bub was doing with Flo.

Bub dropped to the ground, holding Flo there. He hauled
his body on top of hers. She screeched again and struck at
him, but her small arms hardly affected his strong body. She
lifted her head, snapping at him. Then he closed one fist and

struck her in the face, stunning her. She stopped screeching and lay still, her arms and legs relaxing. He hauled his pelvis in close to hers and jammed in between her spread legs.

Suddenly Sam recognized what Bub was doing. He was mating with her. Not in the manner of a male of the home band, sharing joy with a grown female of the band, but as an act of aggression against a foreign female. He had smelled her dawning maturity and done it.

It was quickly over. Bub got up, leaving Flo lying on the ground, her limbs twitching. She turned her head from side to side, and groaned. She didn't know exactly what had happened.

The one holding Sam let go. The others were holding stones they were ready to throw. Sam went to Flo and put out one hand. "Go," he said, afraid that worse was coming.

She groaned, recovering her senses. There was blood on her nose, dribbling down the side of her face. Her eyes were wild. "Hurt," she said.

"Go," he repeated urgently. They had to get away from here, before the members of the hostile band fell on them and killed them all. Sometimes it happened, when band members got too far separated from their home band.

Flo evidently realized the danger. She took his hand, and he hauled her up. She took an unsteady step, and he grabbed her shoulder, stabilizing her. They walked away from the hostile band, and the children scurried along with them, frightened.

A stone landed near them. Sam broke into a run, hauling Flo along, and the children ran too. Soon they were out of range, because the bent-knees did not pursue them.

They slowed, finding a good path, resuming their striding, which was the best way to travel any distance. Sam looked back, but the hostile band members were gone. They had simply driven off intruders, as bands tended to do. Had Flo been older, they might have taken her captive, so that all the men could mate with her, beating her until she stopped objecting. Females often didn't seem as interested in mating

as males were, so had to be encouraged. Sam had seen it
happen, when his band had intercepted a grown female of
a neighboring band who had strayed too far from her own
folk. After every male was satisfied, they had let her go,
and thought no more of it. It was her own fault for straying;
no one had had any sympathy for her. If a strayed female
remained after the first round of mating, and the males liked
her, she would be allowed to join the band as a member.
Then she wouldn't be beaten unless she refused to mate with
a male who wanted to. That was how it was.

But this time it was different. Flo was young, and she
was his friend. She had not really strayed or left her band;
she had been cut off from it by Sam's bad fortune. She
definitely had not sought to mate yet. He wished this hadn't
happened to her. He wished he could kill Bub. But all he
could do was flee.

"Doom," Flo said, trying to wipe the blood from her
face. Her nose was swollen and she looked awful.

"Doom," he echoed, realizing that she thought this was
part of the curse he had seen. Maybe it was. So it was his
fault. Everything bad was happening since that vision in the
sun.

They went on, their pace slowing, because the path was
fading, the children were tired, and so was Flo, weakened
by the attack on her. The sun was no longer beating down
as hotly; it was hidden by a cloud. That helped, but not a
lot.

They rounded another swell of the mountain, and entered
another valley. But soon the band of this valley spied them,
and charged out, screaming threats. They quickly reversed
and walked back into the plain. The bent-knees pursued
them.

This was trouble. Was every valley going to be like this?
If so, they would never get home! They were already very
hot and tired.

Worse, the sun came out again, heating their fur. Sam

remembered what had happened when he kept walking into the sun. The sun would eat them all.

But one thing about the bent-knees was that they had even more trouble in the sun. Sam didn't know why, but it was the case. So he did something desperate. He found a new path and led the way not around to the next valley, where there might be more enemies, but directly into the breadth of the hot plain.

Flo and the children did not question him. They just plodded on, trusting him to lead them somewhere.

When the hostile band saw where the group was going, it turned back. The heat and fatigue were just too much.

Sam looked ahead—and saw something new. There was an outcropping of rock across the plain. Maybe that would do for a camp. So he chose another path and headed for it, striding more slowly now that there was no pursuit. The slower speed was better for all of them; they walked straight-legged and had no trouble despite their youth and tiredness. This was good, because the rocks were far away.

But when they finally approached the rocks, something came out from them. There were several hunched shapes, moving swiftly. Sam couldn't tell what they were. Should he turn back? If they were people, they might throw rocks or mate with Flo again. If they were animals, they might try to eat the whole group.

He paused, considering. The day was now late; they would not be able to return to the mountain before nightfall, even if they had the strength. So it was better to go on to the rocks and see what was there, hoping it wasn't too bad.

He moved on, and the others were with him, crowding closer because they heard the shapes ahead. They were afraid, and so was he.

Then there was a gust of wind, bringing a scent: baboon. This was a baboon lair.

Ordinarily people did not tangle with baboons. The beasts were strong and fast, and could be vicious. But they weren't as smart as people. Sometimes they could be bluffed.

He had seen bandsmen drive off baboons by throwing stones and making a lot of noise. It could work here, if there weren't too many baboons.

"Rocks," he said, casting about until he found a good one to pick up.

The children were uncertain, but did as he said. When all of them had stones in each hand, he led the charge. He lifted his arms and screamed. "Yah-yah-yah-yah!" He ran right toward the rocks.

Baboons were dangerous! Flo hesitated, and so did the children, but they were afraid to be left behind. So in a moment they joined in, screaming in a chorus and waving their arms.

The baboons looked at the charging group, and ran the opposite way. There turned out to be only four of them. This must be a mere fragment of their band, temporarily isolated from it; otherwise this charge would never have worked. When one showed signs of turning back, Sam hurled one of his stones at it. The stone missed, but did spook the creature, and it hurried on after the others. Soon they were gone.

Sam's knees felt weak. It had worked! They had bluffed out the animals. Maybe the baboons had thought that any creatures who screamed and charged like that had to have many more of their own kind behind them. Maybe baboons couldn't count. Regardless, it was a great relief.

The outcropping turned out not to be large, but it did offer a raised section shielded by surrounding boulders. It would be hard for the predators of the night to attack. Sam carried the heaviest stones he could manage, to shore up the retreat, and made a den under the overhang of the largest rock section. It wasn't as good as home, but it would do.

Night was coming. They found good berries all around the outcropping, because no people had foraged there recently, so they were able to eat well before darkness closed. There was a stream not too far distant, so they were able to slake their thirst. Then they entered the den and huddled together for sleep. The children did not seem to be too concerned; they trusted Sam to protect them. They were very tired, and sank rapidly into slumber.

Flo tried to sleep too, beside him, but she was groaning softly. Her bashed nose was probably hurting. Sam reached out to stroke her hair, and she settled down. Grooming always made a person feel better. But who was there to comfort Sam?

The key is heat. The African savanna was hot, and creatures that moved around too much in the heat of the day risked heatstroke. Antelopes have special networks of veins and heat exchangers associated with the nose to cool the blood for the brain; baboons, like cats and dogs, pant, and have enlarged muzzles that facilitate this. But mankind's ancestors had neither device; their noses were too recessed and puny to make panting worthwhile. They had to find another way. That way was bipedalism. Creatures who became vertical presented less than half as much surface area to the blazing sun as those who remained horizontal, and that made a significant difference in heat absorption. So it paid to become bipedal, if they went out into the burning plain at noon. Not just occasionally being on two feet, but constantly, while moving as well as while standing still. Because the beat of the deadly sun was steady. Since this was where chimpanzees were not foraging, because of that heat, it was richer harvesting for bipedal Australopithecus. *Food was the great incentive; a species that might otherwise have been squeezed to oblivion was able to survive, here on the fringe of the Garden of Eden.*

But it was dangerous on the plain, especially at night. So it was necessary to have a safe retreat for sleeping, and forage only by day, in the heat of the sun that restricted quadrupedal predators more than bipeds. It is unknown where Australopithecus *slept, but* it surely was not on the dangerous plain or by a treacherous river. Probably it was in caves or on ledges that were difficult for predators to reach. This was a problem, because the best foraging seems to have been on the open plain, far from the mountains where there were safe places to sleep. How could early hominids have both safety and food?

The answer seems to be that they became commuters. Each morning they left their rocky dens and strode across the terrain to suitable places to eat. Each evening they returned to the dens. Since the two regions might be many miles apart, efficient traveling was essential. Hence the importance of paths—and knees. Bending knees were like constant running, fatiguing to the legs and wastefully expending energy at slow speeds. Lockable knees enabled mankind to stride longer while generating less muscle heat. That made commuting in the heat of the day feasible. It wasn't necessary to seek the shade of isolated trees during the worst heat. Mankind, like mad dogs, could walk in the noonday sun. Thus mankind colonized what other apes could not: the open noon savanna. That greatly extended his foraging range, and was a key survival advantage. It wasn't that he preferred the heat, it was that he could handle it slightly better than rival creatures could, so it paid him to do so.

But becoming bipedal was only the beginning. This turned out to be an extremely significant change, setting Australopithecus on the course that was to lead to modern man, in ways the following chapters will explore. The one most relevant to heat adaptation is the loss of body fur. Though standing vertical cut down the heat from the noon sun, it was at first a marginal advantage; other creatures did have brain-cooling systems. But it enabled mankind to shed that fur, because the bulk of the body was no longer exposed to the sun's rays during the worst of the day. The relatively bare *skin (hair remains on it, just much shorter and thinner) was a more efficient surface for sweat to affect, and mankind developed the most effective cooling system among mammals. Why was this necessary, when bipedalism and lockable knees had already enabled him to survive nicely? Because mankind was later to develop an organ that generated extra heat, and demanded extra cooling, lest it suffer: the giant brain. It probably couldn't have happened on four feet.*

Chapter 2

SCAVENGER

About two and a half million years ago, Australopithecus *gave way to* Homo habilis, *the ''handy'' man,
who was larger in body and brain, fully bipedal, and
probably lightly furred. His occasional use of stones
and sticks to defend himself against other animals was
becoming more regular; he had the foresight to make
collections of rocks where he might need them. In fact,
he probably used a variety of wooden tools or weapons, which are unknown to archaeologists because they
left no permanent residue; stones may have been in-*

*cidental to his life-style. He still foraged, but the sea-
sonal variation of the availability of fruits and tubers
and grubs made for some lean times. His larger brain
was also more demanding for protein. So* Habilis *had
a problem: he needed a reliable source of richer food.
The obvious source was meat, but that presented formidable problems.* Habilis *lacked the ability to catch
and kill large animals, so had to go after the kills of
others. That meant coming into conflict with leopards,
hyenas, or lions: no pleasant business. The chances
were that by the time he located and reached a fresh
kill, virtually all the good meat was gone. There would
be little remaining but gristle and bones.*

Habilis found an answer. It probably took hundreds
of thousands of years, but for convenience of illustra-
tion we shall assume that there was a single early
breakthrough accomplished by a very smart individual.
The setting is the east Rift Valley of Africa.*

JES WALKED BESIDE NED, FOLLOWING their two elder band
siblings. Sam was in the lead, as always, and Flo following.

Flo had a baby in her belly. At first it hadn't seemed so,
but now she was fat in the middle, and she tired easily. She
was always hungry, too, because by the time she reached a
berry patch, the others had already picked it over. Sometimes Sam took her with him to a good patch, and growled
off the others so that she could eat, but usually he didn't
think of it. He was too worried about how they would survive since being cursed with isolation, and about the vision
he had had of warthogs copulating, suggesting that he was
destined to mate with an ugly woman. Jes knew about all
this, having seen it happening and overheard it being told.
The elders thought she didn't understand, but she had seen
the ways of things in the tribe, and knew what was what.
She had heard Sam's awful vision, and she had seen Flo get
raped by the hostile foreign band chief.

When they had first been separated from their band, and

had to forage alone, Flo had tried to help the younger ones. Now the two youngest children were trying to help her. Ned was still not a man, small for his age and not aggressive, but he was smart and quick with his hands. Jes was big for a girl, and homely, and knew it; she would not be popular when she became a woman. The two of them tended to stay together, neither snubbing the other; they might have mated when grown, if they hadn't been band siblings. Jes knew that no other band would treat her as well as this group of band siblings did. As well as Flo had. They had known each other all their lives, and looked out for each other. So when Flo's form and strength diminished, Jes saw her as closer to herself in nature, and associated more frequently with her. Flo was a woman, and Jes was a large child, but Flo was not in a position to protest.

On this day they traveled far in the heat, following the best animal paths and marking their trail so there would be no hesitancy on their return, only to discover that the good berry patch had been savaged and was useless. Saber-toothed cats had made a kill here, dragging down a beast, and in the process flattening the berries. They had come here for nothing. What the cats hadn't eaten, the scavenging hyenas had; a hyena skulked away as the band approached. Obviously it was a laggard, and largely sated, or it would have stood and fought them. Not even the berry squishings remained; the ants were finishing them off.

But the siblings made what they could of it. The good meat was gone, but there were still some bits of flesh sticking to the joints and tendons. Ned had a small stone with a sharp edge he carried with him; now he used that edge to cut away some of the meat left by the animals' teeth. The two smallest children simply put their faces down and chewed directly on the bones, gleaning what little they could.

Ned handed Flo a small string of meat he had severed. She thanked him with a smile and took it. Jes knew it was tough, but Flo had good teeth, and it was clearly much better than nothing. Flo had helped the rest of them so much when she could, that it was natural for them to help her when they could.

Ned picked up a bone and looked at it. Jes followed his gaze. This bone had been crushed, probably by the powerful jaws of the hyena, so that it had split open. Jes smiled; that animal must have been really hungry, to chew on a bare bone. What sustenance was there in bone?

But Ned wasn't satisfied. He poked a finger into the split bone. It was damp inside, and reddish. He sniffed it. Jes watched, having nothing better to do at the moment.

"Hyena," Ned said. "Food."

Maybe a bare bone was food for the hyena, but it wasn't for people. Their teeth were not nearly as strong as those of the hyena, or any other predator. They would merely get aching teeth if they tried to eat that bone.

But Ned still wasn't satisfied. "Why chew?" he asked.

"Meat in?" Jes asked.

Flo laughed. Of course the meat was on the outside, not the inside. But Ned didn't laugh. "Inside," he repeated, shaking the bone. A bit of reddish stuff fell out.

Jes snatched it up and put it in her mouth. She chewed, smiling. There *was* something edible in the bone. The taste was strange, but it seemed to be like meat.

Now Ned got serious. He looked around until he found a large rock with a flat surface. He found a smaller rock, the kind good for throwing, and hefted it in one hand. He put the bone on the large rock, then smashed the small rock down on it. What was he trying to do?

The bone bounced off the rock. Ned put it back, and bashed it again. Of course it bounced off again, so this time Jes grabbed it by the end and held it in place for him. She didn't know what he had in mind, but he was their smartest member, so she might as well help him do it. Ned smiled, thanking her, and bashed it once more. Jes felt the shock, but it didn't hurt, and the bone stayed in place. So Ned bashed again. And again. Finally he managed to crush it so that the split in the end widened. He wedged with a narrower stone, until the bone opened into two parts.

They peered in. There was more of the reddish stuff. Ned pulled at it with his fingers, and it came out in a soft muddy mass. He put it to his mouth. He chewed. Then he smiled, and offered it to Flo. She was doubtful, so he offered it to Jes.

Jes already knew it was edible, though odd. She took it and bit into the softness. She took another bite, liking it better. It was definitely food. Then, catching Ned's warning glance, she paused. He didn't want her to eat it all.

Jes handed the rest of it to Flo, because she was plainly hungry too, and needed food more than any of the rest of them. The woman tasted it, bolder now that she had seen Jes eat it with evident pleasure. Then she ate it slowly, becoming reassured. They had indeed found food in the oddest place, inside the bone. Jes had never imagined anything like that. Only someone as smart as Ned would ever have thought of it.

Flo got up and went to Sam, who had been chewing on a joint, not paying attention. Sam was their strongest member, and a good guy, but not the smartest person. "Food in," she said, pointing to another bone. But he looked blank.

Ned got a larger bone and put it on the rock. He smashed at it with the smaller rock, but it was too tough to crack. So Jes got help. "Sam," she said. "Do."

It took a while to make Sam understand, and Jes and Ned had to demonstrate several times with smaller bones, but finally Sam took the rock from Ned and smashed it down hard on the bone. The bone cracked open, and the reddish stuff showed inside. Ned pried it out and gave it to Sam. Sam tasted it, and his face lighted. "Food!"

After that they cracked open all the bones they could, and all of them ate the stuff inside. It was their first really good meal in several days.

❂

The next several days they traveled and foraged as usual, following their familiar paths, but now they had a new awareness: there was good food to be had at predator kill sites. They had ignored or avoided such sites before, but now they looked for them. The best early indication was the vultures; if they were circling, there was a carcass below. They were easy to see in the sky. So when the gross birds signaled a find, within striding range, the six of them set out in that direction. This time, knowing that they could encounter predators, they carried staffs. These were long poles fashioned from sapling trees, handy for support when walking became tiresome, and more useful when baboons attacked. Stones were good, but there might not be enough good ones in the vicinity. They had caches of stones in convenient places, but they could not anticipate exactly where the kills would occur, and stones were too heavy to carry along with them all the time. A carried staff, however, was an effective weapon.

It turned out to be a wise move, because the kill was recent and a small pride of big tusked cats was still there. Sated cats seldom attacked, but the people didn't care to risk it. So they settled down to wait for the cats to finish and depart, keeping their staffs ready in case a cat decided to rout them. This was a region with tubers, so they found smaller sticks to use to dig the tubers out of the ground. Ned used his sharp-edged stone to make points on the ends of their digging sticks, so that they worked better. Then, thoughtfully, he started carving a point on the end of his staff. Jes, seeing that, had him sharpen hers too.

Several hyenas appeared, and settled down to wait similarly, on the opposite side of the carcass. They knew better than to try to drive the cats off, because it seemed that hyenas did know the difference between one and several, but they would fight any lesser creatures for the rights of first scavenging.

Fortunately the cats soon moved on without attacking. Now the party of people walked in on the carcass. But so did the hyenas. There were six of them, so they were a force equivalent to that of the people.

This was where the staffs came in. They were good for fending off such creatures. Normally it was just a matter of holding the staff out ahead, crosswise, so that it was hard for a creature to pounce and bite without getting blocked. But they could be swung hard to deliver painful blows. And now, Jes saw, Ned was holding his staff with the sharpened end pointing forward, like a tusk of a saber-toothed cat. That could be more effective. She pictured what it would feel like, if she were a hyena, trying to spring at a pointed staff, and maybe getting stabbed in the snout. She winced. She would surely back off. But animals weren't as smart as people; they might see it differently.

The hyenas prowled around, considering. They were hungry; they wanted those bones. They were formidable fighters. But they didn't like fighting aggressive creatures, and they didn't understand the staffs. So they were cautious.

The people advanced on them in a tight formation bristling with staffs. One hyena decided that staffs were not lions, and charged. This was the test.

It came right at Jes. Before she knew it, her staff was thrusting out, striking the creature on the nose and drawing blood. Then Sam's staff came down on its head, hard. The hyena scrambled back, hurting.

But another moved forward. Again Jes's staff thrust out to intercept it, knocking it on the ear, scraping the fur. It snarled and backed off. The staffs were working!

Finally the hyenas lost their nerve, and loped away, leaving the bones to the seemingly stronger force.

Jes felt weak with relief. Had the animals realized that the group consisted of four children, one weak woman with a baby in her belly, and only one strong man, they would have charged and perhaps prevailed. Staffs were good, but not that good. For one thing, if a staff got knocked to the side, a hyena could get in a good bite without penalty. One bite would be more than enough; their jaws were horribly strong.

Yet during the actual fight, she had not been very much afraid. Her weapon had led the way, striking as if of its own volition. She had been thrilled to feel the contact with the flesh of the enemy, and feel the shock of the blow in her hands. Sam had fought more effectively, having far more mass and muscle, but Jes had done her part. She was a fighter too.

They had won the carcass. But this was an exposed place, and a stronger force could come at any time. More hyenas could appear, augmenting the original group, making them bold again, or a large pack of dogs could spy them. The dogs couldn't crack open the bones, but they could scatter them widely as they chewed on them for their external bits of meat. So it wouldn't be smart to settle down to crack open the bones and eat the marrow here, because trouble was bound to come before they got into many of the tough ones. They had known this when they set out for this site.

They took rocks and bashed at the joints connecting the bones, breaking them apart. They collected all the best bones, wrapped their arms around bundles of them, and carried them toward the nearby river. That was safer, because most predators did not like to fight in the water, especially when there were crocodiles there. But staffs would drive away crocodiles too, if the animals weren't too hungry. They had a large cache of stones there, making it far more defensible. The whole business was somewhat chancy, but the reward was great: an excellent meal that would invigorate them for days. Jes knew that Flo, especially, appreciated it, because the first meal of marrow had strengthened her enormously, and she had lived and slept better after it.

They carried the bones to the river, where they drank deeply and set up the stones to crack them open. All of them worked at it, though the two youngest children weren't able to do it by themselves, and needed help. The inner meat was delicious; they all had rapidly developed a taste for its richness.

At last, sated, they marched back to their home cave, following their marked path so that there were no missteps. There they lay down and slept, though it was not yet night. They rarely ate here, because it was too much work to haul food all the way back from the plain. But they did have a pile of stones by its entrance, and a number of staffs inside. They felt secure here.

Jes was especially pleased. Their experiment with the vultures was a success; they had located a fresh kill, and gotten all the marrow from it. Animals were always getting killed, so there were likely to be more such opportunities on other days. In between they could forage, as they always had. Their situation had improved. Because Ned had figured out that there was good food in bones.

Jes woke when Flo got up early and left the home cave. Jes, sensitive to her sister's condition, got up and followed her. Flo had evidently thought to go alone, because of what she had to do, but seemed to be glad to have her younger sibling along. Flo was heavy on her feet, and the descent from the high cave was precarious despite the clear path they had made. Paths were good, very good, but if they made the one to their lair too easy, other animals might use it. Like hyenas. But with Jes helping her, Flo made it down without mishap.

"Baby come," Jes said as they walked out onto the plain, holding their staffs.

"Baby come," Flo agreed. "Keep no."

Jes was surprised. "Keep no?"

"Need man," Flo said.

Because a baby was just too much to handle alone, Jes realized. Flo might die trying to maintain it, and the baby would die too. But if she threw it away, Flo could grow strong again, and live. Jes understood another reason Flo didn't really want to keep the baby: it had been put in her by the rape. It seemed to take a man to put a baby in a woman, and the baby of a bad man was not worthwhile.

They followed the path to the dying place, where old people were left when they stopped walking and breathing, safely away from their normal sleeping and foraging regions. This distance stopped the smell, and allowed the dead to be forgotten quickly. Jes didn't see any bones lying around, but she wasn't looking for them. The hyenas and dogs would have scattered them anyway. She didn't much like death when it happened to people.

Flo found a by-path leading to a forested section, and within that region was a pleasant grassy glade. This was suitably private and comfortable. She put her hands on the trunk of a small tree at the edge of the glade, and held on to it, supporting herself. She spread her feet wide, straddling a declivity between two large roots. She squatted, letting her hands slide down the tree. Then she began to breathe deeply and push her breath out slowly under great pressure.

Jes stood somewhat awkwardly, not knowing what to do. This process frightened her, but she wanted to know about it. She knew that babies came out of people, but had never actually seen it happen. Was it like defecating? It did seem to be the same general region of the body. That was where the bad man had put it in.

For some time, nothing seemed to happen. Flo continued to squat and breathe, facing the tree. Then she started pushing harder, and the cleft between her legs widened.

Suddenly there was a rush of fluid from her, splashing on the ground. Alarmed, Jes stepped forward, but Flo didn't seem to be concerned. Her eyes were closed, and she was still breathing heavily, bearing down. It didn't seem to be blood, so maybe it was all right.

Flo began to groan, and the groans rose in pitch to become small screams, but still Jes didn't know what to do. She stood on one foot and then on the other, as if she could walk to wherever she needed to be to help.

The screams faded. Flo opened her eyes. "Moss," she said, as if this were routine.

Jes ran around the glade, gathering up handfuls of the spongy moss that grew at the bases of trees. She brought back an armful. "Where?" she asked.

"Under."

So she dumped it under Flo's spread bottom, and straightened it, realizing that it was to cushion the fall of the emerging baby. The baby would be left here to die, but maybe Flo didn't want to hurt it directly. Jes could understand that; the idea of hurting a baby appalled her.

As Jes finished, Flo started breathing deeply again. Jes remained on her knees, not knowing whether to retreat. Flo bore down, screaming—and her cleft widened into a circle. Something dark appeared in it, pushing through. It was the baby's head! Jes reached out to catch the baby, so it wouldn't fall headfirst on the ground. Flo screamed again, and heaved, and the head pushed slowly through. It seemed impossible that the hole could open wide enough for a whole baby to pass, but it was happening. Then, much faster, the rest of the baby came, dropping into Jes's hands. It was so warm and wet and slippery that she almost dropped it; she grabbed harder, and must have hurt it, because it shuddered and then gulped and began to cry.

"Cut," Flo gasped, still holding on to the tree.

Now Jes saw the cord extending from the baby's belly back up into Flo. She laid the baby down in the damp moss and brought out her bit of sharp stone. She sliced it across the cord several times until the cord separated. Then, remembering what she had heard, she looped the length of cord around and knotted it near the baby's little belly.

Flo, meanwhile, hauled herself up, took a few steps to another tree, then strained again. More was coming out of her, and now it looked like blood. Jes started to get up, but Flo cried, "No!" So Jes took some dry moss and used it to mop and clean the baby, wiping the blood and waxy smears off it. Now she realized that it was a girl, tiny but perfectly

formed. How awful to leave her here to die! But she reminded herself why: Flo had no mate, and their band was
weak, and so they could not support a child. If she kept it,
the baby would die, and Flo might die too, trying to nurse
it when she was unable to forage enough to feed herself.
That would hurt them all. So it had to be left here. Jes hoped
they would not be able to hear its crying, from the home
cave.

Jes cleaned the tiny feet, and saw a mark between the first
and second toes of the left foot. It looked like a bit of leaf
caught there, and she tried to clear it out, but it was actually
a discoloration of the skin. Well, no one would notice it,
there. Not that it mattered, in a baby destined to die. But it
was sad, somehow, to think of trying to hide a baby's blem-
ish, and it not living long enough for it to matter. Jes felt
her tears starting. She wished that she could take the baby,
but knew that it would be even worse for her to try, because
she had no breasts and couldn't nurse it.

Flo finished her business, and cleaned herself off with
some other moss. She came over to look once at the baby.
She was crying too. Then she turned around and walked
away, back along the path.

Jes took one more longing look at the baby, then got up
and followed Flo. They cried together as they returned to
the cave. As they came in sight of it, Flo paused to wipe
her fur and face clean. Then she put a neutral expression on
her face and marched on. Jes did the same.

But as they were about to enter, Flo stopped. Her tears
flowed again. "Can't," she said, and turned.

Jes didn't argue. She followed Flo back to the glade, se-
cretly relieved. Maybe she could help forage for the baby.
Maybe it would be her child too. At least it wouldn't die.
Not right away.

But when they came up to the place, the baby was gone.
The stained moss remained, but there was no sign of the
tiny girl. Someone or something had already taken her.

Flo uttered a muted sob and searched all around the glade,

but there was nothing. That meant that a person must have
taken the baby, because an animal would have devoured her,
leaving blood and bones. So maybe the little girl would live
after all, having a mother who could support her.

At last Flo gave up her fruitless search and turned again
for the cave. She was crying, but not in quite the same way
as before. There was a tinge of hope in it. Jes hoped that
hope was justified.

Homo habilis *had made a fundamental shift of life-
style. He had found a more reliable source of high-
energy food, but it required special abilities. He needed
to spot fresh carcasses, and to reach them promptly
enough to get whole bones, and to crack those bones
open. This meant fighting off some of the other predators, and represents the first consistent use of tools
we know of: the stone used on the bones. Probably
stones were the least of his technology, as noted before;
wooden tools and weapons would have been far easier
to make and use. Would a sharp stone actually have
been used to cut an umbilical cord? That is a stretch,
but a creature smart enough to carve meat might do
it. Scavenging also meant carrying, so as to be able to
complete the operation safely. Because bipedalism
freed the hands for such things, it was possible; but
more intelligence was needed for such organization.
There was now a greater premium on brains. That
meant the body's mechanisms for cooling body and
brain had to become stronger. Thus sweating increased, and fur thinned further, as it could afford to
do as long as the species remained vertical, catching
the wind while avoiding the noon sun. The prior "Geodyssey" volumes assumed the validity of the Aquatic
hypothesis, wherein a period in water caused mankind
to shed his fur and develop subcutaneous fat; this one*

does not. Mankind appears to have become furless in order to cool his burgeoning brain. But there were further complications of both bipedalism and loss of fur, leading to other remarkable developments.

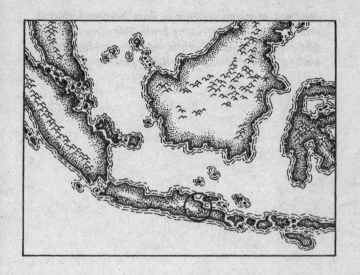

Chapter 3

TRIPLE PLOY

When mankind became bipedal, he surely didn't anticipate the chain of consequences. A major one related to the female of the species. A baby takes perhaps twice as long to learn to walk on two feet as it would for four feet, and this extends the time it is dependent on its mother. She had to carry it much of the time, nursing it as she held it in the crook of her arm. The larger brain and slower development of the child extend that time of extreme dependency further. This places a burden on the mother. As the species progressed, this burden increased—and eventually human women started having babies at shorter intervals than other species did, so that there could be several children dependent on one mother. Nursing drained her physically, and she had to take in more nourishment herself to provide for her baby, while having such a family restricted her from going out to forage. At the same time, Homo habilis progressed, about two million years ago, to Homo erectus, with a division of labor occurring. The male went out to hunt and fight; the female foraged and took care of the children. It was no longer possible for a mother to raise her child by herself. She had to have the regular help of a male, for protection and food for herself and her children. She may have needed a monogamous relationship, or at least a way to be sure of the regular presence of a male, in addition to the support of the tribe. While it made reproductive sense for a father to facilitate the survival and progress of his children, this was not a notion that came naturally to the average male. His reproductive strategy had always been to sow his seed as widely as possible, sniffing out the fertile females, and leave the care of the offspring to their mothers. But it made little reproductive sense to sire many offspring who died because the mothers were unable to support them. Thus it was necessary for the woman to find a way to compel the man's constant attention despite his polygamous instinct, and necessary for the man to modify his ways somewhat. This was, in its subtle fashion, the onset of a battle of the sexes that continues today. Men and women are not really at war, but they do have fundamentally different strategies of survival and reproduction, and compromise is essential. For this engagement, the woman set aside the compulsion of periodic pheromones and developed perhaps the most formidable arsenal of visual, emotional, and behavioral devices any species has seen. It was the triple ploy.

New evidence is pushing the dates of Homo erectus *much further back, as far as 1.8 million years ago in China and southeast Asia. Scavenging may have led naturally to hunting—why wait for your carcass?—and hunting enabled mankind to obtain food anywhere he went, as long as there were animals who could live on vegetation that human beings couldn't eat. So this change of strategy may have opened much of the rest of the world to mankind. However, those groups that lacked the numbers or ability to hunt effectively could still have done well enough by scavenging, the old stand-by, so probably* Erectus *did both. If the forward fringe of settlement advanced just one mile per decade, in a hundred thousand years it would extend 10,000 miles. Thus* Homo erectus *could have colonized virtually all of habitable Asia in that time, and may have done so. The setting is Java, 1,500,000 years ago.*

FLO FOLLOWED THE PATH EVERY day to the glade, but there was never anything. Jes went with her, understanding her need. But in time they had to give it up. The baby was gone.

Sam brought meat and shared it with the others, and Flo recovered her strength. She put more time into foraging, and the foraging was good, and they all did well. Still, she knew that they would not have done well if she had kept her baby; she would have been weaker, and would have needed more, and it would have put an unconscionable strain on the band. She felt guilty for their success, purchased at the price of her baby.

But they were too small in number to be a band. They were six band siblings who had gotten separated from their original band, and now they had their own cave in the vicinity of several other bands. Their time spent struggling to survive on their own had bound them together in a way they had not been before. Sam and Flo were grown, and Ned and Jes were growing, while Bry and Lin remained children.

They were like a large family, and they all looked out for each other, and they didn't want to separate.

In some bands, the males went out to seek females in other bands, and joined those bands. In others, females went out to the other bands. But the six of them had resolved to remain together, bringing both males and females in, if they could. They had a good location, with adequate foraging and hunting, and they knew how to crack open the bones to gain the most from the animals they killed. But they needed more members, so that no other band could come and drive them off.

Sam was big and strong, and had gotten more so recently, but he had a problem. He believed he was cursed to mate with an ugly female, because he had seen ugly animals mating. So he wasn't eager to find a woman. But Flo knew that there had to be mates, because they could never be a true band without couples and children. One day when she was foraging for roots with the others, while Sam was out searching for a carcass to scavenge, she brought up the subject. They were of course busy eating what they found and dug out, but since more time was spent in searching and digging than in eating, there was time for words.

"Sam need woman," she said, speaking each word carefully so that they could understand. When anyone spoke too rapidly, the words ran in together and became incomprehensible, so time had to be taken.

Little Lin put her fingers in her mouth, stretching it wide. The effect was exaggerated because of her deformed hand. "Ugly woman," she said.

"No," Flo said firmly. "No ugly."

Ned agreed. "Sam fear ugly. No mate."

"Tell Sam," Lin said.

That was the problem. Sam believed his vision, and did not listen when Flo or anyone else tried to tell him that he didn't have to mate with an ugly woman.

"Flo need man," Ned said.

"Man no mate Flo," Flo said with resignation. She knew

that she was cursed, because she had been raped and then
lost her baby. What man would want her after that?

"Man mate Flo," Ned said.

"Tell Flo," Bry said, imitating Lin's tone, and the two
laughed.

"Man no," Flo repeated.

Ned faced her. "Tell man baby no," he said seriously.
"Man know no."

Flo was astonished. It had never occurred to her that the
people of other bands wouldn't know of her problem. But
smart Ned was right: How would a man know, if she didn't
tell him? If the others didn't tell him? Her body had resumed
its early form, and her cleft had narrowed, so that there was
no sign that a baby had passed through it. "Tell no?" she
asked, looking at each of the others. This was a phenomenal
new concept: that of pretending to what wasn't true. Always
before, what wasn't true had no meaning; could it now have
benefit?

"Tell no!" they chorused. That meant that none of them
would tell. She would seem to be an ordinary woman, without the curse of a lost baby. Ned had found the way.

They discussed it further, as they completed their foraging, and decided that Sam and Flo should go out together
to look for mates from another band. Sam should have no
trouble, because of his evident size and strength, but even
without the curse, Flo would surely find it difficult, because
she wanted to bring a man back here. So she was resigned
to likely failure. But she would make the effort, because it
was a pretext to make Sam come with her, so he could find
a woman. He wouldn't go alone; despite his size and power,
he lacked certainty by himself, and was largely helpless.
Some woman might talk him into joining *her* tribe.

As they returned from their foraging, with a few extra
roots to share with Sam, they saw him approaching the cave
with an armful of bones. He had found a carcass, and
brought back the leg bones for them to crack open and share.
So it would be a good evening.

Flo broached the subject after they had eaten all the marrow. "Sam find woman. Flo find man. Sam Flo go."

"No," he said.

"Yes!" all the others cried.

Sam was physically strong, but had trouble with intellectual debate. So he shrugged.

Next day the two of them set out. Ned was left in charge of the cave; he was clever at finding ways to make it difficult for any stranger to enter. He could balance rocks so that they fell at the slightest touch, landing on tender feet, and he was adept at putting sharp thorns in unexpected places. He would make any foreign raid during their absence awkward. Even so, Flo didn't like leaving the four children alone, but she saw no alternative. They had to remain to maintain possession of the good cave.

They took a devious path, and walked on past the territory of their nearest neighbor band, because they knew that there were no suitable mates there, and the others knew too much about them. They needed to approach an unfamiliar band. Their band's path linked to the neighboring band's path, becoming less familiar, but it was all right because all people had a common interest in connecting to others. Otherwise how would mates ever be found? As long as they stayed on the path and kept moving, they would probably not be molested.

They did not encounter anyone. That wasn't surprising, because there were not many bands. Their own had come from another place, moving into new territory, and others had closed in around them similarly. The other bands were larger, so could hunt more effectively, and got the best animals first, which was why their own band had to scavenge more often than not. Where the elder generation had come from they didn't know, but Flo's impression was that it was far away. Whenever things got crowded, some people moved; it had always been that way.

Of course the other bands would be aware of their passage. Every band kept watch over its territory. Little Bry had sharp eyes and was always alert for motion or traces; he knew when strangers passed near, but never showed himself. It would be the same with any band. Foreigners were not to be trusted; only when they became sufficiently known were they accepted, grudgingly. That was why mating was difficult; it was not fun for a woman to join an unfamiliar and tacitly hostile new band. Especially at first, when she could be sexually tried by any or all males who desired her, before one decided to make her his own. But it had to be done, if she wanted to breed.

And Flo was making it even more difficult for herself, seeking to make a man come to her band. Yet such a thing was not unknown, if there was a man who wanted to move, or a woman who was uncommonly appealing. Was Flo appealing enough? Her body had matured with the experience of having the baby, and now her breasts were large and her hips wide; she was well fleshed. She remembered seeing adults like that, before the six of them got separated from their original band, and they had attracted the interest of many men. She had learned to walk in a way that accentuated her qualities, attracting male eyes. She had practiced it, before the curse of the rape and lost baby, and Sam had said that if she hadn't been his band sibling he would have found her matable. She had had to cover her head to garner that opinion, because otherwise Sam could not even entertain the notion. Band siblings were family. She knew how it was, because when Sam covered his head, she could see that he was a good mating prospect, but otherwise the question never entered her mind.

She thought again of her lost baby, as she tended to do when not actively distracted by something else. She had had to leave the baby girl to die, then changed her mind, but someone else had taken her. Not anyone in the immediately neighboring bands; it was generally known when a woman had a baby, and all new children were accounted for. But a traveling woman from a more distant band could have taken her. So Flo's eyes were open; maybe she could find her daughter while visiting farther bands. Then—

That was where her mind always balked. She still couldn't take care of a baby. Her milk had dried up, so she couldn't nurse, and without a man to bring her occasional meat she couldn't have supported a baby anyway. So her child was lost, regardless. Yet still she longed for her! Maybe at some point she would see a baby with a scarlike mark between her toes, and know it had been hers.

They strode rapidly, staying mostly on the level paths and in open regions where possible, making no effort to conceal their presence. Of course this warned away game, but that was the point: They were not hunting or foraging for more than they needed to sustain them on the way; they were traveling. The folk of other bands would recognize that, and leave them alone. Since there were few reasons to travel, others would understand their purpose. When they entered the territory of a band in need of mates, contact would be made.

By the end of the day they were near the edge of their familiar range. They foraged for berries and grubs, then made a camp amidst a thicket where no large animal could approach without making a commotion, and slept. It wasn't easy, sleeping in the field, but there was little choice when traveling. Certainly Sam would protect her, if anything came in the night.

In the morning they grubbed for edible roots, drank water from a stream, and resumed travel. Now they were heading into strange territory. Flo hoped that there would be a band here looking for mates.

And in the afternoon contact was made. They approached a fording place in a river, guided by the path, and there was an old woman. She stood directly in their way, and that was signal enough: female meant she was no threat to anyone, and old meant she was not looking for a mate herself.

They came to a halt before her. "What?" the woman asked. It was the general purpose query about their business here.

Sam stared at her, until Flo nudged him. Then he remembered. He tapped his chest. "Sam need woman." He lifted one arm and flexed a muscle, showing his capacity to support a mate.

Then it was Flo's turn. She brushed back the longer fur of her head. "Flo need man." She stood up straight and inhaled, showing her capacity to interest a mate. Then she added. "Man go Flo band."

The old woman looked sharply at her. "Flo go man band."

"Man go Flo band," Flo repeated firmly. "Small band, good hunting." Or at least it would be good hunting, if they had the men for it, so they could be first instead of last after the prey.

The woman peered more closely at her, especially her full breasts and broad hips. Then she shrugged. She turned and walked up the slope, taking a path that surely led to the band camp. They followed at a respectful distance. Due deference was by far the best course, in foreign territory; men would be watching.

The camp was much like their own, with several caves above, and a glade cleared of brush below. The band members had turned out to see them. It was much larger than their own; there were eight grown men, nine grown women, several old folk, and too many children of all ages to count. All of them stared curiously at the visitors.

The band leader stepped forward. "Joe," he said. He gestured to another more slender man who stood beside and a bit behind him. "Bil."

"Sam," Sam said. He indicated Flo. "Flo. Siblings."

"Siblings," Joe repeated, understanding. That meant that they were not mated to each other. Their business here was now obvious. "Where?"

Sam pointed to the west. "Days." That meant they had traveled more than a day from that direction.

Joe nodded. He glanced at the old woman, and he and

Bil rejoined the other men. The formalities of peaceful introduction had been accomplished.

The old woman described their business. "Sam need woman." She glanced at him, and Sam flexed his muscle again. There was definite interest by several of the elder girls. "Flo need man." Flo inhaled again, and spread her legs somewhat apart, and there was interest by all of the men, though that was deceptive because those already mated weren't eligible. "Man go Flo band."

The atmosphere changed. It was clear that the men had a good band here, and no man wished to leave it and be a stranger in a foreign band. "Man go no," Bil said.

"Flo band," Flo said. She had made her decision and intended to stick to it, though it cost her a mate.

But there was a cunning look about the old woman. Sam was oblivious, but Flo could see she was planning something. Not anything hostile, but definitely something. "Wona," she said.

Bil nodded, evidently understanding the ploy. Bil seemed to be the smart member of this band, like Ned in her own band.

From behind the women came one who had remained in the background. This must be Wona. She was a stunningly beautiful young woman. Her fur was light and fine, her breasts large and firm, and her hips were wide. She moved lithely, showing no weakness of body anywhere. Her face was so sweet that it was almost impossible not to like her at first glance. But Flo made the effort, knowing that there was a catch somewhere.

Wona came to stand before Sam. She smiled at him and inhaled. Sam's intake of breath was audible across the glade. He was well impressed. His penis was lifting. He had feared he would have to mate an ugly woman, and here was an absolutely lovely one being offered to him.

The old woman waited until she was sure Sam was hooked. Then she spoke again. "Dirk."

A man hobbled forward, clutching a bamboo staff. He

was not using it as a weapon but for support; he was almost too weak to walk without it. The reason was hardly obscure: he had been badly injured. His ribs were bruised on one side, and were probably broken, and there was a large fresh scar on one leg from a wound that made the use of that leg painful, as each wincing step demonstrated. It would be some time before this man was much good at hunting.

Dirk came to stand before Flo. "Dirk go band," he said, with an apologetic grimace. He knew she would not be interested.

Now the old woman made her point. "Wona Dirk go band."

Sam shook his head. He was not so dull as not to see that Dirk was no bargain. He did not want to stick Flo or their band with him. "Wona yes, Dirk no."

The woman shook her head. "Band siblings. Go, go."

She meant that if Sam wanted Wona, Flo would have to take Dirk—the one man who was willing to join a new band. Because he was no longer welcome in this one, being unable to hunt. He was a liability.

What were they to do? Wona was the embodiment of Sam's wildest dream. Dirk was a disaster.

Yet Flo herself was not as she was presented, because of the secret of her rape and lost baby. And in time Dirk should recover and be able to hunt again. His rueful look had a certain perverse appeal; he didn't like being foisted off on another band like this, but had no choice. He had to do what this band wanted, or be cast out to die. He was not a bad-looking man, apart from the injury. And obviously he would be no threat to Sam's leadership of the band.

Flo knew she was cursed anyway. She had lost her most precious quality, her innocence, and her most precious thing, her baby. Now she would lose her most precious dream: that of a handsome, strong, excellent provider. Maybe it was better to accept her lot, for the sake of the joy it would bring Sam.

She stepped forward and kissed Dirk on the mouth, embracing him and pressing her breasts against him. She was accepting him. She saw his eyes widen with amazement, and heard a murmur of surprise and pleasure pass through the other members of the band. They had expected her to reject the deal, but were pleased that she had not.

Sam, released by that second consent, leaped at Wona and swept her into his embrace. The woman accepted him, returning his embrace emphatically. She wrapped her legs around him, and they dropped to the ground, immediately mating. This was part of the ritual: by mating, they established their commitment to each other in a way that all understood. Of course it wasn't normally done in the direct presence of the band, but at least this way it served as entertainment for the children.

Flo had to mate similarly with Dirk. Fortunately she was female, and so could pretend interest, having no member whose lack of stiffness would give her away. She walked with him to his sleeping site, at the edge of a shallow cave, nominally private. She went down on the ground with him, and as his disbelief faded his penis did stiffen. He winced from his injuries as he tried to mount her, so she mounted him, fitting herself to him in the way that her prior bitter experience had made familiar. But there was one essential difference: this time she was not being raped, even if this was not her ideal of a partner. She was in control, and that enabled her to fit his entry so that it did not pain her, and to govern the motions they made together. Actually, she had little to fear from anything as small as the male member, after something as huge as the baby had passed through the channel. That almost made the act pleasant. She liked knowing that she had this power over a man, to make him respond to her, to do it her way. She liked having a man grateful for her participation, as Dirk plainly was, even if she did not get the same joy from the act itself that he did.

The completion was rapid. She felt Dirk spurt inside her, and knew that Sam was doing the same in Wona, there before the band. She lay with Dirk for a while longer, until he shrank out of her; then she disengaged, cleaned up, and helped him to get back to his feet. They returned to the glade, where Sam and Wona were waiting.

"Eat," Joe said approvingly. The visitors were now welcome here, though soon they would be leaving for their own band.

They had a good meal of tubers and nuts from the band's store of food, then returned to the caves to sleep. Flo knew that Sam was eager for more of Wona, and she couldn't blame him. The weight of his feared curse had been lifted.

But it was different with Dirk. She preferred to talk with him, getting adjusted to his accent. She wanted to get to know him, hoping that he had a good personality, now that she was committed. "Dirk hurt how?" she asked.

He smiled ruefully. "Woman."

Oh. He had fought another man over a woman. Such things happened. Normally mating was by mutual agreement, but sometimes it wasn't. She questioned Dirk further, and learned that a pretty girl had come to the tribe, couldn't make up her mind between two men, so agreed to take the better fighter. Dirk had been doubtful about fighting, because the other man was a friend of his, but the other had had no doubts. So Dirk had lost, as much from conscience as from lack of power. The other man had thus proved to be better. Now Dirk did not care to remain in the band and watch the girl become a woman with the other man and bear his babies.

It seemed to Flo that this spoke better for Dirk than he knew. He had been weakened by indecision, not wanting to hurt a friend, despite his interest in the woman. Flo could live with such a weakness. She had felt it when trying to leave her baby to die. Life was easier for those without doubts, but they were not necessarily the nicest people.

Then Dirk added something that thrilled her. "Flo better girl." He was saying that she was a more attractive woman than the one he had lost.

Flo didn't want to spoil it, but she was getting to like

Dirk; he had a number of ways about him that appealed as they became evident. So she told him the truth. "Flo better no. Man Flo rape. Baby lose."

He stared at her. Then he shook his head. "Flo better," he said, dismissing it.

She was so pleased that she moved into him, kissing him and wrapping her legs around him, inviting him to have more sex. He did so, pleased in turn. It was slower yet better than before. Then they slept.

In the morning they set out on the trail for home. Dirk made a good effort, but his leg pained him with every step, and when the exertion made him breathe faster, his ribs pained him too. Flo could see it; he would not be able to keep any good striding pace. So she took action.

"Sam Wona go band," she suggested. "Dirk Flo slow." She was inviting the other two to move on at speed, while she and Dirk would proceed at whatever pace they could manage.

Sam hesitated, not wanting to leave her. But Wona encouraged him to do it. She smiled at him. "Sam Wona go."

Sam melted. He was soft mud in the hands of this beautiful woman. Soon they were on their way, and Flo was alone with Dirk. "Flo good," he said.

"Flo help," she said. She put an arm around him and matched her step to his, so that their inner legs moved together. That enabled her to take some of the weight of his injured leg on her own leg, and to steady him so that he did not have to struggle for balance. He was considerably larger than she, but well balanced, so she did not actually take much of his mass. It worked well, and they were able to make much better progress.

But it was not possible to come close to matching the pace of healthy individual striders, and they remained far from the home band as night came. So they paused to forage, finding a log with a number of delicious fat grubs. But there were no suitable caves near, and no dense thicket; they would have to sleep in the open, a prospect Flo didn't relish. It wasn't because of the bugs that would come; they could eat those. But there could be predators in the night.

Then Dirk went to a large bramble patch and sat down beside it. His fingers were surprisingly nimble as he took the prickly vines and wove them into a kind of mat. He propped the mat above the ground with several forked sticks, then crawled under it. He had made a shelter! It wouldn't stop rain, but any large animal that tried to poke into it would get stuck with thorns.

Flo crawled in with him. She gave him sex again, carefully, because too much motion would push them against the thorns. And they talked some more. She told him how she and her band siblings had gotten separated from their original band and had to forage for themselves. That was why they insisted on staying together; they had been through hard times and trusted each other. She told him of the other members: how Ned was smart, and Jes was ugly for a girl but loyal and hard-working, and little Bry was very reliable and little Lin was ashamed because she had an extra finger on one hand, but was otherwise very pretty. And that none of them was ever supposed to tease any other about such things.

Dirk in turn told her about the special things in his band. Then he hesitated. "Dirk Joe band no," he said.

"Dirk Sam band," she agreed. He was changing loyalties, because of his mating with her and his agreement to go with her. Band loyalty was important, because lives depended on the cooperation of band members.

"Dirk say bad."

He had something bad to say? But she knew that he was not a mean person. "Bad?"

"Flo tell no."

Something private. Secret. She had better hear it. "Flo tell no," she agreed.

"Wona—" But he didn't finish. He had conflicting loyalties.

"Wona beautiful," she said.

"Wona ugly."

A shiver ran through her. Obviously he wasn't referring to the woman's appearance. But he was from Wona's band; he had to know her well. How was she ugly?

But here the vocabulary failed them. There was something intangible about Wona for which a word did not exist. But it made her ugly.

And Sam was cursed to mate with an ugly woman. Now there was nothing to be done about it. But at least Flo had been warned; she would keep watch, until she learned what it was Dirk knew about the woman.

The thorn shelter served well; no animal bothered them in the night. They slept well, sharing fur in the cool darkness.

In two more days they made it safely to the band camp. The children were glad to see them. It wasn't that they didn't appreciate the way that Sam guarded them, but Flo served somewhat as a mother to them, and they liked her nearness. Actually Sam wasn't in evidence; it seemed that Wona had taken him off somewhere for more delights. The children hadn't wanted to try to go foraging alone, so were hungry.

Well, Flo would take care of that. The day was late and she was tired, because she had been bearing some of Dirk's weight as well as her own, but the children had to eat. She took them all out, Dirk included, to the nearest best berry patch, which had many ripe berries because it hadn't been picked for two days. This also served to show Dirk this key path, so he would know it hereafter. It would take him time to learn all the local paths, but it would happen, because that was part of the strength of a band. Its people knew its paths, while strangers did not.

They feasted. And while they did, the children began to get to know Dirk, warming to him as Flo had. He was cheerful despite his pains, and the quickness of his hands impressed them. He showed them how he could flip a berry up and catch it in his mouth, and soon Bry and Lin were trying it, with less success but more fun. Flo saw that Dirk liked children: another good sign.

Seasons passed, and Dirk healed. They were fortunate that the time of his weakness was in the berry season, when food was plentiful. By the time that passed, he was much stronger, and he was good with a sharpened staff. He actually threw it at small game, and connected often enough to bring in meat fairly regularly. It was clear why the other band had tolerated his weakness; when well, he was an asset to any band. But since he had wanted to leave, they had supported him by forcing the deal to get him mated out. But none of them had thought he would be accepted by as well formed a woman as Flo, he said. Her appearance there had been fortunate for Joe's band.

Flo had not wanted to take him, but soon had become satisfied, and now was quite pleased. It was apparent to all the band siblings except Sam that Dirk was the better acquisition than Wona, who was often irritable and tended to shirk her responsibilities to the group. She got away with it because Sam could see no evil in her, and made excuses for her, or did her work himself. Flo did not remark on it, but she was coming to suspect that Joe's band had wanted to be rid of Wona more than Dirk. How cleverly they had reversed it, demanding that Dirk be taken for the privilege of getting Wona! Certainly that ploy had fooled Sam—and Flo herself.

Both Sam and Dirk delighted in their mates, and before long both women had babies within them. This time the band was strong enough to support new children. With two grown men, hunting was good, and Ned was big enough to help them scare out game.

As both Flo and Wona grew fat with their babies, their

men lost interest in sex with them. This could have been awkward, for Flo knew that grown men never lost interest in sex itself. But Dirk was devoted to Flo, and remained close to her and treated her well throughout, and Sam remained hopelessly fixed on Wona. It was apparent that neither man had any inclination to stray.

Jes, not yet a woman, took more of a hand in managing the foraging as Flo's ability to get around diminished. Jes had had experience at the time of Flo's first baby, so was competent. The children, remembering the hard times of the past, worked hard too. So their band of eight remained viable. In fact, Flo gained more than enough weight. This time she would not be impoverished by the birth of her baby, and she would be competent to nurse it and care for it. She would not have to give it up, this time. That pleased her.

But she did still wonder what had happened to her firstborn. In her mind she saw the baby growing into a beautiful child, with hair as black and glossy as obsidian, and with dark eyes in which knowledge of the spirits lurked. A pretty child, who would surely one day be a beautiful woman, and nice in personality. A perfect child; a joy to her family. One who would always make a good impression.

Flo found herself crying, as she usually did when thinking of her first baby. She knew that the girl was probably ordinary, if she survived at all. But Flo's fancy was free to picture her as ideal, and the image would not fade. She hoped that whatever family had her was a good one, that would appreciate her and love her. As Flo would have, had she been able.

The time of birthing came. Wona was first, which was not surprising considering Sam's eagerness to have at her. She did not want Sam near for the occasion, and Sam, incompetent in any such matter, was satisfied to go out hunting with Dirk and Ned. Flo and Jes attended her, and it was just as well that they had experience, because Wona was difficult to deal with. She screeched constantly in pain when her belly contracted, and accused the two of them of making it worse. She didn't want them to touch her, but she couldn't seem to get the baby out by herself. In fact it was as if she didn't want to part with it; she closed her legs and said she had changed her mind. But she couldn't stop the contractions. Finally Flo and Jes consulted, then acted together. Flo caught Wona's arms and held them up over her head so they could not get in the way, and Jes used her feet and hands to wedge Wona's legs apart and keep them that way. Jes kneeled, watching for the baby, and then took careful hold of its head and pulled it slowly out. Wona's screams must have echoed to the camps of the neighboring bands. But they got the baby, and cut its cord. It was already crying, but could hardly be heard above Wona's cries. Then Jes lifted it clear, and got out from between Wona's legs, and the legs closed again, as if not aware that what they had enclosed was already out.

Flo let go of Wona's arms. "Done," she said. "Girl." Jes was cleaning the baby off with moss and rocking her to try to quiet the crying.

Wona's eyes narrowed. "*Girl?* Boy."

She might want a boy, but she couldn't change what she had. "Girl," Flo said firmly.

Jes brought the baby to her, and they finally prevailed on Wona to let her nurse. But the woman was scowling. She blamed them for letting a girl be born.

Sam was thrilled. He said the baby looked just like her mother. He named her Wilda. He held her and carried her around with him for some time, displaying a devotion that surprised the others. But of course he had never had a baby before, so there had been no chance for him to show such a side.

When the moon cycled back to a similar form, Flo bore her own baby. Wona was nowhere near, which was just as well. Jes attended her, and so did Dirk, and the birthing was easier than the first one had been. Flo neither screamed nor protested, as a matter of pride, and soon had a baby boy.

She was almost disappointed, because she had hoped for

a girl just like the one she had lost. But a boy was good too.

"Good," Dirk agreed. "Flint."

"Flint," Flo agreed as she nursed him. Dirk had done what Sam had, and given a name similar in its initial sound to that of the mother. It was a compliment.

Dirk was no less devoted to Flint than Sam was to Wilda, though he didn't carry him around a lot. Instead he did his best to facilitate Flo's caring for him, bringing her everything she needed. But she did not need much; she had been through this before, and experience was a wonderful guide. How glad she was that she could keep this one!

Thus the triple ploy: sex appeal, romantic love, and attachment. Instead of putting out pheromones to compel the service of all males in the vicinity at the time of ovulation, as most animals did, the prehuman woman shifted to visual signals and reversed her reproductive strategy, actually concealing her moment of fertility. This was not done to make her sexually unapproachable, as most animals are to their mates most of the time, but the opposite: to make her continuously appealing. *Developed breasts became objects of sexual interest, as did the fleshy buttocks and the outline of her body. (Some disagree, believing that only the fact that these parts are normally covered makes them of interest. Nudist camps go far toward nullifying the appeal of concealment. But most men of most cultures are definitely turned on by the firm flesh of young women, and "peepers" do spy on nudists. Why bother to cover those parts in warm weather, if they are not critical?) This meant that a given male did not have to shop among a dozen females to indulge his chronic sexual appetite; he could be satisfied by a single woman, who could accommodate him any time or all the time; there was no limit. That was the carrot. There was also the stick: if he did travel between females, he* could not be sure of siring offspring with any, because no one could tell when it would take. In fact, if he spent time with one, but left her alone for a day, some other male might come and fertilize her that one time—and that one would take. So there was no way to be sure of impregnating a given woman except to remain with her all the time, allowing no other man access to her. And if he couldn't leave her even briefly, how could he go out to sire anything with any other woman? He was locked in. Thus love: complete devotion to one partner, even when she becomes temporarily sexually unappealing in the advanced stages of pregnancy. Such love may seem exhilarating, but nature has a cynical agenda, leading the polygamous male to monogamy, lest his line die out. A contemporary study indicates that such romance typically loses half its force in eighteen months, and most of it in about four years—just long enough for the woman to conceive, gestate, bear, and nurse the resulting baby. Which means that the father gets to know his offspring before his infatuation with the mother fades. Such acquaintance leads to commitment, which is a different kind of love. It has no sexual component, but can be quite strong; men will commonly risk their lives to protect their children, once they know them. Even if their relationship to the mother breaks up, their commitment to their children can remain. Thanks to the triple ploy. Current research indicates that there are actual hormones in the brain that govern these stages; it is not mere imagination. Nature leaves little to chance. Of course women too can be interested in sex, and fall in love, but their commitment to their children always existed, perhaps a woman's strongest emotion; it is the men the triple ploy evolved to handle. It is the men who are most dazzled by sex, and who plunge most heedlessly into love. Even with modern intelligence and knowledge of consequences, men are still governed by it. This is shown also by its *negative aspects: prostitution, rape, stalking, abuse, and murder of a given woman, rather than lose her. A man may throw away his career and life, because of his unwise fascination with a woman who wishes to separate from him. Love is a two-edged sword, and extremely powerful. Sex, love, attachment: there is little else like the triple ploy.*

One possibly confusing sidelight: Homo erectus at this time developed a sophisticated stone tool tradition, notably the Acheulean chipped hand axes, that served him in good stead for more than a million years. Flint was a prime material for this. Thus the name of one character. But as it happens, no Acheulean tools have been found in east Asia, because Erectus migrated there before their invention. Flint as a stone existed, however, so the name is not actually a mismatch, though in this volcanic region obsidian would have been preferred.

Chapter 4

ARMS RACE

The prior volumes assumed that mankind had an aquatic stage, which was when the fur was lost and women became permanently breasted. This volume assumes that there was no water stage, and that breastedness was an aspect of the female family strategy. The increasing size of the brain drove the species to shed the last of his fur, to make his cooling system as efficient as it could be. But this leads to some questions. What happened when the weather got cold? This must have been the original reason for clothing: to replace

*the warming effect of the lost fur. But that stage would
not have been necessary if the brain had not continued
to increase, forcing such an extraordinary measure.
Why did that brain keep growing far beyond the point
required for efficient survival? For the capacities of the
brain of modern mankind, which are still being explored, developed when he was primitive. It seems like
vast overkill, for the life he led at the time. But nature
does not waste her energy. There had to be a compelling reason. And there was: the arms race. The setting
is the southern end of the Great Rift Valley of Africa,
150,000 years ago.*

THEY SAW THE CURL OF smoke in the sky ahead, and veered
to intercept its source. Fortunately there was a good side
path leading that way, for they were in unfamiliar territory.
Small smoke on a clear day, in contrast to large smoke, was
a sure sign of a human being, and they were looking for a
band in this vicinity with which to trade.

It turned out to be a boy of about ten, three years younger
than Ned. He was tending a small fire, over which he was
roasting a tough root. He stood as the two of them approached. He seemed to have a bad scar across his forehead,
as if he had been burned there and the color had not faded.
They stopped at a respectful distance, and Ned spoke. "Here
is Ned," he said, enunciating each word carefully as he
tapped himself. "Here is Jes." He tapped his sibling on the
shoulder. He did not identify her as female, as she normally
concealed her gender from strangers. She was tall, bony, and
homely, like a man, so this was more comfortable for her,
and safer.

"Here is Blaze," the boy said, tapping his chest. "Blaze
make fire," he added with pride.

"Pot make fire," Ned said, showing he understood. Fire
was hard to make, but easy to keep, if a person nested it in
sand and dry moss to keep an ember going. So each band
had its cultivated hearth, where the fire never quite went

out. When it was time to cook something, the fire tender would bring dry leaves or grass and blow on the ember, and get a flame from it. When the fire had to be moved, they would pack an ember with its sand in a hollow stone and carry it. It was surprising, however, to entrust such a responsibility to a child.

"Blaze make fire," the boy insisted. "See." He got down on the ground, where he had several fragments of stone. He lifted one and banged it against another, making a spark fly.

This was intriguing. Could he really make fire without an ember? Ned and Jes got down on the ground and watched closely.

Blaze made a little pile of very fine dry moss, then banged his rocks together so that more sparks flew. At first they missed the pile or faded out before reaching it, but then one landed directly in it and made a little scorch mark. It was possible!

"Blaze make fire," Ned agreed, impressed. "More sparks will make a fire."

The boy glanced at him, perplexed.

Ned realized that he had spoken too quickly. Some people could not distinguish fast sounds, and some did not understand tense. He repeated what he had said, this time carefully separating each word.

Blaze broke into a smile, understanding. "Blaze make fire," he said once more. "Many sparks."

It took many sparks to accomplish it, because of their random nature, Ned saw. But the principle was there. "Show Ned make fire," he said.

Blaze hesitated.

Jes brought out a swatch of fiber net. She stretched it between her hands, showing how it was flexible yet strong, its strands intricately looped to form patterns of circles. Such netting was precious, because few women knew how to do it this way. Their family had learned to harvest, cure, and soften certain tough vines so that they were thin and flexible even when dried out, and could be woven into durable nets. "Trade," she said. "Net—make fire."

Blaze smiled, delighted. Maybe he had simply wondered whether they were serious. Now they had shown they were, for a trade deal was a serious matter.

They turned over the valuable swatch, and got to work on the fire. Ned took the stones, and banged them together, but no spark came. Blaze took them back and showed him how: two shiny sections had to strike each other to produce the spark. Ned took them again and finally got a faint spark, not nearly as big as the ones the boy routinely made. It would take practice. But it was clear that it could be done, with experience, time, and patience.

Ned questioned Blaze about where such rocks could be found, and learned that they were actually stones with flint embedded, from the same mine as the flint used to make tools and weapons. Ned hadn't known about this aspect; he would certainly explore it when they returned to their home band. This was a most significant discovery. While their band had been learning to make fibrous strands and netting that would support moss, fern, and other insulating substances, so that they didn't have to depend entirely on animal pelts for warmth at night, Blaze's band had been learning to make fire, so that they didn't have to depend on cultured embers. That knowledge was at least as important as net, Ned thought.

"May Ned and Jes share Blaze fire?" he asked.

The boy was glad to agree. But he had a qualification. "Root small."

Jes smiled. She got up, looked around, and went on a root hunt. She had sharp eyes, and she had always been good at foraging, as well as finding faint paths. The home band used similar roots, gathering them and bringing them in to the fire, because they were too tough to eat raw. She knew what she was looking for. And soon she found several, and used her pointed staff to pry them out of the hard ground.

Blaze was amazed. "Man good forage," he said as she brought them back.

Jes smiled again. "Secret," she said. "Do not tell."

Blaze looked perplexed, but crossed his arms before his chest, promising to keep the secret.

Jes opened her net cloak, showing her small breasts and furred memberless cleft.

"Woman!" Blaze exclaimed, astonished. "Thought boy."

"Secret," she repeated. "Woman forage."

Blaze nodded. Men typically hunted, while women foraged, so women had the better eye for plants. She had explained her ability to find roots. But she often hunted with the men, and she could use her staff as a weapon when she chose to. But she made no point of that now, as that was a secret of another sort.

They cooked the roots, and shared water from their water skins, and talked, keeping the words slow and distinct. Blaze told how he was his band's fire tender, despite being young, because he had a natural way with fire. He touched his forehead by way of explanation: he had been born with the fire mark. He told how he had a friend who was a girl named Ember, who also liked fire. He liked her a lot, but knew he would not grow up to mate with her, because they were band siblings. That made him unhappy, but he couldn't change it. Jes said she sympathized; she expected not to mate, because she was too ugly to dazzle a man.

Blaze laughed. "When Blaze man, Jes come," he said gallantly, touching his forehead again to remind her that he was ugly too, and also touching his bare penis, not yet furred.

Then Jes did something Ned had not seen before: she blushed. She was touched by the boy's offer, because there was no artifice in it; Blaze liked her. But of course their bands were distant from each other, and it would be two or three years before Blaze was a man, and that was a long time. Nothing would come of it.

Ned explained how they had come to trade net for flint, the precious weapon stone. "Band have flint?"

"Yes." But the boy frowned. "Bub Green Feather band have pelts."

Ned felt a chill. Their band had encountered the Green Feather band once before, long ago, when they were traveling. Bub had raped Flo and then driven them away. But he did not reveal his recognition. He and Jes were unlikely to be recognized, because the episode had been brief, and the two of them had grown since then.

So Bub might not want to trade, as a pelt was better than netting. It was where pelts were rare that net was useful. "No trade, Ned Jes go other band," Ned said.

Still Blaze was uneasy. "Secret."

Ned and Jes exchanged a meaningful glance. There was something they should know. Then both crossed their arms in front, agreeing not to tell.

"Man come, have salt," Blaze said. "Bub take salt, no trade. Man go."

So Bub had been true to form. He had robbed the visitor instead of trading for his wares. Some bands were like that. They might trade fairly with nearby bands, because those were capable of attacking in force, but would cheat individuals from more distant ones, who were powerless. If such a person protested, he could be beaten or killed. This was a grim warning.

But Ned had an idea. "Flint mine near?"

Blaze smiled. "Blaze show path," he said eagerly. He pointed out the direction of the place where the flint was found, and described how it was mostly in scattered chunks amidst chalky rock. They didn't actually need to try to trade with Bub's band; they could find their flint directly.

Ned was pleased. "Let's give him more net," he said quickly to Jes. At that velocity he knew that Blaze would not be able to understand it. He spoke this way so that Jes could demur if she disagreed, without embarrassing either of them.

Jes smiled. "Thank Blaze," she said slowly. She drew a full length of netting from her bundle and presented it to him. "Keep." And she kissed him.

This time it was the boy who blushed, overwhelmed by the gift and the manner of its giving. "Blaze happy," he said, looking dazed.

Now it was late, and they had to go their ways. Blaze doused his fire with sand, and Ned and Jes set out for the flint mine. They would probably never meet again, but it had been a pleasant and profitable interlude.

But they did not go far. "The ashes of that fire are very fine," Ned remarked.

"But cooling," Jes said. "Too late to save any of that fire."

"I want them cold."

"Ned, I'm not stupid, but I can't follow your mind."

"Good. Then others won't follow it either."

So they went back to the site Blaze had left, and found the ashes warm and dry under the sand. They took several handfuls and put them in their tightest leaf-shielded net bag. They smoothed more sand over the place so that there was no evidence that anything had been taken. Then they resumed their trek toward the mine, ferreting out the best paths.

They were cautious. This was unfamiliar terrain, and it was possible that Bub's tribe would have a possessive attitude about the flint mine, though obviously no person had authority over any feature of the land other than the game it supported. So they left the main path and approached the region from a different direction. Here their ability to locate faint paths really helped, because they did not want any stranger to be able to follow them. But darkness was closing, so they found a secluded large tree and climbed into its branches for the night. They put on extra layers of dry grass and leaves bound by netting to shield themselves from the cooler air of night, and from the mosquitos.

"How she feel, being woman?" Ned inquired. Their own

more sophisticated language had words that stood for other words, and these were surprisingly useful in two ways: they eliminated the need to constantly name people, and they made it less intelligible to outsiders. When he had suggested that they give "him" more netting, Jes had understood that he meant the boy. This time "she" meant Jes.

"Nice," she said. Normally no man looked at her as men looked at Flo, because of the angularity of her body, the smallness of her breasts, and her homely face. But the boy Blaze had accepted her as a woman, once he had seen the proof of it. There had been a subtle shift of attitude, perhaps unconscious. A softening of tone, a hesitation of gaze, as if she were a person he wished he could impress. And of course the blush when she kissed him. "Young," she added with regret.

For if Blaze had been older, and if his judgment of her were not different when he had the passions of a man, he would have been a suitable prospect to bring to their band. But as it was, his destiny was elsewhere. So her chance to feel like a woman was fleeting, and she would continue to masquerade as a boy. Ned regretted that, for Jes was capable in the things required of women, and deserved to be treated as one.

In the morning they foraged as they explored the mine area, eating berries that were handy. They found where bits of flint had been pried from chalky sections. When they came to a likely spot, they used their staffs to pry at the stones, and in due course did find several fragments of flint. These weren't useful in their present form, but some careful pounding would produce pieces with sharp edges. They put these in a finely woven net bag. They had accomplished their mission.

Then they set out for home. But they were still cautious, so sought the slightest paths that would allow them to pass unscathed. "Think Bub knows?" Ned asked. They were lapsing increasingly into the full range of their language, no longer needing to school themselves in pidgin so as to be clear to others.

"He saw Blaze with net," she said. "Make him tell."

And the boy would have to tell of his meeting with the two of them. He wouldn't tell that Jes was female, but the rest was regular information. If Bub were inclined to intercept them, he would do so at the place where they had to use a narrow pass between mountains.

But Blaze had also told them of a more devious route from the mine. One that he had explored with his friend Ember. It wound up the mountain much higher, and could be cold, but it was possible to get to the far side using this path.

"Alternate route," Ned decided, and Jes nodded agreement.

They moved swiftly—but not swiftly enough. Because as they found the alternate path, they saw a man on it. Right where it narrowed between rocky ledges so that there was no other way to pass. He had a stout staff, and was not foraging. They did not need to inquire his business. Obviously Bub had anticipated this alternative, and acted to block it as well as the main path.

They exchanged a silent glance. Bub was evidently dangerous, because he was smart as well as unscrupulous. But was he smart enough?

They retreated quietly, until they were safely out of earshot. "We do not know how many men there are," Ned said. "One in view, one or two in ambush, I think. We must make them show themselves."

"They will stop us," she said. "And beat us, or kill us. We can communicate better, but we can't fight better."

"I want you to do two things," he said. "It is warm enough. Give me your netting and bag. Take this." He handed her the small bag of fine ashes.

"You want me to walk naked past those men?" she asked, not pleased. "They may not find me beautiful, but they will put the bag over my head and rape me. Remember Flo.''

"Yes, I think they will. Walk in the manner of Wona, so that there is no doubt of your nature. Stand erect and take deep breaths. I will walk behind."

"Ned—"

"Must I explain?" he demanded with mock severity. "Remember what Lin did?"

A light dawned. "When Bry teased her about her hand? Now I understand!" She quickly removed her net cloak and folded it so that he could carry it. "But I can do better than naked. I'll don the net skirt."

"Wonderful!" he agreed. He helped her wrap the band of netting around her, forming a skirt that hung low on her hips and covered just a bit more than her bottom. "You look truly evocative."

"Thank you," she said, pleased. Then she took two handfuls of ashes.

Soon they resumed their walk, proceeding heedlessly up the path. Jes was bare except for the string skirt, which concealed absolutely nothing. Of course that was the point of it; only available women wore them, to enhance their sexuality. She was swinging her closed hands and her hips with seeming abandon. Her small breasts bounced, calling attention to themselves, and the tassels on the skirt flounced, drawing eyes to her belly, thighs, and bottom. She was not well endowed, but her motion and the provocative skirt made her extremely sexy. She was his sister, yet when he squinted so as to fuzz her familiarity, those strings over her twinkling buttocks almost made him hunger for her. In fact he had to unsquint, lest he suffer a reaction. So Ned followed, several paces behind, carrying all the nets over his shoulders, and their two staffs with them. Obviously the two of them had no thought of encountering anyone on this remote path; they were complete innocents, perhaps looking for a suitable place to indulge in mating play.

The man in the path came to attention. He stared at Jes.

"Woman!" he exclaimed in amazement. Obviously Blaze hadn't told that aspect, as he had promised.

A second man lurched out of hiding. "First!" he cried, staring similarly: first hands on the woman. They hadn't even noticed her homely face, as Ned had hoped. But maybe they wouldn't have cared anyway, as obviously they just wanted to rape her and throw her away.

Ned looked wildly around, as if surprised. "No!" But he seemed to be too stupid to drop his nets and grab his staff; he just watched the two men advance on Jes. They didn't seem to regard him as any kind of a threat.

So there were only two. Jes had sprung the trap. Good.

The first man grabbed for Jes, the second coming at her from the other side. She shrank away, not having to feign alarm, but both of them pursued her. She raised her hands as if to ward them off with her little fists.

Then she flung both hands out, swiping at their faces. But her hands didn't touch them.

Both men cried out and staggered back, clutching at their eyes. She had scored on them with the fine ashes. She ran on past them and up the path. Ned followed with his burdens. The men didn't even try to stop them.

Ned knew that by the time the men got their eyes clear enough to see again, it would be too late for any effective pursuit. Probably the men would report that the quarry had not passed that way, concealing their embarrassment at being duped. Bub might not believe them, but it wouldn't matter; the escape had been made.

When they were sure they were safe, they paused, and Jes donned her more solid netwear and took her staff and her share of the burden. "That was almost as much fun as making Blaze blush," she said. "You do make me feel like a woman."

He smiled, letting the matter pass. His band sister was indeed a young woman, with many qualities to recommend her. But most men could not see beyond the face and the too tall, too thin body, so she had little chance to act the part. Had she not caught the two tribesmen completely by surprise, they would soon have seen how small her breasts were, and that the string skirt covered mannishly slender hips. They would have raped her anyway, but with less gusto. He wished he could help her to find a good man. But maybe she would get lucky, as Flo had, taking a seemingly inferior man and having him turn out to be very good. Flo was now somewhat fat, after birthing her son, but Dirk didn't seem to notice. Was there a good man who would appreciate an angular woman?

They made their way through the high pass, glad of the clothing to shield them from the cutting winds. The path was difficult, and it was late by the time they crested the ridge. They ate from the dried fruit they carried, and drank from their water skins, then bundled themselves in all their remaining netting and lay down back to back to sleep. They knew that no man would come upon them during the night, because it was too cold for others to handle. In any event, they slept lightly, and any suspicious noise would wake them.

"Something I must tell you," Ned said. "You were so much like a woman, it excited me."

"From behind," she replied, calling out the flaw.

"So I could not recognize you as my sister," he said, bypassing the flaw. "If I met one like you, but not you, I think I would not care much about her face."

She twisted in her wrappings and kissed his ear. "You give me hope," she murmured, very pleased.

In the morning they did some spot foraging, finding a few good roots to chew on, and moved on down toward the warmer valley beyond. They got a nice view of it, spread out before them: a grassy plain surrounded by the forest that grew on the slopes. And saw something problematical in that plain.

"A camp of men," Jes said, shading her sharp eyes with one hand.

"Right where we have to cross the valley to return to our

regular route home," Ned said. "They are on the main path.
Dare we gamble on their purpose?"

"No. They are either of Bub's band, or have a pact with
it. There may be others spaced along the valley. I suspect
that someone is really angry with us."

"And really determined that we not show it is possible
for folk to mine their own flint and depart without getting
robbed," Ned agreed. "I think we had better not be
caught."

"They might get confused and rape you and murder me,"
she remarked, smiling grimly.

But they did have to cross that central valley plain, and
there seemed to be no way to do it without being spied by
the lurking men of the camp. That was why the campers
weren't even trying to hide; they weren't the ones being
pursued. They would either catch the fugitives as they
crossed, or keep them confined to the slope beside the plain
until they were spied and caught by other searchers there.
It might be hard to catch fugitives in mountains or deep
forest, because there were alternate paths and hidden ways,
but it was easy in the open.

"I think a handful of ashes will not suffice, this time,"
Ned said, not seeming much dismayed.

"If not the ashes, perhaps the fire?" Jes inquired, following his thought.

"It would be a distraction."

So they worked out their plan in detail, knowing that any
failure could be disastrous. Jes foraged for tinder while Ned
brought out two suitable flint rocks and experimented with
striking them together in the manner he had learned from
Blaze. It took some time, but he was able to start a fire. Jes
made a bed of sand, and they got a small fire going. Of
course the smoke would give them away, but it would take
time for anyone to travel this high up the mountain.

Then Ned damped down his little fire, so that it was
mostly hot embers, and transferred it with its bed of sand
to a section of leaf-and-sand-padded netting. He made a bag

of it that he could carry. The first part of their strategy was ready. His setup was clumsy compared to that of a regular fire handler, but it would not have to last long.

They angled down the slope, leaving the path. This was for several reasons. There might be enemy men coming up that path to attack them, and they needed to get lost in random territory, and they needed to intercept the wind at the right spot.

But when they reached the place where the wind entered the valley, there was a man posted. He wasn't even looking for them; he was just waiting, and watching the plain.

"He will have to be distracted," Jes said regretfully.

"Briefly," Ned agreed. "But you will need a sure escape."

"You get that fire going soon, and I will have it," she said. "You will need it too."

He nodded. Then they prepared themselves. They spread out all their untraded net cloaks, then wrapped them around their feet and legs to the knees. They tied them in place just above the knees, so that the knees could still flex. Their legs looked enormously fat, because of the leaf padding between the nets. Then they took their water skins and poured them carefully out onto the padding, making it wet. They saved a little water for refreshing their leggings later. Of course this left them nothing to drink, but they knew there was a river in the next valley.

Now Jes made her way carefully around the position the enemy man guarded. When she was far enough from Ned, she moved with less caution, until the man heard her. He stood and called out. "Who?"

Jes did not answer. Instead she hurried on away from Ned. The man called again, going after her, trying to get a good glimpse through the trees and brush.

Now Ned went to the edge of the plain, where the grass grew tall, and opened his fire bag. He blew on his embers, feeding more tinder to them, and in a moment had an open fire. He set it down amidst the driest tangle of grass and fed in more fuel. The fire spread swiftly, eagerly consuming the grass around it. It reached up, catching the incoming wind.

Ned stood back, watching the flames eat into the field. Fanned by the wind, they grew and traveled quickly. Smoke billowed up, announcing the fire's presence. The people in the center of the valley would see it soon enough, and would have to move, because the wind was carrying it right toward them.

There was a cry from the man who had been pursuing Jes, as he discovered the fire. He ran back—and spied Ned standing at the edge of the forest. He stepped toward Ned, then hesitated, uncertain whether to chase the man or try to deal with the fire.

Jes hooted behind the man. He turned to go after her again—and Ned hooted. They managed to make the man turn several times in confusion before he got smart and focused on just one of them: Jes. He charged after her. And she ran directly into the spreading fire.

The man stopped and stared. He did not realize that her wetted leggings protected her feet from the heat of the flames. He could not follow her, for his feet and legs were bare. He did not know what to do.

Ned hooted again. The man whirled, reminded of him. He charged. And Ned strode blithely into the fire himself.

Now he held his breath and ran as rapidly as he could, getting beyond the burning section. He found Jes there, waiting for him. The smoke was blowing at them, but they were able to duck their heads low and breathe freely, crossing the plain close to the fire. With luck there would be no man to block their way; all the men should be running for the other side of the plain, to avoid getting cut off by the fire. They would assume that Ned and Jes were still waiting to cross, rather than being already across. Because they would not be thinking very clearly, during the considerable distraction of the fire.

But one man *was* on the far side of the field. Bub had been cunning enough to keep one man back, just in case.

The fire was behind them, the man ahead. He had them—
he thought. He made gestures at them with hips and fist, as
of raping and bashing. He was big enough to handle both
of them.

They paused to pour the last of their water on their leggings. Then they ran back into the fire, holding their breath
again. They knew that the actual region of burning was narrow; the flames ate what they could and moved on, leaving
soot and ashes behind. So they were able to run through the
burned terrain, and the man could not follow. In fact he
could not remain where he was, for the fire was bearing
down on him. He fled.

They ran to the forest edge and hid themselves. Just in
time, for their leggings were hot and charring on the outside.
When the strings burned through, the leaf padding would
spill out even if it remained wet, so they had to watch it
carefully. They retreated into the safety of the forest cover,
then paused to remove their leggings and beat out the smol-
dering sections. They had made it through thanks to their
alertness and readiness to innovate. Ned was, in the process,
coming to appreciate his sister better than ever; he was
known as the smart member of their band, but she was staying right with him. If there ever should be a man who was
interested in courage, loyalty, and intellect, instead of a
pretty face and buxom body, Jes would be a rare prize.

They made their way toward the path that led up through
the next pass, pausing to dig out any edible roots they spied
along the way. They were somewhat worn after their chase
through the fire, for they had been carrying their burdens of
flint rocks as well as suffering the weight and clumsiness of
the leggings. But they knew they had to keep moving, for
the fire would not last long, and then the pursuit might resume.

They intercepted the general trail to the next pass—and
suddenly there was a man ahead of them. They turned, and
there was another behind them. They had after all walked
into a trap. Thinking themselves beyond pursuit, they had

let down their guard when they shouldn't have. What were they to do now? They could try to run back the way they had come, but that led nowhere, and the men were obviously fresher than they were. They couldn't escape.

"Fools. Caught," Ned said with deep disgust, speaking slowly and clearly in the foreign tribe manner.

"Thought. Here. No," Jes agreed in the same mode, for the benefit of the foreign males.

"Move toward the man in front," Ned said swiftly, in a low tone, knowing that the syntax and detail made this unintelligible to the others. "When he grabs you, bite his hand. I will stab him from behind. Then we must turn together on the other, without pause. Without mercy. Without remorse. Only desperate and forceful action will allow us to prevail. You know the consequence of failure."

"I understand," she said grimly. There would be no forbearance on either side. This was a fight for their lives. Then, for the men to hear: "Escape. No." She made a shrug of obvious hopelessness as she walked toward the lead man. Ned followed her, with similar show of resignation.

"Girl," the man said, smiling without niceness. Evidently the word had spread.

"Girl," Jes agreed, opening her netting to show her breasts. She inhaled, to give them more substance. Ned knew she was imitating Wona, who constantly flaunted her nice body. "Spare nice girl?"

"No. Make scream." The man grabbed for her, leering. She caught his leading hand with both of hers and hauled it into her mouth. She bit hard on his fingers, at the same time hauling him around so that his back was to Ned. She might be slight in the womanly curves, but she was strong in the manner of a man.

The man howled with pain, and tried to strike at her with his other hand. But now Ned was on him, thrusting at the man's exposed neck with his flint blade. The point dug in just above the bones and muscles of the shoulder. Ned pulled the blade back, and jammed it in again, trying to cut the tendons of the neck. It wasn't easy to do.

"Ned—behind you, coming fast," Jes said urgently. She still hung on to the man's hand, trying to bend his fingers backward, her teeth bared for another bite. Yet she was evidently looking beyond him, too.

Ned didn't turn his head to look. He jerked out the blade and whirled, throwing himself to the side. The second man lunged in, crashing against Ned's shoulder. And Ned stabbed him in the near eye. He felt the softness of it as the blade sank in, and the hardness as it came up against the bone of the eye socket. Hot fluid spurted onto Ned's hand.

The man fell, screaming, clutching at the other man. The two went down together, both badly injured, neither quite knowing the identity of the other. Ned and Jes drew away and fled, knowing that there would be no instant pursuit by these two.

When they were sure they were beyond immediate danger, they paused to hug each other. "I never did that to a man before," Ned said, his eyes flowing, the horror of it overwhelming him.

"You did what you had to," she said. "You did well. You did well. You are a man." But she was comforting him more in the manner of an elder sister, or a mother, now emulating Flo. Nonetheless, it helped.

In the prior volumes it was assumed that syntax was the key element that multiplied the effectiveness of human speech, facilitating the expression of complex concepts of time and condition: "Tomorrow, if you don't see me here, look for me in the next village." That is probably so, but this volume considers another aspect: velocity of speech. Suppose all concepts are expressible, but in one culture the language is slow, while in another it is fast. The fast one would have a distinct advantage. In fact all human languages are fast, the words proceeding so rapidly as to represent a liquid flow without many interruptions. Try listening to a for-

eign language to realize how confusingly swift it is; words can seldom be distinguished at all. The human brain had to develop the capacity to make sense of this phonic stream so that speech could proceed at jet speed, as it were, instead of walking speed. This was surely a potent innovation, taking time to perfect, and may have marked the difference between modern mankind and all others, such as Neandertal. Even in something as basic as physical combat, this linguistic velocity could make a significant difference, as shown here, and would have been a formidable survival trait. Of course it probably happened over the course of tens of thousands of years, and each increase in speed may have been slight, but the advantage was evidently sufficient. However it happened, there seems to be little doubt that the engine that powered mankind's phenomenal increases in brain size was language.

Clothing was surely also vital. Mankind lost fur and went erect to facilitate cooling, but when the weather changed that could have become a liability. But clothing would have more than made up the difference, because of its versatility. It could shield the human body from cold—and even on occasion from heat. It could be removed as convenient, or bundled on double. Thus it enabled mankind to go further yet in sacrificing his body fur; cold snaps no longer put him into dire straits. In fact, it enabled mankind to travel out of Africa, following Erectus, without suffering unduly from the colder climates there. With enough clothing, he could handle it better than lightly furred Erectus could. Travel to cooler climes had enabled Erectus to handle the excess heat production of his brain without having to sacrifice any more fur, and that was fine, for most of two million years, but not the best strategy for the long term. Thus his body itself had to change to adapt to the brutal cold of ice age Europe, while modern mankind had far less trouble there, or anywhere else.

Because he changed his clothing instead of his body.

With that final loss of fur he also became largely immune to parasites such as fleas, which surely improved his health. He retained hair only on his head, which still needed shielding from the sun, and in the groin, for adults. Why did pubic hair exist, in a region readily covered by clothing? Apparently to facilitate the aeration of genital hormones and odors. Perhaps particular men and women knew each other in the darkness by their individual smells, and were encouraged to make the effort of breeding when those smells were strong. At any rate, clothing may have been far more important to the final evolution of the species than has been recognized. By making it possible for that burgeoning brain to survive both extremes of heat and cold.

Worked furs and hides were surely the first clothing. But in time mankind discovered alternate ways to clothe himself. First he must have figured out how to salvage vines, as described, and work them into baskets, nets, and items of clothing. Later he found thinner fibers, but they were too short, so he found out how to twist them into threads, and threads into string, and then to knot the string into finer nets. This was the first primitive stage of what in time would become the weaving of cloth. Also, string twisted into rope would have been extremely useful, and nets could have served in lieu of skins in the manner shown here. The technology was as yet clumsy, and it left no trace in the early archaeological record because it rotted away, but surely full-fledged cloth did not spring fully developed from nothing. The artifacts of vine fiber may have served for a hundred thousand years before the refinements of cloth developed. The string skirt itself has survived from three or four thousand years ago, but we know it goes back beyond 20,000 years because its semblance appears on the "Venus" figurines (of which

more later). It was as described: a stunningly sexy out-
fit for nubile young women, and a great enhancement
for the triple ploy strategy in the covert contest between
men and women. Who needed cloth, at this stage? But
eventually the marvels of cloth would come. Whether
any such thing as the string skirt was used 150,000
years ago is wildly conjectural, but it is possible, given
the nature of the triple ploy. Today it manifests as the
provocative miniskirt.

But why such a giant brain? Once mankind managed
to forage in the hot savanna, and to scavenge for richer
food, he would seem to have had enough intellect to
survive. Once he adapted his mating scheme to provide
support and protection for women, the better to ensure
survival of offspring, no further intelligence was re-
quired there either. Why keep building the brain be-
yond any likely need to compete with other species?
This is where the arms race figures. Mankind did have
constant competition for the resources of his ecological
niche: variations of his own kind. They were constantly
fissioning off, setting up rival communities, and they
had much the same abilities he did. So who prevailed?
That subspecies that could do it best. For a time it
seemed that bigger and stronger men were the answer,
but in the end it seems to have been the gracile ones
with more versatile intelligence and speaking abilities.
So the race was between brains, and in the end the best
brain won. Ours.

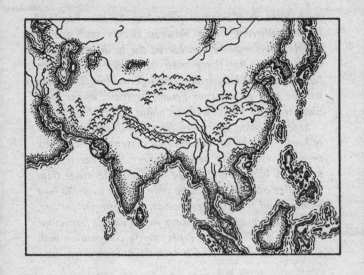

Chapter 5

NUMBERS

Numbers are important. If there are too few members of a given species, it dies out, lacking a viable breeding community. If there are too many for the habitat to sustain, there is apt to be competition and starvation. But even between those extremes, there are dynamics that make a real difference. This is especially true for mankind, a social creature. A lone person may survive for a year. A band of twenty-five is viable for perhaps 500 years if it interacts with other bands so as not to become inbred. A band of 100 is apt to frag-

ment, because of internal quarreling. So most bands of hunter-gatherers range between twenty and seventy people. That may be considered the basic unit of human society. But there must be exchanges between bands, for breeding, trade, and information. Thus they will be part of a larger group, or tribe, whose total number seems most viable at about 500 or 600.

Suppose some way were found to increase the size of human bands, so that internal dissent did not break them up when they became larger than the normal range? A larger band would have more leverage than a smaller one, and might be able to take over the best hunting and foraging territories, and prosper further. Such an advantage of numbers would enable particular bands to survive better, especially in competition with others of their kind. And it seems that such a way was found.

In the prior volumes there was a mystery: why did physically modern human beings emerge from Africa about 100,000 years ago, then remain in the Levant for 50,000 years before proceeding farther? Now it is known that they did not pause, physically, and probably not linguistically. They moved on to southeast Asia, where their traces have been dated back to about 70,000 years ago, and on from there. They seem to have stayed generally clear of the coldest or most mountainous terrain in that 50,000 years, however, which may explain their absence from Europe and central Asia. Perhaps they preferred to follow the convoluted coastlines of southern Asia, whose climate was more like that of the continent they had left. The setting is India, 90,000 years ago.

LIN HELD UP THE FINISHED skirt, pleased. It was a fine piece of work, consisting of a waist cord made of tendon, and long sections of leaves descending from it, with a pattern of alternating colors. She was still a child, but no one could tie leaves as prettily as she could.

"Put it on," Bry said.

Lin put the cord around her slender hips, and wrapped it twice around her small waist before tying it, so that the leaves overlapped, forming the skirt. She adjusted them so that the layers complemented each other. The colors brightened in the sunlight.

"It's good," he said. "Make it move."

She flexed her knees and did a bit of a dance, making the skirt swish aside, showing flashes of her thighs and bottom. Her body wasn't grown yet, so this lacked something, but she enjoyed pretending.

"You must model it at the gathering," he said.

"I couldn't," she said quickly.

"But you made it," he protested. "You should show it. You're pretty enough."

She held up her left hand, the fingers splayed. All six of them.

"Oh, yes," he said. "I forgot. But it's too bad. *Someone* will have to show off that skirt, so we can trade it well."

Lin shrugged, eyes downcast as she removed the skirt. There had been a time when Bry teased her about her hand, and they had fought, and she had flung dirt in his face. But Flo had talked to him, about the need for siblings to defend each other, and Ned had remarked on misfortune, which was Bry's own private dread. Bry believed that each member of their sibling group was cursed in some way, and that his curse was to suffer bad luck in whatever was really important to him. He had taken heed of their concerns, recognizing his affinity with Lin, and now he helped her hide her embarrassment. He had become socially conscious in a hurry, and she appreciated it. She needed a friend who really understood, and he had become that friend. Just as Ned and Jes were friends as well as siblings, and Sam and Flo. The distinction was important, just as it was between friends and lovers.

"I'll ask Ned," he said, and ran off to find their band brother.

Lin carefully coiled the skirt, making it look like a simple bundle of leaves. She was proud of her handiwork, but had never been able to present her art in public. It was hard enough just foraging. It was all right with Sam's band, though Sam's wife Wona would stare deliberately. But when they encountered folk of other bands, Lin always withdrew, even if she had to go hungry. It just wasn't worth the humiliation.

Bry came running back. "Ned says cover your hands! With skirts."

"Skirts?" she asked blankly.

"Little ones to match the big one. It will be a nice ploy. They will laugh, but like it."

Lin went still, which was her way when a revelation came upon her. She could cover her hands with miniature skirts, and her extra finger would not show! Then she could appear in public without embarrassment. Ned, always the smartest member of their band, had come through again.

She took some scraps of tendon left over from prior projects and tied small leaves to them, alternating colors. She wrapped them around her fingers, pinning them with thorns. Now she had two temporary little skirts that would conceal the main parts of her hands, leaving only the thumbs free.

Then she realized that this wouldn't do. "Why should I cover my hands, if there's nothing wrong with them?" she asked rhetorically.

Bry took off again. Lin gazed at her impromptu gloves, wishing she could use them, covering both hands so as not to draw attention to the defective one. She couldn't weave with her fingers covered, she couldn't eat, she couldn't forage, but she could model skirts, and she could even make gloves to match what she modeled, enhancing the effect. It could be so nice, if only she had some obvious reason that wasn't the real one.

Bry came charging back. "Ned says because your fingers

are stained with dye, and you don't want to ruin the impression." He gulped a breath. "Also, make them match the skirt, for the art of it."

And she did use dye, gathered from berries and roots and different kinds of dirt. It was no good for leaves, but it could make the fur clothing distinct, and that appealed to many people. She usually made the body paint for this family, too. It was a job to find out what wouldn't wash out the first time it rained, but some juices worked better than others. And the best ones did stain her fingers for several days. The stain did not wipe off on other things, but most folk would not know that, and anyway, different dyes were different; some might wipe off. So Ned had given her another good answer. And a good backup answer, using the hand skirts to enhance the main skirt. She had actually thought of that aspect herself, before Ned suggested it, which made her feel extremely smart. She could be in public.

She grabbed Bry by the head and kissed him hard on the cheek. "Hey, what's that for?" he demanded.

"For Ned," she replied. "Take it to him."

He laughed. "You'll have to do that yourself. I don't do kisses."

"I will," she said, and set out to find Ned.

They were all there at the gathering: the members of Sam's band, and the members of two other larger bands. Joe's and Bub's bands. Joe's folk were generally all right, but Bub's could at times be mean. Dirk and Wona, the mates of Flo and Sam, had come from Joe's band, so they knew most of the people there. But Bub's Green Feather band had a private grudge against Sam's band, and especially against Ned and Jes, who had outmaneuvered them on a trading deal. So there might be trouble, though there was supposed to be no fighting at gatherings.

The trading was brisk. Bub's band had assorted flints, chipped into serviceable knives and tools. Joe's band had fine pelts from unusual animals, worked until they were quite soft and flexible. Sam's band had assorted dyed hides, leaf skirts, and reed-woven baskets. Lin walked around, with one of her skirts on her torso, and the miniature matching skirts on her hands, and when someone wished to trade for one, Jes would remove the one Lin wore and hand it over, and put another on her. "You are doing well," Jes murmured to her. "You make the skirts look better."

Lin was pleased, because if she could do this well as a child, how much better she should be able to do when she was grown. She was pretty now, and would be lovely then, if she could hide her hand. This was the first time she had been able to model the skirts for trade, instead of letting Woña do it. That was a real satisfaction.

But there was another purpose to these gatherings: women. Young women needed to find new homes, and men needed to obtain mates. So there was a good deal of looking around. Lin looked around too. She was as yet too young, but not by all that much, so she had an interest. Of course no man would consider her, once he saw her hand, so speculation about the future was idle. Still, it was nice to pretend.

As evening came, the trading slacked off, and Lin no longer modeled the skirts. She removed her hand skirts, closed her left hand tight, and looked around. The nudity of her body did not bother her; it was standard for children, but her hand was always a concern. She saw that someone had started a large fire. It seemed to be a boy, which surprised her, because this was normally a man's job. So she went over for a closer look—and was further surprised. It was a girl! Rather, a woman, for she had her baby parked nearby.

The woman saw Lin looking. "Hello, girl," she called. "Do you like fire?"

"Yes," Lin confessed.

"Well, come help me build this up," the woman said. "It needs to be big enough for everyone to sit around."

But if she started using her hands, her extra finger would show. So Lin tried to demur. "I—"

"Or would you like to hold Crystal while I fetch in more wood? I don't like to leave her alone."

"Oh, yes," Lin agreed. She loved holding babies. Then, belatedly, she introduced herself. "I'm Lin, of Sam's band."

"I'm Ember, of Joe's band," the woman replied. She picked up the baby, passed her to Lin, and followed a path out to forage for more wood.

Lin sat holding the baby girl, gazing into the fire. She liked Ember, because Ember trusted her with her precious child. And babies didn't care how many fingers a person had.

But there was a woman staring at her. Lin knew who she was, from memory and descriptions: the notorious Sis, Bub's sister or consort; it wasn't quite clear which. That was one case where the distinctions between sibling, friend, and lover seemed seriously blurred. By all accounts Sis was a beautiful but sharp-edged creature, who would do whatever she thought she had to, to get her way or her brother's way. She must have noticed Lin's hand, and was contemplating some mischief. But she did not approach, and after a while went elsewhere, to Lin's relief.

A man advanced to the fire, carrying a huge armful of wood. He dumped it down beside the sticks already there. He glanced at Lin. "Why, hello, Ember," he said.

"Oh, I'm not Ember," Lin protested quickly. "She went to fetch wood."

He paused, seeming surprised, looking at her more closely. "Oh, I thought you must be Ember, because you are holding Crystal."

"No, I'm Lin, of Sam's band. This isn't my baby. I'm not old enough to have one."

"But pretty enough," he said. "Are you looking for a man?"

"No!" she exclaimed, fearing a frightful misunderstanding. Didn't he see that she was a naked child?

But he laughed. "I shouldn't tease you, Lin. I am Scorch—Crystal's father. I am glad to see you taking good care of her."

Lin just stared at him, flushing, not knowing what to say.

Ember returned with more wood. "Are you teasing innocent girls again, Scorch?" she asked as she set down her load.

"Only the pretty ones," Scorch said. "See what a fine baby this one has."

"But I'm not pretty," Lin said, hopelessly flustered. "My hand—" Worse yet. She shouldn't have mentioned that.

Scorch glanced at his wife, evidently realizing that his teasing had gone awry. Ember squatted before Lin, but didn't take the baby. "Look at this," she said, stretching out one arm. There was a long ugly burn-scar on it. "And this." She showed a knee, blotched with scar tissue. "I have such marks all over my body, because of my trade. Does that make me ugly?"

"Oh, no!" Lin cried. "But—"

"And Scorch has worse marks. But I think he's handsome, and he thinks I'm beautiful. Are we mistaken?"

"But you got those marks from fire," Lin said. "They are normal."

Ember reached out and took Lin's left hand. "I see several perfect fingers here. Who is to say what is normal?" She glanced at Scorch. "Would you mate with such a woman?"

"One as pretty as that?" he replied. "I wouldn't even notice her hands."

"But others—"

Ember nodded. "But I take your point, Lin. There are those who judge by the wrong things. Keep your hand hidden, if you wish; we will not discuss this further." Then she took back her baby.

Lin remained by the fire, liking these folk, who had gone

out of their way to reassure her. Maybe there would be a man for her after all, when she came of age.

When the fire was high, the others took places around it. It was time for the entertainment, while several men roasted a slain ox and carved off hunks of the meat for all present to eat. Others set up a vat made from a hollowed log, filled with water and a number of squished fruits and berries to flavor it. Each person could dip a cup in it to drink. Lin was intrigued by the tang of it, and not long after she drank she felt pleasantly/slightly dizzy. That made the activities that much more fun. The nubile girls came out to dance, forming a ring around the fire, showing their breasts and kicking their legs high so that their leaf skirts parted and showed the men of other bands what they had to offer. Jes was there, and she looked pretty good in the skirt, but she was too tall and spare and homely, compared to the other girls. Which was too bad, because Jes was a really nice person.

"But one is missing," a woman said. It was Sis. "That girl should join them. She's pretty enough." She pointed to Lin.

And Lin didn't have her hand covers now. She would stand exposed to all the folk of the gathering. She would embarrass herself, and her band. Which was what Sis intended: to shame the band her brother disliked. To turn Lin's prettiness against her by exposing her deformity.

She wanted to demur, to get out of this, but all eyes were turning on her. What could she do?

Then Ember spoke. "Isn't that Lin, who modeled the skirts, enhancing them with matching hand sets? Yes, she must dance for us—with the three skirts together."

Lin called down silent spirit blessings on the woman for that considerate suggestion.

Flo got up and hurried across to Lin, carrying the things she needed. Sam followed her, evidently having been advised what to do. "Yes, the dance of staff and hands," Flo said.

Suddenly Lin realized what they intended. They did have

a dance they had devised without hand decorations. Now the little skirts had been made a part of it.

In a moment the skirts were on, and she was facing her band brother, the leader of their band. "We will show them how we dance," Sam said somewhat grimly. He was angry about the spot they had been put in, but his anger was not directed at Lin.

And so they danced, as the nubile maidens gave way to leave them room. Sam was massively muscular, and he carried his heavy staff, potentially deadly as a weapon. But he used it in the way they had when relaxing as a tribe alone, swinging it grandly at her, low, so she could nimbly leap over it. She did so, her skirts swinging around her body and hands as she turned.

Sam swung again, this time at her head. She raised her hands in foolishly inadequate defense—and the staff bounced off her crossed wrists. There was a murmur of surprise from the folk watching; Sam had made it look real, as they did in the game. He could make his muscles bulge with the force of his strike, yet Lin's touch would deflect it. It was part of the game they played. Now it made the miniature skirts seem magic.

The audience loved it. It did not take the people long to figure out the device, but the notion of a little girl having such power against a huge man was hilarious. And Lin realized that the two of them were good at it; it *was* a dance, because their moves were practiced. He had the power and balance of the effective hunter he was, and she had the nimbleness of the child she was.

They circled the fire once, then finished with a flair: He aimed a huge blow at her, but she pranced in close and kissed him on the cheek. He staggered back, as if suffering a mortal blow, while she lifted her hands in victory. Everyone laughed.

Then they sat down, and the regular show continued. Lin had been too nervous to be dizzy while afoot, but now she was giddy with relief and flushed with success. She *had*

danced, and not made a fool of herself. Now she could enjoy
the rest of the gathering without fear.

A hand touched hers. It was Bry, giving her a friendly
squeeze. "You were lovely," he murmured.

"I think I was," she agreed, appreciating his appreciation
and support.

"They were laughing with you, not at you."

"Yes." That was what made it so good.

When the girls were done, a man with a good voice led
the group in singing hunting songs. Then came a storyteller,
who held all the children and a number of adults rapt with
his tales of the history of their tribe, to which all three bands
belonged, speaking the same language. He told how they
had come from a huge wonderful land under the setting sun
so long ago that even the sun hardly remembered it, and
followed the paths along the line between the mountainous
terrain and the great restless sea, until they found this, their
homeland. He told how life had been wonderful, until the
land dried up and the game fled, so that they had to flee too,
staying always near the water. But now they were in the
land the spirits liked, and were doing well.

Lin had heard the tales before, but they always fascinated
her. Normally there was just her band, the women foraging
in their territory while the men hunted, with occasional contacts with their neighboring bands. But this gave her a much
larger view, and she realized that they were part of a people
whose ancestors went way back to that strange good land
where the sun set, and that if that land hadn't dried up, the
people would still be there. That was an awesome concept.

At last it was time to sleep, and the three bands withdrew
to their sections, and the people lay down under their blankets of leaf mat and fur. Some of the young women, Lin
knew, would get under the blankets of men they had encountered today. The men really liked that. Tomorrow the
bands would return to their own territories, and resume ordinary life. Until the next gathering, with other bands.

It was fun, yet routine. But Lin had gained something precious, this time: hope for her own future.

When groups of people exceeded a certain size, the rivalry and quarrelsomeness of the males became disruptive. This effectively limited the size of individual bands, and of tribes. But there was a counterforce that seems to be unique to mankind: the arts. The human species appreciates such arts as song, dance, tale-telling, and tapestry weaving, and this appreciation enables larger groups to assemble without quarreling unduly. People can sit and watch a performance, their attention diverted from their immediate rivalries or grudges, and can participate in group arts, their energies expressed positively. Thus the bands of people who appreciated the arts grew larger than the bands of those without art, and they had more power. If a band of ten encountered a band of twenty, competing for a given resource, the band of twenty would normally prevail. If a tribe could muster more and larger bands than another tribe could, it was likely to prevail. So the arts may have been mankind's secret weapon. Art may be what distinguishes our species from all others, and what enabled us to marshal sufficient cooperating numbers to conquer the world.

Chapter 6

SPIRIT GIRL

Mankind traveled the path of least resistance and best food supply, the boundary between land and sea. There was always vegetation there, and fish and clams. Such association with the water inevitably led to the development of rafts or boats, which were extremely useful for carrying possessions as well as people. Such boats would gradually become more sophisticated with experience, and increasingly seaworthy. Their advantages of convenience and safety could have been such that a culture evolved that was tied into them; women and children would remain in covered boats, rather than in any landbound dwellings, and much foraging could have been done directly from them. When a storm threatened, they would have brought the boats to shore, perhaps beaching them and tying them to trees—and remaining in them as shelters. Such folk could have traveled extremely rapidly, as human migrations go, and quickly traversed all the available coastlines of the world, and explored the larger rivers. They did move on down to Australia perhaps 50,000 years ago; increasingly earlier indications are being found. Since Australia was not connected by land, they had to have been able to cross some open sea. Thus we know they had boats 50,000 years ago, despite having found no direct evidence of them. Similar boats could have taken them on up the east coast of Asia—all the way to Beringia, the land that once connected Siberia to Alaska—and on down the American west coast, and on to the east coast, by circling South America or crossing the narrow land in Central America and resuming water travel on the other side. No barrier of ice would have balked them, because they would simply have boated around it, bundled against the cold and drawing their food from the sea. Until they reached the warmer latitudes, and foraged again from the land as well. It could have happened—but did it? The setting is the east coast of South America, 33,000 years ago.

"STORM," JES SAID TERSELY. "GET to cover."

Bry looked. She was right; clouds were looming ahead, piling high above land and sea. Clouds always seemed unmoving when looked at, but could expand alarmingly when not watched. He grabbed a paddle, and so did Jes. He was a child and she was a woman, but he knew how to use his paddle, and she was much like a man in physical structure, so they were able to help. They stroked from either side, balancing against each other, making it efficient.

Ned turned the rudder, causing the long boat to turn toward land. Sam hauled harder on the oars, driving it swiftly through the water. He had more arm power than the rest of them put together, and was the main propulsive force.

The other boat turned similarly. Dirk was rowing that, while Flo steered. He saw his sister Lin in the other boat, watching out for rocks. She was too small to be of much help with paddle or rudder, but she had sharp eyes and her clever fingers were excellent when weaving baskets or tying skirts. The other women and children stayed out of the way. None of them wanted to get swamped in a storm.

But they ran afoul of a bad current that tried to carry them back out to sea. This was unfamiliar territory, so they did not know the local problems. The water had its paths, just as did the land, and once they were known they were useful; but when they were strange, they were treacherous. Ordinarily they could simply work their way around the adverse current, but at the moment they couldn't afford the time. The storm was advancing rapidly.

"There is a fair current behind us," Ned said. "Turn; it's our best chance."

Sam lifted his oars, panting, while Bry and Jes paddled in opposite directions, causing the craft to turn about its center. The boat looked clumsy, but wasn't; it had an outrigger to stabilize it, and a keel to steady its direction. They had traveled far in it, forging on northward toward new shores. Because the old shores to the south were losing their vitality, getting fished and foraged out. It was always necessary to move on after a time.

They started moving back, while Ned searched for a suitable emergency harbor. He called out the new direction, and the boat moved toward it, followed by her sister craft. But the storm came faster, and now its winds reached out and tried to suck them into the darkness of it. They pushed the craft aside, away from the proper course.

"Rock!" Ned cried in alarm.

It was on Bry's side, almost submerged. He stuck out his

paddle to push against it, to ease them by it without damage.
All of them were versed in such emergency measures, because hidden rocks were a common threat to fragile boats.
But a wave crashed into them from the other side, half
swamping them, and the sudden force of the current jerked
Bry's paddle out of his hands. He was off-balance, his support suddenly gone. He screamed as he fell into the rough
water.

His head went under before he got oriented and stroked
for the surface. He was a good swimmer, of course; all the
shore folk were. But a fierce current caught him and hauled
him around beyond the rock and out to sea.

He had just one lucky break: he saw his paddle floating
beside him. He grabbed it and hung on as the full fury of
the storm struck. He knew his family in the boat would not
be able to help him; they had to make it to shore in a hurry,
or all would perish. So he didn't even concern himself with
that. He simply clung to his paddle, knowing that it would
help him float without wearing himself out. He was in trouble, but knew that the danger would be much worse if he
lost his common sense. Right now he had to focus on staying afloat.

The storm beat down all around him. But he had been in
rough water before. He relaxed, his arms locked around the
paddle so that it kept his head lifted, and held his breath
each time the waves got too bad. He could ride it out, because he mostly floated up and down with the waves, letting
them carry him where they would. He hoped they would
not take him impossibly far out to sea, because if he couldn't
see the land, he wouldn't know where to swim. However,
he did know that the land was toward the setting sun, so he
might find it anyway.

There was a jolt, and pain in his side. He had been swept
into a rock. He looked, and saw no blood in the swirling
water, which was a relief. It was just a bruise, not a wound.
It was not good to bleed in the water, because that attracted

sharks and crocodiles. If one of them came, he would be quickly finished.

Could that be the realization of his curse? To get cut in the water, so that the predators of the sea would tear him apart? Bry tried not to think of that, but it was impossible not to.

As it happened, the storm soon passed, and daylight remained, and the land was not far distant. He looked around, hoping to spy a boat, but there was nothing. He didn't know if they had made it to shore, or sunk, or been carried out of sight. But the boats were tough and stable; probably they were all right, somewhere. All he had to do was find them.

First he had to get to land, because it wasn't safe in the water, now that it was calming. He oriented his paddle for swimming, and started toward the shore.

Ouch! His left side hurt the moment he tried to stroke with his arms. His ribs had been bashed in, and though it didn't hurt much when he breathed shallowly, any greater effort quickly brought warning pain.

He experimented and found that he could still kick hard with his feet without suffering unduly. So he did that, and made slow progress toward the shore.

It was almost dark by the time he waded onto land. Mosquitos formed a cloud around him. But he knew how to handle them. He searched until he found one of the plants that repelled them. He took a leaf, chewed on it to break down its surface, and rubbed it across his face and body. The mosquitos still hovered, and landed, but no longer bit; they couldn't get by the juice of the plant.

He saw no sign of the others. If they had come to shore, it wasn't here. He heard nothing: no sounds of camping, no calling. He knew better than to walk the shore alone at night; his paddle would serve as staff and club, but there were creatures who could come at him in the darkness.

His side was aching, now that he was out of the water; the effort of walking aggravated it. He had to get into a protected place where he could rest and sleep safely. Maybe

the others would come looking for him next day, or maybe
he would see the boats passing. He knew they wouldn't
simply let him go without a search; the family always
looked out for its own, ever since they had been orphaned
four years ago. But sometimes they did get separated, and
had to look out for themselves.

He found a good tree, and lifted his hands to haul himself
up into it. But his side hurt intolerably, and he couldn't. He
would have to find one much easier to climb, or stay on the
ground. He didn't like that.

Bry retied his loin-band and walked along the beach,
peering at trees as the darkness shrouded the forest, but he
didn't see anything suitable. The beach curved, until he was
heading west; he must be at the mouth of a great river. He
dipped his hand in the water and tasted it: yes, it was fresh.
That was good. But fresh water was where the crocodiles
were, and they did not necessarily stay in the water if they
saw prey close by. He had to find a good tree.

Maybe there would be a path leading inland. He did not
want to go far from the shore, but he had to find a place to
safely rest and sleep. The others would know to look for
him along a path; people never strayed far from paths, because paths gave direction and competence to their travels.

Then he saw something. It was an outrigger boat, similar
to the ones his family used, but smaller. Then there was a
figure walking toward it—a woman, in a brief skirt. He had
found his family! "Ho!" he called gladly, walking toward
her.

The woman looked his way—and he realized by her
stance and manner that she wasn't anyone he knew. She
was a stranger, and that could mean another kind of trouble.
He stopped.

Then the woman walked toward him. She was lithe and
lovely, every motion elegant. She had flowing brown hair
and eyes to match. Her breasts were perfectly formed and
balanced. In fact, she was the most beautiful woman he
could remember seeing. He was eleven, not yet of age to

get serious about women, but he was stunned by this one.

"You're a boy," she said, as if surprised. Her accent and inflections were strange, but clear enough. So she was not from a close tribe. "What are you doing alone? Where is your family?"

"The storm—the boats—I don't know."

She smiled understandingly, bringing a thrill to his pulse. "And your ribs are bruised. You floated in with the paddle. I thought at first it was a spear. Who are you?"

"Bry," he said. "Of Sam's family."

She cocked her head, thinking. "I don't know that name. But you could have come from beyond our range, in the boat. I am Anne, of Hugh's family. We have two children."

So she was married and with children: no prospect for romance even if he had been of age. It was amazing how well preserved she was. "I was looking for a tree for the night," he explained. "One I could get into without climbing."

"Lift your arm," she said. When he obeyed, raising it as far as he could before the pain increased, she stepped close and touched his bruised ribs. Her pressure brought a surge of pain, but also pleasure, for even her fingers were beautiful. "Not broken, I think," she said. "But that will take time to heal. You will not be able to paddle for a moon or more."

"Yes," he agreed wanly.

"Come with me." She turned and walked away. Her buttocks under the skirt were as well formed as the rest of her. She was one healthy woman throughout.

He followed, glad that she knew of a suitable tree. But she led him to a path, and followed the path to a shelter built on a rocky outcropping. It was her house.

Two naked children emerged: a boy of about five, and a girl of about three. They stared at Bry.

"This is Bry, of Sam's family," Anne said. "He will stay with us while he looks for their boats." The children smiled in tentative welcome. "And this is my son Chip," Anne continued, indicating the boy, who lifted a hand in formal greeting. "And my daughter Mina." The little girl smiled again, this time brilliantly. She had black hair and dark eyes, and was a beautiful creature in her own right. "Get him some fruit."

Both children scrambled back into the house, and emerged a moment later with ripe fruits. Bry accepted them gladly, suddenly realizing how hungry he was. Mina touched his hand for a moment, staring into his eyes. He was taken aback; there was something special about her.

Anne led him into the house. "Make him a bed," she told the children, and again they scrambled.

He was to stay in their house? "But you don't know me!" he protested. "I am foreign."

Anne turned her gaze directly on him. "Do you seek to harm any of us?" she inquired. In that moment he realized that she was aware of her power over him. His slack expression must have given him away. He could neither hurt nor deceive such a lovely woman, ever. Or those she protected.

"Never," he said sincerely, and all three of them laughed.

"Mina decided you were all right," Chip said. "She knows."

The little girl had made the decision? Certainly Bry bore this family no malice, and much appreciated their help, but this was strange indeed. How could they be sure she wasn't mistaken about a stranger?

"She never is," Chip said, and they laughed again at Bry's expression. "We got her from a dead place, and she knows the spirits."

"A dead place?"

"She had been left to die," Anne said. "We took her, and the spirits have been kind to us ever since."

Bry looked at Mina again. Could it be? Flo had left her first baby, because she had no man and couldn't support a child then. Three years ago. The time was right. Yet that had been far away, south along the coast. So it couldn't be.

Yet if he looked at the child that way, he could see an aspect of his big sister in her. Flo had been attractive when younger, before she got fat, and the dark hair matched. How nice it would be if Flo's child had joined this nice family!

Mina met his gaze again, smiling enigmatically. "Maybe," she said.

This was eerie.

"Bed's ready," Chip announced. "Try it."

Obligingly, Bry lay on the leafy bed. It was quite comfortable. He hadn't realized how tired he was. He bit into the fruit, relaxing.

He woke in complete darkness, realizing that he had slept without even finishing his fruit; it was still in his hand. So he finished the fruit, and went back to sleep.

In the morning he saw that there was one more in the house: a man. That would be Hugh. He must have been out hunting until late.

Hugh was already awake, and beckoned as he saw Bry stir. Bry got up and followed him outside, leaving the others asleep.

"You have a problem," Hugh said abruptly. "We have a problem too. Mina thinks you are the answer to ours. Perhaps we can be the answer to yours."

"I need to find my family," Bry said, somewhat diffident in the presence of the husband of as lovely a creature as Anne. Hugh must have some very strong ability that didn't show, because he was ordinary in appearance and manner. "And my ribs make me weak."

"Yes. We feel you should not travel alone at this time. Your ribs must heal. You can watch the water for boats from here as well as from anywhere, and it is safer. What we offer you is a safe place to stay while you heal and look. Foraging and fishing are good, so you will not go hungry."

"But I thought—only for the night."

"Mina says it will be half a moon before your boats

come. They must make repairs, and there were other injuries.''

"But she's a little child! How can she know?"

"Have you looked into her eyes?"

Bry spread his hands, acknowledging refutation. That little child was like none other he had encountered. "What you offer me is generous beyond anything owed a friend, let alone a stranger who can't work hard to help," Bry said. "What is there I can do for you in return?"

"We are entertainers. We make music and dance, and are rewarded with gifts. We travel in a circuit along the banks of the rivers, from family to family, staying a few days with each, teaching them what we do. When we finish, we have only a short distance to go to return to our house here, which is centrally located. Then we relax for a moon, before starting again. The children travel with us, and help in what we do.''

"They dance?"

"And more. But word has spread of an ailment that is passing through families. It makes children sicken and die. We do not want our children to be visited by these malign spirits.''

"But how—?"

"The spirits seem to move from child to child. They do not move between families that have no contact. So if our children do not go there, they will not sicken. But we are a small family, and have had no one else to protect and care for our children. Now you are here. We ask you to do that.''

"But I am a child myself!" Bry protested. "And with my weakness, I can not protect them."

"Mina believes you can. The spirits give her information. But your boats may appear in half a moon, while our circuit will require a full moon. We ask you not to leave until our return. You will not be able to paddle well then anyway, so perhaps it is not too great a sacrifice.''

Bry was somewhat awed by the prospect. "If you think

I can do it, I will do it until you return. I know my family
will understand."

Hugh clapped him on the shoulder, with a very light touch
so that the ribs did not react with a jolt of pain. "Then it is
agreed. The children will show you where things are and
what to do. And it should not be bad. Mina said there is
one bad time, and a lot of work, but that the rest is good.
And she wants to meet your sister."

Did she mean Flo? What a weird business! "It is agreed,"
he said.

"Now we shall celebrate the agreement in our fashion,"
Hugh said. He brought out a wooden flute and began to play.

Bry was amazed. The man was good—very good. The
notes fairly tumbled over each other, beautifully, like miniature cascades in a steep stream, making a melody as intricate and lovely as the spirits of nature themselves. Bry
had heard music before, many times, but had never known
that it could be that beautiful. The man was a true master.

There was a stir at the house. Anne emerged, in a different
skirt, this one made from grass tied together at the waist.
She was dancing, her bare feet stepping to the music of the
flute, and when she spun the grass flung out and up, showing
her thighs, and her hair spread similarly, showing her dainty
ears. What a woman she was!

Behind her came Chip, his legs marching, his hand beating time on a little drum he carried. And Mina, in her own
little grass skirt, rising to her toes and spinning just as her
mother did.

The three of them made their dancing way down to the
spot where Hugh was playing, and finished with an accelerated cadence of drum beat and feet, and a double whirl
that made the skirts rise until they were almost flat disks
around the woman and the girl. The effect was not only
artistic, it was marvelously seductive; Anne surely had devastating impact on grown men, despite being clearly beyond
her maiden stage. Then suddenly everything stopped, together, and all was still.

Bry realized that his mouth was hanging open. Never before had he seen an act as coordinated and beautiful as that. They were all so *good* at what they did!

"Of course the children are still learning," Hugh said. He played a sudden riff of notes, and Chip brought out a little flute of his own and was able to play only a few of them. Anne moved her hips as if her torso had turned to liquid, then did a high kick with her toe reaching the level of her shoulder; Mina wriggled her body and kicked as high as her waist. That was still better than Bry could have done, on any of it. Once again it made him realize that he would be a man before long.

"Now we must be off," Hugh said. He and Anne fetched hide packs from the house, slung them on their backs, lifted staffs, and walked down to the river.

"Already?" Bry asked, dismayed.

Mina set her little hand on his. "They will return in a moon," she said reassuringly, as the two hauled their boat into the water, put the packs into it, and changed the staffs for paddles. They started paddling efficiently, and soon disappeared upstream. The children waved them bye-bye, smiling bravely.

But in this, too, Mina wasn't perfect. Bry saw the tears in her eyes. He put his right arm around her and squeezed reassuringly, though he had substantial doubts of his own.

"They don't want us to catch fever and die," Chip explained. Then he swallowed and changed the subject. "Let's fish."

There were spears in the house. This was something Bry did know. They went down to the river's edge and waited with spears poised. When a fish swam close, Bry stabbed suddenly with the point of the wooden pole. His ribs gave him a jolt of pain, but he was lucky: he speared the fish. He brought it up flopping. He pulled it off and set it in the basket Mina provided, then used a stone edge to sharpen the point again.

Chip tried for the next fish, with his smaller spear. He

missed, and missed again, but kept trying. "Aim where the fish will go, not where it is," Bry suggested, and next time Chip managed to snag one, off-center. It was another lucky thrust, but it did make it look as if Bry's advice had helped. The truth, he knew, was that no one could be sure of spearing a fish with any particular thrust; much patience was necessary, and if every third or fourth thrust nabbed a fish, that was good.

The children showed him where the best foraging was, along the edge of the forest, where there were fruit trees, nut trees, berry bushes, and herbs. The grubs were fat in fallen wood, too. Paths went to all the good places, showing the truly human nature of this region. It was evident that they would be eating well; the parents had selected this site for its ready access to food, and had prepared it well.

In the evening they gathered wood and brought up the fire. They didn't need it for heat, but for dryness and comfort. They stared into it, and Bry told stories of his family to entertain the children. They were fascinated by the way the six children had been orphaned by a terrible storm, being on land while their parents tried to bring the boats to shore. Sudden storms were the bane of shore boaters. Bry told how the eldest, Sam and Flo, had assumed the job of the lost parents, and after lean times the six of them had finally gotten established as a wider family itself. But he didn't speak of Flo's rape and the child she left; the implications were too uncertain.

At last, talked out, they slept. Chip made a point of sleeping in his own bed, but Mina moved close enough to catch Bry's hand for reassurance. She was a remarkable little girl, but also, after all, very young.

Three days later it happened. Mina woke tense, looking fearfully around. Bry saw nothing, but her nervousness made him nervous too. She was too much in tune with the spirits; her fear might be groundless, but Bry did not care to gamble on that. So he went out and checked all around the house, looking for the tracks of predators or for anything unusual in the water. He saw nothing.

Still, he was watchful as Chip and Mina emerged from the house. He knew it wouldn't help to ask her what she was afraid of; her awareness was not of such a nature. What she knew came to her on its own, and could not be consciously evoked. The spirits could not be commanded by living folk.

They had been improving on their fish spearing, day by day; the fish were good when roasted on the fire, and even when they didn't manage to spear any, it was fun trying. The days tended to get dull, because they never ranged far from the house. Dullness was preferable to danger, while the adults were away. So as the day warmed, they took spears and basket and went to the water's edge.

But the fish were slow in coming. There was only a mossy log floating slowly by. They waited patiently; once the log passed, the fish would fill in the space. Chip squatted, spear posed, and Bry stood behind him, watching.

Suddenly the log opened a huge mouth and lunged at them. Mina screamed almost before it happened. It was a crocodile! Chip, closest to it, lurched to his feet, lost his balance, and fell back on the sand. The narrow snout swung toward him.

Bry brought his spear up and plunged it at the monster. He was only dimly conscious of the pain at his ribs as he did so; the threat was making it fade. The point bounced off the tough green snout without doing any apparent damage. He realized that it was foolish to strike at the hard parts; he needed to go for the vulnerable ones. So he jabbed at the nearer eye. But it was hard to score on; the creature was moving, and the eye was small, and when the point touched it, it closed, and the spear slid on past it.

But at least it was a distraction, for the crocodile did not snap at Chip. The boy scrambled away, leaving his small spear behind. Mina's screaming was continuous in the background; this was surely what she had feared, without knowing its identity.

They retreated from the water's edge, getting clear of the menace. The river had become fearsome, but the land represented safety, in this case.

However, the crocodile was not giving up. Perhaps realizing that these creatures were after all vulnerable on land, it crawled on out of the water, orienting malevolently on Bry. He did not dare turn his back on it, and he was afraid that if he backed away too fast, he would trip and fall. So he kept jabbing at the eyes, forcing the heavy eyelids to close, momentarily baffling the thing.

But something more was needed. Even when fully healthy, he could not hope to hold off a crocodile for long. This was by no means a large one; it was not much longer than Bry himself. It must have been attracted to the fish remnants they had left in the water. But it was big enough to do them real damage, once its teeth closed on flesh. He had to balk it decisively, so as to make it go away. He knew it would be impossible to kill it. Those enormously long, mighty jaws—

Then he had a notion. "A rope!" he cried. "Fetch a rope!" He did not look to see if the children were doing it, because he dared not take his eyes from the crocodile. In the instant he looked away from it, it could loom up and get him, like a storm cloud.

In a moment Chip was back with the cord woven from fibers. "A loop!" Bry said. "Make a big loop!"

Fumblingly, the boy worked the cord into a loop, the kind used to hold on to an outcropping when a person was using the rope to climb. The harder the pull on the rope, the tighter the loop became.

"Now we must get it over that snout!" Bry gasped.

Chip, showing increasing courage, approached with the loop. But Bry realized that it was simply too dangerous for the small boy to get that close to the monster. "Give me the rope!" he cried.

Chip held it out, and Bry grabbed it. He tossed aside the spear, then made a leap in the direction the crocodile did not expect: toward its mouth. Nevertheless, its reaction was swift. The snout came up to meet him, the jaws parting—and he put the loop over and jerked it tight. He knew he had been lucky to do it just right on the first try; he might never have gotten a second chance.

The crocodile whipped its head back and forth, aware of the impediment. Bry hung on, feeling his ribs being wrenched, but knowing that this was his only avenue to any kind of victory. He kept jerking on the rope, and with each jerk the loop pulled more tightly around the snout.

The crocodile lunged at him, the tip of its snout touching his leg. But now it was closed; the teeth could not bite. Still, the animal seemed to think that because its jaws were closed, it must have something pinned between them; it rolled quickly over, trying to drown its catch. But of course this didn't work. Bry kept stepping back, hauling on the rope.

Finally the crocodile had had enough. It righted itself and scrambled back toward the water. "But you've got our rope!" Bry cried, following.

He heard a giggle. It was Mina. Then he realized how foolish he was being: chasing after a crocodile! What was he going to do—go into the water to remove the rope? He let go of it and watched the creature splash away. But it was sad to lose the valuable rope.

It took them some time to relax, after that. Mina led the way, her apprehension gone. "I knew there was *something*," she said. "No more."

But Bry was not at all sure of that. Now, with his relaxation, his ribs were hurting worse; he had done some added wrenching in the heat of the battle. Suppose the crocodile had clamped its teeth on one of Chip's legs? They had overcome the creature as much by luck and blunder as by effort. Suppose another crocodile came—a larger one? They had had so much trouble with the small one, even when fighting it on land, which was the human terrain, that they didn't dare face a larger one.

He came to a decision: he had to make sure that there would never be a larger one. But how could he do that? At the moment he couldn't think of any way. So he asked the children.

They were intrigued by the notion. "Maybe rub on more stink leaf, to make it not bite," Chip suggested.

Bry smiled. That was clever, in its way. If the taste of the bitter leaf on the skin stopped the mosquitos, would it stop bigger bites? But it was a foolish notion. "It would have to bite once, to find out about the taste," he said. "And one bite is too much."

"Make a wall," Mina suggested. "Keep it out." She liked to make walls in the sand, keeping the water back for a while.

Bry and Chip laughed. "A BIG wall!" Chip said, lifting a hand to show how high.

Mina frowned. "Why not?" she demanded.

"Because—" Chip started, then looked thoughtful. He looked at Bry for support.

"It might work," Bry said, reconsidering. "But sand wouldn't do it. The crocodile would knock it down with its tail."

"Stone," Mina said.

"We couldn't move any stones heavy enough to stop the crocodile," Bry said.

"Wood," Chip said, getting into it.

Bry considered. "Maybe if we hammered stakes into the ground."

They liked that. So their project commenced. They ranged the beach and the near paths, always together, searching out pieces of wood and carrying or dragging them back. There turned out to be a considerable number, because there weren't any other families near to search the beach for fire-wood. Some of it wasn't sound, but enough was; they would be able to make their fence.

It turned out to be no easy project. Some of the wood would have been difficult to manage when Bry was in the best of health, and it was almost impossible in his present state. But the children helped, and Bry gritted his teeth and bore as much pain as he could, and they got it moved by slow stages. Then they had to find rocks to use to pound in the stakes, and if the wood pounded in readily, it didn't hold, and if the stakes did hold, it was awful getting them in. Again Bry had to fight the pain as he used his arms for such work. Mina saw that, and came to touch his ribs, and surprisingly the pain did diminish, enabling him to work more freely. There was just something about that little girl! They had to sharpen points on the stakes, as if they were spears, and some had to be braced by lesser sticks that couldn't make fence stakes on their own. These were tedious tasks, and progress was slow. Bry thought the children would soon tire of the effort, but they didn't; the scene with the crocodile must have scared them more than they admitted, and they wanted to be safe. Also, they were good children, remarkably responsible for their ages. That spoke well for their parents.

Their parents. Bry remembered the beautiful music Hugh had made, and the phenomenal dancing Anne had done. That sound and that image would remain forever in his memory.

It became a system. Mina sharpened points by rubbing small rough stones across the narrow ends of the stakes. Chip held each stake steady, upright, while Bry pounded it in. He found that it helped to drag a good-sized rock across to the stake, so that he could stand on the stone and hammer from a greater height. When the stake was down as far as it would go, Chip used a smaller rock to pound in bracing pieces, getting the main stake firm. They had to place half-buried stones around it to brace it, because the sand was never completely firm, but the end result was pretty good. The work was wearing, and they had to rest between stakes, and they got only a few done the first day, but they were highly satisfied with their accomplishment. A line of several crooked but firm stakes extended from the shelter toward the river. Of course it wasn't enough, because the crocodile could simply go around it, but it was the start of their wall.

Next day they did more, extending the line along the side of the path. Bry began to wonder, perversely, whether there was really a point to this hard labor; suppose no crocodile ever came again?

Then, late in the day, the crocodile returned. They had been nervously alert for it throughout. It had gotten the noose off its nose, and seemed as aggressive as ever.

Chip and Mina screamed and ran in different directions. Bry picked up the stake he had been about to start pounding and carried it toward the reptile. The creature was chasing Mina, who darted a desperate look at Bry and ran to the end of the line of posts, then dodged around them and ran on to the house.

The crocodile came to the posts and went up the other side, trying to move directly toward the girl. There was space between the posts, so it could track Mina, but not enough to let it pass through.

This gave Bry a notion. "Chip! Here to the fence!"

Chip, by this time far afield, came in. The two of them stood just opposite the crocodile, who couldn't get at them. It lacked the wit to go around, so kept poking its nose into the spaces between stakes, and as quickly being balked. The tip of its snout was narrow enough to pass, but not its full head or body.

"Go away!" Chip cried, and picked up a handful of sand and flung it at the creature. The sand did no harm, but was very satisfying to throw.

Mina came out, realizing that they had found safety of a sort. She picked up a small stone and threw it through the fence. It bounced off the crocodile's nose.

That set them all off. They heaved double handfuls of sand through, so much that it started piling up around the creature, at one time half burying its snout. But the crocodile couldn't do anything about it, except go away—which, reluctantly, it did. It didn't seem to occur to the creature that it could have come around the fence; once it headed for the water, it kept going. They had won their second engagement more handily and safely than their first—thanks to the partial fence.

That gave Bry an idea. "We don't need to line the path both sides," he said. "Just one side—and be on the other side."

But they realized that this would not necessarily be easy to arrange. By chance the crocodile had come up on the side opposite to the one Mina had taken, but next time it might take the same side. How could they guarantee it would be on the wrong side?

They discussed it, and Chip came up with the answer: climb over the fence. But how could they do that quickly enough? The stakes were high enough so that getting over the fence was awkward. They thought of putting a pile of stones against it, that they could use to get high enough to step over it—but suppose the crocodile did the same?

But that idea turned out to be better than it had at first seemed. Suppose they put stones against one side—and not on the other? People could jump down from that height with no problem—but what about a crocodile? Accustomed to the level water, would it care to tumble off a high fence, to land snout-first? That seemed unlikely. But if it did, it would still surely take some time—time they could use to get clear. Or to cross back to the other side of the fence.

So they set up several piles of rocks, on both sides of the fence, but never right across from each other. Each was like a path leading nowhere, from one side or the other. Would it work? They would simply have to find out.

They resumed work on the fence, pounding stakes between sessions of foraging for food. They did not yet have the courage to try spear fishing again; they went to the water only to drink, and did that as a group, quickly, with two watching the sides while the third drank. But once they completed the fence, and knew that it worked—then maybe they would try for the fish again.

Several days later they had their chance. The fence was now much of the way toward the water, because they were getting better at it as they went. They went for a drink, because the labor made them thirsty, and Mina spied the crocodile. She screamed warning.

"Go on each side of the fence," Bry said, and the two of them ran toward it. Then, just to make sure the crocodile gave chase, Bry threw sand at it.

The creature lunged out of the water, snapping at him. Bry backed away, retreating no farther than was expedient. He had his spear, but merely gestured with it; he had no intention of fighting the reptile if he didn't have to.

It came after him, uncomfortably fast. Bry realized that it probably could outrun him, when it tried. He needed to get farther away from it. He turned and ran for one side of the fence, then paused. Both children made faces and rude noises at the crocodile, daring it to advance. And in a moment it did, going after Mina, the smallest and probably tastiest morsel. Chip, on the other side, made rude noises at it, but it ignored him for the moment.

Mina waited as long as she dared, then ran up the stone stile and paused. The crocodile was still coming. She jumped off to the other side, crying, "Wheee!" She landed in the sand, lost her balance, and fell, but was in no danger: the crocodile hadn't even mounted the ramp.

They stood opposite it, teasing it, as before, but the creature seemed to be unable to figure out what the stiles were for. It tried to get at them through the fence, without any hope of success. When they moved up the fence, beyond the ramp Mina had used, the reptile scrambled over the base of the ramp to get around it, and came back to the fence.

"Crocodiles are stupid," Chip said contemptuously.

"Yes," Bry agreed. "But don't go near it." The boy nodded. Stupid did not mean safe.

The crocodile returned to the water, again not even trying

to circle the fence. It seemed that they had found a good defense against it.

They kept working the following days, completing the fence, which stopped just short of the water's edge. They made ramps at frequent intervals, so that they would never be far from one. And, as an afterthought, they made an extension across the path near the house, so that the crocodile could not ever get inside. They made ramps to cross it, but offset them so that it was still necessary to jump down, whichever way a person crossed. Just in case the reptile one day figured out how to use a ramp.

They remained alert, and that was just as well, because the crocodile did come again. They readily foiled it. "But remember," Bry warned the others, fearing overconfidence. "If it ever gets hold of you, you're done. The fence won't help then." They nodded, appreciating the point.

Now, with the menace of the crocodile somewhat abated, Bry was able to watch for his family's boats again. He had fretted, privately, when he couldn't do that, for fear they would row by and never know he was here.

They got up courage to try spear fishing again. Mina was on watch while the other two focused on the fish. Chip, his arm perhaps stronger after all the practice pounding support stakes, managed to spear a fish through the tail and pull it out of the water.

Then Mina cried out, making them both jump away from the water. But it wasn't the crocodile. "Boat! Boat!" she exclaimed.

It couldn't be Hugh and Anne returning, for only half a moon had passed. Bry had made marks on a wall of the shelter, one little line for each day, and a connecting line for each seven days. Four such larger units would signal the time for return. There were only two.

So it had to be the other. "My family!" he said. "You said they would come now."

"Yes," she agreed, remembering. "I must meet your sister."

Who almost might be her natural mother. Because Mina had been saved from a dead place as a baby, about the time Flo had left her baby. Except that the places had been far separated. So it couldn't be. Yet he couldn't be certain in his doubt.

They waved, and the boat spied them and stroked in to shore. It was Dirk rowing, and Flo steering, and Lin searching from the prow. Trust his sister to spy him first!

The boat heaved part way up on the beach. Lin leaped out and ran lightly to embrace Bry. "I knew you were safe!" she said though her tears. "I just knew it!" Then she oriented on the children. "Well, hello," she said over his shoulder.

"You must have become a man quite rapidly," Dirk remarked, smiling.

Bry released Lin and turned. "These aren't my children," he said, embarrassed though he knew it was humor. "They are Chip and Mina, of Hugh and Anne's family." He turned back. "And this is my closest sister, Lin."

Mina approached shyly. "You have the hand," she said.

Lin's left hand was closed into a fist, the way she normally kept it to conceal her deformity. She glanced at Bry.

"I never said," Bry said hastily. "Mina—she just knows things. The spirits tell her."

Lin extended her arm and opened her hand. Mina looked at the fingers, and nodded. "It's a good hand," she said.

Dirk and Flo came up behind Lin. Flo had Baby Flint, now one year old, in the harness on her back. Bry started to introduce them, but Mina launched herself into Flo's embrace before he got the words out. "Why did you leave me?"

Flo's mouth fell open. "Can it be?"

Mina wriggled free. "Look at my toes." She stood on one foot, lifting her other foot with her hands.

Flo bent to look, and saw the birthmark between the toes. Astonished, she sat down in the sand. "My baby," she breathed. "How—?"

"They found her in a dead place," Bry said. "But it was near here. They have not been far south."

"Then it can't be," Flo said. "Yet—"

"The hair, the eyes," Dirk said. "They match yours. The cheekbones, the chin. She's yours."

Flo began to sob. Mina put her little arms around her, comfortingly. "Why did you leave me?" she repeated.

"I had no man," Flo said. "I could not support you. *Now* I could, but then there was no way. So I left you. Then I changed my mind, and returned, but you were gone, and it was best. Since then I have thought of you every day, wondering, hoping—"

Bry was amazed. It was impossible, yet this did seem to be his sister's child.

"Now you have one of your own," Mina said.

"Yes." Still sitting, Flo lifted him out of the pack and brought him around to the front. "This is Flint."

"Hello, Flint," Mina said solemnly.

Meanwhile Dirk was getting along with the other child, as he usually did. "What is that you have made, my good little man?"

"A fence," Chip explained. "To keep out the crocodile."

"There is a crocodile after you?"

"Yes. It comes almost every day. But we hide behind our fence."

Dirk looked perplexed. "But suppose it comes on your side?"

"I'll show you," Chip said gleefully. "You be the crocodile."

Dirk quickly got into the game. He put his hands down on the sand and lunged at the boy. Chip ran around the end of the fence. Dirk did a beautiful job of almost crashing headfirst into it. Then he paused, pondered a moment, and made his way around it to get on the boy's side.

Chip ran up the nearest ramp and jumped over. Dirk came to the ramp, sniffed it, and then slowly climbed on it. He reached the top, peered over, and stopped. "I'd land on my snout," he said.

"So would the crocodile," Chip pointed out.

Dirk nodded gravely. "So it would. This is a good defense. But how did you make it?" He reached out and took hold of a post, pushing against it. "This is firm."

Bry explained how they all had worked so hard on it.

"With your ribs bruised," Dirk said, looking at him, seeing the way he favored that side. Dirk knew about bruised ribs.

"We had to get it done," Bry said.

"So you did." He seemed impressed.

"Where are your parents?" Lin asked Chip, and the boy explained about that.

Dirk looked at Flo. "We can't take Bry yet; he hasn't finished his commitment here. The other boat won't be back for some time. We'd better camp here until the parents return."

Flo nodded, looking at Bry. "We know what it's like to survive without parents."

"You can stay in our house," Chip said eagerly. "There's room."

Flo and Dirk exchanged another glance. "They surely do have room," Dirk said. "While the parents are away. Let's use their house, and return what favors we may."

So it was done. Dirk and Flo took the section where Hugh and Anne normally slept, and Lin found room at the edge, with the children scrambling to fashion a bed for her. It would be crowded, but could be managed.

Bry was much relieved. He hadn't realized how much tension he had had, until it dissipated. He hadn't known for sure that the rest of his family had survived, or that they would find him. It seemed that the boats had been carried far south, and the others had no idea where he had gone ashore—or if he had. He could tell by the way that Lin was letting go that she had been under similar tension. Now it was all right, and all of them could relax.

The next morning Dirk got serious about return favors. "That crocodile—we are going to take care of it," he said grimly.

They went about it methodically. The spear fishing that had been such an adventure for Bry and the children was inconsequential for Dirk; he quickly speared several fish, and cut them to pieces with his stone knife, and tossed the pieces back into the water. Before long that summoned the crocodile. Then Dirk stood back and let the children lure it out. When it was well up on the beach, Dirk cut it off from the water and went after it with two spears. The reptile that had been so bold against children found it another matter against a competent grown man who had killed crocodiles before. He poked it in the tail, and when it whirled around to snap at the spear, he poked it in the snout. He kept poking it, confusing it, until it stopped reacting and tried to charge him. Then he jammed the spear hard at its face, so that its own momentum added to the power of the thrust. Soon it had been stabbed through eye and belly, and was thrashing on the sand. Dirk looped its snout with a loop, and Bry held the rope taut while Dirk carved open the reptile's throat with a stone blade. Slowly the beast died.

Then came the work of carving it up. Crocodile meat was good, and so was the tough hide; they were not going to waste any of it. By the end of the day sections of crocodile were hanging from the branches of nearby trees. They made a big fire and roasted enough for an excellent meal. They would dry as much of the remaining meat as possible in the sun, and keep it for Hugh and Anne to use when they returned.

The day after that they took the children out for a boat ride. Though Chip and Mina were part of the boat culture, as all people were, their family's boat was small, and used only when they traveled to a new home base, or when on tour. Normally they lived on the shore, in protected houses like the present one. They never went far out to sea; they hugged the shore, so that if any storm or creature threatened they could immediately get to land. So it was a real experience for them to go far out in the big boat with oars.

Dirk rowed and Flo steered, as usual; Dirk and Sam were always the rowers, having the most brute power. Because the rower faced backward—another novelty to the children—and the one with the rudder was at the back of the boat, a young person normally perched in the prow to watch forward. Lin did that, taking the children up by turns to be awed by the prow cutting swiftly through the water.

Bry sat in the middle with the other child and Baby Flint. He faced back, watching the rear and side. "We have to watch all the time," he explained, "because we are crossing deep water and don't want to be surprised by anything."

Chip, with him for the moment, peered over the edge of the boat, down through the water, and then turned his head quickly back to the boat. He looked a bit dizzy. "It's so *deep!*"

"Yes," Bry agreed. "You can see things down there. Big fish, big turtles, sometimes seaweed, looking like a dark forest. It's peaceful."

"And you even sleep in the boat?"

"Yes, usually. We take turns lying down in the center, with one or two people always alert, even when we're not moving. Our boat is the safest place we can be—except when there's a storm."

"I thought I'd be scared," the boy confessed. "But you're right: it does feel safe. It's so big and steady."

"The outrigger steadies it, just as it does on your boat," Bry said. It was nice being the expert on things.

Then Mina crawled to the center. "Your turn," she announced. "There's even a wind up there."

The boy crawled forward, and Mina made herself comfortable between Bry and the baby, facing back. Like girls of any age, she was intrigued by babies.

"It moves so fast," she said.

"That's because of the rowing," Bry explained, nodding back at Dirk right behind him. "He pulls hard with both arms, instead of pulling with one and pushing with the other, the way you do with a paddle. But we paddle too, when we need to.''

Baby Flint got bored or uncomfortable, and started fussing. Mina pulled him on to her lap, and he was quiet.

"You have the touch," Flo said appreciatively.

"Yes. The spirits are with me."

"I wish you were mine."

There was a silence. Then Bry became aware of something. They were all in the boat, and the boat was bearing south, toward a likely rendezvous with the family's other boat. They could just keep going. The children couldn't get off.

Had Dirk and Flo planned this? Bry was alarmed.

Mina lifted her head and looked at Flo. Bry saw only the glossy back of the little girl's head, but somehow realized that she was crying. There was no sound, no motion, but surely there were tears.

Then Flo's eyes changed, and tears came from them. She turned the rudder, and the boat began to turn. They were going back to the children's house.

Bry realized that there had been a tacit contest of wills, and the little girl had won. Mina loved her present family and didn't want to leave it. Flo wanted her baby back, but couldn't take her by force. No one could take anything from Mina by force. The spirits wouldn't allow it.

No further words were spoken. The issue had been decided. Dirk surely understood, and was keeping silent. Bry would keep silent too.

They resumed foraging and fishing, and Dirk explored the nearby forest. They were passing time until the parents returned.

When the moon was done, the small boat reappeared, from the opposite direction; they had completed their circuit, portaging inland to reach another stream.

Chip and Mina rushed out, joyfully welcoming their parents back. Dirk, Flo, Bry, Lin, and Baby Flint waited by the fence. The children would introduce them soon enough.

They did. It took a while for everything to be explained, including the crocodile and the fence, but it got done. Then, as abruptly as Hugh and Anne had done, Dirk and Flo made ready to depart. "We came for our brother," Flo explained. "We have found him. Now we will take him back, and rejoin the rest of our family. We thank you for rescuing him."

"But he rescued us!" Anne protested. "Without him, we couldn't have done the tour alone. We see that he did an excellent job." She glanced meaningfully at the fence. "You must stay and let us repay you for all the trouble you have taken."

But Flo shook her head. Bry realized that she wanted to get quickly away, before she revealed something she thought was best left secret. It was better that Anne not know. So he made a suggestion. "They can reward us with a song and dance. It won't take long. Then we'll go."

Dirk looked perplexed, but shrugged agreeably. So they sat in the sand, and Hugh brought out his flute, and Chip his drum, and the woman and the girl did a dance to music that quickly made Dirk discover the point of it all. Bry was glad to see his impression verified: this was a thing awesome to grown men.

He looked at Flo, and saw her fascinated too, but in a different way. She was seeing how well integrated her baby was in this nice family, learning to be a dancer, bound to become attractive as a woman in a way Flo, who was now fairly fat, was not. Mina belonged where she was; this was now quite clear.

When it was done, they moved to the boat. "Will we meet again?" Hugh asked.

"I think not," Flo said firmly. "We are going far north, looking for new shores. It is our way."

Bry knew that meant that Flo intended to put herself well

away from temptation. He knew that was best. But it was sad to think he would never be with the children again. This had been, despite the pain of his ribs and uncertainty of separation, as good an experience as he could remember. He had been, for half a moon, the man of a wonderful little family.

Mina ran to hug Bry one last time. She kissed him on the cheek. "Never forget me," she said.

"I never will," he agreed sadly, knowing how true that was. And he knew she would never tell their true relationship.

Thus the boat folk may have explored all the coasts of the Americas, proceeding south along the west, circling the tip of South America, and moving north back to North America. Whether they had advanced to the level of oar locks and backward-facing rowing may be in doubt, but certainly mankind had boats capable of such excursions, because Australia was colonized 40,000 to 50,000 years ago by boat. There is some marginal evidence of their presence in South America as long as 35,000 years ago, at sites like Monte Verde in modern Chile and Pedra Furada in Brazil, where radiocarbon dates as far back as 32,000 years ago have been obtained. Cave art there has been dated as 17,000 years old. The site of Meadowcroft Rock Shelter in Pennsylvania, USA, dates to circa 17,000 years ago. The significance of such discoveries is this: Prior wisdom sets a limit for the colonization of America from Asia of about 12,000 years ago. This is because before then the way was blocked by glaciers across part of Alaska and all of Canada, extending to the sea on either side of the continent. Only when the ice retreated could a land crossing have been made. The evidence of the stones suggests that this was the case; the distinctive fluted Clovis points date from this time.

If, however, the continents were settled 20,000 years

before the ice cleared, by people in boats, why is there so little evidence of their presence? Why did the pattern of extinctions of large game animals commence only 12,000 years ago? Why wasn't America already full of millions of settlers, repelling the newcomers from the Asian side of the ice? Well, there is some evidence that when the glaciers retreated, mankind moved north to Alaska from the region of the western United States, rather than the other way. But this is controversial as yet, with archaeologists having some trouble getting such a politically incorrect thesis published in reputable journals. It also does not address the question of why the limited evidence suggests a far earlier colonization of South America than North America. If the boat folk circled the southern continent as described in this setting, what happened to them? Surely they couldn't simply vanish after 20,000 years.

But they may have done just that. The boat folk may have been limited by their life-style to the coast, seldom moving far inland. Culture has strong continuity, especially when buttressed by the economics of survival. They depended on the water for their food, and never penetrated the enormous continental interiors where their home-boats couldn't go. Their numbers were limited, and they came not as a single massive invasion, but as a long series of trickles. Their tribal and band numbers may have been insufficient to enable them to expand their population significantly, as discussed in Chapter 5, so they were always thinly spread. Storms would have been a constant danger, because of the vulnerability of their boats. Then two things could have finished them and their works: a massive invasion of landbound folk 12,000 years ago, displacing or absorbing them without remaining genetic trace in the course of several thousand years, and the waters of the seas rising with the melting of the ice, covering or washing out most of the physical traces of their pres-

ence. So they were gone so completely that they were thought never to have existed. Until little bits of evidence appeared, widely scattered. Such as the chipped stones at the sites mentioned, and the genetic evidence of a tribe living eight thousand years ago in Florida: related to none of the three main Native American groups, but to folk now living in Japan. In short, a remnant of coastal folk. They were the true first Americans.

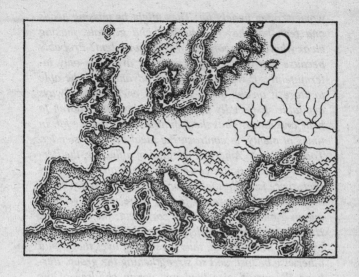

Chapter 7

BONE HOUSE

One frontier was that of the cold northlands. The great glaciers of the arctic had not yet retreated. Much of Europe was covered, but less of Asia; apparently the most massive ice formed downwind from the oceans. Between the ice and the tropic was the vast panorama of Siberia, where bison and mammoths roamed. Here life could be lean indeed, and people were dependent on big animals for food, clothing, and shelter. One indication of the times is the art they left behind: the "Venus" figurines, generally the torsos of naked women, often hugely fat. They might be missing heads and feet, but they had breasts and genitals, making clear what was important. Why so corpulent? Probably because when food was scarce, or available only intermittently, it was a significant advantage to be able to store it on the body, where its energy was always available. Especially for women, who had children to bear and nurse. Thus the feminine ideal became fat. In times of plenty, in contrast, the ideal becomes slender. Today in North America, the land of affluence, the Perfect Woman is supposed to be anorexically thin. However, there is doubt that historically many women could become even moderately fat, so there may have been one in a band who was truly corpulent: the wet nurse. Her huge breasts could feed the children of mothers who died in childbirth, thus preserving lives that would otherwise be lost, and so strengthening the group. Perhaps she would also feed any young children of the group, so that they could be healthy even when their mothers were not quite adequate. Such a service would probably have been very much appreciated, leading to veneration of this type of female body; it enabled the group to preserve its children.

But there was another innovation, similarly striking, in housing. The place is Siberia, 20,000 years ago.

FLO WAS DESPERATE. BRY WAS ill and rapidly getting worse. He had gotten his ribs bashed in a river accident, had been lost for a time, but survived nicely with a neighboring family. Now they had him back—and he had forgotten caution, tried too hard on a hunt, and re-injured himself. He had been able to walk, but it hadn't stopped there; now the boy was feverish. She knew how to care for him, but lacked the facilities.

Normally when they traveled to a new hunting site they cut sturdy saplings to make a framework for a conical house. The poles were tied together at the top, and spread out to form a circle; then the band's cache of hides was stretched over the pole framework and tied tight with cords. Stones anchored the base of the hides, making a nice tight shelter they could heat with a fire at its entrance. Two days of a warm shelter and a steady healing chant would drive out the boy's illness, and he would begin recovering.

But this new territory was a harsh windswept plain. No trees were near, and no natural shelter. That wind was tearing into Bry's clothing, pulling away the heat of his body, draining his vitality when he needed it most. If they had to spend a cold night on the ground, he would be finished. They could wrap him in hides, and lie close around him, but he would still be breathing the chill air. That was no good. The spirits were hovering near him, and they would take him if he did not find physical and magical protection.

She looked around. Maybe they could gather rocks, and make a circle high enough to serve as an effective windbreak, and stretch the hides over the top. They had done that on occasion when wood wasn't sufficient. But she didn't see any rocks; there were surely some scattered around, but clearly not enough to do the job in the time they had. In any event, Sam and Dirk were out hunting, so weren't here to haul the heavy stones. Ned was here, but he was a lean young man, not powerful, not made for heavy physical labor. Jes was very similar to him, though she was a young woman. She was a good forager and a hard worker, but no rock hauler. Flo herself was way too fat for that sort of thing, and Wona too skinny and disinterested in hard work. So rocks were out.

She looked at Bry. He was sitting on the ground, hunched together. Lin was trying to help him, but was plainly inadequate. No, they had to have a good shelter. And there was none to be had.

"We'll camp here," Flo decided, determined to be decisive. There were, after all, the others to see to. They would have to eat and get through the night, hoping that tomorrow would bring the men with fresh meat. Their success had not been great recently, so that the berries and roots foraged by the women served as the main sustenance. Flo had been able to gain weight on that diet, but not the others. Thus Flo was an ideal figure of a woman, with the evidence of her survivability layered on her body. She came closest of her generation to matching the standard of the goddess dolls which for as long as any tale-teller remembered had represented the pinnacle of the female form. But she was lucky; the others needed animal flesh to feed them, as well as foraging.

"I'll forage for firewood," Ned said.

"I'll forage for berries," Jes said.

"Go with them," Flo told Lin. "I'll take care of Bry." The girl looked doubtful, but obeyed. Flo sat down next to Bry and pulled him in to her to her copious bosom to share her warmth. He was shivering despite being well bundled. "We'll get you through this somehow," she told him, but she was afraid she lied.

She bared her huge breast and nursed Bry, as was the custom when the need was great. He was her brother, twelve years old and soon to be a man, but he needed sustenance. The youngest ones could get by on less, for a while. He smiled at her, wearily, and relaxed, reassured. Soon he was sleeping. She hugged him, aware of his burning heat; he would not sleep well, but any sleep was better than none. He was family; she had to help him all she could.

The two children, Wilda and Flint, came to join Flo, as they usually did. They were two years old and mostly weaned. Flo had nursed longer and better than Wona, having the body for it, and so both children seemed like hers now though Wilda was actually Wona's. Wona had never evinced any great interest in sustaining her daughter; she had wanted a boy, and resented the fact that Flo had been the one to get a son.

Wona looked around, then wandered off, theoretically to forage. Flo regarded her as a loss; she seldom pulled her share if she could avoid it, and was generally a force for dissension. But there wasn't much to be done about it; she was Sam's wife, and Sam still doted on her. Apparently Sam could see no further than her beauty, such as it was; she was way too lean to handle a winter properly. But it was better to have her out of sight than here, Flo concluded; but for Sam, she'd have driven the woman out of the band long ago.

She reflected again on the irony of the way things had worked out. At the time Flo and Sam had gotten their mates from the same neighbor band, it had seemed that Wona was the bargain, and Dirk the loss. It was the other way around.

Lin came bounding back, her hair flouncing under the tight hair net. The girl was small for her age, but pretty, except for that hand. Sometimes Flo wished they had simply cut off the extra finger, back when the girl was a baby. But it hadn't happened, and now it was too late. She was twelve years old, the same as Bry, and very soon, food and climate permitting, would become a beautiful if thin young woman. But the years would put some mass on her, when needed.

"Bones! Bones!" Lin cried, excited.

So they had found some bones. Scattered across the landscape there were bones, because when animals died the bones were what didn't dissolve away. Many of their tools and weapons were made of carved bones, including some savagely barbed spears. Why did that so excite the girl?

"Bones!" Lin said again as she arrived. "All over! Big! Dry! Piles of them!"

Flo didn't want to deflate her, but didn't see the point. "We need food and scraps of wood for a fire," she reminded the girl gently. "And poles for a shelter. Your brother—"

"The bones—Ned says the bones will help—they're bringing them. I must go help haul." And she ran away again, following the faint path she had picked out.

What good would old bones do? They would have no usable marrow. But then Flo remembered that some bones would burn, if the fire was hot enough. Not as good as wood, but better than nothing. So maybe it was worthwhile.

Then Ned and Jes came into sight, looking like two young men, hauling on something. Flo strained her gaze, trying to make it out, without disturbing Bry. It was low to the ground and very long, like a pole. Its dragging end furrowed the ground, clearly marking what had been a faint path.

Then her mouth fell open. It was a tusk! A mammoth tusk. Almost as long as two people lying end to end. What a monster!

Panting, they brought it near. "We can make a house with these," Jes said. "There are so many!"

As a substitute for wooden poles. Now Flo saw the logic. "But that thing is curved," she said, getting practical. "They won't make a good point for the top."

"We'll tie them together anyway," Ned said. "If we can just get enough of them here."

Flo had a flash of inspiration. "If there are so many there—we should go there. Easier to move ourselves, than such heavy bones."

Ned paused. "You make me feel stupid," he said. "Of course we should build it there."

Had she really figured out something he had not? Flo wasn't sure. Ned was very bright. Maybe he had simply wanted her to suggest it. "Maybe we'll build another one here, later," Flo said. "But for now, let's go there."

She lifted Bry, who stirred sleepily. "We must move, Bry," she said. "But then we can rest. I will carry you." She knew he would have protested, had he had the strength, but he didn't.

Ned and Jes helped get the boy up in her arms. Then Flo marched after the two of them, following the scuffed line. She was used to carrying her own considerable weight around; she could handle his too, for a while.

The bones turned out to be in a hollow that looked as if it had once been a bend of a river. Perhaps a temporary flood during a heavy rain, that had carried the bodies along with it, then pooled here, leaving the bones when it sank away. There certainly were a lot of them; she had never seen such a white jumble. A dozen mammoths, maybe.

But first things first. She found a clear place and laid Bry down. "Can you build it here?"

"Anywhere," Ned said. "We just need to figure out how to do it."

"Tie the bones together," Flo said. "Lin and I will make rope."

But he hesitated. "These bones are big. The framework will be big. Our hides won't cover all of it."

So he had thought it through. He had a good notion of what to do, and had anticipated the problem. Big irregular bones could not make as efficient a house as straight wood poles, and they had no hides to spare. A house with big holes would be largely useless as shelter, because the cutting wind would keep the interior cold.

She looked again at the vast jumble of bones all around them. They were all sizes, but only the tusks were as long as good construction poles. Unless they made the house entirely of tusks—but there weren't *that* many good ones. They were stuck with an inefficient big bone-pile shelter— or nothing.

"Put the hides inside," Lin suggested.

Jes laughed. Whoever heard of such a thing? But Ned looked thoughtful. "Could we tie them in place?" he asked.

"We can *sew* them in place," Flo said. "Pass threads through the stitches, then loop them over the tusk-poles. It will be clumsy, but it can be done."

"Then it shall be done," Ned agreed. "Lin can work with you on the hides; Jes can work with me."

"What about Wona?" Lin asked mischievously.

"She can choose," Jes said, grimacing. "When she shows up." By tacit agreement they did not openly speak ill of their brother's wife.

They got to work. Ned and Jes hauled bones into a nearby pile and separated the tusks. Lin ran to dig out their supply of twine, but realized that it wouldn't be enough for this. But some distance away from the bones they had seen a

mass of shed mammoth hair, so she went for that and carried
it back. Flo drew out lengths of it and twisted them into a
serviceable cord. They would need a lot.

Wona showed up. She surveyed the situation, then went
to join Ned. Flo was surprised; usually the woman chose
the least rigorous task to work on. But this time Wona threw
herself into it and seemed really to be helping. They did
need the help, because there were so many bones to move,
and some of them evidently weighed more than any two
people together did.

Bry stirred. Flo laid a hand on his forehead. He was still
burning. "We are making a house," she told him. "Soon
it will be warm." He sank back into his troubled sleep.

"It *must* be warm," Lin breathed. She was Bry's closest
sibling, their two mothers having birthed them within days
of each other, with the same father, and the two were also
emotionally close. Just as Jes was to Ned, and Flo herself
to Sam. Lin was in most respects a fine girl, but she would
be a wreckage if Bry died. She had been distraught when
Bry had been lost, and came to life again only when they
found him. There had been a time when Bry had teased her
about her fingers, and she had thrown dirt in his face, but
that was long past; now he was her stoutest defender. The
girl was neither crying nor showing particular concern now,
and that was a troublesome sign, because normally she expressed herself freely. She surely thought that to admit there
was a problem would be to give it power. And, indeed, the
spirits did seem to operate that way at times.

Meanwhile the construction of the house proceeded. Ned
laid out the parts in an expanding pattern that resembled a
giant flower, with the largest tusks in the center. Flo wasn't
sure what the point was, but knew that he had a reason.
Wona continued to labor industriously, even working up
enough heat to enable her to shed her outer jacket, just as
Jes had; what was the matter with the woman?

Then they started assembling it. Ned heaved the point of
one giant tusk up to waist height, which wasn't hard because

this was the light end, and the curve of the thing allowed it
to rest its center on the ground. Jes hauled another tusk up
similarly. They walked toward each other, swinging their
two points around, until they crossed like two enormous
spears. Then Wona took a length of cord and wound it
around the tusks where they crossed, tying them together.
Flo couldn't hear their dialogue, but knew that Ned was
giving instructions, so that their acts were coordinated.

They laid down the tied tusks, which now formed a huge
semicircle. They picked up two more, and bound them together similarly. Then two more, smaller ones. Flo still
couldn't fathom the purpose.

They took yet smaller tusks and used the points to dig in
the ground in several places around the edge of the circle.
What was the point of that?

Then they heaved the first set up again, this time all the
way, until they were holding it up so that it formed an arch
higher than any of them could reach. The two base ends of
it were set in two of the holes in the ground they had made.
Aha; now she saw it. Anchorages, just as they normally did
with wooden poles. They got the arch steady, and two of
them let go, leaving Jes holding it up. The arch weighed
several times what she did, but she was able to keep it balanced. The other two rolled mammoth skulls to the two
bases of it, bracing it in place, and wedged smaller bones
around, until Jes was able to let it go. There it stood, like a
rainbow made of ivory.

Now they hauled up the second arch, which was slightly
smaller than the first. They got it standing crosswise, its
bases in two more holes, so that its highest point was under
the highest point of the first one. They braced it similarly,
until it too stood by itself.

The third arch was the easiest, angled against the other
two, passing under both. They braced it until it stood.

Then they rolled a larger skull to a point in the center,
under all three arches. Wona stood on it and reached up
with cord. But she wasn't tall enough to reach the intersec-

tion, even with that added height. Neither were Ned or Jes. Finally Ned got down, and Wona climbed onto his shoulders, her heavy hide skirt falling around the back of his head. Jes helped him get to his feet with that burden.

Now Wona could reach high enough to loop the cord around the three intersecting arches, without otherwise touching any of them. She made one loop and tied it; then Jes handed her more cord, and she made a second loop, and then a third. She pulled them all snug. The three arches were bound together.

There was a dialogue Flo wished she could hear. Ned seemed to be telling Wona to do something, and both Wona and Jes were demurring. That was unusual; Jes and Wona seldom agreed on anything. But Ned finally convinced them.

Lin was watching too, and she had sharper ears. "He told Wona to hang from the tusks!" the girl exclaimed. "But if she does that, she'll pull the whole works down on their heads! She's not *that* light."

Indeed Wona wasn't. She was entirely too slender for a grown woman, but she was adult, and weighed more than Lin or Bry. What was Ned thinking of?

What happened next astonished them both. Wona took hold of the bound central axis of tusks and held on. Ned dropped down and got out from under, leaving her hanging there. Then he pushed her, so that her body swung back and forth. Her scream was audible across the whole bone yard. Her feet kicked and her breasts stood out as she inhaled for another scream.

And the structure did not come tumbling down. It swayed just a bit, but held firm. What made it so strong?

"She's yelling to him to get her down," Lin said, beginning to enjoy the show.

"Why doesn't she just let go?" Flo asked. "It's not that far a drop to the ground."

"She wants Ned to get her down. She says he put her up there. Maybe it's a test of wills."

A test of wills? Between Ned and Wona? But the two

had nothing to do with each other. They might as well have been in different bands. Flo couldn't understand any kind of contest between them. The useless woman and the brilliant stripling. They had no common ground.

Finally Ned came close, ducking his head as the woman swung toward him, her body turning as she lifted her feet high to avoid kneeing him in the head. Trying to dodge her, he dropped to the ground. Jes and Lin laughed together at the mishap, probably equally delighted by the man's fall and the woman's predicament. Ned looked up, and Flo saw him gape as if dizzy, before he got back to his feet. Flo knew what had happened; he had inadvertently seen right up under the woman's skirt, when her legs were spread wide, a stunning view for a young man. Then he called instructions, and she straightened out her body, and Ned did what he had first intended: he caught Wona around her swinging hips and held her so she could let go of the tusks. She grabbed his head and slid down his front, pressing her bosom hard into his face as it passed.

Lin laughed again. "He played a trick on her. But she got back at him!"

Flo did not laugh. She had a sudden dark suspicion. Wona, however useless she might be generally, remained exactly the kind of narrow-waisted, plush-bottomed, firm-breasted creature young men liked to get hold of—and Ned was a young man. He would naturally not have any notions about his elder brother's wife, and of course he knew Wona's shrewish, idle nature. But young men did not necessarily think with their heads; their interest followed the direction of their penises, and those organs could readily be roused by the proximity of almost any appealing female form. Legends were rife with lovely nymphs whose only seeming purpose was to oblige the lust of whatever men were nearby. Wona had just come to work with Ned, helping him accomplish his purpose. She had enclosed his head with her thighs, and then shown him her bottom and rubbed his face with her breasts. Of course she was clothed in her hide vest and leggings, as all of them were; still, such contact would have its effect. Was she making a play for him?

Flo pondered that as the others resumed work on the bone house. Why would Wona do such a thing? She had never been keen on joining their band; her own band had wanted to get rid of her, and only after she married Sam had it gradually become clear why. Wona simply was no asset to any band, because of her indifferent attitude. She did not pull her weight. But she was cunning enough to know exactly whom she had to please, in order to get away with it. She pleased Sam. But Sam, like Dirk, was away from the band much of the time, because hunting big game was no sometime thing. They might have to track a given herd for several days before finding a vulnerable animal, and then pursue that animal for several days more. The meat and hide were invaluable when they came, but the price of them was the absence of the hunters much of the time. Flo could live with it, and it had seemed that Wona could—but now it looked as if the woman craved a bit of entertainment on the side. That was extremely bad medicine.

So Flo hoped that her suspicion was wrong. Certainly she would say nothing about it. Because if it was right, they would have one awful problem. Better just to believe what the others evidently did, that Wona had for once made herself useful when there was a difficult job to be done, and had suffered a small mishap when testing the stability of the structure, and not intentionally vamped anyone. That was definitely the best interpretation.

Lin took the new cord they had made and went to join the others. Flo stayed with Bry and the children, and worked on more cord. The house was taking shape now, and Ned's design was impressive. The huge tusks served as the framework, and they were piling skulls and pelvises around the base, and weaving the long leg bones between the tusks. It was like a giant basket turned over, with bones instead of reeds. Individually the bones were nothing much, and in small groups they fell apart, but when the design was large enough, they could be woven into a durable structure. A basket of bones!

Finally Flo could remain apart no longer. She picked Bry up and carried him to the new house, calling to the children to follow. She set him on the lee of the structure, shielded somewhat from the continuing wind, and joined in the weaving of bones. This was after all her specialty, though she had never before thought to weave a house.

The work went well, with all of them participating, but there was no way to complete it by nightfall. Jes had to stop to prepare some of their packed dried meat, and Ned had to make a fire by the house's entrance. Lin had to take a hide bucket to the river they had spied in the distance, for water to drink. That left Flo and Wona to tie the hides up inside the house. Fortunately most of them were already linked together; they had simply folded them in large segments after taking down the last shelter. So all they needed to do was use the extra cord to loop around the tusk and bone supports, to hold the mat of hides up. It was weird, having the hides inside the supports instead of outside, but it worked in its fashion. The bones broke up the wind, so that only eddy swirls got through, and the hides stopped most of those.

The fire started to warm the sheltered interior. The smoke blew off to the side, so that little of it got inside. The house was working. Flo brought Bry inside. At last he was out of the wind and in a halfway warm place. Now he could mend—if the spirits allowed it.

They snuggled down inside the bone house, and it was surprisingly comfortable. "You did well, Ned," Flo told him.

"We had to have shelter," he replied, glancing at Bry. But he was pleased. He was also thoughtful. She hoped he was considering the further prospects for building in bone, and not for getting close to dangling women.

The next day they did more work on the house, chinking the remaining gaps with smaller bones and anchoring the hides more tightly. They foraged for roots and berries, and did well enough, considering.

And Bry, warmed in the shelter, improved. The signs were subtle, but Flo could tell that he had turned onto a better path. He would recover. Her gladness was tempered only by her awareness of the way Wona looked at Ned.

Actually, the "Venus" figurines could have been models not of the ideal feminine state, but of the most exaggerated image of fertility. Thus those aspects of a woman associated with reproduction were stressed— breasts, buttocks, thighs, belly, vulva—and those who approached such proportions may have achieved status. The fertility of the land is vital to the success of a human community, and most cultures did their best to encourage it, whether by practical, magical, or symbolic means. But the male taste in females could have remained much as it is today: variable, but remarkably consistent overall. An enormously pregnant woman is not a good sex goddess. So there may have been a distinction between fertility and lust. Most of the Venuses date from about 30,000 years ago for carved vulvas to 22,000 years ago for almost full figures, when the glaciers were advancing. Later figures became more normally endowed, as the climate ameliorated. There is one "Venus" that is just the head of a young woman with an exquisitely sweet face and a hair net. Some have string skirts, definitely an indication of sexuality.

The bone houses were crafted in Siberia and Europe, and later became sophisticated, the bones symmetrically interlocked. But they were braced by wood where it was feasible. The all-bone structure described here would have been an emergency measure. The pictures of such dwellings are quite striking.

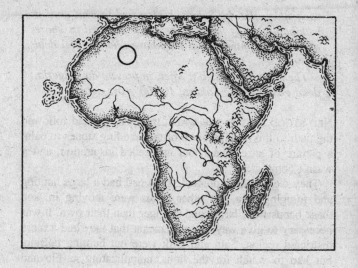

Chapter 8

ROCK ART

Today the Sahara is the world's most formidable desert, but it wasn't always so. The region eased up enough to let Homo erectus out one to two million years ago, and to let modern mankind out about 100,000 years ago. It dried up again about 70,000 years ago in the east, but was halfway habitable in the west 40,000 years ago. Possibly 12,000 years ago the climate ameliorated again, and mankind followed the plants and animals in. Some of the earliest paintings found anywhere in the world are in Africa, on exposed rock slabs. But the Sahara region had to wait until it was habitable by mankind before it received its share of art. Then, however, it may have seen a good deal more.

The setting is Tassili n'Ajjer, in present day Algeria, dead center of the Sahara, 10,000 years ago.

NED STOOD FACING THE WALL, troubled. He had followed the path to this strange place of the standing stones to paint a picture of an elephant, but he needed inspiration, and it wasn't coming.

They were getting pressed. They had had a large hunting and foraging area, but other bands were moving in, and these bands were larger and stronger than their own. It was necessary to give way, but that meant that they had a more restricted region. Sam and Dirk were out hunting buffalo, but had to watch for the lions, complicating it. Flo and Wona were out foraging for sorghum and millet seeds, but these were less plentiful than before, because the group had been over this section too recently. Lin was taking care of the children, and Bry was helping her. Actually she was taking care of him, too, as he recovered from his injury and illness, but for the sake of his blunted pride they did not say that.

That left Ned and Jes. Ned did not like man's work, and Jes did not like woman's work. Ned was slight of build and tended to think too much, while Jes was as tall and lank as a man and dressed so that her breasts did not show. He had once thought he would fill out as Sam had and be a man, and she had once thought she would find the face of a woman, but both hopes had been disappointed. So they were cursed in their opposite ways, and much alike in person.

No formal statement had been made, but times were getting tough, and it was clear that the band needed to find a better way to get through this difficult time. Ned needed to join the hunts himself, or enable the others to hunt more productively. Jes needed to forage or weave or care for children, or find a way to get these things done more expediently. Or they both could go in search of mates, being now of age. As far as that went, little Lin was just about of age, and far prettier than any other in the band. Except for that hand.

So Ned was here to invoke the spirits' aid for more ambitious hunting. The band had never been able to hunt elephants; they were simply too big and strong. But if they could find a way, they would have as much meat and bone as they ever needed. Tradition said that a suitable painting could capture the spirit of any creature and make it subject to the will of the painter. So if Ned could paint the elephant he had observed, and tie down its soul, they would succeed, and the lean times would be over.

But he couldn't just sketch it on the wall. He had to paint its spirit too, or the effort would be for nothing. So he was spending some time in the mountains, wrestling with his thoughts, and Jes was serving as liaison between him and the rest of the band. Because in the past Ned had figured out things that had been significantly beneficial to the band, and enabled it to prosper while other bands suffered. The elder members respected his mind, so they were giving him the chance to use it again. If he could by some magic find a way to help the band despite its problems, find the way to catch the animal's soul from afar—

Magic. He had never really believed in it, but perhaps this time the spirits of the band would commune with him. He stared at the blank wall, trying to see through it, to fathom whether there was any spirit in it he could talk to.

After a time the wall of rock seemed to waver, and it was indeed as if it became like clear water. He searched for the spirit in it, for every thing of nature had its spirit, but didn't see it. Unless—there *was* something inside. A man, standing with a bow and one arrow. A hunter. Watching for his opportunity. Were there game animals in range? Ned stared into the stone, seeking some answer. Could that be his own spirit, ready for the hunt?

Suppose he painted his own image? Would that provide him with spiritual strength for the hunt? So that instead of pinning the spirit of the animal so that mortal folk could hunt it, he invoked the aid of his spiritual self, enabling him to pursue the spirits of the animals out in the field? The notion was amazing, but maybe true.

What special powers might his own spirit bequeath him? Could it show him the path to good hunting? If it could enable him to hunt well, as he had not been able to before, what else might it help him do? There was so much to comprehend that he knew he should not act hastily. He must first understand, then paint, for greatest effect.

There was a sound behind him. That would be Jes, arriving along the path from their camp. Rather than lose his insight into the stone, he remained as he was. His sister would understand.

She came to stand beside him, facing the rock. He smelled a faint perfume of crushed flowers. That was surprising, for Jes did not adorn herself with anything feminine. "I'm looking into the rock," he explained.

"What do you see?"

Ned jumped. That wasn't Jes's voice! It was Wona's.

The spell of the stone was broken. He looked at the woman. "Why did you come here?"

"Flo found a good haul of roots to bring back to cook. Jes has more muscle than I do, so we switched jobs. She will take care of the roots, and I will take care of you. I am better equipped for that."

"Take care of me?" he asked blankly. He had never really liked or trusted this woman, who had been a drag on the band ever since she joined. Oh, he was quite intrigued by occasional glimpses of her body he caught by accident; that was the one thing she had in full measure. She was a truly lovely woman. Once he had seen—but that was nothing he should dwell on. She was after all his brother's wife. The fact was that she was a liability to the band. She took care of no one except herself.

"You have been a stripling. It is time you become a man."

"I don't understand."

"Precisely." She stepped into him, put her arms around him, drew him close, and kissed him on the mouth.

Ned was stunned for a moment. Then he lurched back, pushing her away. "We have no business like that!"

"Not before this," she said, turning his objection into an agreement. She put her hands to her simple hide robe and pulled it open, showing her full breasts.

Ned was mesmerized by them. Women often enough wore no more than skirts, but Wona normally kept herself covered, especially in the sun. Thus her body had not only the appeal of its kind, but that of novelty. She was older than he was, but that simply meant that she was in the full flower of her sexual appeal, while he was, as she put it, a stripling.

She let him look as long as he chose. Her gentle breathing made her breasts rise and fall rhythmically, and they jiggled just enough to call attention to themselves. Her eyes remained fixed on his face, and he didn't dare lift his gaze to meet them.

Finally he forced himself to turn away. "I must return to my business," he said.

"And what business is that?" she inquired.

Suddenly it seemed foolish. "Looking at the rock. To— to find its spirit."

"Of course. We need the help of the spirits."

He turned back to her, and was caught by the sight of her breasts again. "You don't find it foolish?"

"Ned," she said seriously, "I find nothing about you foolish. You are the smartest man I have encountered. You have helped your band many times by figuring out better ways to survive. You will do it again. I have nothing but admiration for you."

He flushed with pleasure, though he distrusted this. "I don't know what better way I can figure out this time. Our territory is too small; other bands are crowding us, and in time they will displace us entirely. I can't make there be more animals to hunt or more wild grains to harvest. Even if I could, the other bands would just move in and take them from us.''

She removed her robe the rest of the way and stood naked. Her body was the stuff of dreams. ''Perhaps not. But if anyone can find a way, you are the one. I believe in you.''

''I have found nothing,'' he said, rejecting something other than her profession of belief. It was in his mind that she was teasing him, trying to make him react, and make a fool of himself. She was probably bored, and this was her entertainment. There had been times before when she had touched him or rubbed against him, by accident he thought, but sending forbidden thrills of desire through him. Once when he had had to lift her down from an upper ledge—it had been days before he stopped thinking about that. She was his brother's wife, he reminded himself again; he had no business thinking of her at all.

''Then let me help you search.'' She stepped into him again, enclosing him with her bare arms and body.

He froze. ''Why are you teasing me?'' he demanded. ''Why don't you go away?''

Her reply was unconscionably direct. ''I have had your brother's child. Now I want yours.''

''But you can't—I can't—''

''No one else will know. But your child will be smart, like you. Give me a smart boy, Ned.''

''But you are Sam's wife!''

''And I will remain so. No one will know. Give me your child.''

''I will not!'' But he didn't move. She was holding him, and he couldn't break away. It was not a matter of physical strength.

''Shall we see about that?'' she asked mischievously. She put her hands to his clothing and began undoing it.

She was serious. He tried to back away from her, but

found his back against the rock face he had been staring into; he could retreat no farther. She soon got him naked, and of course his eager member showed.

Still, he tried to protest. "I must not do this with you. I see your face; I know you for my brother's wife."

"Then I will not show you my face," she said. She turned around and put her back to him. Her posterior view was just as guiltily exciting as her anterior view. "Hold my breasts."

"I can't—"

"I think you can." She reached back and caught his dangling arms. She lifted them up to enclose her, and set his hands on her two breasts. She used her hands to press his hands in to her, so that they made the breasts flatten against her chest. They had a special soft resilience that could be like no other thing. Ned felt as if he were floating; this was unreal. But also wonderful. And awful.

After a while she spoke again. "I think you are ready now. Hold my hips."

"What?"

She reached up and caught first one hand and then the other, setting them on her soft hips. "Hold tight."

Of their own volition, his hands tightened on her evocative flesh. The breasts had been phenomenal; so were the hips. All of her was wondrous. His guilt only enhanced the appeal of the touching.

She bent forward, not falling, because his hands held her bottom in place. She reached under and behind herself, and caught him where he had become involuntarily hard, and guided him, and suddenly he was plunging into her hot slick cleft, unable to restrain himself any longer. Part of him was horrified that such a thing could happen with his brother's wife, but more of him was carried along by the explosive joy of the depth of her. She was, indeed, making him a man.

She held her position until he subsided, then straightened up and leaned her back against him. "You see, you were able to do it, and most admirably. And you did not see my face."

Then she was gone, how, he was not sure. He was so amazed by the whole experience that he hadn't seen her go. Had it happened at all? But he was naked and spent, and he could not have imagined so much. And there was the piece of bread she had left him, that Flo had sent for him to eat. She *had* been here.

He ate the bread, and stared again at the wall, trying to see the spirit picture in it. But all he saw was an image of Wona, slender, with soft breasts and soft hips. Was that her spirit in the wall? Because she had come to him? Or was it just an interference, preventing him from achieving the vision he needed?

He left the wall and walked around the area, staring at the blue sky and the brown rocks, trying to get his thoughts straight. He needed to clear Wona from his mind before he could focus on the proper painting. Why had she come to him? She said because she wanted his child, but she had shown little interest in her daughter by Sam. Maybe it would be different if she had a boy. Maybe she thought she could get a boy from him. A smart boy. That Sam would think was his own. That made sense, perhaps, but Ned didn't much like the notion. He wanted to have his own child with his own wife, when he found a girl to marry. He didn't want mischief with his brother, and this was surely that.

The answer was simple: he wouldn't touch Wona again. She had caught him by surprise, and seduced him, but if she came again he would tell her no. He would try to forget their sole encounter, and pretend it had never happened.

Satisfied, he returned to the wall. He stared into it. This time he saw a herd of giraffes. Should he try to paint them? None had crossed the local territory recently, but maybe they would come if he painted them.

The day was declining. He would wait until morning, and if he still saw the giraffes, he would paint them. He still wasn't sure whether it was better to paint the animal or himself, but maybe the spirits in the stone would guide him.

He heard someone coming. Was Wona returning? He

nerved himself to tell her no. But it turned out to be Jes.

"It's a relief to see you," he said gladly.

"I had to switch jobs with Wona," she explained.

"She told me." Should he tell her any more?

Jes looked at him. "She's been at you," she said.

His sister could read him like a fresh trail! "What could I do?"

"Apart from telling her no?"

"I tried."

"She's just diverting herself, you know. She doesn't care about you or Sam or this band."

"I know. I'll tell her no next time."

She dropped the subject. "Have you figured out the picture?" The blank rock was evidence that he hadn't started it yet.

"I was starting to, when she came. I tried to see what spirits it contained. I saw my own, I think."

"But your spirit is alive," she protested. "There would be only dead spirits in the stone."

"I don't think so, because we couldn't hunt an animal that's already dead. I must capture a live spirit, and pin it to the stone by the painting, so the creature can't escape us. So there must be live spirits here."

She nodded. "I hadn't thought of that. But then you shouldn't have to look *in* the stone for them; they must be outside it, until you pin one down."

He nodded in turn. "That does make sense. So when I saw my own spirit, it was like a reflection in water. But later I saw a herd of giraffes."

"Maybe you should wait for an elephant."

"Yes. But suppose I let the giraffes go, and an elephant spirit never comes?"

Jes shrugged. "Maybe go for the giraffes, then, though I hate to seem them taken. They're so graceful."

"They're tall and lanky, like you." He could tease her about her form, because they had always been close. She knew he loved her as she was.

"Yes. But they have nicer faces."

"Your face is fine," he told her insincerely.

"Fine for a man, you mean."

This time he changed the subject. "I wondered whether to paint my own spirit. Do you think it would enable me to hunt well?"

"It might. Or it might pin you, so a lion could get you."

"That does it. I'll paint an animal."

"If Wona comes again, paint *her* spirit."

"But that would tie her forever to me," he protested, laughing.

"No, it would anchor her to this rock. Then we could move away, and leave her here."

"Except Sam wouldn't leave her."

"Sam's a great man, but an idiot."

"About Wona, anyway," he agreed.

She gave him a direct look. "Don't you be an idiot too, Brother."

"You had better get back to camp, before it gets too dark," he said. But she had broken his mood of doubt and despair, as well as giving him a good warning. She was right. He trusted her judgment, especially in this respect, because though she did not look it or act it, she was a woman, and she had always stood by him.

After she left, he found another crust of bread by his paints. He wasn't supposed to get two crusts in a day, but Jes must have given him hers. She was like that. She was a great person; how sad it was that she didn't have a body like Wona's. Unlike Wona, she deserved it. He knew that she really wanted to be a woman to a man, and only pretended otherwise because no man was interested.

He settled down on his bed of leaves in the shelter of an overhang. He had set up sharpened stakes to block the access, just in case some large nocturnal predator got a notion while he slept. He was remaining here by the wall until he painted the picture; that was the way it was done. Others could visit him, but he could not go back until he had a spirit pinned. It was a lonely business, but necessary. The spirits of the animals had to come to associate him with the countryside, rather than with the human band.

He slept, and dreamed of Wona, naked, backing into him, her buttocks soft yet firm, her wondrous breasts under his hands. The hot wet inside of her. He woke, quivering with desire. Oh, she had known what to do with him, how to make him respond! Even the memory of it brought powerful lust. He knew he should not have touched her, yet what an experience it had been.

He slept again, but the sensations returned. The woman was no good; he knew that. But what a body she had. What joy she had brought him—and what guilt.

In the morning he hiked to the nearby stream for water, and speared a fish. He was allowed to have anything he hunted or foraged near the picture site, as well as very limited supplies from the camp. It was the ritual. The longer he took to paint the picture, the hungrier he was likely to get. The spirits always came to those who got hungry enough. But he preferred to paint it soon, if he could.

He stood before the face of stone and willed his gaze through it, as before. At first his eyes would not cooperate, but then they did, and he stared beyond the surface. Would he find the man, or the giraffes? In time shapes formed, too small to be big prey animals, too low to be men. They were hyenas! Trust them to come and interfere with his vision. They were capable hunters, but often preferred to scavenge what others hunted, including what the band killed. They seldom actually attacked men, but neither did they retreat far; it was as if they were making up their minds about whether to fight. A concentrated charge with spears would make them give way, but they always returned. They were wary about arrows, and extremely hard to hit. They were a real nuisance, especially when the children were close. If a child ever got separated from the adults of the band—

There was a sound behind him. Was it Jes?

"No, it is me," Wona said, understanding his thought.

"Go away," he said, not removing his gaze from the stone.

"In a bit," she agreed. "What do you see in there?"

"Hyenas. They always appear where they are not wanted."

She laughed. "Do you really think of me as such a creature?"

"Yes."

"And you will not look at me."

"You are my brother's wife. I want nothing to do with you." There: he had told her.

"Your words are one thing. Does your body say the same?"

It did not. Her very presence raised a tide of lust. But he did not need to yield to it. "Go away," he repeated. "I am trying to fathom the spirits in the stone, so I can paint them."

"Surely you will succeed. I will leave you to it shortly. I am removing my clothing."

Another illicit thrill went through him. He fought it. "How can you be sure Sam will not see, here in the daylight?"

"I always know where he is. Now I am removing your clothing." Her hands touched him, doing it.

He continued to stare into the stone, lest he give her the victory by being made to look at her. But it didn't stop her. In a moment he was naked. She had at least a half victory, because now his lust was revealed.

"Shall I face away, again?" she inquired. "You do not need to look at me. It is not your eyes I need."

He did not answer. It did not stop her. He found himself staring into the wall past her head, his hands on her breasts, his member between her legs.

"Hold my hips," she said.

"No." So she would fall over when she attempted to do it.

But she merely lifted herself to her toes without bending, and reached back to guide him in, upward. She squeezed her buttocks against him, teasingly.

Suddenly he could stand it no more. He pulled her against him, his hands still on her breasts, and plunged deeply into her. She had made him do it, again, and it was just as intense and guilty as before. Even though his eyes were still fixed on the stone surface.

Then she was gone again, as before, leaving him gloriously spent—and ashamed. Because he knew he had wanted her to do what she had done, wrong as it was.

How was he going to stop this? It couldn't go on, yet he was vulnerable to her approaches as long as he was alone by the stone.

He tried to focus on the spirit animals, but couldn't. He turned away from the stone and walked to the river. He splashed the chill water on his face. He was supposed to be an intelligent man; why couldn't he figure out a way to stop this?

Because he didn't really want to stop it. Wona had sought to have her will with him, and she had succeeded. He might have fended her off the first time, but once he had sampled her delights, he could not deny her again, however wrong he knew it was.

What, then, was he to do? He didn't know. So he put it as far out of his mind as he could, where it hovered like a hyena, and focused on his painting. He did not eat or drink any more, he simply searched the rock, determined to discover what was within it.

The heat of the day intensified. His vision blurred, and he felt oddly light on his feet, but he kept on staring into the stone.

Finally it came: the image of a lion. "What is your business here?" he asked it.

"I am keeping game animals away from this region," the

lion replied. It did not seem odd that it spoke in a human voice; it had always been suspected that animals could talk, if they wanted to.

"But we need those animals to hunt," Ned said.

"I don't care. I will keep them away until you starve. Then this territory will be mine."

"Then I will stop you."

The lion laughed. "Stop me? You? How can you do that, you puny thing?"

"By shooting my arrows into you, and throwing my spears, and cutting your bowels out with my knives."

"What makes you think I will stay still for that?"

"I will pin your spirit to this rock, so that you can't escape us. You may run, but you will not be able to run far enough. You may fight, but there will be one of you and several of us. We will destroy you. Then the game will return here."

"How can you pin my spirit?" the lion asked contemptuously.

"With my paints. I will paint you here."

Then the lion grew nervous. "Spare me, and I will tell you how to get rid of the woman."

That was tempting. But that would be benefiting himself by hurting the band, and he wouldn't do that. "No." It was easier to say no to the lion than to the woman.

"You really should reconsider," the lion said. "I have had experience dealing with females. It is necessary to keep them always in their place. You are failing to do that, and the consequence may be dire. Women are worse than lionesses."

"Not all of them," Ned said, thinking of his sisters. Without removing his gaze from the stone, he made his way to his paints. He had to paint the lion without ever looking away, or it would escape him. If it got away, its spirit would go to warn the physical lion, and it would be twice as cunning as before, and ruin their hunting entirely.

"Are you sure of that?" the lion asked. "One is coming now."

Oh, no! Was Wona returning? She would ruin everything.

But it turned out to be Jes. "Oh, you are painting," she said, pleased.

"A lion," he replied. "I must not look away from him, or I will lose him."

"Of course. I'll help you. Here is your brush. What paint do you need?"

"First I need the charcoal, to sketch him in."

"Oh. Here it is." She brought him the chunk of charcoal.

He began drawing the lion, who had frozen in place when Jes arrived. That was not surprising; normally visions could be seen by only one person at a time.

"Did Wona come again?" Jes asked.

"Yes. I tried to deny her, but couldn't."

"I was afraid of that. She is good only for one thing, but she's very good at that."

"Yes."

"Ned, you must tell the band. That's the only way to make her stop."

"But Sam—"

"He won't like it, but with all of us telling him, he will have to accept it. Maybe he will get rid of her, then."

Maybe it would work. But it would be an ugly scene. Ned sketched a while, each stroke better defining the lion. Then he thought of an easier alternative. "I will tell her I will tell Sam. Unless she stops now. She will stop, because otherwise she will be routed from the band."

"Won't work," the lion muttered.

"But she'll still be here, then," Jes said.

"But there won't be any trouble," he argued. "She will behave herself, and Sam won't be angry or hurt."

"All right," Jes said. "If that ends it. I'd rather see her gone, but you're right, it would hurt Sam awfully, and we don't want that."

"Fool," the lion said.

"The lion says I'm a fool," Ned said. "He says it won't work."

"The lion talks to you?"

"Yes. He offered to tell me how to get rid of her, if I let him go, but I refused."

"Oh—in your vision in the stone," she said. "I can't hear that."

"Maybe when you have your own vision, the animals will talk to you."

"Maybe. Do you need me any more? I had better return to the camp."

"Go. Once I have the sketch done, I'll have him pinned. I'll do the painting right away, so that nothing can happen to the sketch and free him."

"Good. I'll tell the others you are painting a lion." She departed.

"You will regret this," the lion said. "You don't know a thing about dealing with scheming females. You will just make it worse."

Ned ignored him and continued sketching. Soon he had the whole animal outlined. Now at last he could look away. This was just as well, because his eyes were hurting from the strain.

And there was Wona. "I would have come to you sooner," she said, "but Jes was here. So I waited until she was gone."

"Then you can hear this now. If you don't stop coming to me right now, I will tell Sam what you are doing. Then he will drive you from the band."

She met his gaze. "If you tell Sam, I will tell him that you raped me when I brought you food, and threatened to kill me if I told. So I had to keep coming to you, much against my will."

"But that's not true!"

"He will believe it."

"Why should he believe a lie?"

"Because he will want to," she said simply. "The same

way you want to possess me again, though it is the second time today.''

Ned thought about his brother, and realized it was true. Sam loved Wona, and accepted anything she told him. And he, Ned, did want her again, much as he hated himself for it.

"I told you," the lion said smugly.

He faced the wall. "Tell me what to do, and I will free you."

"Too late," the lion said. "I would have made that deal before you sketched me, but now you have injured my pride, and I will let you suffer."

"But you will suffer too! We'll kill you!"

"It will be worth it, to see the mischief that woman does to your stupid band. I shall not speak again." And the lion shut its mouth firmly.

"If you are quite through talking to the wall," Wona said, "let's proceed with our little tryst."

Ned was defeated. "As you wish," he said dully. Yet part of him—the masculine part—was relieved that it had turned out this way.

"Come undress me," she said.

"But you have been doing that yourself."

"That was before we came to our new understanding. Now you will undress us, and you will face me. In fact, we shall lie together, instead of doing it awkwardly on our feet. I think that's more comfortable. Don't you?"

He didn't answer. She had indeed bested him in threats, and now she was in charge. He approached her and started pulling off her clothing.

"Kiss me," she commanded.

He kissed her. The taste of her was forbiddingly sweet. Her real power over him was the same as over Sam: he did desire her.

"Put your hands on my buttocks and squeeze."

He did so, enjoying it, and hating himself for that.

"And after this rock painting is done, and you return to the camp," she said, "I will come to you on occasion, and you will stroke me and plunge me as I indicate, and make no sound. For I mean to have great satisfaction of you, little brother, until I get your child, and perhaps thereafter.'' She took his hand and led him to a suitable place for them to lie down together.

The lion had been right. He had only made it worse. And the worst of it was that any time she tired of him, she could simply tell her husband of Ned's ''rape'' of her, and the worst would happen.

Ned knew himself to be an intelligent and talented man. But he was no match for this merciless woman.

The notion of running streams in the middle of the Sahara, and of lions, giraffes, elephants, and all the rest, may seem strange indeed, but it was so. There are many rock paintings to document it. North Africa was a nice place to live, 10,000 years ago, though still somewhat dry; the running streams would have been intermittent following rain.

As the region slowly dried, the human and animal population became more pressed. Some creatures moved south, and some east, driven by the encroaching desert. People compensated by making several significant changes in life-style. Instead of merely hunting animals, they began to care for them: first short-horned cattle, then sheep and goats. That guaranteed a supply of meat and hides. Instead of merely foraging for wild grains, they began to grow certain types. Thus hunting and foraging gave way, to a degree, to herding and farming, as early in the Sahara region as in Asia. The same is true for pottery; we can not say for sure where it started, or whether it was independently devised. Its ultimate effect was potent; the language of the eastern Sahara folk of that time is now known by its Semitic derivative tongues, notably Hebrew, Aramaic, and Arabic. The folk of the Sahara had to leave the desert; but they didn't leave the world, and the systems they devised were to transform the rest of the world.

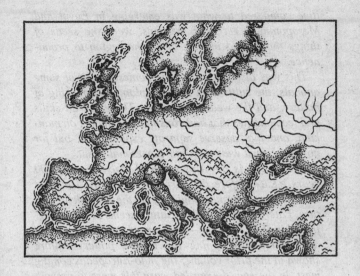

Chapter 9

SNOW

The stone age gave way to the ages of metals relatively rapidly in Europe: one millennium there was stone, the next there was copper, and the next there was bronze, to be followed ever more swiftly by iron and other novelties. Social changes were as significant; collective communities that granted little individual freedom gave way to a society where individual rights were valued. Multiple religions merged into a single religion, unifying the culture to a degree. Still, this was really the cultural and technological backwoods, prim-

itive compared to what was emerging in Egypt and Mesopotamia. Yet here, perhaps, were the seeds of things that would in time bring the region to prominence.

This was also the era of the domestication of some animals, the cultivation of some plants, the making of pottery, and the weaving of cloth. These are all skills and technologies that had considerable impact on mankind, and that deserve separate explorations, but for now they must wait on a more personal event.

The setting is the Alps north of Italy, about 5,300 years B.C.E.—before the current era—at the fringe of what is known archaeologically as the Remedello culture. Later the Bell Beaker culture seems to have originated in Iberia—Spain—and spread north and east, in due course overlapping the corded pottery culture shown in the prior volume: the Indo-Europeans coming west. In the end, the corded ware folk were to prevail, with their battle axes and horses, but at this stage they had not yet arrived in this region. Instead a series of lesser known cultures existed in central Europe. A traveler from the fringe of the Mondsee culture might have crossed the Alps to reach the Remedello culture, where the copper-working tradition was superior, and there he could have interacted in a historically insignificant but personally significant manner with the natives.

SAM TRUDGED THROUGH THE CUTTING wind of the high pass. The mountain range was always a challenge, but he enjoyed it, because the exertion made him fit. His heavy load of good cloth merely added to it, making his muscles strain and his heart pound pleasantly.

Each community had its own rules, and strangers were not necessarily treated kindly. That made trading potentially dangerous. That was why it was Sam who took the cloth out and brought back the goods, instead of one or two of the women. Actually Jes had wanted to come with him, and she could carry her load and defend herself, but the family had decided that she was needed at home to help protect them from marauders during Sam's absence. There was only so much Dirk could do, if several raiders attacked.

There were weapons available to the north, but a hostile tribe barred that direction. So Sam was following the trail to the southeast, open because hardly anyone cared to brave its rigors. He had been here once before, years ago, so knew the general route. But not well. He would have been better off in the company of a native of this region.

However, if this mission were successful, the women would have much less to fear from roving men. For Sam was in quest of the great new equalizer, the weapon that could make a woman as deadly as a man. The copper dagger. So sharp that even the slight muscle of a woman could make it lethal. So small it could be concealed on her body and forgotten until needed. With such knives, Flo and Jes and Lin and Wona would be safe.

Sam did not like to admit it, but this high region was becoming less familiar by the hour. He feared he had lost the way, and would not find the village he sought. But there was nothing to do but plow on.

He crested the pass and gained speed as he descended. There was a settlement of the folk who used the odd wide-mouthed clay pots. It was likely to be somewhere in this vicinity; all he had to do was find it. It was a long trek to reach it, but surely worthwhile this time.

Then he spied sheep. That meant there was a shepherd near. And if there was one person who knew an area well, it was that area's shepherd. So Sam put his hands to his mouth and called: "HALLOOOO!"

This spooked a few sheep, but Sam remained still and in plain view. He wanted the shepherd to locate him, and to see that he meant no harm to the flock. So he raised his hands in a gesture of harmlessness which was more symbolic than real. Sam could take care of himself, and would fight if he had to. But he hoped it wouldn't be necessary.

Soon a man appeared. He was of average size, but had a competent bow. That would be the shepherd, and he could have put an arrow into Sam if he wanted to. And perhaps would have, had Sam not made a point of desiring peace. Because sometimes raiders stole sheep, and sheep were valuable.

"Who?" the man called, in the mountain dialect. Sam had picked it up during his prior travels; he couldn't speak it well, but could understand it well enough.

"Sam, of the northeast," he called back. "Coming in peace to trade cloth for copper. But I have lost my way, and need guidance to recover the trail."

The shepherd came closer. His bow was slung across his back, but he could reach it rapidly. Actually Sam could reach his weapon rapidly too, but he kept his hands raised inoffensively. "You missed it by one peak. Go west and recover it."

"I shall, with thanks," Sam said, and turned to face west. But the mountain slope was plainly impassable in that direction. "Perhaps farther down."

"Easier to pass through my village," the shepherd said, smiling.

Sam returned the smile. "Does your village have copper for trade for cloth?" Sam indicated the heavy burden of cloth bound to his back.

"Yes."

"Then it seems I am not lost after all. I will trade at your village. I thank you again."

The shepherd pondered a moment, then made a significant offer. "I will return there tomorrow. You may travel with me, if you care to help herd sheep."

"It is an honorable profession," Sam said. "I am no expert at it, but I can profit well from instruction." He was saying that he would accept directions from the shepherd without taking offense.

"Then come share my fire this night, and we shall be on our way tomorrow."

"Gladly," Sam agreed. He had half hoped for something like this, but it was not a thing that could be asked for.

"Follow me." The shepherd turned his back and walked slowly east. This was another significant gesture: no one turned his back on an enemy. But Sam knew that the man was well aware of Sam's position and movement; shepherds were said to have eyes on their backs.

So Sam waited a moment, then stepped forward, matching the pace. In a moment the shepherd increased it, and they made good progress.

Only now did the shepherd's dog appear, answering a signal from his master. Sam knew that the dog would have been on him the moment he made a hostile move toward the shepherd. The fact that he had neither seen the dog nor heard him before indicated how well the animal was trained.

It turned out that there was a small cave under a ledge of the mountain. No track led to it, and Sam would never have noticed it, had he passed by it alone. That was no accident, he realized; it was a hiding place as well as a shelter. The shepherd probably had a number of such refuges spread across his region, so that wherever the sheep went, he had a safe retreat.

The dog did not enter the cave. He ranged away, watching the sheep. The connections between man and dog were invisible to others, but Sam knew the animal obeyed his master implicitly.

Inside was a small cache of supplies, including some dried meat, tinder, and wood. The shepherd took his fire cup and soon blew up a small, almost smokeless fire.

"This is unexpected luxury," Sam said, removing his burden and lying down. He unstrapped the sheath for his stone dagger and set the weapon on top of the bound cloth. He was thus disarming himself, signaling his lack of hostile intent. Such continuing cues were important.

In due course the shepherd handed him a section of the heated meat. Sam bit avidly into it. It was tough but good.

And this was the most important signal of all: no man fought with the one he ate with.

Then they talked. "I am Otzi," the shepherd said.

"I am Sam," Sam repeated. But now the introduction was formal. Now they knew each other.

Periodically they went out to check on the sheep, but the dog had things under control. Sam knew that the animal would give notice the moment there was a problem. The sheep were pretty well settled for the night, near a mountain streamlet. Sam and Otzi drank there too, before returning to the cave.

As they settled for the night, they talked, for shepherding was a lonely trade, and so was traveling. Sam told of his tribe, and the manner his family group had formed when it had gotten isolated in a bad storm; times had been rough at first, when his sister had been raped and had to leave her baby in the forest because she could not support it.

But later she had married, and Sam had married, and they both had children they could support, and things were better now.

"Marriage," Otzi said thoughtfully. "I had a good wife, but I lost her to the fever. Now my daughter runs our house in the village, for I am gone for months with the flock."

"What will you do when she marries?" Sam asked sociably.

Otzi shook his head. "I fear Snow will not marry. She's a good girl with a fine healthy body, smart and competent and good-natured, but her face is not pretty."

Sam was sympathetic. "You have described my sister Jes. She's as much of a woman as any man could want, except that she is tall, lanky, and homely of face, so no man wants her." He shrugged. "Beauty isn't everything."

"That's true. But it takes a man time to learn that. When I was young I sought beauty, but few wished to be alone while I was with the flock. Snow is like her mother, and once I knew her mother, I did love her."

Sam pondered for some time before answering. He realized that he would probably never see Otzi again, after he left this region, so it was probably safe to divulge a confidence. "My wife is beautiful like none other. Yet if I had it to do over, I think I would seek a lesser woman."

"You have a truly beautiful wife, and you crave less?"

"She is not as lovely in her nature as in her form," Sam explained.

Otzi laughed, not unkindly. "I have seen it elsewhere. We men are fools about form and nature."

"We men are fools," Sam agreed ruefully. "Yet I can't tell her no on anything."

"That's the way it is, with beauty," Otzi agreed.

In the morning they herded the sheep down the mountain. There were a few ornery goats that gave the dog some trouble; Sam appreciated the magnitude of the job the shepherd had. But Otzi knew the terrain as well as only a shepherd could, and he knew the animals, and he maneuvered them efficiently in the right direction. Sam helped mainly by going to certain wrong paths Otzi directed him to, and waving his arms to dissuade the goats. When the goats went the right way, the sheep followed. Since there were three directions they could go—right, left, and forward—Sam wondered how Otzi and the dog ordinarily managed. He realized that probably the village sent up another man for this drive. Sam's presence enabled Otzi to handle the matter without waiting for the arrival of help.

The herding was arduous, but they couldn't stop, because there was no water for the sheep along the way. Otzi seemed indefatigable, and Sam held up, but he felt the strain. He had the muscle to accomplish heavy lifting or fighting, and the stamina to walk long distances, but this constant running from place to place, with his heavy load of cloths, was wearing.

By evening the outlying fields of the village appeared, to

Sam's relief. The villagers came out to meet the flock. "You're early!" one cried.

"The sheep were ready, the weather was right, and I had help," Otzi explained, gesturing toward Sam.

"Good enough! We'll start the slaughter tomorrow."

Otzi, relieved of his job, guided Sam to his house in the village.

The village itself was formidably situated. It covered a substantial knoll, with a ring of sharpened stakes set around the base. There were piles of rocks inside, that could be thrown, and a few boulders that could be rolled down the steep slope if an enemy breached the palisades. Right now, however, there were no guards; everyone was busy with the rigors of the harvest and preparations for the slaughter. No guards? Sam frowned, disliking this carelessness, but not wishing to criticize the host village. Probably there were lookouts alert to spot any hostile intrusion long before it reached the village.

A woman came out to greet Otzi with a hug. She was much younger, close to Sam's own age, with strikingly light-colored long tresses, in contrast to the man's much shorter dark brown hair. She wore a necklace of amber beads. That meant she was unmarried, probably his daughter Snow. She would cut her hair shorter when she married, giving its fairness to her husband along with the beads. She was well shaped, and would have been pretty except for a somewhat coarse face.

Then Otzi introduced her to Sam, confirming the obvious. Snow smiled, but there was no denying that she was far from pretty despite having a very nice body. She really was not like Jes; she was better in the torso and worse in the face. If only that lustrous hair could cover her face!

She was apt in other womanly arts, though. They ate very well, and Sam was provided with a fine bed of straw to sleep on. Still, when he slept, he dreamed of Wona, the way she had been at first, avid for his embrace. The way she was only in his dreams, recently. He wasn't sure why she had changed, but suspected that she blamed him for giving her a girl baby.

Next day Otzi was busy helping with the threshing. Snow took Sam to the central house and departed, for she had work of her own to do. There were their wares, spread out on a table: bows, arrows, and what he wanted—several fine copper-bladed daggers. He had seen these elsewhere, and desired them, but had not had enough cloth to trade for them. Farther along was one of the necklaces of fine amber beads, that any woman would like, even if they weren't a signal of availability. But he was here for something more useful.

Sam unloaded his bundle and set his cloth down on the clear end of the table, and stepped back, inviting them to inspect it. He knew the workmanship was good; no one could excel Flo at weaving fancy material. She had worked for many months on this, helped by the other women of the family.

A woman came up and checked the cloth with practiced eye and fingers. She glanced at him and nodded, recognizing the quality of the handiwork.

"There is a problem," she said. After his night with Otzi and Snow, Sam was adjusting to the dialect, and knew he could use it well enough to get by.

"This is good cloth," Sam protested. "My sister Flo wove it, and she's the best—"

"No, the cloth is good. It's that we can't trade now. Crockson handles it, and he's busy with the harvest."

The harvest. Sam realized what that meant. Many villages had a policy of postponing all business during harvest time, because all their hands were needed. He should have realized that when he came down with the flock, he would by definition be there for the harvest.

"When will Crockson trade?"

"On our festival day, after the harvest is secure."

That did not mean a day, it meant a week, because they

had to get it done during fair weather, lest all be spoiled. But he was stuck for it.

"The cloth is satisfactory?"

"Yes, of course. But I lack the authority—I merely care for the goods, while the able-bodied work." Sam noticed her hunch, realizing that she was not able-bodied; otherwise she would be out in the field too.

Sam sighed inwardly. "Then I will have to wait upon that day. But may I examine the wares now?"

"Certainly, if you wish."

The woman stepped back. He moved down to the daggers. He picked up the best one and touched its keen edges to his finger. He hefted it, feeling the balance. The handle was of wood, with the copper blade wedged into a split at the end, and bound in place by fine cord. It came with a wooden sheath, superior to the ordinary sheaths of woven grass, with leather thongs attached to tie it in place. A very nice instrument.

He smiled and set it down before him. He picked up the second one. This, too, was nicely made, slightly lighter but no less sharp. He set it beside the first.

He reached for the third, but the woman grunted negatively. "Crockson will not give three," she said.

Sam nodded. The woman might lack authority, but she knew what was what. They would give him two for his cloth, but not three. He considered; perhaps he could bargain. But he wasn't sure, because they were very nice daggers, and surely worth the price.

"Suppose I stay here and help with the harvest?" he inquired.

The woman studied his heft and muscle. "Then I think Crockson would agree to the third knife."

Sam nodded. The deal had in effect been made. "I shall see you again on the festival day," he said, rebundling his cloth and heaving it to his shoulder. She nodded in return.

❋

The following days were busy indeed, as the work of the harvest proceeded. Sam stayed with Otzi and Snow, after making an informal oath of brotherhood to the girl so that it would be acceptable for him to remain with them more than a night. The more he knew of the father and daughter, the better he liked them. Otzi was a competent, hard-working herder and hunter, and Snow was the same in woman's work. It was too bad she was having such difficulty finding a husband. On occasion she removed her clothing so as to wash—something that women thought necessary—and though he studiously ignored her at such times as a matter of brotherly protocol, he was aware of her healthy body. She had breasts and thighs that could certainly put a man into rapture, if she chose. And weirdly lovely hair. Did a face matter so much?

At last the harvest and slaughter were done, except for a few loose ends. Some of the goats had strayed, and now they had to be rounded up and brought in for the slaughter. Sam went afield with Otzi and Snow, for it would take all three of them to catch the frisky animals. But it would be a relatively easy day. Tomorrow would be the festival.

"I'll be glad to make my trade and be on my way home," Sam said. "But it has been nice enough with the two of you."

Snow laughed. She did that often, pleasantly. "You know that Crockson wanted to have you stay this week, because of your strength for the heavy work?"

"I suspected," Sam said. "But it was good work, and I am promised an extra knife."

"We shall see that that promise is honored," Otzi said.

"I am glad you stayed," Snow said. "You are a good man."

Sam, embarrassed by the compliment, did not reply. They continued to the pasture where the goats had strayed.

They went after the goats, catching each one and tying it temporarily while they went after the next. Snow was good at it, for a woman; she seemed to like being out in the field for a change. She sweated as she got hot. Sam liked that; Wona was careful never to exert herself enough to sweat. Not even when having sex on a hot night. Not that she bothered, any more.

Sam spied another goat, and ran to head it off. He needed to get ahead of it and turn it back toward the others. But it was a fleet one, and it surprised him by running right down the path toward the village. By the time he caught up with it, they were almost in sight of the houses. He trapped it in a narrow spot, and managed to lay his hands on it so it couldn't get away. It seemed a waste to haul it all the way back to the pasture; he could take it the shorter distance in to the main village pen.

So he looped his rope around its neck and hauled it along. But as he approached the village, he heard something. So did the goat; its ears perked up, and it snorted.

The noise sounded like human screaming.

Sam's battle reflexes cut in. Maybe it was just a goat being slaughtered; they could scream like children when hurt. But maybe it wasn't. So he hauled the goat off the path, and approached the village under the cover of rocks and brush. He had gotten to know the area in the past few days, and hiding came naturally. The goat, nervous, was silent.

Soon Sam got a good look at the village mound. There was frenzied activity there. For a moment Sam couldn't grasp it. Then he saw one of the village children being carried to the edge by a strange man. The man threw the child to the ground, drew his knife, and stabbed the child in the chest. The child screamed once more, and died. The man turned and went after another child, much in the manner Sam had been going after goats.

Sam was chilled. This was an enemy raid! The village had been taken unaware, and the people were being slaughtered. There would be no mercy; only babies under a year old would be taken, because they could be adopted into the enemy tribe. All others would die.

Sam knew he couldn't help the villagers. All he could do was warn Otzi and Snow, so they could escape before being discovered. He loosed the rope from the goat's neck and let it go; there was no point in keeping it, now. Then he ran back up the path.

In time he heard something. He cocked his head, listening. It sounded like a faint scream ahead.

The girl! Something was happening.

Sam broke into a run. He charged on around a bend and over a small crest. Now he saw several figures in wild activity ahead. They were quarreling or fighting, not aware of his approach. As he pounded on toward them, he recognized the clothing of Otzi and his daughter. They were being beset by two of the raiders, who must have ambushed them. One knocked Otzi down and stomped his ribs. The other grabbed Snow and ripped at her clothing, hitting her in the face as she resisted. He was raping her!

Sam was running swiftly, but it seemed painfully slow because of the distance to cover. He could only see, not stop what the raiders were doing. But his rage was burgeoning, because once he had seen his sister Flo raped, and had not been able to stop it or even protest. Today he had a score to settle with all rapists.

Then at last he was there. He lifted his staff and knocked one man on the head, sending him spinning to the ground. Then, panting, he whirled on the other, who was pinning the girl to the ground. He grabbed the man's hair with one hand, and one leg with the other hand, and heaved him bodily up into the air. Such was the strength of his fury, he whirled around in a full circle, then threw the man into a tree. The man struck the trunk and dropped to the ground without a scream, just two thuds.

Sam turned back to the first raider—but he was already up and running away as fast as he could manage. Sam doubted he could catch him. So he went to Otzi, who was woozily sitting up. The man tried to lift his arms defensively, not recognizing Sam.

"Easy!" Sam said. "It's Sam. I routed the two raiders."

Otzi looked round, seeing that it was true. "Ambush," he said. "I tried to fight them—"

"They had clubs and surprise," Sam said. "I saw from a distance, but couldn't get here fast enough."

Snow groaned, and they both looked at her. Her skirt was half pulled off, and her face was a mass of blood. Blood was in her eyes, blinding her.

Sam went to her, pulling out the cloth he used to clean his own injuries, at such time as he had any. Wary of her reaction, he spoke before he touched her. "Sam. I am Sam. You know me. The raiders are gone. I will help you."

"Sam," she repeated, recognizing the name and voice.

"I will wipe your eyes," he said. He poured some water into his cloth, and used the wet material to clean out one eye and then the other, carefully.

"You are so gentle," she said as she opened her eyes.

Otzi snorted. He had gotten to his feet, and was looking at the raider by the tree. Gentle? The man had been pulped.

Sam cleaned off the rest of her face, then wrung out the cloth and gave it to her to stanch the continuing flow from her nose. "Hold it tight," he said. "I know it hurts, but you must not lose more blood. I think that's your only injury, except—" Then he caught himself.

She caught the implication anyway. Her free hand came up and ripped the amber necklace off. She threw it away. "Except I am no longer a maiden," she said bitterly. "No one will marry me now."

"No, that's not—" Sam started, but had to break off again. Because it was true: most men wanted to marry maidens. The raider had deprived her of her most precious attribute. The only thing that might have made up for her homely face—which now was worse.

She began to cry. Sam, feeling somewhat helpless, lifted her to a sitting posture and put his arms around her somewhat in the manner of a father, trying to comfort her.

"That brigand is dead," Otzi said.

Sam realized that this, too, was probably true. "I was angry," he said a bit ruefully. "My sister—she was—I was then too young to stop it. I have been ashamed ever since."

Otzi nodded. "Justice has been done. Take his things."

Sam shook his head. "No. I want nothing of his. You can have them."

"I want nothing of his either," the man said grimly. He studied the body. "He's of the Green Feather tribe. Those folk are nothing but mischief."

"Yes," Sam agreed. "We know of them too. They plunder and—" Yet again he caught himself. What they did was rape any women they caught alone or inadequately protected, exactly as in this case.

"We can leave him here as he is, to rot without burial," Otzi said. "That is fitting."

"That is fitting," Sam agreed. Then, belatedly, he remembered the main threat. "The village—the raiders have taken it. They are killing all the people. We must flee."

"The raiders!" Snow cried. "The village!"

"Too many to fight," Sam said. "I saw them when the goat led me there. The one who ran just now will tell them of our presence. We must get well away from here, immediately. I was coming to warn you—"

"Then all is lost," Otzi said grimly. "They waited until the harvest to strike, so as to glean the richest spoils."

"Yes," Sam agreed. He did not comment on the village's laxness about defense. "We must go."

Otzi looked at his daughter, whose nose was no longer bleeding badly. It would, unfortunately, never be normal again. Her appearance had not been great before; now it was ruined. "We must go," he agreed.

"Yes," she said, understanding the situation all too well. Sam released her, and she started to get up—and stopped. "Oh!" She fell back flat on the ground.

"What is it?" Otzi asked, concerned.

"The pain," she gasped. "I can't stand."

Otzi winced. Sam knew why; things were already very

bad for them, and would be worse if she could not walk.

"We must find the injury," Otzi said, his voice carefully controlled. Sam knew that the man did not want to further alarm his daughter, who already had more than enough misery. But they had to move out. "Where is the pain?"

She considered. "My back. My legs. I don't know."

Sam turned his back. "You must check," he told Otzi.

"Yes." There was the sound of clothing being moved. "I see nothing."

"I don't feel it now," she said. "Maybe I can get up after all." But then she cried out with pain. "Oh! I can't!"

"But there is nothing," Otzi said.

"There is pain," she retorted.

"Sam, you have the look of a warrior about you," Otzi said, carefully not implying that Sam had any affinity with the raiders. "Do you know of internal injuries?"

"Some," Sam admitted. "But only on men." He did not turn around. Instead he went to pick up the remnant of the amber necklace; it wouldn't be good to leave it here for the raiders. He knew Snow wouldn't take it back, so he tucked it in a pouch.

"Let him look," Snow said. "There must be something. I have no modesty left." Even in her distress, she was politely pretending that Sam had never seen her body. He was her ad hoc brother, having only familial interest in her. On occasion, at need, a brother would view a sister's body, but never speak of it.

But she was unfortunately correct again: the protocols had been savaged, and had become pointless. She had to get moving soon, or the raiders would catch them and kill them all. Sam turned to look at her. She was lying on her stomach now, stretched out.

He kneeled beside her. "I must put my hands on you," he said cautiously. "I mean no harm."

"Yes. Touch me."

He felt her upper legs, which were firm and well fleshed. There was nothing wrong with them. He struggled to main-

tain a brotherly perspective, but it was impossible. He felt
her back and hips through the clothing. They were in good
order too. She was a supremely shapely figure of a young
woman, and his body responded regardless of his mind. "I
find no injury."

"I'll turn over," she said. She started to—then stopped,
with another exclamation of pain.

"In the belly, maybe," Otzi said. He looked nervously
down the path toward the village.

Sam put his hands carefully on her and turned her over.
She winced but did not cry out again. He felt her abdomen,
but it seemed firm, and she expressed no pain. "Unless there
is an injury that does not show—"

"Find it!" she said. "Take off my skirt. Find it." Her
voice was rising with incipient hysteria.

Sam looked helplessly at Otzi, but the man only shrugged,
glancing again toward the village. So Sam carefully worked
her skirt off, laying bare her upper thighs and belly. Her
genital region was in order, not betraying its recent violation. There was no apparent injury. He turned her over. Her
bottom was well formed and uninjured. "Maybe when the
raider—inside—" he suggested hesitantly.

"No. That hurts, but not the same way. This is farther
back. And down my right leg."

He felt down her back. "Tell me when you feel the
pain." He put gentle pressure on her back and hips, but got
no reaction. He pressed her firm buttocks, and all around
her right thigh, with no result other than his own quickening,
guilty interest. Wona would not let him touch her this way.
Actually, Wona seldom let him touch her at all, recently.
That kept coming back to him.

"It doesn't hurt while I'm still," she said. "And your
touch is very gentle."

"I have sisters," he said, embarrassed. "They are not
tough like men. They are—soft." Like her. But he had
never touched a sister this way. "I find no injury. Your body
is—perfect." He felt an embarrassing flush forming.

"We don't have time to delay. We must find out what this is," she said. "I will try again to get up. You watch, and see if you can see where the pain is."

She tried to turn over, but felt the pain immediately. "It hurts when you move yourself!" Otzi said. He was collecting his scattered equipment. He didn't have his bow, because he had not expected to hunt, but he did have his knife and axe. "Not when someone else moves you."

"Yes," she agreed. "I realize that now. It hurts only with my own motion."

"Ah, then," Sam said. "I have had that. Once when I fell and banged my back. A bruise—something inside makes it hurt. It is bad for a few days, then it passes, and is as if it never was. When you were thrown on the ground—"

"Yes," she said. "That must be it. I felt no shock at the time, but I landed hard. So it won't last." She was visibly relieved.

Sam helped her turn back onto her back and put her skirt back on, concealing his masculine reaction to the sight of her inner thighs and buttocks as he lifted her legs for her. In everything but the face she was a most compelling woman. That, too, kept coming back to him.

"You can't walk?" Otzi asked, his hope fading.

"Oh, Father, I would if I could," she said. "But the pain is so bad—it just shoots through me the moment I try."

"The raiders—" he said. "I hear them coming. We must go."

"You must go now," she agreed. "Leave me here." She glanced significantly down the path. "But lend me your knife first." She meant to kill herself before the raiders reached her.

"I can't do that!"

"I—maybe I can help," Sam said. "I think I could carry her to that cave we shared. It's not far. Then she could rest until she can walk, while we forage for her."

"But you have your own journey to make," Otzi pro-

tested. "And the weather is threatening. You have been delayed too long already. You don't want to get caught here."

"I have nothing to take back," Sam said. "My cloths,
and the knives I was to trade for, are in the village. I have
no supplies for the journey." He bent to take hold of Snow.

Otzi nodded. "There are supplies in the cave. Take them,
and welcome."

Sam stood, holding the girl in his arms. "But you will
need them yourself!"

"No. I have other business." He stepped out along the
path, going toward the village.

"Father!" Snow protested.

"The raiders are almost here," Otzi said. "You can't
escape them, carrying her. I will decoy them. Carry her to
the cave, and I will see that they never find you."

"Father!" Snow cried again, despairingly. "You are injured!"

"So I can't fight them," Otzi agreed. "Not without my
bow. I'll make a new one. Until then, I'll lead them astray.
They won't catch me; I know the terrain as they don't."

Sam nodded. "Come find us when it is safe."

"I shall. Now go!"

Without further word, or protest from Snow, Sam started
walking up the slope toward the region of the cave.

He heard Otzi hoot. It wasn't for them; it was for the
raiders, whose heavy tread Sam could now hear. There was
the sound of running. They had spied Otzi, who had of
course shown himself to them. The decoy was being pursued. "He's walking slow," Snow murmured. "He was hurt
too. Worse than he wants to show."

"But he can avoid them," Sam said, hoping it was so.

"Yes. It will just be more difficult."

Sam carried her at as swift a pace as he could manage
without making undue noise. The girl was light in his arms
at first, but became heavier as time passed. He could walk
at only half the speed he had when unencumbered. When
the stress on his arms started to become painful, he knew

that caution was better than valor. "I am tiring. I must set you down for a time, to rest.''

"Yes, of course. You are amazingly strong.''

Sam found himself blushing. He squatted, and set her carefully on the ground. He was able to put her against the trunk of a tree so that she could sit up comfortably. Then he turned away, stretching and flexing his arms, getting them limber again. There was no sound from the direction of the village; Otzi must be causing the raiders to save their breath for the pursuit.

"I must clean your cloth and return it to you,'' Snow said. "My nose has stopped.''

"At the cave,'' he said.

She smiled, fleetingly. The effort was pitiful, considering her ruined face, but he appreciated it. She was still hurting, physically and mentally, he knew, but she didn't complain at all.

That was all. When his muscles had recovered, Sam picked her up again and carried her onward. At her suggestion, he detoured enough to splash through a mountain stream. They both drank deeply of its chill water, then he splashed some distance up it, so that the raiders' dogs would lose any scent.

"The dogs,'' he said. "If they send them after your father—''

"He will club them off the mountain,'' she said confidently. "He can handle wolves with just his staff; dogs are easier. After they lose a few dogs, they'll stop.''

The cave turned out to be farther than he had thought. Snow did not weigh a great deal more than his load of cloths had, but she wasn't balanced on his back, and so distances seemed to be twice what they had been. It was evening by the time they reached it, and he needed Snow's help to find it, because it was more cunningly hidden than he remembered. That was good, because the raiders had little chance of locating it.

Sam did not dare start a fire, for the smoke would give

them away. But the cave was protected from the wind, and he gathered leaves and straw to make a comfortable bed for Snow. He helped her wipe her face again; her nose was swollen and sore, but that was part of the healing process. Then he had to carry her out so she could urinate—another bemusing experience for him, because she needed to be held upright so she would not soil herself. She was surely embarrassed by the procedure, but did not show it. His respect for her nature grew.

Then, as they chewed on the dried meat stored in the cave, they talked in a way they had not in the village. Sam told her of his family, with one sister his age, one Snow's age, and one younger.

"And what of your wife?" she inquired alertly.

"She is a beautiful woman."

"Doesn't it bother her to have you away so long?"

"No."

She wisely changed the subject. In due course she slept. He made sure she was well covered, then curled up beside her to sleep himself. It had been a most wearing day.

On the following day Snow began to walk, gritting her teeth against the shooting pains, because now she knew there was no actual injury there. Sam held her up so she could not fall, his hands on her waist so she could use her hands to hold a staff to help brace her. That worked reasonably well, though her jerkiness as the pain took her caused her body to shift under his hands embarrassingly. "I'm glad you're my brother," she murmured.

When she rested, he traveled to the stream to fetch water for her, and to look for any traces of the enemy. There were none; Otzi was evidently doing an excellent job of leading them astray.

In three days the pains were fading, and Snow declared herself ready to travel. She still winced as she walked, but it was clear that she could handle it. However, they had nowhere to go, because they did not dare approach the village until they were sure the raiders were gone, and they didn't know where Otzi was. So they waited, eating the last of the meat, and foraging for tubers.

On the fourth evening Snow broached an awkward subject. "You have been kind to me, Sam, and I would repay you in some way, now that the pain is fading." She lifted the hem of her skirt. "I can cover my face so that my ugliness does not disgust you, and—".

"I'm married," Sam reminded her quickly.

"Yes, of course. But there would be no need to tell your wife."

"I made you an oath of brotherhood."

"And you have more than honored it. I release you from it. It is not as if I have any virtue to preserve."

"For you, it can be so," Sam said cautiously. "Only your father and I know what happened, and neither of us would tell. No one need know—"

"*I* know."

That ended that aspect. She was firm on that subject. Her bitter honesty might cost her a marriage, but she would not cheat. "Yet I also know I am married," Sam said.

She nodded. "I thought you would say that. You are true to your wife, though I think she is not true to you. It makes you a good man."

Sam stared at her. "She—how could you know such a thing?"

She made a bitter laugh. "I know the nature of lovely women, having so longed to be one. She finds you dull. She is a fool."

Sam did not know what to say. He suspected she was right. But what could he do?

After a time he responded to another aspect. "You are not an ugly woman. Wona is."

She laughed. "Thank you, Sam. I understand what you mean."

That made Sam think of something. "I have two daggers.

Not as nice as the ones I was to trade for, but good enough. You must take one, until your father comes here. So that if we should be surprised—"

"What have I left to defend?"

This provoked him into a statement he hadn't intended to make. "Your life! You are still a nice young woman, with a very nice body."

"Oh, now you are interested in my body?"

"I was always interested in—" He caught himself. "No! I'm married. But if I weren't—"

She was immediately contrite. "I'm sorry. I am bitter, but I know it's no fault of yours. With my face, all I had to offer a husband was my maidenhood, and now—"

"No!" But of course she was right. So he amplified his thought. "My sister was raped, and I could not help her, any more than I could help you. I could not even avenge her against the man. It has been my shame. But her life continues."

"Your sister? You didn't say. Which one?"

"Flo. The eldest. She had a baby, and had to leave it in the forest. I think that hurt her more than the rape did. If I had only been grown, then, as I am now—"

"You would have thrown that man hard against a tree."

"Yes. After that, I might have treated him unkindly."

She had to smile. "At least you did that for me, and I thank you. He just rose up off me and flew through the air! But your sister—what of her, after that?"

"She married when I did. A man who had been injured, so could hardly walk. But when he recovered, he was a good hunter, and a good man. They made her take him, so that I could have Wona. She had a better bargain than I did." He hadn't meant to say that, but it came out.

"So Flo is happy now, and you are not?"

"Yes." Then he paused, surprised to hear himself say it. So he had to try to explain it. "I was cursed to love an ugly woman. So I tried to break the curse by marrying a beautiful one. But it's only her body that's beautiful; her spirit is ugly. So I did not escape the curse."

"Didn't you say you had a daughter?"

"Yes. Wilda is three. But Wona has no interest in her. She wanted a son. So Flo takes care of Wilda and Flint, and Wilda thinks of Flo as her mother. So Flo has a full life, despite what happened to her. You should be able to have one too."

"I wonder."

"I have your amber necklace. Will you wear it again?" He reached over his shoulder, into his pack, and pulled it out. "It can be repaired."

Snow began to cry, as they sat in the cave. But finally she took the necklace, tied its broken ends together, and put it on over her head. Then she settled down for sleep.

Sam was greatly relieved. Snow had accepted the notion that her life, like the necklace, might not be beyond repair.

The next day it snowed. They remained inside the cave, huddling together for warmth. Sam found himself wishing that he had not turned down her offer of sex, yet knew that it remained open, and said nothing. The meat was running out, and so had the tubers, so it seemed best to save their energy, he told himself.

The snow made their tracks visible, and that was dangerous. But it also made animal tracks visible, and that helped. Sam tracked a rabbit and caught it with a stone, and they had food again. This time they risked a small fire, trusting that the smoke would not be visible in the night.

"My father should come soon," Snow said.

"He is making sure he doesn't lead the raiders to you."

"Yes. But they won't stay in our village forever. After they finish feasting and raping and killing all the women and girls, they'll pack up and go home. Then my father will come."

"Yes." They didn't speak directly of the utter disaster that had wiped out the village. They kept the focus narrow, as if this were merely an inconvenience. It was the only way to stop the tragedy from overwhelming them.

The snowfall didn't last; it was too early yet. But was a warning of the coming winter. The cave would not do for that; they would need to find a regular house for Snow, and Sam would have to travel back across the mountains to home before the pass became impassable.

When half a moon had passed, they got bolder. They explored more widely, looking for signs of human presence. There was a column of smoke in the direction of the village, which meant the raiders weren't yet gone. No raiders seemed to be out ranging the land, however. "They must be getting careless," Snow remarked. "They are sleeping off their indulgences, resting for the journey."

"Yes. But we dare not approach too closely."

"Yes."

"Soon they will be gone, and my father will return. He is staying clear to be sure the raiders have no notion where we are."

"Yes." But that rationale was wearing thin.

Otzi staggered through the pass as night came. He was dead tired, but he hadn't dared rest. He had seen two more raiders with dogs, and he knew that if the animals got any whiff of him in his present state, it would be the end. He would have gone to the cave long ago, if it hadn't been for those dogs, because the animals could follow his trail to it even days later. So he protected his daughter by staying well away from her. Soon the raiders would be gone, and then he could check on Snow and Sam. Until then, he had to keep moving through the most difficult reaches of the peak pastures.

He moved out of the pass to a high gully that would shelter him from the cutting wind. It was getting cold again, and he was inadequately dressed for it. But he had handled bad times before. One, two, perhaps three more nights up here; then it would be safe to check on the village, and if that was clear, he could go to the cave to fetch the others.

He leaned his bow against the face of a rock abutment and sat down on the ground. The bow was unfinished; he had been working on it the past ten days while he avoided the Green Feather raiders. If only he had had his regular bow with him when the raiders struck! Then Snow would never have been raped; the two raiders would have fallen before they completed their ambush. He had been stupid ever to let his guard down, even when working around the village, and it had cost him and his daughter horribly. The only saving grace was the visitor Sam. Sam was a decent man who would take care of Snow, even if he wasn't looking for a wife.

He brought out his last scrap of dried meat and slowly chewed it. He had stretched it out as long as possible, but now he had to eat or starve. Tomorrow he would see about netting a bird; that would be better. Tomorrow maybe the raiders would be gone. Tomorrow maybe he would see his daughter again. Tomorrow would be better.

He finished the meat and tossed aside the remnant of gristle. It was dark; time to sleep. He arranged his cloak and lay down on the side that didn't hurt. The air was fiercely chill, but he could handle it. He was so fatigued that he sank immediately into a halfway pleasant daze, and then into sleep. He didn't even notice that his ear was folded over against the ground. Tomorrow . . .

There was another snowfall, heavier than before. Sam knew it would be heaviest on the peaks. If Otzi was still up there, he would have a difficult time.

But after several more days, the smoke died out, and they ventured to the village. It was in ashes; the raiders had burned down every house before departing.

Snow stared. Sam knew she had insulated herself from this reality, but now she had to accept it. There was nothing to return to.

"Father," she said plaintively. "He should be here. He would have seen the smoke."

Sam wanted to argue, but couldn't. She was obviously right. Otzi must have been caught by the storm. That meant he was dead.

"Oh, my father!" Snow cried. "I thought I had lost everything, but it was nothing! I should never have let him go alone."

"We could go back to the pass and look for him," Sam suggested weakly. "He was going to stay in the peaks until—"

"There is nothing there I want to find. I don't want to see my father dead." She looked at him, her eyes abruptly blazing. "Cut my hair!"

The sign of mourning. For marriage it was stylishly cut, but for mourning it was hacked off. She had not mourned for the folk of the village, insulating herself from what had happened there, but the loss of her father was too real. Sam understood, but was loath to oblige. "Maybe he crossed the mountains, leading the raiders far afield—he will return later—"

"Cut my hair."

So, reluctantly, he brought out his dagger he had forgotten to give her to carry, and used it to cut off her beautiful snow-blond tresses. She became a wretched creature of grief, with no remaining asset above the neck.

She took the silken hanks of hair and hung them up on the edge of a stone outcropping. Then she screamed out her misery, beating her little hands against the rock until they were bruised and bleeding. She scooped up dirt and ashes and rubbed them across her face and remaining hair. Sam turned away, unable to watch or interfere. He listened as her grief wore itself out, or at least her voice did, sinking at last to faint sobbing.

As darkness closed, she recovered awareness of their situation and joined him, a miserable creature in appearance and attitude. Her copious tears had turned some of the dirt on her face to mud. "What am I to do?" she asked plaintively.

Sam had been thinking about that. It was obvious that she could not remain here. Snow was in no condition, physically or emotionally, to even make the attempt to survive alone.

"I will take you home with me," he said. "You can do well with my family. My sisters will accept you."

"But you are married."

"But my brother Ned isn't. He is very intelligent, and he doesn't judge people by appearances. I think you would like him, and he would like you."

"But I have no value."

"He wouldn't care about that. I don't; none of us do. Because of Flo. We know it is character that defines a person, and you are a nice and competent woman."

"Then I will go with you," she said, as if it were a simple decision. Perhaps it was, considering the low esteem in which she now held herself. "In the morning."

They foraged amidst the ashes for scant materials, and found some stones and bits of half-burned wood to fashion a temporary shelter of sorts. They lay down together, as brother and sister.

As he drifted to sleep, he felt her sobbing quietly again. The first fury of her grief was ebbing, but it was far from spent. There was nothing he could do about it. Her grief was real, and had to be expressed.

Tomorrow they would set off for his home. Sam hoped Ned would like Snow. Yet that thought was tempered by the realization that Sam liked her himself. It was true that her face was not beautiful, and her smashed nose and shorn hair hardly improved it. But she was a brave, honest, and feeling girl who would never treat a man the way Wona did. In fact, Snow was an ugly woman Sam realized he could love. If only he weren't married. But he *was* married, and there his speculation ended.

What happened to Otzi? As it happens, we know that with considerably more authority than we know about his life or family. He was injured in the rib-cage, and deadly tired, and so hungry that his body was metabolizing its own substance, and the climb to the pass was wearying. As evening came, he decided to rest, hoping to restore himself before going on. He lay down on the ground and sank into a deep sleep. Too deep; he was chilled, and his state became more like a coma. He was in the lethargy of hypothermia. And so he just kept sinking, as the night came on and chilled his body further. The snowstorm came and buried him, and he never roused. He was frozen where he lay.

The snow did not melt with spring. It became part of a glacier. It tried to carry his body down the slope, but he got hung up in a gully and remained. For five thousand years. Until the year 1991, when the snow finally melted in that region, and his body was exposed. This discovery made quite an impression on the modern world. He is now known as the Ice Man.

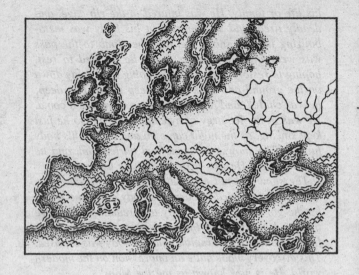

Chapter 10

TRIERES

Circa 430 B.C.E. Greece was one of the centers of advancing civilization. The polis or city-state was the essential political, economic, and social unit. Most were not large, by later standards; populations of 5,000 to 50,000 might have been typical. Athens, with 250,000, was a giant, and thus one of the dominant cities of the region. Its main rival was Sparta, about a hundred miles distant by air, but considerably farther by foot. Most cities were oligarchies, with about 10 percent of their populations having power; Sparta was a monarchy. Athens was unusual, in that it was a democracy—that is, run by male citizens, not women, slaves, or foreigners (there are, after all, limits); each year 500 citizens over age thirty were chosen by lot to govern it. However, the principal power was wielded by a board of ten generals who were elected for one-year terms. Popular generals could be re-elected, so some became quite powerful. An example was the statesman Perikles, who was in power at this time, having been in office for twenty-eight years. He was a clear thinker and a great orator, able to use both reason and emotion to guide his followers. He was one of the factors in the greatness of the city.

But this was now threatened. Athens and Sparta went to war in 431 B.C., and because of their networks of alliances, this meant that most of Greece was involved. Athens was matchless on the sea, while Sparta dominated on land. Sparta marched her army into Attica, which was the home territory of Athens, and ravaged the countryside. The Athenians, outnumbered two to one, had to retreat. The population of Attica poured into Athens, hiding safely within its walls while the Spartan forces ranged outside. But Athens was not in much trouble, because her fleet of ships kept her supplied from elsewhere. Her fleet also launched naval raids against Sparta and her allies. Thus Athens more than held her own despite being under siege, and Sparta had to withdraw. It was a standoff. But the war was far from over; it was merely in remission for a few months. These were surely not great months for the residents who returned to their devastated farms and dwellings.

One family lived on the large long island of Euboea, to the east of the Greek mainland. They were in the hinterlands, and had not had to flee to the city walls, but they, too, had surely felt the ravages of the war. The island had been strategically significant during the

Persian wars, being a staging area for the Greek defense, and was widely regarded as Athens's most important possession. It was a vital region for grain, being better than Attica for farming. When the war broke out, the people of Attica sent their cattle and sheep to Euboea for safety. Yet the association was not entirely easy; there had been a rebellion before the war, and would be another during it. So though there was no enemy invasion of the island that we know of, it was under stress. This family's resources had been severely depleted by the required "voluntary" support for Athens; and its fields had been overrun by poorly tended cattle belonging to others. The neighbors were in similar straits. They had to take strenuous measures to ensure their survival.

JES BROUGHT IN A BUNDLE of wheat stalks she had scavenged from the leavings of the rogue cattle and dumped it down before Flo. "What they didn't eat, they trampled on," she said, disgusted.

"That's the point," Flo said, shrugging. "To starve us out." She squinted at the bundle. "This is good enough; we'll thresh it and get enough."

Lin agreed, opening the bundle. She picked up her makeshift stalk beater.

"We need more." Jes turned to go back to the small coastal pocket of arable land that was their farm. Damn these cattle! She and the men would have driven them off, but the animals had been unstoppable, and they were not allowed to kill them. Three men, a boy, and a woman were not enough; they would have been trampled too. So they had had to hide like cowards, and let the creatures do what they wished. That meant the destruction of their gardens, severe damage to their house, and trampling of their crops. But it was not as bad as an enemy raid would have been; their men had not been killed, their women had not been raped, and their children had not been enslaved. They had been able to come out the moment the cattle left, thus saving some of their things. On the whole, they were well off, compared to those in Attica who had fled to the nearest walled settlements.

"Stay," Flo said, looking around. "We have something to do, while Sam is away fetching supplies."

Jes had heard that tone before. "Wona?" she asked.

"Yes. You know the problem?"

Jes glanced at Lin, who at twelve was becoming a lovely young woman. Except for those fingers. "Maybe."

Lin looked up. "She's seducing Ned."

So they did know. "Ned told me, and I didn't like it, but I kept his secret," Jes said. "We're close. He keeps my secrets too."

"I have no quarrel with that," Flo said. "Trust must not be broken. But I suspected, so I had Lin spy on them to verify it. I think you will break no trust if you tell us the rest of it now. We need full information before we act—and we must act."

"Now, while we can," Lin said. "While Sam is north, and Ned is buying wool in Geraestus." That was the city on the extreme southern tip of Euboea, their closest metropolis. They were country folk, but they did need supplies, and a market for their weaving.

Jes felt a load leave her. "She wants to bear his child, because he's smarter than Sam. She came on to him, and he—he was inexperienced, and didn't know how to stop her. She—he said she had overwhelming sexual appeal. It was like a conquering army, and he was vanquished before he ever tried to fight." She paused, ruefully wishing she herself had appeal like that. Ned had told her about it in excruciating detail, and she was ashamed to admit even to herself that it had driven her into a private sexual ecstasy of desire and frustration. "Then when they had done it—really, when he had stood still and she had done it to him—she told him that if he told, she would tell Sam he had raped her, and that Sam would believe her. He knew Sam would. Sam—"

She shrugged, and both Flo and Lin nodded. Sam was a good man and a good brother, but what he didn't know about women would fill a long scroll. "Ned wants to get out of it, but doesn't know how."

Flo nodded. "That's what I thought. Ned is our smartest member, but a woman with a figure and a will can make a fool of any man when she sets her mind to it. Ned can't free himself. Neither can Sam, if he even suspects. That's why we'll have to do it for them."

"She won't go without reason," Lin said, glancing across to where Wona sat watching the children. The children didn't really need watching, but Wona never volunteered for any hard work, and this was easy work.

"I don't like killing," Jes said. "Not when it's someone I know." Actually, she had never killed a human being. But she had been ready to, once when she and Ned had been caught away from home by men intent on rape and murder. She had distracted them, and Ned had stabbed them, and she felt responsible. Jes had no affection for Wona, but she did know her personally, and that made the difference.

"Neither do we," Flo said. "So we'll have to make a deal with her. I have thought this out. If we can get her a better man, by her definition—one who can put her in idle luxury—she'll desert Sam. Sam may be unhappy for a while, but he'll be better off, and he'll be able to find another woman."

Jes nodded. "With those muscles, he can get a woman. But who would take Wona? Anyone who knows her would know better. Sure, any man would make a wench of her, for a night or a fortnight, but wouldn't marry her."

"So we have to go farther afield," Flo said. "In the big city there should be men who judge by nothing but appearance. That is the one thing she's got. We've all seen how the men stare at her."

"And how she encourages it," Jes added. "It's amazing how her robe falls open when she's near a handsome or powerful man." Jes was again privately jealous of that ability, but would never say so.

"Big city?" Lin asked. "Do you mean Geraestus?"

"No; that's far too close. We don't want her ever coming back. Athens."

"But that's seven days' trek from here," Jes protested.

Flo shook her head. "Three days, if you row across the bay. You can do it; you row every day."

Jes nodded. "I like to row. Yes—and that would avoid Sam, if he is returning."

"That was also my thought."

"So I should take her, and find her a richer man," Jes said. "So she is gone when Sam returns."

Flo and Lin nodded.

"What of her child?"

"Wilda can remain with us. Wona's not much of a mother to her anyway. She wanted a boy."

True. Wona would be glad to be free of her daughter. "But it is not safe for two women traveling out of their territory."

"A woman and a man to guard her," Flo said.

"Her brother," Lin added.

Jes pondered. "I don't like it, but I agree it must be done. Can you talk her into it?"

"Yes," Flo said grimly. "I will give her harsh alternatives."

"I have no stomach for that," Jes said.

"You are too manlike," Flo said, smiling. "You can't bear to hurt a woman."

"A beautiful woman," Lin added teasingly.

"But you keep your word, once given, like a man," Flo said. "She knows that."

They had thought it out. "Then tell her I will conduct her to Athens, and not leave her until she is satisfied with a new man."

Flo and Lin got up without further word and walked across to talk with Wona. Jes picked up the flail and began beating the wheat stalks. But as she worked, she watched, covertly. She saw Flo talking to Wona, gesturing forcefully. She saw Wona's amazement, her defiance, then her capitulation. Jes knew that Flo had threatened to kill Wona if she didn't go—and Flo did have the stomach to do what she had to. So she had offered Wona a less harsh alternative, and Wona had had no choice but to accept it.

Wona got up and went to her daughter Wilda, a child of three. She was saying farewell, and the child hardly seemed to notice. Wilda cared about Sam, who played with her, and Flo, who nursed her; to the child, Wona was just another person in the family.

Then Wona came across to Jes, while the other two remained with the children. She looked grim, and there were tears on her face. So the separation was not entirely easy for her. Jes disliked her less, for that.

"You will guide me safely to Athens?"

"Yes."

"And neither harm me nor allow me to come to harm?"

"As best I can."

"And not leave me until I say it is all right?"

That was harder. "Until you have a satisfactory man."

"No. Until I say it is all right. I want a man satisfactory to me, not to you."

She had a point. She feared that Jes would declare a man to be suitable, just to be rid of her. "Agreed."

"Swear it."

"I swear it."

Wona looked at her cannily. "You will travel as a man?"

"Yes."

"Then make an oath of brotherhood to me."

"I'm not going to be a man to you!" Jes said, embarrassed. She liked to emulate the ways of a man, but she was always a woman beneath.

"But others won't know that."

Jes considered. A non—family man might indeed seek to make sexual use of a woman he guarded, while he had the opportunity. A brother would not; he would be seeking her best interests, and other men would appreciate that. "I swear to be your brother, for this mission," Jes said reluctantly.

Wona smiled. "I trust you, Jes. Others may twist their logic, seeking ways around their oaths. You don't. You hold to your given word without equivocation."

"Yes."

"Then I will travel with you now."

"Now?"

"Flo wants me out of here now."

Jes looked across to Flo. They were too far apart for Flo to have heard, but the woman nodded. Jes realized that she didn't want to give Ned any chance to reappear either. This had to be clean, involving no man. So it had to be now, while Sam was on a distant mission, and Dirk and Bry were out foraging for rebuilding materials. All the men must be innocent of this deed, though they would surely suspect its nature.

"Then get your things," Jes said. "I will get mine."

They went to the half-repaired house and packed their bags. Then they set off together, saying farewell to no one else.

They walked to the shore. They lived near the southern tip of Euboea, and so were part of the Delian League. The stately trieres of Athens, the ships with three banks of oars, protected them from any direct attack by the Spartans, who were not strong on water. It wasn't enough, however; that was why Sam had gone far afield to trade for vital supplies, and why Wona had become too much of a burden to support any longer. Wona was mischief, certainly, and had to be dealt with; but even if she had not cheated on Sam, she would still have been a liability, because she didn't pull her weight.

Jes's small rowboat was one of the things they had that was especially useful. She employed it to get around the long coast, trading supplies (in better times) with neighbors for many leagues around. Jes liked to row; the boat was so smooth, and carried so much, compared to portage across land. She could, and often did, keep it up for many hours at a time, pretending she was an oarsman on a trieres. There was a special joy in sustained moderate exercise that made her forget for a while her general dissatisfaction with life.

They got in. Wona made no pretense of helping; even had she been of such a mind, her thin arms would not have been able to do much. So she sat in the bow, watching ahead, while Jes faced back and took the oars. She hardly needed to see where she was going; she was well familiar with this shore.

They crossed to a small island Jes knew, and another island, heading west as darkness came. Then, at the western shore of the island, they camped. Jes had used this site before, and had no hesitation. She dug out blankets from the cache she kept here, then threw out a line to fish. Then she made a small fire and cooked the fish, sharing it with Wona. There was no point trying to make the woman do anything constructive, and Jes did not bother. Neither did she attempt to engage in conversation; Wona had nothing worthwhile to offer there, either.

They slept, without event, though Jes remained alert for sounds, just in case. It was part of her manly training, never to be caught off-guard, even during slumber.

In the morning she rearranged her homespun cloak, tying it in the masculine way. From here on, she would play the part of a man. Fortunately the clothing of men and women did not differ much; both wore loose-fitting garments that hung from the shoulder. Either a cloak called a peplos, or a sewn tunic called a chiton, made of homespun wool. The wealthy might don a cool linen chiton during the warm months, and have underclothing to alleviate the roughness of the wool. So about all Jes had to do, to change genders, was to tie a band of cloth around her chest to flatten her breasts, and arrange her short hair in the masculine way. And set her face in the somewhat superior mode men affected, especially in the presence of women.

There was one other thing: She used a peplos that had a special property. She had made it herself, and taken considerable trouble. It was reversible, sewn so that either side could be the exterior. The "male" side was rough gray; the "female" side was dull yellow. No man would wear yellow, unless in a play where he portrayed a woman.

They got in the boat, and set out across the channel. Jes stroked tirelessly, not pushing herself beyond her pace, for the distance was what would have been a day's march on land. Now Wona had to participate, because she knew the likely consequence of a wrong direction: much longer time in the water, and possibly getting caught by a wrong current or wind and being borne entirely out to sea. Neither of them wanted that. They were hardly friends, but they had a common mission to travel safely. Meanwhile, in the long silences, Jes could pretend she was alone, and experience some of the deep relaxation of it. She knew that she could never actually row aboard a trieres, because she lacked the huge tough muscles, but by herself she could dream.

In six hours they made it to the mainland shore. Jes had not pushed herself too hard, but her arms knew they had had a solid workout, and she was glad to give her legs a turn. She hauled the boat to a thicket and concealed it carefully. Normally coastal residents respected private property, but after the devastation of the raiders that might have been here, it wasn't safe to make assumptions.

Then Jes slung her bow over her shoulder, made sure of her knife, and was ready to travel. Wona, of course, was rested.

They set out on the hike westward. They were now on mainland Attica, the home territory of Athens. Jes had been here before, when trading on rare occasions with coastal folk, so knew there was a road not far inland. They walked until they encountered this, then Jes turned south.

"But isn't Athens west?" Wona asked.

"It is, as the crow flies. But it will be much easier to follow the road, because it follows the contour and is clear, as well as leading past sanctuaries and settlements. It will curve west soon enough. All roads in Attica go to Athens, ultimately.''

''Oh.''

They followed the road south, and sure enough, within the hour it curved grandly west, passing a defiled sanctuary and a harbor with wreckage. The raiders had certainly been here.

There was something in the road ahead. It turned out to be a human body. Wona averted her gaze, but Jes kneeled to examine it. It was a man, his blood turning brown on the dirt, his equipment gone. Evidently a farmer or laborer, caught and murdered by the raiders, robbed and left where he had fallen.

''I don't like this,'' Jes murmured, a coldness going through her gut. She had hoped it wouldn't come to this. Now she had to steel herself for violence.

''I hate gore,'' Wona agreed.

Jes grimaced. She wasn't partial to human gore herself, but it happened. They had seen the leavings of occasional quarrels on Euboea. ''He hasn't been dead long enough.''

''What does it matter? Two days or five days, he'll still stink.''

''Precisely. He doesn't stink. This man died within hours.''

Wona half turned, nervously. ''Hours?''

''There has barely been time for the ants to find him. He was killed this morning.''

''But that means—''

''That the raiders are still here,'' Jes finished grimly. ''Probably a rear guard, to see that stragglers are collected, and that no Athenian troops are massing for a counterattack.''

Wona was increasingly alarmed. ''They are supposed to be gone.''

''They are gone from Euboea, if they ever touched it. But this is farther in toward Athens. They must have recalled the outlying parties before withdrawing the main force. That's standard practice. An army needs spies ahead and behind, so it neither walks into an ambush nor allows an ambush to close in its rear. The peripheral troops are probably headed north now, after a final sweep. But we had better be watchful, in case some remain in the vicinity. We are following closer than we thought."

"Yes," Wona agreed, looking rapidly about. "What of this one?"

"We'll leave him. We have to reach a safe place to sleep, by nightfall."

Wona nodded. "How far to—to a safe place?"

"There is a walled settlement within range by nightfall, if we travel well. I haven't been there, but I know of it. From there it should be only another day to Athens."

They resumed their trek, faster than before. Wona had been a slight drag, but now she kept the pace very well. She had good legs, and could walk when she had to.

But with raiders actually in the area, would walking well be enough? Jes knew that they would be foolish to gamble on that. She would have to educate Wona for war.

"You have a knife," Jes said.

"Yes."

"Do you know how to use it?"

"Yes."

"Demonstrate."

Wona fumbled inside her garment, hauling out a tied purse-bag.

"You should have it readier to hand than that," Jes said sternly. "If we encounter raiders intent on mayhem, you must be ready to defend yourself instantly. I can't do it all."

Wona nodded, appreciating the point.

"Now pretend I am a man grabbing for you," Jes said, turning to her. "How do you dispatch me?"

Wona lifted the knife up above her head, pointing down.

"No good! He'll just knock your arm aside and take it from you." Jes demonstrated by blocking, then catching the

woman's arm and twisting it slowly until the knife was
about to drop. She took it from the flaccid hand and stepped
back. "Now suppose I am the woman, and you the man.
Come at me."

Wona reached for her. Jes brought the knife up from below her hip, until the point touched Wona's belly. "Fast
and hard, there, where he is soft. Twist as it enters. Then
step back and let him fall."

The woman seemed about to vomit. "I couldn't—"

"You would rather be beaten, raped, and killed?" Jes
asked harshly. "This will not be a nice, gentle man like
Sam whom you can twist around your finger. He will likely
see you as a fruit to be bitten and thrown away. You may
have just one chance to get him, before he gets you. So
keep this in mind, and act when you have to."

Wona nodded wanly.

Jes had mercy on her. "Maybe we won't encounter any
raiders. We just have to be ready, in case."

But in another hour, as the road bore northwest, they encountered exactly that kind of trouble. An enemy party of
five men was marching down the road, toward them. Enemy
mercenaries.

"Spartans!" Wona exclaimed.

"No," Jes said tersely. "Persian mercenaries."

"How do you know?"

"The Spartans generally don't use bows. They have
bronze helms with red plumes. These men use wicker
shields covered in leather, and cloth head wrappings."

"You know a lot about warriors," Wona said, impressed.

The two groups had sighted each other at the same time;
it was too late to leave the road and hide. "This is mischief," Jes muttered, bringing her bow down from her
shoulders. "Too many to fight, too late to escape."

"But they'll—"

"Kill the man and rape the woman," Jes said. "To start.
We don't want that. We'll have to use desperate measures.
I'll flee; you open your robe and scream helplessly."

"But your oath—"

"I'm not deserting you!" Jes snapped. "I can take out two with arrows; you can take out one with your knife, as I showed you. Don't let him see it before you use it. It's the other two we have to finesse. You must distract them, just long enough. Trust me, and do your part. Do you understand?"

Cunning showed through Wona's fear. She did have half a notion of the ways of necessity. She nodded. The knife was in her hand, hidden behind a fold of her robe.

"Wait for my signal," Jes said. "Remember: underhand, hard into the gut, and twist." Her heart was pounding, but she had already appraised the opposition. It was a rag-tag bunch, rather than a disciplined group; they might have been drinking pilfered wine while on patrol. Two had bows; three had spears. She had to take out the bowmen first.

She kneeled, nocking an arrow and taking careful aim. She had never before taken aim with intent to kill a human being, but she abated this concern by reminding herself that the enemy would surely do worse to the two of them if it got the chance, just as she had told Wona. Unless she could bluff them off.

The raiders kept coming, shouting battle oaths in their own foreign language. That was another sign of their rag-tag status; well disciplined Spartan phalanxes often marched silently into battle, not wasting energy. These brutes had little respect for a party of two, especially when one was a fearful woman and the other had the appearance of a stripling boy. They probably expected the boy to prostrate himself and beg for mercy—which he wouldn't get. Stripling boys were preferred by some men to women, and would be treated similarly. Also, a prime means of acquiring slaves was by capturing them in battle, so they might have a continuing use for a stripling.

When the raiders were close enough to see that the boy had his bow aimed, they paused. Then the two bowmen laughed and unslung their bows. They thought this would be easy.

They were well within range. Jes pictured them in her mind as dangerous animals, and loosed the first arrow. It caught one bowman in the chest, a perfect shot. He went down immediately.

Glorious! Jes realized that her fear had left her. She was now a cold fighting machine, doing what she had to do. She was also relieved that these were not first line troops, because their armor would have turned her arrow.

The second raider got off one arrow before she could properly aim her second. But his missed her. The key to success was to take time to aim, and to have one's mind completely clear. She loosed her second as the man was standing, trying to see the effect of his own arrow. He was criminally stupid, and he paid for it by taking her arrow in his stomach. He wasn't dead, but he would be in time.

The three others, realizing the danger in separation, charged forward. They were stupid, but not cowards. They were lifting their long spears and shields. The only good defense against arrow fire was a shield; only drunkenness and overconfidence explained their vulnerability to her first attack.

"Now!" Jes said, running off the road.

Wona screamed on cue, and her robe fell open to reveal her fine breasts. She fluffed out her long hair, looking extremely feminine. She wasn't good for much, but she was excellent at appearances.

The three charging men exchanged shouts. Then two ran off the road, pursuing Jes, while one continued directly toward Wona. Good; they were separating.

Jes ran, not too fast. The two men gained, sure of their quarry. She glanced back. The third man caught up to Wona, whose breasts were flouncing like her hair. "Now!" Jes screamed again.

Then Jes whirled on the two, bringing her bow about,

with its loosely nocked arrow. She aimed as she drew back the string.

Caught by surprise, both men reacted in phenomenally stupid fashion: they came to a sudden halt, staring.

Jes loosed at point-blank range. The arrow transfixed the larger man's chest, and he was done for. She felt another surge of battle glee.

The last man hurled his spear, belatedly. His arm was good, but Jes had anticipated it, and was already moving out of the way and turning sideways to present a narrower target. It missed her, but the man was already almost upon her. There was no time for another arrow.

But she had dropped her bow as she dodged, and was reaching for her knife. She brought it up.

The man paused again, and this time not stupidly. He was, after all, a soldier, accustomed to combat. His own thrusting dagger was in his hand, and it was a monster, far larger than Jes's knife. In fact it was a short sword.

Jes's eyes widened. So did her mouth. Clear dismay gutted her courage. She started to turn to flee.

"Haa!" the man cried, thrusting the sword straight at her. She smelled wine on his breath, and saw the slightly clumsy manner of his attack. He was pretty well inebriated, and that was her great fortune. Her odds would have been much worse against fully prepared troops.

Jes was already dodging back and turning again. The thrust missed to the front as she stepped sideways into him. Her small blade came around and caught him in the throat. "Fool!" she muttered as he went down in blood. He had fallen for one of the elementary ploys: fake fright.

She swept up her bow and turned back toward the road. One figure stood; one lay on the ground. Had Wona been dispatched? Then the figure waved, showing its bare bosom.

Jes ran back to the road. The man lay groaning, the knife still in his chest. Wona was in tears and hysterical. As Jes stepped onto the road, Wona almost leaped at her, flinging her arms around her. "I did it! I did it!" she sobbed. "Just as you showed me. It was awful!"

Jes held her, understanding. She herself had trained for exactly this type of encounter, but she had never killed a man before. Now she had killed four. The sheer need for action had prevented her from realizing its significance, but now that it was done, her battle mindset was fading, and she was shaking.

She realized with surprise that Wona was providing her with comfort she needed. They were comforting each other. She had never anticipated that. She had never been Wona's friend. She still wasn't. But for this instant, they needed each other. The horror of the killing each had done was overwhelming. Now, perhaps, they had a kind of understanding. Because they had both just been blooded.

But it couldn't last, and not just because Jes was no man to hold a woman like this. She pulled back, nerving herself for what else had to be done. "There may be others. We must get away from here."

"Others!" Wona exclaimed, realizing the continuing danger. Her fair bosom heaved. "Yes—we must go. But what of—?" She looked down at the fallen man.

"You're right. We must recover the knife. Help me roll him over." Jes knew that wasn't what Wona meant, but they had to be practical.

They both leaned down to take hold of the raider. Jes glanced across at Wona, noting how her bared breasts hung down in a manner Jes's never would. She could almost appreciate the effect such a sight would have on a man. No wonder this lout had not seen the knife that stabbed him.

As the body rolled over, the knife came into view. Wona had done it right, thrusting hard for the gut and jamming upward. She had scored through the cloth tunic, which fortunately did not cover a metal scale shirt, as it would have in a better appointed warrior. The point had not reached the heart, but had done plenty of damage to the gut. He would die in agony.

She took hold of the hilt and wrenched it out. The man groaned again, and blood welled out of the gash in his belly. Wona turned away, looking ill.

"We shouldn't leave him like this," Jes said, feeling ill herself. "He'll die in hours, horribly."

"What can we do?" Wona asked faintly.

"We should kill him cleanly."

"I can't!"

"I'll do it," Jes said. "It's my job."

She leaned over the man, bringing the gore-stained knife to his throat. His eyes opened, and he gazed at her.

Her hand shook. Her arm became paralyzed. "I can't," she said, echoing Wona. "Not when he's not attacking me."

The man's eyes narrowed. Then, suddenly, his hand came up. It slapped against Wona's knee, making her gasp. It reached up toward Jes.

Jes slashed the blade across his throat, cutting it gapingly open. Bright blood gouted out, soaking his neck. Jes leaped back, horrified at what her triggered battle reflex had made her do. But he was already done for.

Belatedly, she realized that the man had had the courage she lacked. He had acted to make her react, so that he could have a quick death. He was an enemy, a criminal, who had come to grief stupidly, but in the end he had shown a quality to be respected.

"You died bravely," she said, in a kind of benediction. That, oddly, made her feel better. Then, to Wona: "Now we must go."

Wona nodded, not looking. Jes wiped the blade on the ground several times until it was almost clean, then handed it to the other woman. She might need it again.

They left the man there and walked on along the road. After a few steps, Wona took Jes's hand, and Jes did not protest. All they had for the moment to stave off the numbness of the killings was each other.

They passed the other two men, the bowmen. Jes hesitated, then stopped to take one of their bows. "Can you use one of these?"

"No."

"Carry it anyway. And the quiver of arrows. I may need a spare. And we'd better get their knives, too."

They took one knife, but then the other man groaned. Both women stood and hurried away, unspeaking.

They had hardly gotten out of sight of the bodies before there was a sound behind them. Was one of the victims recovering?

"More raiders!" Wona cried, spying the glint of spears. "Three, four!"

They were in for it. They should have hurried away the moment the last man was down, instead of dawdling as they had. This party must have been coming behind them, expecting to rendezvous with the party moving east. "Run!" Jes said. "That walled town can't be far."

They ran, fright giving them energy. They left the new party behind, because the raiders were checking their fallen associates. But Jes knew their respite would be brief.

It was. In moments there was a cry of outrage, and the sound of pursuit.

To Jes's surprise, they kept their lead. Maybe they were fresher than the raiders, who might have been pillaging all day, or maybe desperation accounted for it. Or maybe they were simply more accustomed to running. Jes had always had excellent physical endurance. But Wona—what of her?

As if triggered by that thought, Wona's endurance faded. She was gasping. They had to stop.

"You walk on ahead," Jes told her, slowing to a walk herself. "I'll deal with these." She brought her bow around.

"No, I had better stay with you," Wona gasped.

"You can't help me, and you could get caught yourself. Go on, get ahead while you can."

"I'm not being noble," Wona said. "I'm not that kind of person. If something happens to you, I'm helpless, so there's no point in my going ahead."

The woman was giving a sensible, selfish reason. Therefore it was suspect. "Is that true?" Jes asked her.

"No. I—I find I like you, to my surprise, and I want to help. If I can."

Jes felt an astonishing surge of gratitude. Wona was showing support and courage. But Jes covered her reaction with bruskness, knowing that this was no time to be sentimental. "Then turn with me, and bring about your bow as if you can use it. Maybe we can back them off."

"Yes!"

They stopped and turned together. The men behind were coming rapidly. There were four, and all had bows. If they couldn't be bluffed, this was likely to be the end.

"Imitate my action, but don't loose your arrow," Jes said.

"I can't even draw it back," Wona said. "I will pretend I'm holding the string."

Jes aimed carefully. As the men came to the fringe of bowshot range, they stopped. Evidently they had seen the arrows in the slain men, so knew there was a competent archer here. They were consulting with each other. That was stupid on their part; they should have charged in without hesitation. Some archers were more accurate than others, at the edge of their range, if given time to aim. They were giving her time.

Jes loosed her arrow when she saw their attention was distracted. That prevented them from seeing her shot, so they did not take evasive action. The arrow struck the largest of the four raiders, and he staggered and fell.

Beside her, Wona held up her bow and drew back her arm, slowly. The three remaining men scrambled back out of range.

Jes smiled. "See—they respect you. But there may be more coming up behind them. We had better walk, as long as they let us."

They turned and walked. For a time the men did not pursue, not realizing their advantage. Three against one would surely prevail, but they thought it was three against two—

and that the two were expert. Obviously these men were
rough and tumble archers, whose accuracy was indifferent.

The sun was declining. They had perhaps another hour
of daylight. Then they could either hide in the dark, or gain
the protection of the walled settlement. If the raiders gave
them time.

The raiders did not. Two of the men gathered themselves
and charged forward, spears raised. The third kneeled to take
proper aim with his bow, covering them, before joining the
chase himself.

"I can take out one more," Jes said, turning. "Then it
will be hand to hand. Do your thing." She dreaded this,
because she lacked the brute strength of a man. These raiders would not again underestimate the strength of the opposition.

"First I'll fire an arrow," Wona said, making her pretense
with the bow.

"As soon as I fire, throw yourself to the side," Jes said.
She aimed more rapidly than she liked, and loosed her arrow. "Now!"

They hurled themselves to either side of the road. Just in
time, for the arrow thudded into the ground behind them.
Jes wasn't sure whether it would have struck either of them,
but it certainly was possible.

One raider stumbled. She had gotten him on the leg. Well,
that was better than nothing; she could readily have missed.

The other two paused to help their companion. That was
their mistake, because they weren't following up their opportunity to get to close quarters. Praise the gods for the
errors these brutes kept making!

"Stand and aim!" Jes cried.

She and Wona took the road again and presented their
bows. The raiders retreated, dragging their comrade. They
thought the odds were now even, and they had no stomach
for that. What a stroke of luck!

"Now we can walk again," Jes said. "They have given
up."

"Thank Zeus!"

"Better to thank Artemis, the huntress. She protects arch-ers—and maidens." She made a sarcastic gesture at Wona.

They walked swiftly away. "I must learn to use a bow," Wona said.

"It takes muscle, and years."

"You showed me how to use the knife, and it saved my life. What other weapon can I learn?"

Jes considered. "Maybe the light club. A fast stroke can set a man back, even knock him out. If he has a knife, you can hit his knife hand before he can stab you. It's less deadly than a knife, but more versatile when there is more than one enemy. It won't get stuck in someone's gut."

"The light club," Wona agreed.

As evening came, they spied the wall of the settlement. They had made it!

But as they approached, men appeared above the ram-parts. They had bows aimed.

"They think we're raiders!" Jes cried in dismay.

"But we wear Delian apparel."

"We could have stolen it from people we killed. Not that Delian differs much from any other everyday clothing in Greece. But they can see we're not armored or fully armed. They're being ornery."

"Then now must be the time to do my thing." Wona stood up straight and opened her robe as she flounced out her hair.

There was a pause. Then a hand beckoned. They walked forward, though several bows remained trained on them. They stopped before the main gate, which remained closed.

"Who are you?" a man, evidently an officer, called from above, while the bowmen stared avidly at Wona's open bosom.

"Wona from Euboea, traveling with my brother Jes," Wona answered. "We have encountered raiders, and seek safety for the night."

"I don't think so," the man replied. "Go your way."

"But the raiders are behind us!" Wona cried.

"Exactly. They can't force the gate, so they want to get an infiltrator inside to do it for them, at night. It's an old Spartan trick. We are not deceived."

"But we're Delians! We had to kill raiders to get here."

"Of course," the man said, with rich irony. "Like the Gorgon, you stunned them to death with your aspect." The bowmen laughed uproariously.

Furious, Wona closed her robe. There was a murmur of dismay from the wall.

"Now go," the officer said. "In deference to your beauty, we are letting you and your brother depart alive. But don't test our patience; we are already on edge because of being besieged. My men will kill you if I give the order. That would be a shame."

"But the siege is over!" Jes protested.

"So you say." He lifted his hand as if to signal the archers.

"It's no good," Jes murmured. "They think we're spies."

"Then we must go." Wona opened her robe to give them one more flash, then closed it and turned away.

Jes smiled. Wona had just made the defenders regret their decision. How could they know what might have been, had she been admitted? The town could have admitted two stragglers without serious risk, but evidently the officer was a martinet more interested in asserting his authority than in anyone's convenience. Now their situation was bleak. Had the raiders known they would be suspected? So there was no hurry to catch them?

"We'll have to hide in the hills, in the darkness," Jes said. "At least we have the night."

"At least," Wona agreed bitterly.

They made their way south, where they found a burial ground. "This is good," Jes decided. "They won't bother us here."

"But there are evil spirits!"

"No, there are honest Delian spirits," Jes said firmly. "They will protect us, not harm us."

Wona seemed doubtful, but she was even more tired than Jes, so acquiesced. "I hope so."

They ate the last of their food, attended to natural functions, and lay down among the burial markers to sleep. But though they were weary, sleep did not come immediately. Too much had happened, of too much significance. When Jes closed her eyes, she saw the bodies of the men she had killed. How many had there been? Seven, she thought. It was sickening.

"Why do you hate me?" Wona asked.

This was a ploy to make her deny it. So she resisted. "You don't work enough, you made a fool of Sam, and another of Ned."

"It is true. It is my nature. I envy you yours."

Jes was startled. "Me?"

"You are strong and honest and courageous."

"You value these things?"

"I value what I lack, yes."

"You, with the body to make men stare?"

"Do you envy me that?"

Jes had been brutally direct before. Now she had to be again. "Yes."

Wona laughed. "I would trade with you."

Jes snorted, not believing it. But as she drifted at last to sleep, she wondered.

She dreamed of bodies and blood and horror. The killing she had done might have been justified, but it was as if she had been raped. Whatever innocence she had had was forever gone. Her tears of remorse wet her face. The gore she had made was now part of her soul, a well of horror she could not escape.

Once she heard sobbing. For a moment she was afraid it was her own, but it turned out to be Wona's. Jes reached out and found the woman's hand, squeezing it in silent support. That sufficed.

In the morning they cleaned up as well as they could, and made their way west cross-country. It was slow and uncomfortable, but had some advantages: the raiders weren't prowling here, and there was some foraging to be done. They found a little overlooked grain in a battered shed, and there was some fresh water in a buried well, and a few usable arrows scattered around abandoned farmsteads. Some grapes had ripened, in the absence of people to pick them. Those helped a lot. The inhabitants were still sealed inside the walled settlements, and wouldn't come out until the last raiders were gone.

Jes found in the tangle of a wreckage a stout stick of suitable length. "This will do for a club," she said, whacking it solidly against a tree. "Take it."

Wona took it, holding it awkwardly. "If I tried to use this, I would bash myself in the leg," she said ruefully.

"Any weapon takes time and practice to master. Strike it against tree trunks and rocks as we pass. You will get the feel of it."

The woman nodded uncertainly. "I'll try."

"We may be as well off here as in the settlement," Jes remarked as they resumed their westward trek. "At least we have freedom to travel without hindrance."

"And freedom to sleep in peace," Wona said.

"We would have had that in the settlement."

"*You* would have that, there," Wona retorted. "What did you think would have been the price of our admission?"

The bowmen would have wanted to use her body, Jes realized. "I thought you liked it."

"The way you like slaying men."

A telling thrust! "I do that only when I have to."

"Exactly."

"But you so readily show your body to men," Jes said. "Why, if you don't want them to have it?"

"Why do you keep your bow and knife ready for immediate use, if you don't want to use them?"

Jes nodded. "I do what I hate, because the alternative would be worse."

"Exactly," Wona repeated. "And you make sure you are good at it, for the same reason. My breasts and thighs are instruments of another kind."

Point made. Except for one thing. "But what of Ned?"

"How else was I to get a smart child?"

Jes was taken aback. "You did that only for the child?"

"Which I didn't get. Why would anyone want to go through all that, with a stripling, if she didn't have to?"

"I would," Jes said defensively. "If any decent man were interested."

Wona turned to her in surprise. "Have you done it with any man?"

"No."

"Then how do you know you would like it?"

That set her back again. "Because—because I'm interested. I want—to do it. To enjoy a man. I know I'd like it."

"This is weird. I've got the body, you have the passion. I could live years without sex, but men will never let me be, so I use it to gain favors I need. You, who actually have desire—"

"Am not desired," Jes finished. She was surprised at herself for telling Wona her secret. She normally spoke with candor, but had not expected any such dialogue with this particular woman.

Wona pondered. "Last night I asked you why you hated me, and you answered. But you also said you envied me my body. I thought you meant so that you could befuddle men and gain ready advantage. But now I think that wasn't it."

"That wasn't it," Jes agreed. "I would like to—to have a man enjoy being with me."

"I think we can make a deal. I have after all something you want."

"A deal?"

"You teach me the use of this club. I will teach you how to make men notice you."

Jes laughed. "With my body? My face? Impossible."

"No more so than teaching me to wield this weapon effectively. We both have weapons; they merely differ in nature."

Maybe she had a point. "If you could teach me that, I—I would be amazed and grateful."

"I can teach you. But you must be able to learn."

"Like you with the club?"

"Yes. I think it is a good analogy."

Jes paused. "It occurs to me that we have no rush to reach Athens, because it may still be under siege. We are finding some food out here, while the people are gone. Is this a good time to exchange skills?"

"I think it is. I want to get to Athens, but I don't want to fight any more men. Neither your way nor mine. We should approach it cautiously."

"Then we are of one mind. Let's find a place to instruct and practice."

They searched out a farmstead that was in better shape than most, and settled in for the time being. They made sure that there was no ready access without discovery—so that no raiders could come on them by surprise. Then they foraged for more food, and excavated a chamber in the collapsed house for their temporary residence. This would do, for a few days. Jes felt slightly guilty about taking what was not theirs, but reminded herself that the laws of hospitality decreed that any man open his house to travelers in need. So they were simply discharging their host's duties for him, since his absence prevented him from doing it himself. Certainly they were not doing any harm to the premises.

By the time they had done all that, the day was over. They made a final check of the premises, and almost as an afterthought set a trap by the main path: a small pit covered over with a thin layer of sod, that would cause an intruder to take a fall and give his presence away. Then, satisfied, they retired to their chamber for the night.

"I am sorry about what I did to your brothers," Wona said. "They deserve better."

Jes didn't answer. She did not want to be friendly with this woman, but neither did she want to antagonize her unnecessarily. That would only interfere with her mission. She was not inclined to forgive what Wona had done. So what was there to say?

"That was why I agreed to leave without a fuss," Wona continued. "It was the cleanest way to end it. Your family will be better off without me."

Again, Jes didn't answer. The woman was speaking truth.

"If I should ever have opportunity to make it up, I will do so. But we both know that this is unlikely. So all I can do is leave my apology with you, and hope that both Sam and Ned will have better times hereafter."

"I hope so too," Jes agreed, glad that she finally could speak without offense.

"And tomorrow you will show me how to use the club, and I will show you how to use your body in a new way."

"Tomorrow," Jes agreed. Then they slept.

The next day they traded expertise, starting with the weapon. Jes showed Wona how to swing it so that it put little stress on her wrist and arm, yet developed formidable clout. She showed her how to block with it, by anticipating the opponent's likely attack and countering it before it really got started. How to gain advantage, by being ready at the moment of the countering, then to strike with precision while the other party was still pursuing his wasted move. "Keep your head, and watch his body and his weapon," she said. "You can prevail using a fraction of his energy, if you are cool. One well placed, well timed blow can finish it almost before it starts; you don't need a lot of muscle." Wona was clumsy, but eager to learn, and she soon got the essence, if not the expertise.

Then it was Wona's turn to instruct, and Jes was surprised

to discover just how much science there was in Wona's feminine art. When she walked, she didn't just walk, she swung her hips. Jes had thought it was natural to Wona, but in due course she herself was walking similarly. When Wona spoke to a man, she didn't just speak, she murmured with a certain lilt. When she stood still, she didn't just stand, she put her weight on one leg and angled the opposite knee in to half cover it, so that the line of her hip and thigh was accentuated. Her breathing was controlled, so as to make her bosom rise and fall noticeably. Every action was studied, for a single purpose: to make an impression on any nearby man.

"Of course you would have to adapt your clothing," Wona said. "You are small-breasted, so you need to have a halter that lifts and compresses. It can be done, if you wish."

"To what purpose? No matter what I do, I'm not going to impress a man."

"Yes you are," Wona insisted. "Many men like plump, but as many like slender. The way you look at a man can make most of the rest irrelevant."

"Look at?"

"Picture yourself as a man for a moment, and look at me."

Jes did that. Wona met her gaze sidelong with half-lidded eyes, and a trace of a smile. And Jes felt the lure of it. That amazed her, for she had no interest in actually being with any woman. How much stronger that look must be with a genuine man.

She practiced that too, and though it seemed highly artificial, Wona said she was getting it.

So they continued, for the day, alternating instructions. Betweentimes, they foraged, and rested. They saw no other raiders, so concluded that the Spartans had vacated this area. Soon the local citizens would emerge from their walled settlement and reclaim their lands.

"They are Delians, as are we," Jes said. "But I think we had better be gone from here."

"Yes. They don't trust us."

So on the following morning they resumed their travel, but did not hurry. They remained alert for people of either side, and continued their exchange of information. It was clear that Wona would not be a very effective warrior, and that Jes would not be a very effective seductress, but both were making progress. Wona was acquiring the extra twitch of the wrist that made the clubhead swing with extra force just as it connected to the target, and Jes was learning how to use her hair to cover enough of her face to make the rest seem dainty. Both of them were discovering the pleasure of mastering new skills.

"I can almost believe that I could knock out a man, if he didn't take me seriously," Wona remarked with wonder.

"And I might almost seduce a man, if he didn't get too clear a look at me," Jes said with similar wonder.

"Should we look for two men to practice on?"

"No!" Jes replied with sudden alarm. Then they both laughed. Jes realized that it was the first time they had laughed together, at the same thing.

They continued cross-country, crossing over the mountain range rather than following the more convenient road. The trek was considerably rougher, but the foraging was equivalently better. They found a spring, and camped near it another night, then followed its trickle down into the valley, where it became the River Ilissos, leading right to Athens. They knew the city by its massive wall, looming ever higher as they approached.

And there the people were emerging in force. Streams of them were moving outward along several great roads that converged at the city. That meant that the last of the raiders was gone. They had timed it well. Not only that, they were better rested and fed than they would otherwise have been, and had learned things from each other that might or might not benefit them in the future.

But for now they were brother and sister. Brother Jes was here to find a suitable husband for his lovely sister Wona. Great Athens was the place to look.

They rehearsed their roles, and stepped onto a road leading to one of the mighty open gates. The fact that they were going the opposite way from the overwhelming majority might attract attention, but more likely they would be taken for two who had turned back for something forgotten in the city. Attention was something they did not want, at present.

Athens was huge. It dwarfed the walled settlement they had approached before. The great outer wall was three times the height of a man, and the gate was guarded by several armed men. But this time there was no challenge; they were admitted without fuss, when there was a break in the stream of people leaving the city.

Inside, it was reasonably chaotic. It looked as though the majority of the refugees from the raiders had camped just inside the wall. The region stank. The two of them hurried on toward the center of the city.

They passed the Acropolis, which was a rocky citadel on which stood the great monuments of the city. It rose well above the surrounding plain, overlooking everything else. They saw the Temple of Athene, and the Parthenon, built of shining marble, including even the roof. Jes was amazed by its grandeur, and would have liked to walk through it, but Wona was more practical: they had to find a place to stay. She hardly cared about monumental architecture; she preferred creature comfort.

They circled the Acropolis and walked on to the Agora, where there was a structure that did impress Wona: the immense two-storied colonnaded market called the Stoa of Attalus. "I could shop there forever!" she breathed.

"Not without gold," Jes muttered. She was aware of how little of that they had. They would have to find work to sustain them, while searching for a suitable man for Wona to marry. They couldn't forage, here in the city.

Now they made their way to the nearest residential suburb. There were no towering marble buildings here, just close set dwellings that jammed in together so tightly that there was little or no space between them. Some were larger, containing a number of little chambers. These were the rental units for visitors.

For one of their few silver owls they rented a house for half a month. It was a modest brick structure with a court-yard but no windows and no furniture. But it was a base of operations, not far from the market, and that was good. It was dirty, because it had just been vacated that morning, but they knew how to clean it.

Now they went to the market and bought bread and wine. There were many fancy things on sale, and Wona would have liked to buy them all, but Jes knew better. "We have to earn more money before we can eat well. Otherwise we will soon starve. Remember, we can't forage here." Wona reluctantly agreed, and they bought a bag of dry beans. They would swell when soaked in water, and would last for some time.

They returned to their house. Jes used her knife to carve off slices of bread, and Wona poured wine into clay cups. They dipped the bread into the wine, to soften it and flavor it, and chewed. It was a good, if ordinary, meal.

"Now we must consider," Jes said. "We shall need to become familiar with this city, in order to ascertain where the best prospects are. You don't want a man of the streets, you want a citizen. You don't want single nights, you want marriage. That means not only locating the good men, but getting to know them. This may take time."

Wona nodded. "There should be some at the Acropolis."

"Yes. But to impress them, you will need better clothing. That means more silver. So our first priority is to earn it. How can we do that?"

"You might join their military force."

"Then I'd be shipped away to wherever they were fighting a battle, leaving you here alone."

"No."

Jes nodded. "I suspect we should get a job together. Maybe weaving; we both know how to do that."

"But that's woman's work."

Jes grimaced. "I may just have to be a woman, here in the city, until I can go home."

"But two women alone—would it be any safer in the city than in the countryside?"

She had a point. "Maybe not." Jes considered further. "We could carry weapons."

"Not a bow. No woman carries a bow."

"The knives. The clubs. There won't be any distant hostilities here anyway, only close ones."

Wona touched her knife. She had it in a sheath on her thigh, so it was concealed. "But the club—"

"I noticed that some men here have been injured. They wear braces on their limbs, to strengthen them while they heal. Some of those braces are crude. Suppose we wore such braces on our legs?"

"But we aren't injured."

"How would anyone know?"

Wona shook her head. "Why should we want to—"

"Like this." Jes took her club and laid it along the outside of her right leg. Then she tied it there with a band of cloth. "See—a splint." She stood and walked around the chamber. "It chafes a bit, but some padding should ease that."

Wona's face brightened. "And if some man attacks—"

Jes reached down and quickly untied the club. "Then I am armed."

"I like it." Wona tied her own club similarly. "But this wouldn't do at the Acropolis."

"At such time as we have finer clothing, we'll seek some other way."

"But maybe, for such work, I should not be beautiful," Wona said thoughtfully.

"As plain as you can be," Jes agreed. "That won't be a problem for me."

They settled down for the night, satisfied. The house was bare and chill, but no worse than camping outside. They would get by well enough, for now.

In the morning they ate more wine-soaked bread, used the refuse potty and dumped it in the trench behind the house, and strapped on their braces. Then they went out to seek employment at the nearest weaving establishment. Jes was garbed as a woman.

The proprietor hardly glanced at them. "If you work well, you get paid. I will be the judge of your merit."

Jes shrugged. "If you are not fair, we will seek work elsewhere."

"I am fair. My name is Crockson."

"I am Jes. This is my sister Wona."

He led them to the working area, where several women labored at small looms. "You are familiar with such equipment?"

"We have a similar loom at home," Jes said with satisfaction. "Give us your pattern."

Thus directly, they were working. The work was long and tedious but familiar, and they were competent. These were standard weighted warp looms, with the vertical strands suspended from a cloth beam and held taut by decoratively molded baked clay weights tied at their bottoms. The alternating warp threads were divided into two sections, which hung on either side of a wooden bar: the shed. The weft, or horizontal threads, was woven in between the descending warp at intervals, according to the pattern. The patterns were simple, requiring no particular attention. Jes got no special thrill from weaving, because it was traditional woman's work, but she could have handled a much fancier design than this.

At times they shifted off to help prepare the threads, which were of two types. Wool was the common fiber, and it came in several natural colors: black, gray, brown, tawny, beige, and white. It was easy to dye, and was warm. Flax was rarer, because it required rich soil to grow and much water for its initial processing, but it was softer next to the skin, and much stronger. So the finer weaving was done with flax. But most of the work in the shop was on the wool, which had to be untangled, cleared of burrs and debris, and combed out into long, fluffy sausage-shaped bundles for spinning. They used drop spindles for spinning, patiently forming the thread. There were always women on the looms, and others "working the allotment," as the cleaning, combing, and spinning of the wool was called. This was the most tedious chore, and there were normally two women spinning thread for each one working the loom. Most of their production was for export, because Athenian women were expected to fulfill the modest needs of their own households.

Days passed, becoming routine. Crockson was as good as his word, paying them fairly for their production. Soon they had enough money to improve their life-style somewhat, with better food and better blankets. Loom work was no quick path to riches, and they still had to live frugally, but they were no longer at risk of starvation.

Jes was interested in the things of the big city, and really appreciated its beauties. Wona was indifferent to those, but was alert for the places where wealthy men might be found.

One day they visited the Agora again. This time they toured the Painted Stoa, a handsome colonnaded stone building in which many paintings were hung. These showed scenes of Athenian military exploits, done on removable wooden panels. Jes's eye was caught by those depicting sea battles. How she wished she could step into one of those scenes, and be there on a trieres, a ship with three levels of oars, the ruler of the seas. But alas, it was just a foolish fancy.

There were no rich citizens in attendance on that day, and Wona was soon eager to visit elsewhere. So they went to the Monument of the Eponymous Heroes, one of the newest structures. Ten new tribes had been formed, and the names of a hundred early Athenian heroes were sent to the oracle at Delphi. The oracle picked ten, and it was after these ten that the tribes were named. Now there were ten statues honoring these heroes. The monument served a practical as well as an esthetic function, because public notices were posted here, concerning upcoming business of the tribes. But no really likely prospects were reading the notices at the moment, so Wona soon lost interest. Thus their visit was a failure, in one sense, but Jes was glad to have done it. She would have liked to see all the monuments of Athens.

Crockson had seemed indifferent to their presence; they were just two weavers among a number. Then he surprised them. After a few days he spoke privately to Jes. "I lost several good employees recently, because of the disruption of the war. I see that you are competent in all the aspects of weaving, and do not shirk. I will promote you to manager of this section, at higher pay, if you will commit to remaining here for at least a year."

Jes didn't question why he knew that her commitment would be good; he was clearly a competent judge of character. He had made the offer to her because he saw that her work was better, and that she had discipline and integrity. Unfortunately, she couldn't oblige him. "I am here only until my sister finds a suitable man to marry. Then I must go home to my family."

"Your sister is a beautiful but inattentive woman." He squinted at her. "Sister-in-law?"

He was observant indeed! "Yes."

"If I help you find a man for her—"

"I will go home that much sooner," Jes said firmly. "I have prior commitments."

"And you honor them. You are a good woman. I will help you anyway. I will tell you the best and most honest merchandiser of clothing, and where to encounter citizens."

"We would appreciate that. But why should you bother?"

"Because if ever your situation changes, and you need to

return to Athens for a prolonged stay, you will take the job I have offered you.''

She considered, and nodded. ''I do not expect to return, but if I do—it is a good offer.''

He told her what he knew, and in due course she and Wona went shopping with their new obols and drachma coins where Crockson had recommended, and were treated fairly. They were ready for the next stage.

But excellent prospects turned out not to be as common as they had hoped, and one section of the city after another failed to yield Wona's prize. Jes chafed as months passed, taking through the winter, without resolution. Meanwhile she worked in the position Crockson had offered, running his shop. She had to admit it was a comfortable interim situation. If only it didn't seem so permanent!

Finally, they went to the Acropolis as brother and sister, because unaccompanied women were frowned on here. Wona was well dressed, a splendor to behold, catching male eyes in exactly the manner intended. The market place was one thing, but the seat of government was another; women needed to know their place. Jes carried a short staff, which she used as a cane, as if somewhat uncertain of her footing. They ascended by way of the Propylaea, an enormous sloping ramp, and went to make an offering at the Temple of Athene.

There were indeed men there, for Athene was the goddess for whom the city was named, and many wished for her favor as the goddess of war, fertility, handicrafts, and wisdom. Wona flirted shamelessly, apparently on the theory that more prospects were better than fewer. Jes tried to caution her, but could not speak openly in public, lest their purpose become too obvious.

No man, however, made a direct approach; this was after all a pious place. But when they passed a dark alcove, a hand reached out and caught Wona by the elbow, hauling her in. It took Jes a moment to realize that she was gone, for Jes's attention had been on the grandeur of the temple.

Then she whirled, and spied the action in the alcove. The man wore the robes of a citizen. These were of the ordinary style, simple in cut and material, but fine in workmanship. Ostentation was frowned on, but quality in clothing did show. However, in this case, no quality of manner was showing.

The man was groping Wona hungrily, sliding one hand into her décolletage while the other drew her in closer. Wona was trying to extricate herself without screaming or being unladylike, but it was clear that more was needed, and quickly. What the man had in mind was something other than courtship and marriage.

Jes stepped in. "My sister is not interested in this relationship," she said politely but firmly. "Please desist and release her."

"Get out of here, stripling," the man grunted, getting hold of Wona's breast.

So much for politeness. Jes lifted her staff and rapped the man smartly across the back of the head. He grunted and his grip slackened, allowing Wona to wrench free.

"We had better flee this region," Jes muttered. "Hurry."

They hurried, but it was already too late. "That man attacked me!" the citizen cried. "Kill him!"

This was no time to argue the niceties of provocation and reaction. They broke into a run.

The temple guards quickly took up the chase. Jes knew there would be no mercy, for the guards would take the word of the citizen over that of noncitizens. They had to hide immediately—but where?

"The priestesses' quarters!" Wona said, pointing to an offshoot archway.

They dodged into it, and then around another corner. There was a great loom with a partly done tapestry.

They paused. "Can we masquerade as two women?" Wona asked with half a smile.

"We had better," Jes agreed wryly.

Hastily Wona simplified her robe, removed her limited

jewelry, and adjusted her composure to fit the style of a temple woman. Jes hid her staff in an alcove and quickly removed and reversed her robe so that its yellow side was out, then donned it and adjusted her style to be feminine as they scrambled for the stools before the tapestry.

The thing was huge, and very finely wrought. A pattern was being made according to a picture, and a scene was being woven in. They only glanced at it as they completed their adjustments, quickly loosening and binding back their hair in the temple mode. Wona had to rub off makeup, while Jes tried to make herself look more submissive.

Only now did they have the chance to really examine the loom. "Look at this!" Wona breathed. "Brass thread weights—with owls."

Jes peered at one. Indeed, it was metal, imprinted with a design showing an owl with human hands spinning wool from a basket in front of it. "Athene's bird," she agreed. "The same as on the silver coin."

The picture was about half-complete, showing a series of horizontally oriented scenes covering the entire cloth. The design was exceedingly intricate, in two colors, each requiring its own special threads: saffron-yellow and purple. Such a tapestry would require months to complete.

"This isn't just an incidental project," Wona said, awed.

"This is the peplos," Jes agreed. "The Peplos of Athene."

They gazed at it, overwhelmed by the significance of their discovery. Every summer the Panathenian festival was held in Hekatombaion, the first month of the Athenian calendar, and it was the biggest event of the year. The culmination was the presentation of the richly woven robe that was the peplos to the statue of Athene, and the sacrifice of a hundred cows on Athene's altar, which was then set afire by the prize-winning torchbearer.

The weaving of the peplos was reserved for specially chosen women, a great honor. The colors were expensive and significant. Saffron associated with women and femininity;

indeed, a poorer grade of that color was what Jes and Wona
wore. The purple was "sea purple," the color of kings, its
rich dye derived from the murex shell. Unlike most natural
dyes, both of these were colorfast in both water and sunlight.
Athene rated only the very best.

The scenes on the tapestry had as yet only their top
halves, but this was enough to show that they portrayed
Athene and Zeus leading the gods to victory in their epic
struggle with the Titans. The design differed somewhat each
year, but the essence was the same. The peplos would dress
the life-sized statue of Athene Polias—"Goddess of the
City"—on the Acropolis.

"It would be almost sacrilegious to weave even one
thread of this sacred work," Wona said. "We are not *er-
gastinai*, the approved matrons."

"So let's do it," Jes said wickedly.

But before they could properly orient on the pattern and
find the correct thread, the pursuit burst in. The delay had
not been at all long; their amazement at their discovery had
made it seem more. Two guards stopped to stare suspi-
ciously at them. Probably other chambers were being
checked at the same time, so the guards had no way of
knowing which one held the fugitives. That didn't mean that
Jes and Wona were safe, just that they had a chance. If they
could bluff well enough.

They both paused with their hands lifted, as if interrupted
amidst their joint labor on the tapestry. Both stared at the
intruders with startled innocence. Jes had just recently
learned the expression, and hoped she had it right.

One guard studied Wona, who still looked ambitiously
female despite hunching down to seem less so. "That one
could be the woman." He turned to stare at Jes. "But that's
not the youth."

"He's beardless," the other said. "Might be him."

Jes took the initiative. "Why are you staring at me?" she
asked. "Don't you louts have better things to do than intrude on the work of temple matrons?"

The first guard hesitated, but then decided. "You could be him. We'll take you to the head priestess."

That would be disaster. Jes knew she had to act quickly and decisively to avert such a step. That meant either grabbing a weapon and trying to disable them silently, which was surely a hopeless effort, or satisfying them that she really was a woman.

They stepped toward her. She set one foot on her own hem and stood up suddenly, in alarm that was genuine, though not for the reason she wished to convey. The foot anchored the robe, preventing it from rising with her, and it pulled down off her right shoulder, exposing her breasts.

"Oh!" she exclaimed, in only half-feigned mortification. She quickly hauled her robe back up as she inhaled and arched her back, making her modest bosom stand out just before it was covered.

The men stopped. "That's no stripling," one muttered. Then, embarrassed, they turned and exited the chamber.

Jes sat back on the stool, weak with relief. Her heart was pounding, and she felt her face flushing. In that moment she remembered an episode with Ned, when they had taken wares for trading to a distant city and she had distracted bad men by wearing a string skirt. That, too, might have been fun, had there not been peril.

"Well played!" Wona said. "You showed them just enough, in a brief flash, so that their male eyes exaggerated the effect, and you also forced a maidenly blush."

"Half of it was accident," Jes said.

"Then make sure it's not an accident next time. Show men only flashes, not the full display, until such time as they are committed. You could also have remained sitting."

"But then the robe wouldn't have come off."

"Like so." Wona swung her legs around toward Jes, and her robe failed to follow perfectly, so that one thigh and the dark crevice between thighs lay open to view. It was very clear that Wona was no man.

"Oh." That might indeed have been easier.

"But your way was good too," Wona said. "With that maidenly exclamation. In that instant you seemed as female as it is possible to be."

"Thank you." But Jes knew that they weren't safe yet. "How do we escape before the real priestesses return?"

Wona reflected. "We may just have to walk out as we are. But it's too soon to make the attempt; the guards are still searching. So let's weave our thread."

Jes nodded. They addressed the tapestry, studying the pattern, and solemnly wove in one thread. No one would notice, but they would know that they were part of the most famous garment in Greece.

By then, enough time had passed. They went to the corner and recovered their hidden things, and also strapped their daggers back on to their inner thighs, just in case.

Then they heard someone coming. They dived back to the stools and addressed the tapestry again. Jes's staff made a clatter as she hurled it back into the corner.

A single, mature woman entered. She wore a tiara bearing an owl, and a necklace of beads carved in the likeness of olives, another symbol of Athene. Her quality saffron robe identified her clearly: she was the head priestess!

The woman's glance was imperious. "Come with me," she said. "Bring your things."

Jes exchanged a wary look with Wona. Did the priestess know? Or were there so many novice priestesses that she simply didn't recognize them all? But then why was she ordering them to go with her? Was she going to turn them in to the male authorities?

There didn't seem to be much choice. They stood, and Jes fetched her staff. They followed the priestess out of the chamber.

She led them through convoluted passages to an opulent chamber in another part of the temple. "The goddess saw fit to shield you from the guards' eyes, and we will not presume to go against her will. But you must leave. We can not afford scandal in the Temple of Athene. There has been no episode. The guards were confused. Depart by this rear exit.'' She opened a door that led directly outside. ''Never speak of this. Agreed?''

Jes and Wona exchanged another glance. Then both nodded. The head priestess was letting them go!

The woman left by the internal door. Alone, they quickly changed back to their original aspects, Jes becoming male. Then they walked out the back way as man and woman.

''She knew,'' Jes murmured as they got clear of the temple.

''She knew,'' Wona agreed. ''She saw that we were harmless, and she did not want blood on her floors. So she got rid of us much the way we got rid of the guards, with minimum fuss. She is not our friend.''

''But neither is she our enemy. To that we owe our lives.''

''We owe our lives,'' Wona agreed soberly. ''I think I will not look for men any more there, lest she change her mind.''

They walked back to their apartment. The day was a failure, in the main sense, but perhaps not entirely.

Another day they visited the port city of Piraeus, which was connected to Athens by a set of long walls that enclosed the road to north and south. The walls were fortified throughout, and there were cross-walls so that even if an enemy force got between the main walls, there would be no easy access to the cities of Athens or Piraeus. The bowmen on the walls were relaxed, now that the enemy was gone, but it was clear that they could devastate a hostile force if the need came.

Piraeus was much smaller than Athens, but interesting because of its harbors and the ships in them. The stately trieres were there, moving out on their two sails, their oarsmen resting. Jes was fascinated. She was familiar with the type of ship, but had never actually been on one. ''To think they have to pay oarsmen to serve on those," she said. "I would do it for food."

"How much do they pay the captain?"

"The trierarch? Nothing, usually. It's a public duty for citizens of high standing, lasting a year. He has to outfit the ship and pay the crew. The city is supposed to pay for it all, but that can take time, and meanwhile he has to cover it all himself. That's why so few ever volunteer for this duty."

"No wonder, if it costs them a fortune instead of making them a fortune!" Then Wona's mind fixed on another aspect. "That means the captains have to be rich to start with."

"Yes. That's why it is limited to citizens of high standing. Others would not be able to afford it."

"So such a citizen would be a good one to marry."

Now Jes got her drift. "Yes, if he needed a wife."

"Suddenly I am interested in trieres."

Jes shook her head. "It's the wealthy or prominent citizens you are interested in. During the year they serve on ship, they aren't available at home. You need to catch one before or after his public service."

"But by the same token, he will be in need of female companionship during that year, and perhaps less choosy about it. It is surely a good time to make the acquaintance."

"There are hetaerae in plenty for such needs." Those were the women of easy virtue. It was an honorable profession, but not what Wona was looking for.

"When the ship is abroad?"

Jes considered. "I suppose not when it is between ports. But you don't like roughing it in the country, any better than any other woman does."

Wona sighed. "True. So Athens remains the best hunting ground."

Jes agreed. She hoped Wona would find a suitable man soon, because she was getting homesick for her family. Sam should have returned by now, with his trading goods, and

would be adjusting to the loss of Wona. Ned would be free
of her. New things would be happening. Even if life was
lean, it was her life, and she wanted it back.

Sam viewed his home farm with evident joy. "This is where
I live," he told Snow. "Now you can marry my brother
Ned."

Snow smiled, though she was oddly sad. "I haven't met
him yet. He may not like me."

"Any man will like you, once he knows you. You are
beautiful."

How she wished such words were sincere! "You are kind
to say so, Sam."

Soon the approaching pair was spied. A young girl
sounded the alarm and charged across the landscape to meet
them. Then she halted, realizing that one of them was a
stranger.

"My little sister Lin," Sam said, beckoning to the girl.

"She is lovely."

"Like you," he said.

"No, I mean she really is. She is about to be an outstand-
ing woman."

Sam did not reply, but his jaw tightened. That was odd.
He clearly loved his sister, but there was something he
wasn't saying. The girl certainly was beautiful in face and
body, unlike Snow, who had only body. What was his reservation?

Shy, now, Lin approached. "Who—"

"This is Snow," Sam said. "She has come to marry
Ned."

"To meet Ned," Snow said quickly. Sam was a wonderful man, but somewhat short on social finesse.

Lin turned an abruptly appraising gaze on Snow. "Maybe
so," she said after a moment. "Flo will decide."

"Flo will decide," Snow agreed, relieved that there was

someone else to make such decisions. What would be, would be.

"Snow is really nice," Sam said, defensively. "Ned will like her."

Lin considered a moment more. Then she smiled brilliantly, as if something wonderful had just happened. "I'll tell Flo!" She spun about and ran back toward the farm, exuberantly leaping across rocks and plants.

"Lin's a great kid," Sam said as they followed more sedately.

"Any moment now she will be a lovely young woman," Snow said firmly. What was the mystery about her?

Sam stared hard at the ground. "I think I must tell you. Did you see her hand?"

"Yes. Her fingers are delicate and well formed." Then she realized that she had seen only the girl's right hand. The left had been kept out of sight. "Something is wrong with the left hand?"

"She has six fingers."

Suddenly it came together. "You say Lin is lovely, like me. You mean that one feature spoils all the rest."

Sam looked everywhere but at her. "I didn't mean—"

"She has a deformed hand. I have a homely face."

"I don't care about either!" Sam exclaimed. "I love—" He balked, flustered. "I love my sister."

He was socially clumsy, yet of good motive. Snow wished that he weren't already married. She would marry his brother, who was surely a fine young man, but she knew already that he could never be the same as Sam.

Now two figures appeared: Lin and a massive older woman. That would be Flo, the true leader of the family. Snow felt suddenly nervous. Where would she go, if Flo rejected her?

The four of them came together. Flo took the initiative. "Hello, Sam. Hello, Snow. We must talk."

"I brought her home for—" Sam started.

"Of course. Sam, you go catch up with the others. This way, Snow."

Sam hesitated, then shrugged and followed Lin away.

Bemused, Snow followed the woman to the station where she had been scraping a sheep hide. It was a messy, tedious job. "I can do that," Snow said quickly. "I am a sheep-herder's daughter."

"We'll both do it," Flo said, handing her a bronze scraper.

They got to work on the hide. Snow expected the fat woman to ask about her background and reason for coming here, and she would answer directly, without dwelling on her grief. But Flo surprised her.

"Sam isn't married anymore."

Snow stared at her. "But he told me—"

"He doesn't know it yet. Lin's telling him now. His faith-less wife has gone to Athens to find a richer man. We will not see her again."

Snow fumbled for words. "She left him? Without word? What kind of woman would—?"

"We arranged it. She wasn't pulling her weight, and she seduced Ned. We had to be rid of her. While Sam was away. You understand."

Snow nodded. Sam would never have agreed to such a thing, yet if his wife were faithless, and with Sam's brother, it had to be done. So this was no simple family situation. "You want me to go elsewhere? I never intended to com-plicate things."

"Do you love Sam?"

Shaken, Snow could only confess the truth. "Yes. But I never told him—we never—I thought he was—"

"Married. And Sam is an honorable man. We want him untouched by scandal. Never speak of what his wife did with his brother."

"I will never speak of it," Snow agreed. "It would hurt him to know. He spoke very well of Ned, recommending him to me. He said Ned wouldn't mind that I had been raped.''

Flo's mouth tightened, and Snow remembered belatedly that Flo herself had been raped. ''True. We understand about such things.''

''And that Ned judged by other things than—than faces. I'm sure he is a fine—''

''Ned is. He is a brilliant man, and a kind one. Sam meant well. But you will marry Sam. You are obviously the woman for him.''.

A dam within her burst. Flo had put things together so quickly, so well. Snow's tears flowed.

''Sam is not brilliant,'' Flo continued. ''But he has fair judgment. We know he would not have brought you home for Ned, were you not a fine woman, and I can see that you are. You would have been very good for Ned. But it would not be fair for Sam to lose a second woman to his brother. Lin says Sam loves you. Lin is very sharp about such things.''

''I think he does,'' Snow agreed.

''This solves our problem. We feared that Sam would be upset. Now he will not be. You will share his room tonight, and marry him when convenient. It will be clear to all that you had no guilt in his loss of Wona, because she left before you came.'' She stood and laid one heavy arm across Snow's shoulders. ''Welcome to the family. These are lean times, but I think you will like us well enough.''

Snow nodded, trying to wipe away her tears. It was so sudden, so unexpected. She had been so careful not to compromise Sam, and now she could love him openly. She had indeed been aware of his growing feeling for her, and his guilt about that feeling, and she had felt guilt for returning it. But she had never said anything, respecting his determination to do the right thing. She knew that Sam would gladly marry her, and would not much question the disappearance of his former wife. The sisters had efficiently put it together, wasting no time.

Things went well enough, in Athens, except for one thing: Wona still couldn't find a man. She wouldn't take anything less than a full citizen, and citizens had their choice of women of the lower echelons, so there was a good deal of competition. She could, and occasionally did, spend the night with a prospect, and it seemed that she impressed such men favorably, but they were not looking to marry. For one thing, there was the war with Sparta, and everyone who was anyone was making desperate preparations for the resumption of hostilities. It was not a time for making long-range commitments.

Sure enough, in the spring, the Spartan army marched into Attica again. Athens did have ground forces, but they were outnumbered two to one, and could not stand against the invaders. So the Athenian soldiers retreated, delaying the Spartan advance as much as was feasible, while the population of the countryside poured into the city. The people actually dismantled the wood structures of their homes and used the material to build crude huts within Athens. These had poor ventilation, and were called "swelterings" in summer. It was not yet summer, but already they stank. As more and more people crowded in, the shelters spread onto holy ground normally reserved for the temples, and many squatters took up residence in the temples themselves. The priests didn't like it, of course, but there was not a lot they could do about it. These were, after all, supporters of Athens, seeking succor in their time of need, and theoretically the temples were for the benefit of the people.

Fortunately the competent statesman Perikles, who had lost his position as a *strategoi*, as a member of the governing board of ten generals, earlier that year, was back. Popular opinion had rebounded in his favor, because his enemies had turned out to be far less capable, if not actually incompetent. Maybe, the common folk thought, this siege would not have occurred if Perikles had been at the helm. So Perikles had returned to power.

Now Jes and Wona saw what it was like from inside. The city doubled in size, and there was hardly room for all the refugees. Extensive camps formed just within the walls, and strangers thronged the market places. Rental units became precious. The landlords raised the rent, knowing that if the renters didn't pay it, someone else would. Prices rose, especially for food.

There was also more crime. Jes had to assume her masculine form and carry a weapon in an obvious manner; otherwise they would have been assailed by robbers who were looking for food and silver, but would not be averse to a bit of rape on the side. Even with the weapon, they had to be careful, and stay clear of certain regions, lest they be overwhelmed by disreputable groups of hungry men. On occasion there were mobs of women, too; they robbed for silver and food and clothing, but didn't rape.

Crockson was very good about it. He hired guards to protect the workers, and sometimes when the mobs were bad, the guards would see the women home. He hired women from the refugees. Jes assumed some managerial duties, because it was not possible for Crockson to monitor the larger number by himself, and she was paid extra. She had not made the deal to stay a year, but she saw how easy it would be to make that deal, should she ever change her mind.

But what she really wanted was to be back home. She hated this crowded city, where the forest was not even visible, and neighbor had to be wary of neighbor. She had thought this would be a fairly brief mission; instead it was dragging out interminably. She couldn't really blame Wona for that; in any other times, the woman should have been able to land a citizen. It was this disruptive war that changed everything. What could be worse?

Too soon, they found out. One of the new workers developed a rash. "You must go home immediately," Crockson said, alarmed.

"But I haven't finished my work," the woman protested. What she meant was that she hadn't been paid yet, and she needed the money.

Crockson gave her several small silver obols. "Go home and get well. There will be work for you then."

"But it is not safe alone on the street."

Crockson was beginning to look desperate. Jes didn't understand why he was making such a fuss, as the woman's illness did not seem to be serious. But she stepped in to help. "I can take you home."

"A woman?" the woman asked doubtfully.

"She will suffice," Crockson said, bringing Jes's outdoor cloak.

Jes did her best to mask her shock. Her club was concealed in the cloak, and he had to be aware of its presence. He had, it seemed, caught on to her masquerade, and not told. The man did have discretion. She had been foolishly sure she was undetected.

Jes donned the peplos, and they stepped out onto the street. Wona remained working, knowing that Jes would return. The moment they were out, Jes paused to redo her hair and make herself into a man. The woman, evidently feeling worse, seemed not to notice.

They walked to the camp where the woman lived. A rough-looking man eyed them, but Jes lifted her club in a nominally friendly salute, and he turned away. Had she been seen as a woman, he would not have. Then she would have had to club him, swiftly, before he could do damage, perhaps attracting attention. Attention, in such a situation, could be deadly, because it summoned ruffians in the manner of hungry sharks. This way was better.

The woman was fading rapidly. Jes had to take her by the elbow to steady her, lest she fall. Crockson was right: this was more than an incidental malady.

They reached the woman's temporary hovel. She collapsed on her dirty straw bed. No one else was there. "You have a family?" Jes asked, concerned.

"Yes. Working. They will be home soon. Thank you."

Not entirely satisfied, but anxious to get away from this unpleasant section and back to work, Jes left her lying there and made her way down the alleys. Obviously Crockson recognized the illness; she would ask him about it.

"It is the plague," Crockson told her grimly. "I have seen it elsewhere. First the rash, then sickness in the gut, and it can get so intense there is blood in the refuse. Many die."

"It is that bad?" Jes did not like the sound of this, as she had been exposed to it.

He nodded gravely. "I think I won't get it, because I survived it before. I never felt worse in my life! There was swelling under my arms and in my groin, and—never mind. I heard rumors of an outbreak a few days ago, but did not want to believe it, and did not want to help spread false panic. After all, there are many illnesses in these crowded conditions, and most are not serious. But now there is no doubt. I have some advice I hate to give you."

"Advice?"

"Get out of here. Out of Athens. So you won't catch it. Believe me, you don't want it. Come back when it's gone."

"But the city is already under siege! How can we—?"

"At night, perhaps. The Spartans can't watch every cranny all the time. If they see you, Wona may have to— you know. Distract the men for a while. But you may be able to get away."

"But my work here—"

"I value your work highly. But you will be of no use to me if you die from the plague. Take your friend and go today. Here is your pay." He gave her a small bag of silver coins. She could tell by the heft of it that it was worth far more than he owed them.

"I think your advice is good," she said. "I think you are a decent man."

"It's a business decision," he said, embarrassed. "And

I'm not doing it for the others. I want you to return to run my shop.''

She knew better. The silver was really a gift. ''Thank you,'' she said, touched by his generosity. Then she collected Wona, and they left.

But the news of the plague was already circulating. Crockson was not the only one who had heard rumors. It seemed that the fever had appeared in several parts of the city. People were starting to panic. The already-stressed veneer of law was rupturing, and brigands, ready to ply their trade the moment any opportunity arose, were openly attacking people, as if not concerned about any penalties. They were probably correct.

They went to their apartment and gathered up their things. Then, as evening approached, they headed for the nearest gate.

''Magic amulets for sale,'' a street hawker called. ''Protection against the plague.''

''I want one of those,'' Wona said. Before Jes could protest, she signaled the hawker, who came right over.

Jes clenched her jaw. It was the woman's right to waste a coin on magic if she chose to.

They resumed their trek to the gate. It was closed. ''Go back,'' the guard called. ''The city is under siege.''

They knew that. But the guard wasn't amenable to their logic of going out under cover of darkness. ''You think it's some kind of picnic out there?'' he demanded. ''They're slaughtering first and asking questions second. Go back into the city, you fools.''

Jes cursed herself for not realizing that of course it would be this way. She and Wona should have left the city before the plague, not after it struck. Before the siege. They had indeed been fools.

''Maybe we can go to Piraeus and catch a merchant ship,'' Wona said, horrified. ''They're full when they come in, but empty when they go out, aren't they?''

"Maybe," Jes agreed doubtfully, still cursing herself for her lack of foresight.

They made their way to the doubly walled road to the port city. But as soon as they reached it, they saw it was hopeless. The region between the walls was jammed with the temporary structures of the refugees, and they could hear the groans of a number with the plague. There might or might not be a ship out, but they would have to go through the thick of the illness to reach it.

Well, if that was the way it was, they had better brave it now, before it got any worse. "How is it in Piraeus?" Jes asked a guard at the gate between the walled channel and Athens proper.

"That's where this curse started," the man replied. "I'm glad I've got my magic amulet." He touched a wooden charm strung around his neck. "I don't want to die of that thing."

Jes had little faith in amulets for protection. She had experimented with one as a child, and found that she was as likely to get hurt with it as without it. But maybe she hadn't had a good one. "So it's worse in the port city?"

"For sure. The ships are coming back with it too."

That did it. They turned away, and returned disconsolately to their apartment in Athens. It was too late to go back to work, but they would do so the next day. Crockson's generous gesture had not helped them after all.

"I don't want to catch the plague," Wona said, looking nervously around. She dug out the amulet she had bought and put it on.

Jes didn't comment. But she was not easy as she sank into sleep that night.

The next day they went to work. "It was too late to go," she explained to Crockson. "But we thank you." She gave him the bag of silver, which she had never opened.

"May Athene preserve you," he said simply.

Jes did not have a great deal of faith in the beneficence

of the gods, either, but it wasn't politic to say so. "Thank you."

More women came down with the plague, and Jes saw them back to their hovels, one by one. But there was hope, because the majority of people did not come down with the malady. Maybe the siege of illness, like that of the Spartan army, would ease without becoming total. Stories abounded, accounting for it. "The Peloponnesians poisoned the cisterns," a woman whispered fearfully. "I don't dare drink from one." She was referring to the mechanism that collected rainwater, because no new wells had been sunk to provide water for the massive influx of people. Jes didn't believe that, because there should be no Spartans inside the city. "It is the wrath of the gods," another woman said. "Especially Apollo. He did it to the Greek host before the city of Troy; now he's doing it to us. The oracle said it would be so!" But Jes remembered no such pronouncement by the oracle. The woman was insistent: "My grandfather recalls it from the time of his youth." She went into a singsong. "The Dorian war will come, and death along with it."

"No, it was 'dearth,' " another woman protested.

"It was both," a third said. "And we will pay the price. We should never have gotten into this war."

With that Jes was inclined to agree. She had learned from Crockson, who had an interest in contemporary politics, that Athens had been arrogant. Sparta had committed sacrilege against the god Poseidon, who had punished the city with a series of earthquakes a generation ago, sending it into decline. Athens had taken advantage of the situation to increase its own power. It had built a large navy to defeat the dreaded Persians, and expanded it thereafter. Other cities in the Delian League were nominally equal, but Athens had increasingly treated them like subject states. Athens had used the money from the League treasury as her own, claiming it was to ensure their protection. Three years ago Athens had banned Megaran traders from Aegean markets and instituted an embargo against Megaris itself. Athens had also intervened in disputes between Corinth and Corcyra, and forbade Potidaea from choosing its annual magistrate from Corinth, as had been the custom. So Corinth had made it clear to Sparta that they must go to war, or face the dissolution of the rival Peloponnesian League. Thus had the war been joined. "And it wouldn't have happened," Crockson concluded, "if Athens had not gotten too pushy. You can't do that to other cities, without building resentment. Now look where it's gotten us."

Indeed, they were in trouble. Jes was sure that the refugees had brought the plague with them. If there had not been war, there would not have been refugees, and then there might have been no plague. But of course it was too late to complain.

The moment the siege lifted, they would leave Athens and seek a husband for Wona in a city that was free of the plague. It wasn't just that the war had siphoned off most of the worthwhile men, but that the plague had caused an almost complete breakdown in order. Jes would have much preferred to walk alone through a forest infested with vicious wild animals, than on a city street. Almost every day she had to use her club, and sometimes her knife, to defend Wona and herself from ruffians. How she longed for the calm island of Euboea!

Then Jes abruptly felt strange. She found herself blinking repeatedly and rubbing her eyes, which were stinging. She felt cold and unsteady. Then she smelled her own breath, which was unnaturally fetid. "Oh, no!"

Crockson heard her exclamation. He came over to check. "Dust blow in your eyes?"

"I think I've got the plague." For she had seen the symptoms often enough in others, during the past few days.

He put a hand on her forehead. "Fever, inflamed eyes, bad breath. I agree. You have the plague."

"I must go home before—"

He shook his head. "I think not. You must remain here."

"But others will catch—"

"We don't know how it spreads, but it isn't necessarily from one person to another, or all my workers would have it now, instead of only a quarter of them. I suspect it is bad water. In any event, if it spreads from person to person, you got it from someone here, so it is my responsibility. I will take care of you. You can stay in the back storage chamber."

"But Wona—she can't go home alone."

"She will remain here too, to bring you food and water and change your clothing." He smiled, very briefly. "I think you would rather have her do some things for you, than have me do them."

Wona came up. "Yes, I will do them. I can't go out by myself."

Jes was too distracted to protest further. She allowed herself to be guided to the back room.

Her fever got worse. She lay on a pallet, shivering though Wona piled blankets on her. Her tongue swelled until she feared she would choke on it, and her throat became so sore that breathing was verging on painful. Wona brought a basin of water and sponged her face, but it didn't make her feel better. Then, by uneasy stages, she stumbled her way into sleep.

She woke sneezing, and each sneeze burned her throat, mouth and nose horribly. The room looked red, because of the inflammation of her eyes. She tried to speak, and her voice was hoarse. "I hate this!"

Wona appeared. "Rest, Jes. That is all you can do."

Indeed, that was all she was capable of doing, other than suffering. Wona gave her water to sip, and she managed some, but had no appetite for food. Wona helped her use the pot, because she was too unsteady to manage it on her own. Then she sank back into a tormented haziness that lasted the night. Her dreams were scattered and senseless, with inexplicable things like the cracking open of bones to reveal horrible jelly inside, and seeing a woman crack open similarly, jelly squeezing out of her, that assumed the form of a baby. But it couldn't be, because they left it there on the ground and walked away. Then a fire blazing across a valley, and she was running right into it, her legs strangely thick. Huge Sam and little Lin dancing together, making people laugh. Paddling strange long boats along an unfamiliar shore. Building a house made of monstrous bones. Ned painting a picture on a big rock. And Ned again, trying to run, and Wona, pursuing him.

She opened her eyes, and there was Wona. "You stole my brother!" Jes exclaimed in a fury.

"Yes. I owe you for that." Wona held a cup of water to her mouth. "Drink."

"I should have killed you!"

"Instead you protected me. You are a better person than I am. Drink."

Jes drank, and faded back out.

She wasn't sure how much time passed, but it could have been several days. The plague reached into her chest, making her have a hard cough. Her chest got tired, but she couldn't stop coughing. She had seen it in others, and wondered why they didn't just stop coughing when it hurt; now she knew.

She thought the malady was passing, but that was illusion. It was merely retrenching. It reached into her belly and twisted her gut. She retched, vomited, and vomited again, spewing out whatever remained inside her, and when that was gone, she continued heaving dry. That wasn't enough, and she kept heaving until it seemed she would turn inside out, finally managing to spit out foul-looking and -smelling bile. Wona cleaned it all up without comment.

But the worst had not yet passed. After more scattered intervals of sleep, she developed the characteristic rash. It was awful. Her skin turned reddish, and was spotted with pustules and small sores. She hated the look of it.

Wona put a hand on her forehead to check her fever— and Jes screamed. She was so hot that she couldn't bear to be touched. "I'm burning, burning!" she moaned.

"But you're not at all hot," Wona protested.

That was what she thought. Jes's heat increased, until she could not bear the touch of anything. Not a blanket, not even the lightest clothing. She threw everything off and lay naked, not caring whether Crockson might come in and see her. In her fevered memory, he had been in and out many times already.

She woke again, intolerably thirsty. Wona was absent, but she couldn't wait. "Water," she gasped.

After a time, Crockson did come in, carrying a jar of water and a cup. "Can you drink it yourself?" he asked, extending the brimming cup.

She snatched it from his hand, spilling some, and jammed it to her face. She gulped it avidly down, but her terrible thirst was not quenched. Crockson poured more from the jar, and she drank this too, and then a third. Still she was not quenched.

"That is enough, for now," Crockson said.

"But I need more—much more," she protested, reaching for the cup again.

He held it away. "You will drown in water, and never get enough. Trust me. I have seen it before. I will give you more later. Now rest."

She looked down, and saw her stomach distended from the water inside her, and realized it was true. This thirst could not be quenched.

"Where is Wona?" she asked querulously. "Why isn't she doing this?"

He gestured to the far side of the chamber. There was Wona, asleep. "She has served you well, but she too needs her sleep," he explained.

"That's more than I expected," Jes said.

"She needs you," he said. "If you die, she is alone without having found her man. So she has done the best she can for you."

It did make sense. "And you—why do you help us so

freely?'' she demanded. "You know I will not stay to run your shop.''

"I like you, Jes,'' he said seriously. "You are my employee, but I regard you as a friend. There are thousands of people in this city more worthy of dying than you, so I hope to keep you among the living.''

"But you are too generous. That bag of silver—''

"You returned it.''

"Because we didn't go.''

"How many others would have done that?''

Jes couldn't answer, because she couldn't think of any she knew here in Athens.

He stepped back. "Now try to rest. This malady is not yet done with you.''

"I can't rest!''

"That is part of it. But you must try. I will bring more water soon.'' He left the room.

Only then did she remember that she was naked. She hadn't noticed, in her inordinate thirst. She suspected that he hadn't noticed either. It wasn't because she wasn't much of a figure of a woman, especially in this grotesque illness; it was because he had no designs on her.

But what about Wona? Had she bought his favor?

Jes tried to sleep, but could not. She tried at least to rest, and could not. She knew that she would never be able to relax, no matter how tired she became. The plague simply would not allow it.

After a time, Wona stirred. "Oh, you are alert,'' she said, getting up.

"Did you pay Crockson?''

Wona laughed. "With what? We owe him silver already.''

"In your way.''

"Oh. No. I offered, but he declined. He said he preferred to be your friend.'' She shook her head, bemused. "He doesn't even want your body, just your respect. He is strange.''

"Very strange," Jes agreed. Some day she would find a way to repay Crockson for his kindness.

She managed to eat a little, and of course she drank all the water they would allow her. It was more than she needed, because what she didn't throw up or sweat away she urinated away. More than once she overflowed the pot; it seemed impossible to empty it as fast as she filled it. But her thirst remained.

The violent spasms passed, but Jes did not feel very much better. She must have gotten snatches of sleep, because sometimes it was light in the chamber, and sometimes dark. Wona told her that seven days had passed since she first felt the fever. That seemed impossible; it was either far too long, or far too brief.

The plague stopped bothering her skin so much, and her cough eased. But the malady moved deeper into her gut. Now she had diarrhea, and it was like the heaves, in that it wouldn't stop. It turned black, and she knew there was blood in it, but she couldn't stop it from coming. Wona took the pot out repeatedly, not complaining.

Then Jes lost her strength, as she had not during the violent stage. She became so extremely weak that she could hardly stir herself to move. She lay there and felt her life fading away.

At one point she heard them talking, but she lacked the strength to react. "What can we do?" Wona asked. "She's so near death."

"This is the point at which she will die, if she is going to," Crockson's voice replied. "I am not a doctor, but I think it is the bleeding in the bowels that takes away the life energy. She must heal by herself—or fail to. We can only watch."

"I hate this!"

"So do I. But there can be worse. So though I hope she lives, I would rather see her die, than—"

"Than what?" Wona demanded, alarmed. "What could be worse than death?"

"Some recover, but leave parts of themselves behind. The distemper can fix itself on some particular member."

"I don't understand."

"It ruins the hands, making them permanently useless. Or the feet, so that the person can't walk. Or the genitals, or the eyes, leaving them blind."

"Oh," Wona said, appalled.

"Or even the mind, so that they remember nothing, and neither know themselves nor recognize their friends."

"You are right," Wona agreed. "Better she die, than that."

"But she is strong," he concluded. "I think she will survive, and be herself again." But he did not sound confident.

"May I speak frankly?" Now there was a certain edge to Wona's voice.

"Of course. We have a common cause, in the saving of this person."

"Do we? I am not her friend, but am bound to her until I find a suitable man. She will be very glad to see me placed, so she is free. So the relationship between the two of us is understood. But you—why are you being so generous to us?"

"I am generous to those I feel are deserving."

"By that you mean Jes."

"Well, I mean no offense to you. You are a beautiful woman, and you have done your part."

"I offered my body to you, in payment for our debt to you. Why did you refuse?"

"It would not be right to take such advantage—"

"And you have not taken such advantage of any of the other women who work for you. Many are married, and many are not pretty, so maybe that is understandable. But I am another matter. I owe you, and I am unmarried, and beautiful. You could legitimately take me. Yet you do not."

"You must remain chaste for the man you will marry."

Wona spat in negation. "You know chastity is not a word that ever applied to me."

"Still—"

"Do you hold my nature against me?"

"No, I understand it. You are as you are, and you use what skills you possess to forward your security, just as others do."

"Why don't you marry me? Then Jes will be immediately free."

"But you don't want an old trader, you want a citizen with status."

"I am realistic. You are a good man. You would take good care of me."

"This is not feasible. You must seek a man better suited to you."

"Would you prefer Jes? She is slender where I am not. Some men like their women lean."

"I value Jes as a friend and a fine person. I would not—"

"Because your true passion is not for girls at all," Wona said. "It is for boys."

There was a silence.

"And you took Jes for a boy, at first," she continued relentlessly. "She passes for a stripling man, so that was understandable. But she needed no weapon to impress you."

"It is a respectable association," Crockson said defensively.

"Yes, in the cities. Less so, in the countryside. I am not condemning you, merely making sure I understand. You do for her what you would do for a young male lover."

"Yes. I wish I could have had a relationship with her. But I can love no woman, and she is a woman, no matter how she garbs herself. But if you feel you owe me anything, repay me in this manner: do not speak of this to her. I love her in my own fashion, which is not hers, and my love can never be consummated. I would not for all the world cause her the kind of distress such a revelation would bring her."

"As you wish. I make no claim to being any fine person, but I pay a price when it is fair. I will spare her this."

"Thank you."

"But if you married me, I would be tolerant and discreet. I have no more actual interest in sex with men than you do in sex with women. Except as an exercise in power over them. All I want is a secure, wealthy life."

There was a pause, as Crockson considered. "In another culture, I think I would find your offer attractive. But here in Athens there is not such need for concealment. I can sponsor my lovers openly, so long as I do not pursue the relationship past the age of maturity, which is thirty. The only exception is when I do not wish to hurt one I respect like Jes. I think I am better off single."

Wona sighed. "Surely so."

Jes faded out. But now she had something to think about. What she had learned distressed her. She was more attractive as a boy than as a woman? But what could she do about it?

More time passed. Sometimes she was conscious of being picked up and moved, so that her soiled bedding could be changed, and she doubted that Wona had the strength to do that, so it must be Crockson. Someone was cleaning her body and putting her back down. She lacked the strength to protest, so kept her eyes closed and let it happen. She faded in and out.

Then she woke feeling not as bad. She still lacked the will to move, but thought she could do so if she tried. She heard the others talking.

"It is awful out there," Crockson said. "I have heard the reports. Neither priest nor amulet retards the spread or mitigates the intensity of the malady. Physicians are helpless before it; they themselves are dying from it. All through the city, Athenians are abandoning themselves to despair. The space between the walls leading to Piraeus is a scene of desolation. Every man attacked with the malady loses his courage at once, and lies down and dies without any attempt to seek for preservatives. At first friends and relatives lent their aid to tend the sick, but so many of those attendants perished themselves that soon no man would thus expose himself. The most generous spirits, who persisted the longest in helping others, were carried off in the greatest numbers. So the sick ones are left to die alone and unheeded. Sometimes all the inmates of a house are swept away one after another, no man being willing to go near that house. Half-dead sufferers lie unattended around all the springs and reservoirs.''

"But if you are right," Wona said, horrified, "aren't they then giving the plague to the water others must drink?''

"That is my fear. But I found a clean supply, so that no bad water comes into this house."

"That must be why I didn't get it," Wona said. "I know of no reason the gods would protect me.''

"The gods protected no one," Crockson said. "I understand that bodies are piled up in the temples. I dare not go there to check myself, of course.''

"Why not?" Wona asked ironically.

But he answered her seriously. "You know why not! As if the physical suffering isn't bad enough, those who survive the plague are filled with reckless despair. They have cast away the bonds of law and morality, amidst such uncertainty of every man both for his own life and that of others. Men care not to abstain from wrongdoing, because punishment is not likely to overtake them, and they fear that they will not live long enough to reap any further benefits of life. So they take advantage of that brief interval to snatch what joy they may, however ill-gotten, before the hand of destiny falls upon them. They steal, they kill, they rape—and the women are hardly less loath to participate, so many cannot be raped, being all too eager to experience what they might otherwise never feel. So, for some, it is a weird orgy of despairing pleasure. But I prefer to remain inside, my door barricaded.''

"And you shared your hoarded food and water with us," Wona said.

He laughed, not unkindly. "Jes did not eat much."

"If any deserve to live, she does. She hates me for what

I did to her brothers, and she had a hundred chances to kill me or leave me to die, but she was true to her word.''

''That is another reason why she is so precious to me. I see so few truly honest and decent folk. They are like coins of gold.''

Perhaps the dialogue continued, but Jes faded out again. When she woke, it was another day and this time she felt strong enough to open her eyes.

Wona was there. ''Are you feeling better?''

''Yes. Weak, but better.''

''Can you move your hands? Your feet?''

Jes understood her concern, and shared it. She moved her hands, then her feet, then her head. ''I am whole.''

''May the gods be praised!''

Recovery was not swift, but as Jes ate and drank her strength seeped back. In due course she was able to stand and walk, and to attend to her own functions. She had recovered without permanent loss, thanks to the care and protection she had received.

It was just as well, because Crockson was running out of food. Soon they would have to go out to get more.

When Jes felt able to walk a distance, and to swing her club, they went out as a tight group. The city was desolate. A stench hung over it. Bodies littered the streets.

But there was some activity. Men were hauling the bodies away. Crockson recognized one. ''He is an indifferent sort, never one to do a favor that promised no swift reward,'' he remarked. ''Yet not a criminal either. I wonder what he is up to?''

''Maybe he is being paid to bring in bodies,'' Wona suggested.

''Hail!'' Crockson called to the man. ''How is it that you risk this grisly contact?''

''I am recovered from the plague,'' the man replied. ''When I felt the awful weakness, and knew I was dying, I begged Athene to spare me, and promised I would make a better thing of my future than I had of my past. Athene spared me, so now I am doing public service, knowing I will not get the plague again. Do you wish to help?''

Crockson looked at the others, then answered. ''Yes, as soon as we have found food.''

''Go to the Temple of Athene. They will give you good food if you help them clean up.''

So it was that they found themselves, in the ensuing days, hauling bodies out of the temple. Wagons took them to funeral pyres, where the fires raged continuously. They still had to be watchful for maddened or indifferent ruffians, but a kind of macabre order was returning to the city.

''Where are the vultures?'' Wona asked.

Jes looked around. Wona was right: there should be scavengers throughout the city, but there were none.

''I think I know,'' Crockson said. ''They preyed on contaminated bodies, and died themselves.''

Wona laughed. ''Served them right!''

In a few days Jes's strength had largely returned. She knew it would take time for her to achieve her former health, but she could manage well enough for now.

She reconsidered what she had heard during her illness, and found that it no longer bothered her. What did it matter that Crockson, like many Greek men, preferred to associate with boys rather than women? He was not forcing his way on anyone else. She had encountered such boys elsewhere, on occasion, and understood that they valued their associations with wealthy elder benefactors, and often remained friendly with them long after passing on into manhood and founding their own families. There was no force, only agreement. And Crockson had been extremely good to her despite knowing that there could never be the kind of association he had craved. If he had taken her at first for a boy—well, that was a misunderstanding she had invited by her masquerade. He had never reproved her for deceiving him. Thus he was indeed being generous in the manner of a friend, and she respected that.

Should she say anything to him? It would be easy to avoid

the subject, but not entirely honest. So she broached it, when there was opportunity for a private dialogue. "I was extremely ill, and I know you cared for me, so that I survived instead of dying or becoming maimed."

"I am glad you recovered."

"I heard what you said to Wona. About boys. Now I understand why you offered me a permanent position."

He looked as if expecting a blow. "I wish you had not."

"I would consider it an honor to be your friend."

He stared at her. "You are not revolted?"

"I was disturbed by the notion that I might be more attractive as a boy than as a woman. That you might have seen me as such. But I learned better, as I pondered your generosity to us. We all are as we are, and there is no fault in that. I thank you for increasing my understanding."

"Oh, Jes, you have gladdened me immensely. I very much want to be your friend."

"Then we are friends. There is no need to speak of this again."

"No need," he agreed, visibly relieved.

The next day Jes decided to go back to work at the looms. Wona had been working on them, when the burden of Jes's care ameliorated. For the time being Crockson had no other workers; they had either succumbed to the plague, or were caring for sick relatives. There was a considerable backlog of weaving to be done.

The siege lifted. It was rumored that the Spartans were afraid that the plague would spread to them. It was now possible to leave Athens.

"You must go," Crockson said before she could bring the matter up. "Wona has escaped so far, but the plague is not over; others fall prey to it daily, in no pattern I can ascertain. If she gets it—her constitution is not as robust as yours—"

"Yes," Jes agreed. "We must go to a city that doesn't have the plague. But we can't leave yet. Neither of us has worked in a fortnight, and we owe you silver."

"Consider it a loan. And take this." He proffered the same little bag of coins he had before.

"But we couldn't possibly—"

"When Wona marries a rich man, she can send you with repayment," he said, pressing the bag into her hand.

"But I might not get the money, or might not survive to return it to you. You are likely to lose it despite my best intentions."

"Please. It is a thing I need to do for you. For what might have been, had it been possible."

She considered that, understanding. "With that understanding, I can accept your generosity. I think, considering what you have done for us, I owe you my life, and would have repaid you as you desire, had it been possible."

"I very much appreciate the sentiment."

"Do you have advice about our destination?"

"Calydon, on the Gulf of Corinth. It is a member of the Delian League, and far from Euboea."

He understood her need perfectly. "And Athens is on the route back from there to my home."

"I hope to see you again, before long," he said.

"Would you take it amiss if I kissed you?"

He looked uneasy. "I prefer to remember you as I once thought you were."

Jes nodded. The magic would be absent, because he knew she was not a boy. "Another time, perhaps."

They made preparations for their renewed journey. Wona donned reasonably nonprovocative apparel, and Jes assumed her masculine form, complete with the two bows and their arrows, and a club and dagger that showed. They would be traveling through some hostile territory, and of course any territory could be dangerous for a woman alone.

But the morning of their start, Wona felt bad. She was blinking and rubbing her eyes. "Oh, no," Jes muttered.

Crockson took one experienced look. "The plague," he said, confirming it. "She did not escape it."

"But I can't get the plague," Wona protested. "It will ruin my looks."

"Not if you are well cared for," Crockson said. "And you shall be. We'll put you in the back room."

"But you have already taken much trouble to take care of me," Jes protested. "I should care for her on my own."

"Making those dangerous trips alone? Leaving her alone? That won't be practical or safe."

Jes knew it was so. So they put Wona in the back room, and began the siege of her illness. Now Jes saw how it was from the perspective of the caregiver. Sometimes when Wona felt awful, she did not look that bad, while at other times she looked far worse than she seemed to feel. Much of the time she was unconscious or delirious, and sometimes she unknowingly said things she never would have uttered when in control. Jes found some of them wickedly fascinating. Wona had evidently had a lurid history before marrying Sam, and she liked to make men react. Her sexuality was merely a tool she used to achieve her objectives. Wona had explained that before, but her confidences of delirium suggested how cynical the process was. Jes wished she herself had such ability.

It also occurred to her that if Wona died, the family problem would be solved. Feeling guilt for the thought, she did everything she could to ensure that the woman survived.

The disease wended its course, and though Wona was extremely ill, it became apparent that she was not suffering any permanent damage. She would recover and be as lovely as before.

But after the stages of the illness passed, Wona remained quite weak. It took her a long time to recover strength. "That is the way of it, with some," Crockson said. "They look well, but their resources are slight. It may be months before she is back to normal."

"Months!" Jes exclaimed. "I have been away from home too long already!"

He shrugged. "Do you wish to remain at home all your life?"

That set her back. "Yes and no. Our family stays together. We try to marry outside, and bring our spouses in to the family. So I want to bring a husband in to the family."

"Then you should be looking for a man to bring in."

That was a difficult point. She knew her prospects in that respect were so slight as to be not worth pursuing. "First I have to get Wona placed."

"But while she is recuperating she does not need constant attention. You could go out to search for your own man."

She laughed bitterly. "What point? I am not man-finding material."

"I think you are. You simply haven't looked well enough."

"How should I look?"

"What do you most want to do or be, in your life?"

"A sailor. On a trieres. I love the ships. I love seeing new shores. I love the water. But—"

"But they don't take women. So sail as a man." She had a tacit understanding with Crockson: neither betrayed the secret of the other, so she could change identities at the shop. He would even check to make sure her details were correct.

"I can fool most people when afoot and on my own, but how long could I do it on a ship? The moment I had to urinate—"

"You would do that on land. The ships put in to shore twice a day."

"Or swim—"

"Few sailors swim. The water's too cold."

"Or when asleep, if my clothing should—"

"Not if you garb yourself carefully."

"Or when there is contact with a man, as there sometimes is in close quarters. There are so many ways—"

"And if you are found out, what then? Will they execute you?"

"Rape me, more likely."

"In the presence of the captain or an officer? That seems unlikely."

"The captain would curse me and put me off the ship without my pay."

"And meanwhile, you will have had your adventure. And have met two hundred healthy men, one of whom you might find worthwhile. And there will always be another ship."

She reconsidered. "You make it sound possible."

"Possible, if dangerous," he agreed. "If your ship saw battle, you might be killed or injured, and injury could betray your nature when they stripped you for care. But maybe you would get through without discovery, if you were careful. If you prepared well."

"How could I prepare?"

"Go down to Piraeus and study the ships. Learn their ways. Then you will know how to avoid mistakes, at such time as you board one."

She nodded. "That might be."

So on her next day off from work, with Wona resting comfortably, she assumed her male guise and walked down to the port city. Now that the siege was gone, most of the campers had departed and the road was clear. Traveling alone, she was able to walk swiftly, getting good exercise. She was glad of it, because she had not yet recovered her full strength either, and this should help.

The port city was in constant activity. There were ships coming in and departing every day. Because it was war time, and the ships were on constant patrol, some were damaged and were being repaired. She was even able to go aboard one as it lay in dry dock, awaiting the attention of the overworked repair crew. It was fascinating. She was able to step more than thirty paces along its curving main deck. She saw the covered places for oarsmen, their stools on three levels beside the holes for the great long oars. The highest was actually a special kind of outrigger; the oarsmen on that file were called thranitai. What phenomenal coordination was required to ensure that no oars banged into each other! No one person would be able to see all the oarsmen at once; there were a hundred and seventy of them, allayed along the length of both sides of the ship. How did they coordinate? It was a detail that hadn't occurred to her, before actually looking at this layout.

Then she heard someone coming, and quickly got off the ship. She didn't want to answer any awkward questions.

When she returned, Crockson was grim. "Perikles has got the plague."

"But surely there are others to govern Athens," she said.

"Not the way he does. He is largely responsible for the building of the Parthenon and other temples on the Acropolis. He pledged extra funds from the treasury to the goddess Athene. He has been very good for the city."

"But isn't he as unscrupulous as any other politician?"

Crockson nodded. "Politics is not child's play. Thirteen years ago, when he was facing vociferous criticism for his policies, such as the massive building program, he used a device to eliminate his chief opponent."

"He had him killed?"

"Not physically. Politically. He arranged for an ostracism."

"A what?"

"The people meet in the Agora once a year and take a vote to determine if anyone is becoming too powerful, and is in a position to establish a tyranny. If a majority conclude that the danger exists, they meet again two months later. This time each person brings an *ostrakon*, a potsherd, along, on which he has scratched the name of the person he wishes to get rid of. The man with the most votes gets ostracized, and is exiled for ten years. That time, Perikles's opponent was exiled. He didn't deserve it; it was a political ploy. But he had no choice; he had to go. So Perikles is not a man to fool with. But that is exactly the kind of man we need in power today. Now that he is ill—if he doesn't recover, Athens will be in bad trouble.''

Jes appreciated his point. She hoped Perikles would recover. Unfortunately that hope turned out to be vain; the man remained too weak to get off his bed.

During other visits to the harbor, over the course of the fall and winter, Jes learned a great deal about the ships. They looked massive, but were actually very light. So light that they would not sink when rammed and holed; they would merely bog down in the water, becoming too sluggish to be effective. So nobody drowned when a ship went down, unless he got knocked into the water and couldn't swim. That didn't mean that nobody died; if an enemy force caught a ship, there could be a slaughter. So sea battles were dangerous for the same reason land battles were. Of course each ship carried ten hoplites and four archers whose job was to see that no enemy overran the ship. That might not be enough in a major battle, but probably sufficed for routine missions, such as reconnaissance.

Four archers. Now there was something she could do. She had a good bow, and good aim. Maybe she could sign on as a bowman, after demonstrating her capability.

But then she found a better prospect. Each ship carried one pipeman. That was the one who played the musical beat that enabled the rowers to coordinate by ear. The pipeman sat amidships or toward the front, facing back toward the captain's deck, taking his cue from the captain. The pipeman did not have to be a great musician, she learned, but he had to have a strong sound and a good sense of rhythm. And he had to understand the operation of the ship, so as to give no miscues. The pipeman, almost as much as the captain, was the heart of a well functioning ship.

Jes was no expert piper, but she had played a wooden flute at family festivities and could remember a tune. In any event, she understood that the tunes played for ships were quite crude, performed for the cadence rather than for entertainment. They related to real music about the way a

baby's cry did to adult communication. She suspected that
this was a job she could do.

She went back to the shop and told Crockson. "Now I
believe you are right," he said, pleased. "You have found
a way. And I happen to have a flute, given me by one of
my lovers; I don't believe he would be offended if I lent it
to you."

"Oh, I can buy my own—"

But he was already digging it out, and she couldn't refuse,
though it turned out to be a finely wrought instrument,
surely of considerable value. He clearly liked the idea of her
playing it. So she accepted it, and began to practice.

She was rusty, but soon enough she was getting it straight.
They discovered that the loom workers became more efficient when they heard the music, and Wona was more alert.
So periodically Jes played instead of working on her loom,
and the work went well. She perfected several tunes that she
could play with feeling and without hesitation. When she
strayed beyond these, she became less apt, so she knew her
limits. But the familiar ones seemed to be good enough for
this group.

She continued to visit the shipyard and harbor, now listening as well as looking. She learned that though the tunes
of the pipemen were simple, there were several different
ones, and these were used to guide the oarsmen in different
maneuvers. One tune was for straight ahead; another for
reverse; others for turning, when the oarsmen on one side
had to stroke more powerfully than those on the other side.
She practiced these tunes, closing her eyes and imagining
that she was playing on a ship as it forged through the water
during maneuvers. It was a wonderful feeling.

By the time Wona was well enough to travel it was winter. "It will be cold out there," Crockson said to Wona.
"Your prospects would better in spring, when you can don
light clothing and allow it to fall open."

"You have an eye for the ways of women," Wona replied without rancor.

"They are in some ways like the ways of young men."

Jes would have preferred to get moving, but they did owe Crockson money, though he never pressed them for it, and the winter's work would go far to making it up.

Thus they passed the summer of Wona's slow recuperation, and the fall, and winter, and Crockson's shop did prosper with the management and work Jes accomplished. The surviving women returned, and were augmented by others, and there was a good market for the cloth. Crockson was quite satisfied, and actually Jes found herself satisfied too, because the shop was compatible. It was Wona who wanted to get on with their quest for her man, after their year's delay. However, she was resigned to the situation and, having nothing better to do, did work reasonably well on the loom. Her endurance was not great, but that was also true for some of the other recovering victims of the plague. They rested when they had to, and learned to work efficiently, and accomplished about as much as the healthier but less attentive women. Jes filled in for them during those rest periods, so that there was no actual delay, and the women appreciated that. They liked Jes's style of management, and this contributed to harmony. Crockson, assured that the shop was in order, felt free to go out to make deals, instead of having to watch every worker closely. It was a reasonably comfortable situation.

In the spring it was time for them to move on, before the Spartans besieged the city again; they needed to get well clear of Athens and into neutral territory, or at least some region where they could be anonymous. Wona dressed for travel rather than sex appeal, but remained an appealing figure of a woman. Jes dressed as a young man.

Crockson put on his formal robe to bid them farewell. He smiled, but he looked sad. "I wish you the best health and success," he said.

Wona stepped into him. "Thank you for your kindness

to us,'' she said, and kissed him on the cheek.

Then Jes approached him. "Thank you for your generosity," she said—and kissed him on the mouth.

Then they departed, leaving him stunned. They had rehearsed the little ritual, and realized that it was the best way to handle it. The man would have a memory of being kissed by what looked very much like a stripling youth. Jes realized that if she impersonated a male, she could afford to impersonate him in this manner also, considering the considerable assistance Crockson had been to them. They were departing Athens in reasonable order; it might well have been otherwise, had they worked for someone else.

They left by the Sacred Way, passing without challenge out through the main gate to the west. They followed the road to the coast, where it fringed the Bay of Eleusis. They spent the night in the city of Eleusis, renting a room for the night. They had traveled barely half a normal day's hike, but were being careful, because Wona was not yet up to full strength. It was better to take easy hikes, building up gradually, so as not to risk a relapse of the illness.

When Jes opened the bag of silver coins, in order to extract one to pay the proprietor, she made a discovery that astonished her. She quickly masked her reaction, but Wona caught it. "What's in that bag?" the woman demanded as soon as they were alone.

Jes shook her head, bemused. "Gold." She opened that bag and poured out its contents on the floor.

There were a number of silver coins, and three small gold coins. The three were worth as much as three bags of silver would have been.

"That man really likes you," Wona breathed, awed.

"I had no idea," Jes said, half in chagrin. "I would never have accepted it, if—"

"That's why he gave you no hint."

"But he can't like me that well, because—"

"I am more cynical than you in this respect," Wona said. "I have seen men, and I think I understand them somewhat.

Most desire women; some desire men; some desire boys. I think those last bestride separate steeds, unable to accept one or the other completely. So they seek partners of their own gender, that most resemble the opposite gender. When those beardless boys become too much like men, they lose their appeal and must move on. So the passion the elder men feel for them is of limited duration, but perhaps more powerful for that. They love without seeming limit, for those few years, and then love the next one similarly. You are just across the line, being like a stripling male, but female. You thus represent the ultimate in desirability: forbidden love. You are clearly worthy, in form and nature. He wants so much to love you, and tries to persuade himself he can love you, but he cannot. In guilt for this, he treats you even more generously than he would a true male youth. And your tolerance for this he appreciates more than he can say in words. So he says it in gold. This is the way of men who are truly smitten.''

Jes was amazed, but recognized the likely validity of Wona's conjecture. It made sense. ''But still—so much—''

''You can do him no kinder favor than accepting it. By that token you indicate that you accept him—or would, were you able.''

''I do accept him! As he is, though it is not the way I am.''

''This is the way he wants it.'' Wona pondered a moment. ''There may be one advantage to this. You will never grow a beard. You will never become a man. You will always be like a stripling boy. His dream boy. So his love for you need never fade. It will endure well beyond the time when it would have faded, were you a real male.''

''I do not want to take any advantage of him!''

''Nor do you need to. Merely visit him on occasion, and be his friend.''

Jes nodded, relieved by this solution. ''That I can do.''

They ate some of their food, and retired for the night. But it took Jes some time to sleep. Before this excursion it had never occurred to her that she could ever have a friendship of this nature, but now it seemed appropriate. Crockson was a good man, merely different in one key respect. Her awareness of that type of relationship would remain with her for the rest of her life.

Actually, she had never thought to have as close a relationship with a woman like Wona, either. She now realized that the contempt in which she had held Wona had been based largely on ignorance. The woman did have her points; she was merely unsuited to the type of life the family offered. So Jes had learned much about tolerance, and that was worthwhile.

The next day they crossed the mountains into Boeotia, which was hostile territory. But this was between sieges, so the troops were not out; the two of them should be taken for neutral travelers. They expected to cross it in two days, at their present pace, barring problems.

The road they were on turned out to be ill-chosen; it followed a river into the mountains and faded out. It took them some time to find a trail going their way on the other side.

Then they encountered a group of people walking north. They were carrying food, belongings, and wooden planks. What was going on?

So when they spied a solitary man, they inquired. "The Spartans are coming!" he exclaimed.

"Already? But surely they will be attacking Athens."

"They are turning north, not south! We just got word. We are fleeing to Plataea for protection."

Jes exchanged a glance with Wona. They had been planning to stop in Plataea for food. The city was in Boeotia, but was an ally of Athens; it had bad relations with the chief city of the region, Thebes.

They got off by themselves and discussed it. "If we go there, we may get caught in another siege," Jes said.

"Normally I much prefer a room in the city to a stall in

the country,'' Wona said. ''But the last time I got caught in a city, I got the plague. We had better stay well away from Plataea.''

Jes agreed. ''But where will we be safe from the invaders?''

''Maybe we can go to the water and get a ride on a ship.''

''Sparta isn't helpless at sea, in this region. Corinth is her ally, and Corinth has the second strongest fleet in Greece. And Corinth is right there on the Gulf of Corinth.''

''But there are Athenian allies along the gulf too, aren't there? We can try for one of their ships.''

Jes wasn't sure how feasible this would be, but it seemed to be their best chance. So they traveled northwest, cross-country, avoiding further contact with other people. They wanted to disappear, so as not to fall prey to the ravaging forces of Sparta.

They had no trouble avoiding the Spartans; their main force had not yet arrived. It had nevertheless been a close call; the women had assumed that they would be well ahead of any such expedition.

They camped for the night in a deserted hay shed, keeping an ear alert for any approach. The discipline they had practiced during their approach to Athens the year before came readily back to mind.

So did other facets. ''I need to practice with the club again,'' Wona said. ''And you should practice being a woman.''

''I have been a woman for a year, weaving,'' Jes protested.

''That was drudgery, not femininity,'' Wona retorted. ''There was no point in trying to impress Crockson.''

She had a point. Femininity was a talent worth cultivating, just in case Jes ever had occasion to make use of it. Crockson was a good man, but no amount of feminine wiles would impress him. Some other man, however—

So next day, as they resumed their careful trek to the sea, they practiced. Jes made Wona a light club, and Wona cri-

tiqued Jes's walk and breathing. Jes was in masculine garb,
but as long as no one saw, she could still practice swinging
her hips. It helped allay what was a generally dull day, for
they did not encounter any Spartans.

The Gulf of Corinth was considered to be a long, narrow
inlet into the heart of Greece. But from its shore, it seemed
an enormous expanse of water.

There were ships on it, too. But not Athenian. "Corinthian," Jes said. "Enemy vessels."

"Does it make a difference? They have rich men too."

"Maybe it doesn't make a difference to you, but it would
to them. They would know you for Athenian, and despise
you."

They proceeded along the north shore of the gulf, avoiding roads, because at any time Spartans might appear on
them. They foraged in deserted fields, and slept in deserted
houses. Until they got beyond the danger region, and area
life became normal. But it was normal Boeotian life, and
Boeotia was allied with Sparta, so they still couldn't risk
discovery.

They passed through Locris, another Spartan ally. They
avoided the city of Delphi, though they would have liked to
go to see the oracle there; they probably lacked the price of
such advice, and it was generally incomprehensible anyway,
but the experience might have been interesting. Then they
crossed into the territory of Phocis, an Athenian ally, and
were finally able to walk openly. Here the ships were Athenian, and not to be feared.

Indeed, when they saw a ship coming to shore for a meal
stop, they stood at the beach and waved to it encouragingly.
It came in close, its oars in perfect synchronicity, then
swung about and faced away from the land. The oarsmen
reversed their stroke and propelled the craft backward to the
beach, until it slid partly out of the water and came to a
stop. The hoplites and archers jumped off, followed by the
oarsmen. Half of them headed for the bushes.

Wona started to walk toward them. "Wait a moment,"

Jes cautioned her. "They have full bladders."

Wona paused, then walked toward the ship, where the captain was the last to disembark. Jes saw that she was using her siren walk. She had quietly rearranged herself to accentuate attractive traits.

"Never mind," the captain called, laughing. "I promised my wife to stay clear of incidental booty. But if you want to deal with any of the men—"

Wona glanced meaningfully back at the bushes. "Too dirty for me. Do you give rides on your ship?"

"Not while on duty. You would distract the oarsmen anyway, and start a fight among the hoplites."

Jes nodded agreement. "My sister is looking for a husband," she said. "We thought this might be a good region."

"Naupactus is," he said. "We're based there, this season, and there aren't enough beautiful women to go around."

"Thank you," Wona said, flashing him a brilliant smile.

"But one word of caution: there has been some plague there, brought by the ships from Athens."

"We have had it," Jes said. "Now we are immune."

"Good for you. You have nothing to fear except the Spartans."

"Not as long as we have bold men like you protecting us," Wona said with another smile.

He laughed again. "Get away from here, siren, before my wife regrets it." He patted her on the bottom and moved out to join his crew.

"It is good to get in some practice," Wona murmured. "That is exactly the type of man I would like to capture, but it's too public."

"Well, he's married."

"That, too. He would bed me, but not marry me; he gave me fair warning."

"I didn't hear him say that."

"Didn't you see him pat me? He's interested."

"Oh. I suppose I don't know all the signals."

"I am teaching them to you one by one, just as you are

teaching me the use of the knife and club. It is still a fair exchange, I think.''

It probably was. Jes wasn't sure she would ever become proficient at such social interaction, but she would learn what she could.

"As we depart, watch the eyes of the men we pass. A lift of both eyebrows means they notice; a lift of one is asking me. I should be able to bring any one to me.''

"Any one—and not the others?'' Jes asked. "I don't see how—''

"I will demonstrate. I will bring the third one we pass. Then you must cut in, so I don't have to follow through.''

Jes wasn't sure she liked this, but did not object, as she was curious to see how much substance there was to the woman's claim.

The men were strung out as they returned from the bushes. Each raised both brows, and then one. The first two passed on by, but the third one stopped. He was an oarsman, with solidly muscled arms. "Hello, lady,'' he said to Wona.

"My sister is not to dally,'' Jes said quickly.

The man eyed Jes somewhat contemptuously. "So you say.''

Wona made a moue. "My little brother guards me carefully, lest our father beat him. I would not want that to happen. We must be on our way.''

"As you prefer.'' The man moved on.

"Point made,'' Jes said when they were clear. She was impressed.

"There are surely similar signals when two men consider combat over a nonessential matter.''

"Yes. It is pointless to fight unless you really want to, and sometimes one man can demonstrate ability that cautions the other. It never occurred to me that men and women could fence similarly.''

Wona tensed, and spoke without turning her head. "Oops. I did not signal this one. You will have to back him off.''

Indeed, a hoplite was forging toward them. He had muscle, weapons, and swagger. "Haven't we met before?" he demanded of Wona.

"No," she said sharply.

"Well, then, we must remedy that forthwith."

"My sister is not to dally," Jes said.

The soldier ignored her. He reached for Wona's arm. She neatly drew it back, clearly trying to discourage him.

Jes tapped her club. "I said—"

Now the man glanced at her. He tapped his own club. "Depart, stripling, before I give you reason."

He was too burly and experienced to handle with a club. So Jes went to the next stage: a demonstration.

Her hand went for her dagger so swiftly that it was a blur. The point came up and the tip almost touched the man's nose. Now she had his full attention. After the briefest pause, she flipped the knife into the air, and caught it again by the hilt, before his nose.

"Maybe some other time," the man said, and moved on.

"I never saw you do that before," Wona said, impressed by herself.

"I never had to, before. I probably couldn't take him in a fair fight, and he knew it, but I could have cut off his nose then, with the element of surprise, so he knew it was merely a warning. He returned a warrior's courtesy by leaving the field to me. But if I had cut him, even slightly, or if any of his companions had seen, we would have had to fight."

"I'm not sure he would have taken you," Wona said. "I have seen you kill."

"There is a difference between battlefield conditions and a formal encounter. I would have had to meet him formally, or a bowman would have shot me. Soldiers don't like ambushes."

"What bowman?"

"That one." Jes indicated a man standing by a tree. As she did so, and Wona looked, the man waved.

"Then someone did see the encounter!"

"Not a companion. Bowmen and hoplites belong to separate clans, socially. Anyway, the bowman was behind the hoplite, so wasn't visible to him."

"But you saw him. Why didn't he call to the hoplite?"

"Professional courtesy. I carry a bow."

"Which you do know how to use." Wona took a deep breath. "Let's get out of here."

"Gladly." But just as Wona had liked demonstrating her abilities, Jes had rather liked demonstrating hers. There was indeed a camaraderie of arms, and it did facilitate things when armed strangers met. She appreciated the way the bowman had given her the chance to settle her quarrel on her own. He had accepted her, in a way that counted, though they were strangers.

They made their way without further significant event to Naupactus, which turned out to be a small but vigorous city. It had been settled by Messenians, implacable enemies of Sparta who had been exiled from their homeland by Sparta.

They sought an apartment close to the harbor, because Wona wanted the best chance to meet any and all officers. They were able to get one close to an inn that served the personnel of the ships. There seemed to be a high turnover in both workers and clients, because this was a war zone, and Wona was able to get a job as a serving wench: exactly what she wanted.

"But won't they pinch your rear and make lewd remarks?" Jes asked.

"And give me silver if they like me enough," Wona said. "It's a fine way to meet people, and the gossip will be first rate. In a few days I'll know exactly who among the captains is married and who single, and will be able to chart my course."

"But what do I do while you're doing that?"

Wona considered. "We're not destitute, thanks to Crockson's generosity to you, but we can always use money. This is your opportunity as much as mine: get a position on a ship. I don't have to have you constantly at my side, now that I have a good residence and position. If things work well for me, you will soon be free to go home.''

"I would like nothing better than to be aboard a trieres,'' Jes agreed. "Even if only for a few days. If you don't think I'm running away—''

"Jes,'' Wona said seriously. "You have so much honor it's spreading to me. I am a better person than I have been, because of you. I have no concern about your running away. Just don't get yourself killed!''

Jes was so flattered that she was in danger of blushing. "I'll try not to.''

So Jes went down to the harbor each day to inquire whether any ship was in need of a piper.

"I need an oarsman,'' one officer told her. "But I doubt you have the heft for that.''

"True. I have rowed all my life, but only in small craft. I'm not muscular.''

"That will come with time,'' he said. "You're not yet grown.''

This was typical. Each ship needed 170 oarsmen and only one piper, so her chances were small. But there were twenty ships here, so one might be able to use her.

On the third day Wona's gossip mill bore fruit. "There's a ship with a bachelor captain—and it's in need of a piper!'' she exclaimed. "You can hire aboard, and introduce me to the captain.''

"But that isn't the way it's done,'' Jes protested. "Captains don't socialize with the men.''

"Then make it a business deal: you'll be his piper if he dates me. Play your pipe for him; he'll want you.''

"And if you play your body for him, he'll want you,'' Jes echoed. "Maybe it will work.''

"This is our best chance yet; it has to work.'' Then Wona frowned. "Though it does seem almost too easy. Do you think it could be a setup?''

"I don't understand.''

"We met that captain before, and now we have been talking with many people. Word of us will have gotten around, just as we pick up word of others. Maybe someone wants to bed me, so he says he's single. Men do that all the time. A captain of a trieres is a wealthy citizen, by definition, so has had ample opportunity to marry. By the time I verify his status, he will have had what he wants from me.''

'But the pipeman position—what about that?''

"That's probably legitimate. The word is that the plague took out several crewmen, and there may be a battle soon, so he can't wait for them to recover. But he knows he can hire you; it's me he can't have for hire. So that's what he charges.''

"Charges?''

"A job for you—if I let him into my skirt. I'm paying for you.''

She could be right, Jes realized. ''I can look for some other ship.''

"No, take the job. Maybe then you can find out whether he is really single. Then introduce him to me—as we thought before.''

On reconsideration, this did seem best. ''Very well.''

Jes located the ship and approached the trierarch, or sea captain, a weathered, burly man. ''I hear you are in need of a pipeman.''

The captain squinted appraisingly at her. ''One drachma a day, half payable as earned, remainder in Piraeus. Bonus when we see action, if warranted, and a share of whatever plunder. Paid to your father if you die on duty.'' This was his acknowledgment of Jes's youth.

And nothing said about getting into anyone's skirt. This seemed legitimate. ''It will do. Do you want to hear me play?''

"I have a practice run this afternoon, to try out new oars-men. You will play then.''

"I will be there.''

The captain nodded. ''I am Ittai, of Athens.''

"I am Jes, of Euboea.''

Ittai walked away. Their business was concluded, for

now. Jes was impressed; the man wasn't much to look at, but he spoke to the point. He surely ran a no-nonsense ship. That was the best kind.

She returned to the apartment, then went to the dining hall where Wona worked. "I play this afternoon, tryout," she said as Wona came to bring her bread and wine. "Trierarch Ittai is gruff but competent. He said nothing about skirts. I think he doesn't know I have a sister."

"He surely *does* know. I like him already. But make sure you get the word on his marital state."

Jes brought the flute Crockson had given her to the ship. Captain Ittai spotted her immediately. "Jes! Report to the helmsman." He turned away, attending to other business. He had the facility, useful in a leader, for recognizing a person in a group, and remembering the name. Jes was further impressed.

The helmsman was easy to spot by his bright robe of command. All the oarsmen had to see the helmsman, who ranked next below the captain, and the boatswain, who implemented his orders. Jes would take her signals from either man, but probably the boatswain unless the helmsman stepped in directly. How well she responded, and how well she played, would determine her future with this crew.

She brought out the flute and held it before her as she approached the busy officer. He was directing new oarsmen to their seats, but oriented on her immediately. "You are of course familiar with the essential tunes?"

"Yes. But I need to know the signals for them."

His eyes narrowed slightly, but he demonstrated the signals for each one, and she fixed them in her mind. She had not anticipated this awkwardness; of course an experienced pipeman would know the signals. "The boatswain will indicate the cadence, so," he continued briskly, making a circular gesture in the air with one forefinger. "Pick it up and keep it until he changes it. This means accelerate it." He elevated one palm slowly. "And diminish it." His hand turned over and moved slowly down. "During distance travel at constant velocity, the melody can be your own, but vary it occasionally so the grunts don't get bored. Take your place.''

He assumed that she knew where her place was, as any experienced pipeman would. Fortunately she did. She walked the gangplank to the gangway along the center of the ship, and made her way to the main mast. There was a built-in stool just behind it. She sat on this and rested.

Her heart was pounding. She was actually on a trieres, as a crewman! She knew what to do, but the reality of actually doing it was fantastic. She gazed at the backs of the oarsmen, sitting at three levels. Those on the lowest tier of oars were farthest into the center of the ship, and those on the highest tier were almost against the hull. They were fitting in so close together that they almost touched, but each had free play for his oar.

The ten hoplites boarded together. Each was well armed with knives and spears, and all looked tough. They were, of course, the most privileged class aboard, aside from the officers. They spread out along the length of the gangway, glowering at the oarsmen and sailors. They were there to protect the ship—and not just from external enemies. Any oarsman who got rebellious would find himself skewered.

The commander of this guard took a central position, which meant he stood close to Jes. He looked down at her and grimaced. It was clear that he did not like her. That made her nervous, because he was a large, powerful, and possibly dull man.

When all the oarsmen were seated, the seamen hoisted the two sails and took the ship out to deep water. Sails were normally used when there was no hurry, and evidently the captain did not want to risk a foul-up in the harbor. So he was taking the ship out to where he had some privacy, to work out the kinks. Once the new crew members were functioning properly, he would take it under power back into the harbor.

Sure enough, when they were well clear of the harbor,

the helmsman strode to the center of the ship, right near Jes. He raised his hand so that both the bow officer and the boatswain could see it. Then he brought it down. The boatswain made a loop with his hand. Jes started playing the Prepare melody on her flute, as loudly as she could without distorting the notes. It was not the strong beat of traveling, just a preliminary. The oarsmen could not see the boatswain well, but they could all hear the music. They unhooked their oars and lowered them to the water.

Then, in time to the beat of the boatswain's fist, Jes went into the Forward rowing beat. "Go!" the boatswain yelled, and the oarsmen pulled together. Now it was her flute that governed them; she suspected that many had their eyes closed, depending on it alone.

The ship moved forward, which meant in the direction of the backs of the oarsmen, and Jes's back too. It was not their business to see where they were going, but to propel the ship as efficiently as possible.

The helmsman let them row for a while, as he walked up and down the central gangway, looking at individual oars. "Pick it up!" he snapped at one whose oar was lagging a trifle. "Shorten your stroke!" at another.

The boatswain lifted his palm, slowly. Jes accelerated the cadence, slowly. She continued her slow increase until the boatswain put his hand out again, level. Then she leveled it at that pace.

The boatswain lifted his hand, not in a signal, but in a warning of a coming signal. He made sure he had Jes's eye. Then, suddenly, he rammed his fist down.

She played extra loud, slowing the beat precipitously. The oarsmen followed.

The commander of the hoplites turned to sneer at her. What was the matter?

The helmsman was right beside her. "Wrong," he said, calmly. "That was a 'Dead Halt' signal he gave you. Try it again."

Oops. She had indeed misunderstood.

They got the ship moving rapidly forward again, while the helmsman cautioned individual oarsmen on their errors. Then the boatswain gave her the warning, and the dead halt. This time she blew a single loud note and stopped.

The oars froze in place, rapidly braking the ship.

The cadence resumed, slower than before. Then there was another maneuver. "Starboard," the boatswain shouted. "Double cadence!" And he signaled Jes with a short, sharp jerk of the hand.

This time she wasn't sure what to do. She hesitated, while still playing. Again the hoplite commander grimaced, as if in the presence of an utter fool. "Mark and keep the beat," the helmsman murmured.

She played one beat loud and high, and kept the existing beat. At that, the oarsmen to her left, the ship's right, suddenly increased their pace, while those on the other side maintained theirs. The ship swerved. They were making a turn.

She saw the helmsman signal the boatswain. "Port—half cadence reverse!" Now he was describing the orders, instead of depending on Jes to play the right tune. The helmsman was standing right by her, murmuring instructions. That was not the best sign. They had all too quickly caught on to her inexperience.

The boatswain gave Jes the Mark gesture. This time she was on it immediately, playing her pipe loud and low, following with the correct tune. The oarsmen to her right abruptly lifted and reversed their oars, stroking backward.

The ship, propelled at double speed forward on its right, and half speed backward on its left, fairly whirled around, turning almost in place.

The boatswain brought his fist sharply down. Jes played a loud note and stopped. The oars stopped in place, dragging against the water, and the ship halted its turn.

The helmsman nodded with satisfaction. The maneuvers were falling into place. He walked away, to her immense relief, because that meant he did not expect to have to instruct her further. She had more than enough black marks already.

They practiced for the rest of the afternoon. Jes made other mistakes, and each time she did was rewarded with a glare from the hoplite commander, but made sure never to repeat one. She was gaining confidence. She could handle this job.

At last they stroked back to port. The men were given leave to disembark, but the helmsman spoke briefly to Jes. "Wait." So she waited, hoping she was not in trouble. She had made several mistakes, but surely they allowed for that, on the first day out. She hoped. She watched the men file past the ship's purser, who gave each a small coin: the day's half-pay.

After a time the captain came down. "I am told you lack experience, but play well." Actually he had heard her himself, but was going through channels, taking the helmsman's report.

"I missed several signals, sir," she confessed, embarrassed. Was he going to fire her?

"You have an excellent sense of the ship. Have you had other experience?"

"None on a trieres. I have rowed my own little boat all my life. I like the sea."

"That explains it," Ittai said. "Your position is confirmed. Go to the purser."

Relief flooded through her. She had not realized how worried she had been, until that acceptance came. "Thank you, sir."

"I feared I would have to settle for incompetence," he said gruffly. "In that I was disappointed." He walked away.

She got up and went to where the purser sat. He glanced up at her. "Name and post?" Of course he already knew her post, but was also following the forms. That was the way of a well run ship.

"Jes. Pipeman."

He handed her three silver coins.

She looked at them, startled. "This is too much! I was told half a drachma."

He checked his list. "That is the correct amount. One drachma. None is held back pending completion of the tour, because you have joined it halfway along. Plus two obols, for maintenance of your equipment. You are not actually being paid more." Then he smiled, briefly, becoming human. "But you evidently have the trierarch's favor, if not the hoplite's. You piped well."

"But I made mistakes!"

"Perhaps he expects you to live up to his expectation."

"I—I will try." She was amazed by this development. The fact that they were paying her full wage now meant that they had no hold on her; she could leave at any time without penalty. So though the pay was standard, this was indeed a sign of the captain's favor.

Back at the apartment, she told Wona about it. The woman nodded. "I told you that your playing would impress him. You are good, Jes—very good. You must have made the crew row unusually well."

"It did seem good. But the oarsmen are experienced. I assumed—"

"Did you find out his marital status?"

"No. I hardly talked to him."

"Well, I did. He is single. His wife died in the plague. I think this tour with the ship is a relief for him, because he doesn't have to face his empty home. I want an introduction."

"I will try," Jes said.

The next day was more practice. This was mostly, Jes suspected, to build the oarsmen up so they could row all day, and sustain speed in battle conditions. Today, too, the full crew was aboard, including the ten hoplites and four archers. The hoplites were ranged along the gangway, sitting on anchored stools, staying very still, because any movement could disturb the equilibrium of the craft and interfere with the efficiency of the oars. They were there to defend

the ship from enemy boarding, and to fight on land when
the ship was beached, but Jes suspected that they had a
secondary purpose: to maintain discipline among the oarsmen. If any oarsman seemed inclined to protest anything, a
sharp glance by a hoplite served to quell the notion. The
four archers were grouped at the stern around the trierarch
and helmsman, and would be bodyguards for them during
combat. The seamen were completely idle while the ship
was being rowed, but when the lunch break came, they
sprang to their positions at bow and stern, hauling on the
lines that anchored the foresail and mainsail. It was clear
that a good wind could take the ship any distance, but for
battle that was not feasible, because the ship needed to move
rapidly in any direction.

"Ho!" an oarsman cried during the afternoon session.

The nearest hoplite scowled in his direction. "What?"

"There's a leak on my foot."

The hoplite caught the eye of the helmsman. "Leak," he
called, pointing.

The helmsman signaled the boatswain, who signaled Jes:
glide to a halt. She slowed her beat until the boatswain gave
her the complete Halt signal. The oars lifted from the water,
and the ship drifted.

Now the shipwright appeared from belowdecks and made
his way to the indicated spot. Sure enough, a jet of water
was coming in. The commander of the hoplites grimaced
steadily in Jes's direction, as if blaming her for this mishap.
Why did he hate her so? But the shipwright quickly pegged
and tarred the leak, and bailed out a few buckets of bilge-
water. The ship was reasonably tight again.

At the end of the day, Jes dallied after the men had been
paid, nerving herself for what she had to do. Captain Ittai
spied her. "You have a problem, piper?"

"No, sir." She took a breath. "May I speak candidly,
sir." It was a request, not a question.

"You may."

"My attractive sister would like to meet you."

He laughed. "Now why would you have to speak for her?"

"She asked me to. She is seeking—"

"Clear enough. But at the moment I am not looking for female company."

"I will tell her, sir." Jes turned away, embarrassed.

"Hold, piper." She turned back. "Are you comfortable with this?"

"I would rather never to have brought it up," she said, striving not to blush. "I apologize."

"So I thought. But you had to do what you were told to do. It occurs to me that I was perhaps hasty. My wife is never going to return, and my nights are lonely. Take me to your sister."

Jes tried to control her surprise. "As you wish, sir."

"About the hoplite commander," he said. "His name is Kettle, the son of Pot, a repatriated slave. He is not the brightest of men, but he makes up for it by the ferocity of his combat and his loyalty to those he respects. The prior pipeman, taken by the plague, was his friend. He resents any replacement."

Oh. That explained that aspect. "I will try to do well enough to please him, in time."

"Only your abject failure would please him. But he is a good man, and dedicated to the welfare of the ship. He knows there must be a pipeman. You need have no fear of him."

"What about away from the ship?" she asked nervously.

He shook his head. "Then stay away from him. He will not come after you, but it would not be wise to provoke him."

They walked to the hall where Wona served. "She works here," Jes explained. "I can tell her—"

"No. I am hungry anyway. We shall eat."

"Sir?"

"You and me and your sister."

"Yes, sir," Jes agreed faintly. She was not at all comfortable with this developing situation. For one thing, she really liked her position as piper, and didn't want to risk forfeiting it because of some social complication. The trierarch was clearly accustomed to being obeyed by those he encountered, and Wona did not necessarily respond well to such imperatives. Sparks could fly—and Jes could be caught in the middle.

They took a table. Wona soon came over. She gave no sign that she knew Jes. "Your best wine and bread, for three," Captain Ittai said, proffering a silver coin.

Wona flashed a smile at him. "Immediately."

"You will join us."

"Oh, I am not allowed to—"

"This is Captain Ittai," Jes said quickly.

Wona, startled, nodded. She must have mistaken him for a lesser officer, not expecting so high a personage to walk right into her hands. She would get permission from the proprietor, who surely did not have many trierarchs as patrons.

"She is attractive," Ittai agreed, watching the swing of Wona's hips as she departed.

Jes felt awkward. "There is no need for me to remain—"

"Stay. I have not been with a woman in some time. I am not adept at trifling dialogue. When it lags, you provide it."

Worse yet. "Yes, sir." Her tension did not ease.

Wona returned with an excellent meal. "I thank you, captain," she said, flashing him a smile as she took the third seat. "I have wanted to meet you."

"So your brother informed me."

Things progressed rapidly, as Wona utilized her considerable array of charms. Jes did not need to attempt to fill in dialogue; Wona kept it going without seeming difficulty. When the good meal was done, the captain invited Wona to spend the evening at his residence, and she accepted. They departed together, leaving Jes to finish off what remained of the bread, which she was glad to do. It was good to eat really well, for once.

So it had been a success, after all. Wona had finally found a suitable man, and she would make sure he did not escape. But Jes's feelings were mixed. Because while she was glad to see the near end of her long mission, she was not easy about inflicting a woman like Wona on the captain, who seemed to be a decent man. Yet maybe it would be all right, because Ittai had the wealth to afford a woman like that, and would not expect her to do manual labor. If she had children by him, there would be servants to care for them. Wona was a bad deal only for a poor man. In any event, the trierarch was surely capable of making up his own mind.

She consumed the last crumb, pleasantly full for the first time in several days, and went back to the apartment. She still had most of Crockson's largess remaining in her hidden purse-bag, but she was hoarding that for a time of real need. She was existing for the moment mostly on scraps Wona brought back from the inn.

She lay on her pallet and slept. Her sleep was undisturbed; Wona did not return to the apartment in the night.

The next day the activity on the ship was normal. They continued to practice maneuvers, becoming ever faster and sharper. The helmsman nodded with satisfaction as the ship became a finely functioning unit.

At the end of the day, the trierarch approached Jes. "It was a good introduction." He turned away.

Later, back at the apartment, Wona echoed the sentiment. "I believe he is the one. He is wealthy, mannered, undemanding, and in a few months his term of service will end and he will retire to a rich estate. What more could a woman want?"

"Love?" Jes asked.

Wona laughed. "Maybe eventually. A man has to earn my love."

"How does he do that?"

"By treating me the way I like, for several years. It is not smart to sell love cheaply."

Jes didn't argue, but she winced internally. She would

have liked to have love on any terms, and wealth hardly mattered. Captain Ittai was a good man, and Wona was using him. It didn't seem fair. But it was not her place to object. She had, after all, introduced them.

She thought of Sam, who had been similarly used. Did Ittai have a sister? A little brother? Would they suffer?

She put such thoughts from her mind and focused on the training at the ship. She liked being its pipeman, and she liked being part of a smoothly functioning crew. The men treated her courteously despite considering her a stripling, because she was doing the job well. They accepted her, and that was worth a great deal. When they participated in coordinated maneuvers with the other ships of the fleet, their ship often was assigned the lead position, and she knew that was because it was among the fastest and surest. And that was because the oarsmen were responding well to her piping.

She didn't even mind spending many nights alone. She had lost her earlier dislike of Wona, after the woman cared for her well during the plague, and they had taught each other some worthwhile things, but the memories of Sam and Ned remained. She could survive quite well without the woman's company.

"He is a real catch," Wona remarked on one of the nights she was home.

"He is a good man," Jes said.

"That, too." Wona glanced at her. "He likes your piping."

Jes nodded. At least it seemed that her job was not in peril. But she remained uneasy about the relationship of the two. Wona could bring such grief to a good man.

"Something's up," Wona said another evening. "There is going to be a battle. The gossip is rife."

Jes discovered that the fear she had expected to feel at such news was lacking. "We have a good ship, a good crew, and a good fleet. We are ready for battle."

"They have fifty ships."

Jes stared at her. "Fifty?" There were only twenty ships in Phormio's fleet.

"From Corinth, stroking this way. Most are troopships. They are going to Acarnania."

Troopships. That was better. They would be heavily laden, and sluggish in the water. No match for the Athenian vessels in speed or maneuverability. But if contact was made between the ships, those troops would overrun the scant troops on the Athenian side. This was dangerous.

The next day Captain Ittai assembled the crew and confirmed the news. "The Corinthians are attempting to sneak past our blockade of the gulf," he announced. "They have forty-two troopships and five fast ships. We have to stop them. We shall do so."

"Yes!" the members of the crew agreed. But their enthusiasm was tempered by realism. They were overmatched, and this was likely to be a grueling campaign, with substantial losses.

They set out eastward, toward the mouth of the gulf. The masts of the enemy fleet were visible by the southern shore. The enemy was proceeding in plain sight by daylight, seemingly contemptuous of the lesser Athenian fleet. They knew that if Phormio tried to engage them near the south shore, the maneuverability of his fleet would be limited, and any ships that were disabled would be subject to attack by Spartan forces on that shore. Only in the open sea, far from land, could the Athenians make their superiority in fast ships count. The Corinthians were not giving them that chance.

All day they paced the slow enemy fleet, staying north, but not engaging. In the afternoon the Corinthians passed the narrowest section, alert for attack, but Phormio did not attack. Was he letting them get away?

By nightfall the Corinthians landed at their harbor at Patrai, where it was not possible to attack them. The Athenian fleet landed on the north shore and bivouacked. This would have been a problem for Jes, because she could not urinate in the bushes in the way of a man. But it was dusk, and she was able to lose herself in the shadows for the necessary time.

Supplies arrived from Naupactus: food, bedding, even a hardy corps of prostitutes. Jes was relieved to see that Wona was not among them. This was too much like a final fling before execution.

They ate well, and sang some rousing songs. But Jes knew that it would take more than such encouragement to prevail on the morrow, when they would have to fight—or suffer the shame of letting the Corinthians have their way.

Jes had learned, from the attitude of the crewmen and the gossip Wona culled, that Phormio was considered to be the smartest admiral Athens had. The ships of Athens were generally conceded to be the fastest and best-managed in Greece. But there were limits. Twenty against forty-seven? Expertise could not make up for lack of power. The Corinthian admiral was surely no fool. If he maintained a tight formation, how could anyone stop it from going where it wished? The main Athenian technique was ramming; when a ship jammed into another ship from the side, the ram would puncture and disable it. But if one Athenian rammed one Corinthian ship, the men of a second Corinthian ship would grapple, board, and destroy the Athenian ship before it could pull free of the wreckage. So even with a perfect score, they could take out only twenty enemy ships—while losing all of their own.

It was time to sleep. Jes headed with her blanket for a suitable spot, then spied Kettle, the hoplite commander, there, and quickly changed course. But he saw her, and sneered before turning disdainfully away.

It was one gesture too many. Jes was tired and her temper was worn. So she did something foolish. She changed course again, and went to lay her blanket down near the man.

He stared darkly at her. She stared back. "Have you something to say, Hoplite Kettle?" she inquired.

He reached for his spear. But before his hand could grasp

it, she had her knife out and cocked, ready to throw.

His jaw dropped. "You threaten me, stripling?"

"I merely suggest that I intend to sleep in peace, sir." He was not in her chain of command, but he was an officer, so she gave him that token courtesy of recognition.

Kettle lifted the spear. He was sitting on the ground, but could throw it hard and accurately from that position.

She refused, again, to be intimidated, though she was distinctly nervous. She had to make her stand now, or forever be wary of him. "If you will hold up your shield, sir, I will show you my aim."

He made a sound of contempt, and lifted his shield part way.

She hurled the knife into its center, hard.

Kettle looked. It was clear that she could as readily have put the knife into his face. She had given fair warning that she was not to be held in contempt. He laughed and jerked it out, flipping it back to her hilt-first. "Sleep in peace, pipeman." He lay down and closed his eyes, not at all concerned.

It was a small and dangerous victory, but perhaps she had won a modicum of respect. At least he had addressed her by her title.

The trierarch was going among the men of his crew as they settled for the night, talking briefly with each before moving on. He came to Jes. "Bed down now," he said. "We may be roused early, and must be ready."

"Yes sir," she agreed uncomfortably.

"You have doubts?"

"I fear for our success."

He squatted beside her. "Jes, do you question my competence?"

"Oh, no sir! I didn't mean—"

"At ease; the question is rhetorical. Of course I am competent in my position, as you are in yours. I will perform well tomorrow, and so will you. Admiral Phormio is not merely competent; he is a genius as a strategist. If it is possible to destroy the enemy fleet, he will enable us to do it.''

"But is it possible, sir?''

"Not only possible but probable. We are bound to take some losses, but theirs will be far heavier. Have faith in that.''

"I will try, sir.''

He leaned close. "Jes, I know the admiral's strategy. It is brilliant and feasible. All we need is discipline and performance in our crews. I have faith in both the strategy and the crews. I ask you to accept my word: we have victory within our means. Do you accept that?''

Somehow she had to believe. "Yes, sir. Thank you, sir.''

"Welcome.'' He tousled her short hair and stood. He glanced at Kettle. "Good to see you guarding my piper, commander. I will stand in great need of both of you, tomorrow.''

The hoplite nodded noncommittally.

And now Jes did believe. The situation made no more sense than before, but Captain Ittai had made her confident that their fleet had the advantage. Somehow his confidence and his touch of camaraderie had transferred his faith to her. He had transformed her fear into assurance.

She knew that he was doing the same for every other crewman. Intellectually she remained in doubt about the outcome of the coming engagement, but she no longer feared it, and she was now quite sure of the leadership of their ship. Captain Ittai was quite a man.

One thing still bothered her, though. Her brother Sam was quite a man too—and Wona had made a fool of him. How great was Jes's guilt for bringing Wona to the trierarch?

So even if the Athenian fleet was completely victorious, with no losses, what mischief lay ahead?

A hand tapped her shoulder. "Pipeman.'' It was Kettle, but this time he didn't sound angry. He could have dropped a clod of dirt on her face, by "accident,'' but hadn't; he had his own honor. If he ever attacked her, it would be with the same fair warning she had given him. "Up, pipeman. Clear your bladder and go immediately to your post."

It was still dark. She did as directed. All around her she heard others doing the same.

The helmsman checked the roster. The ship slid into the water. Other ships were moving similarly. "Faint pipe," the helmsman said. Jes played just loud enough to be heard in the hush. She knew her music was vital, because the oarsmen could not see the boatswain in the darkness. Neither could she, but the helmsman was directing his orders to her. As dawn came, the full fleet was rowing almost silently out to sea.

And there, in the middle of the channel, was the Corinthian fleet. It had been trying to sneak past without notice. Admiral Phormio had anticipated that ploy, and acted to catch the enemy ships away from the shore, in open water. That was where he wanted them, Jes knew.

But that fleet was still more than twice the size of this one, and packed with fighting men. What strategy could prevail against it?

Yet as the two fleets closed on each other, it was the enemy who blinked. The Corinthians formed their ships into a large circle, their bows pointing outward. The smaller supporting vessels and merchantmen, which weren't counted as part of the fighting fleet, were sheltered within that circle. But also there, oddly, were the five fast ships—the only ones that might match the Athenian craft in speed.

Then she remembered her history: a formation like that had been used successfully against the overconfident and surprised Persians at Salamis. The fast ships would rush to support the outer circle wherever it was attacked, so that it would not be breached. They would have only a short distance to go, and would be almost instantly in play. So this made maximum use of them. It was a good formation. If the Athenians tried to envelop the circle, in the standard tactic of periplous, the vulnerable beams of their ships would be exposed to a sudden outward rush by the Corinthian rams. That could virtually destroy the Athenian fleet in one move.

So what could be done? The enemy position seemed impregnable to attack by even a much larger fleet. What was the source of Captain Ittai's confidence in victory? Jes played her pipe, automatically following the directives of the boatswain, while her mind struggled with the mystery. Were they simply going to try to hold the Corinthians in place indefinitely, so they could not get where they were going? That didn't seem feasible; the enemy should be able to wait as long as the Athenians could.

The Athenian fleet formed into a single line, and circled the enemy formation at a distance. The Athenian ships were too far out for a sudden thrust to be effective; by the time an enemy ship got there, the Athenian ships would have changed position, and the Corinthian formation would be broken.

The enemy admiral was too smart to fall for that. He kept his ships in place, not only pointing outward, but making constant adjustments so as to orient on the closest Athenian ships. The Athenians would have to approach to have effect, and then they would be vulnerable to the outward rush. This was like circling an angry bear: its swift paws would strike when anyone came within range.

The Athenians did not approach. Instead they circled continually around the Corinthian formation. It seemed to be an impasse.

Then Jes realized that the circling wasn't static. With each pass, the Athenian fleet was slightly closer. The approach was so gradual that there was no point at which the Corinthians could act to resist an attack, but an attack seemed constantly imminent. So the enemy oarsmen had to keep stroking and backing, staying clear of their neighbors without allowing a gap to open in their defensive ring, aiming outward.

As the Athenian ring tightened, individual ships would

change course slightly, as if about to turn inward for a
thrust. The enemy ships oriented on them, ready to counter.
But no thrust was made. The Corinthians were clearly becoming uncomfortable. This was becoming a war of nerves.

The helmsman walked along the gangway, speaking to
the oarsmen in a low tone. When he came close to Jes, she
overheard his message: "Maintain present cadence. Do not
respond to the piping. Wait for my signal. Ignore the piping." Then he turned to Jes. "Play the full repertoire,
loudly, until I signal Stop."

She abruptly went into the Turn melody, loudly. They
were now close enough to the enemy formation so that the
nearest ships could hear the music. They knew its meaning.
They thought the attack was starting. One ship started to
move forward, before countermanding. Then it had to reverse and recover its position. But others were out of position, and there was almost a jostling of oars before they
got it straight. There was a low chuckle among the Athenian
oarsmen. They liked the joke.

Jes realized that the Corinthian oarsmen lacked the skill
to maintain such a difficult formation for long. They were
being cruelly teased. But still, even a ragged formation was
more than the Athenians could safely penetrate. So all this
was doing was making the enemy angry. Something more
was needed.

The helmsman signaled Jes to silence, and walked the
gangway again. "Resume honoring the pipe," he told the
oarsmen. "The joke is over." He made sure they understood
before moving on. Then he signaled Jes to play the normal
Forward tune. They continued in their line, circling the enemy formation.

The wind freshened, as it normally did at dawn. And suddenly Phormio's strategy became clear. The Athenian vessels had no problem, being under oar and with room to
maneuver. But the Corinthian ships were in a compact formation, pointing in every direction; they could not turn to
ride with the wind. They were getting blown out of for-

mation, or sideways into each other. The deckhands had to use poles to push them apart. As the wind continued to gain strength, this got worse. They tried to take evasive action to avoid their neighbor ships, but there was nowhere to go. Seamen and oarsmen were shouting at each other, and soon cursing each other. They were no longer listening to the words of command, or to the boatswains. The oarsmen, not well trained, could not recover their stroke in the increasingly choppy water. The helms became unresponsive.

Now, at the worst possible moment for the enemy, Admiral Phormio gave the signal to attack. Jes saw him waving his flag on the flagship, and saw Captain Ittai acknowledge. Then Ittai turned and spoke to the helmsman. Now was the time.

The boatswain gave Jes the Turn signal. She went into the melody, and the ship swung sharply around. Almost simultaneously, all the other ships of the fleet did the same. Like ferocious birds of prey, they swooped in.

The enemy ships were helpless. Their flagship was caught broadside, unable to turn in time, and Jes heard the crash as it was rammed. Her own ship did not catch one in ramming position, but did manage to sheer off a row of oars. The Corinthians were in utter confusion, not even trying to fight.

There was a brief period of intermeshing. The oarsmen kept rowing vigorously, while the hoplites stood and hurled their spears at the enemy craft. Some even threw from a seated position, surprising her with their power and accuracy. Then the Athenian ships passed each other in the center and moved on out to clear water. They turned, ready for additional ramming runs. But the Corinthians were already reorganizing, in their fashion: to flee back to Patrai. Not one ship tried to fight.

It became a rout and pursuit. Ittai's ship overhauled a troopship, and made a wide sweep so as to come at it from the side and ram it. But by the time the position was right, they were close to shore. The enemy troops jumped into the water, deserting their ship as they swam for land. So did the oarsmen and hoplites. In a moment the Corinthian ship was deserted. So there was no point in holing it. They drew up alongside, carefully, and transferred a limited crew to take it away. It had just become an Athenian ship.

Most of the enemy ships escaped, but when the action was done, one had been sunk—it wasn't as light as the fast ships—another disabled, and twelve captured. It was a stunning victory, with no Athenian losses.

They made their leisurely way home, towing some of the ships that they hadn't manned. The men were still under orders, but they were smiling and joking, and the officers made no objection.

During a break, Captain Ittai ambled by Jes's station. "Now you know," he said with satisfaction.

"Indeed I do, sir," she agreed.

Kettle, nearby, nodded. He had not scowled at her all day.

There followed a bout of repairing and refurbishing, as they got the captured ships into shape. They would not be used for some time, because they lacked captains and crews, but they bode well for the future of the Athenian navy in these waters. The crews were given leave time for a few days; they had earned their rest.

Then Captain Ittai approached Jes when she reported for duty, as she had to to be sure of her pay. "We are not going out today," he said. "But come aboard anyway. I have been meaning to tell you something, and to ask you something."

She joined him on the otherwise deserted ship, uncertain what this was about. He gave her the helmsman's vacant seat in the stern, and took his own. From this deck they had a good view of the surrounding harbor.

Ittai looked around, seeming vaguely uneasy. "May I speak candidly?"

"Sir?" Because of course a captain had no need to ask permission of any crewman for anything.

"I have in mind a matter that does not relate to business. It is personal and private."

Oh. "Of course, sir. I will not repeat it elsewhere."

"Thank you." He hesitated, then plunged in. "I will not be marrying Wona."

Oops. "If I offended you by introducing—"

"No offense. She is a beautiful woman, and most obliging in the female way. She made me realize that I am after all ready to consider marrying again. But she is also vain, faithless, lazy, and inconsiderate of those of whom she believes she has no need. I believe I would regret marrying such a woman, who is not at all in the class of my former wife."

He had Wona precisely targeted! Jes could not in conscience argue the woman's case. "I am sorry, sir."

"Don't be. There are many men who would be quite satisfied with such a woman. Perhaps I was spoiled by my wife, who was no beauty, but a creature of sterling personal qualities."

This remained awkward. "Surely so, sir."

"So I wanted to make clear to you my decision in that respect, before asking you my question. Wona and I have no future, regardless."

She looked at him questioningly. What else was on his mind? This hesitancy was unlike him.

"As I mentioned before, I am not adept at social relations," he said after a pause. "I command men, but I do not know how to speak to a woman in a truly courteous manner. I am a man of the sea."

She waited. She felt much the same when dealing on a social level with men, but she couldn't say that.

"So I ask you to understand that no affront to you is intended, and to hear me out before you answer."

"Of course, sir."

He set himself, and spoke again. "I know you are a woman."

Oh, no! He was going to fire her. He would have to,

because women were not allowed on warships. So he was apologetic because he didn't like having to do it.

She held her chin up, determined not to cry. "If I may ask—how did I give myself away?"

He smiled. "You didn't. You play your part so well that I could not be sure, though I fancy myself an astute judge of crewmen. I marveled that a stripling should pipe so well, with such feeling for the sea and oars. Usually it takes a man some time and experience to develop that spirit—yet you lacked experience. Your explanation of rowing alone sufficed, but the matter did not quite leave my mind. It was a minor mystery. Then when you introduced me to Wona—"

"She told you?" Jes asked, appalled.

"No. She did not betray you. She does have loyalty to you, a person she respects beyond others. But I made a connection. There had been a story of a beautiful woman traveling in the company of a stripling brother who nevertheless could handle weapons; it was said that he killed several Persian raiders last year, and did not brag of it. That was why that story remained in my memory, another minor curiosity. As a manager of men, I have an awareness of details that don't quite mesh; sometimes there is a larger pattern. I concluded that you must be that stripling."

"I did not realize how news travels," Jes said ruefully. "I take no pride in killing, but I had no choice."

"So I gathered. One of my suppliers is a trader named Crockson. He—"

"Crockson!"

"I do not know him personally, but I know of him. He fancies stripling males, and treats them well. He is currently without one. There was a story that one with a beautiful sister came to work for him, but that he did not take that particular stripling as a lover. Not, I think, because of refusal, for he gave that stripling money and a flute, and the lad played well."

Jes brought out her flute. "Yes, it is his flute. He helped

me practice, and had me study the ships, so that I could do—as I did.''

"That third memory finally enabled me to see the larger pattern. But though I could fathom a reason why you were not his lover, I still wasn't sure. So I verified it.''

She looked at him questioningly.

"One of my bowmen has exceptional night vision. I asked him to spy on you in the night, during the bivouac. He reported that you found it necessary to squat to urinate. He was instructed to tell no one but me, and he obeys instructions. I was then satisfied with my diagnosis.''

He had certainly been careful and competent in his investigation! "I—I will go without fuss, sir, so as not to embarrass you. I—''

"No. You are an excellent pipeman, and I want to keep you. You did not panic under stress in the battle. It is my prerogative to hire whom I please, regardless of gender. But it would be better if the remaining crew did not know. The oarsmen, in particular, have their superstitions, and the hoplites might seek to take advantage, the moment you left the protection of the ship.''

"Yes, sir." She thought of Kettle, the commander of the hoplites, who would surely be furious to learn he had been backed off by a woman. She had been on the way to earning his grudging respect; this would destroy it.

"So keep your secret, and so will I, for the duration of your service on my ship.''

"Oh, thank you sir! I love it on your ship. I—''

"Do not be grateful yet. There is worse. I don't know how to make this sound appropriate, so I won't try. I want to marry you.''

Stunned, she stared at him. "What?''

"By the time I had ascertained your gender, I had learned a good deal about you. You are a fine person. You possess all the qualities Wona lacks. You have courage, integrity, constancy, discretion, and ability. And I think you could learn love. You are the kind of woman I want. A woman who could replace my wife without seeming inferior.''

''But I'm not beautiful!'' she blurted.

''You are not buxom, agreed. Your face is not pretty. But you are slender and graceful. In any event, you are quite attractive to me in personality, and I think in body too, were you appropriately garbed and coifed. Much lies in the way a woman presents herself.''

That was true, as Wona had taught her. She could act like a woman, if she tried. But she was still so amazed by his offer that she could not truly believe it. ''I—I can't—''

''I realize I am old,'' he said. ''And stout. I can't blame you for not finding me desirable as a man. But I can offer you an excellent life in other respects. A life that will continue well after I am gone. That should be some compensation.''

''Oh, it isn't that, sir. I respect you as a man. I just never thought—''

''In any event, there is no need to make an immediate decision. All I ask is that you consider the matter for a fair period, and give me your answer, of whatever nature, before this tour is done.''

''I think I am dreaming this,'' she said. ''But even in a dream, I have to say that I came here with Wona to find a husband for her, not for me, and I am honor bound not to desert her until she finds a suitable man.''

''I will obtain another officer for her. One who will satisfy her, and be satisfied by her. You can assure yourself on that score before saying anything further to me.''

''And I—I never even thought of marriage. Not to a man of your stature. I—I like being a crewman. I don't think I could be a gracious woman, confined to a house. I would always want to put on mannish garb and go out for more adventure.''

''If that is the price of you, I will gladly pay it. I would ask only that I be allowed to accompany you on your adventuring, so as to be assured of your safety.'' Then he frowned, reconsidering. "Unless you are saying that your taste is not, after all, in men."

"Oh, no, sir! I want to be with a man when—I mean, I try to look like a stripling male, but that's to enable me to go about my business safely. I am a woman. I long to be—to be a woman with a good man. To be desired as a woman."

"I am very glad to hear it. Then I trust we are agreed: You will continue your position here, in male guise. But you will also think about the role I offer you as a female."

"I will certainly think about it. But—may I speak candidly, sir?"

He laughed. "There is another level? Speak; I will not be angry."

"You—in your position—you can command women, any women you desire. You can—can command me. As a woman. I am young and inexperienced in this respect, but I—I would do whatever you asked, just to keep my position on your ship. And I would not—not find it unpleasant, though I would lack the ability Wona has. You surely know this. You could use me and discard me, without commitment. Why do you speak of—of marriage?"

"That is easy to answer. Because I don't want easy passion, or experience. I can get that from women like Wona. I want a true relationship. I want love. That cannot be compelled, and I would not compel it if it were possible. You are young, but you understand honor. I know you would not speak love to me unless you meant it. If—if it is your desire to marry me without the commitment of love, I will accept that, hoping love will come in due course. But I would much prefer to have your love, and give you mine. I realize that this makes me a foolish man, but it was the way it was with my wife. So you must come to your own conclusion, and if you realize that you can never love me, I will let you go without rancor. But I sincerely hope that is not the case."

Jes found herself flattered as well as surprised by his of-

fer. But marriage? It was so far beyond any notion she had
ever entertained that she simply could not assimilate it. "I
will think about it, sir," she finally said.

"Thank you." He stood, in that manner dismissing her.
"In the interim I will see about placing Wona."

"Thank you, sir." She turned to go, and felt him pat her
bottom. She remembered what Wona had said about that:
proof that a man was interested. That little token impressed
her almost as much as his words did. It wasn't a purely
intellectual thing.

She made her way numbly to the apartment. What was
she to do? What Ittai asked seemed inconceivable, yet she
knew he was serious. She had to decide, and give him an
answer. But what would be her answer? She was not close
to a conclusion.

Wona showed up when her shift was done. Jes wasn't
sure what to say to her, so said nothing. That turned out to
be easy, because Wona was full of news of her own. "I met
this new man," she said. "He says word got around about
Trierarch Ittai's new woman, so he wanted to see for himself. He's a citizen too, and younger and handsomer than
Ittai. I'm free tonight, so I'll give him a try." She perfected
her appearance and breezed out.

Jes had not had to say anything. That seemed best. Evidently Ittai had been as good as his word, and spoken to
another officer. Wona was not even aware that she had been
passed off. She thought she was just being her normal faithless self, choosing among options.

The training sessions resumed. It was clear that the war
was not over, and the power of Sparta and Corinth had been
set back, not broken. There would be other encounters. In
fact, the enemy had not given up its designs on Acarnania
and was determined to dislodge Phormio and open the
blockade. More Peloponnesian ships were being mustered.

Phormio, alarmed, sent to Athens for more ships. Word
was received that a fleet of twenty fast triereis was on its

way. But then they were diverted south to Crete, and were indefinitely delayed there.

"The idiots!" Wona exclaimed as she relayed this gossip. "Don't they know we have a war on here?" Apparently she was coming to identify with the war effort, now that she was dating a younger and more communicative officer.

Jes was concerned too. The news was that a fleet of at least seventy-five ships was coming, and these were not an expeditionary force loaded with gear and troops, but were cleared for action. They were intent on destroying the Athenian fleet. And they had a new and talented commander named Brasidas. Not only was this fleet larger and deadlier, its commander would not be making the foolish mistake of allowing the wind to mess up his formation. This time the odds seemed truly overwhelming.

"Oh, by the way," Wona said as she made ready to go out. "I believe this young citizen I am presently seeing will do. You may go home now."

Amazed by the suddenness of it, Jes could only protest. "But you aren't married yet."

"I will be, in due course. He has asked me to join him in his quarters, and I know when a man is serious. Only idiocy will deny me this rich union, and I am not stupid in this respect. I will never let him go. So I thank you for your patience, and you are no longer my brother."

"But what of Trierarch Ittai?"

"I told him I had found another. I think he was not sufficiently taken with me, after the first couple of nights. Maybe it's guilt about his dead wife; he doesn't believe he should be allowed that much pleasure. No fault of yours, Jes; it was a good introduction you made. But I have a much better prospect now."

Amazing. Wona had no idea what was on Ittai's mind. "Then—then I wish you well," Jes said. "But I will remain to finish out my service, because I like being a member of the crew of a trieres."

"Obviously so. I'm glad this service you did for me is not a complete waste for you. Fare well."

"Fare well," Jes echoed as the woman breezed out.

At the door, Wona paused. "But take his offer, Jes." Then she was gone, leaving Jes stunned. That had been happening to her, recently.

Captain Ittai was summoned for a strategic conference by the admiral. He took along one crewman as an aide. Jes. She walked behind him and kept silent, taking and holding his peplos when they entered the assembly chamber. He said nothing to her about anything personal. She knew he was giving her a chance to overhear important business, and she appreciated that.

She also wondered how Wona had caught on to the relation between Ittai and Jes. Then she realized that the trierarch might have confided to the other officer that he had another woman in mind for himself, so the other would not be concerned about the chance of Ittai wanting to take Wona back. And Wona could have wormed that fact out of the man. Since Ittai was seeing no other woman, Wona could have added up the ciphers and come to a correct conclusion. Probably Jes had given unconscious hints when she spoke Ittai's name, too.

For the idea of the trierarch was growing in her mind. She had never experienced wealth, but it certainly did not seem like an evil. She did appreciate his company. And his offer was most flattering.

But now there was more important business. She put away her idle thoughts and paid attention.

Admiral Phormio minced no words. "Admiral Brasidas is encouraging his men by claiming that their lack of skill is compensated for by greater daring and numbers. He also reminds them that whereas in the previous action their fleet was not prepared for battle, in the coming action they will be seeking it. He is correct." He paused. "They have seventy-seven ships. We have twenty. We are at a severe disadvantage. I shall not stage the contest in the gulf if I can help it, nor will I move into it. I see plainly enough that a confined space is a disadvantage to a few ships, even if they are used with skill and are faster, against many ships inexpertly used. The fact is that one cannot properly move against a ship to ram it, if one cannot get the enemy in one's sights from some way off, and if one cannot retire if need be in a difficult situation. There are no opportunities for carrying out a breakthrough or a sharp turn, which are the maneuvers of a faster-moving fleet; but in a confined space it would be necessary to turn the sea-fight into a land-fight, and in those circumstances the larger fleet wins.''

That certainly covered it, Jes thought. But what did he propose instead of those bad alternatives?

"Now I want you to have your men stay near the beached ships in good order,'' Phormio continued after a pause. "Make sure they act on the words of command with alacrity, particularly since there will be little room between the fleets for embarkation and attack. They must be able to get off the beach and into a defensive formation quickly. In the battle they must regard disciplined movement and silence as the most important things. These are necessities in most warlike operations, and not least in fighting at sea. And they must repel the onslaughts of the enemy in a manner worthy of their former actions.''

Jes was disappointed. She had hoped to learn of some brilliant strategy, and all she was hearing was elementary instruction.

Then the admiral talked with individual captains. "Ah, you brought your pipeman,'' Phormio said, nodding at Jes. "Your ship is, I believe, the most readily maneuverable in the present fleet, thanks to your piping and the responsiveness of your oarsmen.''

"Perhaps, sir,'' Ittai agreed, pleased.

"If we should have to retreat, you will cover the rear.''

"Yes, sir.''

Jes was appalled. That meant that they would be the last ship, in front of the first ships of the superior enemy fleet. It was a likely death sentence.

"It is a position of honor," Ittai told her, as the admiral moved on to another captain. "One ship may save several others, by interfering with the pursuit. But it must be able to maneuver very cleverly, if it is not to be destroyed."

It was an honor that could destroy them. Jes brooded on that as they made their way from the meeting. Finally she could stand it no more. She broached a subject she had never, before this month, dreamed she would.

"Sir, I fear we are going to die. Do you wish me to—to be with you tonight?"

"Under duress? No."

"I—I am volunteering. I would be pleased to—to do it. If you wish it."

"Do you love me?"

"No, sir. I am only intrigued. But there may be no other—"

"Jes, there is nothing I would like better than to be with you tonight, or any other night. But it is your love I desire more than your body. I will not have you when you are hostage to the fear of death. Sleep in peace."

"But I am considering—it is not that I dislike you, sir—I think I would like to be with you. I just don't feel worthy of marriage to you. So maybe it is better to—"

"A compromise," he said gently. "Be with me, but without any touching. We will talk and sleep separately."

"Yes, sir." Her feelings were mixed. She had really hoped to have sex with him, but couldn't say that. He assumed that she was offering to oblige him solely from a sense of obligation, so he was being decent.

His quarters were far more comfortable than the room she rented with Wona, a clear signal of his wealth and status. There was an older woman there. "Serve my pipeman and me a good meal," he told her. She nodded and set about her business.

Jes realized that he had been serious about the nature of this night. He had a maidservant, and he wasn't sending her away. That was reassuring, but also frustrating.

They ate well, served by the maid, and talked of incidentals. "I miss Athens," Ittai said. "But as it was, not as it is now, ridden by the plague. I believe I shall retire to some outlying province, where the crowding is less. Perhaps I shall purchase a boat that can be rowed by two or three, and explore the by-paths of the shore."

"That sounds beautiful, sir." She spoke the truth, but remained in doubt, because she didn't know whether she could agree to share such a future with him. What he offered was ideal in every respect, yet somehow she could not accept it.

Ittai did not look directly at her. "Do you suppose a woman of the provinces would appreciate a life like that?" he inquired. "I am thinking of marrying one, but I am not of the provinces, and don't know what such a person would wish for."

He was being careful to protect her identity, lest the maid overhear. She appreciated that, too. "I think she would," she agreed cautiously. "I am of the province of Euboea, and though the women there mostly stay at home and work, there are some who do like the sea."

"But would such a woman care to do it with an old city man?"

"I don't know." And there it was, again. What was holding her back? Why couldn't she take what was offered, which was so much better than any future prospect she might have?

He shrugged. "Perhaps because she would think that the offer was not sincere. Or that he would tire of her, and make her a kitchen servant while he took a mistress, as some men do."

"Oh, no sir!" she said. "I—I don't think she would think that. I don't—don't know what she would think."

"She's a mercenary fool," the serving maid muttered. "And so are you."

Ittai smiled. "You must forgive my maid. She has been in the family for decades, and has forgotten her place."

"No I haven't," the maid said. "I just don't want to see you ruin your later life with that wanton wench from the provinces. Why can't you settle on a decent woman?"

She was thinking he meant Wona! Jes began to like this servant, who obviously had been treated well. There were men who beat servants for speaking out of turn, and it was clear that Ittai did not. This servant had a motherly or sisterly protective interest in his welfare.

"I shall have to seek a decent woman," Ittai agreed. "One my maid approves of. It would not be safe in the household, otherwise."

"Hmpf." The servant moved away, theoretically annoyed at being mocked.

They finished the meal. "The piper will stay the night, and go to the ship with me in the morning," Ittai told the maid. "He will use the spare room."

That room turned out to have an internal toilet and a fabulously soft bed with a voluminous quilt. Jes had never before experienced such affluence. And this was just his temporary lodging while he was on duty away from home. Such a life could be hers—if she could simply accept it. So why couldn't she?

And the answer came to her: because she was not a creature of affluence. She had toyed with the notion, but now that she saw the reality, she knew it was beyond her. She liked the lean country style of living. Having servants, getting soft—it just wasn't her way. Such a life would drive her crazy.

And so at last she knew her decision. She would have to decline. That would be painful, but rational.

Yet she could not quite settle on that, either. So she went out of the room and sought the trierarch. "I—"

He saw immediately that she had something serious on her mind. "Shall we take a walk while the maid finishes here?" he inquired.

"Yes, sir."

They left the house and walked along the beach until they were alone. "You have decided," he said.

"Yes, sir. I—I think I could not endure the life you lead. I—I wish you were poor!"

"That is a novel rejection."

"I am trying to be rational, so as not to hurt—not to make a decision I would later regret. But I do feel I owe you, sir. I—I would like to—to spend this night with you, and go my way tomorrow."

"So as to give me some payment for my courtesy."

"Yes. And to taste what might have been."

He walked in silence for a time. Then he spoke in a very low and controlled tone. "I dislike gambling, but sometimes it becomes necessary. I am declining your offer."

"Sir?"

"I suspect that your mind is not yet firmly decided. I am refusing your small offer, for the sake of the large one I want from you. Were I sure of your resolve, I would accept this night, for my desire for you grows stronger by the hour. But I do not care to win one ship, if it costs me the battle. I want you to take more time to be sure of your decision."

"But we may die!" she cried.

"And if we live, we may live fulfilled. What is a night, compared to a lifetime?"

"But I know your life-style is not for me. Please, sir—"

"Think for a moment, Jes. If you bear a baby—do you want to be out on a mountain? Or would you prefer to be in comfort inside, with your needs attended to?"

"I—" She paused, realizing what she was saying. "I think I do not want to bear a baby. I would not be a fit mother. Children need constant attention."

"And they can have it. In a poor home, the mother is bound. But in a wealthy one, there are servants to relieve the mother. You could have a child and still be free to row across the sea, returning at the end of day. I offer you not restriction but increased freedom."

He had a point. "I—I will consider further, sir."

"Thank you, Jes."

They returned to the house, and slept apart. Jes discovered that she was relieved, not because she had not given her body to him—he surely knew what to do in that respect, so she would not have been unduly awkward—but because the prospect of marrying him had not been ended. He was correct: she was as yet of two minds about the matter, and could not be sure she would decline again. But it did seem likely.

In the morning she woke early, as she normally did, and used the facilities to wash herself. Then she discovered something she had missed before: a feminine dress. One of Wona's, probably, purchased for her by the trierarch, now forgotten.

She stared at it for some time. Then she lifted it from its peg and pulled it on. It fit her somewhat loosely, but a few adjustments fixed that. She stood before the metal mirror, admiring herself as that rare creature, a woman. She turned about, watching the skirt flare outward.

Then a strange urge overtook her, and she did something she feared she would regret. She walked out of the room, wearing the dress.

The maidservant was already working at the hearth. She turned as she heard Jes, then her eyes widened. "Keep my secret," Jes told her, and marched on into Ittai's room.

She stood in the center, waiting until his eyes opened. Then she began to dance. She did know how to do it, having shared in family activities from childhood on. She whirled, making the skirt flare out and up, showing her legs right up to her bare crotch. She moved her knees and hips in the way Wona had taught her, making her body flex. She made graceful leaps, landing softly. She stepped forward and back, as if she had a partner.

And then she did have one. The trierarch joined her, matching her steps. Then he held her and turned her. Then he kissed her.

"Will you marry me?" he asked.

"No. I am still thinking."

He stepped away from her.

"But I offer myself to you, this day."

"I want that. But I want more."

"How can I decide, if I know only part of you?"

At that he chuckled. "You are teasing me, you lovely creature."

"No! I really am trying to decide. But it's not fair to make me decide without knowing—what it would be like."

He nodded. "Perhaps it is my groin speaking, but you have a point. So I will gamble again, bedding you without commitment. Come to me, if you really wish it."

She hauled off the dress, flung herself into his embrace. They turned around, kissing, and then they were on the bed, and she was under him, wrapping her legs around him, and he was suddenly pushing into her with a sharp pain. She bit her lip, realizing that it was like this, the first time.

He pumped, and pumped again, and grunted as he swelled inside her, and erupted, and relaxed, panting. His weight was heavy on her, but she could handle it. She hugged him close, and stroked his head with one hand, loving being a woman despite the stinging in her groin. In any event, that discomfort was fading.

"You didn't tell me you were a virgin," he said, admonishing her.

"I said I lacked experience," she reminded him.

"All women say that. I apologize; had I realized, I would have been far more gentle. There was no art in this, only my burgeoning desire for you, that I could not hold back. Another time, I promise, it will be different."

"No, it was better to do it without art, the first time. I am glad to have this slight pain, of you."

He kissed her face, wherever his lips would reach. "Oh, Jes, I know I can love you, if you let me. You are— everything."

"Don't speak in the passion of the moment," she said. "Such decisions are not wise at such times." She was actually speaking for herself, because she knew that if he asked her again to marry him, she would agree, regardless of the wisdom of it. He, not she, had had the sexual climax, but it was her passion that was burgeoning. She reined in her emotion, as she would during a battle. She still needed time to consider.

He got off her. "Then I will make one statement I know is rational," he said. "That was the best bedding I have had since I lost my wife." He turned away, evidently embarrassed to have made the comparison.

"Thank you." She could not trust herself to say more. She knew she could not rely on anything she felt at this moment. She got up, recovered her dress from the floor, pulled it on, and returned to her own room to clean up. Again.

"I'm glad you are a woman," the maid muttered as she passed.

The woman had feared the trierarch would take a boy to his bed? "So am I," Jes agreed.

The bleeding wasn't too bad, but she feared it could spot her uniform and betray her on the ship, so she stuffed in some cloth and hoped for the best. Then she donned her uniform, made sure she looked masculine, and went out to have breakfast.

"My maid approves of you," Ittai said as they ate.

"How does she know I am worthy of approval?"

"I don't know, but her judgment is infallible. After she critiqued Wona, I realized she was correct."

So that was how he had targeted Wona so accurately. A woman could see through a woman in ways a man could not.

After that, they went without further comment to the ship. Ittai addressed his crew in the manner Admiral Phormio had recommended, and the routine cautions seemed to have good effect, because they all knew that a severe test of their skills was coming up. They had shown that they could row rings around an enemy fleet, and they hoped to do so again.

But there was one significant difference, this time. In the

prior battle, the Spartan fleet had had to travel to a particular destination, and the Athenians had been able to make an ambush of their choosing. This time they had to defend their base of Naupactus. Should the enemy advance on that city, their own fleet would have to stand and fight, regardless of the odds against it. They were pinned down. It seemed very bad to Jes. If only those other twenty Athenian ships had arrived in time! With forty good ships against seventy-seven, they might have made a good fight of it. But as it was, the enemy could bring almost four ships to bear on each Athenian ship—and this time the Spartans were fast, cleared for action, and competently commanded. They would not be giving away any easy advantages.

However, it was not Jes's place to brood about strategy. She just had to focus on her piping, and do the best she could. And hope that disaster was not close upon them. So she fixed instead on her feeling for Captain Ittai, but it had not yet settled into any measurable format. Her body longed to be in his embrace again, but her mind derided this as the folly of a girl without experience. A man in combat who was swept off his feet would soon be dead; similarly a woman who lost her bearings in passion would make a bad decision. Wona's cynicism was surely well justified. Jes still needed time to get perspective. So she returned to consideration of the tactical situation of the ships.

The Spartan fleet was there, practicing maneuvers. The ships were so numerous that from a distance they seemed to form a dense cluster. Several came out to look at the Athenians, and they were indeed fast. The description did not apply to their actual speed in the water, but rather to their type; sometimes a speedy "slow" ship was faster than a poky "fast" ship. But these were fast in both senses of the word, and perhaps almost a match for the Athenian ships.

The enemy did not offer combat. It was merely showing off, teasing the defenders. The Athenians could not afford to attack; they would go right into disaster. So all they could do was watch and wait. There was no point in remaining out in the water; they needed to conserve their strength until the Spartan fleet made a move. So Admiral Phormio ordered his ships to land, where they beached. Now his cautioning about staying close to the ships counted; at any time there could be action, and any delay at all could be disastrous.

For several days the Spartan fleet practiced its maneuvers. Even from the distance of the full width of the gulf, they were impressive, and more so when the Athenian fleet moved up for a closer look. There was nothing clumsy here. But the Athenian crews were becoming restive; they did not like holding off from action so long.

Jes did not return to the trierarch's house, though she longed to. Slowly her disciplined mind was gaining ground, reminding her of the difference in their stations, and of the enormous change in her situation an association with him would mean. As if in the distance, the sensible decision was taking shape.

During one of the frequent pauses, Jes happened to be near Captain Ittai; perhaps it was by his design. "The admiral is determined not to be drawn into the narrow confines of the gulf for battle," he murmured, not facing her. "But I fear he will have no choice."

"My fear, too," she agreed.

"At times I wish I had accepted your offer. Then, if I die, I would at least have had that much."

"Sir?"

"Or did I forget something?"

He was teasing her. She liked it. "Perhaps it was only a dream."

He nodded. "A phenomenal dream. So there is no help for it but to win this battle and survive. Then perhaps we can try reality."

"Yes, sir." Once more, it was all she could utter.

He moved on, but her sensible decision was now out of sight over the horizon. His little ways charmed her. She tried to remember Wona's cynicism, but that, too, was far gone.

Prospects for close combat she could assess; the sense or nonsense of love defeated her.

The next day at dawn the Peloponnesian fleet moved out. It formed into four columns and turned east, into the gulf. The fastest ships were on the right wing.

"Damn!" the helmsman swore.

So the enemy was going for Naupactus. This was serious mischief.

The Athenians hurriedly embarked and moved east along the north coast, while the supporting force of Messenians made a similar move along the land. The Athenians formed into a single line, stretching out their formation so that the enemy could not make a sudden lunge and cut them off, beginning an envelopment. Ittai's ship was in the middle; it would not seek the rear until it had to.

The Spartan fleet abruptly turned from its "line ahead" formation to "line abreast," four ranks deep. It was a savage and brilliant maneuver, and it almost ended the battle right there. But the eleven leading ships of Phormio's fleet stroked valiantly forward. "Play, piper!" the helmsman shouted as the boatswain lifted his palm.

Jes played, speeding the cadence, as the enemy fleet bore down. The ships ahead were pulling clear, thanks to their speed, but it looked as if Ittai's ship was about to be caught. A Spartan ship's ram was coming right at it.

"Go!" the helmsmen cried, shooting his own hand upward.

Jes increased her cadence as rapidly as she could without outstripping the best beat the oarsmen could match evenly. The oarsmen, spooked by the threat of the ram, responded with a final surge of power. The ship pulled just clear of the enemy vessel, so close that some of the opposing oars collided.

The boatswain brought his hand down part way. Jes slowed the cadence, allowing the oarsmen to get their stroke back. Now the ship pulled rapidly away from the enemy, because of the time it took for the Spartan ships to turn and pursue.

Jes, facing back, could see the carnage behind. All nine ships caught by the sudden charge were driven in flight toward the land; they had no room and no time to maneuver to get into fighting position. They were quickly overrun and made useless. The Athenians dived into the water and swam to land; any who didn't escape were killed.

With one exception: the Spartans managed to encircle and capture one ship with its crew intact. The Athenians on that one did not dare move, lest they be summarily slaughtered; enemy bowmen had them completely covered.

The Peloponnesians wasted no time; they tied ropes and started towing away the empty ships. The one captured entire they required to row itself where they directed; only by obeying could its crew hope to survive. The spoils of war were already being taken.

But the battle was not yet done. The Messenian land force arrived and went immediately into action. The Messenians hated the Spartans, and were eager for battle. They charged into the sea in full armor, overtaking several of the captured ships as they were being towed, and threatening the enemy crews. There were far more Messenians than Spartans, but the Messenians could not effectively reach the ships in deeper water. They did board several of the towed ships, and recaptured them in fierce fighting on the decks. They also recovered the ship with the full crew, a significant prize. Jes had not before fully appreciated the importance of land support; she had thought it was only to assist the crews as they took their meal and comfort breaks. Not so!

Meanwhile she continued playing the Straight Ahead tune. They were the last in a line of eleven ships, now being closely pursued by twenty fast Peloponnesian ships. It was apparent that the enemy ships were not quite as fast as the Athenian ships, not because of any inferiority of design, but because their crews were not as well honed. The ten ships before Ittai's were pulling slowly away, reaching the harbor at Naupactus in time to range themselves in the "Line Abreast by the Temple of Apollo" formation, ready for defensive action. Their bows faced seaward as they waited for the onslaught.

All except Ittai's ship. The boatswain was signaling with his palm down, bidding Jes to slow the cadence. She did, cautiously, and now the ship lost distance ahead of the pursuit. The enemy fleet, believing that it could catch the laggard, was putting forth all due effort, and the twenty ships were spreading out as the faster crews outpaced their neighbors. Soon the leaders would flank Ittai's ship and attack it from either side with bow and spear.

What was the captain thinking of? She remembered Admiral Phormio's directive that Ittai perform rearguard action, and this he was doing—but the force behind was overwhelmingly greater, and would soon destroy the single ship. What was to be gained by offering up this sacrifice?

Well, maybe it wasn't entirely futile, because one Leucadian trieres was now significantly outpacing the others. It might be possible to fight it alone, before the others caught up. Still, even if they won, it was only one ship, with many more rapidly closing. Much more was needed, if there was to be any chance to save Naupactus.

Their ship reached the harbor barely ahead of the Leucadian. Jes could hear the Peloponnesians singing the paean for the final attack. Normally the crews were silent; noise was the mark of an ill-disciplined crew. But this was the exception; they were working themselves up for the final slaughter.

Ittai's ship passed a merchant ship that was anchored in deep water, as such vessels normally were. Such noncombatants were normally ignored in battle; they were part of the booty, not capable of fighting.

But as they passed it, the boatswain gave the Hard Right Turn signal. Surprised, Jes played it, and the oarsmen obeyed automatically. The ship made an exceedingly tight turn, going behind the merchanter, as if hiding. There was laughter from the pursuing ship.

But there was no Slow Cadence signal. What were they doing? The ship continued its turn, looping entirely around the merchant without slowing more than it had to to make the turn.

And suddenly there was the pursuing ship—exposed in profile. The boatswain gave the Straight Ahead signal, followed immediately by the Ram signal. Jes played the tunes, and the oarsmen evened their strokes and propelled the ship ahead. The Leucadians were unable to move out of the way; they could only watch in amazed dismay as their doom closed on them.

Just before the strike, the boatswain signaled Lift Oars. Jes played the tune, and the ship completed the maneuver on inertia. They all braced for the impact.

It came. Jes would have been thrown from her seat, if she had not braced herself. The collision holed the enemy ship, immediately disabling it. Ittai's crew cheered.

Then the Withdraw signal. Jes played, and the oarsmen reversed their stroke and hauled the ram back out of the hole, leaving the other ship floundering and filling with water. It would not sink, but it was useless for combat. The crew could not even desert it, because this was Athenian water, and any swimmers would be easy targets. So they just sat and waited in evident despair. How quickly their fortune had reversed!

The following Peloponnesian ships were similarly dismayed. Their line had become ragged in the close pursuit. So their leading ships backed their oars and halted, waiting for more ships to catch up. However, some did not halt in time, and ran aground in the unfamiliar harbor. Their enthusiasm for pursuit had blinded them to common sense.

Now Phormio made a single shout. The ten remaining ships of the Athenian fleet surged forward in attack. The distance was small; in a moment they were on the stalled enemies. The Spartans were in a poor position to defend themselves. The integrity of their fleet had been lost, and they had little room to maneuver. They had foolishly surrendered their momentum, close to the Athenian line. Because of all the mistakes they had made, and their state of disorder, the advantage of their superior numbers had been forfeited.

Ittai's ship turned and rejoined the Athenian formation. It was no longer the laggard. Jes played the Forward tune, and they closed on the enemy in proper style. She felt exhilarated by the elixir of battle, not at all afraid. This was glorious!

The Peloponnesians fought only briefly, before turning to flee. That was yet another mistake on their part. The Athenians had easy pickings, choosing their targets. They went after the easiest ones and let the others go. Their discipline, maneuverability, tactics, and courage in adversity had enabled them to win the day despite the enormous odds against them.

All that remained was mopping up. Their ship went after one of the grounded ships, taking advantage of its inability to maneuver. Troops on the ground were wading out to capture it, but it seemed about to free itself and escape.

Instead of ramming a ship they could capture and salvage, they cut off its escape and crowded against it from the sea side. They grappled it, holding it firm. That prevented it from avoiding the Messenians, who came on, waving their spears and shouting.

But the ship did not surrender quietly. Their hoplites made a desperate lunge, leaping aboard Ittai's craft and engaging its hoplites. For a moment there was fierce fighting.

An Athenian hoplite fell in front of Jes, wounded in the leg. The enemy hoplite stood over him, raising his spear for the finishing thrust.

Jes acted without thinking. She drew her knife and hurled it at the enemy soldier's face. The blade penetrated his left eye. He screamed and fell backward off the ship.

But another was coming. Jes dived for the Athenian hoplite's shield. She hauled it up and held it over the man's body, protecting him from further injury.

Then Kettle appeared. He intercepted the enemy hoplite and dispatched him with a single thrust of his spear.

The Messenians arrived, and the remaining crew of the captured ship surrendered rather than be slaughtered. The fight was over.

The commander of the hoplites turned to Jes. "You have lost your knife," he said. "Take mine." He drew his dagger and offered the hilt to her.

She accepted it, realizing that by this token he had finally accepted her position on the ship. He must have seen her defend the wounded soldier.

There was a pause while the other ship was secured. Jes looked around—and saw that Captain Ittai was down. The helmsman and boatswain were attending to him, while the bowmen looked crestfallen; they had not succeeded in protecting him. Yet how could they? He had been struck by an arrow.

Something tore apart within her breast. Before she knew it, Jes was there, throwing herself down by the captain even as the helmsman pulled out the arrow in his shoulder. "Oh my love, don't die! Don't die!" she cried, her tears flowing. She kissed his pale, still face. "I love you! Don't die!"

Ittai's eyes opened. "Does this mean you will marry me?" he asked with a weak smile.

"Yes! Yes!" All her doubts had dissipated. She no longer cared where or how she lived, as long as it was with him. He was an honorable, valorous, decent man, and fully worthy of love.

"Good." His eyes closed, and he sank back into unconsciousness.

"It is a flesh wound, painful but not lethal," the helmsman said. "We will take care of him." Indeed, he held a bandage in his hands.

Then Jes realized where she was. She looked up at the

boatswain and bowmen, all of whom were staring. "It's a woman!" one of the bowmen said.

"A woman!" the nearest oarsman echoed, amazed. "Bad luck!"

She had given herself away. Now she was in trouble.

The helmsman stood up straight. "On the ship, the captain makes the rules. I serve the captain."

"We all serve the trierarch," the boatswain said, and the four bowmen nodded agreement. But the oarsmen were scowling rebelliously.

Kettle was close. "I see no woman," he said. "I see our pipeman, who has served the ship well in two hard battles." He glared at the thranites, his hand on his blood-soiled spear. "And will continue to serve. As will the rest of us."

The oarsmen looked away, not daring to challenge him.

The helmsman smiled. "Pipeman, return to your station."

Jes got up and went back to her chair. The boatswain gave her a signal, and she began to play her flute. The oarsmen, encouraged by the glares of the hoplites, bent to their task. The ship moved out.

The Athenians captured six enemy ships, and recovered all of their own. This battle, like others, showed the reasons for the Athenian command of the Greek seas: Their crews were highly disciplined and competent, and their captains refused to accept the logic of numbers or a tactically unfavorable situation. No ship panicked. They retreated when they had to, but not in disarray, and reacted quickly and decisively to take advantage of a sudden change of fortune. Even when they lost almost half their force, they did not give up. Their tactical professionalism was decisive. They wielded the ram with a deadly precision that was beyond that of the opposing forces.

The captain of the Leucadian ship, Timocrates the Spartan, killed himself as his ship began to fill with water. The Spartan fleet still outnumbered the Atheni-

ans, but it retired to the south, surrendering control of the gulf to Phormio. Thus the blockade of Corinth remained in place for years, crippling that city's economy.

The plague, which was probably typhoid fever, ravaged Athens for two years, skipped a year, then returned for one more year, as virulent as before. It reduced the orderly existence of the city to chaos. The rule of law became fragile or absent, as few people there thought they would live long enough to pay the price of their actions. Perikles fell victim to the plague, surviving it, but he never regained his strength and was reduced to lying abed wearing a protective charm.

In the end, in 404 B.C., Sparta defeated Athens, but the prestige of Athens remained until the city was sacked six centuries later. The power of Greece in time gave way to that of Rome, to whom it bequeathed much of its culture. The greatness of classical Greece is honored even today.

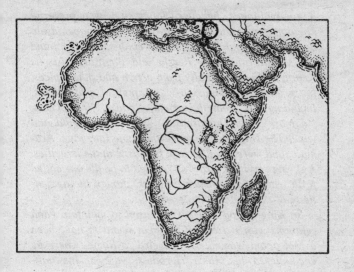

Chapter 11

PRINCESS

In the year A.D. 36 Herod Antipas was tetrarch, or governor, of the Roman territories of Galilee and Peraea. A Roman procurator governed the main part of the province of Judea. Thus Herod was, by default, the preeminent Jewish authority of the time. But he was not considered to be a good man. In A.D. 27 he had John the Baptist killed, fearing his influence among the people, and Herod was the one who saw to the execution of Jesus Christ. He married the daughter of the king of the Nabataeans, Aretas IV of Petra. This was

a good alliance, because Nabataea was a powerful
kingdom that controlled most of the Arabian peninsula
and the principal trading routes connecting Egypt and
the Mediterranean to Persia and the Far East. Its
wealth derived originally from myrrh and other spices,
but grew to encompass a wide range of trade goods,
including silk from the orient, "gauze" from Gaza,
"damask" from Damascus, as well as grain, gold, and
wine. The Nabataeans spoke the same language, Ara-
maic, and were usually close friends with the Israelites.
A spring serving Petra was reputed to be the one called
forth when Moses struck the rock, though the authen-
ticity of this belief is uncertain.

So King Herod had every reason to maintain good
relations with Petra. But the man seems to have been
a fool about women. He traveled to Rome, where he
encountered his niece Herodias, wife of his half-
brother Herod Philip. That led to significant mischief.

BRY WAS HELPING LIN TEND their terraced garden. It was
little, but it was vitally important, and every day they had
to carry crocks of water up to irrigate it so it wouldn't burn
away in the hot sun. Without it, they would soon be hungry,
because they had almost no reserves of grain or meat. They
existed largely by the tolerance of the king of Nabataea, who
accepted them as immigrants from the north but had not yet
seen fit to grant them citizenship. At such time as they had
citizenship, and the right to graze sheep and goats on a section of Nabataean pasture land, they would be much better
off.

They carefully poured out the water so that it ran between
the rows, none of it being wasted. Then they stood, straightening their tired backs. Water was heavy, especially when
hauled uphill.

Bry straightened and looked around. He saw something
in the distance. "Lin! A caravan!"

She was as excited as he was. Caravans passed regularly

through Khirbet Tannur on their way between the capital city of Petra and points north, but that did not mean they were a daily occurrence. They always stopped to make an offering—it was not nice to call it a toll—at the Shrine of Atargatis, the goddess of love, beauty, fruitfulness, vegetation and much else. Also of war, and the underworld. It would be very bad form to incur her ire.

"Maybe it's Jes," Lin said.

But Jes had been gone more than a year. She had left with Wona, and would not return until that faithless wife had been placed, preferably far away. Maybe in Jerusalem, in Judaea, or maybe in Gaza. Maybe even somewhere in Phoenica, really far away. So it was bound to take time. But Bry worried secretly, as the months passed without her return. There were so many dangers along the way!

Lin glanced sharply at him. "Don't say it."

That brought him out of his morbid reverie. "Right. Maybe it's Jes. She's due."

Without further word, they left the garden, scrambled down the steep path, and ran for the shrine.

The shrine stood alone inside the juncture of two canyons that branched out from the Dead Sea, seven leagues to the northwest. It was on an isolated stone rise, visible from the primary caravan route through the area, though still below the rim of the canyon. It was a singularly impressive structure, facing east and dominating that region of the canyon. It was left open to the sky, with a broad flat stone platform for worshippers and supplicants to stand on, flanked by two stone obelisks triple the height of a man, carved from the native rock of the ridge. One pillar represented the god Dushara, ruler of the mountains, and of all this land, and the other Al-Uzza, goddess of springs and water, so vital in this dry land. But the Shrine Tannur was for the goddess Atargatis; the others were merely guests at this site. The altar was for offerings to her.

The caravan made good time, because it was arriving at the base of the shrine the same time Bry and Lin did. Lin gave a scream of sheer joy. "Jes!" she cried, running to fling herself into her big sister's arms.

Bry was just a bit more cautious. He had no doubt of Lin's identification, for he recognized Jes too, despite her male attire. But she was in the company of strangers. If she was concealing her identity or gender, they could be causing her real mischief.

But his concern turned out to be unwarranted. Jes set Lin down and strode forward to hug him too. "You look wonderful! Both of you! How are—?"

"They're all fine!" Lin said. "Sam brought home a new wife, Snow. She's nice. He thought she would marry Ned, but Flo said—"

"Of course," Jes agreed, probably not grasping all of that but satisfied that it was all right. "Wona has remarried. And I am married too."

Bry and Lin froze, astonished. "You?" Bry asked.

A portly older man standing nearby laughed. Jes turned to face him. "This is my husband, Captain Ittai, retiring from the sea. This is his caravan."

Bry stared at the array of camels, horses, and attendants. A number of them were armed.

"Our caravan," the man said, putting his arm around Jes as she came to him.

"But—" Lin started.

Jes leaned toward her. "Yes, he's rich," she whispered loudly enough to carry through the canyon. "And these are my siblings, Bry and Lin," she said to the captain.

"I am glad to meet both of you," the captain said.

They still could not believe it. "How—?" Lin asked.

Captain Ittai smiled. "It is a long story, but I will make it short. Jes signed on aboard my ship as a man, but I penetrated her disguise—"

"That wasn't all you penetrated," Jes said archly.

"And after that, we just had to marry," he concluded smugly. "So here we are, to rejoin the family."

Lin tried again. "But Jes is so—"

"So much more woman than I may deserve," the captain said, patting her bottom. "She wanted to love me and leave me, but I persuaded her it wasn't fair to take advantage of an old man like that."

It was becoming clear that the two were not going to tell their full story all at once. "Sam is doing construction nearby," Bry said. "And Ned is designing it. Flo—"

"Why don't you go to let them know we are here," Jes suggested. "While we make our offerings to Atargatis. Then we can go together to meet Flo and Dirk. We have something important to discuss with them."

"More important than getting married?" Lin asked. She still seemed as amazed as Bry was that angular Jes could have accomplished such a thing. She was acting almost like Wona.

"Well—" Jes said, glancing at her husband.

"Equivalently important," Ittai said. "And somewhat urgent."

"Oh, come on," Jes teased him. "We did it just an hour ago. It can't be that urgent."

"This is weird," Lin muttered.

"I'll tell Sam," Bry said to her. "You tell Flo."

"Yes." They ran off in different directions, while Jes and the captain climbed the long steps to the shrine.

As it happened, Sam and Ned were together, consulting about the placement of a significant block of stone. This was to be a shelter for high-ranking travelers, well above the base of the canyon. It was being built on commission by the king of Nabataea, and the family was allowed to occupy land in this vicinity and to farm on it as long as progress on the construction was satisfactory. Bry knew it was, because Ned was good at designing things, and Sam was good at heavy work. Still, the favor of kings was notoriously fickle, so nothing was certain until they were granted citizenship.

"Jes is back!" Bry cried as he saw them. "And she's married! A rich captain!"

He saw Sam and Ned exchange a significant glance. But they didn't doubt him openly. They concluded their business and accompanied him back to the farm.

Jes and her old rich husband were already there. Flo was better prepared, having been briefed by Lin. But there was another surprise. "You have an urgent mission," Flo told Bry. "Talk to your sister while we get things ready."

Without waiting for him to react, Jes took him by the elbow and led him to a shady spot by the wall. "Flo says you're the only one who can do it. You know the terrain, you speak the dialect, and you're small enough to slip by unnoticed."

"Do what?" he asked blankly.

"Travel to Galilee alone."

"What?"

"My husband is Judaean. He has contacts there, especially relating to events of the sea. He learned that when King Herod Antipas of Galilee traveled to Rome, he met his niece Herodias, said to be a most attractive young woman. She was married to his half-brother Herod Philip, but didn't like him, so she agreed to marry Herod Antipas if he would get rid of that Nabataean princess. He was so smitten with her that he agreed, and he is about to do the deed."

"But that's Princess Aretania, King Aretas's daughter!"

"Precisely. She will die, if she doesn't get out of there in a hurry. Herod will be there in another three days. She must be warned before he gets there."

The gravity of it sank in. "You want me to go warn her."

"Yes. We hate to ask this of you, Bry, but—"

"But I don't know the princess! And she doesn't know me. Why should she accept the word of a stranger?"

"I wish we had an official letter to give you, Bry, but if we did, you still couldn't risk carrying it. If you were caught with anything like that—" She shook her head. "You will simply have to be persuasive. Her life depends on it."

"But I'm not even a citizen! And her father—"

"We will proceed on down to Petra while you go north.
Our mission is ostensibly to request a land grant, which will
likely be granted, considering my husband's wealth. But we
will seek immediate private audience with the king, and tell
him what we know, and what you are doing. We'll ask him
to send a force to the border to escort the princess when she
crosses it."

"But—"

"You will have to get her safely across it. Can you do
that, Bry?"

His head was spinning with the suddenness and urgency
of the mission. "I guess I'll have to."

And so he found himself traveling alone that night, instead of sleeping, for night was the best time to move
swiftly. It was cool, and there was no one to observe. He
had a pack that Flo had prepared, with figs, bread, hard
cheese, and strips of dried goat meat. He had a change of
cloaks, so as to be able to shift his appearance quickly. And
he had his message.

He knew the way well, for he had spent his young life in
the vicinity of the Dead Sea and Galilee. Drought and
changing politics had forced his family to move south, seeking a better situation, but he hadn't forgotten the old haunts.
He could follow the trail all the way north to Peraea. After
that it would be less familiar, but he could find his way.

He walked swiftly through the starry night, using his staff
to check any dark objects in his path. He didn't tire; the
urgency of his mission propelled him. He passed the city of
Kerak and by morning he was at Dhilban, ten leagues north
of his starting point. This was excellent time, but he reminded himself that it was illusory, because now he faced
the heating day, and the possible curiosity of strangers.

He continued as long as he could, slowing. Now fatigue
was catching up with him. He had done a lot of errand
running, but this was a much longer haul than any before.
At the border of Peraea he found a private grove and hid in
it, lying down to sleep during the heat of the day.

He was lucky. The palm trees kept the sun off him, and no one spied him. It would have been too much to say he was refreshed by his hot sleep, but at least he wasn't utterly worn out. As evening came he ate sparingly from his pack, took a good drink from a local well, and resumed his trek.

The border of Peraea was not well guarded, for this was a time of relative peace. Merchants and tradesmen crossed all the time. He walked down the road as if he had business ahead, and no one challenged him. But he was now in potentially hostile territory.

The road moved along the northeastern shore of the Dead Sea. The barren land sloped down to the salty water, with massive pieces of dark basalt rock lying scattered as if by a giant's hand. Salt crusted everything near the shore, turning it white. If Bry slitted his eyes, those coated rocks looked almost like clouds in air. But he knew it was a dead region; there were no fish, no plants, because of the poisonous thickness of the brine. There once had been life here, though, because he saw the seashells lying high up on the slopes.

The darkness closed in, and he could see the sea no more, but he could hear its waves lapping the shore, and smell the thickness of the air. He would be glad to get beyond this desolate region.

In due course the sea curved west, away from the road. The Jordan River came in from the north—and along its banks the ground grew green again, for it was fresh water. There were grass, and wheat, and olive trees, and the air became sweet. The smell of plowed fields wafted in on the night breeze. What a relief!

The river ran straight north, following the cleft between mountain ridges, and the road ran straight beside it. Bry's fatigue actually diminished as he walked, because of the pleasure of the environment. He was making good time. Still, he had a long way to go, and little time. He had to get there before King Herod did!

By dawn he was near the northern border of Peraea. The

two sections of Herod's domain were discontinuous, with a portion of Decapolis between. Herod, an arrogant man, did not necessarily get along well with his neighbors, so it would normally be better to travel through Samaria instead, going around Decapolis. But that would take him a full day out of his way. So he had to risk the direct route. But not by day.

He found another grove, selected a secluded spot hidden within it, ate, and slept. Bry was good at finding paths, and good at hiding, having done both all his life; no one discovered him.

In the evening he resumed his trek. He had about half a day's travel left, if he could find the way.

He had no trouble locating the city of Beisan; it was right across the river. The bridge was guarded, as it represented access to the city from a foreign territory, but the guards were evidently asleep. Good enough; he moved silently across and to the gate.

It was closed for the night. He couldn't get in without waking the guards, and he didn't want to do that, for any number of reasons. So he slid around to the side, circling the city until he reached the gate on the other side. That was closed too, but before long it should open to admit routine vegetable venders bringing their wares from the surrounding fields. Cities were hungry things, and needed huge amounts of food. So Bry settled down against the wall to nap until the day began. Any activity at the gate would wake him.

Sure enough, soon there was the approach of hooves. Several mounted men charged up to the gate. "Open for His Majesty King Herod Antipas!" one demanded loudly.

The sleepy guard was unimpressed. "I see no king. Where is your authority?"

"Here, you lazy scoundrel." The man handed across a scroll.

The guard perused the scroll, then gave the order. This was indeed the advance party for the king.

Bry scrambled up. The king was already arriving? He barely had time to warn the princess.

He walked around to the gate. Sure enough, it remained open, because there wasn't much point in closing it when dawn was so close and the king would soon arrive. He walked in unchallenged.

The houses were densely packed inside the city: simple cubic flat-roofed dwellings with dung-colored walls. The palace wasn't at all difficult to locate: it was a two story stone structure of considerable size, containing chambers for the city elders to gather after the day's work, and where citizens could come to receive judgment and make legally binding declarations. This was where the princess would stay.

Now came the hard part: getting in to see the princess, before the king arrived. He couldn't take a day to scout out the situation and find the best way; he had to do it immediately.

He decided that a bold course was best, in this situation. He went to a public scribe and bought a small blank scroll. Few folk were literate, but he could write a few words. He wrote four, then made a deliberately indecipherable signature, and rolled and sealed the scroll so that it looked official. Then he put on his better tunic, brushed his hair back, and approached the main entrance.

The guard here was not asleep. He wore the badges of some rank, and had arrogance to match. "What's your business, boy?"

"I bear an important message for Princess Aretania."

"What is the message?"

"It is only for her ears."

"Don't fool with me, boy! I will be the judge of what is or is not important. Now speak, or get out of here."

"As you wish. I was told to allow no one but the princess to see this, on pain of severe punishment, but I'm sure you have the necessary authority." He handed the sealed scroll to the man.

The guard considered the scroll. Messages to royalty were special; a person could readily get his head lopped off for snooping. So he did not open it. Instead he snapped his fingers for a servant. ''Take this message to the princess.''

The servant took the scroll and disappeared into the depths of the palace. Bry waited, doing his best to maintain a calm mien. The princess could summarily order his own head off, if she thought the matter an unkind joke. But he hoped she would be curious enough to inquire.

The servant returned. ''The princess says to admit the messenger to her presence.''

The guard never blinked. ''Of course. Guide him there forthwith.''

The servant turned, and Bry stepped briskly forward to accompany him. He felt weak with relief. His gamble had paid off.

The princess's apartment was well back in the labyrinth. The servant brought him to the curtained door and spoke loudly enough to be heard inside. ''Majesty: the messenger is here.''

''Enter, messenger,'' a woman's voice replied.

Bry stepped through the curtain and found himself in a richly decorated suite. There were rugs on the floor and carpets on the walls. A woman stood alone in the center. She was not old, but neither was she young, and she was somewhat plain of feature. Her robe, however, was ornate, and she wore jewelry that looked quite precious. She was clearly the princess. Accordingly, Bry dropped to his knees and bowed his head, waiting for her to acknowledge his presence.

''Rise.''

He got back to his feet, but remained silent. He knew that a common person never spoke to a royal person, but only responded to direct orders or queries.

''What is this message?'' she asked.

He looked around. ''Your Highness, it must not be overheard by anyone else.''

"Where are you from?"

"Nabataea, Your Highness."

"Speak to me in that dialect."

"Gladly, Your Highness," he said in that variant. It was mainly a matter of accent and inflection, but was almost impossible to fake. Bry, living between the two kingdoms, had learned the dialects of both.

"Ah, you really are! From the northern province, no?"

"Yes, Your Highness. Near Tannur."

"Follow me." She turned and went to a small garden courtyard where a fig tree grew. He followed at a respectful distance. She picked a fig and offered it to him. "Eat."

He accepted it and put it in his mouth. It was delicious. He understood the significance of this, too: he had eaten in her presence, and by Nabataean custom would not hereafter betray her or speak falsely to her.

"Now the message. Dispense with the formality and speak plainly."

"King Herod has found a new love, his niece Herodias, and will marry her. But she demands that he get rid of you first. Princess, you must flee this kingdom before he returns!"

She blanched. "How came you by this news?"

"My elder sister married a ship captain. He has connections, and learned the scuttlebutt of a ship coming from Rome. They say that Herodias is fair of feature and form, and is given to making demands of men. She has entirely fascinated the king, and—"

"Yes, I'm sure. What says my father?"

"He has not yet been informed. We—we deemed the matter so important that I was sent to warn you, before Herod returned. My sister is even now informing King Aretas. We beg your forgiveness for our presumption, but—"

"Why should I believe you?"

Bry was appalled. "Oh My Lady, I beg you—"

She smiled. "I do believe you. I know my husband, and I have heard of Herodias. I must return forthwith to my father. But I know Herod will not let me go."

"You must go before he returns!"

"Too late. He is already here."

"Then if you can flee before he—"

"No, I will not be able to leave without his approval."
Now she looked grim. "What is your name?"

"Bry, of the family of—"

"Bry, you show a certain resourcefulness." She glanced
at the scroll she still held. "All this says is BEARER HAS
SECRET MESSAGE."

"I could not risk writing it down."

"To be sure. What would you recommend?"

This surprised him. "I—I—maybe if you could go with
his permission. If he doesn't know that you know. If you
visit your father—"

"He would not allow that."

"Then maybe a city near the border, in Peraea—"

She smiled. "That, I may be able to manage. I have been
before to the fortress of Machaerus, at the southern end of
Peraea. That would even be a suitable place to dispatch me,
in some seeming accident of which he has no official knowledge. He won't want to antagonize my father by being open
about it. So he may agree."

"And from there you can sneak across the border and be
safe," Bry agreed, relieved. "My mission is done."

"By no means," she said. "You will see me safely across
that border, because you know that terrain as I do not."

"But I can't stay with you! I mustn't be seen with you,
lest suspicion—"

"You are young. You will become my maid."

"I—"

"Wait here." She walked from the garden.

Bry waited. He knew how Jes often dressed in male clothing, and sometimes Lin joined her in that. It was safer to
travel as boys. But to dress as a girl—

Yet it did make sense. Who would suspect a personal
maid? Unless someone made the connection between the

arrival of the messenger boy and the new maid.

The princess returned with an armful of female apparel. "We shall make a fine girl of you," she said with satisfaction.

"But others will know, if I don't depart after delivering my message."

"You have already departed. I sent a servant who resembles you. He masked his face. The guards saw him go. I get new servant girls all the time; they have no enduring value. Now change."

She was catching on quickly. But this remained difficult. "I don't know anything about being a girl. I will make mistakes all the time."

"I will teach you."

"But—"

"Get on with it," she said briskly. "Take off all your clothing. I will prepare you suitably."

"But—" he started, alarmed at the thought of being seen naked by a woman.

"If I am to trust you to deliver me through the wilderness, you must trust me with the preparation of your body. I'm sure you don't have anything I haven't seen before." She reached out and caught hold of his tunic. "Do it now, or I will do it for you."

Bry hastily got out of his clothing. In a moment he stood before her, bare. She studied him for some time, considering. Then she nodded.

"These are the undergarments," she said, presenting him with silk slip and sash. He put on the first, but had no idea what to do with the second. "This is padding," she said. "It belonged to a maiden who was less endowed than she craved. It will give you the form of a maiden. But be sure you keep it in the right place." She put the thing around his chest, wrapping it several times, tying it behind. It did bulk up his front somewhat.

Then he donned a cotton underskirt, and frilly vest. Over these went a solid dress. There were slippers, too, that made his feet look surprisingly delicate. Finally the princess fussed with his hair, arranging it in a female manner and fixing it in place with a large curved comb. She tied a colorful scarf over his head.

"There," she said, satisfied. "Now see yourself." She held up a large brass mirror.

Bry was amazed. The face in the mirror was that of a rather pretty young woman. He angled the mirror down, and saw a slender but definitely feminine body, complete with dainty feet.

"But I don't know how to act, or what to say," he said. "I can't even—when I have to—the clothing is wrong."

"You will be mute to all but me. You will do whatever I tell you. If you don't understand, I will call you stupid. No one will suspect." She smiled fleetingly. "And you will squat to pee, as all girls do."

Oh. She seemed to have worked it out. He nodded, mutely.

"Now I will go and charm my loving husband into sending me to Peraea," she said. "I am not entirely lacking in the wiles of my gender."

That was becoming clear. But what was he to do, meanwhile?

"Wait here," she said. "Take this mirror and this sponge and wash your face and arms—and your legs, where they show. Girls are cleaner than boys."

She departed, and he got to work as directed. He was not thrilled to become a girl, but it did make sense, and certainly it would be even less thrilling to get caught and executed along with the princess. He found that there was indeed a fair amount of dirt caked on him; he hadn't noticed, before. But with the help of the mirror and a fair amount of work he succeeded in becoming more feminine.

After that things moved swiftly. That afternoon the princess and her maid boarded a horse drawn wagon with a sunshade and curtained sides for privacy and protection from insects. There were horsemen before and after, to en-

sure that no one interfered with the princess and that she
didn't go anywhere by herself. They were almost alarmingly
protective.

That left a lot of time alone in the carriage. The princess
insisted on having her maid ride with her, and the maid
fetched anything the princess might need in the course of
the ride. When the maid did, sometimes a guard would try
to steal a kiss. Since Bry was playing the part of a mute,
they assumed that he would be unable to tell. Bry had to
get advice about how to deal with that. "Just try to stay out
of reach," the princess advised. "They figure to start with
kisses, then proceed to more, and if you try to protest, they
may try to rape you, and deny it if challenged. This is the
way of men with women."

He was coming to appreciate the situation of women in
a way he had not, before. "My sister Flo was raped," he
said. "And my brother's wife Snow. We thought it was just
ill fortune."

"No, it is standard practice," she said. "Men conspire to
separate women from their protection. A girl must be ever
on her guard." Then she reconsidered. "Or maybe you
should kiss him. Hard."

"But—"

She brought out a tiny spice box. "This is the foulest-
tasting stuff I know of. Smear it on your lips. Just keep your
tongue off them."

Bry touched it with a finger, and tasted it with the tip of
his tongue. It seemed as though he had just bitten into camel
manure that had grown too ripe. He smiled.

It took only one kiss. Thereafter, no one bothered him,
even when the taste faded. It had been worth it.

Betweentimes, they talked. Bry was surprised to discover
how much they had in common. He was the youngest boy
of an orphaned family, so had felt somewhat isolated from
the regular community of people. She was the only daughter
of a busy king, used to make a political marriage to a neighbor king who didn't really care for her, and she felt isolated

too. Both of them loved the rocky countryside of Nabataea, and its impressive cliffside architecture. Bry realized that isolation could happen to anyone, whether royal or common. He missed his sister Lin; Aretania missed her brothers.

In due course they reached the fortress Machaerus. "We must not wait, even for a night," the princess said. "My husband's assassins can strike at any time, and I have obligingly put my head on the block. I will send you out on an errand, and you will explore the best route out. We must act at nightfall, before they expect it."

"Yes."

So even as they arrived, Aretania went into her act. "Oh, this is so wonderful!" she exclaimed as they were escorted to the mountain fortress. "Girl, go out and pick me some posies! I want a nice selection of fresh flowers for my room."

Bry nodded, picked up his skirts, and hastened out to the countryside. The guards shrugged. Nobody cared about the bad-tasting mute servant girl.

It didn't take long. He picked flowers on the slopes and scouted out a path suitable for women in skirts, that avoided normal paths. Soon he had an excellent route that would get them efficiently away from the fortress.

And someone spied him. It was a lone boy, probably returning from an errand. It was just bad luck that their paths had crossed.

The boy stared at him as they passed each other. "Bry?"

Startled, he paused. He recognized that voice. "Lin!"

"I thought it was you," she said as they embraced. "But I never expected a girl. With posies, yet. I had to verify it before speaking."

"Well, you're a boy!" he said defensively.

She smiled. "For sure."

"But how did you know I would be here?"

"Our spies tracked the royal tour. You have the princess?"

"Yes. I'm scouting her escape route."

"This is it. I know the way from here. Bring her here and we'll be ready."

"Just as soon as we can get her out of the fortress. But suppose guards come along? They follow her everywhere."

She glanced significantly around. "We have bowmen ready. Bring the guards here too, if you have to. By the time their bodies are found, we'll be gone."

"Right. I never expected to see you here."

"Someone had to make contact, and I said I'd know you anywhere." She eyed him again. "But I almost didn't. You make a fine girl, Bry. Maybe you'll grow up to be a good wife and mother."

"The same time you become a husband and father!"

She laughed and kissed him on the mouth. And rebounded. "You taste like camel manure!"

So some of the taste remained. "Of course. Next time keep your lips where they belong, you fresh boy."

"Aw, do I have to?" She patted him on the bottom.

"Your hands too!" he exclaimed, but he couldn't help laughing.

They separated, both quite satisfied.

He returned at dusk with a nice bouquet of wildflowers. "But these are not enough, you stupid girl!" the princess cried imperiously. "I need more. Many more."

Bry spread his hands, indicating that he had found all he could.

"You idiot!" the princess screamed. "Do I have to do everything myself? I'll show you where there are flowers! You just haven't looked in the right places." And right then, extemporaneously, she walked out. To show him where to look.

The guards, caught off-guard, were slow to follow. The princess looked back at them. "Hurry up!" she called. "You can pick flowers too."

For some reason the guards lagged even farther behind. It wasn't difficult to lose them in the crevices of the mountain. Then the two of them hoisted skirts and ran along the route Bry indicated, knowing that the pursuit would soon be hot.

He led her, panting, to the place he had encountered Lin. She was there, with a small hooded lamp in the dark. "This way," she said, offering a helping hand to the princess, who evidently wasn't accustomed to exercise this strenuous.

"Guards in pursuit," Bry warned Lin.

"They won't pass this spot."

They slowed to a walk. Soon they reached the border. There were troops from Nabataea, and a curtained wagon with horses. "Your Highness," the captain of the guard said, bowing low.

"Never mind that!" the princess gasped. "Just get me out of here in a hurry!"

They got to it, and soon the wagon was moving south. Bry assumed that he could now leave the princess's side, but she had him join her again. "But my sister can—"

"I know you, Bry, and everyone else thinks you're a girl, while she looks like a boy. There are appearances to be maintained. Help me change; I'm soaking in sweat." She gestured to the clothing thoughtfully provided in the wagon.

"But you know I'm not," he protested.

"I saw you naked. Now it's your turn. Anyway, it's dark."

So, while the wagon bumped along through the darkness, she stripped off all her clothes, and dried off, and he helped her get into new clothing. It was indeed dark, and he was almost sorry he wasn't able to see anything. She was not a beautiful woman, but it would have been interesting.

"Thank you, Bry. Now you may rejoin your sister if you wish. Or, better, bring her in here, and we'll all sleep."

Thus Lin joined them, and they talked briefly, and then slept.

As dawn came, they were at Khirbet Tannur, and went in a group to give due thanks to the goddess Atargatis, who had surely guided their successful effort.

Bry thought that now he would be free to return to his

family, but the princess had a different notion. "I want you to meet my father, who will surely reward you for your heroism."

"I'm no hero," he protested. "I just did what I had to do."

"Same thing," she said. "Get in the wagon."

Now they had new horses and a new guardian force, and rode by day, making good time. But it was nevertheless a tedious daylong trip. They halted only for rest stops. The princess questioned Bry about his family, and seemed genuinely interested in his answers. They also snoozed some more.

In the afternoon they reached the region of the Nabataean capital city of Petra. Bry had not been there before, and was interested, because he had heard that it was a city of amazing splendor. The princess drew aside the curtains so that he could goggle all he wanted. She evidently enjoyed his anticipation.

They were surrounded by towering cliffs of many-colored rock, the bands showing red, yellow, white, and mauve. But that was only the beginning. The way narrowed, with the rock rising up on either side as they followed a winding wadi, where a river ran when there was rain but disappeared in normal times.

"I told them to enter by the east, through the Wadi Musa," the princess said. "So as to provide the most impressive tour."

The wadi deepened and narrowed, becoming a gorge. "This is the Bab as-Siq," Aretania said. "Oh, it's so good to be home!"

The gorge became alarmingly deep and close, with the walls towering almost vertically on either side. In some places the rock actually leaned out over the road. Bry was afraid some rock would dislodge and crash down to crush them. The walls were sculptured by nature, forming crude patterns that could be taken as statues or arches. A channel had been cut into the south base, where water flowed. He could see only a short distance forward or back, because of the continuing curving.

Then it grew so tight there was barely room for the wagon to pass, and the guards had to ride before and after. The slanting sunlight no longer penetrated; they were in deep shadow. Still it squeezed in, until it seemed they would have to stop, lest the wagon get stuck between the closing walls. He found himself shivering, though it was not cold. He didn't like the feeling that it could all collapse inward on his head.

"Look ahead," the princess said, enjoying his unease.

Bry looked, and saw a narrow vertical line of light extending from the bottom of the gorge upward to the sky. Then they made a turn, and the gorge opened out to reveal a truly splendid monument. It was two stories high, with six tall stone columns on each level, and intricate carvings between them. It was built against the mountain wall, and steps led to an antechamber within the mountain. Further steps led beyond it into the dark interior.

"This is Al-Khazneh, the Pharaoh's Treasury," Aretania said, "because of the vast treasure contained in the urn at the top. It is said that he who breaks open that urn will reap a showering harvest of gold and silver coins."

"Is that true?" Bry asked, staring up at the huge stone urn.

"It is true that it is said," she replied with a faint smile. "We arrange not to investigate too closely, lest the gods be annoyed and drop the urn on our heads."

Bry could appreciate the concern. He could also appreciate the usefulness of the legend. Many folk would come to see the urn, and they would bring business to the city. But it was definitely carved stone, not a real urn. It looked to be more than twice the height of a man in itself. Only a god could actually use an urn of that magnitude.

"Actually it's a monument to my ancestor, King Aretas III," she continued after a pause. "His coffin is there."

"Was he the one who conquered Damascus?" Bry asked, surprised.

"Yes. He imported Damascan artisans to craft this monument, which is unlike the others in our city."

"I am awed," he said candidly.

"Would you like to go inside?" the princess asked as they drew abreast of it.

"Yes! But is it allowed? I mean, if his coffin is in there—"

"For me, it is allowed. I am of his blood, and I have nothing but respect."

"But don't you want to get home as fast as possible?"

"This is home." But she looked pensive, and he realized that she could be concerned about her reception. She had evidently failed in her marriage, and her father might not be pleased. So she was taking the pretense of obliging Bry's curiosity, to delay her arrival a bit.

The wagon stopped, they got down, and walked up the three steps between the central pillars to the vestibule. The two guards bowed, recognizing the right of the princess and her servant girl to enter. There were large door-frames to either side, with smaller (but still large) wooden doors. The central steps led up to another doorway. This one was huge; the frame was quadruple the height of a grown man. The guards quickly pulled open the doors and lit torches so that the interior could be seen.

Bry had thought it would be shallow, because carving chambers out of rock was no easy thing, but it was a full-sized square room a dozen paces across, with three more alcoves off its walls. The one farthest in contained an altar three steps up, in front of a great stone coffin. Aretania went to this and kneeled, bowing her head. Then she stood and dropped a gold coin on the altar. She was giving thanks to the gods for her deliverance. And perhaps also to her ancestor, after whom she had evidently been named.

Bry turned away, not wanting to intrude on this private matter. He looked at the painted walls, discovering all manner of carvings and statuary. The interior and exterior of this grand temple contained every kind of representation, including dancing Amazons, eagles, sphinxes, lions, satyrs, and other animals. His eyes shied away from the snaky-locked Medusa, lest her stone stare transform him to stone, and lingered on the bare breasts of human priestesses. This was a marvelous monument.

Aretania turned away from the alcove and came to join him. "I think it will be all right," she said. "My ancestor would not have approved the treatment I received in Galilee."

"Surely not," he agreed.

They left the monument and returned to the wagon. The princess's step seemed lighter now; she had received reassurance. The wagon turned north, then northwest, where an enormous semicircular arena opened out against the western slope. "Oh, my!" Bry exclaimed, awed.

"This is the main theater," the princess said with justified pride. "It seats three thousand people. We have some of the finest spectacles in the world here."

It was surely so, for nothing less would justify such a magnificent setting. A huge colonnaded building closed off the semicircle, where the personnel and displays were housed, and they led onto a raised stage area. It was easy to imagine a huge crowd filling the theater, cheering as the show was put on.

"I will command your presence, next time there is a show," Aretania said. "You will be my guest, in the reserved section in the first row."

"Oh, I couldn't—"

"You won't have to be a girl, for that."

"Thank you, Princess." That had indeed been his concern.

Then they moved north again, passing a number of lesser tombs. They finally emerged from the gorge to reveal the broad expanse of the central city of Petra in its phenomenal splendor.

Bry's head turned from side to side as he tried to take it

all in. On to the northeast a fantastic array of tombs were built into the mountain face; to the west the city itself nestled in the bowl-like hollow of the mountains. There were houses dotting the slopes, and larger structures in the center. He was awed all over again.

They turned west and rode into the busy city. The main street had been cleared, but the people were thronging to see the returning princess. Bry tried to fade into invisibility, but could not avoid the cynosure. "Wave to them," Aretania said mischievously. But he knew better, and sat as still as he could, while she smiled and waved to the onlookers.

"There is the Colonnaded Street," she said, indicating a row of tall columns ahead. The street ran right along beside the columns, and it was paved with clean stone blocks. "And up ahead is the market section." He saw countless stalls set within the shelter of the open structures, with their wares laid out enticingly. The smells of breads and meats wafted across to them. He discovered he was hungry; they had not eaten much during the day.

"There is the palace," Aretania continued, pointing out an impressive structure on the north side. "We will go there to meet my father, after the tour."

"But don't you want to see him first?" Bry asked.

A shadow crossed her face. "These things must follow the proper form." He realized that she still was not certain of her welcome. Her rejection by King Herod of Galilee could cause much political mischief.

"There are the public baths," she said, shaking off the mood as she pointed ahead and to the south. "You won't have to take one of those, either, right now."

"Thank you." It was bad enough being in such a public eye, but worse being taken for a girl.

She turned to the north. "The Temple of the Winged Lions, up there on the slope. We shall have to go there, too, another day."

"We?"

She gave him a serious glance. "You saved my life, Bry;

I want to show my appreciation.'' Before he could try to protest again, she added: ''You understand my situation; I value your support. I regard you as a friend. I will not keep you long, just a few days. Until things settle down.''

He appreciated her moment of candor. She had known him only a few days, but they had been together in Galilee and for the journey south; he was a witness to her activities. He could support what she had to tell her father. ''Of course, Princess.''

''And the Tenenos Gate,'' she continued as they passed through a massive portal girt by four enormous clusters of columns, some with flat contours, others rounded. Stone carvings traveled up those contours to the lintel above. ''Leading into the Sacred Courtyard.''

The sounds of the city faded as they moved through that courtyard. This was lined with impressive sculptures of every description. There were the busts of gods, both bearded men and clear-faced women. There were eagles with wings outspread, and griffins, and a sphinx, and pediments with full human figures, including bare-breasted women of inhuman perfection. It was also a garden area, with nicely shaped trees and bushes. ''The gods surely come here to relax,'' Bry murmured.

''They surely do,'' Aretania agreed. ''Certainly I do. But now we are coming to the greatest of temples, the Qasr al-Bint.''

This was indeed the most magnificent of the free-standing buildings he had seen here. It was at the end of the court, and was about thirty paces on a side, and similarly high. About a dozen broad steps led up to its base, where four enormous pillars supported its roof.

''Close your mouth,'' Aretania murmured. ''The gods already know it is awesome.''

Bry closed his mouth. ''It's so big,'' he said.

''My grandfather Obodas built it. It took twenty years and depleted the treasury, but it was worth it. Now we shall say a prayer at the altar, then go to the palace; I think the tour of the temple will have to wait."

They mounted the steps of the open-air altar that stood before the temple, and the princess bowed her head and gave another gold coin as an offering. Bry didn't have any gold or even silver, so he gave what he had, a copper coin, embarrassed.

"The gods don't judge by the material value so much as the spirit of the supplicant," Aretania said. "I'm sure your spirit is good."

"I hope so."

They returned to the wagon, and now rode to the palace. Now it was dusk, and the market place was clearing. A separate honor guard emerged to escort the princess inside. Bry tried to hang back, but she signaled him imperiously forward, and he had to follow her. "Just stay two steps behind me, and stop when I stop, eyes downcast. Don't say anything; just be there."

That was about all he was capable of doing. He had never expected to meet the king himself.

The guards formed a square around them. They marched as a unit into the palace. At least Bry didn't have to go; all he had to do was stay in his place in the formation, and try not to trip over his skirts.

They mounted the steps and passed the columns of the entrance. Inside were more steps, and an anteroom, and a great hall. Therein, on his grand stone throne, sat King Aretas. Bry kept his eyes downcast, but was able to sneak peeks past his eyelashes.

The king stared at the princess for some time before speaking. Bry could see her shaking; he knew she was afraid of her father. She was afraid she had brought shame on him. She was afraid of his wrath.

Finally the king spoke. "It is an outrage!" he exclaimed.

Aretania's head bowed lower. "I am sorry, Father. I tried my best to—"

"Yes, I know." He looked around. "I am going to do

two things. First the one who brought me this ill news. Where is the foreign sailor?"

"I am here, Your Majesty." It was Captain Ittai's voice. Bry was startled; he hadn't realized that the man was present. There was a woman behind him: Jes.

"You are hereby granted citizenship in Nabataea. You may choose an estate to possess, and your wife and family are granted tenure to share it with you. Where is the boy who carried the message to my daughter?"

There was a pause. Bry couldn't speak up! Then Aretania turned. "Here, Sire." She indicated Bry.

"But I was told—"

"I required him to don female garb, Sire, so he could guide me home without suspicion."

The king stared at Bry. Then he burst out laughing. "Good work, boy! You have earned your family favor in this court. Take this in partial token of that favor." He brought out a small purse and handed it to a courtier, who walked to Bry and presented it.

Bry knew the moment he hefted it that it was filled with gold; nothing else had such heft. "I—thank you, Your Majesty."

But the king was already turning to other business. "Second, I am going to punish Herod for this treachery to my daughter and affront to the Kingdom of Nabataea. That miscreant will learn to respect my disfavor. This hearing is ended."

The courtiers bowed and backed away. The princess was starting to do the same, when the king signaled her with a slight twitch of his fingers. Then his eye caught Bry's, and his fingers twitched again. So Bry followed the princess forward.

As they approached, the king smiled. Then Aretania threw herself into her father's arms. "Oh, Sire, you aren't angry?"

"I am furious," he corrected her. "But not with my innocent daughter. That misbegotten oaf sought to have you killed, just to make an incestuous liaison with his slut of a niece! He will pay, I swear.''

"I feared I had failed you, Sire.''

"My favorite daughter never failed me.''

"I am your only daughter,'' she reminded him, smiling. Then she burst into tears.

"I will not send you away from this city again,'' he reassured her. "Foreign barbarians are not to be trusted.'' He glanced again at Bry. "Now put this fetching young creature back into his natural attire. No man should have to endure what he has.''

"Being garbed as a woman?'' she asked.

"No, suffering your company for three days.'' Then he laughed again, so that they could be sure it was a joke.

King Aretas did indeed raise an army, and sent it toward Judea under the command of his generals. Herod sent his army to battle without taking personal command. In the engagement, some of Herod's forces joined the Nabataeans, who won a resounding victory.

This had several consequences. The people of the scattered parts of Israel sought for some divine reason for their defeat, and remembered Herod's prior crime against John the Baptist. The later Gospel writers then connected this somewhat anachronistically to the request of Herodias's daughter Salome, who danced the Dance of the Veils and beguiled Herod to promise her anything. She asked for John's head, because John had condemned her mother's marriage as adulterous, Herodias still being married to Herod's half-brother. It seems that incest—she was Herod's niece—was not the issue. Surely John the Baptist would have condemned the marriage on similar grounds, had he been alive at the time.

Meanwhile, in history, the Emperor Tiberius of Rome was annoyed by the affront such a defeat meant to a Roman province. He sent Vitellius, his commander in Syria, to conquer Petra and bring Aretas's head back to Rome. Vitellius set out at the head of two legions and their auxiliaries. He began his march through Judea, but was persuaded by priests to take an alternate route, because of all the religiously offensive graven images the Roman army carried. However, Vitellius himself accompanied Herod Antipas to Jerusalem, to offer sacrifices and take part in a religious festival that was about to begin.

According to legend, which may have been generated after the fact, when King Aretas learned of the approach of the Roman army, he consulted his diviners. They told him that it was impossible for the Romans to enter Petra, for one of the three rulers involved would die to prevent it. That is, he who gave the order for war, or he who marched to implement it, or he who defended against it.

Sure enough, Vitellius stayed at Jerusalem for three days. On the fourth day he received word that Emperor Tiberius had died. Thus bereft of the authority under which he marched, Vitellius ordered his army back to Syria and dispersed it to winter billets. Petra was saved. In another generation it would indeed be conquered by Rome, but not while Aretas ruled.

The legend of the gold and silver coins in the great urn exists among the Beduins today. It probably postdated the actual residence of the Nabataeans, but seems appropriate to the spirit of the time.

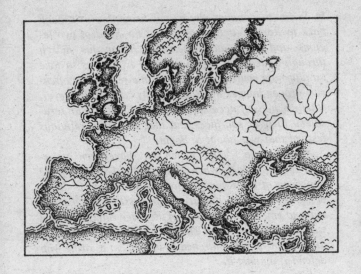

Chapter 12

QUEEN

It is a common perception that the Roman Empire represented a bastion of civilization, in contrast to the barbarians surrounding it. This was not necessarily the case. Rome did possess resources and military capacity that were formidable, and it was these that normally carried the day, rather than any superiority of culture. Julius Caesar invaded Britain in 55 and 54 B.C., but did not stay. Rome did not actually occupy Britain until the first century A.D., taking over most of it in campaigns dating from A.D. 43 to 84. But it was not an easy island to keep pacified, and even those regions nominally under Roman control could be restive. Roman arrogance and avarice hardly helped the situation.

The kingdom of the Iceni in southeast England rebelled against Rome, but was defeated. A new king, friendly to Rome, was installed, and for a dozen years the kingdom thrived. But in A.D. 59 that king, Prasutagus, died, and things changed. In his will he left the kingdom to the emperor Nero and his own two daughters as co-heirs. He may have been trying to avoid strife, knowing that Rome could not be denied. But his caution was wasted. The Roman procurator, responsible for administration and collection of taxes, was greedy and corrupt even by the standards of those who supported Rome. He ruled that the country of the Iceni was wholly the property of the emperor, and that money given to the leaders of the Iceni had been a loan, not a grant, and was now due for repayment. This was of course not the understanding of the Iceni, and they resisted what seemed like a betrayal of prior understandings.

Meanwhile, the tribe immediately south of the Iceni, the Trinovantes, was chafing because for a decade retiring Roman legionnaires had been driving Britons off their lands and claiming their estates as land grants. The original landholders were being treated like prisoners and slaves. This was colonialism at its worst.

Rome had also issued an edict disarming the Celtic tribes. This was enforced in the client kingdoms as well, and was a further source of anger.

By A.D. 60, relations throughout Britain were severely strained. Most of Rome's British forces were tied down in Wales, where guerrilla attacks were chronic. It would have been a good time for Rome to tread softly. But the tyrannical procurator Catus Decianus

had other ideas. He intended to show the difficult na-
tives their place, once and for all.

"THIS IS MISCHIEF," CENTURION ITTAI said as he read the proclamation he had just received. "I shall have to try to reason with Decianus before he brings the whole Isle of Britain down about our ears." He glanced at Lin. "Summon the family; we must have a conference."

"Yes, sir," Lin said, leaving the chamber. She didn't know what was in the scroll, because it had been sealed, but she was sure that trouble was brewing.

First she found her closest brother, Bry. He was her age, twelve, for they were twins. They told each other everything, just as Ned and Jes did, though they did not yet have any secrets as great as those of their older siblings. Bry was in the garden, picking bugs off the cabbages.

"Big family meeting, right now," she cried. "You fetch the men; I'll fetch the women."

"No, we'll fetch together," Bry said, standing and brushing off his shirt. "So you can tell me what this is all about."

"It's because of some official Roman letter Ittai got. A mounted messenger delivered it; I just showed him in to see Ittai. He says it's mischief, and he'll have to go to reason with them. That's all I know."

"Where's the messenger?"

"Jes took him to the kitchen to feed him. He has to wait for Ittai's response, so he can take it back."

"Ittai's treating his wife like a servant?" Bry asked with the hint of a sneer in his voice.

"He had to. She was male." They both laughed, appreciating how Jes fooled visitors by acting like a boy. The not-so-long-married couple had been preparing to ride out around the estate when the messenger arrived.

"You know," Bry said, "I'm glad she married him. We'd have been in trouble, otherwise."

She nodded. Their family had fallen on lean times, and when their big brother Sam's estate had been taken over by the conquering Romans, things had looked bleak indeed. But Jes had found Ittai, and gotten him to ask for this particular estate as his land grant. Because he was a prominent Citizen of Rome and a ranking military officer, with solid military credits, his wish had been granted without question. So he had come as the new owner, but instead of running them off or requiring them to serve him as slaves, he had simply asked for their loyalty. A loyalty he was prepared to return, as a family member. They had sized him up and quickly agreed. As a result, there were no Roman soldiers to enforce estate discipline; Flo and Dirk ran things as they always had. That left Ittai free to ride around with his wife, whom he clearly loved regardless of her dress, and to participate in Roman politics. When any Roman appeared, they all deferred in an obvious manner to the centurion, and indeed he was the head of this hierarchy, but there was no friction. They had nothing to fear from the Romans, in contrast to their neighbors, and Ittai's connections and wealth brought them benefits they would otherwise have lacked. So Ittai was actually no liability; he was contributing in his fashion to the welfare of the family. Jes had not only gotten rid of their liability, Sam's former wife Wona; Jes had become their salvation by marrying surprisingly and extremely well. She had seemed the least likely prospect for such a thing. That was part of what was in the centurion's favor: he had recognized Jes's worth, and accepted her as she was. A woman who liked looking like a man, at times, but who was very much female inside.

They arrived at the wall that Sam was constructing. There had been some depredations by wild pigs and so they were walling off this section, to protect their delicate vines. Snow was helping him, placing small stones in the chinks to hold the big ones in place. Sam liked this heavy work; it gave him brute exercise. Lin liked Snow; she was a nice person, and she shared this family's propensity for a prominent defect: her body was lovely, but her face was downright homely. It was Lin's hand rather than her face that was defective, but she related well.

"Family meeting," Bry called as they approached. "Ittai thinks there's going to be trouble."

Snow grimaced. "We've seen enough of that already." It was an understatement, for her own life; her entire village had been destroyed in a raid, and only Sam's presence had saved her from death. Sam had unknowingly done himself a giant favor when he saved her. He had in effect exchanged a woman who was ugly inside for one who was ugly of face, and became far happier.

They ran on to locate and notify Dirk and Flo, then found Ned. Before long all of them were assembled at the main house.

Ittai was quite serious. "The brute procurator is set to make an example of the Iceni," he said. "He intends to cow them into complete submission by destroying their royal family in the course of the provincialization of the kingdom. Their queen Boudica will be demoted to servitude. I am directed to attend, as a gesture of Roman unity in this matter."

Jes shook her head. "Queen Boudica will never submit to that. There'll be rebellion if they try. The Iceni are fierce."

The others nodded. Their own tribe, the Trinovantes, had had their brushes with their neighbors to the north, before the Roman conquest, and knew their mettle. There had been peace only because the Iceni had remained nominally independent as a client kingdom, with their own leadership in place. Roman support had enabled the Iceni to gain advantage over other neighbors and to prosper. But if the Romans now proposed to humiliate Boudica, the widow of their king, there would be mischief indeed.

"I shall try to persuade the procurator of the folly of this step," Ittai said. "But he is a greedy and pig-headed man, and I fear I will not be successful. So while it would be a betrayal of my status as a Roman to suggest that any royal

Iceni try to escape while they can, it may be that someone will convey some such warning to them.''

Lin saw Ned smile, and Jes, and then the others. Someone would certainly warn the queen of the Iceni, if she had not already gotten news.

"I must attend, but there is no reason to let the estate be idle," Ittai continued. He glanced at Sam. "I trust you and Flo can handle things in my absence." He always gave Sam nominal precedence in the family, though they all knew that it was Flo Sam listened to, and Dirk who made most of the decisions, after consulting with Ned.

"Yes," Sam said.

"I think Bry and Lin should come with me, along with my wife, of course. But it is probably best to travel as a party of four males."

Lin smiled. She could pretend to be a boy readily enough, as she had not yet flowered into a woman. She had done so before. She knew she would enjoy the adventure.

Ittai wrote out a message, rolled and sealed the scroll, and gave it to Lin to give to the messenger. They would set out on the next day, and be there by the end of the third day hence.

Lin was excited. She had never before been to the capital city of the Iceni. She knew that Bry was similarly thrilled. It should be a great adventure, even if they only tagged along to act as servants to Ittai and Jes.

"We'll have to be the ones to warn the queen," Bry said.

That was right, because most of the rest of the family wasn't coming. That made it twice as exciting.

They rode out next day, all garbed as males, riding good horses. Ittai wore his centurion uniform, and looked very bold. He was retired, but Lin knew that no Roman ever retired completely; he could always be recalled to service in an emergency. As he had been, in effect, this time. He surely had not been required to attend just for his appearance; the procurator wanted a competent officer present, just in case the situation got complicated.

Soon enough the long ride became dull, as they passed

field after field, and forest after forest, and village after village. Lin managed to snooze on the horse. She was glad when they paused for a luncheon from their saddlebags, and glad when they came to an inn for the night. Ittai and Jes got a good room, posing as a Roman traveler and his lackey. Bry and Lin had to sleep in the stable with the horses, of course, but there was a point to that: to be sure that neither their goods nor the horses themselves were stolen. They did get a good supper inside, at least. Bry covered for Lin when she went out back for a natural function; she was garbed as a boy, and didn't want anyone seeing her where it counted. He had a good deal of sympathy, she knew, because of the time he had had to masquerade as a girl.

In three days they came to the Iceni capital. Now Jes had to resume female aspect, so as to be introduced to the procurator with her husband. Bry and Lin took the horses to the stable reserved for the Romans, and saw to their well-being. There were many other horses already there; a surprising number of Romans had come in. Then they returned to attend the centurion.

"The formal meeting is tomorrow," Ittai said, glancing at them. "Perhaps you boys have other business in the interim."

Oh, yes: they had to warn the queen that there was real mischief afoot, in the off chance she didn't already know it. They went back out into the town.

The queen's residence was clear enough; it was the grandest structure in the settlement. But it was well guarded, and the guards were not about to let two stray boys in. However, they were prepared. Lin changed into female garb, with gloves on her hands to cover her fingers, and they approached in humble fashion.

The gate guard frowned. "What do you want, child?"

Lin smiled. She was young, but knew she was very pretty in the face. "My brother and I have a gift for the younger princess," she said. "May we see her?"

"No." The guard turned away.

"Thank you," Lin said sweetly, and slipped by him. Bry followed.

"Hey!" The guard turned, but the two were already well inside the compound. He surely realized that it could be difficult to catch two children, and he didn't care to make a scene for nothing. What could they do? There were other guards inside; let them stop the intruders, who were probably harmless anyway.

In this manner they passed a second guard. But the third would have none of it. Lin smiled again, most winsomely, she hoped. It was fun practicing her womanly wiles, which she hoped would be truly effective when she matured. "We have this fine necklace for the princess. Please, sir, let us give it to her; then we will be on our way, we promise."

"No! Begone before I cudgel you."

But another figure appeared, and the guard hesitated. It was a richly garbed young woman not far beyond Lin's own age. Lin could not help admiring her dress and hair. This was clearly a person of note, despite her youth. "What is it?" she inquired.

"Oh, Princess!" Lin exclaimed, making what she hoped was not too great an assumption. "I have a gift for you!" She held up the necklace.

"Why thank you," the princess said, accepting it. "I am Wildflower, daughter of Queen Boudica. Who are you?"

"Lin, servant to Centurion Ittai."

The princess glanced sharply at her. "A Roman?"

"And I bring a message," Lin said quickly. "I hear things, because they don't notice servants. The Romans are planning mischief. You and the queen must flee."

The princess laughed. "They wouldn't dare."

Lin shook her head. "Please, Princess Wildflower! I heard my master say that the procurator was a greedy and pig-headed man who wants to make an example. Please get clear of him while you can."

"I don't care how greedy and piggish he is," the princess said with a toss of her locks. "All Romans are that way.

Mother simply will not allow any foolishness. The Romans are here by our sufferance, and if they get difficult, we'll throw them out. Mother will establish that at the meeting tomorrow. She will be very firm.''

''But—''

Wildflower smiled patronizingly. ''I'm sure you mean well, and I thank you for the nice necklace; I'll wear it tomorrow. But you haven't seen Mother in action. No one tells her no.''

Lin saw that it was hopeless. ''Please, at least tell her,'' she said. ''So she will be prepared, just in case. I hope you're right.''

''Of course I'm right.'' The princess turned away and disappeared into a hall.

''Well, we tried,'' Bry said consolingly.

''We tried,'' Lin echoed.

They walked on out, and the guards ignored them.

The next day the big meeting was held in the public square. The Romans were there first, and Lin was in attendance on Centurion Ittai, who looked appropriately splendid. He also looked grim, because the procurator had indeed not listened to reason. An added signal of mischief was the fact that Jes was back in male garb, and armed. They were just spectators, but they just might have to fight their way out.

Lin looked around. There were many Roman troops present, armed and armored, with their long spears held vertical and their massive shields reaching from the ground to their waists. One of the things about the Romans, Lin knew, was that they were well equipped and disciplined.

The royal kinsmen of the Iceni walked down the street. They were men of middling age in good cloth robes. They took their places around the square, forming a kind of central enclosure.

It was only a short distance from the royal mansion, but Queen Boudica arrived in style. She rode a fancy wagon drawn by two spirited horses, with her two daughters flanking her. One was Wildflower, fair and smiling, and Lin saw with pleasure that she was wearing the necklace. The other girl was about a year older, dark-haired and sullen. Both were pretty and richly garbed, wearing diadems.

The queen was another matter. She was huge of frame, with a glowering aspect. A great mass of dark red hair fell to her knees, seeming to curl around her body like a separately living thing. She wore a great necklace of twisted gold, and a many-colored tunic under a thick mantle fastened by a brooch. She glared around at the assembled Romans, as if to destroy them with her mere gaze, but they were impassive.

The wagon halted, and servants hastened to assist the queen and her daughters down. Boudica marched to the throne set up in the center of the square and took her place, while the daughters stood on either side. "Well?" she demanded. Her voice was harsh.

The procurator stepped forward. "Are you prepared to repay the loan Rome gave to your people, and turn over the reins of government to Rome, according to the treaty?"

"By no means," the queen said imperiously. "My husband King Prasutagus left the kingdom to Emperor Nero and my two daughters. Until they are of age to reign, I act in my daughters' stead, and my word is law among the Iceni. You will have no money, and no reins of power. Now that that is settled, begone; your presence annoys me."

"This is not the correct answer," Catus responded. "If you will not turn over the money and the reins voluntarily, I shall take them regardless. Now I ask you again, are you ready to do your duty by Rome?"

Boudica stood. "I have no duty by Rome. I spit on Rome!" And she spat at the procurator. The gob missed, but the Roman flinched. "Now get away from here before I have my minions flog you for your impertinence."

"Oops," Jes murmured, next to Lin.

"It is you who are impertinent," Catus said. "And now

you will feel the consequence of your arrogance.'' He turned and lifted one hand in an evident signal.

Suddenly more Roman troops appeared, pouring out of the surrounding houses. They charged into the square, shoving the kinsmen aside. In a moment they took hold of Boudica herself, and her daughters.

"What is this?'' the queen shouted. "You can't touch the royal persons! I'll have you sacrificed to the gods!''

"Strip her and flog her,'' Catus said coldly.

"What!'' the queen screamed piercingly. "I'll see you flayed for this!''

The kinsmen tried to come to her rescue, but the Roman soldiers lifted their spears threateningly. It was clear that the Roman force was overwhelming.

Lin watched with horror as the men systematically stripped Boudica of her clothing and threw it aside. Both daughters screamed and tried to help her, but this only attracted attention to them, and now they too were stripped. Then the men tied the queen's wrists together with rope and hauled them up over her head under a temporary wooden frame so that she was hoisted almost off her feet. One soldier brought out a whip and laid it across her back and bottom.

Boudica screamed, more in outrage than in pain. "I'll kill you! I'll kill you all!''

"Ten lashes,'' Catus said, and turned away.

Lin was too appalled to watch further. But when she looked to the side, she saw what was happening to the two daughters. They were both naked and struggling, the elder with nascent breasts, the younger without—and both were being raped by the soldiers.

"No!'' Lin cried in absolute horror. She started to run toward them, but Jes turned and caught her in both arms, lifting her off her feet. "Don't get yourself raped too!'' she hissed.

In a moment Lin realized that it was true. She would only

get herself similarly stripped and brutalized. She had to stand and tolerate this atrocity.

Soon it was done. The Romans marched off, taking several of the kinsmen with them, to be sold into slavery. Boudica and her daughters were left behind, dumped on the pile of their clothing, all three of them suffering similarly. "After this, you will behave," Catus said smugly as he departed.

"I must go to them," Lin said.

"No," Jes said. "You want no association with this. We must leave this area swiftly."

"For sure," Ittai agreed. "There will be Hades to pay."

They made their way back home with all due haste. Because they traveled swiftly and mostly incognito, the ominous stirring of the folk of the region did not touch them. But a dark tide was rising.

That tide continued through the winter. There was news of Queen Boudica and her daughters visiting the various tribes of Britain and enlisting their participation in the coming rebellion. The Romans might not recognize her as queen of the Iceni, but other tribes clearly did. There were meetings with the Coritani, Cornovii, Durotriges, Catuvellauni, Brigantes, Dubunni, and others, and of course the Iceni and Trinovantes, where Lin's family lived. There was no rebellion, yet, but everyone knew it was coming. Everyone except the Romans.

"I don't want to know!" Ittai protested. "I am a Roman officer; my loyalty is to Rome, however shabbily her minions may behave. If war comes, I must serve with Rome."

"Then why don't you go warn Rome?" Jes asked in the presence of the other family members.

"Because the idiots wouldn't heed me before, and won't next time."

"So there's nothing you can do anyway. So what's the harm in knowing?"

Ittai stared at her. "Are you thinking like a man or a woman?" he demanded.

Everyone laughed. But then Jes got serious. "I'm thinking like a settler who doesn't want to see her lands ravaged by either side. How can we avoid being regarded as an enemy by someone?"

Ned nodded. "We need representatives in both camps. I think we are protected from the Romans, but not necessarily from the Celts."

"So maybe we should attend the secret meeting they are having next week in—"

Ittai stood. "I have business elsewhere," he said gruffly. He was serious about not wanting to know.

Jes shrugged. "Of course, dear. I will join you." She got up and followed him out. But at the door she paused, speaking over her shoulder. "Just give me time to get my clothes off."

They all laughed again. The centurion was preserving his official ignorance of anything un-Roman, and his wife was supporting him in that, as she, too, was now legally Roman. She had let the others know that the two would not be returning for a reasonable time. As long as it took to make leisurely love.

"She really likes being a woman," Flo remarked appreciatively. They all knew how little chance Jes had seemed to have of such a relationship. Now she was reveling in it.

Ned shook his head. "I envy my sister her happiness." Then he glanced significantly at Snow. "And my brother his." Snow obligingly blushed, as the laughter continued. They all liked her very well. "But about that meeting: they know us all, and that we do get along with our Roman proprietor. They won't trust us. It may not be safe for us to attend."

There was a pause. Distrust could indeed be dangerous. The outrage of the Britons was great, and anyone they perceived as enemy or spy could be summarily killed.

Lin steeled herself and spoke. "I could do it," she said, her voice tight with nervousness.

Flo shook her head. "They know you as well as any of us. You were at the flogging."

"Yes. I met Princess Wildflower. And saw her raped. But I tried to warn her. Maybe she—she will protect me. If I go. If she's there."

"Even so, she will know you for a spy," Ned said. "She has no love at all for Romans."

"But maybe—maybe she wouldn't want to see me hurt, any more than I wanted to see her hurt. So if I told her I just wanted to try to keep it from happening to us—" She saw the doubt in their faces, and halted.

There was a pause. Then Flo spoke. "Still, we do need a connection. If Lin is willing to take the risk—"

"A risk of death!" Bry protested.

"A risk we all may face, if Queen Boudica's forces deem us an enemy," Flo said.

There was another pause. Lin knew that they did not want to push her into taking such a risk. But she knew the possible consequence if she didn't. The Celts would be no more gentle than the Romans had been, and they had a keen sense of justice. How well they all knew that, being Celts themselves!

"I'll do it," she said, more firmly than she felt.

Flo nodded. "You have courage." That was a considerable compliment, because Flo did not make empty statements.

The meeting was in the nearby town, Camulodunum, the major settlement of the Trinovantes, where Lin was not well known. That helped. Because if she were recognized, she could be in trouble. The Romans governed the town, but a number of prominent Britons had reassured the officials that all was well, so they were not alert to the real nature of the gathering. All known associates of the Romans were rigorously excluded, unless they had suitable credentials as true patriots of the land.

It turned out that though Boudica herself was elsewhere, her daughters would indeed attend the meeting. It seemed that these things carried more conviction if one of the victims of the Roman atrocity was present. That was what Lin needed to know. She dressed in male guise and had no trouble getting in; she was obviously a young Briton.

The hall was crowded. There was no formal program; instead there was a rising tide of emotion. Lin realized why: they did not dare speak openly of rebellion, because word would get out to the Romans, who would then ruthlessly suppress it. But they were fomenting a general emotional state that would make rebellion easier to accept when the time came.

An old woman cried out dire prophecies of doom and desolation. "Have we not seen the statue of Victory fall and lie face down on the ground, presenting its back in surrender," she cried, in a thinly veiled allusion to the Romans. "Have we not seen apparitions in the Thames? Blood-red tides, washing things ashore that resemble human corpses?" She spoke metaphorically, for the Thames did not flow through Camulodunum. But they had all heard the spooky stories. It was easy to believe that there had indeed been such omens elsewhere.

"Yes! Yes!" others echoed.

Then a man started speaking in tongues, sing-songing unintelligible words. Others hummed, and keened, and the level of sound rose. Lin felt herself being tugged by the feeling of it, but fought it, because she was here for another purpose. Her sympathies were with the Britons of course, but before she could yield to them she had to accomplish her mission.

She moved among the people, searching for the princess. Apparently the girl was taking no active part in the event, merely lending it authenticity by her presence.

Lin spied her, standing between two stout men. She approached diffidently. "Princess—" she began.

One of the men reached out and caught her arm. "What's this? A spy?"

"No!" Lin cried. "I'm a friend of Princess Wildflower! I tried to save her! I gave her a necklace!" She tore off her close cap and let her hair fall free.

Now the princess's eyes widened with recognition. "You were the one! You warned me, but I did not listen." She glanced at the guard, and he immediately let Lin go. "But why do you come to me now? Is there a spy here to kill me?"

"No," Lin said quickly. "None that I know of. It is for myself I come. I must beg a favor of you, Princess."

"You come to one who was ravished and demeaned and made powerless, for a favor?"

"Oh, Princess, you know I serve a Roman master. All other Romans deserve destruction, but this one has been good to us. Please, please, spare him."

"What authority do you think I have, that I can help a Roman?"

"If your mother tells them to bypass his estate, which is our estate—"

Wildflower pursed her lips. "It is hard for me to speak favor of any Roman."

"I know. I—I saw what they did to you. I don't want it to happen to me. But it was our Roman who bid me warn you of the danger."

The princess's mouth fell slightly open. "*He* bid you?"

"He said the procurator was out to make an example. He said he, as a Roman, could not speak against it, but if some-one else did—"

"So you came to me," Wildflower agreed, nodding. "I dismissed your warning, and paid a hideous price. It was a folly I will never forget. Very well: this time I will heed your words. I will speak to my mother. But tell your Roman to stay on his land, because if he ventures from it, there will be no recourse."

"I will! I will! Oh, thank you, Princess! Thank you!" Lin

dropped to her knees and kissed Wildflower's hand.

"Don't thank me," Wildflower said, embarrassed. "My mother may not listen." Then she drew her hand away. "What is his name?"

"Centurion Ittai."

"I will see. But I don't know. Mother is extremely angry."

But Lin was satisfied. She had obtained the commitment she had come for.

The revolt came suddenly, while Governor Suetonius Paulinus was campaigning in Wales, conquering the Druid stronghold at Mona. Most of the Roman forces were with him in the west, leaving almost nothing to counter the uprising in the east. The Roman forces were caught wildly unprepared. The family received news from the Britons who rushed to join the fray, and Romans who were dismayed by it.

Centurion Ittai had sent word to the authorities in Camulodunum to expect trouble, and to shore up the Roman defenses, but he had been ignored, as expected. Now the Romans were desperate. They sent to Londinium for reinforcements, but Procurator Catus sent only 200 men.

Meanwhile Queen Boudica's army marched on the city, numbering perhaps a hundred thousand men. The town was without fortifications, and had few strong points. The Britons quickly captured it and burned it. The defenders made a final stand in the Temple of Claudius, holding out for two days before the building was stormed. They were slaughtered.

As soon as the sacking was finished, Boudica's army prepared to move southwest toward Londinium. But first it moved northwest. It bypassed the region where Lin's family lived, and Lin knew that Princess Wildflower's intercession was responsible. Instead it went to meet a force of five thousand Romans from Lindum, all that they could muster on short notice. The Britons ambushed the column along the margin of the fens. The Roman infantry was cut to pieces. Only the cavalry managed to return to Lindum. Thus the only force in eastern Britain capable of meeting Boudica in the field had been decimated.

Then the action got more immediate. Centurion Ittai received orders from Governor Suetonius: he was being reactivated, and had to join Suetonius in Londinium forthwith.

"I was afraid of this," Ittai said ruefully. "That idiot Catus set off an uprising that is a major embarrassment to Rome, and now I must participate. I am a naval officer, not a commander of land forces, but when Rome is in peril, all must serve as they are able. I will deed the estate to my wife, in the event I do not return."

"Oh no you don't!" Jes protested. "I'm not sending you out alone to die! I'm going with you."

"But women are not allowed in combat."

"But officers have young male squires."

He looked at her. "I will die in the service of Rome if that is required of me, but I do not want my wife put at unnecessary risk. You are young, and—"

"You are part of my family now," Jes said. "You have saved our estate; we look after you too. Someone must go with you, and it ought to be me."

"But—"

"Suppose you are killed in battle, and we get no word? We would not know what to do. One of us must be with you."

It was clear that Ittai did not want Jes along, and not because he did not love her. He wanted her well away from danger. "There is merit in what you say," he said slowly. "But have you considered this: If you are with me, you are at increased risk of dying too. If we both die, the estate will be lost, because I can deed it only to my wife, not a native. Rome recognizes such rights only for its citizens. Then your whole family will suffer. Have you the right to put your brothers and sisters at such unnecessary risk?"

Jes froze. He had scored. This was the one time she should not be with him. The others were nodding agreement.

"Another family member can accompany me," Ittai said, following up his advantage. "One who can be spared, no offense to any of you. Perhaps Bry."

"He is working on the wall with Sam," Flo said. "In these troubled times, we need that wall finished soon."

"I'll do it," Lin said.

Both Ittai and Jes frowned. "A girl in battle conditions—" Ittai started.

"Untrained in weapons—" Jes continued.

"A boy. A squire," Lin said quickly. "And I know the princess."

"What has that to do with it?" Ittai demanded.

"I got her to have her mother bypass this region," Lin said. "If you get wounded, maybe I can get her to get her mother to spare you." It was far-fetched, but all she could think of at the moment.

But Jes accepted it. "That just might work. Anything that promotes my husband's likely survival—"

"I don't want to share close quarters with my wife's little sister," Ittai said. "The propriety—"

"She's a child," Flo said. "There is no—"

"She's a lovely nascent young woman."

That caught Lin by surprise. She blushed.

"She is that," Ned said.

The others looked to Jes. She considered for a moment, then decided. "I trust my husband, and my sister. Go."

But now Lin wasn't sure. "I never—"

Ittai lifted his hands in surrender. "We have no time for such debate. Perhaps I spoke inappropriately. Pass as a boy, Lin, and I will treat you as one."

"And don't let him be seduced by any camp followers," Jes said with a rueful smile.

Now Ittai was embarrassed. "I never—"

Then they all laughed. It was decided.

They rode out next morning, on good horses. Lin was

garbed as a squire, and Ittai referred to her as male from the outset, so as never to slip and give her away. Londinium was a day's easy ride distant, so they did not have to hurry, but they did have to keep moving.

"We must establish some rules of association," Ittai said as they paused to eat and to water the horses. "I must keep you close, which means we must share quarters, but I prefer that there be no embarrassment to either of us."

"Treat me with the unconscious contempt due a young servant," she said. "It's the only safe way."

"In public, yes. I'm glad you understand. But in private—"

"The same. The land has ears."

"And if there is violence, warn me and get clear. You will guard my possessions and carry messages, and otherwise be invisible."

"Yes, sir." She knew this mission was dangerous, but she was rather enjoying it. Had it been like this when Jes first met him?

"And keep your gloves on. By my order, if anyone asks."

"Yes, sir." This went beyond possible embarrassment. If any stranger saw her sixth finger, in this troubled time, it might be taken as an omen of evil, leading to instant mayhem.

They reached Londinium in the evening. It was a huge city, bigger than anything she had seen before; it just spread out and out. It was also a worried city, because the people knew that Boudica's terrible army was on its way. Would the Romans be able to defend it?

They rode to the garrison headquarters. It was in near panic. Ittai identified himself to the harried magistrate there. "Where is Procurator Catus Decianus?" Ittai demanded. "I must report to him."

"Sir, he departed this morning for the continent, with his staff, family, and belongings."

Ittai swore a mighty oath. "So the rat deserts the ship, his own folly holed!"

"If you say so, sir," the magistrate said, trying to suppress a bitter smile. He could not speak thus of his superior, but he could appreciate it when a higher officer did.

"Where is Governor Suetonius?"

"On the way, sir. We expect him tomorrow."

"Who is your ranking officer?"

"I am, sir. Or rather, you are, now."

Ittai swore again. It was a delight to listen to. "I know nothing of the defenses or apparatus here. Carry on as best you can, and I will report to Suetonius when he arrives. Just assign me a room for the night."

"There are plenty available, sir. Perhaps you should take Catus's former residence."

"That surely will be considerably more than adequate."

Indeed it was. The procurator's residence was palatial, with a frightened staff left without order. Ittai gave some, and they obeyed eagerly, glad for some semblance of restored order. He and Lin had a fairly good evening meal, with her tasting each item of his food first. This was a standard precaution against possible poisoning, and it showed the servants the nature of their relationship. Should she get suddenly sick, there would be a savagely enraged officer to fear. Not because of any value of the squire, but because of the effort to assassinate the officer.

Fortunately there was no problem. After the meal, Lin managed to talk with some of the servants, who naturally took her for one of them, and learned that the wife of one of the fleeing officials had been a beautiful woman named Wona. Lin concealed her surprise. It was surely the same woman they had known, once Sam's faithless wife. Wona was evidently in the kind of company she liked.

Ittai stretched, and retired to the sumptuous bedchamber suite, followed meekly by the squire. "Disgusting," he muttered as he looked around. "The toad certainly treated himself well."

"I'll sleep on a blanket by the door," Lin said.

"No, just block it with something, and take the bed in

the other room. It has its own bath facilities.''

"But—"

"When Queen Boudica gets here, all this will be burned. We might as well get some use of it.''

She nodded and took the alternate room. This meant that she was able to strip and wash without concern. This continued to be a fine adventure, heightened by the tension of coming violence.

The cavalry arrived next day, led by Governor Suetonius. Ittai reported, but the governor was tired and distracted. "Is Poenius Postumus here?" he demanded. "He was supposed to rendezvous with me outside the city, but we didn't see him.''

"He is not here,'' Ittai said.

"And the procurator?''

"Fled to the continent yesterday, with his family and possessions.''

"What are our resources?''

"Only those you bring with you, sir.''

"And the enemy?''

"Closing fast.''

Suetonius made a gesture as of tearing his hair. "We have neither time nor resources to organize a defense. Do we have even the capability to evacuate?''

"No, sir.''

"Then we must abandon the city. It's a black day for Rome.''

"Black, indeed,'' Ittai agreed. "And for Londinium.''

"I will assemble those citizens who can provide their own mounts, and take them into my column. Take some men and burn the city's grain stores. Anything beyond what you can carry conveniently out with you. Then join me in my ignominious retreat.''

"Done, sir.'' Ittai saluted and got to work.

They loaded grain on their horses, then lit torches and set fire to the granary. Lin felt horribly adventurous and evil as she wielded her torch, knowing that this act meant likely starvation for many, but this was the nature of war. She watched the fire rise, fascinated despite, or because of, her horror of its significance.

They rejoined Suetonius as the smoke piled into the sky. "Just in time," the governor muttered. "The woman's minions are already entering the city. Had they been one day earlier, we would have been done for."

As they made their way out of the city, it seemed to Lin that she could hear the angry roar of the Britons, furious that their prey had escaped. And in the following days, the reports of the savagery Queen Boudica visited on the city were horrendous. It was apparent that vengeance and violence, not wealth or power, were the chief goals of the Celts. There had been some hope that the queen would hold the city for ransom, therefore not harming it much, but she did not. The population, guilty because it had been satisfied under Roman rule, was slaughtered by gibbet, fire, and cross. There was a mass sacrifice of women in the sacred groves of Andrasta, the goddess of war and fertility. Nearby cities were also sacked. It did not matter if the inhabitants were Celts rather than Romans; they received no mercy at the hands of the rebels.

Lin had had much sympathy for the Britons, who were after all her people, especially since she had seen the Roman brutality toward Boudica and her daughters. But this faded as the dreadful reports came in. At least Romans had not slaughtered Romans, and their brutality had been narrowly targeted. In contrast, anyone of either camp close to Queen Boudica was in deadly danger. Her violence had become pointless, as there was no vengeance to be had from the actual perpetrators, Catus and his guards.

By the time Boudica's forces moved out of Londinium, reliable estimates put the total number of those slaughtered at 70,000 people. And of course immense damage had been done to the physical city. All because the queen had been flogged, and her daughters raped.

Meanwhile Suetonius had been marshaling his scant

forces. Between the defeats already suffered, and the abdication or mutiny of lieutenants, he was able to gather only the pitifully small force of 10,000 infantry and cavalry. Boudica moved out of Londinium with a force perhaps ten times that size, intent on catching the Romans and destroying the last vestige of their power in Britain. This was to be the final showdown.

"Perhaps it is time for you to return home," Ittai told Lin. "You have been a good squire, but there is no need for you to participate in what is coming."

He wanted her to carry word of the disaster back to the family, so that they would know which side to back, and thus avoid likely mischief. He also did not want her to see what was about to happen.

But she couldn't do it. "The battle has not yet been fought," she said bravely. "So my job is not yet done."

"But once it starts, there may be no escape. You know how the queen's army is."

She knew. But she couldn't simply flee, leaving him to his likely fate. "I must stay until I know."

He sighed. "You remind me of your sister."

"Thank you."

"But perhaps I have an alternative. You may be able to witness the battle from a safer vantage."

"Safer?"

"You know the princess. Go to her."

"But—"

"The queen has kept her daughters with her during the campaign. They suffered as sorely as she did. Their presence incites the masses to further mayhem. They share her command tent."

"I know. But—"

"The princess will want you to watch the battle. She will reject your plea, but she will accept your presence, because of what you tried to do for her. Her mother should spare you, to carry the news home. It will represent vindication for the Celts."

"But not for me!" Lin protested, tears flowing.

He shrugged. "What will be, will be. At least we will be better assured that you will return safely home."

She had to go. It did make sense. Her mission was to report to her family, whatever the nature of the news, and this would facilitate it. It was risky, approaching the princess, but not as risky as remaining with the Roman force.

So that night she left, going quietly in the boy role she had perfected. The Roman sentries did not challenge her.

The Celtic camp was a far more boisterous thing. It had sentries, but they were drinking and carousing, hardly paying attention. Indeed, what did they have to worry about? A surprise attack by the tiny Roman force? So it was easy to enter the camp, and to locate the palatial tent of the queen. It was in a separate compound in the center of the camp.

She approached the guard. This one was alert; Boudica was taking no chances with her own person. "I need to see Princess Wildflower," Lin said timidly.

"She is too young to accept a lover," he said.

But not too young to be raped. "I am no lover," she said, drawing off her cap as she had before.

"The Roman's girl!" he exclaimed, recognizing her by reputation. "You she will see."

Princess Wildflower came out. "Lin! What are you doing here?"

"I come to plead for the life of—"

Wildflower's mouth turned hard. "No. I told you he had to keep to his own demesnes. All Romans in Britain must die."

"I had to try," Lin said. That was no lie; she wished she could have gained her brother-in-law another reprieve. But there would be no reprieve here.

"Come in," the princess said. "But you may not bring a weapon inside. I must search you."

"I have only a knife," Lin said, bringing it out and proffering it hilt first.

"Even so. I believe you, but my mother has strict orders.'' She drew Lin into a lesser tent, where a candle burned. "Strip."

Lin complied. In a moment she stood naked. She wished her body had developed, because she felt worse naked as a child than she would have naked as a woman.

Wildflower brought out a feminine robe, which Lin donned. Then she noticed the gloves. "Them, too."

Reluctantly, Lin drew them off. Her malformed hands was exposed.

The princess stared. "Oh, I didn't know! I'm sorry. There could have been a weapon—a spike or something. But you will have to leave the gloves off. My mother will have to see."

"I—I would rather not meet your mother."

Wildflower laughed. "Nobody wants to meet my mother. But it must be. Come." She drew Lin after her, to the larger tent.

Queen Boudica was there, huge and fearsome. Her red hair swirled about her, and her eyes glittered in the candle-light.

"Mother, this is Lin—the girl who tried to warn us."

"The Roman girl!" the queen exclaimed, looking ferocious. Her voice was loud and harsh. Lin quailed.

"The Celt girl who begged us to flee the Romans," Wildflower said firmly. "But we wouldn't listen."

"So what is she warning us about this time? To flee the battle lest we be destroyed?"

Lin tried to speak, but could not.

"She came to beg mercy for the Roman."

Boudica laughed. "Plead mercy for yourself, girl; you were a fool to come here." She drew a knife with a wickedly shining blade.

Wildflower stepped in front of her. "Mother—I granted her sanctuary. She's my friend."

"She's a creature of the Romans!" Boudica made a threatening step.

"Mother!"

The queen relented. "Oh, very well. But she must make an oath of peace and friendship."

Wildflower turned to Lin. "See, she likes you." Even the queen had to smile, briefly, at that. "Will you make the oath?"

"But—but I am loyal to—"

"Yes. If you are loyal to your own, you will be loyal to those you oath. You would never have come here, if you did not have courage and honor. My mother must be assured that you mean no harm to us."

Lin was amazed. "I—I—yes, I can make that oath." There was a pause, and she realized that she hadn't phrased it properly. "I do make that oath."

"Then take back your knife," Wildflower said, proffering it.

"But—"

"You are no threat to us now, are you?"

"No, of course not. But—"

"Take it," Boudica said impatiently.

Lin accepted her knife. "I—I thank you for your trust, Queen Boudica."

"Sit down and tell us why you are really here," the queen said, sitting herself. "As a friend would."

Lin took the indicated cushion. "My—the Roman didn't want me in his camp. He said that once the battle began, there would be no escape. I am sister to his wife, and he feared that harm would come to me."

"Centurion Ittai is bearing arms?" Boudica asked sharply.

"Yes. He was summoned, and he had to go."

"We spared him once, on condition that he stay clear of us," the queen said gravely. "Now he must die."

"He—he knows that. He said the procurator was an idiot who had set off the uprising, and a rat who deserted the ship his own folly had sunk. But he had to obey the order."

The queen did not seem fully displeased with this news. "There are qualities to be respected, even in a Roman. But if you went back and told him to depart tonight, avoiding the battle, would he go?''

"No. He obeys his orders."

"So he must die. He is too competent to spare."

Lin nodded sadly. "Yes."

"But he arranged for you to be spared," Wildflower said.

"Yes."

"You will watch the battle tomorrow," Boudica said. "If you see him go down, and if you can reach him before he dies, stand over him with this tassel, and he may yet be spared." She produced a large red section of intricately woven cloth.

"Oh, thank you, Queen Boudica!" Lin exclaimed, her tears flowing.

"It will probably be too late," the queen said gruffly, and turned away.

"Come," Wildflower said, and led Lin to another section of the compound tent.

Lin gazed at the tassel. "Why—?"

"Because you came before with the knowledge of the Roman. He knew what we did not, and tried to spare us. And when it happened, he faced away in disgust."

"How could you know that?"

"We saw you with him. We knew who he was. We saw how he hated what was happening. We saw that none of his party participated. We suffered for our own folly, not heeding him. My mother remembers her friends—and even her enemies, if they show conscience."

"So does Centurion Ittai."

"Yes. So probably he will die, but it will be with honor, and your estate will not be ravaged." Wildflower paused. "And I do thank you for what you tried to do for me. I was a fool, and I paid for it. Now no man will marry me, unless he is forced. My mother will not say that, but she knows. We will see that you return safely home."

"Thank you," Lin said faintly.

They settled down for bed and sleep. The tent was not as

opulent as the quarters in Londinium had been, but was much nicer than the ground outside would have been.

The next day the two forces arrayed for battle. Wildflower guided Lin to a large wagon set up behind the arrayed force of the Britons. It was in the center of a long line of carts and wagons and standing women. The wives of the soldiers had gathered to watch the slaughter of the hated Romans.

It took some time for the Celts to array their forces. There was much cursing and jostling. Lin also overheard complaints about the food: it seemed that there was not much to be had, because the Romans had destroyed the granaries before the Celts could occupy Londinium. But they were sure that there would be plenty, once the Romans had been dispatched.

Lin got up on the wagon as high as she could, trying to peer over the Celts to see the Romans. Wildflower and her sister joined her. They piled additional planks, making a taller platform, and then they were able to see all the way across the field to where the Romans were assembled. Their array looked pitifully small, backed up against a forest.

"They don't even have anywhere for their wagons to flee," Wildflower remarked.

"They don't intend to flee," Lin said.

The princess glanced at her with compassion. "They are brave, at any rate. It will be over soon."

Surely so. But now Lin remembered things about the Romans. How tough they were in close quarters, or on a field of their own choosing. How their equipment and discipline counted. She knew that Ittai, though not trained for land combat, was a competent commander of men, and excellent general strategist. Jes had told of his proficiency and courage in sea engagements. Lin remembered how Ittai had complimented Suetonius's ability in the field. These Romans were no longer fleeing; they had elected to stand on ground of their own choosing, and they would be tough.

But could they be tough enough? Could 10,000 Romans, no matter how well equipped and disciplined, possibly hold their own against a hundred thousand savage warriors? It didn't seem likely. Especially since the Celts wouldn't give any quarter. They were out to kill every Roman in Britain. Except possibly Ittai, if he fell and lay still, but wasn't killed outright. If she could get to him in time. And the queen hadn't promised him freedom, just life, maybe.

"I'm glad we aren't close enough to see the blood," Wildflower said. "We've seen enough of that already."

Surely so! This whole business had been so unnecessary, such a waste. All because of the arrogant coward Catus.

At last the Britons were ready. They were divided into tribal contingents. Their several forces of chariots charged forward, whooping savagely, eager to draw the first blood. Lin saw them sweep in several masses at the Roman lines, to hurl their javelins, trying to cause fear and confusion among the enemy troops. But the Romans didn't budge. They simply stood there at the top of a slight slope, evidently dispersing the chariot changes with concentrated fire from the archers in their auxiliaries. The chariots tried to get around the Roman flanks, but those were too well protected by rough terrain and the close forest. So there just didn't seem to be much way for the chariots to have effect. All they could do was swoop by, taunting the Romans, daring them to come out and get chopped to pieces, and retreat.

Finally the Celts decided to charge in a mass. Lin quailed, knowing that the troops on foot would not be turned aside by slopes or trees or even arrows; there were too many of them. They could take losses of thousands, and still overwhelm the defenders by sheer numbers.

The Romans did not move. Their lines remained still and straight as the ragged swarm surged close. Then, as the two forces almost converged, there was a hesitation.

"What happened?" Wildflower asked, perplexed.

"The Romans discharged their javelins at close range," Lin said. "They waited until the enemy was too close to avoid them."

Indeed, the front of the Celtic line seemed to shake, and

shake again, as the second barrage of javelins was hurled.

Then the Roman lines moved. "What's happening?" Wildflower asked, this time somewhat plaintively.

"The Roman infantry is advancing to attack," Lin said, relying on her memory of Roman tactics more than anything she could actually see. For now the two forces were merging, and the center was a mass of nothing distinguishable. But she knew that the Romans were charging in wedge formation, striking the Celtic lines in much the manner of a hammered peg, splintering it. Such contact was devastating, and the Celts would not be able to fight well. The Romans had short swords which were very good for stabbing in close quarters. The Celts had long slashing blades which were good when there was space, but almost as dangerous to friends as foes in tight places.

For a moment, Lin visualized a sea battle Ittai had described, where the more numerous enemy ships had gotten crowded together, unable to fight properly. The distantly seen motions of the land forces seemed to resemble that.

Then the Roman cavalry charged the Celtic flanks. The Celts, jammed in together, were unable to maneuver well, and could not effectively face the enemy.

"What's happening?" Wildflower asked once more, confused.

"The Romans are winning," Lin said, amazed. She was seeing it happen, yet she could hardly believe it.

"But how can that be? There are so few!"

"Better discipline, better equipment," Lin said wisely. These had been mere concepts to her before; now she appreciated their reality. Centurion Ittai would probably survive!

"But we have so many!"

"That's the problem. They are getting in each other's way." Then Lin saw something else. "Oops."

"What is it?" the princess asked, distracted.

"The Roman cavalry is coming here. We had better get clear in a hurry."

"But we can't go! Mother said—"

"She'll have to look out for herself. We're in trouble. Come on; jump off the wagon and flee away from the Romans. Both of you," she called, including the other princess.

"I'm not going," the other protested. "We *can't* lose."

"Then come on, Wildflower!" Lin cried, tugging the princess along with her as the horses charged up.

The two of them ran as fleetly as they could, hearing the thunder of the horses' hooves. Soon, breathless, they paused to look back.

The Romans were overturning the wagons and carts. The women were running and screaming, but they weren't being chased. That was another sign of a disciplined army: no plunder or rapine along the way. They were intent on winning the battle first. But why did they want to prevent the women from riding away?

Then it came clear. The Celtic army was now in confused retreat. It surged back toward the wagons—and couldn't pass them, because Roman archers were firing at them from the cover of the wagons, and the horsemen were patrolling immediately behind. It was a deadly trap.

A woman screamed. Lin looked, and saw her fall. The Romans were killing the women too!

"We must get away from here!" she said, and half dragged the princess into a second run.

They were not pursued, and soon were able to slow to a walk. They were safe, for the moment. But where were they to go now? No place would be safe for the princess, now that Rome had triumphed.

The decision was as swift as the question. "You must stay with me," Lin said. "We must get male clothing. When night falls, I'll take you to Centurion Ittai. He will protect you."

Vacant-eyed, Wildflower nodded. Lin realized that the princess had just suffered a second shock, perhaps as bad as when she had been raped and seen her mother flogged.

They were able to find clothing at a nearby deserted

house—possibly its master had been killed in the battle, or
merely fled the dangerous scene—and after dark Lin took
the princess to the Roman camp. A guard challenged them,
but she called out the password, and they were admitted.

"Lin!" Ittai cried, recognizing her as soon as she came
in sight. He was not even wounded. "I feared for you."
Then he paused, looking at Wildflower. "Who—"

"Another boy, just like me," Lin said quickly. "I promised sanctuary."

"Just like you," he repeated thoughtfully. "Then he had
better stay close to you, until we return home in a few days.
The family will decide."

By that token, he indicated that he knew the identity of
the princess, and would allow her to seek sanctuary with
the family. He had not approved of her raping, and would
not approve of her killing. And Lin was sure the family
would not turn her away, knowing that there would be no
safe place for her in Britain. Any more than there would
have been any safe place for Romans, had the battle gone
the other way.

But there was something they needed to know. "What
happened to the queen?" Lin asked him.

"She got away. We don't know what happened to her
daughters; they may be with her."

Lin saw Wildflower relax a trifle. At least she knew that
her mother still lived.

*The Roman historians reported 80,000 Celtic deaths,
compared to 400 Roman deaths, and a greater number
of casualties. The rebellion was over. The remaining
pockets of resistance were hunted out and extermi-
nated. The Iceni Queen Boudica escaped, but died soon
after; it is uncertain whether she poisoned herself or
was taken by disease. The fate of her two daughters is
unknown; they may have died, or may have faded into*

*anonymity. Rome maintained power in Britain until the
Roman Empire fragmented in the fifth century A.D. The
Angles, the Saxons, and the Jutes then invaded, and it
became Angle Land, or England.*

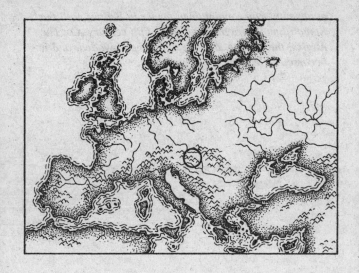

Chapter 13

SLAVE

In the sixth century A.D. the Roman Empire fell apart and was settled largely by "barbarian" tribes. But the Eastern Roman, or Byzantine, Empire survived, extending its hegemony over most of the eastern Mediterranean region. The westward surge of Mongol and Turkish tribes continued, and Slovenoi or Sclavini tribes moved west and south.

The Romans were as adept at playing barbarian politics as were the Chinese in the east. The emperor in Constantinople incited the Avars into action against other tribes that were harassing the borders of the empire. The Avars, nothing loath, quickly conquered the Bulgars, who were descendants of the Huns, and assimilated them into their own horde. Then they moved against the Antes and the Slavs. They defeated the former, but rather than war against the latter they made peace, because their real objective was to raid the richer Frankish kingdom beyond. Thus the Avar power extended through the large Slav territory, amicably. The Avars met the Franks to the west, but the Franks, under Sigibert, defeated them in battle. The Avars, under their new Khagan Bayan, beat the Franks in a second pitched battle, but Sigibert fared well enough to negotiate a peace and obtain Bayan's agreement to withdraw beyond the Elbe River.

The Avars then focused their attention farther to the east, allying with the Longobards (Lombards) to destroy the Germanic Gepid tribes in the modern region of Hungary. The Lombards then migrated into Italy, while Avars and Slavs filled in their former territories. Meanwhile the Slavs were raiding and looting Byzantine settlements in the Balkans, north of modern Greece, so the Roman emperor persuaded Bayan to march against his sometime allies. Bayan first asked them to submit willingly and pay tribute, but they rejected the notion and killed his envoys. This was of course asking for trouble. The Avars crossed the Danube and sacked several Slav villages. The Avars were horsemen, and the Slavs, fighting on foot, could not match them. But they avoided heavy losses by fading into the marshes and forests.

Later the fickle nature of politics made the Avars and Slavs allies again, as they raided Byzantine provinces. Some Slav tribes were independent, while others were treated as tyrannized subject peoples. Overall, they were definitely in the shadow of the Avars, forced to give way to them and pay tribute. It was not a situation the Slavs enjoyed, in the early seventh century. But what could they do?

The setting is just north of the Adriatic Sea, at the fringe of what is nominally the Eastern Roman Empire, in the mountains of what came to be modern day Austria, in the year A.D. 623.

THE FIRST THING SAM NOTICED about the prisoner was that he was a Frank. He was bedraggled and downcast, of course; he wore a collar of tough rope and his hands were tied behind him. His Avar captor would have yanked the rope tight enough to choke, at any sign of resistance. Captives learned very quickly to behave, or they died.

Sam himself had a nice gold vase, his booty from the successful raid on the Byzantine town. He had learned to be choosy, taking only what he could conveniently carry some distance home without tiring. Gold was the best for that. So he was well set.

Now he did something stupid. He joined the Avar, whom he did not know personally; Slavs as a rule did not cultivate the acquaintance of Avars, though they were nominally allies. "Mind if I share your fire a moment, before I trek home?"

The Avar looked up with annoyance, then his eye measured the size and muscle of the intruder. "Suit yourself, Slav." The Avar was chewing on dark bread.

Sam set his vase carefully in front of him, in the process turning it so that it reflected the light of the flames. He dug out his own dark bread and began to gnaw.

The Avar stared at the vase. "Where'd you find that? I couldn't find any gold."

"I poked into the crevices of a burned-out house. I thought something good might be hidden there, and I was right."

"You sure were! That thing is beautiful." He meant in terms of riches, not art; Avar raiders didn't care about art.

"But it's pretty heavy. Be a burden to carry all the way home. I see you don't have that problem."

The Avar laughed. "Right! My booty is mobile. But you got the better deal, Slav. You don't have to feed your gold."

Sam glanced at the prisoner, as if only now becoming aware of him. "I don't know. Sometimes they have skills that bring a good price on the slave market. Where's he from? He doesn't look Roman."

"I don't know. I didn't ask him. He speaks some foreign language."

"Maybe I can find out. May I question him?"

"Sure."

Sam addressed the prisoner. "What are you?" he asked in Slavic.

There was no response. "Answer him!" the warrior snapped, jerking on the rope.

The prisoner winced; it was clear that the rope chafed his neck, and he did not want more punishment. "Frank," he said. That meant that he had understood the Slavic words.

Sam spoke a little Frankish, learned from his wife.

"What is your skill?" he asked in somewhat halting Frankish.

"I am a trader."

"What's he saying?" the Avar asked.

"He says he's a trader."

"He's probably lying. Traders are smart."

"A trader?" Sam asked the prisoner. "How did you get taken captive?"

The Frank grimaced. "I was in the wrong place, the wrong time."

Sam translated that.

"For sure!" the warrior said, laughing. "Still, it would be nice if he is a trader; better price. Can you verify it?"

"I'll try," Sam said. "A trader should be able to put a fair price on this vase. You judge it, and we'll see if his price matches."

The Avar squinted at the vase. "May I heft it?"

"By all means."

The warrior picked up the vase, and tapped it with a knuckle before setting it down again.

"If you are a trader," Sam said to the Frank, "you should be able to price this vase. What is it worth?"

"Four bushels of wheat," the man replied promptly.

"But you didn't even heft it, or really look at it," Sam protested.

"Ask the Avar," the Frank said.

Sam turned to the Avar. "He says four bushels of wheat."

The man was surprised. "By Svarog, he's right!" the Avar said, swearing by a Slavic god. "That's how I priced it."

"How could you tell, without hefting it for weight?" Sam asked the Frank.

"I know my business. I have handled many such vases. I know such goods well."

Evidently so. "Are you literate?" Sam asked.

The Frank looked thoughtfully at him. "Are you pricing me?"

"My wife's Frankish."

The Frank nodded, understanding Sam's interest. A captor with a Frankish wife would likely be a better master than one who didn't even know the language. "Yes, I am literate."

Sam turned to the Avar. "He says he's literate, and has handled many such vases. That's how he knows the value."

The warrior nodded. "I heard."

"You understand his words?" Sam asked, surprised. "Then why did you have me translate?"

"To see if you were straight. Want to trade? Him for the vase?"

"Yes. We could use a literate man. But he may be worth more than the vase."

"Are you?" the Avar asked the Frank in Avarish.

"Yes," the Frank replied in the same language.

"He may be lying," the Avar said.

"A literate trader who speaks three languages? He's worth a lot." For now Sam was sure the Frank knew both Slavic and Avarish.

"Maybe to you, if you manage the sale right. He's too smart; he makes me nervous. When will I sleep, with a cunning prisoner? I'll settle for the gold; it's sure."

"Done," Sam said.

"Done." They shook hands. Then Sam picked up the vase and proffered it, and the Avar handed him the end of the rope.

When they were on their way back to Sam's village, the Frank spoke again. "Why did you want me?"

"Are you trustworthy?"

"No trader is trustworthy. He has to make a living."

"To your friends."

"You are not my friend. You are my captor."

Sam handed him the end of the rope. "I swore to my wife not to abuse any Franks. I love my wife. I give you your freedom, asking only that you repay me your value if you ever have opportunity."

"You surprise me, Slav." He considered. "I accept your bargain. I will call you friend." He picked up a clod of earth and set it on top of his head, in the Slav manner. This made the oath binding.

"Then go, friend," Sam said, impressed by the way the Frank knew the Slav culture. But of course traders made it their business to know about those with whom they dealt. The oath might not mean as much to a Frank as to a Slav.

"But I have not yet repaid you my value."

"You haven't had the chance. We may meet again some year."

"And we may not. I prefer to remain with you until I make the repayment."

"As you wish. My wife will be glad to meet you."

"I would be helpless alone, without money or weapon."

Sam reached for a knife to give the man, but the Frank

demurred. "I am already too much in debt to you. I'll manage."

Sam shrugged. He hoped he had done the right thing.

The Frank put his fingers to the rope, but the knot did not readily yield. "Will you help me with this?"

Sam drew his sword. He put it carefully to the rope by the man's neck, and sawed until the strands separated. The skin beneath was red and raw from the chafing.

Sam brought out a small jar of balm he carried in case of injury, and proffered it. The Frank scooped out some and smeared it on his sore neck. "I thank you, friend."

They walked on toward the village. When night came, Sam shared the last of his traveling food, then lay down to sleep. The Frank lay a reasonable distance away, and did not stir. Sam could sleep lightly when he chose, and he trusted no one completely when out on a raid; associates could be almost as dangerous as enemies. But the Frank made no effort of treachery. He was being true to his oath of friendship.

The next morning they arrived at Sam's village, which was nestled in the protection of a dense forest. Several clans were there, their family houses set close together. They went to Sam's family house—where little sister Lin spied them. "Sam!" she cried, loudly enough to alert the others, and flung herself into his arms.

Then she looked at the Frank, turning abruptly shy. "I am a friend of Sam's, owing him a debt," the Frank said. "I am glad to meet you, pretty maiden."

Lin blushed. Her long braid and bare head signaled her status as maiden.

Snow appeared, and embraced Sam ardently. "You are uninjured," she said with evident relief. "What did you get?"

"Nothing, this time," Sam said.

"He got me—and freed me," the Frank said.

Snow stared at him, surprised. "You are—"

"Another Frank," he said. "A trader, captured in a raid,

enslaved, freed for the price of my value—which I have yet to repay. But I assure you, I will repay it.'' He did not pay her a compliment, because her kerchief and short hair signaled her married status, apart from her obvious relation to Sam. A compliment to another man's wife could be taken as desire for her.

After that, the Frank became part of the family for a time, while his neck and bruises healed. Flo gave him a piece of amber to trade, and a day later he brought her back a fine copper necklace. Ittai gave him a larger piece of amber, and he returned with a healthy sheep. Uncertain about the legitimacy of this, Jes had him take her along the trading chain he had managed, and discovered that all those he had traded with were satisfied. The Frank was simply very good at judging values, and at persuading others that they needed what he had to offer. The right item at the right time could be worth more to a particular person than it seemed.

Soon the Frank was managing the family trade, and the family prospered. The size of the family collection of cows, sheep, horses, goats, pigs, dogs, and chickens doubled. Everyone came to know and like the Frank. But the Frank, meanwhile, adopted Slav attire. He donned a coarse wool shirt, leggings supported by a rope belt, and leather sandals. He shaved away his beard, but kept his mustache. Women found him attractive, and he found them attractive, but he avoided any suggestion of interest in any woman of Sam's clan. In short, he behaved well.

The family had come upon difficult times, because their tribe was not closely allied to the powerful Avars, and was forced to pay tribute of barley, wheat, millet, rye, and oats—a hefty share of everything they were able to grow. If they did not produce enough, and pay enough, Avar raiders would come and take it by force, and perhaps take a few of their women too. Ittai had once been a Roman, but had moved to these hinterlands when he married into the family, and his wealth had been leached by the raiders. That was why Sam had had to turn to raiding himself; it was better to join the raiders than to be raided by them.

Sam tried to suggest that the Frank had repaid his value, because of the improvement of family circumstances brought about by his flair for trading. But the man demurred. "You gave me my freedom; I owe you yours."

"I am free," Sam protested.

The Frank did not argue, but neither did he depart.

In due course they built a house for him, square in the conventional manner, submerged more than a meter into the ground. The walls were wood, and the roof was covered with sod for insulation. It was mainly a single room, with a stone hearth in one corner. It was said that a number of fair women shared nights by that hearth.

Ned became friends with the Frank, who openly admired Ned's intellect. The Frank made no claims to being the smartest of men, but he had a power of persuasion that was at times uncanny. Ned was in turn fascinated by this. "The man is a genius in getting along," he said.

Then the Avars came. It seemed that the clan tribute was not enough. The levees had been raised, leaving the clan in arrears. They had to give up half their stores for the winter. They would be hungry long before spring.

"Something must be done about this," the Frank said angrily. "You are being treated like slaves. I have a notion what that feels like."

He surely did. But what could anyone do?

"We can't beat the Avars," Sam said. "Hunger is better than death."

"But independence is better than hunger."

"For sure!" Sam agreed. "If only we could achieve it."

"We can achieve it if we unify."

Sam shook his head. "We Slavs have never been able to do that."

"I believe it is worth trying. Failure would leave us where we are now. Success could benefit us greatly."

Sam laughed. "Persuade Ned."

The Frank nodded. "I shall."

And to Sam's amazement, he did. That same day, Ned asked Sam and Ittai for a family meeting.

"The Avar strength in this region is slight," the Frank said. "It is Slavic force that prevails, if we but knew it. We serve as allies to bolster the Avars, answering to them. Yielding the bulk of our winnings to them. If we unified and reserved our forces to ourselves, we could profit from our own power."

"Are you speaking of Slavs or Franks?" Flo asked.

"Of Slavs. My origin is Frank, but now I am Slav."

"It does happen," Snow remarked, and the others smiled.

"Listen to him," Ned said. "He may be able to do us much good."

"I would like to go to the leaders of the other clans and tribes," the Frank said. "To persuade them that if we can unify, we can oust the Avars and rule ourselves. But I can't do it alone, because—"

"Because they won't listen to a Frank any more than they will listen to a Roman," Ittai said. "Unless supported by a native Slav leader."

"Sam," Snow murmured.

And so Sam found himself traveling again with the Frank, and with Ned, to make the case to the leaders of other Slavic tribes of the region. Sam was not good at public speaking, so he yielded that job to Ned, nodding as Ned spoke, and Ned introduced the Frank.

They went first to the leaders of the Visians, the tribe to which their own clan belonged. Sam's family was in good repute there, so it was not hard to gain an audience.

At first the others were cynical. "What is your name, Frank?"

"I speak for Sam," the Frank said. "My foreign name does not matter."

"Then we shall call you Samo, in lieu of Sam." A chuckle went around the circle. They were not taking him seriously.

"Call me Samo," the Frank agreed with a smile. "Sam

gave me my freedom. It is a name I honor.''

They did not argue with that. He had answered well, without either taking or giving offense.

Then the Frank spoke of the power of unity, and the inherent greatness of Slavs, and the indignity of taking orders from any foreign power. His persuasiveness manifested, and soon they were nodding, and agreeing. He played upon their prides and their prejudices with an art that Sam could only envy from the depths of his inability to speak similarly.

In the end, they yielded to the Frank's vision. ''If you can get other tribes to join, the Visians will stand with you, Samo,'' their leader said.

''I hope they are as perceptive as you are,'' Samo replied. There were smiles; they knew he was idly flattering them, but the dream was catching hold.

They went next to the Moravanians, the most powerful Slav tribe of the region. This was a more difficult audience, but in the end it was the same. Later they managed to bring the leaders of the Czech, Slovak, and Polabian tribes together for a common meeting, with a Moravanian leader attending, for news was spreading, and the Frank persuaded them all. They would unite and throw out the Avars.

But who would lead this effort? The Slavs suffered from the same problem as always: they could agree on no single one of them to govern others for more than a single battle. There were too many rivalries and resentments.

''You must speak,'' Ned told Sam. ''It is the only way.''

Sam knew what to say. He was shaking as he stood before the group, for he was a man of action, not speech. ''I am Sam,'' he said. ''I am no leader. But I know one who is. It is the Frank. He has no history with us; he has not fought against neighboring clansmen. He was a trader. But he knows what to do. Follow him.'' He stopped, knowing he had spoken clumsily. He hated that.

''Well spoken, Brother,'' Ned said. ''Follow the one who knows. Follow Samo.''

"But he is foreign," a leader protested. "How can we know he has our interests at heart?"

Ned turned to the Frank. "How do you answer?"

"I am of foreign origin," the Frank said. "But I was taken captive by an Avar, and given freedom by a Slav. I swore to restore to him my value. I will not leave his people until I have done that. My value is what he gave me: freedom. I will stay with him until I have given him freedom. And since he can not be free until his people are free, I will try to give his people freedom. And I will join his people. Every person I work with will be Slav, and I will marry a Slav woman. I will become Slav to the best of my ability. All that I do will be for the Slavs."

"Even if the Franks should oppose us?" a leader demanded.

"Even then," he agreed. "I make my oath on it." And he took up a handful of earth and put it on his head.

They were impressed. They debated among themselves, and they set certain conditions, but they accepted him as their leader for now. He would have to be adopted into a Slav tribe, and heed the council of representatives from all the tribes. Samo agreed, and began by appointing Sam and Ned as his chief lieutenants, and asked for the daughter of a Slav leader to marry that same day.

This time there was less hesitation, because women were well regarded among the Slavs and were heeded by their husbands. All five tribes offered women.

"If I may take them all as equals, I will marry them all," Samo said gallantly.

They considered. This would mean that each tribe had a ranking woman close to the leader. None would be slighted. They agreed.

A protocol was issued: the Slavs would no longer tolerate foreign interference in their affairs.

They proceeded immediately to organization and training for war, because they knew the Avars would not ignore this rebellion. Their best war leaders and men labored to form a unified force. Certainly it was the largest force they had assembled, because it was drawn from five tribes instead of one. But the Avars were brutal fighters; would this new Slav army be able to prevail, or would it collapse under the Avar onslaught?

Samo was concerned about that too. He consulted long hours with the war leaders, and with Ned, and with Ittai, who knew of Roman tactics. Thus there were military schools to draw from: Slav, Frank, and Roman. They devised solid new strategies, considering the ways of the Avars. The leaders were impressed; Samo himself was not a military expert, but he knew how to get the best advice from all sources.

The Avars marched. They were contemptuous but careful. They obviously expected to win, and they maintained good military discipline. But their contempt nevertheless betrayed them, because they allowed the Slavs to select the battle site. The Slav leaders shook their heads. "They are fools. We will destroy them."

It turned out not to be that easy. The ground was hilly, with alternating bare slopes and forests, so that the action was somewhat dispersed. They had intended it that way, so as not to have to meet the Avars on open, level ground, but now it was interfering with them almost as much as with the enemy. There were problems of organization and coordination, and a certain disinclination to go to the aid of a usually rival tribe when it was hard pressed. One group had overrun an Avar contingent and taken booty, but other Avars were closing in and it was about to be in trouble.

Samo, watching from the height of a protected hill with his lieutenants, cursed. "Ned, go tell that Czech force to go to the aid of that Slovak force, and to the netherworld with their damned rivalries! We all fight together, or we are all doomed."

Ned went to his horse. He was being sent because the leaders knew him, and knew he could be trusted.

"Sam, go to the Slovaks and tell them to retreat until the Czechs arrive. They know how to do it."

Sam nodded and went to his horse. He galloped down through the forest, staying out of sight of the action until he reached the Slovaks. "Retreat, by order of Samo!" he cried to the commander. "Until the Czechs arrive to help."

"What? Does he think we are cowards? We're just getting started. We don't need any Czechs."

"He said that you know how to do it," Sam said, with a meaningful look.

"Of course we know how to do it! That's why we don't need any Czechs!"

That damned fractiousness was getting in the way again. The Slovak commander thought he could handle it alone. "Samo has given the order," Sam said firmly. "Shall I tell him you choose to disobey it?"

The man paused, considering. "Ah, yes." Then he gave the orders.

The retreat began. The Avars, taking this as the turning point, eagerly surged forward. The Slovaks' retreat became a rout; they overran their rear formation, whose members dropped their booty and ran away.

The Avars broke their formation, going after the booty. Their expectations were being met; at the first sign of real battle the Slavs were fleeing. They began to quarrel over the spoils. The discipline they had shown under combat evaporated.

Then the Czech contingent arrived. The Slovaks turned, quickly resuming their formation, and charged back to the attack. Sam was in their midst, glad to get in a bit of real action while he could. The Avars were caught flat-footed by one of the oldest tricks in the Slav combat manual. They fought, but they were at a double disadvantage, in poor formation facing fresh troops. Soon they were the ones in retreat.

But the Slovak commander spotted him. "Did Samo give you orders to fight?" he asked pointedly.

Sam sighed. He broke off and started back to Samo's headquarters to report.

So it went. The battle was brutal, but in the end the merged Slavic army defeated the Avars. It was not a rout, but the enemy force took solid losses and was forced to withdraw. Victory was theirs!

Slavs had won battles before, and always then separated into their separate tribes with their loot. But this time that did not happen. "If we let our alliance dissolve, the Avars will take vengeance on us separately," Samo said. "We must maintain our power and vigilance.

He was right, and they saw it. Grateful for the victory, and still unable to back any individual leader among their own ranks, they named Samo king. Thus came to be the Kingdom of Greater Moravia, also called the Kingdom of Samo.

In due course Samo issued a royal decree: the family of Sam's clan answered to no one but the king himself, and he made an oath that he would never give an unreasonable order to that clan. "Sam gave me my freedom and my name; now I have returned my value to him."

Of course it was not that simple, historically. But the Kingdom of Samo endured, even defeating the Frankish king Dagobert in 632. Thus it maintained its independence, answering to none of its powerful neighbors, the Avars, the Franks, and the Byzantines. It survived intact, about the size of modern Germany, until Samo's death in 658. Then it was absorbed back into the Avar empire, and was largely lost to history, but still served as the kernel around which later Slavic unions and nations were formed. Samo had shown the way.

This was, however, only a brief respite in the fortunes of the Slavs, who were overrun by many other peoples, and whose very name was taken by some to mean "slaves." Today their presence manifests in such

names as Czechoslovakia and Yugoslavia, which names
are fragmenting as their nations do.

Once again, the tribes are fragmenting after unifi-
cation brought them victory or economic success. It has
ever been thus.

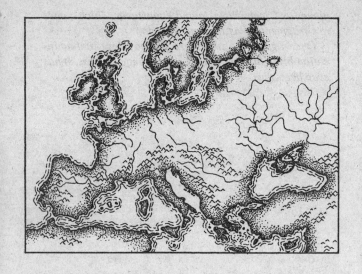

Chapter 14

PLAGUE

The second millennium A.D. was a time of generally rising levels of civilization and warfare. One of the largest empires of human history, that of the Mongols in Asia, was formed and dissipated, and later came the European global expansion. But some of the more interesting by-paths of history occurred on smaller scales. Among these was the trade rivalry of two north Italian cities, Venice and Genoa. Venice was on the northeast coast, at the northern end of the Adriatic Sea; its influence and trade expanded through the Adriatic region and the Aegean, and even as far as the coasts of Egypt and Asia Minor. Genoa was on Italy's northwest coast; its trade was westward as far as Spain and south to the African shore.

But there was an exception to this pattern: in 1201 the Genoese settled at Kaffa on the Crimean peninsula at the north coast of the Black Sea, in rival Venetian territory. This was a connection to an overland trade route from the far east, so was potentially a rich one. The Venetians established a trading post at Azov, in the same area, north of the Crimean peninsula. Thus the rivalry of the major Italian cities was echoed in the far-flung minor ones.

Then politics took a hand: in 1261 Genoa backed a revolt that placed a friendly emperor on the Byzantine throne, and was granted a monopoly on trading rights to the region. In 1266 the Mongol Khanate of the Golden Horde ceded a piece of land there to the Genoese. Thus the tiny trading port became the center of European trade with Asia. A burgeoning Christian city grew up around the central fortress.

Later, the winds of political favor changed, and the Venetians returned in force. In 1296 a fleet of twenty-five Venetian ships attacked and laid waste the port and fortress at Kaffa. In 1307 the khan was angered because the Italian merchants were supplying Turkish slaves for the Mamelukes of Egypt. He felt this deprived the steppe of potential soldiers. He sent an army to besiege Kaffa. The Genoese had to abandon the city. They took to the sea, burning the port and city behind them.

But in a few years the situation changed again, and the Mongols allowed the Genoese to rebuild Kaffa. Perhaps they missed the trade, from which they, too, profited handsomely. By 1316 Kaffa was flourishing again. The Venetians were also allowed to return, and they built a trading colony at Tana, which may have

been a restoration of the prior one they had had at
Azov. The exact nature of the relationship between the
colonies of Venice and Genoa in this region is uncer-
tain; probably it blew hot and cold as local politics
shifted. There is evidence of both quarrels and coop-
eration.

   In 1343 an Italian merchant encountered a Mongol
in the market place of Tana. The Italian insulted the
one he termed a Tartar. The Mongol responded with a
blow. The Italian drew his sword and killed him. This
set off other street fights, and a number of Mongols
were killed. The khan, not one to take such affront
lightly, then drove the Venetians from Tana. They
sought refuge in Kaffa, which was better defended. In
1345 and 1346 Genoa and Venice combined their fleets
to enforce a blockade of the Mongol coast. Meanwhile
in 1344 and 1346 the Mongols besieged Kaffa. They
were unable to take the city, and the Italians blockaded
the Black Sea, preventing all foreign traffic from en-
tering or leaving Mongol waters. It was a stalemate.

   Then came the plague.

FLO WAS BUSY ORGANIZING THE day, so it was some time
before she became aware of Wildflower's proximity. The
girl was actually of a high-born Mongol family, but complications of politics and vicissitudes of battle had stranded
her amidst enemies. Lin had saved her by garbing her as a
boy and bringing her to Captain Ittai, who had stashed them
on his ship and brought them home to Kaffa. Because Mongols were not in good repute at the moment in the city, the
girl was confined largely to the house for the duration of
the siege. Normally she kept to herself, doing whatever was
asked without complaint, and doing it well. She had once,
Flo understood, been imperious, but the loss of her position
had entirely changed her nature. She was really a very good
house guest, and Flo rather liked her. But now something
was evidently bothering her.

Flo paused in her activity. "What is it, Princess?"

"I—I—do not wish to give offense."

There had once been a day when she wouldn't have cared about giving offense. But maybe that had been a schooled royal attitude, and now the real nature of the girl was showing. "You haven't given any of us any offense yet. What do you have in mind?"

"I—I am about to be fourteen. In my—among my people, that is considered an age to—to—to be betrothed."

"Oh, my," Flo breathed. "Let me look at you, girl."

Wildflower stood up straight. Flo saw that she was indeed coming into womanhood, with a nice face, nice legs, and breasts verging on nubility. Her hair was long and braided in the Genoese manner for young unmarried women. She wore a fitted robe laced down the front, with elbow-length sleeves whose back sides descended down past the elbows. She was an attractive girl, without doubt. But she was Mongol, and Genoa was at war with the Mongols. Her prospects for marriage within the city were nil. If she even went out on the street with her race and gender showing, she would be raped and killed in short order.

"I know I am not of good repute—because—"

"Among your own people, you would be quite attractive," Flo said quickly.

"No."

"Oh, I'm sure of it! In time of peace, even Genoese have taken Mongol brides. Especially when they are pretty. And you are pretty. How much more likely that one of your own would, especially considering your royalty. When this war is done, and you can go out—"

"No. I was—was—"

Oh. "You were raped by Venetians, when they captured you. But we understand about that. I myself was raped, long ago, and Snow—"

"Yes. You of Sam's family do not condemn. And the one I—the one I wish—"

Flo felt an expectant shiver. "Who?" But she already knew.

"Ned. But he—"

"He thinks of you as a little sister. Like Lin."

"Yes."

"Do you really like him, or is it that he is your only prospect?"

Wildflower looked at her, and tears started from her eyes. Answer enough.

Flo considered further. Wildflower was a good girl, with many skills and a sweet disposition. She was young, but old enough. She could make Ned a good wife. If he ever noticed her in that manner.

"I will do what I can," Flo said.

Then Wildflower ran to her and hugged her. She was a young woman now, but had not yet given up all of her delightfully youthful ways.

"But it may take time," Flo warned her. "A man can't be forced in such things."

"I know. I will be patient."

Flo returned to her preparation of the big meal of the day, and Wildflower returned to her washing of clothing. It seemed a shame to have a princess doing such menial chores, but it did help conceal her nature, and the girl didn't seem to mind.

Snow returned, carrying a bag of vegetables from the market place, with her son Sid. Flo looked up from her work, smiling. The woman was well dressed, for she was the wife of the head of the family and needed to maintain appearances. Her hair was finely coifed, tied into an intricate braid, or rather, twin braids coiled over the ears, contained by woven netting. She wore a loose surcoat whose sleeves were buttoned from the shoulder to the wrist.

Flo liked Snow, and it wasn't because the two had a fair amount in common; it was that Snow truly loved Sam and would never play him false. Sam was working on the constant but essential shoring up of the city wall, to be sure that no weakness developed. The city depended on that wall for its security. If the Mongols ever breached the wall, there would be great wailing and gnashing of teeth for sure, not to mention wholesale raping and killing. Flo wasn't worried; the wall was massive and high, and was constantly guarded; the enemy didn't have a chance. But Sam and Dirk made sure that nothing happened to it.

"All is well?" Flo inquired.

"All is well," Snow agreed. "But Dirk says something is going on out there. We don't know what. There aren't as many catapults operating as before."

"Maybe they are running out of rocks to hurl," Flo suggested.

"Dirk doesn't think so. He says there seem to be plenty of rocks. They just aren't hurling them."

"That certainly saves us work," Flo said. "Fewer rocks, fewer repairs." But she wondered. It wasn't like the Mongols to give any battle less than their best, and a siege was a kind of battle. Of course the Mongols weren't good at siegework, despite illustrious exceptions, because the tribes tended to become restless and dilatory when faced with long, dull sieges. Still, this sudden cessation of activity was surprising.

Snow put Sid to sleep, then stripped to her close-fitting underdress and got to work beside Flo, preparing the produce she had brought in. It wasn't especially good, but that was because it all had to be imported by ship and spent too much time in the hold. It was still much better than nothing, whatever the children might think.

In the afternoon, Bry and the children charged in. "They are—" Bry cried.

Flo blocked them off. "Don't come in here all dirty!" she exclaimed. "Get those filthy things off!"

"But they are—" Bry protested as Flint and Wilda grimaced. They were close to six years old, and loved dirt.

"You know the rule! I'll tolerate no city dirt and no vermin in this house."

"I must be one or the other," Bry muttered, and the children giggled. They started stripping off their clothing, which was indeed badly soiled. Wildflower delicately turned her back, to allow them to stand naked and wash at the tub, also dumping in the badly soiled clothing. Flo, of course, didn't matter; she had seen everything times beyond counting.

When they were all clean and in fresh outfits, Bry was finally allowed to blurt out his news: "The Mongols! They're falling sick! It's the plague!"

Flo felt a chill as she exchanged a glance with Snow. She knew of the plague; Jes had suffered it two years ago, and reported that it was deadly. The Mongol siege was bad enough, but a siege of the plague could be worse.

"If it is out there," Snow murmured, "it will soon be in here."

"Yes," Flo agreed grimly. "We had better hold a family council."

"Why?" Bry asked. He was thirteen, and curious about everything.

"We might find it expedient to get on the ship," Flo said quietly. "Soon."

"Oooooh!" the children exclaimed, clapping their hands with delight. They usually went aboard Ittai's ship only to visit when it was in port.

"Yes, that might be fun," Flo said, with a warning glance at Bry.

But the ship was not in the harbor at the moment, so that was not an immediate option. They would have to hope that the plague did not come to the city before Ittai and Jes arrived home. Meanwhile they quietly stocked up on all supplies they could, because Flo knew that once the plague entered the city, there would be panic, and it would not be safe to set foot outside the house.

But meanwhile it was best to act as if nothing was out of order, so as not to precipitate that panic. So Bry and Lin and the children went out to play as usual, but more carefully than before, and not far from the house. If the plague came, Flo wanted everyone safely in the house as long as possible.

The news from outside was that the Mongols were being ravaged by the plague, and would soon have to abate the siege. That seemed like good news to many townsmen, but Flo knew better. Nobody knew how the plague spread, but it surely could penetrate the walls. Whatever the Mongols suffered, the city well might suffer too. If only Ittai's ship would get back in time!

Sam and Dirk, in their hooded cloaks, coarse wool trousers, and working aprons, brought grim news from the wall: the Mongol catapults were active again, but now they were not hurling rocks. They were hurling bodies. The bodies of enemy warriors killed by the plague.

"We don't want those bodies with us!" Flo said at the impromptu family meeting. "Maybe the dead can't give it to the living, but—"

"But maybe they can," Sam said grimly.

"Maybe they can, indeed," Ned agreed. "We must get those bodies out as fast as they come in."

"Yes," Wildflower said faintly. But Flo saw that Ned didn't notice her.

The city authorities agreed. Crews were organized to haul out the bodies, street by street. Every able-bodied man not already active in the defense was expected to participate, however ugly the chore.

"For once I'm with the authorities," Flo said. "Our men are busy, but we have other hands. I will haul bodies, and—"

"So will I," Ned said. He was the best dressed of the men at the moment, because he worked more with his mind than his hands. He wore a close-fitting tunic that tied up at the front, with a leather belt and pointed shoes.

"So will I," Wildflower said.

Ned shook his head. "You should stay inside, girl. That plague is ugly."

Flo was about to agree with him, but managed to stifle herself. If the two could work together . . .

"If you get the plague, you will bring it inside anyway," Wildflower said. "We all may get it. Unless we get those bodies out quickly. So I might as well help."

"But if the city folk see a person of your race—"

"I will shroud my head in gauze, to stop the plague. No one will see me."

He looked at Flo. "Are you going to let this child take this risk?"

Flo saw Wildflower wince. She considered. "As she says, we are all at risk. Our best hope is to get those bodies out as quickly as possible. And she's not a child."

"Yes she is."

Flo smiled. "Ned, girls grow up to become women. She has done so."

"No she hasn't."

Flo kept her face neutral. "Wildflower, if you will, show him your figure."

Wildflower was glad to oblige. She unlaced her robe and removed it, standing straight in her close-fitted underdress. She took a deep breath so that her small but definite breasts were accented. She unbraided her long black hair and let it fall to her waist. She met Ned's astonished gaze, and smiled.

"I think he remains unconvinced," Flo said mischievously, noting the way his pupils had dilated. She herself was surprised by just how far Wildflower had developed. She was slender, but her hips and thighs were solid, establishing her capacity for childbearing. "Perhaps you should take off some more."

"No need," Ned said quickly. He knew as well as she did that there wasn't anything under the underdress. "I yield the point, little sister."

"I'm not your sister."

"Well, it's the same thing. You and Lin—"

"I live here by the sufferance of your kind family," Wildflower said carefully. "It is no affront to be taken as Lin's sister. But I am not."

He shrugged. "As you wish." He turned away.

"So we three will go out and haul bodies," Flo said briskly. "Snow and Lin will take care of the children. But we must wear gloves."

They did not argue. No one knew how the plague was spread, but physical contact seemed the most likely vector.

No bodies landed in their street that day or the next, but when one did come, they were ready. Gloved and masked, the women wearing baggy borrowed men's trousers, the three went out to the gruesome corpse.

The thing stank. The man had evidently fouled himself before dying, and no one had cleaned him up. That suggested the intensity of the siege of the disease. His clothes reeked of urine, feces, and vomit. On his neck was a horrible swelling sore. His eyes were staring and bloodshot; he must have suffered terribly before dying.

"The feet," Flo said, suppressing her rising gorge. "Drag him by the feet. Don't touch anything but his boots." She leaned down to grab one boot, and Ned took hold of the other. "Wildflower, see if you can signal the corpse wagon."

The girl nodded and ran ahead of them down the street. They hauled the corpse along. No one else came out to offer help; the majority of the people of the city had such fear of the sickness that they would not get close to a corpse even to try to save themselves from the plague. At least that made it easy to do the job; the street was clear.

The body was heavy, and they were panting by the time they brought it to the end of the street where it intersected the main road. Wildflower had succeeded in signaling the wagon, and it was approaching. The key to rapid disposal of the bodies was rapid location and movement to pickup points; it was well organized, because of the importance of the task.

They waited while the wagon arrived. Two men jumped down and picked up the body, heaving it onto the back. Like Flo and the others, they wore gloves. "Good job," one said. Without delay they got back aboard and started the horses onward.

That was all there was to it. Except for the cleanup. Neither Ned nor Wildflower argued when Flo said they would wash both themselves and their clothing immediately upon re-entry to the house. They had seen the festering corpse, and wanted none of that for themselves.

Snow had already set out the washtub, full of water. She took the children and retreated, giving them privacy for their act. They stripped as quickly as possible and dumped their clothing in a pile. Then they took sponges and cleaned themselves, rapidly but efficiently, doing their hair too. They helped each other with their backs, wanting to miss no places, lest the plague fix there.

Flo was mature and fat and Ned's true sister, so she knew he had no problem with her. But she watched surreptitiously to see whether he had any problem with naked Wildflower. She saw him wince once, as he scrubbed the girl's back and got a good view of her rounded bottom, but he suffered no masculine reaction. Evidently he still regarded her as a sister. Too bad. Wildflower was almost as pretty as Lin, and her body looked even more feminine naked. She really would be a fine mate for a man.

Only when they were clean did they dump the clothing into the tub. Flo started to wash it, but Wildflower stayed her hand. "I'll do it; I know how."

Flo nodded. "We'll go get dressed," she said. "I'll bring you clothing." For by prior agreement, they had had no new clothing in the room, lest it become contaminated.

She and Ned went to the next chamber, where Snow had laid out the things. Flo was glad to get dressed again; she did not much like showing off her body. Ned seemed the same, though he was a fine figure of a young man. "Good job," she said, echoing the wagon man.

"Yes," he agreed.

That was all. She left him and took Wildflower's clothing

to her. But she had noticed a trace of blood in Ned's mouth as he spoke. She knew its significance.

"Thank you," Wildflower said, accepting and donning the clothes. Then, after a pause: "He really does regard me as a sister."

Flo shook her head. "There was blood in his mouth."

Wildflower looked at her, alarmed. "Not the plague!"

Flo smiled. "No, dear. He bit his tongue."

"To stop from retching, out there?"

"No. While washing your back."

The girl stared at her. "He hated doing that?"

"You know better than that. He saw you, when he thought no one observed."

Slowly, Wildflower smiled. "Do you think it took much pain, to stop—it?"

"Yes."

"Thank the Christian God!" Now there were tears of relief on her face.

"Next time you can ask him to wash your front. He'll be in danger of biting his tongue off."

Wildflower giggled, then sobered. "Why doesn't he want me to see his interest?"

"Because his feelings are mixed. For the past year he has seen you as a virtual sister. Now he sees you with an appealing body. It feels like incest. So he fights it. But give him time. He will come to see you as a separate woman."

"I hope so."

No more corpses landed on their street. Flo was almost disappointed, as was Wildflower. But all too soon they had another concern, for the plague appeared within the city. First in scattered houses, and the bodies were taken out by the wagon for dumping in the sea. Then it became endemic, striking in almost every house.

"We must get out of Kaffa," Flo said. "We have been lucky so far, but there is too much of it; we're bound to be caught if we stay."

But they couldn't leave, because Ittai's ship had not yet

come in, and there was no passage on any of the others. Everyone wanted to get out of the city!

A neighbor came. "Please—my husband—he will die. You are a healing woman; you can help him!"

"All I know is caring for my family," Flo said.

"And they are all healthy."

What could she do? "I'll try."

The man had a huge black swelling on his neck: the bubo. He was writhing and groaning continuously. Flo put her hand on his head, but couldn't keep it there because of his motion. One touch sufficed, however: he was burning hot. He smelled, too; he had defecated in his clothing.

"Get him clean," Flo said. When the woman seemed not to understand, Flo tackled the job herself. She drew the clothes off the man, stripping him naked. The woman did not protest. One advantage of being fat was that one had no sexual attraction, so was considered no threat to anyone else's man. She fetched a bucket with water, and used a large sponge to wash the soiled region.

The man relaxed, and fell into an uneasy sleep. Flo realized that the coolness of the water must have done it. So she rinsed out the sponge and washed his whole body. His sleep became less troubled. "Keep him clean, keep him cool," she said. "Maybe it will help."

The woman nodded, and Flo returned to her own house. But she visited the neighbor man several times thereafter, mainly to offer moral support to the distraught wife.

The man's fever continued, and he sweated copiously, and the sweat carried its own stench. So did his very breath. The woman was keeping him clean, now, but everything about him stank of the plague. The discoloration of his skin spread out from the bubo, the splotches ranging from red to black.

On the third day the bubo on the neck broke open and thick pus welled out. Flo clenched her teeth and mopped it up. After that the man seemed able to relax better, as if the illness was draining from his body. In two more days the fever faded, his skin cleared, and he began to take an interest in food.

"He is mending!" the woman cried. "You did it! You saved him!"

Flo shook her head. "I just tried to make him more comfortable. He threw off the malady himself." But she was glad to have helped.

Meanwhile the city was in a siege of another kind: terror. Everyone wanted to escape, but could not. Panic was endemic. The overland route away was too dangerous; even with the Mongol siege lifted, the terrain was hardly safe from the wrath of the khan, and anyway, the plague was there too.

Then Sam got the plague. He developed a swelling in the armpits, and ran a high fever. He made it home under his own power, and to the bed, then collapsed.

"I can take care of him," Flo said grimly, knowing how horrible this was going to get.

"No, it's my job," Snow said.

Flo didn't argue. She had made the offer, expecting it to be turned down. "Then Lin should take care of Sid."

Snow paused, then nodded. They knew that there was no point in exposing the baby to the plague. Snow would continue nursing him, but at other times he would be kept away from her. There was no problem; Lin had cared for him before, when Snow was busy.

They closed off the chamber where Sam lay. Snow was the only one to enter it. So far the plague did not seem to travel from person to person, but there was no point in taking chances.

The next day Dirk fell ill. Did he, too, have the plague? They moved him in with Sam, and now Flo entered the chamber, because it had become her business.

They used clothes and cool water to bathe their men constantly, trying to ease the fever. It didn't seem to help much. Both men just seemed to get sicker.

Sam's armpit swelling expanded, turning deep red. He

flung his muscular arm out, groaning. "What is it, my dear?" Snow asked helplessly.

"The bubo hurts," he said, grimacing. "Cut it out!"

Snow looked helplessly at Flo. "What can I do?"

Flo considered. When the neighbor's bubo had suppurated, he had started mending. Maybe that was the key. "We will drain it," she said.

She fetched a sharp knife with a thin, almost needlelike point. She sponged off the swelling. "This will hurt, a moment," she said. "But it may help."

"Do it!"

"Snow, hold his arm," she said. "So I can work."

Snow took hold of Sam's arm, clasping it to her generous bosom. Flo aimed the knife point, then stabbed it precisely into the center of the bubo.

Sam grunted. His arm swept down, hauling Snow with it, so that she landed across his chest. Flo barely got the knife out of the way in time.

Then Sam relaxed, and Snow recovered her balance. Flo lifted the arm away, and he did not resist.

Her aim had been true. Blood and pus were welling out of the hole she had made. "The pressure is off," Sam said. "It doesn't hurt as bad."

"It is draining," she explained. Then, to Snow: "Let it drain. Keep it clean. Better that poison come out, than stay in his body."

Dirk was more fortunate. His fever broke, and there was no bubo. He was ill with something else, and was recovering. That was a relief.

Sam mended, and Dirk did. The draining of the bubo seemed to have been the turning point for Sam. Flo knew that it might be coincidence, but she was glad that her experience with the neighbor man had given her the hint.

Then Ned came down with the plague. He had gone to the wall to see to the unfinished work of the other two, because though the Mongols appeared to have given up the siege, that could be a ruse. Now he had the swelling in the neck, and the fever.

"We know how to tend him," Flo said.

"My turn," Wildflower said. "Please."

"Girl, this is ugly business," Flo warned her.

"I know. But if I stand idle, and he dies—"

"We'll do it together," Flo decided.

They moved Sam out. He remained weak, but could walk, and was no longer in danger. They left Dirk for another day or two; his illness was routine, but debilitating. Ned took his brother's place.

Wildflower had been somewhat prepared by the body they had hauled out of the street, and by discussion of Sam and Dirk's illnesses. But Flo feared she was not ready for the malady in Ned. So she kept a close if unobtrusive eye out.

"We shall have to strip him and bathe him," Flo said. "I can do it—"

"No. I will do it."

"He will stink. It is the odor of the plague, coming from his breath, skin, spittle, and all else. It must simply be endured."

"The smell carried through the house," Wildflower said, wrinkling her nose as she smiled.

"He will foul himself. We must simply clean it up."

"I will do it."

And Wildflower bravely did the required jobs, leaving Flo to tend to Dirk. Flo hoped it wouldn't extirpate her feeling for the young man, because the more this former princess buckled to the noxious task, the better respect Flo had for her.

Ned's fever was high, and in the throes of it he cried out in delirium. "Wona, no! Don't make me do it!"

"Who?" Wildflower asked, perplexed. "Do what?" But he was lost in some other realm.

"It may be time for you to know," Flo said. "But you must never repeat it."

"Repeat what?"

"Ned was seduced by Sam's first wife, a beautiful and faithless woman. He could not break her hold. So we sent her away, and Sam found Snow instead. Sam does not know, and Ned feels guilt. So if you have a relation with him—"

"That could be a problem," Wildflower agreed. "But if he didn't rape her—"

"She raped him, really."

"Then I understand well enough," the girl said grimly. "Better than someone else might."

"We do understand about rape," Flo said.

Then at last the ship came in. Ittai and Jes arrived home in style, as befitted their status as proprietors of a merchant vessel. He wore a short buttoned tunic of intricate pattern, divided down the center into opposing colors, with a fringed collar and a long pointed hood. Beneath it was a long-sleeved shirt with decorative buttons and armbands with descending cloth streamers. He wore a jeweled girdle about the hips, and hose with each leg a different color. His pointed shoes buttoned at the ankle and the top of the arch. Jes's hair was too short to be braided, but she wore a pretty tiara. Her gown was sideless and sleeveless, and laced with fine ribbons from shoulder to hip. Flo knew they hadn't worn those elegant outfits on the ship; they had changed just before disembarking.

The family made immediate arrangements to embark. But Captain Ittai balked. "We can't take a man with the plague on the ship! The crew would mutiny."

Flo realized that it was true. "Then we shall have to wait."

"The crew is not eager to remain in port any longer than necessary. We can't delay more than a few days."

"It will have to do."

For several days Ned's outcome remained in doubt, as the bubo on his neck swelled and his skin spotted. He stopped fouling himself after the food that had been in his system cleared, but the stench of his body was awful. Flo and Wildflower took turns going out so as to have the relief of fresh air. They took turns sleeping too, because Ned's case was worse than the others. Flo lanced the bubo, but it didn't seem to help. His body seemed to be wasting away.

"I can't hold the crew much longer," Ittai warned them.

Flo shook her head. "I think we had better prepare ourselves. Ned is going to die."

"No!" Wildflower protested. "He must live!"

"You don't know that he will value you, if he lives," Flo said, trying to soften the blow rather than to be cruel. "Maybe he doesn't really want to live."

"I understand that too. But he is my hope. I must save him!"

"Girl, I wish you could. But I don't know how."

Wildflower's face was desperate. "By loving him!"

Flo did not argue. It seemed that the strain of this siege was affecting the girl's mind.

Wildflower sponged off Ned's face. "You think you are evil, because of Wona," she told him. "But you couldn't stop her. You are not evil. You think no one will love you, but someone will. I will love you. I will love you." Then she kissed his wasted lips.

Ned's eyes opened. "But you are my sister!" he protested.

"I am not your sister!" she retorted. "Could a sister do this?" She kissed him again.

Flo kept her silence. There was no real logic to Wildflower's words or actions, but they were probably as close as she would ever come to the love she craved.

Yet they did seem to have some effect on the man. Ned relaxed, and fell into what seemed to be a less tortured sleep. Flo marveled, wondering whether it was possible. Was Ned expiring from guilt as much as from the disease?

It was, indeed, the turning point. The next day Ned's fever was down somewhat. He took water and a bit of food. The day after, he took more.

Then he became conscious of his surroundings. "Who

has cared for me?" he asked Flo, for Wildflower was now sleeping in the next room.

"We have," Flo said. "Wildflower and I."

He looked wary. "I had a strange dream. Did I say something?"

"Yes."

"Did she say something?"

"Yes."

He shook his head, electing not to pursue the matter.

Now they could depart this cursed city. The crew might not like it, but Ned was obviously recovering. So probably he would not spread the plague to anyone else, even if it did pass from man to man, as seemed doubtful. Two of them had been stricken, and been lucky enough to survive; Flo was sure that luck would not hold much longer.

Unfortunately, the very ships seeking to carry people to safety from the plague carried the plague to other cities of Europe. The crews might not knowingly take aboard sick people, but the delay between infection and symptoms made it inevitable. In 1347 it spread to Constantinople and Turkey; in 1348 it spread to Greece, Italy, Spain, and France; in 1349 it spread to northern Europe. Thereafter it moved on into Russia and faded out. It killed 60–90 percent of those infected. But not everyone caught it. The manner of contagion was a mystery to the people of the time, but today we understand it. We also know that there was not one, but three forms of it. The first, which was at Kaffa, was bubonic: spread by rat fleas when they bit human beings. It could not be transmitted directly from human to human. The reason Flo's family was largely spared the plague was her unnatural fetish about cleanliness; there was little dirt, and no rats, and therefore no rat fleas in her house. Its course and symptoms were as described. There is no evidence that draining the bubo helped, however; indeed reports are mixed on whether a draining bubo led to recovery or immediate death. It may be that the best course was to have the bubo subside naturally, a symptom rather than a cause of recovery. Possibly those who had good health before being stricken had better survival odds; that is the assumption here. Later in Europe the second form was encountered: pneumonic. This occurred when a person infected with the plague also caught pneumonia. It attacked the lungs, causing violent, bloody coughing. The bacilli infected the breath, so that it spread by air. It was more deadly than the bubonic form, being said to be universally fatal in three days. When a person coughed blood, he was doomed. This did not improve with time; an outbreak in the twentieth century was fatal, on average, in 1.8 days. Buboes did not appear, perhaps because there was hardly time. The third form was septicemic, and was even swifter: it infected the blood, and the victim was dead in a few hours. The plague, in its three forms, may have killed a third of all Europeans during the first great siege. It recurred irregularly, and still exists today. But the contemporary world has seen little to compare to the horror the plague held for the folk of the fourteenth century.

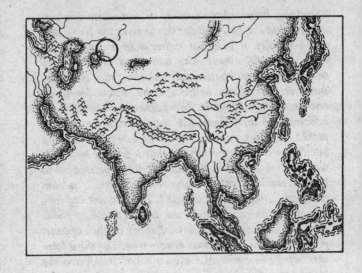

Chapter 15

KHAN

One of the most notorious conquerors in history was Timur the Lame, otherwise known as Tamerlane. But that was what his enemies called him; he called himself Sahib Qiran, "Lord of the Fortunate Conjunction." He was a Turk in Transoxiana ("Across the Oxus" River—now the Amu Darya), in central Asia north of modern Afghanistan. He seems to have been a genius in battle but a poor governor, so that his battles always had to be fought over. But his impact on central Asia may have been second only to that of the Mongols, whose mantle he claimed.

One day a Mongol prince came to Tamerlane's capital of Samarkand to beseech his aid against kinsmen who were displacing him. This was Toqtamish, a descendant of Genghis Khan and pretender to the throne of the White Horde. Timur was glad to receive him, as this royal Mongol might prove useful, and gave him three cities: Otrar, Sabran, and Signakhi on the north bank of the Syr Darya, the northern of two rivers feeding into the Aral Sea. This was between the territories of Transoxiana and the White Horde, claimed by each, so needed strong defense.

Unfortunately Toqtamish was not apt in this respect. His relatives invaded and defeated him in battle, driving him out. He returned to Timur, who sent a force to back off the Mongols, installing Toqtamish in Sabran again. But when Timur's troops departed, the Mongols came back and ousted Toqtamish again without difficulty. This time Timur himself came into the steppe and in 1377 severely defeated the White Horde, putting Toqtamish back in power in his cities. But as soon as Timur went home, the Mongols routed Toqtamish a third time. So Timur gave the hapless prince further support, and in the winter of 1377–78 not only beat the enemy, but enabled Toqtamish to become khan of the White Horde. How long this would last was doubtful, as Toqtamish seemed to have as much of a genius for losing battles as Timur had for winning them.

Then something odd happened. It remains a mystery to history, but an exploration of the events following Toqtamish's second rout may resolve it. The time is 1376.

NED, RANGING OUT AHEAD TO scout the way, heard a distant clamor. That could be trouble. He rode up on a bluff overlooking the Syr Darya and peered forward.

To the north, across the river, the remnant of a battle was proceeding. He could see the colors of Timur, and those of the White Horde. The standards of the Turks were in disarray, while those of the Mongols were organized.

"Oh, no," he breathed. "Toqtamish lost again."

He was about to ride back to carry the word to his commander, when he saw a special eddy current in the larger swirl of the battle. A lone horseman was fleeing a group of riders. He had evidently gotten isolated from his troop and was about to be killed.

But why would they pursue an ordinary cavalryman? Where could he go? He was caught between the enemy and the river, evidently unarmed, no longer a threat to the Mongols. They would do better to mop up the remaining pockets of organized resistance. Unless—

Could it be? Yes, that would explain it. It could be Toqtamish himself, the one the White Horde was after. The pretender to their throne. They would not let *him* go!

Fascinated by the distant interplay, Ned strained to see it unfold. He remembered how rival royal factions among the White Horde had vied for power, and Urus Khan had risen to dominance five years before. Opposed by his cousin Tuli Khoja, he had acted forthrightly: he had attacked and killed his rival. Khoja's son Toqtamish had had to flee for his life. He had gone to the one power capable of reversing his ill fortunes: Timur of Transoxiana.

Ned, as an apprentice strategist in Timur's court, had studied the activities of the White Horde, because Timur's generals were keeping a wary eye on the rise of a potentially dangerous power to the north. Urus clearly had large ambitions, which included reuniting the White and Golden Hordes under his own leadership, and possibly Persia too. Since Persia was Timur's sphere of endeavor, this bore watching. Ned was one of a number of strategists assigned to watch and advise about such developments, so that Timur would not be caught unprepared. What use to conquer Persia, if the White Horde then swept down on his flank? So

the appeal of a legitimate pretender to the Mongol throne
was of considerable interest.

He remembered the fanfare with which Timur's General
Uzbeg had escorted Toqtamish to Samarkand. Timur himself had hastened back from the front to meet him, greeting
him as his son. There were lavish gifts of gold, gems, robes,
silks, furniture, camels, horses, tents, drums, banners, and
slaves.

He had installed Toqtamish as ruler of the borderlands
between Transoxiana and the White Horde, and given him
fresh troops with which to defend his territory.

Of course Timur's generosity was calculated. A genuine
and loyal Mongol prince was a fine buffer to have on that
perilous border. It solved the problem of the ambitions of
the khan of the White Horde. For now.

But as soon as Toqtamish settled in, Urus Khan sent an
army commanded by his son Qutlugh-buka to rout him out.
Toqtamish was forced to flee, but the victorious Qutlugh-
buka was severely wounded in the battle, and died the next
day. This surely did not please the khan.

Ned had watched with wonder as Timur greeted the Mongol prince with even greater honors than before, and supplied him with a fresh army. Toqtamish had set out to
reclaim his lost domains. But spies had brought news to
Samarkand of another Mongol army moving south, this one
commanded by Urus Khan's eldest son, Tokhta-qiya, who
was determined to avenge the death of his brother. So Timur
had sent the ranking official Idiku Berlas to counsel Toqtamish and assist him in ruling his limited kingdom, so that
he would not be ousted again. Ned was part of that party.

But now it was apparent that they were too late. Tokhta-
qiya, perhaps spurred on by his grief, had not waited for
Toqtamish to enter Sabran. He had intercepted Toqtamish
on the way, and probably caught him by surprise, and routed
him. Now Toqtamish was fleeing for his life, and his prospects looked bleak indeed.

The lone rider reached the river just ahead of the pursuit

and drove his horse into the water. But the animal might have balked—Ned couldn't tell from this distance—and the man had to shed armor and swim. The troops of the White Horde drew up at the water, not caring to try to ford it in their armor, and took deliberate aim with their bows. Several arrows missed, for it was a fleeting target; the man was holding his breath and swimming under the surface as much as possible. Also, the river's current was bearing him along, further confusing his irregular appearances. But then there was a cry, and Ned saw the faint discoloration of blood in the water. The fugitive had been struck!

But the man made it to the far bank. He staggered from the water, entered the forest, and threw himself into the underbrush, evidently exhausted. The archers were running down the river, trying to get into better position for loosing their arrows more accurately, but their target had disappeared.

Now Ned turned his horse and galloped back to report to Idiku Berlas, as he should have done before. But he had wanted to see whether the fugitive escaped, because if it was Toqtamish, and if the prince died, then their mission would have become pointless. Now he knew that there was still a chance. But he had to hurry, because he had to reach Idiku and return with aid before the Mongols could reach a fordable spot in the river, cross, and locate their prey.

Soon he reached Idiku. "There is a battle beyond the river!" he cried. "Mongol, Turk. The Mongols won. I think I saw Toqtamish escape!"

"Where?"

"By the river woods. I marked the place."

"Lead the way."

Idiku and his troop followed Ned to the region he had seen. They plunged into the woods flanking the river, forging on through.

"He could be anywhere along here," Ned said. "And the Mongols could be crossing the river in pursuit."

Idiku signaled, and the men spread out to approach the

river in a line. They reached it, and saw Mongols carefully fording it with roped horses. But the moment the Mongols spied them, they retreated. The river was no place to defend against arrows from the land.

Meanwhile Idiku and Ned ranged through the brush.

"Prince!" Ned called. "We are friends!"

There was a groan nearby. Ned went there, and saw the fugitive lying under a bush. He dismounted and ran to him. It was indeed Prince Toqtamish. "Here!" he called to Idiku as he kneeled beside the fallen man.

In a moment Idiku was there. "He is wounded in the hand," he said. "Nonlethal injury."

Ned bound the hand, and they helped Toqtamish to a horse. He was too weary to ride competently on his own, so Ned rode with him, keeping him from slumping out of the saddle as the horse walked.

"We'll take him directly to Timur, at Bukhara," Idiku said.

They camped for the night, posting guards. Toqtamish began to revive, eating bread and drinking wine. He inquired about the identity of his rescuers, and Idiku introduced himself and Ned. "Ned spied you crossing the river, and led us to the place," he said.

"What is it he wears?"

"A cross," Ned said. "I am a Christian."

Toqtamish nodded, evidently losing interest. "I will remember." Then he found a place to urinate, and retired to the tent to sleep.

In the morning, rested, the Mongol prince was able to ride on his own, and they made better time.

Timur welcomed the prince again, and gave him more riches and honors. Ned marveled at this extreme generosity to one who had proved to be of questionable competence, but of course did not speak. He was just an incidental functionary, beneath the notice of royalty. He stayed close to Idiku, his immediate superior, and tried to remain part of the background. It was the first time he had been allowed into even the incidental presence of Timur, and he felt the thrill of the honor. He saw that Timur walked with a slight limp, and he, too, had an injury in the hand. Stories abounded about how he had received the wounds to his right appendages, varying with the regard in which the tellers held him. Supporters told of his ferocious appetite for combat, in which he had been injured during pitched battles with enemies who greatly outnumbered him; detractors spoke darkly of botched cattle raids or even single combat with his own father. But all conceded his legendary prowess on horseback and personal valor in battle. Certainly his lameness did not slow him in those pursuits.

This time the Mongol khan did not simply let the fugitive go. Within days word came that Urus was marching south with a larger army to punish Toqtamish. Soon two envoys arrived bearing his ultimatum: "Toqtamish has killed my son, and has since sought refuge with you. I demand the surrender of my enemy. If you refuse, we must choose a battlefield."

"Oooh," Idiku murmured for Ned's ears only. "That is the wrong tone to take to Timur."

Indeed it was. Timur glowered at the envoys. "If the khan's son had stayed where he belonged, instead of infringing on my territory, he would be alive today. Return to Urus Khan and tell him that I not only accept his challenge, but also that I am ready, and my soldiers are like lions, who do not live in the forest but have their den in the battlefield. If he is smart, he will hasten out of my territory before his own life is forfeit."

Then, when the envoys had departed, he turned to Idiku. "Follow them by secret patrols. I want to know exactly where the khan is camped."

Idiku turned to Ned, his mouth quirking. "Christian, get your horse. You know what to do."

"Yes, sir." As Ned turned to obey, he saw Toqtamish smile. They all knew what was happening. The khan's arrogant message had made the matter personal for Timur.

Ned was one of several who trailed the envoys, staying always out of their sight. It was easy to track the prints of their horses, or to lie hidden near their likely trails and see them pass. When he was sure of their trail, he marked it so that Timur's scouts could follow it.

Timur himself marched soon after. Now Ned became a scout, leading the troops along the trail he had helped mark. The khan was in for an ugly surprise, for he would find himself surprised before he was organized for battle.

The White Horde force was camped near the city of Signakhi, one of those from which it had displaced Toqtamish. Timur brought his own army to the plains of Otrar, twenty-four leagues away.

But the weather interfered. There was a terrible rainstorm, followed by such intense cold that lasted so long that it prevented any action though that winter. Timur chafed at the forced inaction, but would not act until he was sure he could do so effectively. The men were given rotating leave to visit the city, but remained always on ready alert. That meant that Ned could not visit his home city of Sabran, or attend the Nestorian church there, though it was only a few leagues away. In any event, it was uncertain under whose control the city was at the moment. He hoped his family was not suffering unduly.

Food became so scarce that Timur commanded his generals and lesser officers, on pain of death, to see to it that no one in the army should bake bread for himself. All the food was redistributed, the generals and princes getting precisely the same rations as the private soldiers and servants. No one was allowed to eat anything more than thin gruel. One bag of flour, together with a few herbs, supplied sixty dishes: one dish of broth for each soldier, each day. The soldiers searched for eggs of waterbirds, for animals, for edible plants—anything to supplement the ration of gruel.

Finally, after three months, the weather eased. Timur sent a detachment of 500 men out under two commanders to attack the enemy in the night.

But the Mongols had spies too. They were met by a force of three thousand commanded by the khan's third son, Malik. The fighting was fierce, and one of Timur's commanders was killed, but Malik was wounded in the leg and had to retreat. The victory went to the Turks.

Then Urus Khan sent out a scouting force of 200 men. This force stumbled on a smaller force of Turks that was returning from Otrar after provisioning troops there. The Turks fled. When the Mongols got spread out in their pursuit, the Turks whirled around on them and cut them to pieces. The Mongols had fallen for the oldest trick in the Mongol book, the mock retreat.

Discouraged by these failures, Urus Khan returned home, though the bulk of his army was untouched. Timur also retired from the field, having won back his territory by default, though that was not his preferred way.

Now at last Ned got to visit his family in Sabran. His little sister Lin kissed him. So, to his surprise, did her companion Wildflower, who had once been a Mongol princess. The girl had helped take care of him during a severe illness, and did seem to like him. He found them all in good health, but somewhat worn by the long threat of a siege by one side or the other. Food was scarce, because the two armies had raided the supplies.

But he could not stay long, because as soon as the weather turned favorable, Timur set out once more. This time he advanced into the territory of the White Horde, giving Toqtamish command of the advance guard. The Mongol prince knew the way, and guided the army so effectively that in fifteen days they reached the interior town of Geiran Kamish, "The Reeds of the Deer." They had attracted little or no notice.

The inhabitants were taken completely by surprise, and put up no effective defense. The army pillaged the town and captured large numbers of sheep, camels, and horses.

Best of all, they learned at this time that Urus Khan was dead. Apparently he had been ill, and that was one reason he had retreated. The rigors of the campaign had worn him down beyond recovery.

Timur, well satisfied with these successes, decided to return to his other campaigns. He was, after all, in the process of conquering Persia from the remnants of the former Mongol khanate there, and the job couldn't wait indefinitely. Now that he had protected his flank, he left Toqtamish with enough troops to uphold his pretense to the throne of the White Horde and gave him a fine horse. This was Kunk Oghlan, sired from Timur's own stallion, and famous for his speed.

Now that the Mongol prince was settled in, Idiku Berlas was settled too, and no longer needed Ned's help in the field. So Ned was given leave to rejoin his family in Sabran, though subject to recall at any time. He rode south with his share of the booty: several fat sheep.

He was welcomed again by the enthusiastic embraces of his little sisters, Lin and Wildflower, and Flo was much gratified to have the sheep. "Wool and meat," she said. "Exactly what we need."

Ned settled down to do what he most enjoyed: designing military architecture. He had had experience formulating city walls, and had once advised a local leader in the design and use of such defenses. He had learned much during the recent campaigns against the Mongols and enjoyed analyzing and trying to improve on them in retrospect.

But he wasn't given much time to himself before something astonishing came up.

Ned looked up from his architectural draft to see the solid shadow of his elder sister Flo approaching. It was unusual for her to come to his place of work, so he suspected she had some serious concern.

"We must talk," she said.

That confirmed it. He gave her his full attention.

"I have two concerns. One you surely know of: there is agitation against the Nestorian Christians in the city. We arrived here at a bad time."

He knew it. They had fled physical illness only to discover the emotional illness of religious persecution. The majority of the city's inhabitants were Moslem, and they resented having what they called infidels among them. The Mongol rulers of old had been largely indifferent to religious matters, and did not persecute anyone for his faith, but much went on that was beneath the notice of the rulers. Now the Mongols themselves were becoming Moslem, and their attitudes were changing.

"They choose to blame us for the ills war has brought to the city," Ned said. "This is nonsensical. It is the warring between Mongol factions that has done it, and the ineptness of Timur's governance." Here in the privacy of his family he could speak freely. He had nothing but admiration for Timur's prowess in the field, but the man paid almost no attention to the ordinary running of his empire.

"It is easier to blame a small minority than to blame either Timur or the Mongols," Flo said darkly. "The minority can't strike back."

He nodded. "You wish to move to a more comfortable city? We might find good work in Samarkand."

"No. I prefer to gain protection by seeking the favor of the khan." She meant the pretender, who held power in this region only.

He laughed. "How long do you think Toqtamish will last? The plotters and rebels will soon bring him down. Again."

"Maybe not." She paused, then changed the subject. "Wildflower loves you."

"And I love her. She's a nice girl, just like one of the family. She tended me when I was deathly ill."

"You misunderstand. She's a woman, and she wants to marry you."

Ned's jaw dropped. "She's my little sister!"

"No. She is not your sister. We took her in when she was caught between Mongol family feuds, and saved her from likely death."

"But not from rape," he agreed, remembering. "Lin smuggled her out of danger, but too late to spare her that. But she has adapted very nicely. She might as well be a sibling. She's almost as pretty as Lin, when allowance is made for her Mongol heritage, and quite fair of form." He had noticed that several months before, when the girl had had occasion to strip in his presence. He had felt guilty for noticing.

"Indeed. She is a princess, cousin to Toqtamish. Now that he has power, he is no longer a refugee, but a person of note."

"Good for her! She can take her place in his court, as long as it lasts."

"Yes. But she won't go."

"Why not? She would be better off there, than with a persecuted minority."

"Because she loves you."

Again he took stock. "And you don't mean just as a sibling. She has a crush on me. But surely it will pass. I assure you, I have never given her any encouragement of that nature."

"You have been largely oblivious, except for your guilt when you see her naked."

He had hoped that Flo had not grasped that awkwardness. Flo believed in cleanliness, so they all had to wash periodically, and sometimes he saw his sisters naked. It could not be helped, but they did have breasts and fur, and looked like women, and at times it was hard for him to remain properly neutral. "Well, it is not proper to lust after one's sister."

"She is not your sister," Flo repeated.

"You know what I mean. I have treated her with all proper deference, and never sought to indulge in anything untoward."

"Ned, you are our smartest family member, but you can be monumentally stupid about women."

"To my everlasting shame," he agreed. "When Wona—"

"Forget about Wona! She's gone. You are of age and maturity to marry, and you could do infinitely worse for a wife than Wildflower."

He stared at her. "Are you suggesting that I—take advantage of a girl's passing fancy, to get into her skirt?"

Flo met his gaze with a hard intensity he seldom saw in her. "No. I am suggesting that you marry a young woman who is worthy of you."

"But why? I agree that she is a nice girl, with an appealing body, but that's no reason to—"

"You need a more practical reason than the love of a woman who could make you happy?"

"Yes! Because it would not be fair to her, to prey upon her naivete. I know the evil of that. Wona—"

"Wona preyed on yours," she agreed. "And you found ecstasy amidst the guilt. Your determination not to do that to another person is worthy. But this is not that. Wildflower truly loves you, and will give you her body without guilt. We of the family approve."

"The family has discussed this?" he asked, appalled.

"We had to. Bry and Lin were attacked in the street this morning. For being Christians. They got away without suffering harm, but it is an evil signal."

Ned felt a cold and angry shiver. "Sam knows of this?"

"Yes. But we agreed that violence is not the answer. We need protection."

"I will certainly agree to move! I don't want anything to happen to my siblings. Or to Wildflower."

"Then marry Wildflower."

He looked blankly at her. "What has this to do with danger in the streets?"

"If you marry her, you will be related to the future khan of the White Horde."

Now at last he understood her import. He could at one stroke bring the family unparalleled protection. Nobody harassed kinsmen of the Mongol khan. Not in this city. Not anywhere within the domains of the pretender to the throne of the White Horde. Not as long as he retained power.

"But it would be using her!" he protested. "Not merely sexually, but politically. She is a Mongol princess. We have no right to do that to her."

"She suggested it," Flo replied evenly.

"She—" He broke off, astonished.

"She really does want to marry you, Ned. And she brings a dowry we can not decline. We can be safe—if you only oblige her love."

"If I only seduce an innocent girl! Flo, where is the honor in this?"

"I said it would be a good marriage. I know you, Ned; I know she is right for you. Your idiocy is in refusing to see it. If you will not do it because of love, do it to save the welfare and perhaps the lives of your siblings. It will not be an unkind or difficult relationship, I promise you. You can love her, if you allow it."

He shook his head. "Surely Wona used a similar rationalization when she decided to prey on a naive lad." Then he thought of something else. "She *is* a Mongol princess, and needs to hide it no longer. What would Toqtamish think of this? Of her marrying an infidel?"

"We are about to find out. She is traveling to see her cousin now. If he gives her leave, she will marry you."

"And you are telling me to marry her."

"Yes. We believe it is best, all things considered. It will help the family survive, it will satisfy her love, and it will fulfill your life in a way you don't yet appreciate. It is an unusually good solution to a combination of problems."

"I'll think about it," he said shortly.

"You have until she returns from her visit to her cousin."

She seemed so sure he would agree!

Meanwhile, there was their situation in an environment becoming increasingly hostile. They were careful, but the mood of the city was bad and getting worse. Scapegoats were needed, and Christians were the most likely candidates. Their little Nestorian church was suffering defacement. If it hadn't been built of solid stone, with thick walls and small windows, the damage would have been worse. It was clear that they would have to leave soon, if they didn't get protection. Yet it would probably be about as bad in other cities. Moslems were many, and Christians few, in the Mongol and the Persian realms.

Ned wrestled with his mixed emotions. It was true that Wildflower was unrelated to him, and that she was attractive. But she remained a sister in his mind, and he felt guilty even thinking about her sexually. How could he marry such a girl? Yet he feared he had to. He wished he could talk to her, to try to make her see that this was not a good thing to do. But she was away, and anyway, he wasn't sure his arguments would be persuasive. Flo and the family thought it was right to do, and they generally did know. So was he the one who was wrong?

In the end, he concluded that the need of the family probably outweighed his personal scruples. He would have to marry her, and try to consummate the union, though he knew that the guilt spawned by Wona would interfere. Logically the situations were not really analogous, but in his feeling they were. With Wona, it had been a betrayal of the family; with Wildflower, it would be in support of the family. So they were different. If only he could believe that!

Then Wildflower returned. "I'm going to marry him!" Lin reported overhearing.

"She's hardly older than you," Ned said. "Do you think it's right?"

"She's a full fourteen. That's old enough. And she's got the body." Lin passed one hand down her front, disparagingly. She was still thirteen, and of rather slight development. But her face was pretty, and when her body followed, she would be the loveliest girl of the family, as long as she wore gloves.

"If you liked a man, and he had sex with you, would it be right?" he asked her. "Just because you were willing?"

"She's more than willing, Ned. She really does love you.

Besides, you're not just romancing her; you're marrying her." She paused, glancing at him sidelong. "Aren't you?"

"Yes," he said heavily. "Yes, I am." And that was his point of final decision.

"Then maybe you had better go propose to her. A girl likes that."

That hadn't occurred to him. "I have no idea what to say!"

Lin assumed a pose. She took his hand and gazed into his eyes. " 'Wildflower, please marry me.' Then kiss her."

He had to laugh. But it was serious. That was exactly how he should do it. Except for one thing: "You are confusing popular fancy with Nestorian practice," he told her. "There is supposed to be no direct contact or conversation between the prospective bride and groom. The families negotiate the financial aspects of the wedding, bride-gift, dowry, and so on. It is a business proposition."

"I knew that," Lin said, remembering. "And once it's all agreed, the father of the bride gives a feast."

"And a priest or bishop consecrates a ring and gives it to the groom, who arranges to have it delivered to the bride, via a trusted matron who has the confidence of all parties."

"Yes, it would be too bad if she ran away with the ring!" Lin agreed, giggling.

"And if the bride agrees to the marriage, she puts on the ring as a symbol of their betrothal. From then on the bond between them has all the force of marriage, and any infidelities incur similar punishment, though they still live apart."

"Yes, isn't it romantic!" she agreed. "And the wedding festival takes a whole week. The bride looks great in her rich veil, and friends throw raisins and small coins so she'll be fruitful." She giggled again. "Fruits to the fruitful. I love that."

"We all live together in this one house," Ned said. "So how is any of that to be accomplished here?"

She considered, mildly crestfallen. "Oh."

"It would be impossible for bride and groom to live apart, even if we had the resources for gifts and all," he concluded. "And neither bride nor groom has parents to negotiate the deal."

Then Lin brightened. "So maybe you'll have to do it my way after all."

Ned sighed. "I suppose so. Certainly I wouldn't arrange anything like this for Wildflower unless I was quite sure that she, herself, really wanted it."

"So ask her, just the way I told you."

He nodded. He rehearsed it in his mind, so that he wouldn't flub it.

Then Flo appeared, with Wildflower at her side. She looked meaningfully at Ned. He realized that Flo must have sent Lin to prepare him, and been waiting close by for him to get ready. They had organized this like a military campaign, and he was the target.

He walked across the room and took Wildflower's hand. "Wildflower, please marry me."

"Yes!" the girl exclaimed. She flung her arms around his neck, pulled his head down, and kissed him soundly on the mouth. The funny thing was that it was quite pleasant. She was a sweet creature.

There was polite applause. The other members of the family had quietly arrived and witnessed the exchange.

"We must do it quickly," Flo said. "I will prepare for the ceremony next week."

So soon! But Ned knew why; they needed the protection the marriage afforded immediately. They also could not be sure when he would be called back into military service.

They compressed the ritual to make it fit their resources. Sam, speaking in lieu of the groom's father, talked with Dirk, who spoke in lieu of the bride's father. The bishop at the church consecrated a ring and gave it to Ned. Ned gave it to Lin, who was absolutely thrilled to play the role of "trusted matron." She took it to Wildflower, who immediately put it on.

The following week they held the ceremony. It was done without great fanfare, because of the likelihood of persecution, but it was done according to the rites of Nestorian Christianity. Sam and Bry celebrated as companions of the groom, and Dirk and Ittai represented men of the bride's family. Wildflower was ushered into the church, completely shrouded by her heavy veil and gown. The bishop performed the ceremony, and then they all changed back to street clothing so as to avoid possible mobbing on the streets by Moslems.

Back at the house, Wildflower donned her gown and veil again, and Jes threw raisins at her, and one tiny coin. "Be fruitful and prosperous!" she cried, and the others cheered. Then they scrambled to pick up the raisins, for they were too precious to be wasted as food.

Then, all too soon, they were alone together in their nuptial chamber. Wildflower stood expectantly before him in her wedding robe, quite pretty. She removed her veil, smiling.

Ned hesitated. What should he do now?

"Aren't you going to undress me?" she asked.

Of course. He went to her and fumbled with her apparel. He didn't accomplish much.

"Maybe if I do it," she murmured. She was so young, yet she seemed more competent than he was.

"Yes," he said, relieved.

Carefully, she dismantled her apparel, and stood at last naked before him. He averted his gaze.

"Don't you like me?" she asked.

"Yes, of course," he said, forcing his eyes to bear on her. "Your body is very nice."

She looked disappointed, and he realized that he should have been more emphatic. But she rallied. "Aren't you going to undress yourself?"

Oh. He tried to remove his own clothing, with no better success than he had had with hers. His fingers, normally nimble, seemed not to want to cooperate.

"Maybe if I do it," she said again.

"Yes."

She gently stripped him of his clothing, until he stood naked too.

"Would you like to embrace me?" she prompted him.

He took her in his arms.

"And kiss me?"

He kissed her on the cheek.

She lifted her hands, took hold of his head, and brought it down so that his mouth met hers. She kissed him, hard.

He pulled away.

Her eyes brimmed. "Do you hate me so much?"

"No! I—I like you. Love you," he said without conviction.

"Am I so ugly you can't take me?" Now her tears were flowing down her face.

"No! You are beautiful."

"Your limp penis gives you the lie. You have no desire for me at all. I should never have forced you into this."

"That's not true. I do desire you. I—my body—just hasn't caught up."

"Are you biting your tongue?" she demanded accusingly.

"No!"

"I'm not as good as Wona was. I don't have the breasts, the hips, the face." She ran her hands over herself, disparagingly, in much the manner his sister Lin had. That bothered him, for a reason he did not care to explore at the moment.

"There is nothing wrong with your body," he said quickly. "Wona was voluptuous, you are slender but by no means ill-formed, and to my eyes you are lovelier than she, because you are good. I would much rather embrace you than her."

"But you did embrace her, and not me."

He did not quibble with technicalities. He *had* embraced Wildflower, but not shown desire for her. "I could not resist her. I have been ashamed ever since."

She organized herself with a visible effort. "What did she do that you could not resist? Tell me, so I can do it too."

He felt himself flushing. "Please, I would rather not speak of it."

She shook her head. "You owe me this much, Ned. To let me try to be at least as much to you as she was. What did she do?"

She had a point. Reluctantly, he summoned the memory. "She was my brother's wife. She wanted my child, to be smart. I said I saw her face, that of my brother's wife, and could not do it. She turned away from me, so as to hide her face, and put my hands on her breasts." Guilt and shame surged with the telling; it was his deepest secret, for all that Flo had somehow found out, and acted to solve the immediate problem by exiling Wona from the family.

Wildflower turned away from him, so close her buttocks touched his thighs, and reached back to capture his hands. She brought them up to rest on her breasts. He knew this was hard for her; her hands were cold, and shaking. "Squeeze," she told him.

He did, but experienced no reality of sensation. He hated reenacting what he had done with Wona. He hated having decent Wildflower be any part of this association. "There is—there is nothing wrong with them," he said. "You are not inadequate in any respect." That was the truth, but not the whole truth.

"I must be deficient, somehow. What else?"

How could he end this, without being unfair to her? He was supposed to be smart, but he couldn't think of any way. "She bent forward, making me hold her hips so she would not fall."

She paused, evidently nerving herself again. "Do it."

"Please, Wildflower—"

"I must be a woman to you. My love is not enough."

He wanted to flee this travesty, but could not. He transferred his hands to her hips, which were very nicely rounded. Why couldn't he react to them as he should? She bent forward so that her buttocks pressed tightly against him. He should be wildly excited, but instead was numb in that region. "And?" she prompted.

"And she—she put my—put it inside her—"

She reached around to grasp his member. Her touch was very light and fumbling. There was a pause. "But it must have been ready to go inside her."

"Yes," he said, doubly ashamed for his impotence.

She straightened, giving up the futile effort, and faced him. Her tears still flowed. He understood what an effort this had been for her. She had forced herself to most actively seek the instrument that had ravished her, and had failed to find it. Her face was flushed with a shame that mirrored his own. "You just don't desire me."

"I do! I just can't—I don't understand why I can't—"

"It's that rape!" she flared. "I am unchaste, and you are revolted. I am dirty in your eyes, filthy, forever soiled, a thing of horror!"

She was calamitously wrong. "No! My sister was raped."

"I'm not your sister!" she screamed.

He flinched. "Yes, you are not." Now, to his added embarrassment, his own eyes overflowed. "I am sorry, Wild-flower. I wish I could—could—"

"Your sister," she repeated, coming to an understanding she had resisted. "You still do see me as your sister. And a man does not lust after his sister."

"Yes." That was the essence. "I know you are not, but my body doesn't know."

"And you do feel for me. I see your tears."

"Yes." It was a perverse relief to speak the truth. "Wild-flower, I know you are everything I should want. I have no shame in marrying you. I would—would do anything to please you. I just can't—this part of it—"

She seemed as relieved as he was. "Come lie with me on the bed, and we'll talk."

So they lay, embraced, and talked, and kissed, and agreed not to tell the others of this problem. He found himself quite comfortable with her, now that there was no expectation of sex between them. She seemed more relaxed too, now that she did not have to try to play the part of a seductress. He loved her, in an ironic manner, for that ineptitude.

"I'm glad I understand," she said. "And of course I don't mind that you didn't—I was afraid of it, because of the rape. You could never be like that."

She was trying to console him. She had shown no fear of sex, just of rejection. Maybe she would have feared sex with another man, but she wanted it with him. Yet indeed, even were her statement about being afraid true, she had nothing to fear from him in that respect. "Oh, Wildflower, give me time. It must change, in time."

"Of course. Meanwhile, we must say the words, until they become real. I love you, Ned."

"I love you, Wildflower." And it was true, to a degree. But she meant it completely, while he fell somewhere short. He loved her without sexual passion.

Then she thought of something else. "What of the time we were naked, washing up, and you had to bite your tongue?"

So she did know of that. "A man does not lust after his sister," he repeated. "You were—interesting—and I could not afford it."

"But now you *can* afford it."

"Now it is not a guilty peek. Now it is legitimate. That changes it, somehow. I knew, then, that there could be no sex. Now I know there can be, and it prevents me."

"I don't understand that. But I believe you. Will you be with me like this every night, so that if you ever are able, we won't lose the chance?"

"Anything you want," he agreed.

"I have heard that pretense can become real. Ned, if you care for me at all—"

"I do! There is no pretense."

"Then hold me and kiss me and speak love to me, for I

truly do love you and would do anything for you. Please don't turn away from me."

"I will never turn away from you!"

"I fear you will tire of my kisses."

"I want your kisses." That, again, was true. He wanted very much to love her in all the ways she desired. He knew her for a fine and lovely person, deserving of everything.

"And I will try not to torment you unduly with my attentions."

"Stop it, Wildflower! The failure is mine, not yours." Then he drew her in and kissed her repeatedly, and she responded avidly, and he almost felt a stirring of answering desire.

In due course they slept, and he woke in the night with her arm across his chest and her breast against his side, and started to react, until he remembered her identity.

He woke in the morning before she did, and gazed at her face in repose. She was lovely, and her body was lovely. If only, by some magic, he could forget she was his sister, for all that it was a lie.

He bent his head down and kissed her mouth. Her lips were flaccid in sleep, but then they woke and became firm.

Her eyes opened. "Oh, thank you, Ned! I love you."

"I love you," he echoed, glad that he had awakened her in this way.

She caught his hand and brought it to her breast. "Can you—?"

Regretfully, he shook his head.

She brightened. "Maybe if I cover up my face, so you don't know it's me?"

"That would be unfaithfulness, at least in spirit. I can at least be faithful to you, Wildflower."

"That's the loveliest answer, Ned! I will cherish it forever."

She should be so easy to love! And he did love her, behind the barrier of his impotence. So he kissed her again, and it was good. At least he was trying.

In due course they got up, cleaned, and dressed. Wild-flower gave him a straight look. "Let's not speak of this night to others."

"It is a private matter," he agreed, once more relieved. She was being so loyal and supportive! Exactly as a good wife should be. "Let them assume what they choose."

She reconsidered. "I can fool them. But maybe you can't. So you should refer any questions to me."

"Yes." He knew she would not lie, but neither would she let slip the truth. She would protect his privacy in a way others would misunderstand.

The more he reflected on that, the better he liked it. Flo was right: Wildflower was the perfect match for him.

He saw her glancing at him, wondering at his silence. So he spoke. "Wildflower, I want you to know that I am doing this simply because I want to." Then he embraced her and kissed her several times.

"I thank you for that gift," she replied. Then she returned the favor.

Soon it was time to go out and meet the others. "Now I must return to see the khan," she said.

"The khan? Why?"

"Because you married me to save your family. I must tell the khan we are married, so that the word spreads."

"But you just visited him, to get permission. Isn't that all that is necessary?"

"No. I must tell him myself. So he can appoint you to a good position."

"A good position! I did not marry you for such a commercial reason!"

"I know. But I love you, and I want you to have it."

"I have just failed you, and you want to reward me?"

She stroked his cheek. "When you love me as I love you, you will understand."

"I truly do not deserve such love."

"You truly *do* deserve it. You are the smartest, nicest, handsomest man I know."

He didn't know how to argue with that, so he just stroked her dark hair.

But before Wildflower could travel again, the political situation changed. The news spread rapidly through the city: Urus Khan had been succeeded by his eldest son Tokhtaqiya, but the new khan had died almost immediately, leaving the throne of the White Horde to the surviving son, Malik. This had seemed like easy prey to Toqtamish, who had marched to attack, but once again the Mongols had proved to be superior in battle to the mixed forces of the pretender. Toqtamish had been driven from the territory of the White Horde, and had fled a fourth time for refuge with Timur. And once again Timur showered his vassal with riches and honor.

But Wildflower's trip had become pointless. However well her cousin was being received by Timur, the fact was that he had proved to be repeatedly inept in battle, and lacked any real power. Timur's patience must be about exhausted. "I have failed you," Wildflower said dispiritedly. "You married me for nothing."

"You have failed in nothing," Ned told her.

But Bry and Lin did not dare go out in the streets without Sam to guard them. The persecution was back in force.

They endured for several months. Wildflower turned fifteen, but it made no difference to their marriage; Ned could embrace her and kiss her and talk to her, but he could not be potent with her.

Then as fall came, things changed again. Ned was abruptly recalled to service. He suspected that he knew why: A refugee from the White Horde had arrived at Timur's court and told stories of how Malik was losing the support of his tribes. He had gained a reputation for debauchery. He lay abed until midmorning, delaying the main meal of the day, and no one dared disturb him. He was oppressive, and the people were weary of his rule. Many wished for the return of Toqtamish, who had had a better sense of the duties of a leader.

Ned kissed Wildflower. "You may yet be a princess again," he told her.

"Just keep safe, my love," she replied. "You are all I want."

That made him feel guilty again. She offered him so much, and he gave her only the semblance of a marriage. He rode to join Idiku Berlas at Signakhi, where Toqtamish was camped. He became a scout again, as Toqtamish marched north against Malik with troops provided by Timur. He had his own equipment, for each warrior had to provide himself with his own bow, thirty arrows, a quiver, and a shield. Armorers were at work, providing harnesses and shirts of mail. There was a spare horse for every two men, and a tent for every ten men. Each complement of ten had two spades, a pickaxe, a sickle, a saw, a hatchet, an awl, a hundred needles, thread, casting nets, and a big iron saucepan. Each chief gave a written undertaking, to assure that troops would arrive at a given rendezvous.

This time Toqtamish paid close attention to the counsel of Timur's military advisers. They caught Malik at his winter camp in the hills, and defeated him. Malik fled with the core of his followers, and Toqtamish ascended the throne without further opposition. He was at last khan of the White Horde.

They arrived at the capital city. The khan was not in the royal tent, but in a magnificently decorated pavilion, as was his custom every Friday after prayers. It was constructed of wooden rods covered with plaques of silver gilt, their bases inset with precious stones. Beside it a huge tent had been erected, its supporting columns gleaming. There were awnings of cotton and linen cloth, and it was carpeted with silken rugs. In the center was an immense couch made of inlaid wood whose planks were covered with a large rug.

The khan and his principal wife would sit on cushions here when receiving visitors. But at the moment that couch was not in use.

Wildflower kissed Ned, suppressing her extreme nervousness. "I must leave you for a time," she said.

"Why? Am I not your husband?"

"It is a ceremonial thing. I will return to you as soon as I can."

"But we are about to see the khan."

"I must see him alone, my husband. Then he will send for you."

"This is not protocol."

She looked him in the eye. "Please, Ned."

Bemused, he yielded to her requirement. She walked to the entrance of the pavilion.

One of the guards stopped her. "No one enters the presence of the khan unannounced."

"I am his cousin, the Princess Wildflower. Announce me for a private audience."

"You are garbed as a common scullery maid."

"Look at me and tell me I am not a Mongol." She removed her kerchief to show her glossy black hair and dusky skin, and turned on the imperial visage. She had schooled herself in the way of a lowly peasant girl, but she had not forgotten her origin.

A guard went in to check. Soon he emerged, looking slightly dazed. "He will see you."

She brushed past him. Toqtamish was seated on his couch, alone, facing south. He was tall and handsome, as she remembered him, a man of her dead father's age. He did not move as she approached.

She stopped at the proper distance and dropped to her knees, bowing her head. Then she went down farther, into a full prostrate obeisance.

"Cousin, what is the meaning of this?" the khan demanded after a significant pause.

"My lord, you forbade me to marry the Christian. I disobeyed. I have come to receive my just punishment. You may slay me now for my insolence."

"You have nerve, Cousin. I thought you would not tell me."

"I am of your blood. Courage runs in the family."

"Get up from the floor, you scoundrel."

She got slowly to her feet. She put her hands to her neck and pulled out the collar, baring somewhat more than her neck for his gaze. "Here is my neck for your blade."

He ignored that. "Why? Why did you bring this shame on the family?"

"I love him."

"That is not enough. A royal Mongol does not allow love to interfere with expediency. Why did you do it?"

"His family saved my life, after I was ravished. Now they are being persecuted. They must have protection."

"So he prevailed on you to marry him?"

"No, Lord. He did not want to marry me. I prevailed on him, using this argument."

"Not good enough. No man would *not* want to marry a Mongol princess. Why did you do it?"

He had asked her three times. Now she had to give her most genuine reason. "I want you to give him a good position. One fitting a royal relative."

"A position! For a miscreant Christian?"

She remained silent, eyes downcast, in what she hoped was the picture of maidenly innocence and disappointment.

The khan let her remain that way for a number of heartbeats, then relented. "Oh, stop it! You know I'm not going to kill you. Your mother was always my favorite cousin, and you do take after her, even in your mischief."

She raised her eyes. "Thank you, Lord."

"I will do it. But you must pay me, as your mother would."

"Anything, Lord." She didn't mind that her tears of relief and gratitude showed. He could indeed have killed her, despite his protestation. But it had been a gamble she had to take.

"Tell me your darkest secret."

And she had to do it, according to the private protocol between them. Her mother had told her of the secret games that she and Toqtamish had played as children, and the minor yet sacred trysts they had kept. They had been ready to deceive anyone else, but never each other. "My husband is impotent with me."

"Impotent! How can this be?"

"He sees me as his sister."

The khan shook his head. "The man's an idiot."

"No, Lord. He is a genius. And a man of honor. That is part of why I love him. He just isn't very smart about women."

"True words!" The khan rose from his couch and came across to embrace her. "Were you not my cousin, I would make you my choicest wife, you delightful creature. How well you understand our nuances. We will not speak of the substance of this dialogue elsewhere." That was part of the protocol; her mother had told her of the games, but not revealed any actual secrets. "Send him in."

"Thank you, Cousin!"

She started to back away, but he stopped her with a gesture. "If you are to be married to the lout, it must be by a proper Moslem ceremony. He must not remain a Christian. I trust you informed him of this?"

"I saw no point, Lord."

Toqtamish glowered. "No point! No Moslem woman can marry out of the faith, and it would be intolerable for a princess to take up with an infidel. You know this. How could you neglect such a requirement?"

"There was no point, if I was going to die before consummation," she explained.

He gazed at her for a time. "You gambled heavily, Cousin."

"Sometimes one must gamble, if one is to win."

He nodded. "And suppose he refuses to convert?"

"I will persuade him," she said.

"If you can't persuade him to plumb you, how can you hope to persuade him to do something important? Christians can be obstinate."

"I will do it," she said, hoping it was so.

"Your daring compels my admiration, Cousin. You say he really has not penetrated you?"

She blushed. "I'm sure he will, in time. He wants to."

"Of course he wants to, you beautiful siren! But he hasn't."

"He hasn't, yet," she agreed.

"So you remain pristine for the wedding."

That was another awkward point. "Not exactly. I—"

"Do not speak of the past. No one here knows of it. You are pristine."

"If you say so, Lord." It was true that no one in this court would speak of what the khan decreed unspeakable. She was now legally virginal, as a Mongol princess should be. Actually Mongols considered fifteen to be a suitable age for a girl to marry, but she was acceptable for sexual congress from age ten on. So most brides were well experienced by the time they married, albeit only with the men they married. So the khan was holding her, as a princess, to a higher standard than usual, officially. So that no one would dare whisper of her shame of getting raped.

"So you must remain aloof from him until the wedding, so that there will be no risk of scandal. Go into seclusion."

"But I must persuade him!"

"I will do that."

She was startled. "You, Lord? But—"

He frowned. "You doubt my ability?"

She paused, to phrase her response carefully. She could afford neither to insult him nor to trust him too far. "I fear your ability, Lord."

"Don't. I will accomplish it without bloodshed."

She remained wary. "If he dies—"

"He will not."

"If you threaten him—"

"I will not threaten him. I will merely reason with him. You say he is smart. He will appreciate my point."

That seemed tight. This was more than she had hoped for. No reprisal against Ned, and a formal royal wedding! She bowed her head. "Thank you, Lord."

"And if he does not consummate that marriage promptly, he will be executed for treason."

She stared at him in horror, discovering the loophole in her deal. She had not protected Ned *after* the wedding. "My Lord—"

Then he smiled, to a degree. "My little joke."

But she wasn't sure it was. Her cousin sometimes delighted in unusual cruelty. "Lord, the hour after he dies, so do I." Then, after a pause, she smiled, emulating his smile exactly. "My joke, too." Perhaps that would be enough to dissuade Toqtamish. If not, she would make good her threat, on schedule.

He snapped his fingers. A woman appeared at the east side of the tent. Wildflower went to the woman, and followed her silently out a side exit.

Ned saw a guard emerge from the royal pavilion. The man beckoned. "What happened in there?" Ned asked. "Where is my wife?"

"The khan has granted you an audience. Leave your weapons here."

Perplexed, Ned stripped himself of sword and dagger, setting them on the ground to his left. "As you wish." He approached the door, and the guards let him pass.

The khan was seated on his couch, resplendent in royal robes.

Ned stopped at a suitable distance from the couch and bowed his head, waiting to be addressed.

"Who are you?"

"Lord, I am Ned, of the family of Sam, a sometime scout in the service of Timur." It was clear that Toqtamish did not recognize him as the one who had found him by the river. Ned was just one of thousands the khan had routinely dealt with.

"My cousin tells me she married you, according to Christian rite."

"Yes, Lord."

"She tells me you are a man of honor."

"Yes, Lord."

"She required me to give you a position."

"I did not ask for this, Lord."

"Will you serve me with absolute loyalty?"

"If you require it, Lord. So long as it does not conflict with my personal code of honor or my prior loyalty to Timur, whom I would never treat treacherously."

"I do require it."

"Then I hereby give you my oath."

"How can you be of best use to me?"

Ned hesitated. "It is not for me to say, Lord."

"Is this how you honor your recent oath of loyalty?"

"I fear giving offense."

"Then brave your fear."

He had to answer with candor. "Lord, I believe I could give you better military advice than you have had before."

"How so?"

"You have suffered military reverses, so that Timur found it necessary to aid you. I know something of military strategy."

"A Christian architect? What could you know of military matters?"

"A military architect, Lord. I have had some experience advising a military leader. I believe I could improve your defense—and your offense."

"I have experts for these things—men who have trained all their lives. You must be a relative amateur. You feel you know better than they?"

"I mean no offense, Lord, but it is possible that they are too set in conventional ways. I have studied some of the campaigns of Timur. He is a military genius. He seldom does what others expect, and so he brings them down."

Toqtamish was thoughtful. "He does have the touch. He may have lost some battles early in his career, but he suffers reverses now only when a general goes counter to orders and botches it. He has certainly helped me."

"Yes, Lord. If you could follow similar strategies, you should be similarly successful—without requiring his help."

"Without again requiring his help," Toqtamish said. "This has considerable appeal."

Ned was silent, realizing that the comment was not an invitation to speak further.

"How is it that you did not try to remind me of what you did for me at Syr Darya?"

Ned was startled. "I did not think you remembered, Lord."

"I told you I would remember. I do not encounter many Christians who are not seeking my blood. Did you doubt my word?"

"Oh, no, Lord! But it was hardly my place to seek favors for doing my duty."

"Your duty may have saved my life. You brought a party to my rescue when the enemy was about to catch me. Now my cousin swears by you. These are good recommendations."

Ned was silent. Now he understood that the khan had had reason to interview him, and to trust him. Otherwise Ned might never have made it to the city. It would have been easy for the khan to have a party kill him on the way, rendering his marriage to Wildflower academic.

"That cross you wear—I remembered that, of course. Is it true that the cross is a symbol of the manner your religious leader was tortured to death?"

Ned thought it best not to argue theology. "It is true, Lord."

"He must have been a brave man."

"We consider him so. He remained true to his way despite all his enemies could do."

Toqtamish nodded approvingly. "We Mongols value courage. What is the distinction between your brand of Christianity and the variety the Byzantines practice?"

"It is somewhat technical, Lord. You may not be interested—" He broke off, seeing the khan's glance of irritation. "I apologize for presuming, Lord. The Byzantines believe that Jesus Christ was either the son of God—that is, Allah—or God Himself. Nestorians believe that Jesus was mortal, and experienced life fully in the manner of a human man. But he also partook of the Godhead, being vested with that eternal spirit. Thus his mother Mary was not the mother of God, but of the man in which God manifested. Jesus died, but God of course continued."

"Just as Mohammed, the prophet of Allah, died, but Allah remains eternal."

"Yes, Lord." Again, it seemed better not to quibble.

"And for that trifling theological distinction, the Christian pope banished your sect as heretical?"

"Yes, Lord."

"It is similar with Moslem sects. I think politics occur within religion as well as outside it."

"Yes, Lord."

The khan came to a decision. "I will give you a try. Now understand, I can't give you an official position, because you are a Christian. My ancestors were indifferent to religion, but the people here are Moslem, and it would foment dissension in the ranks. I may privately find it a nuisance, but I have to acknowledge the passions of the people. Have you a way around that?"

"I agree, Lord. I shall be satisfied if you listen to what I have to say, and give my notions what trial you deem fair. I need no official position. Could you make me your body servant?"

"To tend my clothing? To dump my chamber pot? These

functions are fulfilled by slaves, not free men! Wildflower would never forgive me for demeaning her husband so."

"Maybe if you put a better title on it. Chief valet, perhaps. To ensure that your slaves do not err, perhaps causing you embarrassment. Then we could converse at your convenience, and you can send me away when you tire of me."

"I will try it. But understand this: if your advice puts me into difficulty, I will banish you to another city."

"Of course, Lord."

"One other detail. You will have to convert to Islam."

Ned was amazed. "Lord, I thought you accepted me as adviser as I am."

"Yes. As adviser. But not to marry my cousin. A Moslem woman may not marry outside the true faith."

"But we are already married!"

Toqtamish stroked his beard. "That does complicate it. Then I shall have to execute her for violating the word of the prophet. That will free you from that awkwardness, so you can serve me as a Christian. Too bad; I rather like her."

Ned realized that he was being put to a test. "If one of us must die, it should be me. Wildflower is blameless."

"No, I need you. You did not violate your honor; she violated hers. So it must be her."

Was the khan bluffing? Ned was much afraid he wasn't. The Mongols were famous for solving problems with brutal efficiency. Wildflower could indeed die. "I will convert."

Toqtamish pulled on a cord, not even acknowledging his victory. Ned heard nothing, but in a moment a commander appeared. "I am appointing this man chief of my personal arrangements. He will be with me often, and will have complete freedom of my presence. If he speaks to you with a message from me, honor it."

The man nodded respectfully, and backed away. It would be done.

"Have you any questions?"

"Lord, I know little of royal Mongol attire, let alone the

requirements of the Moslem faith. If there could be someone to instruct me, at first—"

"It will be done. Anything else?"

"No, Lord. I shall be happy to rejoin my wife now."

"That is not possible."

Ned stared at the khan, not knowing what to make of this. Toqtamish smiled. "No, nothing has happened to her. Nothing will. She must be married according to Moslem rites. She has therefore gone into seclusion until the wedding. You will see her then."

Ned realized that any protest would be dangerous. He nodded.

The khan snapped his fingers. A servant appeared. "Conduct this man to my apartment and see to his comfort."

The servant nodded, and waited for Ned. Ned bowed again to the khan and backed away. When the khan averted his gaze, tacitly recognizing that the visitor was now beyond his awareness, Ned crossed to the servant, and followed him out the back. He wasn't sure what would happen to his sword and dagger, but knew that they would be attended to.

The servant brought him to an elegant tent suite in the city. The Mongols simply didn't use buildings the way others did; they were always ready to move on at short notice. But that did not mean that the royal ones suffered privation. This tent was the virtual equivalent of a palace wing. "Sahara will see to your needs," he said, turning away.

A strikingly lovely young woman of Mongol stock appeared. "You are the new valet?" she inquired in a dulcet tone.

"Yes. You are Sahara? I will need instruction in that office, and in the Moslem faith." Ned remained bemused at his sudden conversion, but with Wildflower's life at stake he had had no choice. Now he would have to follow through, for he would not cheat in this, however forced the decision had been.

"First you must dress appropriately. The khan must not be seen in the company of a peasant."

"These clothes are all I have with me."

"I will attend to it. This way."

He followed her through several corridors walled off by hanging carpets and tapestries until they came to a huge bronze tub decorated with the stylized Mongol representations of predators and birds of prey. Ned looked into the hot water, uncertain where to go next.

"This is for you," Sahara said. "I will take your old robes."

"But this—this must be the khan's bath," he protested.

"It is. So you had better be finished before he returns."

"But I can't use his bath!"

She eyed him. "I suppose I could wash you standing beside it, but that would not be as effective. I prefer to wash you in it."

"Wash me in it!" he exclaimed. "I don't want you present."

"Khan's orders," she said. "It would not be wise to evade them."

"You're sure? That he wants this?"

"Quite sure, Lord Valet."

Still he hesitated. "Who are you? I mean, what is your position?"

"I am one of the wider pool of women who serve the khan in whatever manner he wishes."

"A concubine?"

She frowned. "Unfortunately, I did not achieve that honor. I am a dancer who learned the necessary arts, but was chosen for other purposes. But I am glad to serve in whatever other manner he chooses. Now he has decreed that I prepare you and instruct you in the rudiments of the position to which you have been appointed."

"Rudiments? I should learn it properly."

"There is no need. His regular staff will attend to it."

"But—"

"You are of course aware that you hold this position in

name only. The khan wishes merely to converse with you when he finds it convenient.''

Evidently the instructions had been a good deal more detailed than had seemed possible. "Then I must trust you to guide me correctly. But is it really necessary that you attend to me in this particular fashion?"

"Yes."

It occurred to him that the khan was testing him. Did the Mongol want him to be diverted by this comely woman, and change his mind about remarrying Wildflower? That would be a convenient way to salvage a princess from marriage to an infidel. But the very notion of hurting Wildflower that way appalled him. So he would brave the khan's temptation and remain true.

He stripped his clothing efficiently and stepped into the huge bath. He had to admit it was a pleasure, for he was grimy from travel, and unlike many, he did prefer cleanliness. It was probably a legacy of Flo's attitude in that respect. He sank into the water, reveling in its comfort. There was a broad stone bench set at a level to allow him to sit with the water up to his chest.

Sahara disappeared with his old clothing, then reappeared with what looked like a costly robe. She set this on a counter. Then she stood before the bath and began to remove her own clothing.

Ned was about to ask her what she was doing, but feared she would give an honest answer, so stifled it. He proceeded to wash himself, staying mostly submerged.

Sahara stood directly before him, stripping to the waist so that her large and well formed breasts were prominent. Then she stripped the rest of the way, and turned around so that he could see every part of her. He looked, determined not to give her or the khan the satisfaction of making him retreat, figuratively. She was as appealing a figure of a woman as he had ever seen. Even Wona had not been this generously endowed. The khan was certainly able to get the best.

"Now I will wash you," she said, and stepped into the bath with him.

How far would she take it? Just as far as he allowed, he suspected. So he tried to ignore the provocation and act as if this were routine.

She stopped before him, her breasts floating. She reached out and massaged his shoulders and neck. Her touch was expert, and the sensation was wonderful. Then she moved around behind him and went over his back.

"You know your business," he murmured.

"Yes." She drew herself close to him so that her slick soft breasts pressed against his back, and reached around to massage his chest. She lifted her legs and sat behind him on the bench, her firm thighs embracing his hips.

Ned had controlled his reactions somewhat up till now, but this contact overwhelmed him, and he was suddenly fully aroused. Fortunately the water concealed his state.

Her hands worked down to massage his belly. He remained still and silent, determined not to protest.

Then her hands found his member, and grasped it with authority. Now there was no secret; she knew what she had accomplished. "Would you like to face me?" she inquired in his ear. "I will do whatever you wish."

"I wish simply to finish this bath and get dressed." It required effort to keep his voice level.

"Would you prefer to have me on a bed? I serve completely at your convenience."

"I am a married man. I prefer to be only with my wife, in that manner."

"Your wife is surely fortunate." She finished washing him, and allowed him to emerge from the bath. His erection had not diminished, but she took no further note of it as she used towels to dry him. He had either passed a test—or failed it.

The robe was quite warm and comfortable. Sahara tied his belt and brushed out his hair, making him presentable. Just in time, for now the khan arrived.

The woman disappeared. Ned, uncertain what to do, followed his best judgment. "Lord, may I help you with your clothing?"

"Don't bother. The staff already knows you are to be my companion, not a servant. Only in public will you stand ready to carry my coat."

"I hope I can live up to your expectation."

The khan led the way through a bewildering maze of interconnecting carpeted corridors and tents until they came to another pavilion. "Now we shall eat." Without seeming signal, servitors arrived with steaming platters. The khan indicated the table where they were being set. "You will sit always at the foot. In public you will sample my food first, but in private don't bother. I have many guards against poisoning."

"As you wish, Lord."

"The title—only in public. Likewise speech: You need not wait to be spoken to. If there are things you feel I should know, mention them, and I will decline if I wish."

Ned experimented. "This seems like unusual favor for a stranger whose presence is imposed by the whim of a willful girl."

Toqtamish laughed. "I think I like you already. I tell you privately: I was close to Wildflower's mother, who did me many favors, and I was sorely grieved by her death. Her daughter favors her, as I remember her as we both emerged from childhood, and I can deny her nothing within reason. Both seem to have had good judgment in people."

"My family felt that Wildflower was a good match for me. They are surely correct."

"Ah—so it was an arranged liaison."

"To a degree."

"You have reservations?"

Ned hesitated, and caught a sharp look from the khan. "I dislike the notion of marrying for social or political advantage, but I seem to be guilty of it. I am here because of it."

"But my cousin surely loves you."

"She is fifteen. Love comes readily to that age."

"This interests me. A lovely young princess throws herself at you, and you hesitate?"

"I hesitate to use her for commercial purpose. I respect her too much for that."

"I have one chief wife, a dozen secondary wives, and I have lost count of the number of concubines. All of them came to me for political or commercial advantage. I have no problem with it, so long as they are beautiful, accommodating, and loyal."

"You are the khan."

Toqtamish nodded. "A fair answer. Why did you not take Sahara?"

Ned had seen no dialogue between the woman and the khan, yet clearly the khan knew what had happened. "I am married."

"She knows that. She would be discreet."

"I would die before I would be false to my wife."

"You could have Sahara as a second wife."

Ned felt a chill. This was potentially considerable mischief. "Is this your desire?"

"Is it yours?"

This remained treacherous ground. "I mean no affront to your hospitality or to the charms of Sahara, who tempted me sorely. But a Christian takes only one wife."

"You are no longer a Christian."

Ned had lost track of that, in the welter of new impressions. "True. Though as yet I know too little of my new faith."

"Sahara will instruct you. She is well versed in scripture and protocol. By Moslem law and custom, you are not yet married to Wildflower."

"By Christian law and custom I was married to her, and my loyalty to her remains. I would not hurt her for anything."

"Neither would I. That is one reason you are here, instead of without your head." The khan made a gesture, indicating that the matter was of little consequence. "But you must marry her by Moslem custom, if you are to have royal favor."

"I am prepared to do that. Once I have mastered the requirements."

"She made a sacrifice, indulging your Christian ritual. She knew she was agreeing to prostitute herself. But for you, she was willing."

"She is no prostitute!"

"I speak figuratively. She is a princess. But Mongol passions run strong." Toqtamish shrugged. "Speak to me of strategy."

Ned did not question this abrupt change. He plunged in. "You have recently won your kingdom, because of the help of Timur. If you could organize and fight as he does, you could greatly magnify your domain."

The khan's interest quickened. "How so?"

"To your west is the khanate of Kipchak, the Golden Horde, whose domain is greater than yours. You can make it yours, if you act expediently, thus reunifying the territory of your forebears."

"I am not so great a fool as to tackle a superior army. The territory would be unified at my expense, and my head would top a pyramid of heads of my family and supporters." He smiled grimly. "I have had some experience against superior armies, as you know."

"The key term is expediency," Ned clarified. "There is a time to wait, and a time to act. I believe that you have an opportunity now that will be lost if you delay. The Golden Horde is struggling to quell the revolt of its Russian vassals. Khan Mamai has his hands full at the moment."

"Mamai is a Mongol and a kinsman."

"So were the chiefs you vanquished in order to assume your present position."

"I see you do understand politics. But Mamai is more competent than those who governed the White Horde."

"He can defeat the Russians. He can defeat the White

Horde. He can not defeat Timur. He can not defeat any combination of those forces. If you move against him now, coordinating with the Russians, you can prevail. But you must be careful. You must make certain that Timur approves your effort. You must never cross Timur.''

''Because he is my benefactor.''

''Yes. And because he is matchless in the field.''

''I see we understand each other. Even so, the resources of the Golden Horde are greater than mine.''

''Yes. You must not meet it directly in battle, yet. You must have patience, and wear it down, while the Russians continue to distract it. You must have military forces that are responsive in the manner of Timur's forces. You must practice the art of strategic retreat, though it may look like cowardice.''

''I am no coward!''

''Neither was Genghis Khan. He was master of strategic retreat. When his enemies thought they had prevailed, and lost their formation, he turned and destroyed them. He did not care what they thought at the time; he made them fools.''

''I like the way you think. We will speak more of this at another hour.'' Toqtamish snapped his fingers, and in a moment an extremely comely young woman appeared, evidently a concubine.

''I should depart,'' Ned said.

The khan didn't answer. A hand touched Ned's elbow, making him jump. It was Sahara.

He followed her back to the bath, and beyond it to a separate chamber. ''This will be yours for the duration. Take your ease, but if this bell rings, report immediately to the khan's chamber.'' She gave him a sharp glance. ''Immediately.''

''I understand.'' He had seen how quickly others had responded. If he was in dishabille, he would have to repair it as he could on the run.

"And for anything you require, I will serve. Do you prefer me with you, or in my own chamber?"

"Where is your chamber?"

She indicated a smaller one opening onto his from the east. Mongol women were always on the east, and the men on the west. "I will always be at your service, in any way you desire."

He was getting on top of this situation. "You understand, Sahara, that though I find you desirable, I do not wish to use you in any way other than ordinary. I am married."

"I understand."

"Then retire to your own chamber. But if you feel there is something of which I should be advised—"

"Of course." She hesitated. "May I comment?"

"Yes."

"I think Wildflower is marrying well." Then she turned and entered her chamber.

Ned found himself quite pleased by her flattery. It meant that she appreciated his forbearance. She had to accommodate him in any way he wished, but understood his stance. Perhaps she had a man of her own, for whom she preferred to reserve her favors, if given a choice.

But in a moment she emerged. "It is time for the ablution."

"The what?"

"We Moslems pray to Allah five times a day."

Now he made the connection. "Of course."

She showed him the ritual posture, wherein each person of the true faith bowed in the direction of Mecca, the Moslem holy city, getting down on knees and hands, touching the head to the ground. He had seen it done, but it was different actually doing it. But the physical forms were the simplest to follow; it was the intellectual forms he considered to be the challenge.

Thereafter there were many conferences, and the khan seemed to be increasingly influenced by what Ned had to say. He formulated careful plans for a sustained campaign against the Golden Horde, but did not announce them. Now was the time for quiet preparations, the training of good officers and good troops, and the acquisition of accurate information on the disposition of the enemy.

Betweentimes, Sahara acquainted him with the intellectual aspects of the Moslem faith and practice. She took him to elders of the faith, who explained the nuances and showed him the sacred texts. Ned found himself enjoying this. He loved to learn, and there was much to learn here. Much of the Moslem faith was similar to the Christian faith, for both derived from the foundation of Judaism. But while the Christians believed Jesus Christ to be the Savior, the Moslems believed him to be merely another prophet, while Mohammed was the true prophet. Thus Ned did not have to renounce his faith, merely amend it.

Then came the day for Ned's Moslem wedding. It was to be a royal ceremony, with full honors. Ned hesitated to demur, though he would have preferred something less conspicuous. He just wanted to get back together with Wildflower, for he felt most comfortable with her.

The bell sounded. Ned hastened, half-dressed, to attend the khan. The man was lying comfortably amidst the fair nude torsos of several concubines, but seemed to take no note of them. "Something I thought you should know," he said without preamble. "Wildflower offered her life on your behalf."

"But she had no need to—"

"Ah, but she did. I had forbidden her to marry you. She disobeyed me, then came to pay the penalty."

"But she indicated to us that you had acceded!"

The khan nodded. "She truly loves you, Ned. When I intimated that I might have you killed, she intimated that she would die the hour after you did. She is a Mongol; she was not bluffing. So I made the best of it, and gave you the chance to prove yourself. You have done so. But you owe it to her. Remember that."

"I shall." Indeed, Ned was shaken. He had had no idea that Wildflower had done such a thing.

The khan waved him away, then slapped the bare bottom closest to his hand. The woman stirred, more than ready to do his business.

Sahara was waiting to complete·his dressing. "You look dismayed. He told you?"

"Yes. I never suspected."

"My instruction was to ascertain whether you were potent. I don't see how there could have been any doubt."

She had misunderstood, but this was also relevant. "The khan thought I might be impotent?" Had Wildflower told?

"I think he just wanted to be sure. Some men are not partial to women. It would be extremely awkward to have such a man marry into the family."

"I thought he wanted to wean me away from my wife."

She shrugged. "That too, perhaps. But I think he was not disappointed when I failed."

"Did you really try?"

"There was no need, once I had fulfilled my mission."

That explained why she had let him be, after he had turned her down. Her instructions had been limited. He was relieved; he wasn't sure how long he could have held out, had she persisted. "And you would have married me, as a second wife, had I been inclined?"

·"Yes, of course."

"Have you no life, no wishes of your own, apart from the will of the khan?"

"No."

"What, none?"

She smiled wistfully. "I hope that some day he marries me to a noble who will value me as you value your wife, and who will be as true to me as you are to her. To love and be loved, as it is with you. But Allah's will be done "

Suddenly he felt affection for her. She was a human being, rather than a mere body. And perhaps she could be of real use to him. "Sahara, may I confide in you?"

"You may do what you like with me, as always."

"No. Not by order of the khan. This must be by your own choice."

She looked alarmed. "Please do not say anything treasonable. I would have to report it, and we both would suffer."

"No, nothing like that. I have a personal question you might help me with. But I ask for your confidence, in the manner of a friend, if you feel any friendship for me."

"I am a creature of the khan's. I—" Then her expression changed, and her eyes became bright. She had been sorely flattered. "I would not have minded marrying you, though you be Christian. You are a fine and brilliant man. But I am glad I could not sully your love for your wife. I will be your friend, to the extent I am able. What do you wish of me?"

"The reason the khan tested my potency is because I was impotent with my wife. I love her, but she is too much like my sister."

Her mouth formed an O of astonishment. "I never suspected! You were so virile. Yet you resisted me."

"It was difficult. Extremely difficult. But what I want more than anything else is to be potent with her. I know she is not my sister, and that she is worthy. But what I could do with you, I can't with her. Can you help me?"

She laughed. "It is an irony, that I must enable a man like you to be potent with another woman. But there is lore. Sometimes with political marriages, when the woman is unattractive, or when a husband is troubled and unable to do what he wishes to—there are love-herbs. I can give you one that would make you potent with your own grandmother, for an hour. You must take it an hour before the need."

"I think that is what I must have. You are sure of it?"

"Oh, yes. Had I put that in your food, you would have plunged me raw, regardless of your aversion."

"Thank you for not doing that."

"Thank the khan, that he did not direct me to." She fished in a hidden pocket and brought out a tiny silk pouch.

"You keep it with you?"

"I must always be ready to do the khan's bidding, whatever its nature. But have no concern; had I used it on you, the test would not have been valid. Your potency would not have been natural. In any event, there was no need. Your potency was quite evident."

To be sure. "How do I take this?"

"In your wine, or water, or food; it does not matter. But make sure that she will be with you, because you will be in pain if she is not."

"In pain?"

"Your urgency will become unendurable in the second hour after you take it, so that you will grasp whatever offers, even if you must rape the scullery maid. You would not like that, for she is twice your age, and ugly as a toad."

"I will make sure to be with my wife. You mentioned an hour of potency; what happens after that?"

"The body becomes exhausted with the savagery of repeated indulgences, and sinks into sexual lethargy. You will not be able to achieve potency for the following twelve hours, and thereafter only with effort. So the love-herb is not wise to take unless you really require it."

Ned thought of something else. "Does this love-herb work on women too?"

"Oh, yes! That is how it is usually used. There are no reluctant maidens in the khan's palace, unless they have the wit to avoid the wrong foods or drinks. Or the wit to flee to the nearest frigid pool the moment they feel the first surge of lust." She smiled. "Sometimes several lovely girls dive mysteriously into icy water at odd hours, occasionally in their dresses. No one professes to know why."

Ned laughed. "Has that ever been the case with you, Sahara?"

"Yes. I can speak for the power of the love-herb."

"The bath you shared with me was hot."

She smiled. "I would have needed no herb with you, Ned. It would have been a pleasure."

"And if I should take the herb, and then through some foul mischance not be able to be with Wildflower for that hour?"

"Then come to me, Ned, quickly, and I will abate your ardor and keep your secret, as a friend would."

He tucked the bag into his own pocket. "Thank you, Sahara; this is exactly what I needed."

"She will surely be most pleased, for an hour, and then rather tired," she said wistfully.

He kissed her, a thing he had not done before. "I hope so." He was vastly relieved.

Then he thought of something else. "The dowry! By Moslem custom, the man gives it to the woman, or her family. But I am poor. I have nothing worthy of a princess."

"No need to be concerned. A small dowry is in order, in a case like this, because a princess needs no enhancement. I have a bauble of little worth, that will do as the symbol." She fetched a tiny closed box. "Do not open it. Merely give it to her at the appropriate time. She will understand."

"But won't it insult the khan?"

She smiled. "He told me to give you this. Now the trinket is yours, and it will be hers. Be guided by our judgment; the gift will not be taken amiss."

He accepted it. "Thank you again, Sahara."

"It is a pleasure to assist so good a man." She squeezed his hands around the box, and then departed.

Ned learned that Moslems did not take marriage as seriously as Christians did, or at least not in the same way. They adapted to whatever cultural rituals existed in the local population. A man could divorce his wife simply by declaring publicly "I divorce thee" three times, and of course a man could have four or more wives. So he did not expect much,

on the day the khan had decreed for his marriage to Wildflower.

He was surprised. It was not a wedding at all; it was a
dance. Was he being mocked? Sahara had dressed him carefully in a formal robe, then disappeared. The khan was
seated on his throne, watching several appealing young
women gyrate. There was a considerable audience also
watching the show.

"Ah, there you are," Toqtamish said, spying Ned.
"Come stand by me. This will surely be worthwhile."

Had the khan forgotten about the wedding? Ned went to
stand by him, disturbed. He hadn't seen Wildflower in a
month, and missed her. He wanted to be with her again.

The women cleared away, and another appeared. She was
of statuesque proportions, and she moved with singular
grace. She did not remove her heavy veil, but Ned recognized her: Sahara. The Mongols belonged to the Hanafite
school of Sunni Islam, which sect did not require veils for
women. But veils were often used for decorative purpose,
or in dances, where they enhanced the mystery and made
the dancers more alluring.

"Ah yes—you are to be married today," the khan said
to Ned. "But who would be a suitable bride for you?"

Ned did not dare answer the rhetorical question. Was
Toqtamish playing one of his jokes? Did he intend to make
Ned marry Sahara?

"I think it should be she who dances best," the khan
decided. "So let us compare." He snapped his fingers.

Sahara beckoned offstage. A woman appeared. She
danced well. But the khan shook his head after a brief interval, and she was replaced by another. That one in turn
was replaced by a third, and so on in a chain.

"No, these are not good enough," Toqtamish said. He
glanced at Sahara. "Show these amateurs how it is done."

Now Sahara danced, and she was indeed superior. Her
limbs and body were matchless, and her skill was phenom-

enal. Ned knew that no one was going to dance better than she did.

Then there was a commotion at the far end of the hall. A guard appeared. "What is this interruption?" the khan demanded irritably.

"Lord, a royal procession approaches."

"But this is not my time for visitors," Toqtamish said. "There is no appointment. We are engaged in private business here."

"Do you wish us to drive it off?"

The khan hesitated. "I need more information. Ned, go out and ascertain what's going on."

Ned obediently went out with the guard. Beyond the pavilion there was indeed a procession of wagons: several small ones, and one large one. The main one was covered with rich blue cloth, with several curtained windows. They walked out to intercept it.

The wagons halted. Lovely girls got out of the small ones, each wearing a finely worked robe and a silk veil, along with a cap encrusted with jewels. They walked to the large wagon, where they opened its door and helped an elegant woman descend to the ground. She was completely shrouded in a voluminous cloak, with a hood surmounted by peacock feathers and set with precious stones. She had such a long train that the comely young women clustered around her to catch hold of loops on her robe and lift the skirts clear of the ground. In this manner the lady proceeded toward the palace.

"But who is she?" Ned asked, daunted by this evident affluence.

A guard associated with the procession approached them. "Make way for the khatun," he said bruskly.

Oh—one of the khan's chief wives. Satisfied, Ned returned inside, where Sahara was still dancing. "The khatun," he reported.

Toqtamish frowned. "None of my wives are attending this function. This has to be a stranger."

Ned realized that he had made a mistake by not seeking positive identification. Embarrassed, he began to go back out. But the khan stopped him with a gesture. "We might as well discover what she is up to, since she is here anyway."

Now the strange woman was escorted to the main chamber. All heads turned to face her, evidently impressed by her royal attire.

Sahara paused in her dance, and the khan looked across the hall. "Who is this who interrupts our amusement?"

The woman strode forward, surrounded by her attendants. She lifted her arms, and the girls quickly removed her cloak. Beneath it she wore a dancer's attire, with a tasseled halter and flowing skirt. She struck a pose.

"Oh, you came to dance," the khan said, surprised. "You heard of this contest and decided to participate. Then do so."

She danced, and her body came alive in a marvelous way. The ranking wives of the khan had become fat, and were no longer used in bed, but this one was completely lithe. She dipped and whirled, so that her skirts flung out, and her jewelry sparkled. She leaped, and landed, and flung off a tassel at intervals. Her body was slender rather than buxom, but her balance and poise were excellent, and the effect was quite nice. She was good, very good, and Ned saw heads nodding. This stranger was dancing better than Sahara had. But who was she? How could she have such a procession, if she was not really a khatun?

She came at last to face the khan, and finished with a whirling flourish, bowing down before him, her bosom heaving.

"You danced very well," the khan said. "But we have important business here. You must not be anonymous. Who are you?"

The figure removed her hood to reveal her head. Her face was veiled, but a bright golden crown set with gems spar-

kled above it. There was a murmur of awe in the hall. This
was a princess!

"So you are of royal blood," the khan said. "Show us
your face."

Slowly she removed her veil. It was Wildflower!

Ned was astonished. He had never seen her like this. She
was exquisite, and truly a princess.

Something changed in him then. It was as if the world
changed colors, and what had been familiar became newly
unfamiliar. He had known she was a Mongol princess, but
still thought of her as his little sister. Now he knew she was
the same girl Lin had befriended, but he thought of her as
a princess. He had seen her in her royal Mongol splendor.

"So you are my cousin, the Princess Wildflower," Toqtamish said. "And you have won the dance. Now you must
marry my valet."

Wildflower nodded, smiling.

"Then let it be done." He looked around. "Who will
bear witness to the validity of the contract?"

Sahara spoke. "I will, Lord. I know this man to be competent and honorable."

"Who else?"

Idiku Berlas appeared. "I will, Lord."

"And where is a group of righteous people to establish
the validity of the ceremony?"

A man stood in the audience, one of the ranking officers.
"We are here, Lord," he said.

"Where is the dowry?"

There was a pause. Then Sahara's eyes flicked toward
Ned. Oh—he had forgotten.

"I have it here, Lord," Ned said, producing the tiny box
he had been given. "It is a thing of no great worth, as my
family is not wealthy."

"It will do," Wildflower said, accepting it with a smile.
She opened the box to show a single bright faceted diamond.

Ned was amazed. This was the "mere bauble" he had

been carrying? It was of enormous value. The khan had played another little joke.

"Such a small dowry suggests that the groom is extremely desirable in his own right," the khan remarked with a straight face. He glanced at Ned as if in doubt. "Can this be the case?"

"It is the case, Lord," Idiku said gravely. "He is a loyal, gentle, and intelligent man. In any event, the bride needs little, as she is lovely, she is royal, and she carries the favor of all the Mongols." He glanced significantly at the audience, and it responded with a low chorus of agreement.

Ned was coming to appreciate how carefully this play had been crafted. This was public recognition of the status of the bride, and of the marriage. Every one of the khan's questions was rhetorical, with a rehearsed response. It was no conventional wedding ceremony, but it had considerable authority. The khan had had his bit of fun with Ned, leaving him in doubt about the nature of the marriage, but now it was serious.

"Is your father present?" the khan inquired of Wildflower.

"My father is dead, Lord."

Toqtamish stood. "Then I, as your nearest male relative, will do the honor." He took her hand. "Praise be to Allah and blessings be upon His prophet!" He turned to Ned. "I give you my cousin Wildflower in marriage."

Now he could speak the line he knew, which was religiously ambiguous. "Praise be to God, and blessings be upon the Messenger of God. I accept her in marriage."

Then they kissed. He had kissed her before, but this time there was magic in it. He had thought of this second ceremony as a formality, but knew that it had made his marriage to her real.

The wedding was done.

"Now the important part," Toqtamish said. "The feast."

And it was some feast. The food was brought in on tables of gold and silver, each table carried by four men. There was boiled horsemeat and mutton. There were drinks and pastries. The carver came wearing silken robes overlaid by a silk apron, with a number of knives in their sheathes. He cut the meat into small pieces, together with the bones, and served it on small silver platters in which there was salt dissolved in water.

Ned fed Wildflower tidbits, and she fed him tidbits, and they both drank too much qumys, which was fermented mare's milk, and honeyed mead. Alcoholic beverages were forbidden by most sects of the Moslem religion, but fermented liquor was held to be lawful by the Hanafites. There must have been something strong in the drink, because both of them got too dizzy to walk straight.

At last it was done, and they were allowed to leave. Wildflower donned her veil and cloak, becoming the anonymous woman again. Several members of the group saluted them in parting. Ned had no idea where they were going, but she did.

They came into the nuptial chamber. It was sumptuous, but he hardly noticed. All he could see was Wildflower, the vision of loveliness.

"I missed you," he said, taking her in his arms. "I hated being separated from you."

"Yes," she breathed.

He lifted aside her veil and kissed her. "I think I did not know how I loved you, until I was separated from you."

"Yes."

They were beside the huge bed. He clasped her and fell upon it. She fell on top of him, her gown flaring out, her legs straddling him. "I do love you, Wildflower! I know it now."

"Yes."

"And I desire you most ardently. If you—may I—?"

"Yes!"

Then he was driving through her clothing, searching for the flesh beneath. She used her hands to make way for him.

They rolled over, and he drove on into her explosively, heedless of anything but the need.

"Yes, yes," she said, clinging close, squeezing him with internal muscles.

The bliss of it transported him. "Oh, Wildflower, oh Wildflower," he gasped, buried within her.

"Yes." She held him close, as if unable to get enough of him.

Only as he subsided did he realize the full implication of what had happened. "I was potent!"

She laughed. "I hoped you wouldn't notice, until too late."

"It is definitely too late," he said, half ruefully. "I have creased and soiled your wedding gown." Actually it was her dancing costume, but that didn't matter.

"Then take it off me and do it again more cleanly."

"I think I shall."

They disentangled and got their clothing off. He realized that she still wore her little crown. Naked, they looked at each other. Ned's member had lowered, but now it rose again. "I asked Sahara for a potion to make me potent," he said.

"You what?" she demanded with a sudden regal flash of anger.

"But I forgot to take it."

She considered that. Then she burst out laughing, her whole body shaking. "You didn't need it!"

"I thought I would, and I wanted to please you. But the moment I saw you, there was nothing in my world but you. I love you, Wildflower."

"You must, because you converted to the Moslem faith for me."

"Yes."

Then she seemed to think of something. "I was going to ask you to, but I wasn't sure you would. My cousin said he would persuade you."

"He did."

She turned sober. "*How* did he persuade you?"

"That doesn't matter. I am glad to be with you in this."

"I made him promise not to hurt you or threaten you."

"He didn't."

But she was suspicious. "How did he persuade you?" she asked again.

Ned saw that she was determined to have the truth. "He said he would execute you for betraying your faith."

"He wouldn't do that!"

"Oh, Wildflower, I couldn't take the chance. He told me how you protected me by threatening to die the hour after I did. Even though I had been no kind of a husband to you. I couldn't let you die!"

"You were all the husband I wanted."

"How could I be the beneficiary of such love, and not return it?"

She flung herself upon him, bearing him back on the bed. He felt her breasts and thighs against him, and this time they were mounds and columns of ecstasy. "I love you, Ned! I always loved you! But you saw me as a little sister."

"You are not my sister!" he said with mock seriousness as he cupped her tight, soft bottom with his hands. "You never were. I know that now." He tickled her buttocks, making her squiggle. Then they dissolved into further laughter.

Somewhere in the middle of it, they coupled again. "So strong a passion," she said. "Are you sure you didn't take that potion?"

"Absolutely. Do you want me to?"

"No."

"Do you want to take it yourself?" he asked mischievously.

"No! I want only you, with me like this, forever."

"You can *have* me like this, forever."

Her own face turned mischievous. "Was it like this with Wona?"

"No. It's much better with you."

"Really, Ned?" Suddenly she was the wondering child again, wanting reassurance.

"Really. With her it was guilty and forced. With you it's fulfillment. My only guilt with you is waiting so long to take what you offered. I really was a fool, and I thank you for bearing with me so long. You truly are all that I ever needed. Ever really wanted. I know it now."

She sighed, loving the news. They fell somewhat apart, but she snuggled up against him, within kissing range. "What changed?"

Ned tried to analyze it. "I think it was a combination of things. The separation—I saw myself as such a fool for not—I mean, you *are* a lovely girl, Wildflower—"

"Thank you." She kissed him. "Go on."

"Then there was Sahara. She tried to seduce me—"

She stiffened. "What?"

"But didn't succeed." She relaxed. "But she did get me, you know, excited."

"I know." She stroked him where he was excitable.

"And I thought, how can I be so—so ready to do this with her, and not with you? It didn't make any sense."

"Yes."

"And the khan told me how you risked your life for me. That frightened me. If you had died—oh, Wildflower!" The horror of it burgeoned anew.

"I love you," she explained. "I did what I had to do."

"And the khan admired that." He paused. "Did you tell him about—?"

"Oh, Ned, I didn't want to! But I had to. He asked for my deepest secret, and I had to give it to him. It's part of our protocol. But he shouldn't have told anyone else."

"I don't think he did. But that's why he sent Sahara. To see if I was potent. She reported that I was. And that I was loyal to you. And I knew that I had to be with you again. Then when I saw you—you were nothing like my sisters. You were so regal, so beautiful, so wonderful! The way you danced—I never knew you could do that!"

"I practiced. Sahara helped me."

"It was as if I had never seen you before, and yet I had. In that moment I really desired you."

She kissed him again. "As I desired you."

"Yes. You truly are a princess."

"I truly am."

"And I truly love you."

"And now we are truly married."

"Yes."

"And you won't need Sahara in your bedroom any more."

"I never needed her there. Now stop being jealous and kiss me some more."

"I'll do better than that." And she did.

❂

There were many discussions, and Toqtamish heeded them, and soon developed a force to be reckoned with. Timur supplied advice and help, but now the khan was becoming increasingly independent. Good commanders were being promoted, and good men recruited and trained. The khan called in levies to raise a considerable army.

It was not long before his leadership was tested. Malik had been defeated and driven out, but he was not dead. The Mongol prince of Serai had refused to ally with Malik against Toqtamish, so Malik had killed him and claimed his lands. Now, using Serai as a base, Malik raised an army to attack Toqtamish. By his side was his companion Balinjak, whose prowess and honor were famous, lending strength where Malik alone would have been weak.

But Malik faced a far more disciplined and powerful force than he had reckoned with. In just a few months the White Horde had become not only strong but savvy. Toqtamish had a number of advisers, and he consulted them all—and chose the course that most resembled Ned's private advice. He met Malik in the spring of 1378 and destroyed his army.

Malik was killed, and Balinjak was captured and brought before the conqueror's throne.

"How should I deal with such a hero?" Toqtamish asked Ned before the meeting.

"Spare him, if he will make his oath of fealty to you," Ned said. "You could have no better defender by your side, and he can really help rouse the troops and compel the loyalty of those who once served Malik."

Toqtamish nodded, then led the way to the audience chamber. Ned followed, carrying the khan's cloak. By this time Ned's true place was widely known, but because he was newly converted from the Christian faith it remained unofficial. He was satisfied, because the lowliest position, with the khan's favor, was more exalted than the highest with the khan's disfavor. He had married the khan's cousin, which was a root of favor, but now he had that favor on his own merit.

Balinjak was a fine figure of a man, and he walked with his head upright despite his bonds. He seemed hardly daunted by his circumstance. He ignored the people in the court, and met the khan's gaze without flinching.

"What do you expect of me?" Toqtamish asked the prisoner.

"A swift death." He did not grant the khan a title.

Toqtamish made a show of considering. "I am told you are a man of honor."

Ned remembered a similar remark, when the khan had first interviewed him. The subject did not come up unless Toqtamish was already prepared to deal.

"I am, and I serve my master loyally, or his heir."

"I am Malik's heir."

"You are not his heir. You are his conqueror, because of the support of Tamerlane."

There was an angry murmur in the court. "We do not call Timur by such a name," Toqtamish said.

"I do."

The man was in effect daring the khan to kill him outright. Toqtamish glanced at Ned, then back to Balinjak. "Will you make your oath of fealty to me?"

"No."

Toqtamish shook his head. "You are a good man. I would like to have you in my service. But if you will not serve me, I will still spare your life and set you free, if you will swear never to conspire against me."

Balinjak looked surprised. "You would spare me?"

"Men of honor are rare," Toqtamish said, glancing again at Ned.

Balinjak shook his head. "I have spent the best years of my life in the service of Malik. I cannot bear to see another on his throne. May his eyes be torn out, who wishes to see you on Malik's seat." Then, surprisingly, he dropped to his knees and bowed his head. "Lord Toqtamish, if you would be gracious to me, cut off my head and put it under that of Malik, and let his corpse recline on mine, so that his delicate body may not be begrimed with dust."

Toqtamish glanced a third time at Ned. Ned shrugged. The prisoner was honorable, but would not yield. He had used an honorific title only when pleading for a special death.

"So let it be," the khan said with regret. The gallant prisoner was escorted away, to be honorably executed.

Ned regretted it too. He would have liked to come to know Balinjak, who was a much better man than the master he had served. But if he would not give his oath, he was too dangerous to spare. Ned realized that he himself could readily have suffered a similar fate, had he made a similar demand. As a result, he was one of the few men the khan truly trusted. As Malik had surely trusted Balinjak, with good reason.

Later, with Wildflower, Ned confided his deep regret at the outcome of that encounter. "That's the trouble with honorable men," Wildflower said. "You won't bend at all." Then she kissed him passionately. "It is one of the thousand reasons I love you."

"You have reasons?" he inquired with mock surprise.
She struck him with three more kisses.

Toqtamish's second campaign of that year was much
grander in scale and purpose. He moved against the Golden
Horde. Timur's emissaries were surprised; they had expected Toqtamish to be a relatively unambitious ruler, once
he had secured his kingdom. Instead he was acting much
the way Timur himself would have. They did not object,
though they evidently feared that the khan would misplay
his hand and soon come to grief, as he had so often before.

But it was Ned's job to see that Toqtamish did not do
that. There was nothing haphazard about this campaign.
Toqtamish did not seek open battle with the unified forces
of the Golden Horde, but rather campaigned against the
weaker local khans and princes who had aspirations for the
top position. The strongest of these was Mamai, the leading
claimant for the throne of the Blue Horde, the major faction.
Mamai was too strong to meet openly, and Toqtamish had
to suffer a number of taunts about his supposed cowardice,
but he stayed with Ned's program and avoided a definitive
battle. There were times when Ned feared the khan would
listen to his more violent advisers and seek one glorious but
ultimately disastrous battle, but as long as Ned's way won,
Toqtamish remained with it.

Thus it went for two years. Ned spent a lot of time in the
field, surveying situations, because the key to victory was
in timely, accurate information. He also spent much time
with the khan, and was often home in Sabran with Wildflower. She did not like the frequent separations, but she
remained with the family, and was especially close to Lin.
The fortunes of the family prospered in this period, by no
coincidence. Sam had good work building siege engines,
and Jes and Ittai had a good ship and trade route on the
Caspian Sea.

Toqtamish's chance came late in 1380. Mamai was in

firm possession of the western tribes, including the Kip-
chaks, but now he faced a united uprising of the Russian
princes to the north. The Russians were commanded by
Dmitri, Grand Prince of Moscow. They had never been very
orderly vassals, and constantly desired independence. Mamai found it necessary to petition for Lithuania's aid against
the rebels. But Dmitri, acting to prevent that, marched out
quickly to force a confrontation with Mamai in the region
of Kulikuvo. This was hilly country south of Moscow, by
the headwaters of the Don, the river that flowed south into
the Sea of Azov and thus connected to the Black Sea.

But Toqtamish did not strike. He waited, letting the Russians make their move. He had spies out to watch the action
and keep him current on it. As Ned had advised him, it was
best to let the two other sides bleed each other dry without
distraction. Then the pieces would be easier to pick up.

The Russians, as it turned out, were not stupid about war.
Their men had spent a century serving as conscripts in Mongol armies, and they had learned how to fight the Mongol
way. They anchored their lines in positions that could not
be flanked, extending from the bank of the river to a steep
forested slope.

The Mongols were stuck with a battle site chosen by their
adversaries. "Idiocy!" Ned remarked, smiling. "Genghis
Khan would never have tolerated that." But of course this
was not the day of Genghis, or of his genius generals.

The Mongols had little choice but to try to pierce the
Russian front. After fierce fighting and heavy losses, they
finally buckled one wing of the Russian lines. But Dmitri,
with cunning worthy of a Mongol, had a cavalry troop hidden in ambush in the forest. The Russian cavalry caught the
charging Mongols in the flank, decimating their ranks. He
had used their own tactics against them, employing a ruse
of weakness to lure them into a trap. Mamai's army was
routed, and he had to retreat to the lands between the Don
and the Volga to gather a new army and exact his vengeance.

Ned nodded. He had predicted something like that. A straightforward attack at a site chosen by the enemy was stupid. Once again he had shown Toqtamish the wisdom of caution.

The Russians, victorious but exhausted, lacked the strength or supplies to press their victory, and returned home. They had accomplished their purpose, defending their independence.

"Now!" Ned said.

Toqtamish made his move. He pounced on Mamai while the khan's forces were weakened, at Kalka, near the Sea of Azov. It was hardly a fair situation, and the remnant of the Golden Horde was routed. Mamai fled to the Genoese colony nearby, but the Genoese, who had suffered from his arrogance, slew him. Toqtamish became khan of the Golden Horde, which now encompassed all the territory of its ancient days.

"But you can't afford to leave the rebellious Russians on your flank," Ned warned him. "Should they ally with the Lithuanians, they could become too strong to handle."

"But we lack the strength to properly subdue them now," the khan protested.

"True. So you must maintain relations with them. But don't relax. They are potentially more dangerous to you than Mamai was."

Toqtamish nodded. But for once it seemed that Ned's caution was wrong, for the Russians immediately sent sword-bearers with their homage. They recognized the fact that their princes held their positions only at the khan's pleasure. The advisers who had opposed Ned's strategies claimed that he had led the khan into foolish concern about an enemy too weak to cause him any mischief.

However, when Toqtamish summoned the Russian princes themselves to come in person to his court, and to pay tribute, the Russians sent excuses.

"You were right, as always," Toqtamish told Ned. "They proffer only lip service, not substance. They think that because they beat Mamai, they can beat me. We shall have to teach them a lesson.''

But it was necessary to recover and prepare. So for a year the khan left the Russians alone, while he mustered and prepared his army. Then in the summer of 1392 he moved against them. His army was massive and well trained; the only thing it lacked was siege equipment, because that would slow down progress. Ned rode with the khan, and this time his sister Jes came too, garbed as a man, to protect Ned in the field. She loved her husband, just as Ned loved his wife, but her hunger for travel and action remained. The khan knew her nature, but pretended not to; he enjoyed this incidental secret.

The Mongols seized Russian boats and used them to ferry troops across the Volga River. They enlisted Russian guides to lead them along the best route to Moscow. The Mongol army was overwhelming, and some Russians lost hope. They sought to curry Toqtamish's favor with gifts. Prince Dmitri's godfather in Novgorod sent his two sons with presents. And spies reported that Prince Dmitri himself abandoned Moscow and went northeast to Kostroma to raise a larger defensive force.

Toqtamish continued his march on Moscow. Flames and smoke from burning villages and fields marked his advance, visible by day and night. He was making his point. Ned did not enjoy this aspect of campaigning, but Jes did. ''The Russians showed their contempt of us,'' she said. ''Now they are learning respect. In the future they will consider more carefully before holding back on tribute. This is what war is all about.''

''I prefer peace.''

''Then you will have to find some other khan to advise, because Toqtamish is out to conquer the world.''

''All except Timur's domain.''

She glanced sidelong at him. ''Oh?'' But she did not comment further.

The news of the scouts continued. Many people were fleeing Moscow, but those who remained were organizing a defense. Prince Dmitri sent a young Lithuanian named Ostei to take charge, and his competence instilled confidence in the people. The Lithuanians were formidable because they understood the significance of the campaign. Peasants from the countryside poured into the city for shelter. The walls were manned by brave but largely untrained militia. Even monks were bearing arms in the defense of their city. But, the spies said, there was a feeling of doom.

"Well justified," Jes remarked with satisfaction.

"I gather you are not much interested in staying home and having babies," Ned said.

"I will get to that in due course." But she looked thoughtful.

On August 23, 1382, the Mongols arrived at Moscow. Toqtamish sent envoys who spoke Russian to ask about Grand Prince Dmitri. They were told that he was no longer in the city, and it seemed to be true, as it confirmed the news of the spies. Ostei, the Lithuanian, was now in charge, and no, he would not yield the city. So the envoys returned to report to the khan, and the siege began.

For three days the Mongols punished the defenders of the wall with deadly storms of arrows. Jes was among them, firing at any head she saw on the wall. Soon no heads showed; the Russians were afraid to fire back.

But when the Mongols attacked the walls directly, they were repulsed by heavy stones and boiling water. Ostei did know what he was doing, and his amateurs were learning professionalism in a hurry. This was likely to take some time—and Ned had already advised the khan not to get embroiled in a winter campaign. They needed to take Moscow without undue delay, or the war would become considerably more difficult.

Toqtamish was thoughtful. "Do you know of any way to cut this campaign short without sacrificing our objectives?"

"Bring the siege equipment."

"It will take a month to get here."

Ned refrained from reminding the khan that he had urged that the siege engines follow closely after the main army. Other advisers had belittled the notion that the cowardly Russians would actually stand and fight in the face of the overwhelming Mongol army. But they had not reckoned on the unexpected: the expertise of the Lithuanian commander. Ned had known to expect the unexpected.

"It is Dmitri you need to nullify," Ned said. "Maybe you can make peace with the city, since he isn't here, and move on to capture him before he raises a big army. Once you have him, Moscow won't matter."

Toqtamish nodded. "I will consider it." That meant that he would consult with his formal advisers, and see whether there was a consensus.

That day a new adviser arrived, summoned from a far province. This was Ormond, who had a reputation for getting the job done by whatever means he deemed expedient. Ned did not like the man's reputation, nor the man himself, when he met him; sneakiness seemed to surround him like a noxious cloud. Rumor said that his conniving had brought shame to the man he had most recently served, so that he had had to depart in haste lest he be quietly executed. Thus he had been available for a new position.

The formal introduction was in the khan's tent, which could have held 500 people. It was covered in white felt and was lined inside with silks, cloths, and pearls. This, for the khan, was roughing it in the field.

The visitor touched the ground with his right knee. "I hastened at your beck, Great Khan," Ormond said, bowing his head low before Toqtamish. "I apologize that it was necessary to bring my good Moslem Turkish wife with me, lest the infidels mistreat her."

"We regret in turn that we lack proper facilities for a woman of quality," Toqtamish responded graciously. "But when we take the city, she shall have fitting accommodations. Present her to me now."

Ormond bowed low again, then signaled to the side. A

cloaked and veiled woman stepped forth. Despite her complete shrouding, Ned could tell by her proportions and the way she moved that she was beautiful. No wonder Ormond had not cared to leave her behind.

The woman bowed as low as her husband had, unspeaking. Her poise and grace spoke for her. Ned's curiosity was aroused. How had this loutish man won such a creature?

"Show your face," Toqtamish said, similarly intrigued.

She lifted her head, and then her veil, allowing the beauty of her countenance to shine forth. And Ned froze. *It was Wona!* His brother's former faithless wife. Who had seduced him, and tortured him with her power over him, until Jes had taken her away.

"This court is blessed by your presence," Toqtamish told her. "You and your husband must join us at our repast today."

Wona nodded, properly grateful for this significant sign of favor by the khan.

The formalities concluded, but Ned was hardly aware of them. He had never expected to see Wona again. Now she was here, instantly complicating his existence. He hoped she had not seen him or recognized him, where he stood as one of several of the khan's attendants. As soon as he could, he left the tent, so as to rejoin his sister.

"Wona!" Jes exclaimed. "What is she doing here?"

"She is the wife of the new adviser, Ormond."

"Ormond! He's the one Ittai sent her to. But he lives far away. I was sure he would never cross our paths again."

"He fell out of favor where he was, and the khan summoned him to be an adviser. He just arrived."

"This is mischief."

"This is mischief," he agreed glumly.

"Did she see you?"

"I don't think so. But she will eat with the khan today, so she is bound to see me then."

"Toqtamish shouldn't miss you for one meal. Find business elsewhere."

That made sense, because the last thing he wanted to do was have any further interaction with Wona. Just the single sight of her had stirred a complex both of guilt, shame, and desire in him. She was still so infernally lovely! So he busied himself with his equipment, and tried with notable unsuccess to blank her out of his thoughts.

But that afternoon as he went to the latrine trench to relieve himself, he heard a dulcet voice. "Ned."

It was Wona. He didn't turn. What was she doing at a place like this? The stink was terrible.

"Ned, I must speak with you," she said. Her voice was low and urgent. "We must not be seen together. If my husband knew—"

"Then don't leave his side," he said gruffly. "I want no part of you."

"How do you know? You once liked that part well enough."

He turned, but didn't see her; she was hidden behind a tree. "I am married now. You mean nothing to me."

"Congratulations. I'm sure she is a nice girl." Her tone suggested that "nice" equated to "uninteresting." "But I have information you will want."

"I want nothing of yours. Share it with your husband."

"It is *from* my husband, who doesn't know I know. I overheard—but I can't tell you here. Meet me tomorrow morning at the red farmstead down the trail three leagues east of here."

"I'll not meet you anywhere! I don't want to be near you." But that was true on only one level. The very sound of her voice had given him a guilty erection.

"Ned, be sensible! There is a massive, terrible treachery in the making. You must tell the khan, for I cannot. My husband would—Ned, you must hear me out!"

"Treachery?" It was not difficult to believe that Ormond would be involved in something dirty. For whom was the man's real loyalty?

"The red farmstead, tomorrow morning," she repeated. "Don't let anyone see you go there."

"I'll not go—" he started. But now another man was coming to the trench, and he couldn't continue talking. So he walked away, not looking at the tree.

He found Jes and told her. "And she wants me to meet her tomorrow at a private place."

"I think she just wants to seduce you again."

"Yes. She probably has no information."

Jes cocked her head thoughtfully. "Yet suppose she does? If there really should be something, and you passed it by, and then Ormond leads the khan into an ambush—"

"You think I should see her?"

"She'd have you back in thrall in a moment."

"No she wouldn't." But his doubt showed.

"Ned, I know you love Wildflower. But you are a mouse before that snake. Wona will consume you."

"So I can't see her," he said, half-relieved.

"You will have to see her, to be sure there is no betrayal she knows of—and I will have to go with you. I'll kill her if I have to."

"I don't think I could do that."

"I know you couldn't. But I can. Probably it won't have to come to that, because she knows me, and will back off. I will protect you."

And she would, in two senses: physically and emotionally. "Thank you, Jes."

"I'll get horses. You go to the trench—and on beyond it, when no one is looking. I'll be there at dawn."

Ned nodded. He profoundly appreciated his sister's support. She understood him perfectly, weaknesses and all, and would see that he handled this matter properly.

In the morning he met Jes beyond the trench, and they rode out to the east. In three hours they spied the red farmstead, nestled at the edge of the forest. It looked deserted, but there was a horse grazing beside it.

"Just in case it's a trap," Jes said, drawing her knife and

holding it against the side of the horse away from the house. She could hurl that blade swiftly and accurately.

He dismounted and walked to the door. It opened as he approached. Wona was there, wearing a tight woolen dress that concealed nothing of her proportions. "Come in quickly, Ned; don't let anyone see you."

"My sister brought me."

Wona glanced beyond him, frowning. "Then she must hide too. It is death for all of us, if my husband learns."

"Tell me, and we'll be away from here," Ned suggested.

"No; it is too long in the telling. Let the horses graze; maybe it will be all right."

Jes dismounted and led the horses to the pasture beside the house. She tied their reins up on the saddles. They were well trained; they would not stray, and would come when called. Ned waited until she joined him, before stepping into the cabin.

It was empty, except for Wona. Jes had known that, or she would not have entered. She had a warrior's senses about such things.

"You thought I would ambush you?" Wona inquired disdainfully. "I would never hurt you, Ned."

Jes snorted.

"Or you, Jes," Wona continued. "We have meant too much to each other. I'm glad you took Ittai; he's a good man."

"What's this?" Ned asked.

Wona smiled. "You didn't know? Captain Ittai left me for her. But I think he would not have, had I not shown Jes how to use her body. Had I not been willing to go."

Ned looked at his sister. "What did she show you?"

"We exchanged information," Jes said tightly. "I showed her how to kill, and she showed me how to appeal to a man." But she turned a hard glance to Wona. "Just tell my brother what you have to tell him, and we'll go. We don't want to see you again."

"Then we had better settle into some comfort," Wona

said. "It will take some time in the telling. I have some food. Take a stool."

"We didn't come here to eat," Ned said.

Wona shrugged. "Please yourself." She fetched bread and a jug of wine from a bag in the corner, and set them on the wooden table. "I have something special: caviar. It greatly improves the flavor of the bread." She lifted her right leg so that her comely thigh showed, and revealed a sheath strapped there. She drew a knife and cut off some bread.

Ned pretended not to have noticed that deep flash of thigh. But he was sure Wona had angled her leg deliberately to give him the most compelling view. Knowing her ways did not prevent him from reacting to them. Emotionally he despised her, but physically he desired her.

"I don't eat on a mission," Jes said.

"But surely you will want to sample this." Wona proffered the bread.

Jes paused, then accepted it. She dug out some of the caviar and put it on the bread. She took a bite.

"You see, it is good food," Wona said. "I am eating it too." She cut off another slice of bread.

Jes nodded. "It is good food."

"You and I do not want to interfere with each other," Wona said to Jes. "We have tended each other in illness. Give me one hour."

"What are you talking about?" Ned asked.

Jes paused, then answered. "Wona and I came to know each other, when we traveled together. We are different creatures, but we do not see each other as evil. If she led you into an ambush, I would kill her. But she means you no harm, by her definition. She has asked me to allow her to deal with you without interference."

"All I want is the news of that treachery."

"But there is a price to that news," Wona said.

"Why should he pay it?" Jes asked, as if negotiating.

"Do you think I could not have held Ittai, had I chosen

to? When I learned that you were the other woman, I let him go because I would not hurt you.''

"You let him go!" Jes repeated, astonished. "No—he left you!"

"There were sides of me I did not need to show him or his housemaid. I could have fascinated him, blinding him to all else. You know that. I know my business, as you know yours." Wona paused, letting that statement sink in. "He was worth more to you than to me. Because of what we meant to each other, I gave him to you."

Jes's surprise slowly turned to acceptance. "You could have held him," she agreed at last.

"What would be the price of him?"

Jes nodded reluctantly. "One hour."

"This is not making any sense at all!" Ned protested.

Jes angled her head. "Is someone coming?"

"No one followed me," Wona said. "And I'm sure you wouldn't let anyone follow you. So anyone who passes here must be coincidental."

"All the same, I'll check." Jes started for the door, carrying her bread.

"Don't leave me!" Ned cried.

Jes sighed. "Ned, I think this is one battle you must after all fight yourself. She's not going to say anything until she has settled with you, one way or the other. My time is better spent making sure there is no mischief abroad." She went on outside.

"See—she trusts me alone with you," Wona said as she used the knife to spread caviar on the slice of bread.

"She knows I'll call her if there is trouble." Ned, feeling awkward, sat on a stool.

"What have you to fear from me? She knows that you are the very last person I would hurt. I would much rather make love to you." She handed him the slice of bread.

Bemused, Ned accepted it. "What is this treachery?"

She cut off another slice and smeared caviar over it.

"Have you lost your feeling for me? I have not lost mine for you. You're such a brilliant man."

And such a fool about women, particularly this one. "You held me like a captive bird. What is this treachery?"

Wona took the stool opposite him, drawing the skirt of her dress up above her knees so that it would not stretch out of shape. The knife-sheath got in her way, so she slid the skirt up farther and removed it. She seemed to be wearing nothing underneath.

She picked up her bread and bit delicately. "Do try this, Ned. Caviar is a rare Russian delicacy, said to enhance potency." She let her legs spread.

Ned looked away from her clearly revealed thighs, ashamed of the sexual urgency they generated in him. He chomped his bread almost savagely. The taste of it was surprisingly good. "What is this treachery?"

"Do you know what I want of you, Ned?"

"If you are loyal to the khan, you will give me the information."

"The khan is a Mongol. I am a Turk, as are you. My loyalty is to myself and my friends. I do not simply give away my wares; I make the best deal I can."

"I don't care for your deal." But his sincerity was being undercut by the sight of her body. He didn't want to desire her, but his body took no more note of his mind than it had when he had been impotent with Wildflower.

Wona stood, found cups, and poured some wine. She offered it to him. "Would you like me to sip from it first?"

She was teasing him with the notion that he might suspect her of poisoning him. He grasped it almost roughly and drank. It was fine and strong; he would have to be careful lest it cloud his judgment. Wona was doing everything to distract him, and succeeding admirably. So was that her only purpose? To try to seduce him again?

"Oh, there really is a conspiracy," she said, as if fathoming his thoughts. "You will need to tell the khan. Would you like more bread?"

"No." It seemed that she was determined to make him wait for her information.

"More wine, then?"

"No."

"You are a hard man to please." She took his empty cup and set it on the table. But instead of returning to her stool, she began to dance. Her motions were languorously slow, and her body became like liquid. Her breasts quivered under the knit dress, and her hips flowed out and in as if possessed of their own agendas. He had not seen a dance like that since Sahara performed at his wedding. She let down her hair so that it joined the sway, and smiled at him.

Ned swallowed. He was married, and he loved his wife, but he desired Wona with an intensity he would not have believed. He wanted to protest, or at least look away, but did neither.

She circled close to him, and he smelled the appealing musk of her body. She turned and danced with her back to him, so that he could see the flexing of her buttocks under the tight knit. She bent forward, projecting her bottom, and he remembered how she had received his explosive entry, so long ago. He wanted to leap up and take hold and plunge in, and knew she would not only let him, but make it as good for him as was humanly possible. Wona had faults, but was matchless at that particular type of performance.

One hour: that was how long Jes was giving them. If he could hold out for that time, the sexual siege would be over. He tried to close his eyes, and could not; he tried to focus his mind on Wildflower, and could not. He had carelessly walked into a battle of her choosing, and was at a severe disadvantage. He was caught in the storm of Wona's desire, and could only try to ride it out.

Wona turned again, and now her living breasts almost brushed his face. Then she abruptly sat on his lap, flinging her arms around him and pulling his face into her bosom. His arms involuntarily went around her midriff. "I still want your child, Ned," she said.

"I don't want to give it to you," he said into her warm woolen left breast. Her body was so soft and light!

"No one need know. Just give it to me, and go your way, and I will go mine." She tensed her buttocks rhythmically, sending a hidden message to the most interested part of him.

"No." But he heard the weakness in it. He knew he should throw her off and depart, but he couldn't. He couldn't even let go of her. Her body was so exquisitely formed, and so close and pliable!

"We can do it right here, right now," she said. "Open your trousers, and I will hitch up my dress."

"No." Yet he knew he was on the verge of doing it.

"Here, this is better." She got up, hoisted up her skirt, spread her legs, and sat on him again, her thighs clasping his waist. Even through the clothing, he felt the compelling magic of their touch. "I can bring you such joy, Ned! You know I can. Just let me do it."

And he knew she *would* do it, if he let her, as she had before. She had already excited him almost beyond endurance, and she would set him inside her, and he would give her all that was in him. Still he did not move.

"Or I can give you something to kiss, first." Wona reached around herself and pulled further on her dress. It slid upward around the curves of her body, shaping itself to them as it moved, until her fine breasts popped out beneath it. She wore nothing underneath, as he had known would be the case. "I want you to be satisfied, Ned." She leaned into his face.

He turned his face aside, but it still rested between her breasts. She used her hands to lift them up for his closer appreciation. "I know you want me, Ned, as I want you."

He could not deny it. He was ready to give himself up for lost. He fought to summon an image of Wildflower's face, ashamed of the betrayal in which he was indulging. But his wife was far away.

"And I will give you my information, after," Wona said, bending her head to kiss his ear.

Why was she still bargaining, when she had already won? Apparently she didn't know of her victory. Then he realized that there were limits to what Wona could do. He could not fight her, or throw her off, or even speak out against what she was doing, but he could resist her. So he remained unmoving.

She took his silence for assent. "Now let me make the connection," she murmured, reaching down to open his trousers.

He moved his arms. He caught her wrists and held them.

"Why, how nice, Ned; you are responding at last!" She moved her breasts against his face. They were twin mounds of desire, perfectly formed.

Ned simply sat there, with the naked woman on his lap, and held her wrists. He had found his only weapon of defense. Could it possibly be enough? How much of the hour remained? How much of it did he *want* to remain?

"But we can't proceed if you don't let me," she said after a moment. She tried to move her hands, but he tightened his grip.

"You are hurting me, Ned," she said.

He knew he wasn't. He did not let go.

"Of course I can give you more." She bent her head and brought it down to kiss him. He turned his face to the side, but she pursued it and managed to capture his mouth with hers.

Then Ned felt his grip weakening. Her kiss transported him, making him heedless of any consequence. But he forced strength into his hands, and maintained his grip. Had she been a man, she could readily have broken it. But physical strength was not her way.

She kissed him again, and this time he turned his face into hers and returned it. But he maintained his hold on her wrists. She could inflame his desire, but could not open his trousers, and therefore could not complete the act.

At last she sighed. "I fear you have beaten me, Ned."

He didn't answer. He knew he had merely nullified one

ploy. She would have others. In fact this was probably one: to make him relax in seeming victory, and then be lost, in the manner of troops that lost their formation pursuing a fleeing foe, and then got cut to pieces. Wona was just as devious and dangerous in her domain as any Mongol army in its domain.

She gazed into his eyes. Then her own eyes turned wet. Her tears flowed, silently but copiously. "Oh, Ned—I love you so!"

Again, he felt his strength dissipating. The fluid of her eyes was melting his resolve. He knew they were deliberate tears, but they still had their effect. If she tried to free her hands now, she would succeed, for his fingers were numb.

But she didn't know that. She was waiting for him to let her go. So he waited for the next ploy.

It came with mercurial suddenness, like a summer storm. "Then the hell with you!" she flared, her anger like a suddenly ignited thatch fire. "I don't need you."

"Then tell me of the treachery, and let me go," Ned said.

Instead she kissed him again, savagely. But they remained in their impasse, her hands imprisoned.

She lifted her head and gazed into his eyes. It was as if he could see through her eyes into some other realm, a Moslem paradise, infinitely beckoning. "Do it, Ned, I beg you, and I will tell you everything."

"No."

She sighed, and the sound stirred a wave of mixed feeling in him. "Then I must tell you first, and then you will do it."

"No." He knew better than to be trapped into her seduction. Because the first would not be the last.

"Ned, you are being unreasonable. You must meet me part way."

Even seeming reason was part of her repertoire! "All I came for was the information. Give that to me and go."

She stared into his eyes. Moonlight and clouds danced in

her depths. "I have what you want. You have what I want. It seems fair to trade."

"I want to protect the interests of the khan. You want to have me in thrall to you again. I don't think you have what I want, and I won't give you what you want."

She shook her head. "You are wrong, Ned. You think you know, but you will have a crushing disillusionment coming. This is something you really do need to know."

She seemed sincere. It could be a ruse, but he feared it wasn't. "Tell me, and let me judge."

"I will, but first you must agree that if my news is worthy, you will give me my desire." She kissed him again. "Your baby. That means a number of sessions, most likely."

An extended affair. Which would bind him to her, and destroy his marriage. His body was urgent to agree, but his mind was in control for the moment. "No."

"Even though you know it is no onerous chore I ask of you, while the news I have will affect you profoundly?"

Again, he wavered. She seemed so sure! If she were bluffing, she wouldn't offer to tell him her news first, letting him judge its merit. She was sure he would complete the deal, once he heard her information, if he agreed on the terms beforehand. So he could afford to make the deal only if he was sure she was bluffing. And if she was bluffing, there was no point in making the deal.

"No."

Wona shook her head sadly. "Ned, you are going to regret this."

"I already regret coming here."

She laughed. Her upper body shook, especially her breasts, and it was all he could do to prevent his face from kissing them. "I think you just need a little more persuasion."

But it was an impasse. He would not let go of her wrists, and she would not cease her efforts to persuade him. Slowly his resolve was weakening. It would be so easy to yield!

And maybe her information really was what he needed to know.

"Yes, I think when you say no, you mean yes," she murmured, conscious of her increasing power over him. "We have meant so much to each other in the past, and will in the future. Kiss me, my precious. My body hungers for yours."

Somehow he hung on to her wrists, but his hands were feeling paralyzed. At any point she would try to free her hands, and would succeed, and then would complete the act despite his passive resistance. And she would have him. This was a siege in which the besieged was running out of strength and hope. It was only a matter of time.

There was a sound to the side. "Oh, no," Wona muttered. "I forgot about Jes. The hour has passed."

Ned had forgotten too. It hadn't seemed like an hour. Strength returned to his hands. Wona had not seduced him in time. The rescue troops were coming to the aid of the besieged city.

Jes entered the room. "I watched carefully, but there is no threat from outside." She looked at the pair of them. "I think my brother has defeated you, Wona. If you couldn't seduce him in an hour in that position, you couldn't do it in a year."

"Yes I could," Wona said. "Give me just a bit more time."

Jes drew her knife. "I think not. Don't make me use this on you, Wona."

Wona scrambled off Ned's lap. He let her wrists go as she did. "You caught on," she said.

"I suspected."

"Caught on to what?" Ned asked. Despite this victory, his desire for Wona was not abating.

"She put love-herb in the food."

Suddenly it came clear. "That's why my resistance was weakening! That herb—it takes an hour."

"That's why," Jes agreed. "I ate her food to be sure it

wasn't poisoned. Then when I thought about it, I realized that there could be another way. I came in, knowing what she was up to."

"You waited too long," Wona said. "Ned desired me anyway; now he will have to have me. This goes beyond reason; it cannot be denied."

"No!" Ned said. "I know the remedy. Jes, take me to cold water."

Wona winced. Evidently she had hoped they wouldn't know about water.

"This way. I ate too; I need it too." Jes led the way out.

That intrigued him, passingly. Was the love-herb so powerful that it would cause a brother and sister to merge? He didn't care to find out.

"But I took it also!" Wona protested.

"Too bad," Jes said tersely. "There is no other man close by."

Behind the house there was a stone cattle drinking trough fed by a tiny stream. Ned and Jes tore off their clothing and climbed into it. The water was devastatingly chill: exactly what was required.

Then Wona was there, still naked. "Make room for me," she said.

Jes laughed. "I have half a mind to keep you out." But she took no action, and in a moment all three of them were shivering in the trough.

"Well, I tried my best," Wona said. "It would have worked, had you not caught on when you did. Just a few more minutes—"

"So did you really have any information of treachery?" Ned asked.

"Oh, yes. And I will still make the trade, if you care to get warm with me now." She inhaled, shivering.

"No." Her persistence bothered him, though the cold water was effectively damping his ardor. Also, shivering cold flesh was not as appealing as soft warm flesh, however well formed. He could not believe that she truly desired him, other than as a confirmation of her power over men. Yet she had gone to extraordinary effort to seduce him, and was still trying. Why was she bothering?

"What is your interest in this?" Jes asked Wona, echoing his thought. "Obviously you are not motivated by patriotism, and you could have seduced any man you wished, with your body and the love-herb. Ned hardly seems worth your while."

"But his child would be mine," Wona said. "So when I learned what I learned, I decided to make good use of it."

"And you will let the treachery happen?" Ned demanded. "Just to spite me?"

"If I gave things away, I would never be able to bargain. So I give nothing, without its price."

"To you, love and war are much the same," Jes said.

"I'm glad you understand."

Ned shook his head as he shivered. Something was missing, but he couldn't figure out what. Why hadn't Wona chosen to seduce some other man in exchange for her information, or traded it for gold? Any of the other advisers could have borne the news to the khan. Why had she fixed on him, so soon after seeing him? He did not believe that it was all for the desire to bear his child; she had not shown much interest in her prior child. Yet she *had* fixed on him, most determinedly. Where was the key?

"I can't stand this," Wona said. "I'm getting out."

"We'll take turns," Jes said. "One at a time."

Wona climbed out, then danced on the ground, recovering her warmth. Ned watched her bouncing body, almost wishing he could feel the desire he should. But the cold was too compelling.

When Wona was warm, she reluctantly got back in the water, because Jes would not let Ned out otherwise. Ned got out and danced around, while Wona watched, no doubt with similar thoughts. Then he returned, and Jes got out. Ned noted that his sister had put on some feminine flesh, and was no longer as lanky as he remembered her. Marriage had evidently been good for her—or maybe it had simply caused her to fight less and love more.

In due course the hour passed, and they were able to get out and stay out. They carried their clothing to the house, drying off in the air. All of them were shivering and somewhat blue of lips and skin. Ned found that the information Sahara had given him was correct: his desire had waned, and he no longer cared who had clothing. He had not indulged sexually, but evidently the cold water had depleted his energies similarly, and he just wanted to rest.

"I had thought to have had my will of you, and be alone to recover, by this time," Wona said as she dressed.

"Will you tell me your real motive for all this?".

"Of course not. That deal must wait until we are able to consummate it."

She was one tough negotiator. Ned realized that he would have been no match for her, without Jes to support him. As it was, it had been a close thing.

Jes looked around the cabin. "We should be getting back to the camp, but I feel depleted. I would prefer to rest until my strength recovers."

"So would I," Ned agreed. "But this is Wona's house."

"How can that be, when she and her husband just arrived from far away? It is merely a place they saw was empty when they passed by it."

"We are like combatants after the battle is over," Wona said. "Stay here and rest; I don't mind."

Ned looked at Jes. She shrugged. Why not? Their battle had been fought and ended. So they found separate spots on the floor and lay down to rest. Ned woke as dusk was closing. He hadn't meant to sleep, but evidently had done so. That love-herb had a wearing effect on the system.

"Too late to return," Jes said, seeing him stir. "We'll have to stay the night."

"I have food," Wona said. "The herb is in the caviar; the bread and wine are good."

They shared the bread and wine, and talked about old

times, and slept again. It was strange being together like this, but Ned's lethargy was slow to wear off, so it was easier just to accept the situation. Wona seemed like a different person as she inquired about her daughter Wilda, seeming truly to care.

At dusk Ned performed his ablution toward Mecca, and Wona joined him. Jes abstained, making no comment. She knew why Ned had converted; it was no issue between them.

In the morning Ned's interest in sex was returning, and he knew that this was true for Wona also. But he knew better than to dwell on that. They rounded up their horses and rode back together. A league before they reached the camp, they separated. "My husband would not understand," Wona explained. Surely so!

"She professes to be a good Moslem now," Jes remarked after they separated. "But she made her obeisance to Allah only when you did, and never mentioned Him otherwise."

"That's right! She gives only lip service to Allah, when with Moslems. I hadn't noticed."

"She gave you other things to notice."

"Yes." He wished he could feel good about his victory, but it had been more luck than skill, even with Jes's support.

"Be alert for that treachery," Jes told him as she took the horses, leaving him to make his way quietly into the camp afoot. "Wona obviously doesn't care about the khan's welfare, but we do."

He nodded. "Thank you for saving me, again," he said.

"I did it for Wildflower," she said, looking down.

Wildflower! How eager he was to return to her embrace.

He made his way to the khan's tent. "Ned! We missed you," Toqtamish said. "We feared something had happened."

"I was told of some terrible treachery," Ned said. "I went to investigate, but could not ascertain what it was, and was unable to return to the camp yesterday. I do not know whether it was a false lead, or whether there is some great threat to your person. I am concerned."

The khan nodded. "I appreciate that. I am glad you are safe. I will be alert, and will keep you close by my side until we know more."

"I hope I was not needed," Ned said. "I did not mean to be derelict."

"Have no concern. That new adviser, Ormond, developed a great new strategy to implement your suggestion that we make peace with Moscow so we can go after Prince Dmitri elsewhere. The problem was in convincing the Muscovites of our good faith, as we have not been kind to other Russians. We sent some chiefs to meet with them and tell them that we bear them no ill-will; it is only Dmitri, the rebellious prince, that we seek. If they will send me presents, open their gates, and allow me to tour this ancient city and see its curiosities, I will then withdraw and let them be."

Ned was surprised and gratified, but wary. "I don't think they would believe that."

"That's the key. We sent the two sons of Dmitri of Nijni Novgorod, Vasili and Simeon, with our messengers, to pledge on their swords as Russians and Christians that we will keep our word. Mongols they would not believe, but Christian princes they will."

Still Ned doubted. "If there is some great treachery planned, the Russians could agree, and it could be a ruse. If you go into that city, they could abruptly close the gates, then turn on you and slaughter your retinue and take you captive. Perhaps this was the plot I was unable to track down."

Toqtamish pondered. "I value your caution, Ned. Suppose we reverse it, and ask them to come out to visit us? Ostei can come to see me in my tent. That way I will not enter the city, and can not be cut off from my forces."

"That would be better," Ned agreed. "But take care that they sneak no arms into your presence."

"Of course." The khan smiled. "Then it is settled. We

may soon be finished here." Toqtamish glanced at him. "But stay in my sight, my valued friend, and keep your militant sister by your side, just in case. We can never be too careful."

Indeed, it seemed that they had worked it out. The Mongol camp waited while the officials of the city consulted. Then the gates were thrown open, and Commander Ostei emerged, with his retinue bearing rich presents. He was followed by priests bearing a large Christian cross. These were followed by the boyars, the nobles. Finally the common citizens of Moscow trooped out, wearing decorative colors. It was a fine procession. The Russians were so very glad to be relieved of the siege.

Still, Ned worried. Where was the great treachery Wona had warned of? Should he have submitted to her passion, for the sake of the information she had? Yet if she had overheard it from her husband, Ormond, the treachery must be associated in some way with him, rather than the Russians. Unless he was a secret agent for the Russians.

Ned looked around. He did not see Ormond or Wona in the throng around the khan. There were a good number of armed troops close by, abridging the normal proscription against arms near the khan, but that would be because of the concern about possible betrayal. So Toqtamish should be safe. But why was the adviser who had arranged this encounter not present? He should be claiming due honor. Instead Ned himself was here, when he had not been responsible for the settlement. That was odd.

Treachery. Oddity. Something did not add up. Ned glanced at Jes, and saw that she was similarly concerned. Now he wished that he *had* made a deal with Wona. Could he have offered her anything other than his child? He wasn't sure, but he should have tried. Now all he could do was wait and watch, hoping his instincts were mistaken.

Ostei was escorted directly into the khan's tent. He was smiling. "O great Khan," he said, his words decipherable though they were in Russian. He bowed his head.

Then Ormond appeared, carrying a sword. He stepped right up close to Ostei and swung the sword. Ned saw it as if the motions were slow. He could not believe it. Ormond was attacking the leader of the city, who was here under the flag of truce? There must be some mistake!

The sword struck the man. Ostei fell, his blood spurting, amazement rather than pain on his face.

Then Toqtamish gave a signal, and mayhem erupted. The Mongol guards fell upon the citizens of Moscow, slaughtering them without mercy. Screams sounded as the victims discovered their fate.

Now at last Ned understood the nature of the treachery. Not against the khan—*by* the khan. Wona had heard her husband planning the conspiracy, and knew that Ned would want to know it. But he had refused to deal on her terms, and paid the price.

He felt a tugging on his arm. It was Jes. Numbly he followed her. How could Toqtamish have agreed to such an evil ploy? He should have had Ormond executed for even suggesting it. Yet it was plain that the khan had agreed to it.

Jes hauled him along to where she had two horses. "Follow me," she said, mounting.

"But—" But she was already starting off. All he could do was mount and follow.

They rode rapidly out of the camp. No one paid them any attention. The Mongols were too busy cutting down the Russians. Already troops were charging into the city, where more screaming sounded. The city was doomed.

Only when they were well away from the action did Jes pause so that Ned's horse could catch up with hers. "But we should not be fleeing the carnage," he said. "We should be trying to abate it."

"You fool," she said gently. "That woman took you— and what's worse, deceived me too. We are done here."

"Wona? But she would have warned me, if I had only—"

"Don't you see, innocent brother: she was part of it. Her job was not to *tell* you, but to *distract* you, so that you would have no chance to learn of the treachery. She kept you away from the camp for a full day and night, while the thing was set up. She accomplished her mission."

He realized it was true. Wona had used her attempted seduction only as a means of distraction, so that he would not guess her true purpose. While her husband arranged the grand deception. They had known that Ned would never agree to it, so they had kept him well clear of it—until too late. Toqtamish had conspired too, making sure Ned had no suspicion, keeping him and his sister close by so they could not question anyone or spy anything going on. They had been deceived exactly like the two Russian princes. How cunningly it had been accomplished!

"I can not serve Toqtamish any more," he said, grim and heartbroken.

"That's why I got you out of there," she said. "He would have had to have you killed. I think he thought you would see reason, by his definition, once the deed was done. But I knew better. He does not understand honor; he thinks it means merely that you will not betray *him*. Honor to an enemy is an alien concept for him."

She was right. "But what can we do now?" he asked plaintively.

"We can gallop home and get our family to safety before the khan's minions come for all of us," she said.

He realized it was true. The family's years of affluence and favor with the Golden Horde were through. "We shall have to return to Timur," he said. "He will protect us, and send us somewhere safe."

"We are, after all, Turks," she said. "And it will not annoy him that you are now Moslem."

"Yes. Perhaps I can continue to help the family. All is not lost."

"All is not lost," she agreed.

So it was that Toqtamish, the lackluster Mongol pretender, became one of the two major figures of central Asia. In four years, 1378–82, he showed considerable savvy, so that he came to rival Timur himself in power and influence. How could he have so suddenly changed?

He must have gotten a smart new adviser, who understood the politics of the day and knew what pitfalls to avoid, and he must have paid attention to that man. How such an adviser came to him, and precisely what he said, are unknown to history, but it could have been as presented here. The fact is that Toqtamish was surely neither as stupid in the early days nor as smart in the middle days as he seems. The prior khan of the White Horde pursued him relentlessly because he knew that Toqtamish was legitimate, competent, and ambitious; he gave the handsome young pretender no chance to get established. Only the generous and patient intercession of Timur enabled him to survive. But once he was established, Toqtamish knew how to use the reins of power, and did so with dispatch. The Golden Horde had been losing its control over Russia; he restored it for another century. Moscow was looted and burned, and after it the other Russian towns were destroyed. Dmitri never actually took the field against Toqtamish.

But what happened after he lost his good adviser? Toqtamish surely thought he could do well enough without him. And he did, for a while. He sent a conciliatory letter to Prince Dmitri, proposing peace and reaffirming Dmitri's position as Grand Prince of Muscovy, under Toqtamish. Dmitri, yielding to the reality of Mongol power, sent his son Vasili as a hostage. Vasili was well treated, and there was no more trouble on the Russian front. Meanwhile Toqtamish consolidated his power among the Kipchak tribes ruthlessly and effectively. He dominated central Asia from the *border of Europe to the border of China.*

Then he went wrong. He did the one thing his Turkic adviser would never have countenanced: he cast eyes on the territory of his benefactor, Timur. In 1385, while Timur was busy in Persia, Toqtamish invaded Azerbaijan, the territory southwest of the Caspian Sea, with an army of 90,000. He sacked its chief city, and returned home before the winter intensified.

Timur was annoyed. He wrapped up his business in Persia and moved to retake Azerbaijan in 1387. Toqtamish, despite a sensible reminder from some advisers: "Who knows whether, in some change of fortune, you might have to go again to Timur for help," marched his own army to meet him. A Mongol party made a sneak attack on the Turks, only to be countered by a second force and defeated. Yet Timur sent his captives back with a gentle and deserved reproof. This enraged the khan, and the war continued for several years. Timur quelled rebellions and drove off the invaders, then invaded the Golden Horde. He defeated Toqtamish and drove him from power. The Mongols remained in control of Russia, but the faithless friend had paid the price of his foolishness. Too bad he didn't stay with his good adviser.

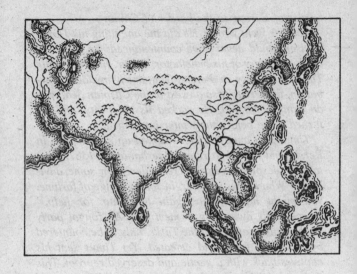

Chapter 16

WALL

The Mongols dominated Asia for centuries, slowly losing territory to the cultures of the west, south, and east. The Chinese were especially hard hit by their depredations. The Mongols conquered China in 1280 and lost it in 1368 when the Ming dynasty was established. Thereafter the Mongols periodically raided China, as before, and at one point even took the emperor captive. The Chinese realized that there had to be some better way. Thus their efforts to build walls, to protect them from the invasions from the north.

However, the three thousand mile long Great Wall of China, existing from the Ch'in Empire in 221 B.C. on, is a myth. Walls existed, but these were mainly local, made of earth packed around wooden supports, and they were not maintained well. They served more as boundary markers than as defense. Land within the walls was regulated and taxed; land beyond the walls was wilderness. Only when the walls were actively defended were they effective, and the money and manpower for this were usually lacking. The frontier was actually guarded by widely spaced forts. The invading nomads had no trouble going around, through, or over the walls. A single, unified, manned, stone wall defending China as a whole simply did not exist, despite cultivated mythology. Only after the Mongols were expelled did more impressive bulwarks develop, but even then there was no unified project. There was a series of smaller building projects, each designed to shore up a weakened section of the northern perimeter. Even these relatively modest efforts suffered from lack of planning, design, funds, and manpower.

In 1470 an official named Yü Tzu-Chün surveyed and repaired the western defenses. He had 12,000 troops to defend an area more than 500 miles long, protected by twenty mud-brick forts. He convinced the emperor that this was hopeless, and was given 40,000 men and over a million silver pieces, and he built a wall about 550 miles long with some 800 watch towers and sentry posts. This was effective. But Yü knew that the barbarians would simply go around it, so he petitioned the emperor for funds and men to greatly expand the defensive perimeter. This could have been the first true Great Wall. But he annoyed the bureaucrats, who surely felt they had better uses for all that money, and was forced to retire. The barbarian raids continued.

In the 1540s Altan Khan succeeded in unifying the Mongols of the region. He made several attempts to establish peaceful trade relations with the Ming, but was continually rebuffed, and often his messengers were killed. This has never been smart policy when dealing with Mongols. The Chinese emperor of the time was Chia-Ching, who reigned from 1522 to 1566, but was not much interested in the actual business of governing. He preferred to indulge his lifelong quest for the secret of immortality. Fortunately for China, his disinterest allowed more rational heads to handle the border fortifications. The far-west fortresses and walls were massively rebuilt, though this consisted mainly of bricking over the original earth walls. A network of signal towers was set up, so that messages could be sent quickly, by flame, smoke, or cannon-blast. This helped.

But the main threat was farther to the east, where Altan Khan was ambitious. Yü's original construction had been allowed to erode, but periodic repairs and new construction had maintained that portion of the border defense. But nearer the capital city of Peking was where the Mongols repeatedly raided. There were two lines of defense, enclosing two garrison cities, Ta-t'ung and Hsan-fu. They had once been formidable, but early in the sixteenth century had fallen into decline. The soil of that region was dry and unproductive, so the military supply farms suffered continual shortages and the local diet was poor. The troops consisted of hereditary soldiers and prisoners exiled to the frontier for life. Long winter hours manning the towers often led to frostbite or worse. Officers were cruel, and morale was terrible. There had been several mutinies, including a major revolt in 1524. Now the region faced its worst threat yet, in the form of the unified Mongols under Altan Khan.

In 1544 Weng Wan-ta was named commander of this disaster area. It was his job to make sure that the formidable Mongol forces did not get through to ravage *the rich countryside of the capital region. Weng was competent, but this was almost too much of a challenge.*

The time is 1549; the setting is the two garrison walled loop northwest of Peking.

IT WAS NICE, RIDING WITH her brother, Jes thought, because then it wasn't so deadly dull. She craved adventure, while Ned craved intellectual challenge. Theoretically they had both, here, because there was no more dangerous region than the one where the Mongols liked to attack, and there was plenty of architectural design and construction. But in practice, all they saw was walls and towers and bleak stretches of wilderness.

She and Ned were on a routine scouting mission, making sure the defenses had not broken down or been breached. Sometimes a stone fell out of place, or a storm washed a gully under a support. She spotted such problems, and Ned considered them, and then designed superior replacements. But in the long stretches between such minor discoveries, there was nothing much to do but chat.

"So did you give Wildflower a baby yet?" she inquired brightly.

"I'm trying," he said. "And she's trying. But so far all the joy has been in the effort, not the success, as with marching." She appreciated his grimace; they much preferred riding to marching, but the common soldiers had no such choice. "But what about you? You've been married longer than I have."

"I don't want a baby. That would interfere with my free life."

"Odd how a sister thinks she can lie to a brother," he remarked to the wind.

"All right, I lied," she said crossly. "I want a baby. We've certainly tried. But it doesn't come. If you can tell me what's wrong—"

"You're lean," he said. "Not much female flesh on you."

"Ittai doesn't complain. He finds what he likes readily enough."

"Oh, you've got it," he said quickly. "More than you used to. But not as generously as some."

"I wouldn't want to be fat. Some of those cows—"

"My point is that, in my limited observation, girls with some flesh on their bodies get babies faster. They don't have to be fat, just reasonably female. I'm trying to get Wild-flower to eat more, but she's young."

Jes ran the women she knew through her mind. Ned was right; the plump ones had the children. Could the secret be that simple?

Meanwhile her eyes were constantly surveying the wall they paralleled, as were Ned's. "Oops," she murmured, reining in her horse.

"Mongols!" he exclaimed, keeping his voice low. "They've broken through."

"That's not hard to do, because we haven't yet completed the extension of the wall," she said. "I don't see a break, but there's no doubt they're through."

"Cover me while I get an estimate," he said, dismounting.

She remained on her steed, keeping trees between it and the Mongol force, while Ned crept closer afoot. She unslung her bow and nocked an arrow. She would shoot any Mongol who came after Ned. But she hoped he would not be spied, because outrunning Mongols was chancy at best, even with a head start and familiarity with the terrain.

Ned was soon back. "Too many to count," he said. "They are here in force. Full-scale alert."

Jes nodded. They guided their horses quietly back the way they had come, until well enough clear to be able to risk the sound of galloping. Then they moved at full speed west, toward the nearest signal tower.

"Full alert!" Jes called as they approached. "Mongols through the wall!"

"How many?" the guard captain asked as his men blew up the signal fire.

"We couldn't count," Ned said. "But by their organization, I'd guess at least 10,000. This is no skirmish squad."

The men threw damp leaves on the fire, and a big cloud of smoke went up. Unfortunately, the wind was wrong, and the cloud blew toward the Mongols. "This is mischief," Jes muttered.

"Our men will spy it," the captain said.

"But the Mongols will spy it first," she said. "They're not idiots. We'd better carry the message directly."

"Too late to call back the smoke," Ned said. "In any event, the signal system will far outpace any riders."

"But General Weng will want more detailed information than the signals can transmit, and with the Mongols alerted, there won't be much time to provide it."

"So we'd better hurry," he agreed.

They set out again, moving at the maximum sustainable pace for their horses. Probably the Mongols would not be in pursuit, because they would fear an ambush. But the Mongols would certainly be ready.

As they rode, Jes thought about the Mongols. Ned's wife was a Mongol princess, but she was loyal to Ned and the family. Ned had at one time worked for the Mongol prince, but that had ended badly. Their experience with Mongols helped them here. Indeed, General Weng had hoped to use Ned as an emissary to reestablish trade that would benefit both the Mongols and the empire, and defuse hostilities. But the eunuchs who ran the empire distrusted the Mongols, thinking they would only spy and cause trouble if allowed into the country, so that sensible option was closed. Thus the far more expensive and dangerous option of military defense was the only feasible alternative. But Weng's massive and necessary wall extension project had been underfunded from the start, delaying and weakening it. It was too bad. Now they were about to suffer, again, the consequence of the empire's multiple follies.

The horses were lathered despite the cold March air, but they made it to a larger fort by dusk. The commander assured them that the message had already been relayed, and that the general would be expecting them. They pinpointed the location of the enemy on the commander's tactical map so that he could prepare more specifically. Now Jes and Ned could relax, briefly, and get some needed rest. They were given supper and bedding for the night.

"Why couldn't you have been Wildflower?" Ned complained as they settled down under a joint blanket.

"Same reason you couldn't be Ittai," she returned archly.

They snuggled close together, sharing warmth, as they had done from childhood. They had always been best friends as well as closest siblings. They didn't mind seeing each other naked, and they shared and kept each other's secrets. On occasion they had problems with their spouses, which they could discuss with each other and ameliorate. When Ned was hurt because Wildflower declined love one night, Jes reminded him about the female cycle. "Cramps are bad enough, without that." When Jes was furious because Ittai didn't remember the date of their first meeting, Ned told her that he remembered when Lin brought Wildflower home, but he couldn't tell the date of the month that had happened. "We men don't mean any harm. It's just not the way our minds work," he explained, and she realized it was so.

The next day they rode the rest of the way to the main camp, where General Weng was hastily assembling his forces. They were ushered immediately to him to make their report.

"They seem to have circled the end of the wall," Ned said. He did the talking, being the man. "Now they are coming this way, in force."

"Damn those empire bureaucrats!" Weng swore. "If they hadn't cut our funds, we would have had that wall complete by this time." He was right, of course. Sam and

Dirk were out of work at the moment because the money to pay the wall builders had run out. Fortunately they could also fight, or work on the farm. "How strong are they?"

"I didn't see their full force, only a contingent. But the nature of their formation is suggestive of a full-scale invasion." He was being cautious, but he would not have said that much without being almost certain that there was indeed a full army following the Mongol vanguard.

"Go secure your premises and report to Hsan-fu." Weng turned away, already barking orders at lesser officers.

They left. The general was nothing if not efficient.

Another hour brought them to the farm, which was by the Nan-yang River near the Hsan-fu fortress. It wasn't much, and this was the fallow season, but Flo was doing her best to instill some fertility in the soil. They were working to divert some of the river water to flow to the farm for irrigation. Sam and Dirk had dug a contour channel most of the way to the garden. But that work had to stop during this crisis.

They hastily closed down their operations and took their valuable horses and supplies to the fortress. Hsan-fu was large and well situated, guarding a pass through the hills. The Mongols would have to take it to secure their route; otherwise they would be vulnerable to harassment from their rear. Despite this certainty of attack, it was the safest place to be, because the countryside would be governed by the Mongol horsemen. Once sure of the safety of the others, Sam and Dirk armed themselves and went to report to their combat units.

By nightfall they were safely in the fortress, crowded into their makeshift temporary billets along with the other farming families of the region. As a general rule, the farmers did not mix with the troops, because the officers considered themselves above the farmers, and the prisoner conscripts were apt to be rough and uncouth. That was one reason the farmers were being given shelter within the fortress: the military discipline kept the troops from molesting them. Many soldiers were also farmers, on the military farms, but these were often unsuccessful, because the soldiers lacked the desire, patience, and aptitude to make the soil productive. Their own family was unusual in its mix, with warriors, designers, and builders all part of it. But that was because they had made it a point to keep the family together, never allowing it to fragment. It traveled as a unit, finding strength in its internal variety. Many Chinese families were unified through the generations, but their own mixture of classes was remarkable.

Jes found herself seated beside her younger sister Lin as they ate their gruel. Lin was fifteen, and blossoming into by far the loveliest member of the family. Ned's Mongol wife Wildflower was somewhat better developed in the torso, and had lustrous black hair, and Sam's wife Snow was much better endowed, but Lin had a youthful delicacy of face and feature that made men and women alike pause. She ran errands among the troops without trouble, because men were inclined to protect her rather than molest her, and for any man who might feel otherwise, there were several who would come quickly to her rescue if any hint of a need arose.

But Lin was plainly unhappy at the moment. She was silent, and her eyes were somewhat puffy; she had been crying.

Jes did not look at her directly. "I don't wish to pry," she murmured.

"It's Li," Lin said, sniffling.

Jes sorted through her memories. Li was a neighboring youth of relatively good family, husky and handsome. Evidently there was a romance in the offing. "Li," she agreed.

"He saw my hand."

That said it all. Jes freed a hand and put her arm around Lin's shoulders. The girl turned into her bosom and quietly sobbed.

Lin was beautiful, but that six-fingered left hand might as well have been a third eye, considering the effect it had on the superstitious. She usually wore a mittenlike glove on that hand, and in winter that was easily justified. But it was hard to hold hands with a boy without evoking an unkind reaction. The members of the family were used to it, and thought nothing of it; all Lin's fingers were functional, and she could work cloth quite well. Yet outside the family—

Then Jes had a notion. "There are men who are not handsome, yet who are worthwhile," she murmured. "Look at Sam. Look at Dirk."

"Look at Ittai," Lin said, a glint of humor interrupting her misery.

"All right. My husband's not young or handsome, but his wealth makes our lives halfway comfortable, and he's certainly a good man. Suppose you considered someone like that?"

"Oh I wouldn't want to take Ittai from you." The mood was definitely lifting, in the rapid way possible to youth.

Jes closed her hand and gave Lin a light punch on the shoulder. "Thank you for that favor, Sister dear. You know what I mean. Suppose there were a good man, who had some fault not of the mind or personality, but of the body, that made other girls reject him? He would be like you, in that respect. You would know exactly how he felt."

"Yes, I would," Lin agreed, wonderingly. "I never thought of that before."

"He might be a future Sam, or Dirk, or Ittai. Or Ned. You need to learn to see beyond the superficial."

"I'll try," Lin agreed. Then she disengaged and ate her gruel with more gusto. But she glanced back at Jes, mischievously. "You need to have a baby."

Jes was careful in her reaction. "Why?"

"Because then maybe you'd have enough bosom to cry into, as Flo does."

Jes laughed. "I'll try."

Next morning Weng's troops massed outside the fortress, bracing for the onslaught of the Mongols. The incursion had happened so suddenly that the Chinese force still was not complete or fully organized. The signal system had allowed Weng to track the Mongols' progress into Chinese territory, but they were moving so swiftly that the scattered defensive forces had not had time to gather. The Mongols, inveterately clever warriors, had surely planned it that way, quietly slipping through and massing until discovered. The Mongols understood the signal system perfectly; in fact they destroyed the towers at every opportunity. It was a sign of its effectiveness that the clever enemy had not been able to nullify it more than partially.

Sam and Dirk marched, but neither Ned nor Jes was allowed to join the main army. "You are too competent to risk in the field," Weng had said gruffly. "I need your designs for construction." That was Ned. "And an accurate bow to defend the fortress." Jes. The general knew her nature, but saved her face by not mentioning it. She suspected that her husband had made a deal with him, to keep her out of mischief. Ittai was of course too old for combat. That was a private comfort. But not too old for command, so he was in charge of one of the outlying forts.

However, the fortress did need defending, and she was good with the bow, so she didn't object. She reported to the wall foreman, who assigned her to the crew defending the north gate. The packed earth ramparts had been enclosed by stone and topped by small towers, just as in the walls themselves, and seemed formidable enough. But Jes had seen Mongol attacks before, and took nothing for granted. With luck, Altan Khan had not brought siege equipment along this time, and would not make a really determined effort. Not while being harassed by Weng's army. Otherwise the fort could be in real trouble, because the Mongols knew how to take down a wall by pulling out a few stones and mining out the dirt that was its core. The point was to prevent the Mongols from ever having the chance to do that.

So why hadn't they built all the walls out of solid stone? Because it was said that it took a hundred men to do in stone what a single man could do in packed earth. The walls needed to be done quickly, before the Mongols attacked again, and there simply was not enough manpower to accomplish that. Even if there had been more men, there was not the money to pay them, because only a fraction of Weng's sensible estimate was actually provided by the stingy empire. So most of the work was in earth, just as it had been in the past.

Jes wished that the emperor could be sent out here for a few months, to endure the hardships and see the impossibility of accomplishing enduring construction with the resources provided. But the emperor was too interested in Taoist mysticism to bother with such practicalities. So those in charge of the defenses had to struggle through inadequately, hoping they could stave off the Mongols one more time.

Well, the family had sought protection from the Mongols. This frontier post had not been their preference, but the present Chinese administration simply did not trust them enough to let them farther in. Jes actually liked it well enough, because there was adventure and responsibility here, but the others would have preferred a farm in the rich river delta to the east. Maybe once the walls were finished, it would be allowed.

Extra arrows from the armory were distributed, because it would not be feasible to recover expended ones. If the enemy charged the wall, there would be flaming tar poured out, too. It would be expensive for the Mongols to take this fortress. But not as expensive as it would be for the defenders, if the Mongols succeeded. It would be better to die to a man—and woman—before that happened. Certainly they would not trust any Mongol assurances about a truce. Not out here in the combat zone. If the emperor ever got sensible and made a trading pact with the Mongols, as they wanted, then it might be all right. But the Ming dynasty had been founded by those who drove out the Mongols from the rule of China, and that animosity might take centuries to fade. So common sense gave way to abiding hatred and contempt.

Nothing happened on the first day. But the second day, the Mongols drove back Weng's army. Ned was right: they were here in force. Weng had to retreat to the fortress. His losses were not great, but he did not have enough force to defeat the Mongols in open battle. However, more of his troops were arriving daily, and his reserves were growing.

The Mongols were aware of this. They knew they had to take Hsan-fu quickly, or be at an increasing disadvantage. Now they laid siege to it.

The arrows came in sheets. Jes and the other bowmen took cover behind the towers. They would fire back when the Mongols tried to charge.

But a number of the arrows were blazing. They arched high, their target the interior of the fortress, where they would set anything flammable afire. Their burning pitch was almost impossible to extinguish; the arrows had to be grasped by their shafts and buried in sand. There were crews for that purpose, and they were busy now. But it was dangerous, because many regular arrows still rained down, catching those who were exposed. So it was necessary to have a shield-bearer protect an arrow-fetcher. This slowed down the work, and some blazes did start.

The Mongol horsemen charged the wall, under the cover of another ferocious volley of arrows. This was what the defenders had been waiting for. Protected by their shield-bearers, they stood and fired at the men outside. They had the advantage of height, and of being stationary, and of planning. They made their arrows count. The closer the Mongols came, the easier targets they and their horses were. The fire from the fortress became punishing indeed.

The Mongols swerved away before reaching the wall. But the defenders did not cease. Jes took careful aim at the back of the nearest horseman, and put an arrow through it. He had light armor, but at this range it wasn't enough; her arrow penetrated, and he fell from his horse. She was already orienting on another.

The Mongols set up catapults and hurled heavy rocks into the fortress. These were dangerous, as there was no way to stop such missiles. But Weng sent a detachment out to attack the catapult crews specifically, and soon those were silenced.

This was the pattern for two days. But by then the rest of Weng's forces had assembled, and were closing in on Altan Khan's army. The Mongols had battered the fortress but failed to take it, and now they were forced to withdraw.

They tried the old Mongol trick of false retreat, but it didn't work. Weng brought sufficient resources to bear to defeat the enemy when it turned, and the retreat became real.

Reports came constantly back to the fortress. Weng's forces were still getting stronger as units arrived, while the Mongols had no backup. It became apparent that this was not a major Mongol invasion, but more of an exploratory incursion. Had it been able to take the fortress, then Altan Khan would have been well situated to invade China at his convenience. Since the surprise raid had not succeeded, all he could do was go home and plan something else.

There were several other engagements, and Weng's forces prevailed in them all. The Mongols were definitely being driven out. The defenses had held.

Jes chafed at the inaction. She had few enough chances to fight, and with the fortress no longer under siege, there was no action here. So when one of the messengers collapsed from a wound, she slipped in and took his place. The commandant didn't see her, or perhaps pretended not to. Thus she ''returned'' to the general's camp, riding a swift horse. This was more like it; there might yet be some combat.

But there was not. Scouts had verified that the Mongols were circling the wall to the east, going back to Mongolia. The Chinese would remain vigilant until quite sure, but the chances were that this raid was over.

Disconsolate, Jes prepared to be sent back to the fortress. But as she dawdled near the edge of camp, looking for any pretext not to check in properly and be discovered, a motion caught her eye. Someone was firing an arrow at her!

She turned her horse as she brought out her own bow. But the Mongol ambusher was already in full gallop, streaking away. She would have little chance to catch him, and he would only lead her past an ambush anyway.

Besides, she realized that he hadn't intended to strike her with the arrow. The range had been such that he could have winged her; no Mongol was that bad a shot. The arrow had landed in the ground right in front of her horse. It had a peculiar thick shaft. Almost as if—

She hastily dismounted and went to fetch the arrow. It was! It was a message. There was a scroll wrapped tightly around the shaft.

She knew better than to unwrap it. She remounted and took the arrow directly to General Weng.

"What are you doing here?" he demanded as he spied her.

"Bringing you a message arrow," she said serenely, presenting it. "It landed in front of my horse."

He took it and unwrapped it. " 'If trade is not resumed, I will attack Peking in the autumn. ALTAN KHAN,' " he read. Then he looked up. "It has his seal. It's authentic. The man wants to trade. So do I. But will the emperor listen?"

The question was rhetorical. None of this warfare would have happened, if the emperor had been willing to listen to reason. But the message would be sent on to Peking anyway.

The question of whether only plump women can conceive babies is not simple, but studies have shown that the truly lean ones, such as athletes or the malnourished, do have that problem, and may suspend menstruation. There does have to be a certain minimal amount of body fat, or nature shuts down that particular apparatus. With the poor local diet of the time, the poorer women could have had a problem, while the better off ones did not.

The message to Peking was not heeded. Like many other leaders, the emperor preferred to fight, at whatever internecine cost, than to make a reasonable settlement.

Within three months Weng was promoted to minister of war, so he never saw the end of his building project. Then his father died, and he retired to his home in Kwangtung, in southern China. The Mongols attacked again in 1550, coming through a broken section of wall north of Ta-t'ung. They drove away all forces arrayed against them, and came again to the fortress Hsan-fu. But once again they were unable to take that fortress city. There is a suspicion that they were bought off by bribes by Weng's less-competent successor. At any rate Weng's double-wall frontier had held.

So Altan Khan went around the walls—a long way around. He took his army east all the way to the sea, where he was able to skirt the defense. Then he descended onto the plains around Peking. He drove away the Ming cavalry arrayed against him, and raided and ravaged within sight of the city walls. The sky was filled with the smoke of burning fields and estates. Only when they were good and ready, did the Mongols return to the steppe.

The emperor really should have agreed to resume trade.

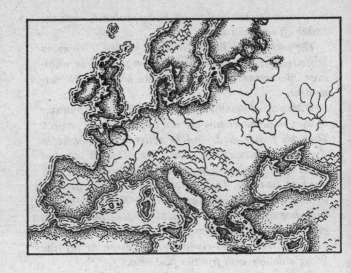

Chapter 17

MELODY

France was a major player in the New World in the late sixteenth and early seventeenth centuries. Driven by the lucrative fur trade, her territories in North America came to include most of what is now southern Canada and most of what is now central United States. But this was mainly on paper; the actual French population was exceedingly thin, and strongly contested by the American Indians who had a prior claim on the land. In the end, Britain and Spain were to prevail in North America, at the expense of France.

But this was not evident in 1661, when King Louis XIV assumed actual control of France, after a number of years of regency by his mother and dominance by Cardinal Mazarin, successor to the infamous Cardinal Richelieu. The young king studied governance and learned his lessons well, and was to become one of France's longest-reigning and greatest monarchs. The court of Louis XIV was the most magnificent in Europe. The Thirty Years War had exhausted much of continental Europe, and England was still struggling to regain its strength after the collapse of Cromwell's Puritan state. But while Louis XIV was the closest thing to an absolute monarch in Europe, his authority was still constrained by the wealth and power of the nobility. His common sense and diligence enabled him to gauge the temper of potential adversaries, and to achieve his ends without arousing their overt opposition.

In 1661 the colonial governor in Canada, Baron d'Avàuger, sent a messenger to the court at Versailles to plead for aid, because the colony was being severely pinched by naval weakness and the Iroquois Indians. The emissary he sent was Pierre Boucher, the governor of Trois-Rivières in Quebec. Boucher met with Louis XIV and impressed upon him the benefits that a thorough exploitation of the New World's resources might bring. Louis and his excellent new finance minister Jean-Baptiste Colbert favored this, but a number of powerful nobles did not. Therefore the extent of the help the king might provide was in doubt. Unless Louis found a way to nullify some opposition, the French presence in Canada could be in trouble.

LYNNE STOOD AT THE PROW of the great ship, gazing ahead. There it was: New France! The great land some called Quebec, and some called Canada. It was covered with green forest. Some of that forest would be theirs. They would make a farm more wonderful than ever, and have the very best and richest furs, here in the great New World.

Then they were at Quebec. The Fort St. Louis de Quebec sat on a promontory dominating the St. Lawrence River. There was the colonial governor's residence and administrative offices, and the Chateau St. Louis, the cathedral, the Jesuit college, the Ursulines convent, and the Hotel Dieu, which was the hospital run by nuns. There were several wealthy private houses on the promontory, but most of the homes and warehouses for the merchants were at the foot of the cliffs, along the edge of the St. Lawrence and St. Charles rivers. A few were built of stone, with steep pitched roofs like those of northern France, but most were of wood or wood and plaster. There were, in all, about 800 people living there.

But they would not stay there. The best land was farther inland. They would carve it out of the virgin territory, and commute to Quebec for trading, or when the Iroquois made it too dangerous. But maybe that problem had been exaggerated. Because some of the horrors that had been described were simply too horrible to be believed. So she didn't believe them. Quite. Nevertheless—

Lynne woke. She had been dreaming again. She wanted so much to see the land that Jessamine and Ittai had described. The family would be going there on the ship's next trip. She just knew that everything there would be so much better than it was here in France. After all, Jessamine and Ittai had laid claim to a suitable farmstead in Montreal. The soil was rich, and the fur trade was richer. All the region needed was more people. But it was hard to get more people, because the Iroquois had gotten guns and ammunition from the dastardly Dutch traders at Fort Orange, and were dedicated to driving the French out of the St. Lawrence River Valley. But with the help King Louis would provide, that should not be too bad a threat. She hoped.

"Come on," Jessamine said briskly. "We must be ladies today."

Lynne suppressed a smirk. At age fifteen—almost sixteen—she liked dressing up in skirts, but her big sister didn't. Jessamine would much rather be garbed as a sailor on her husband's ship, passing for a male sea hand. But today Ittai had to play the part of the rich merchant seaman he was, and Jessamine had to be a lovely lady. And so did Lynne. The others were closing down the farm and packing the ship, but Lynne was coming to the court because a pretty face just might incline the king toward their cause. Their mission was to support Pierre Boucher's plea for aid for New France. So that it would be safe for them to move there.

They helped each other dress. Both of them had free-flowing gowns with laced bodices. When the laces were pulled tight, the bodices squeezed the breasts, making them swell out the top. Jessamine had put on some weight in recent months, and was more buxom than Lynne had thought. Lynne swelled similarly, though the bodice was uncomfortable and restricted her breathing.

They did each other's hair, adding perfume and ribbons, making it curl just so. Jeweled combs made it sparkle. But the worst of it was the high-heeled shoes. They had to walk carefully, lest they stumble. "I feel like a clown," Jessamine muttered. "I wish Snow could have done this instead. She has the bosom for it."

"She would swell right out of this bodice!" Lynne said, giggling as she glanced down into her forced cleavage.

"Precisely. The king would surely like that."

When they were fully prepared, Lynne drew on her gloves. The left one was specially made to conceal her embarrassment.

Ittai arrived. "Are we ready for the court?" he inquired from outside the room.

"Come on in," Jessamine said. "We're bedecked."

He entered the room. He was wearing a long and ornamented vest, culottes gathered at the knees with buckles, lace stockings, and boots. Overall he wore a long open coat, whose wide sleeves were trimmed with lace, and a wide soft hat tilted up on three sides and sporting a plume of feathers. He had shaved his face, except for a great mustache. "You look lovely!"

Jessamine grimaced, but Lynne spoke up. "You're really handsome!"

He doffed his hat to her and made a little bow. "Clothes make the man, fortunately." He gave her a second glance. "You have grown, Lynne."

"No I haven't. It's this squeezing bodice. Everything I have is outside it." She tapped one of her bulges just above the lacing.

"It will do." He turned to Jessamine. "Bear up, my love; soon we shall be free of this nuisance."

"I'd rather fight a duel," Jessamine snapped.

He smiled. "Dueling has been forbidden, fortunately for any knave who might cross you."

"I've got my knife anyway."

"But you couldn't draw it without lifting your skirt, and showing the knave more delight than he deserves."

"Stop making me miserable." But Jessamine finally did return his smile. Jessamine did have good legs, because she was so active, and she liked having her husband appreciate them. In fact Lynne suspected that Jessamine really didn't mind being required to dress up and prove she was a woman. As long as she got chances betweentimes to adventure in the fashion of a man.

They went out to the coach. Ittai gallantly assisted them both in boarding, before joining them inside. "Remember: ladylike throughout," he said gravely. "No fighting." He glanced at Jessamine. "And no cartwheels." He glanced at Lynne.

They both had to laugh. The thought of turning a cartwheel in this outfit was hilarious. "That knave's eyes would pop out," Lynne said.

"So would our breasts," Jessamine added.

"And you would never get them crammed back in," Ittai

agreed. "Pregnancy becomes you, my love."

"What?" Lynne asked, astonished.

"All the more reason not to get bound up like this again," Jessamine said. Then, to Lynne: "Yes. I have missed two periods. I think I am with child. At last."

"Great! Now you'll really have to be a lady."

"A woman."

"A lady today, a woman always," Ittai said.

The palace at Versailles was southwest of Paris. It was the biggest, fanciest building Lynne had ever seen. She was dazzled by its great brick walls and multiple stories. She knew it had started as a hunting lodge, some thirty-five years before, built by the king's father, but it had been almost continually expanded. Indeed, there were signs of construction now, as outlying buildings were being added.

They introduced themselves to the gatekeepers, who checked their roster and verified that these visitors were expected. A page guided them to the breakfast chamber of the king. Pierre Boucher was already there, in his best clothing, along with a number of courtiers Lynne didn't recognize. There they waited until Louis completed his breakfast and acknowledged their presence. The king was a handsome man in his early twenties, quite well dressed and surprisingly free of affectation. He wore a magnificent head of golden curls, his hair surrounding his face and covering his shoulders. Lynne might have mistaken him for a woman, as he wore neither beard nor mustache, had he not been so obviously the king.

"Ah yes, Monsieur Boucher," Louis said. "From New France. I am so pleased to meet you. And your fine merchant captain, Ittai, of whom I have heard good things. And—" He glanced meaningfully at the women.

"My wife, Jessamine," Ittai said quickly, and Jessamine made a curtsy. They had practiced, to be sure to do it correctly. "And my wife's sister, Lynne," he continued after a moment. Now Lynne curtsied, relieved to accomplish it without mishap.

"Charming, charming," Louis said. "Come with me to the council chamber, and we shall see what all this is about."

He meant only the men, of course, as women had no place in governance. The two of them had ceased to exist.

But as they turned to leave, a woman approached them. "Lynne," she said. "We have met before."

Startled, Lynne looked at her. The women was indeed somehow familiar. She was beautiful, but that wasn't it.

"We knew your brother Bry," the woman said. "When he was lost in the storm."

Then it registered. "Annette!" Lynne exclaimed. "You danced!"

"Yes, I am here with my husband to instruct courtiers in the new dances," Annette agreed. "He is busy elsewhere at the moment, so I thought I would tour the palace, which I understand is a marvel. Would you and your friend care to join me?"

Lynne realized that she had been guilty of a breach of etiquette by not thinking to introduce her companion. "This is my sister, Jessamine. Her husband is with Pierre Boucher, of New France."

"How nice to meet you," Annette said.

"Likewise, I am certain," Jessamine said politely.

"She wasn't with us, on that trip," Lynne said. "She was in the other party, looking for Bry."

"A fine young man," Annette said.

"You should see her dance," Lynne said to Jessamine. "It's wonderful!"

"We shall be holding a class in dance this afternoon," Annette said. "Perhaps you would like to join us then."

"Yes!" Lynne said eagerly.

Jessamine shrugged. Annette smiled. Then she guided them to the marvelous chamber of the palace. There were magnificent paintings on every wall, and statues in every hall. Even the tables were richly ornamented, with glistening surfaces. In fact the floors, too, were tiled with repeating patterns. A number of other people were touring too, admiring the phenomenal display of art.

But after two hours, Lynne was getting bored. She realized that she was not yet of an age to properly appreciate such a display. Fortunately they were able to go to the kitchen and get some rolls of sweet bread to eat.

Then Annette took them to the chamber reserved for practice. There were a number of ladies there, and a few men. One of the men turned out to be Annette's husband Hugh, who Lynne noticed was left-handed. It didn't matter, as he was putting together a nice wooden flute. In a moment he was playing, and the melody was sprightly. Lynne already felt like dancing.

"Today we have a new dance," Annette announced. "The dance itself is a variant of ones you may be familiar with, involving a couple, but the music differs. Now my husband will play the music, so I will need a partner to demonstrate with." She looked around smiling. She was a lovely woman, so several of the men were interested.

But before any of them stepped forward, there was a voice from the entrance. "I will do it, if you please."

Lynne looked—and was amazed. It was the king! He was surrounded by the courtiers who had the daily honor of walking with him. There was a murmur, and the men bowed and the women curtsied.

Louis paused to allow them to complete their devotions, then nodded graciously. He was every inch the monarch.

"This is a simple demonstration of the dance, perhaps beneath your notice, Your Majesty," Annette said, seeming slightly daunted herself.

"No dance is beneath my notice," Louis said, striding forward. He was resplendent in a voluminous robe, which he doffed and handed to a courtier in order to free his body for the dance. His legs were in snug white stockings, showing their perfection halfway up the thighs, and his delicate feet were in high-heeled sandals. "This is a dance lesson. Treat me as you would any other partner."

"As you wish, Sire," Annette said respectfully. "But I shall have to presume to give you direction."

"I take direction well, from lovely ladies," he said, with a slight bow. There was an appreciative chuckle among the courtiers. The king had a reputation, and evidently fostered it, for no such notice would have been taken without the knowledge of his approval of it. The courtiers struck Lynne as fawning sycophants.

The music started over, with a new cadence and melody, and Annette stood beside the king. "The motions are very small, even delicate," she said. "In fact we call it the 'minuet.' This dance is stately rather than active, but it gives a nice effect for spectators. Now you will hold my hand, so, and we shall turn around each other, facing, in measured step, so." She demonstrated, smiling at the king, and Louis moved with her, following her motion so perfectly that it seemed he had always known it. "You are apt at this," she said approvingly.

"I like the art of dance," Louis said. "I believe it to be one of the most important disciplines for training the body."

"I certainly agree."

They continued with the demonstration, and Lynne was enraptured. Annette was a perfect dancer, and so, it became clear, was the king, whose poise and grace were phenomenal. It was as if the two had always danced together. Taken as a whole, the little dance was a work of art.

The demonstration must have taken some time, but to Lynne it was only an instant before it ended. The music stopped, and Annette and Louis made token bows as the small audience burst into applause. Everyone was taken with this charming little dance, and it would surely be popular at court.

"Now we must teach the rest of you," Annette said. She glanced at the king. "Your Majesty, if you would be so kind as to choose another partner—"

Louis nodded. As Annette selected another man to dance with, the king looked over the women. Every one of them was eager to be his partner, for not only was he a monarch, he was a handsome and exceedingly graceful man. Then he strode across and proffered his hand, making another little formal bow to the one he had chosen.

"Go, girl," a woman murmured behind her. Lynne jumped. The king was asking *her*!

Dazed, she tried to curtsy, tripped, and stumbled forward toward the man. Horribly embarrassed, she realized she was about to crash into him. There was nothing she could do about it, though she seemed to be falling ever so slowly.

Then his hands were on her shoulders, steadying her with a power that shot right through to her ankles. "That is not the step," he murmured with a smile.

She tried to speak, but her tongue was stuck in her mouth as the flush spread across her face. What a fool she was making of herself!

"Face me, and step so," he said, taking her right hand and guiding her. He made a mincing step. She mimicked him, feeling unreal.

Then, slowly, it worked. They stepped together, she following his lead, and they were dancing the minuet. Near them Annette and her new partner were dancing too, the man following the woman's lead. He looked as uncertain as Lynne felt. But her concern was fading, as the reassuring competence of the king guided her, and after a while she was matching his steps with increasing competence.

Then the little dance was done, and she was finishing with a twirl under his hand. She saw her skirts spread out as she turned, showing her legs; it was as if she were watching from across the room. Then she finished, with a curtsy that worked just right this time, matching Louis's token bow. There was another round of applause from the audience. She had done it! She had danced the dance.

After that, it multiplied. The king danced with other ladies, and Lynne danced with other men, showing them the nice little steps. She had always liked to dance, and this was hardly a complicated or demanding one, but she was amazed at how well she had picked up on it. Louis's guidance had really helped her. She was having a wonderful time.

In due course the multiplication had taken all the men, including the courtiers who had accompanied the king, and Lynne found herself without a partner. She stood at the side, watching the others, admiring the niceties of the minuet, its little mannered moves. It was easy to do, yet also wonderful to behold. Jessamine was dancing with a courtier, and seeming to enjoy it.

Then Louis himself dropped out and came to stand beside her. "I know about your hand," he murmured.

Lynne's world imploded. "Oh!"

"Be at ease, pretty maiden. I speak not to disparage you, but to ask a favor."

"A favor," she echoed numbly.

"The politics of the court can be difficult. There is a noble for whom I would like to do a favor, so that he will not oppose support for New France. His word carries considerable weight in certain quarters. I think that if you, a lovely maiden from that province, were to dance with his son, it would be effective."

"Oh, I'm not actually from—"

"I speak figuratively. It is your dream, is it not?"

She nodded numbly. "His son?" She still had trouble accepting the fact that the king was asking a favor of her. Kings didn't ask, they commanded!

"The youth has sterling qualities and excellent breeding, but is extremely awkward with women. It would be good for him to be seen with one as beautiful as you."

He was complimenting her! This great man. "I—of course, Your Majesty. But how—?"

"I will introduce him to you. He has a club foot."

It came together. "His foot—my hand—"

"Neither infirmity reflects any defect in character or accomplishment. But I think you could reassure him. Other women have mocked him; therefore he is shy."

"Yes," she agreed, on more than one level.

"I must return to council. You may accompany me." He held out his arm.

Surprised again, she obliged, putting her right hand in the crook of his elbow. They left the dancing chamber and walked through the halls. A number of courtiers followed; it seemed that the king never went anywhere alone. She felt like a princess. Was this the way Wildflower felt, when she visited her home court?

At the council hall there was already a group of people. It was a chamber of considerable size, with many ladies in attendance, each finely garbed. Lynne realized that they must be the wives or girlfriends of the nobles, having no part in governance, but there for decorative purpose. All eyes seemed to fix on Lynne as she entered on the arm of the king. But by this time she was largely inured to embarrassment. She thought she should let go of Louis's arm, but wasn't sure, so she held on, trusting that he would tell her when.

Louis greeted several courtiers by name. Lynne heard the names, but they meant nothing to her. Until they stood before a stout, bejeweled man with a young man at his side. The young man seemed ill at ease.

"And this is Lynne, who will be traveling to New France with Captain Ittai," Louis said, straightening his elbow so that her hand slid down and away. "Lynne, this is Jacques."

This was the one! Lynne smiled at the youth. "Hello." It seemed inadequate, but was all she could think of.

"Tonight at the ball, perhaps you will dance with her," the king said to Jacques. His tone was polite, but Lynne realized that it was an order. She saw both the elder man and the younger one stiffen, almost imperceptibly; they thought the king was trying to embarrass them. She was suddenly glad that Louis had forbidden the practice of dueling, because otherwise someone might have had such a notion. But she was learning the way of court intrigue, and allowed none of her thoughts to cross her face. She just made sure she would recognize Jacques when she saw him next time.

Then the king turned away, leaving Lynne standing there before the angry courtier and his son. She had no idea what to do, so stepped back, hoping to get out of sight.

The attention of the room followed the king, so in a moment Lynne was suitably anonymous. The king took his seat, and the courtiers began a discussion of a technical matter of governance that was beyond Lynne's comprehension. Oh, she could have followed it if she had cared to put her mind to it, but what was the point? So she let it slide by her. Pierre Boucher was part of the group, as was Captain Ittai; they were surely waiting their turn for the king's attention. The ladies around the chamber began to converse with each other, quietly, so as not to interrupt the main business. Every so often one would turn an appraising glance in Lynne's direction. They were discreet, but she felt naked. Could she return to the dance class? She was afraid it might be a breach of court etiquette to depart after the king had brought her here.

"So the king threatens to humiliate the opposition's clumsy son," a lady murmured loud enough to be heard. "By having a foreign darling do it."

Lynne suffered a flash of utter rage. The tone and the implication were as clear as the words. She was being damned along with Jacques. In that moment she resolved to see that the youth suffered no shame at all because of her. In fact, in a perverse wash of feeling, she suddenly liked Jacques, because of what she knew he was suffering at the court. How well she understood that sort of prejudice! Just because a person had some physical infirmity—

Then Hugh and Annette appeared, and Jessamine, so it seemed the dance class was over. Lynne walked across the chamber to join them, relieved to find familiar faces.

But before they could settle into the background, a child entered the chamber. It was a girl, perhaps five years old, well dressed; she was probably the daughter of a noble who had lost track of her mother. She carried a small piece of parchment.

The eyes of the ladies of the court turned to this new arrival. Lynne saw more than one pair of eyes roll expressively; it seemed this child was mischief. But no one went to take the child in hand, to usher her out, which indicated that she was of royal birth.

The girl oriented on Hugh. "There you are, musician!" she exclaimed happily as she dashed up to him. "I have composed a melody. Play it for me!"

The bright, high voice cut through the murmur of the court. Now all the ladies were watching, some with masked smirks, enjoying the royal embarrassment. The king himself paused, glancing toward the sound. Lynne saw a fleeting frown cross his face; evidently he, too, recognized the child.

Hugh hesitated, then glanced at Louis. The king made a tiny nod. So Hugh took the parchment, read it, and smiled. "Of course," he said. He gave the parchment to Annette, and lifted his flute as the child waited expectantly.

The melody was simple, brief, and rather crude, as might be expected from a child. The masks were coming off the smirks; someone's parents were being royally embarrassed. Lynne saw the king frown again; apparently the embarrassment attached to him, too, peripherally. Maybe this was one of his love-children. Maybe this awkwardness would somehow solidify the opposition to the New France petition. Lynne wished she could do something, but she had no idea what.

Hugh paused, then spoke. "But this is only the theme," he said. "Now we must embellish it."

He played again. This time the melody was recognizable, but there were added notes that filled it out, making it stronger and more consistent. The child clapped her little hands, delighted. Hugh was an expert musician, and he was making the melody into something significant.

In a moment that rendition, too, was done. But Hugh was

not. "Now let's give it full play," he said. "I think this is properly a dance piece."

He played the melody a third time, and now it had the sprightly cadence of a dance. It was lovely, and it invited feet to move. The little girl began to dance, in her fashion, enjoying it.

Annette joined her, smiling, doing a variant of the minuet. Suddenly what had been, perhaps, a joke became lovely: the woman and the girl stepping around each other in the stately manner of the dance.

Lynne saw Louis nod appreciatively. The embarrassment of the situation was fading, thanks to the courtesy of the musician and the dancer.

Lynne had a sudden notion. She crossed the chamber to approach the club-footed youth. "Dance with me, Jacques," she said, flashing him a winning smile.

He looked like a trapped animal. "You mock me!" he muttered.

He didn't know. "No. Let me show you something." She caught his left hand with her right, and drew the sullen youth to an alcove. Sheltered by that, she had him face toward the wall beside her. Then she drew off the specially tailored five-fingered glove on her left hand. It was cunningly designed to mask the extra breadth of one of the fingers, so that two of hers could fit within it. "Believe me, I wouldn't mock you," she said, wiggling her fingers. "Please do not tell."

He stared. "But you're so pretty!" he protested.

"And you are handsome. Come—the dance is simple, and you will not have to move much. I know you can do it." She pulled her glove back on and drew him from the alcove.

He seemed dazed. Then he took her hand. "Very small steps, slow," she said. "Then turn me." She lifted his hand and turned under it.

He nodded. He could do it, and the smallness of the motions masked his incapacity of the foot. He understood how to dance, and adapted readily to this variation. All he needed was a supportive partner.

They moved out on to the main floor, dancing with increasing competence. Lynne saw that courtiers and ladies alike were staring, astonished by this sight. "They think I showed you something else," she said, giggling.

Jacques laughed. "I won't tell."

Now others were joining the dance, somewhat in the manner of the dancing class. Lynne realized that Louis himself had left the meeting and chosen a partner; that was why everyone was suddenly doing it. What had been an embarrassment had become an occasion.

Then, after a glance from the king, Hugh brought the music to a halt. "Delightful piece," Louis said. "You must play it at the ball tonight." He glanced at the child. "And you must go tell your mother how well you have done as a composer."

The child ran off. The king turned back to the meeting. The interruption was done.

But Lynne remained with Jacques. "You did beautifully," she said.

"I did, didn't I!" he agreed, amazed. "Because of you."

"The king said you were a good man."

"The king is just trying to get support for the New France project."

"Yes, of course. That's why he introduced me to you."

"And now you will go there, and I will never see you again."

She glanced at him. "Would you like to see me again?"

"Yes. You understand."

"I understand," she agreed. "Could you come too?"

He was surprised. "To New France? How could I?"

"It is a hard trip of three or four months across the sea, and a difficult, frontier life, with many dangers," she said. "But a man can use an axe, or a gun, or a spade. I understand there is a fortune to be made in the fur trade. He doesn't have to run or dance."

He considered, amazed at the prospect. "With you?"

"Well, I hardly know you," she demurred. "But why don't we get better acquainted, and see?"

Then she leaned forward and kissed him, lightly. She had a feeling that this would work out.

> *Louis XIV authorized 100 troops and 200 indentured laborers to join Boucher on his return trip to Quebec in 1662. This was small, but represented a compromise with the conflicting forces of the court. Though the fortune of France in the New World was less than that of England and Spain, the French presence in Quebec remains significant today, and French is one of the official languages of the region.*
>
> *The little dance, the minuet, became quite popular in all the courts of Europe, and remains a staple of the dance form today.*

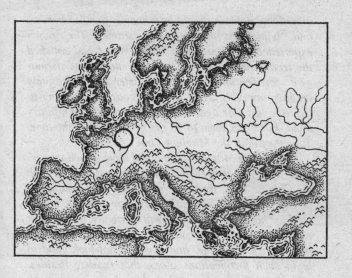

Chapter 18

MAGINOT

World War I devastated Europe. France suffered horrible casualties: 73 percent of her total forces mobilized, including almost two million men dead or missing. France was on the winning side, but it was a Pyrrhic victory; another such victory would finish her as a nation. Yet another such war was already threatening, as Nazi Germany gained strength and brutality. With manpower at a premium, France's military strategists turned away from the idea of aggressive response and counterattack. They believed that the key to national defense should be a heavily fortified border, and "battlefields prepared in peacetime." The French experience with Verdun in World War I had satisfied the leaders that a strong line of trenches and permanent fortifications could be defended indefinitely against any odds. They were, of course, preparing to fight the last war again, a classic error of the military mind. But it did seem to be the best choice at the time. Thus they built the Maginot Line.

Actually the Maginot Line could have served its purpose well, had it been fully implemented. But as with the Chinese Wall, its builders suffered from insufficient funds, and politics got in the way. For example, it covered the border France had with Germany, but was not extended to the sea, because Belgium was an ally, with its own defensive line, and it would not look good to build such fortifications along that border. Besides, they decided, the forested Ardennes region through which German forces would have to pass was virtually impenetrable. A few blockhouses and some ready forces would pinch off any invaders as they emerged from the forests. In retrospect this was sheer folly; the Germans simply forged through with tanks and aircraft, and thus avoided the Maginot Line in much the manner the Mongols avoided the Chinese Wall. But hindsight is a cheap shot; at the time it seemed reasonable. At the time the line was designed, both armor and air force were considered to be curiosities rather than strategic weapons. No country in the world had formed an armored brigade or an offensively effective air force. Even so, had the line been completed as originally envisioned, it well might have repelled the Germans, because their costs in penetrating it would have weakened them too much for the conquest of the remainder of France. Actually they did penetrate it—but that was after its purpose had become moot because of the Belgian bypass.

So what was the Maginot Line actually like? It was activated once, before the war. In March 1936 Adolf Hitler moved German troops into the Rhineland, violating the demilitarization of the region agreed by treaty. France, in response, ordered a full mobilization of its defensive perimeter. The Maginot Line was fully manned for the first time.

SAM WAS LOADING AMMUNITION ONTO a railroad car when he got the call. "Sam—your brother is on the phone."

That would be Ned. There were those who thought Sam should be resentful of the fact that his little brother was an officer while he was an enlisted man, but Sam could have been an officer if he wanted command. He preferred to exercise his muscles and leave the management to others. Ned had the mind for tactics and strategy, so was an officer. His only problem qualifying had been his German wife, Wildflower, who the officials suspected was potentially disloyal. But she had finally been cleared, and he was doing well. Sam was glad. After all, his own wife, Snow, was Austrian. What counted was not a person's origin, but her loyalty to family and nation.

He picked up the receiver. "Sam here."

"Ned. I have a problem. I brought Bry in to see his friend Jacques, but there's a problem down the line and I have to investigate it. Can you take Bry instead?"

"Bry shouldn't be here during an active alert!" Sam protested. "Don't you know that? He's underage."

"Officer's prerogative. If it comes to war, we could have women and children manning our bulwarks, so they had better be prepared. Bry's sixteen, old enough to learn the way of it. But I have to go to a region not cleared for civilians. So if you could take him on to Jacques—"

Something was going on. Ned wouldn't have called him about a routine thing that he could have assigned any private to do. "Where are you?"

"At the command post nearest your block. I'll wait for you."

"Yes, sir," Sam said, with the faintest edge. How could Ned have brought Bry in during this activation, when there were bound to be emergencies?

He checked with his subaltern, who took his word; that was an advantage of being reliable. If his brother the captain needed him, he was available.

He rode the ammunition train down the tunnel to the main depot, then reported to the personnel section. There was Ned, quite striking in his uniform, and his younger sibling.

Sam's face froze. It wasn't Bry—it was Lynn! She had a heavy hat over her bound hair, and wore male coveralls and shoes, but he had no problem distinguishing his brothers from his sisters. Suddenly he knew why Ned had called him. If word got out that there was a girl here . . .

"Sam will get you there, Bry," Ned said. "I must be on my way." He nodded to Sam, and walked away.

"Well, *Bry*," Sam said, slowly shaking his head. "How did you ever talk Ned into this?"

"Wildflower did it," Lynn murmured.

Wildflower. Lynn's closest friend, more sister than sister-in-law. Ned had taken time to notice her, thinking of her as a little sister, but once she had succeeded in making an impression on him, her slightest wish had become his command.

"And why did Wildflower do it?"

"I asked her." Then, before he could question that, she added, "I haven't seen Jacques in two weeks."

Two weeks. And at her age, that was like two years. So, dying for romance, she had prevailed on her brilliant but in some ways soft-headed brother to bring her in to visit her boyfriend. New love was heedless of consequences. And now Sam was stuck with this treacherous chore.

"Snow sends her love," Lynn added.

How could he be mad at her? Lynn had always had his number. She was such a small, pretty thing, in such need of protection because of her hand, that they all served her in their ways. She took advantage of that, and they all knew it, but it remained almost impossible to say no to her. She had reminded him of his own romance, kindled during a trip to Austria at the time when his first marriage was breaking up. Second love had proved to be better than first love. He didn't like being separated from Snow, but because she was his wife, he did get leave time to be with her. Lynn and Jacques lacked that avenue, being merely in love.

"This way," he said gruffly.

"Thank you, Sam." She wasn't fooled; she knew he was glad of her company despite the circumstance. Family members always liked to be together, whatever the circumstance; they watched out for each other.

Another ammunition train was going out. Sam waved to the diesel engineer, and the man slowed the engine enough to let them hop on to a car. Cooperation was essential, in order to get the confusions straightened and the work done. Sam lifted Lynn up onto a rack of shells, then stood beside her.

"You're so strong," she said.

"And you're so light," he said. "Save your charm for Jacques. But make sure you answer only to the name Bry."

She laughed. She was enjoying this adventure, heedless of the inconvenience to others. She kicked her feet against the metal below her.

"I wouldn't," he said. "That's high explosive."

The feet stopped. "It must really be fun, here in these tunnels all day."

"It's dull." But now, seeing it through her eyes, he realized that the scene was remarkable. The train was following its tracks down the lighted tunnel, which was six meters high and seven meters wide, with a power line running along its ceiling. The half-circle dome of concrete was bleak and dirty, but for a young person, surely thrilling.

"Ooooh—a turnoff!" she exclaimed.

"That leads to the main magazine of the ouvrage, the

main fort,'' Sam explained. ''But this load is going farther down the line.''

''How deep down are we?''

''About fifty meters.''

She laughed. ''Fancy a whole train going through the ground!''

''It's to ensure that German bombs can't interfere with our communications.''

The tunnel narrowed. ''Are we there?''

''No, just passing through a section where the tunnel can be closed off by a seventeen ton blast door.''

''Ooooh,'' she repeated, suitably awed.

Beyond the narrowing, the tunnels split again. ''That goes to the barracks,'' Sam explained. ''But we have to go on to Jacques's block, some distance down the line. He is stationed at one of the smaller casemates.''

''Jacques,'' she breathed, her eyes shining.

Sam thought again of Snow. How could be begrudge that delight to his little sister?

The train slowed. It was reaching its exit to the surface. ''We'll have to get off here,'' Sam said. ''And walk on down. It's not far.''

He helped her down to the base of the car. Then as the train emerged into the light of day, they both jumped off. Sam waved to the engineer as the engine disappeared into the landscape.

''There's an incomplete shunt going in that direction,'' Sam said. ''We can follow that a way, if you like the tunnels.''

''I love them. Besides, it's cold out here in the wind.''

So they turned back into the tunnel, and took the turnoff that led in the right direction. The isolated casemates were not connected in the way the major forts were; there was simply too much terrain to cover. Sam would have liked to show off one of the cannons that could rise to the surface to fire, and descend into the depths at other times, but the authorities would never allow such a breach of security.

They moved on down the passage. Lynn walked along a rail, spreading her arms for balance. She got little joys from everything.

"By the way, Hugh knows Guillaume," she remarked.

Sam was lost by this non sequitur. "Who knows whom?"

"Hugh, the musician with the lovely dancing wife." She paused, giving Sam time to make the connection. He did remember that wife. "He knows Guillaume—Jacques's commanding officer. That's how Ned got clearance for Bry's visit to the block."

"But what about a girl?"

"That would be more complicated."

To be sure.

Then they came to another turnoff. "What a labyrinth!" Lynn remarked, loving it.

"It's less complicated than it seems. The tunnels connect the magazines where the ammunition is stored, the main barracks, the cannons—"

"It's still fun to explore."

They followed the tracks through an airlock. It was open at the moment, but the massive panels could be seen. "That's so that nothing can get at the defenders," Sam explained. "Especially not poison gas."

"Poison gas! Would they do that?"

"They might. We can't presume too much on the good graces of an enemy."

Then they came to a region where water dripped from the ceiling. "This shouldn't be," Sam said, disgusted. "How can it be airtight, if it's not watertight?"

"Somebody's going to get in trouble!" Lynn said in a naughty sing-song.

"No, we'll just have to get it fixed. Meanwhile, this is our only way through. We'll just have to avoid the drips."

But the drips got worse. At one point there was a veritable sheet of water coming down, and the floor of the tunnel was flooding. Sam tramped through, his boots protecting his feet. But Lynn, walking on the rail, lost her balance and fell full length into a puddle. There was a great splash.

Sam leaped to help her. "Are you hurt? Oh, Lynn—"

"Bry," she said wryly. "No, I'm all right. The water cushioned my fall. But I'm all wet."

"We'll have to get you changed. It's cold in here."

"I know." She was turning blue.

"The block barracks is right ahead. They'll have clothing."

"Sam." Her tone made him stop. "I can't change here."

Oh. Of course. She would be revealed as a girl.

Sam pondered, but couldn't think of an alternative. "You need to strip, to get dry, and put on new clothes. And get warm. I might bring some clothing out here, but—"

"Someone might come," she agreed. "I guess I better not change."

But her teeth were chattering. If she caught cold, and it led to pneumonia, and—what would Flo say? "We must get you warm," he said.

"No, I'll get by. It's my own fault. I shouldn't have come."

How could he blame her, when she blamed herself? "Come on. There has to be a way."

"Let's just hurry there."

They climbed endless stairs to the surface, where a guard checked Sam's credentials and let them out. Now they were beside an ordinary road, with a path leading through hills to the rear of an almost buried bunker. Sam wished their destination were closer, but at least the fast walk helped warm her.

He led her the rest of the way to the casemate, which was the combat block where Jacques was stationed. It had fifteen men and a lieutenant, with barely room for them and the supplies. They entered it from behind. Sam had to get permission to enter from the officer in charge before a metal grate dropped across a deep ditch and the armored door opened to admit them.

Sam saluted. "Sam and Bry reporting, sir."

"This is highly irregular," the lieutenant said, returning the salute. "We are on alert; no visitors are permitted."

But he had admitted them. "The musician sends his appreciation," Sam murmured.

The lieutenant nodded curtly. Evidently he was repaying a favor, but was not completely comfortable with the matter. Then he saw Lynn. "But the boy's soaking wet!"

"There is a leak in the transport tunnel," Sam said. "We must notify the command post."

"We already have. They say they will get to it in due course." The lieutenant grimaced. "It seems that there are many such leaks. No one noticed, until the alert came." He looked again at Lynn. "He is shivering and blue; he must be changed immediately."

"He—prefers not," Sam said. "He has no other clothes."

"We have supplies. I will have a man attend to it." The lieutenant turned, about to give an order.

"Please, sir, no," Sam said quickly.

The man frowned. Officers did not like hearing the word "no" from enlisted personnel. "No?"

Sam wished he had Ned's ready mind. He couldn't think of a suitable explanation. "He—he is uncomfortable changing in the presence of others."

"But he will have to. We have no privacy here, no spare space at all."

"Still, sir," Sam said awkwardly.

The lieutenant's eyes narrowed. "What are you concealing?" Then, as Sam hesitated: "That is an order, sergeant."

Worse and worse! But what could he do? Sam leaned forward and whispered, "He's a girl. Lynn. Bry's sister."

The lieutenant's look of astonishment was abruptly replaced by a cold mask. "Come with me." He made a military turn and descended a curving flight of steps.

They followed him to the basement, where the troops bunked. The lieutenant led them into his tiny separate room and closed the door. "Explain."

Sam looked helplessly at Lynn.

"I just had to see Jacques," she said. "I love him! I didn't know I was going to get wet." Her face was wet with more than the puddle; she was crying.

The lieutenant reacted in the classic French manner. "Ah, love." He faced Sam. "I will fix this. But there will be no word of it outside."

"No word," Sam agreed. No one wanted a scandal, least of all the officer who would be held responsible.

The lieutenant spoke into his phone. "Jacques—bring a complete change of clothing to the CO's room. Small size."

"Jacques!" Lynn echoed, brightening.

In a moment there was a knock on the door. The lieutenant opened it. A smartly uniformed young man was there. "Jacques, you will have precisely ten minutes to handle this matter in complete privacy before we return." Then he stepped out, his eyes signaling Sam to follow.

Jacques looked confused. Then he saw Lynn. "Yes sir!"

Sam exited, and Jacques entered, limping, and the lieutenant closed the door behind them. "Perhaps you can return with a personal report, possibly eliciting some action on the flooding tunnel," the lieutenant said, showing the way into the adjacent barracks, where several soldiers were sleeping. Because the block had to be vigilant twenty-four hours a day, the troops worked in three shifts. One soldier was awake, but studiously ignored them; Sam suspected that standing orders were to pay no attention to the commanding officer unless he asked for it. "It isn't simply the leaks; supplies are incomplete, so that we could withstand a genuine siege of only a few days. Our block is inadequately heated, as your little brother has noted. Lighting is sparse, and no provision has been made for decoration." He gestured at the triple-decker metal frame that held fifteen bunks. "No paint on ceiling or walls, no pictures, no decent floor covering. No privacy. This is bleak indeed. We are patriotic, but I believe we are entitled to at least minimal amenities while we serve our country."

"Yes sir," Sam said with feeling. "I will tell them."

"And Hugh—you have seen him recently?"

"Actually, Bry is the one of us who knows him best. Bry stayed with their family for some time, when he was young. But I think I would know Anne anywhere, by Bry's description."

"You would," the lieutenant agreed. "It has been some time for me also. We were neighbors, and our children mingled. Perhaps we shall meet again, in due course."

"I think Bry was somewhat smitten with her, though he was only eleven at the time."

"She is that type of woman. And her daughter Mina is even more so, despite being adopted. A truly winsome girl."

Sam had not met the lieutenant before, but found himself liking the man. There was a certain aura of intelligence about him that Ned would have related to.

"And I understand that in addition to your brother Bry, you also have a little sister, said to be a similarly lovely creature," the lieutenant continued after a moment. He spoke obliquely, because they could be overheard.

"Yes."

"Understand, I have no wish to intrude on the affairs of your family. But my men are a personal concern to me, and I wish to see none of them hurt, other than in the line of duty." He smiled briefly, indicating the fleeting humor; of course he didn't want anyone hurt in the line of duty either. "This little sister has an interest in someone?"

"Yes."

"Even if someone has an infirmity?"

"Yes."

"Not just because he is the son of a general?"

"No. She understands. She has her own infirmity."

"I am glad to hear it, no offense intended."

"I am glad you have an interest in the welfare of your men, sir."

The lieutenant shrugged. "I have an interest in surviving an attack. Every man must be at optimum performance. The

Germans are devising horrors we little anticipate."

"My brother Ned believes that we are preparing to fight the last war, while the Germans are preparing for the next war."

"Precisely. Therefore I hope it never comes to war."

In ten minutes they returned to the lieutenant's office. Lynn had changed, and was now in a baggy but dry uniform, seeming happy. She looked like a twelve year old boy rather than a sixteen year old girl.

"Now that your friend has taken so much trouble to visit you, Jacques, why don't you give him a tour of the block?" the lieutenant inquired. "Let's see how much you really know of our business."

"Yes, sir!" Jacques agreed eagerly. "But my station—"

"I will cover for you. I could use the practice."

"Yes, sir," Jacques repeated. Then, to Lynn, "I will show you everything."

"I suppose that's fair," the lieutenant murmured so that only Sam could hear. "He has already seen everything his friend possesses."

Sam had to smile. Lynn was a beautiful girl, with one exception, and in the course of changing and drying she had surely showed all of it off.

They went to the firing chamber on the upper floor. This was right above the crew room. A soldier stood there with a two barrel machine gun pointing out an armored window. Sam saw that he had a good view of the terrain outside; he would be able to riddle anything approaching on this side of the block. Except a tank.

"I read your thought, sergeant." The lieutenant spoke to the man. "I am substituting for Jacques at the moment. What would we do if we saw a tank charging us?"

The man immediately swung his machine gun away to the right, clearing the window. Meanwhile the lieutenant unstrapped and pushed forward a larger gun suspended from a rail on the ceiling. "This is our forty-seven millimeter anti-tank gun," he said, looking along its sights. "I think it would be a bold tank that charged directly into this field of fire.''

Sam had to agree. Tanks were deadly, but the gun was designed to take them out.

Jacques and Lynn appeared. "And this is my station," the young man said. "We have a twin machine gun, which is our main anti-personnel weapon, and an anti-tank gun. So if the enemy tries to flank us, avoiding our weapons turrets, we can mow him down. No one will get past this post.''

The lieutenant turned to Sam. "Makes it all seem worthwhile, doesn't it," he remarked wryly.

Sam had to agree. "But my brother Ned wonders what will happen if the enemy goes around the line.''

The lieutenant nodded soberly. "I hope your brother has the ear of the higher authorities. We shall do our part, here, but will they do theirs?''

The question gave Sam a chill, as it always did.

Indeed, the French were completely unready for the German blitzkrieg in 1939, the highly mobile tactics that bypassed the Maginot Line with its underground cannon, formidable anti-aircraft guns, and well secured bunkers. The German forces came through the supposedly impenetrable Belgian forest and spread out too rapidly to stop. France was effectively conquered in days, the Maginot Line largely untouched. It is now thought of as folly, but it would have served well enough if made complete.

Later, of course, weapons like the atomic bomb made all such defenses obsolete. But for its time, the Maginot Line concept was worthwhile as a stop-gap measure. It was the implementation that was inadequate.

Chapter 19

DREAMS AND BONES

As population increased, and resources decreased, the squeeze affected human societies in at first subtle, then more obvious ways. The third world nations suffered waves of starvation and illness; the first world nations suffered financial and economic disruptions. Politics became turbulent, and elections were supplemented by assassinations. The hearts of the cities became arenas for increasingly random violence by ever-younger gangs. It was clear to some that the end of the current way of life was approaching, but the

majority refused to recognize the deadly underlying
trends. What, then, were those few to do? The setting
is eastern America; the time is 1995.

"LOOK AT THAT," BRY SAID. "They've got that new game
on CD. Let's get it."

"No you don't," Lin protested. "We've got a budget."

"I'll buy it," Jack offered.

Now Bry backed off. "No. She's right. We don't need to
sponge off you."

"Wildflower's at the checkout," Lin said.

They walked to join her, and Bry took the bag as she
cleared the cash register. They went out of the store and out
of the mall, walking home at a leisurely pace so as not to
embarrass Jack. It was a nice summer afternoon in Wash-
ington, D.C.

But as they neared the housing project, a group of youths
appeared. "Hey, bitch!" one yelled at Wildflower. "You
trying to play white?"

Bry felt a chill. The gangs were getting worse. They were
ranging out farther, and looking more constantly for trouble.
These boys evidently took Wildflower for black, and wanted
to make something of it. She was a Moslem from Egypt,
and her skin was darker than some. So the gang was trying
to reserve this territory for whites only.

"Just keep moving," Bry said. "Maybe they're just passing by."

"Routine insults," Lin agreed. "But we'd better hurry,
just in case."

But when they picked up their speed, Jack's limp showed.
The gang members turned to follow. "Hey, gimpy—what
you want with that black slut? How much you paying her?"

"Don't respond," Bry advised. "Just keep walking."

But it did no good. With two targets, the gang kids had
enough to interest them for a while. They followed more
closely, hooting, and some ran ahead to block off the entrance to the project. "Hey, doll!" one called to Lin.

"Wanna make it with a real man?" He was evidently the leader, though he could not be more than sixteen.

They came to the intersection and tried to make the turn, but the gang kids stood squarely in the way. "Pay the toll, troll," one said, reaching for the bag Bry carried.

Jack stepped across and knocked the hand away. The four of them shoved forward, brushing by the kids, entering the street leading into the project.

"Oh, gimpy's tough!" one cried mockingly. "I'm scared!" Then he drew a knife.

All around them knives appeared.

It could be worse, Bry realized. Guns were increasingly common on the street. The main advantage of knives was their silence, but it was getting so that juvenile thugs no longer cared about noise.

"Run for it!" Lin cried.

They tried, but immediately two gang kids went after Lin, catching her by the arms. The others closed on the other three, their knives held forward menacingly. "You ain't going nowhere, you turds," the leader said. "You wanna get cut?"

They had to stop. Even if the other three made it to the project, Lin was caught and would pay the price. Bry noted that the inexperience of this gang was showing; many of the pejorative terms used were childish rather than savage. There was about as much bluster as action. That made it worse; if amateurs were getting this bad, what were the hardened professional gangs up to?

"That's better," the leader said, enjoying his power over them. "Okay, black bitch, you first: take it off."

Bry realized that there was a protocol: humiliate the black woman first, while the others watched. To send the message: stay out of white territory. They might not be able to justify raping a pretty white girl, but a black one was fair game.

"No!" Lin cried.

"Make her scream," the leader said without turning.

One of the kids holding Lin twisted her arm. She screamed.

Wildflower flinched. She knew what rape was like. She didn't want Lin to suffer it. She started to take off her clothes.

"Hey, hey!" the boys said, smiling. They had seen that Wildflower had a nice figure; now they were eager to confirm its details, feeling very naughty. They were nevertheless working themselves up, and some of them would indeed try to complete the rape.

Bry looked desperately around, but there were no police near, and no one else was coming to their rescue. That was par for the course, at night. Now it was happening in broad daylight. What could they do? Even without the knives, the four of them would have been no match for the gang. Jack had a bad foot, Bry was holding the bag, and the two girls couldn't fight.

Wildflower pulled off her red blouse, standing in skirt and bra. At age eighteen, she was a fine figure of a woman. "Yeah, yeah!" the kids agreed, ogling. They were young enough not to have had much actual sexual experience. They would have seen pornographic videos galore, but reality was much more compelling.

Wildflower waved the blouse over her head, like a flag. "More, more!" the boys cried gleefully.

There was the whistle of a bullet, followed by the sound of a shot from the project. The boys wheeled to look—and another bullet struck the road almost at their feet.

"Another time, bitch!" the leader cried as the gang members fled.

"You signaled Jes!" Lin exclaimed, catching on.

Wildflower nodded as she pulled her blouse back on. Then the four of them resumed their walk to the project.

Flo met them at the door. She was grim. "If I hadn't heard you scream—"

"And if Jes wasn't a dead shot with that rifle," Lin said, relieved.

"You did nothing to provoke them?"

"We were just walking. But they didn't like Wildflower's color."

Jes appeared, carrying her baby. She had fired from the upstairs window. The sound of the shots must have awakened the baby. But she had done what she had to do.

That night, when the men were home, they had a family meeting. "We can't have this," Ned declared, furious because of the threat to his wife.

"We can't afford better housing," Flo reminded him. "Anyway, the trouble is spreading to the 'good' neighborhoods now. The city isn't safe. Soon no city will be safe."

"And no town," Dirk added. "Violence isn't just for ghettoes any more."

"Where else can we go?" Snow asked. She was foreign-born, like Wildflower, and was having trouble finding work.

"I saw something," Bry said, remembering. "An ad. Maybe it's for us." He dashed to find the newspaper, searching out the section. "Here." He gave it to Flo.

" 'Planned community looking for skilled personnel in the following occupations,' " she read. Her eyes skimmed across the listing. " 'CAD—Computer Aided Design.' " She looked up. "That's you, Ned." She returned to the list. " 'Heavy construction.' That's you, Sam. 'Project organizer.' That's you, Ittai. 'Large-scale cook.' "

"That's you!" several others cried, laughing.

"What's the small print?" Ned asked.

"There isn't any," Flo said. "There's only a blind box."

"A what?" Sam asked.

Flo smiled, briefly. "Sam, your age is showing. It's a newspaper box, protecting the anonymity of the advertising party. There's no way to find out who is behind it except by answering."

Snow was interested. "But suppose you are looking for another job, and the ad is by your present employer? You could get fired, because—"

"Then you list a 'destroy' address: if your response is

headed for the named company, destroy it instead of delivering it. You can list any number of such addresses, to avoid past and present employers, estranged spouses, aggressive creditors, government agencies—''

"Hey, neat!" Lin cried. "Let's list that juvenile street gang." But no one laughed.

"So this is an essentially anonymous ad," Ned said. "With no indication of rates of pay, location, working conditions, duration, or benefits."

"So maybe we'd better ask," Flo said. "We don't have to sign up for anything we don't like. But we could certainly use some of these jobs, especially if they are together."

"It does say 'planned community,' " Dirk said. "That suggests something out of the city, with a lot of setting up to do. I rather like the notion, if it's valid."

"There certainly isn't much to hold us in *this* city," Ned said, with a glance at Wildflower.

"There isn't much in this *culture* to hold us," Ittai said grimly. "Companies are downsizing, jobs are scarce, and the average wage earner is making substantially less in real terms than he made twenty years ago, with no sign of improvement in the future. The welfare roles are increasing, while benefits are being cut. Things are worsening on every front. People are getting mired in debt they can't escape."

"Company store," Ned said. "The pay is such, and the prices such, that most folk can only sink lower. That's the beauty of it, by company logic: the subtle creation of a virtual slave class, while the owners reap record profits."

"St. Peter don't you call me,'cause I can't go," Lin singsonged, echoing an old song she had picked up in the schoolyard. "I owe my soul to the company store."

Ittai nodded. "We do seem to be in a company store society. But I suspect it's not as simple as a conspiracy by the haves to further deprive the have-nots. The resources of the world are being depleted, and there simply is not enough to go around. So everyone is scrambling for what remains, and an increasing number are losing out."

"Musical chairs," Bry said. "There's always one chair too few, so someone loses."

"A nice enough analogy," Ittai agreed. "I believe that when the livelihood of families is strained, with both parents having to work outside the home, or single-parent families with that parent working or forced onto welfare, the children are inevitably neglected. They turn to their peer groups, and we get street gangs. The next stage will be what we already see in third world countries: mass starvation, food riots, class warfare, and revolution that accomplishes little other than intensification of the misery."

"We have to get out of this game," Lin said. The others nodded soberly.

"So maybe this planned community has the same idea," Flo said. "Get out of the city, get self-sufficient, get independent of the company store, have enough chairs."

"It works for me," Lin said.

"So let's answer this ad," Flo said, looking around. No one objected.

✥

Two weeks later they were on their way to Dreams, a planned community in southern Pennsylvania, near the Maryland border. They drove in both their vans, a convoy of two, watching out for each other in case one broke down. It was the family way. Counting the baby, the full family now numbered fifteen, because Jack had elected to come along. It wasn't just that he was engaged to Lin and wanted to be with her; he felt at home with a family that accepted him without reservation. His family was wealthy, and Jack was prepared to be generous with money, if asked. But he was never asked. So he lived as they did, fitting in, and liked it.

Jack and Lin and Bry rode together in the rear seat, Lin in the middle, her left hand holding Jack's right hand, their fingers interleaved so that hers fell outside his on both sides, and her left foot touched his clubbed right foot. Bry was privately jealous of their intimacy. It wasn't that Jack had come between Bry and his sister, for he had not; it was that Bry lacked an equivalent girlfriend. Someone beautiful but in some way tainted or marked. He knew that a psychiatrist would consider his taste to be warped, but Bry understood his own dream. Marked people could be like pearls among swine, real bargains for those who looked.

In three hours they were in the Appalachians, looking for the turnoff to Amaranth, a town so small that it wasn't on their roadmap. It was supposed to be about ten miles north of the Potomac River's northernmost loop, where it almost pinched off the western tip of Maryland. Then they explored the back roads until at last they found the entrance to Dreams. The scenery was phenomenal; this was true mountain country, largely forested, and barely touched by the works of man.

An elder man came out to meet them as they climbed out and looked around. "Greetings. You would be the visiting family?"

"We are," Flo said.

"I am Marc, with a c. I am one of the elders of the community. We have a house for you, but regret that it is as yet unfinished."

"I'm sure we'll make do," Flo said. "Where do we check in?"

"There is no checking in as such. You will introduce yourselves at the evening meal, and any community members you meet will introduce themselves to you, until you know them. I will conduct you to the various working sites. I think you will know soon enough whether these are compatible, and we shall come to know you too."

"So we'll know whether we really want to join Dreams," Flo agreed. "But we'd like to learn more of the community philosophy and outlook."

"There are informal community meetings every evening, where discussion and group activities occur."

"Well, that's fine. But I understand that this is a religious community. We aren't sure that we—"

"The project is founded and funded by volunteers associated with the Religious Society of Friends, commonly called Quakers, in conjunction with the American Friends Service Committee, or AFSC, a globally charitable organization. So we do have weekly Meetings. But attendance is not mandatory, and we don't require that others join. But I must advise you that pacifism is a tenet of our religion, and those who profess or practice violence will not be welcome here. This is something you will have to judge as you work with us. We are short-handed because others have found this aspect unsuitable. We do not require that you adopt pacifism as a philosophy, just that you practice no violence of word or action on these, our premises. Similarly, no flesh of animals is served here; you will have to seek that elsewhere."

"Understood," Flo said for all of them. "We will behave appropriately while here. So you don't have a problem with, for example, non-Christians. Ned and Wildflower are Moslem."

"As long as they do not proselytize. We encourage discussion of religion in all its forms, and they are welcome to clarify their belief for us, but we frown on efforts to convert. We will not try to convert you."

"Fair enough," Ned said.

"However, those of you who elect to remain with us will be expected to convert to the extent of becoming familiar with our essential philosophy, and supporting it. We would ask, for example, that the young lady refrain from wearing a weapon while in the community."

Jes nodded. "What about during this trial period?"

"Thee is free to do as thee wishes, as thee is uncommitted."

All of them were startled. "Thee?" Jes asked.

Marc smiled. "I apologize for not clarifying this earlier. We who are committed tend to use the plain talk, which derives from the manner the Quakers—that is, the Religious

Society of Friends—spoke in an earlier age. It fell gradually out of favor in recent times, but we regard Dreams as a new beginning, and so the use of plain talk seems appropriate. This affectation is not required of thee.''

"But you weren't doing it before.''

"Second person singular is 'thee.' Second person plural is 'you.' I was addressing the group of you before, not thee personally.''

"Oh." Jes was evidently intrigued, as were the rest of them.

They trouped to the house, which turned out to be of the modern log cabin type, a sturdy and large two story structure with a number of rooms, but unfinished inside. "There has been so much to do, that this lacked priority," Marc explained. "We hope that in winter, when outdoor work— gardening, and so on—is not feasible, we will be able to catch up on interior work.''

"It will do," Flo said. "Those of us with skills for you will see to those now; the others can unload the cars and set up the house." She looked around. "Snow and I will head for your kitchen. Ned and Bry will go to your computer designing facility. Ittai will go to your organizing section. And Sam will help with your brute work.''

Soon Ned and Bry were in the Dreams computer room, adjacent to the machine shop. A man looked up from the computer. "These are Ned and Bry, our visitors," Marc said. Then he left.

The man stood and came over to shake hands. "Bill. Does thee know CAD?''

"Yes," Ned said. "But not necessarily your particular program.''

"It varies. How is thee on the Stirling engine?''

"Archaic external combustion engine," Ned said. "Intriguing, but it lost out to the internal combustion engine because of the problem with bearings and low mechanical efficiency.''

"Suppose it could be hermetically sealed, with no external piston?"

"That would solve one problem, but generate several others. Such as how to make it perform work."

"Let me introduce thee to the Solar Stirling engine, which we propose to use for generating electricity."

"Solar! For electricity! That would do it. But the technology—"

"Can be tricky in detail. Right this way."

In the shop was a squat device somewhat like a bomb. Bry tried to look interested, but engines weren't his specialty, and this one seemed comprehensible only to Bill and Ned. It didn't even seem to have any moving parts.

Bill glanced at him. "This must be pretty dull for thee, Bry. Why don't thee go on out back and ask my daughter Faience to show thee around? It may be hours before we're back on the computer."

"Okay," Bry agreed gratefully. He went out in the indicated direction.

There was a girl of about fourteen working on basket weaving. There were mounds of fibrous material around. She looked up as Bry approached. "Hello. I'm Faience."

"I'm Bry. My family just arrived for a trial visit. Your father said you might show me around."

"Glad to, unless you'd rather learn basket weaving."

"No, computer games are more my style."

"Mine too. But we have to wait for off hours. Thou shalt not waste prime computer time, and all that." She put aside her materials and stood up. She was a plain girl with freckles, but seemed pleasant. "Right," she said as if reading his mind. "I'm not much to look at, but I've got personality. Or something."

"I didn't say—"

"You didn't have to. Come on. I'll show you the pump. You know what a hydraulic ram is?"

"Either an animal or a machine, I think."

She laughed. "Right! Do you like to run?"

"For about a hundred yards."

"Then follow me." She set off across the field at a run, her shortish hair fluffing out. She was lean, and ran well; it was a job to catch up with her, and then he was out of breath.

She slowed somewhat. "Sorry, didn't mean to tease you. I just love it out here so well I can't help myself."

"I just wanted to stay behind to watch your jeans," he panted.

She laughed again. "That's a lie I can live with." She slowed to a walk.

"But I wasn't—"

She turned to face him. "Don't lie for real. That would ruin our friendship, and it has hardly begun. No one considers me romantic; I'm too young and too plain. But I do make a good friend."

"Okay. I'm new here, and I don't know if we'll stay more than a month. I could use a friend for that month."

"Done! Do you like movies?"

"Yes."

"We can get a ride into Hagerstown tomorrow and see one. I like company when I leave Dreams."

"But don't we have to work? I understood that in a planned community, everybody has his job."

"That's true. But tomorrow's Saturday. We work during the week, we attend Meeting on Sunday and relax in quiet, cultural, or educational ways. Oh, it's not bad, and I do like the folk singing, but Saturday's my chance to be a regular irresponsible teen. Do you have any sisters?"

"Three. The elder two are married, but Lin's my age and she still likes movies. Maybe she and Jack will join us. Jack's her boyfriend; they're pretty serious."

"Great!" They were now descending a steep forested slope, following a pipe that made a knocking sound every second.

"Um, Faience, if I may ask—I notice you don't use the plain talk."

"Well, that depends. Mom and Dad do, in the community, but not outside. I'm just here because they are; I'm not committed on my own. So Bille—that's my brother—and I figure it would be, well, not exactly a lie, but misleading to use it, until such time as we are committed on our own. But when someone uses it to me, I do tend to respond in kind. It's no big deal."

"So if I said thee to you, you would say thee to me."

"Yeah," she said, smiling. "I would say thee to thee."

"Something else: Marc said that no meat is served here. Why is that? Because they consider it violent?"

"Not exactly. It's that it takes something like twenty pounds of grain to make one pound of meat, when you run it through the animal first. So it's inefficient. If things get tight, and people get hungry, our gardens will go twenty times as far if we cut out the middleman, as it were."

"I guess that makes sense. But don't you have animals here?"

"Oh, sure, lots of them. We believe in biodiversity. But not for meat."

"Suppose an animal dies coincidentally? Would that be eaten?"

Faience made a face. "Would you want to eat your pet dog? We have pet llamas. But I guess they would be eaten, yes, if not diseased."

They came to the bottom of the hill, where there was a stream.

"This is the hydraulic ram," Faience said, indicating a round tank sitting on top of the pipe. The knocking sound was loud.

"Where's the motor?"

"This is the motor. It's like this: Water comes down this pipe in the stream. The valve in the end of it lets out some water, but that motion makes the valve slam shut. That's why it knocks. Then the valve opens again, and lets a bit more water out, until it slams shut again."

"But that's not a motor!"

"Yes it is, in its fashion. See this connecting pipe? There's a valve inside that. When the first valve knocks closed, the water moving inside comes to a sudden stop, and the pressure jumps. That forces some water up through the inside valve. The air tank is to ease the shock, so it doesn't pound itself apart. That water keeps nudging into the pipe and on up the hill. It's slow but sure, and it uses no external energy, and it pumps all the water we need."

"With no fuel?" Bry asked, surprised. "Free pumping?"

"Free pumping," she agreed. "That's sort of our philosophy: renewable energy, environmentally friendly, durable, cheap. All our machines are like that, except maybe the computers. But they help too, really, because with things like E-mail and the Internet folks don't have to waste so much energy commuting to work."

Bry was impressed. "The water gets moving and knocks at the valve, like a hammer, and keeps driving a bit more water up the pipe. But doesn't it lose as much water as it pumps?"

"More. But this is a river. Plenty of water here. But not enough up the hill where we are. We have all we need. The water really pumps itself up to us. The hydraulic ram should last indefinitely, with no maintenance, unless a valve should get jammed."

"I never knew there was such a thing. I like it."

"They say that thirty years ago there was a problem translating the term from a Russian paper. It came out 'water sheep.' "

Bry laughed. "So maybe I was half-right. It is an animal."

They made their way back up the hill, following the pipe. Then Faience paused. "I just realized: I have a date to go in tomorrow with Tourette."

"Who?"

"I need to explain about her. She's really nice. But there are two things. Can I tell you something in private?"

"You mean a secret?"

"Not exactly. It's something you need to know, but not to bruit about, as it were."

"To use discretion."

"Yes. I don't want to embarrass anyone."

"Sure, yes. I'll be discreet."

"Tourette's from the Bones community."

"The what?"

"Our nickname for it. It's a neighboring community we don't like, settled by survivalists. Gun nuts. Militia men. Every one of them is armed and dangerous. We wish they would go away, because—"

"Because you're pacifists. And vegetarians. What a combination!"

"Yes. They don't much like us, and we don't much like them. But neither group is moving; we both have too much invested in our land and development. We don't speak to each other. If we see one of them on the road, we go right on by in silence. They do the same."

"You snub each other."

"Yes. And Tourette's one of them. So I don't speak of our acquaintance."

Bry considered that. "I don't want to give offense, but is that honest? You said you like straight speaking."

She looked pained. "I do. But this is difficult. She's nice. And there aren't a whole lot of girls my age around here. Actually she's sixteen, two years older, but that's close enough."

Bry spoke carefully. "Sometimes there is a conflict between truth and decency. My sister Flo is really fat, but we don't go up and call her fatso. So maybe if a person has a friend that others might not approve of, for no good reason, it's better just to keep her mouth shut."

"Yes!"

"So I guess I can keep my mouth shut. But how did you get together with her, if the two communities don't associate?"

"I was out looking for berries, alone, and there she was.

We sort of struck it up. She's lonely too. Her folks are really overprotective. So we're secret friends.''

''But if you go into town together—''

''Mom drives. She understands. So Mom shops for supplies, and we see a movie. It's nice. I sort of watch out for Tourette.''

''But if she's older than you, and armed—''

''That's the other thing. Tourette's not her real name. It's just what I call her. She—when we met, she was shy, almost afraid of me. I couldn't think why. I mean, she carried a gun and a dagger, and I was unarmed, so it couldn't have been any thought that I could hurt her. Then she started twitching, sort of, and I was scared. I asked whether anything was wrong, and she said Tourette. I thought it was her name, so that's what I called her. Later I learned it wasn't, and I was really embarrassed, but she said it was okay, she knew I didn't mean anything by it. So that's her name, to me.''

''I don't understand. Why did she give you a wrong name? And why did she twitch?''

''It's a disease, or at least an affliction. Tourette's syndrome, named after the doctor who described it. Mostly boys get it; only about 20 percent are girls. They vary. Some just twitch, and they can suppress it for a while, if they try, but eventually it will happen. Others are worse, and they grunt or even say things, like cusswords or obscenities, and they can't help it. Tourette—I mean my friend—is sort of in between. It comes and goes, and she can hold it down some, but sometimes it really gets away from her and she'll grunt and hiss something awful. It passes in a moment, and she's okay, as if nothing happened. But she doesn't like to do it in public.''

''I can appreciate why. Maybe it's like epilepsy.''

''Maybe. I don't think anybody really knows. What matters is that it's not her fault, and it's not contagious, and it has nothing to do with how else she looks and acts. So if she twitches, just ignore it. Give her a break.''

"You're afraid I don't understand?"

"Yeah," she agreed, embarrassed.

"I do understand. But I'm not free to tell you why. That's another confidence I keep. But maybe you'll find out. Then you'll know how well I understand."

"Okay," she said, looking relieved. "So if you come over to my house tomorrow morning, early, we'll go in. We use the community van; there's room in there for any number of teens, sitting on the floor. Only, if your sister and her friend—"

"They are discreet. May I tell them?"

"You'd better. But I'd really rather it didn't go farther."

"It won't. We'll be there, and we won't embarrass her."

"She's really a very nice person, and smart as anything. She's read just about every book there is, and knows so much. I'm sure you'll like her. Apart from that one thing."

He saw that she feared he and Lin would treat her friend with that polite disdain reserved for those one could not blame but really did not want to have close by. So it was time to change the subject.

Bry looked around, noticing something he had missed when running through this field before. There were strange plants growing taller than his head. "What is growing here?"

"That's hemp."

"Hemp? But isn't that illegal?"

"The stupid law is changing. Anyway, it's not for drugs. Quakers don't use things like that; in fact they don't much like alcohol or cigarettes either. A true Quaker is almost without vices." She grimaced. "It must get dull. Hemp's great for fibers; you can make rope or cloth or paper from it, and it grows just about anywhere. It produces three to eight tons of fibrous dry stalk per acre per year, depending on climate and variety, compared to two or three tons of fiber for southern pine, and it's easier to process. So it represents a way to save all the trees that get pulped for books and newspapers. Sure, some species are used for narcotics, but that's not what we're after." She paused. "But maybe it's best not to talk about it elsewhere. We grow a lot of stuff that some folk wouldn't understand about. Rare medicinal herbs, exotic food plants, biomass for alternate fuel, and so on."

"Agreed."

"We're experimenting with kenaf, too. That may be even better than hemp, because it's not illegal, if we can find a frost-resistant strain."

"What's that again?"

"Kenaf." She accented the second syllable. "It's a variety of the hibiscus, a cousin of cotton and okra, and it has a similar flower. It grows over twelve feet tall and yields five to ten tons of fiber per acre per year that's relatively easy to process for paper. This could revolutionize the pulp industry. Think of it: great fields of pretty flowers that provide all the paper the world needs, more cheaply than wood. Beauty and economy together. So that trees will be for the birds again."

She was really animated, and it was contagious. Bry liked the new directions this community was exploring. It wasn't retreating from the world so much as trying to help save the world from its own folly. This was exactly the kind of thing he would like to be a part of.

They reached the shop. "I'd better get back to work on the baskets," Faience said. "But at least I've shown you something, and I don't mean my jeans. You'll get to know all the parts of Dreams soon enough, I'm sure."

"Maybe it's time for me to learn basket making," Bry said. "Will you teach me?"

"Sure!"

So they settled down, and he learned how to make a basket from hemp fiber and reeds. It was both more challenging and more fun than he would have thought.

That evening he got Lin aside and explained. "I thought maybe, if something happens, you could, you know, if you want to," he concluded a bit lamely. "So she knows it's okay."

Lin nodded. "Maybe. I'll tell Jack."

In the morning the three of them went to Faience's house. They met her mother Fay, and piled into the back of the van with Faience.

"But where is Tourette?" Bry asked.

"We'll pick her up along the way," Faience explained. "I guess her folks know what's she doing, but she keeps it pretty quiet. I think maybe they'd tell her no, if she asked, so she doesn't ask and her mom doesn't say anything."

The van got moving. Before long it stopped, and Faience threw open the side door and jumped down. Bry saw a rather pretty young woman in blue jeans and heavy shirt standing beside the road. "We have three friends along this time," she said. "It's okay; they're visitors: They want to see the movie too."

Hesitantly, the girl stepped into the van and sat down beside Faience. She wore a sheath at her hip, with a solid knife. "This is Tourette," Faience said. "And this is Bry, and his sister Lin, and her friend Jack."

The van moved out. "Hi," Bry said.

The girl looked at him somewhat in the manner of a frightened deer. She was clearly not at all at ease. Her hair was parted in the center, passing down to frame her face before falling across her shoulders. It gave her an elfin look. Then she began to twitch, and then to grunt.

They looked away, trying to defuse the awkwardness. In a moment the girl settled down. But she looked as if she wanted to scramble out of there.

"It's okay," Faience said. But clearly it wasn't.

Lin glanced at Jack, then at Bry. Then she spoke. "Tourette, I want to show you something." She lifted her left hand, which was clutching her purse. She set the purse down. She opened her hand, so that all six fingers showed clearly.

Tourette stared. Then she reached out. "May I?"

"Yes."

Tourette took Lin's hand and touched every finger, verifying that all were real. Then she nodded. "I have read of it, but never expected to see it. Most such cases get corrected surgically at birth. I'm glad that wasn't the case with you. It's a good hand."

"Good enough for me," Lin agreed. "I just don't like a hassle, so I mostly hide it."

"You said you understood," Faience breathed, looking at Bry. "Now so do I."

"And Jack has a club foot," Lin said. "We don't make fun of anybody, in our family. We know how it is."

Tourette smiled, visibly relaxing. "Yes. Thank you."

After that they talked of other things, feeling increasingly at ease with each other. Bry discovered he rather liked Tourette; she had a very quick mind, and she smiled often, now that she was at ease. She soon elicited descriptions from Bry and Lin of their travels.

"It must be wonderful to be in such far places," she said.

"It really wasn't all that much," Bry demurred. But her ready interest flattered him. At the same time, he saw how well read she was, because she knew details about the places he had been that he would have thought only a traveler would have picked up on.

When they reached town, the five of them walked together to the theater, and found grouped seats. Lin and Jack sat beside each other, of course, then Faience, Tourette, and Bry.

After a time, in the darkness, Bry touched Tourette's right hand. "May I?" he whispered.

She turned her hand over, and he took it, interleaving their fingers. After that, when something interesting or meaningful happened in the movie, he squeezed her hand, gently, and she squeezed back. It had become a date.

When they returned to the van, Bry sat beside Tourette. "Why don't you hold her hand again?" Faience asked mischievously.

Tourette blushed, and Bry felt his own face heating. They had thought that business had been unobserved. But he lifted his hand, and Tourette lifted hers, and they clasped hands. Thus it was official: they had dated.

"I'm sorry," Faience said. "I thought I was joking. It wasn't funny."

"These things happen," Lin said, snuggling closer to Jack. "Your turn will come."

Again, they talked about many things, compatibly. Tourette suffered a minor series of twitches, but Bry held firmly on to her hand, and they passed. He continued to bask in the glow of her interest in all the things he had done. It was as if he were far more important than usual. He had always regarded himself as somewhat of a nonentity, and it was a real pleasure to be regarded as otherwise by this smart and pretty girl.

The van slowed, and stopped. It was time for Tourette to leave. Bry made as if to get out with her, but she shook her head. "They would not understand."

"Maybe—next week?"

"I hope so." Then she turned and walked into the forest. He watched her go, feeling strange emotions.

"So how do *her* jeans look?" Faience inquired.

"Just great," Bry answered.

"Their whole compound is wired and guarded like the Maginot Line," Faience remarked. "But she knows a safe route through. That's how she gets out without passing the guard station. But she has to go alone."

"You really like her?" Lin asked Bry.

"I guess I do. There's something about her."

"She's got a pretty potent figure under that clothing," Jack remarked. "If she ever dressed to show it off, she'd be something."

"Oh, you were noticing?" Lin asked him.

"Don't be jealous, wench. You've got something she doesn't."

"A sixth finger," she agreed, and they laughed.

"Maybe that's it," Bry said. "Maybe I've been looking for someone with a sixth finger, or something."

"Or something," Lin agreed, nodding. "She's got plenty."

"I told you she was a nice girl," Faience said triumphantly. "You two really hit it off, once she knew you were for real."

Lin agreed. "I think she's the one for you, Bry."

He realized that she might be right. What a day it had been!

That evening there was a community gathering, where the family was introduced. There were too many people to assimilate all at once, but all were friendly. Several complimented Flo on her cooking; she had, in her fashion, dug in and made something good happen. It was a nice way to get acquainted. But Bry was distracted by his memories of the day, and thoughts of Tourette. Yes, she had an awkward syndrome, but it was indeed part of her appeal for him. He knew how precious the roses could be that others did not appreciate. And Jack was right: she was a comely girl. Her face and figure were nice, and so was her nature. Faience was right too: she was as bright a girl as he could remember encountering. He liked that. In fact he liked all of her.

Sunday morning they all dressed up and went to Meeting. It wasn't required, but they wanted to understand this community, because it wasn't just a question of finding employment. They were not being paid for their work in money, just in kind: their residence was free. If they decided to join, and the community of Dreams wanted them, they would continue to work without pay. Membership was the only reward. They needed to know whether they could fit into this religious community, and whether they wanted to.

Quaker Meeting was not exactly like a regular church service. There was no minister, and there were no songs or readings. The people filed in quietly and took the pews and seats. They sat in silence.

After a while, one of the men of the community stood.

"We live in perilous times," he said. "The world is becoming more difficult. It is good to find refuge in the field and forest. I pray to the divine spirit that is within all of us that our effort will be successful. We hope to achieve an island of peace that will endure though troubles come elsewhere. I see it being realized, but I don't know whether it is enough. May amity and fellowship prevail throughout." He sat down again.

Later another person stood, and spoke of the beauty of the day and the countryside, and the joy of the experience of harmony with nature. Another person did not stand, but leaned forward and spoke a prayer for peace in all the world.

Bry wasn't sure what to make of it. This was a religious service? It seemed like a meditation session, with occasional comments thrown in. Yet he rather liked the atmosphere. There was a certain quiet good humor throughout. These people were quite serious, without taking themselves too seriously.

In due course the meeting ended, and people chatted with each other. Jes discovered an old friend of hers named Crockson. "I must repay that loan!" she exclaimed.

"What loan?" the man asked blankly.

"Don't pretend you don't remember! It enabled me to travel on until I found my husband."

Bry moved on, not much interested, because he didn't know Crockson. Faience came up. "What did you think of it?" she asked Bry.

"It's different, but nice," he said.

"Like Tourette?"

He laughed. "Maybe so."

They adjourned to a nice lunch of fresh vegetables that tasted better than anything Bry had eaten recently. "We do our own gardening," Faience explained. "We can use another gardener, if you're interested."

Offhand, Bry could not think of anything he would be much less interested in. But his recent experiences with the hydraulic ram, basket weaving, and Tourette had shaken his certainties. Maybe there would be more surprises. "Okay."

In the evening there was a song session. The harmonies were not perfect, but were enthusiastic, and Bry found himself joining in as he learned the songs. One especially struck him: "The Garden Song." "Inch by inch, and row by row, Going to make this garden grow." There was a wholesome optimism that was contagious. "Pulling weeds, picking stones, We are made of dreams and bones." The image caught hold of him. Dreams and bones—that was indeed what this community was all about. It was personal for Bry, because this community was called Dreams, while the nickname for the other community, where Tourette lived, was Bones. Bry and Tourette, dreams and bones. He had nice dreams, she had nice bones. But it was more than that. Much more.

The next day, Monday, Bry started the day with Ned and Bill, who were trying to design a refinement for the Solar Stirling engine. Bry realized that if he wanted to be of any real use with the computer, he would have to learn to understand the principle of the Stirling engine. But its mechanism was weird; it had a piston, but it wasn't like a gasoline motor. For one thing, he had heard it was a free piston, connected directly to nothing. How could that accomplish anything?

"Maybe I can help," Faience said. "I have a general notion, because Dad has explained it to me about half a zillion times. I can tell you what I know while we work on the garden."

He had forgotten: he had agreed to go to the garden with her. "Okay."

It turned out that they had a number of gardens, ranging from old-fashioned outdoor dirt to hydroponic. They had to pull some encroaching weeds from a tomato patch without damaging the garden plants. This was reasonably tedious work, which was ideal. While they worked, Faience explained the Solar Stirling engine as she understood it.

"First, you have to understand that it's an external combustion engine," she said. "It can run on anything, but we're using the sun as much as we can. We have huge reflectors set up to focus the sunlight on the engine, making it very hot."

"I didn't see those."

"They're portable, and made of shiny cloth or foil stretched on frameworks; no point in setting them up until we get the kinks out of the engine. We can also use a series of Fresnel lenses—named for a French physicist—which consist of very thin optic lenses of short focal length layered in concentric rings. We can get square Fresnel lens panels commercially, and they can generate a lot of heat—up to 3,000 degrees Fahrenheit. They're less sturdy, but resistant to minor pocks or scratching, and much more efficient, and that's important here where we can't be sure of intense sunlight."

She obviously had more than a "general" notion. She was comfortable with terms he had never heard of. "Okay, *I* understand how a lot of heat can translate into power. A gasoline engine does that. But there the explosions push the pistons, and the pistons push the wheels, ultimately, making the car move. Your Stirling engine has just a loose piston that stays inside. I don't know what makes it move, and how it can do any work when it does move."

"Those are easy questions to answer," she said. "The heat focuses on a chamber and heats the air inside. Actually it's not air, it's helium, what we call the working fluid, but you can think of it as air if you want to."

"Isn't helium a gas, rather than a fluid?"

She smiled. "Sure it is. But under high pressure at high heat, it acts just about like a fluid, so that's the technical term. It heats and expands, and pushes the piston out. Then the heat is cut off, and it cools and contracts, and the piston comes back in. So that's what makes it move. Of course the actual cycle is way more sophisticated, with a regenerator, a piston, which is actually connected to the alternator, not exactly 'free' in the way you thought—it's what we call a 'kinematic mechanism'—and a displacer, and the piston and the displacer take turns moving as the helium changes volume and moves about. The displacer is to make sure it doesn't lock up at the extremes, I think. I could draw you a diagram in the dirt—''

"No, I get the message: it gets hot and pushes the piston out, then it gets cool and pulls the piston back in. But since the piston isn't connected to anything solid—''

"How does it do any work," she finished for him. "You'll kick yourself for this one. You know how they generate electricity from big dams or whatever?''

"They pass iron wiring through magnetic fields. The motion generates electric current that—'' He paused, seeing it. "Electricity! The piston generates current. It doesn't need to go outside the engine; all it needs to do is move."

"Right. So it moves a tenth of an inch, sixty cycles a second. The helium varies only a few degrees in temperature, at about 670 degrees Celsius, but it does the job. And we have power. Or will, once it is properly set up."

"What's the matter with it? Don't they deliver these things ready to operate?"

"They do, but it seems that the tolerances are extremely close, and it has to be adjusted just right. That's what Dad's been working on. He's checking the computer to get the settings exactly right for the job we have, and, well, he says the devil is in the details."

"That's what Ned says, too. They'll work it out."

"They'd better. We're on commercial power now, but when the crash comes, we'll have to be on our own power."

"The crash?"

"You know, when society collapses and civilization ends. That's why were out here. So we won't be taken down with it, and humanity won't expire."

Bry was amazed. "Do you really think that's going to happen?"

"Oh, sure. We just don't know when. Isn't that why you folk are out here? To save your skins?"

"No, just to find decent work and living conditions. We don't much like it in the big city. But I guess you're right: We know that things can't go on as they are. Something's going to give, and maybe pretty soon."

"Yes. So it's best to be well away from the bomb before it explodes. And not to be dependent on the rest of the world for anything, so we don't get dragged down with it."

"Isn't that a rather selfish philosophy?"

She nodded, unsmiling. "I guess it is. But I don't see too many others trying to protect themselves either. They find it easier just to ignore the handwriting on the wall."

"How about the survivalists?"

"Bones. Yes, I guess they are doing it too. But we don't like their guns. In fact, they make us pretty damn nervous."

"Why? Aren't they just trying to be ready to protect themselves?"

"From what? From us? More likely they figure to come in and take what we've got."

Bry was silent, pondering that. It did seem like sheep living next to the den of wolves. "But Tourette—she's not like that."

"Yes she is. Ask her."

"But then why are you friends with her?"

"The crunch hasn't come yet. So there's no problem. But when it happens, we won't be friends any more. We both know that."

"I can't believe that."

"Well, you're half in love with her."

"I am not! We've only dated once."

She shook her head. "I'm jealous, I admit it. Not of you personally. I knew you weren't for me. I mean of your relationship. You saw her, and she saw you, and it was like two magnets getting charged. And not just because you're handsome and she's pretty, though I guess that doesn't hurt. I wish I could meet someone and have that happen. I'm a little annoyed I didn't see it coming, but of course I was afraid you'd be turned off by her syndrome. You said you understood, but I didn't really believe that. Tourette was almost afraid of you, despite being fascinated. Then when your sister showed her hand—you've been waiting all your life for someone like Lin, only who's not your sister, and there she was. And Tourette—she's never had a boyfriend. She saw that hand, and she knew. You two were destined for each other." She looked at him challengingly. "Now tell me it's not so."

Bry considered. Could he be in love with Tourette, after just one day with her? And she with him? "I don't think love happens like that. Fascination, maybe, but not love. Sure I like her. But—"

"What's the big distinction between fascination and love, except that the one happens fast and the other slow? You two are in mutual orbit, spiraling in together. Maybe if you never see each other again, you'll get over it. But next week—do you even want me along?"

Bry reconsidered. "I think maybe you'd *better* be along. If she feels the way I do, we're in free fall. There's no telling what might happen."

"Would it be wrong?"

"Yes! We're not ready for that. My family may not even stay here, and anyway, if I'm a Dream and she's a Bone, how can it be?"

"Okay, I'll be there. But I think you'd better have that Dreams and Bones discussion with her right away."

"I'd better," he agreed, with uncomfortably mixed feelings.

The week passed, and with every day it looked more as if the family was fitting in, and would stay. Flo liked the big kitchen, and the community members liked her cooking. Dirk was an all purpose handyman, doing good work. Sam was finding plenty of outdoor hard work to do, the kind he liked, on a crew that Ittai organized, and it was evident that they were making a difference. Ned and Bill were working well together, each appreciating the intellect of the other. Snow and Wildflower and Lin were mixing with the women, doing everything from baskets to painting walls, compatibly. The children loved everything about the community. Faience showed Bry around the rest of the garden area, including the heated greenhouse, which could be kept at over a hundred degrees Fahrenheit if required. It seemed that some of their rare medicinal herbs liked that kind of environment. Only Jes seemed a bit out of sorts, but that might be because she was still adjusting to new motherhood.

But there was no avoiding the fact that the community of Dreams did not like the community of Bones, just as Faience had said. The weekly trips into town to see the movie were the only contact between any members of the two, and that was quiet, perhaps unknown to any but the mothers of the two girls. And to Jack, Lin, and Bry, who were not talking about it. There just might be hell to pay if the news got out.

Saturday came. Jack and Lin did not go; they had other things to do, being well wrapped up in community activities. So it was just Bry and Faience—and Tourette.

This time Tourette wore a skirt and blouse. She was indeed a nice figure of a woman. She had done something with her hair, and looked lovely. This time she wore no visible weapon.

Faience jumped down. "I'll ride in front, this time," she said, and climbed into the front seat. That left Bry and Tourette together alone in back. There was a screen separating the front seats from the rear of the van, so they had reasonable privacy.

They closed the door and settled down, leaning against opposite sides, their knees up. Tourette's skirt fell away below, so that her thighs showed. Bry tried not to look, but failed. Actually the van was dark enough inside so that it was mostly shadow down there, but his imagination ran rampant.

Her very presence made his pulse accelerate. He was suddenly shy. "You're beautiful."

"Thank you."

"I think—I think we have to talk," Bry said.

"Before we do, would you kiss me?"

"If I do that, we may never talk."

"That's okay with me."

Bry came to a pained realization. "You think I'm going to—to break it off?"

"I would, in your place."

"You think—the syndrome? That's not—"

"Please. Before we get into it. Then I will listen, and there will be no trouble. I promise." She looked at him, beseechingly.

He moved across, kneeled, and kissed her. The van lurched at that moment, and he caught only half her mouth before he fell over. But she joined him on the floor, laughing. Lying there, they kissed again, hard and long.

Then, embraced, they remained there. Her body against his was wonderful. He felt the motion of her breast when she breathed. "Faience says it's love," he murmured.

"She may be right."

They kissed again. Then she spoke. "I'm not apt at this. I have no experience in romance. But the way I feel— maybe it's better to be clumsy than silent." She took his hand and set it on her thigh where the skirt rode up. "Anything you want, Bry. Please."

"Oh, Tourette, I want everything. I think you're the greatest girl. But—"

"I know. Two different worlds."

"We're—we're joining the pacifists. Do your folk really go armed all the time?"

"Yes. And we are trained to use our weapons."

"But you aren't—"

"Yes I am. Here." She guided his hand up under her left arm. There, next to her breast, was a flat holster. "Knife. In this outfit, a gun's too hard to conceal."

"Why did you dress this way, then?"

"For you. Because I wanted to look nice for you. And to

make it possible for you to do anything you might want to do with me. But I still had to be armed.''

"For self-defense," he said. "Because it's not safe for a girl alone."

"You understand?"

"My eldest sister got raped. And my brother's wife, too. And—well, Lin needs protection. My sister Jes is always armed, even now with her baby."

"But you can't be that way, in Dreams."

"But I don't mind if *you* are. I mean, each person makes his own decision, doesn't he?"

"No. At Bones, you train in martial art. You go armed. Always. Even when sleeping."

"So if I visited, I'd have to have a gun, or something?"

"Yes." She moved his hand across her blouse, so that it touched her warm breast. "Anything you want, Bry. But I am what I am."

"You mean you think I'll dump you, but you'll give me everything anyway?"

"Yes. Now, while I can. I think I love you."

"I think I love you, too. But I know these things take time. Sometimes it doesn't work out. My brother's first wife was beautiful, but—it just takes time. Maybe I should meet your father, or something."

"No. He would see to it that I never saw you again."

"Oh, Tourette, I couldn't bear that!"

"He may find out anyway. He has ways of knowing. I love him, but he's a hard man. I don't mean he's bad; he's tough but fair. Mom can stand up to him, but I can't. So this may be our only chance. I hope not, but I don't want to gamble."

"You want—to have sex—because you may never see me again?"

"Please. I might twitch a bit, but that will pass. As I said, I dressed to make it possible."

She had actually planned for this! Yet he balked. How much of this was love, and how much was desperation, if she thought she would never again be with a man? Any man? "I can't do that. I must see you again."

"You don't know. Dad's away now, but when he returns in a few days, he'll know. Then I won't go to town any more."

"But don't you have any choice?"

"Not in such a case. We—we aren't a democracy, Bry. My father is the headman. What he says, goes. I will have the chance to embarrass him only once."

"If you don't come out," Bry said with sudden resolve, "I will go in to find you."

"Oh, Bry, don't do that! You have no idea! Please, just love me and let me go, if that's how it has to be."

"I can love you. I can't let you go. Not while I know you love me."

"I do, Bry." Then she kissed him with such passion that there was no point in further dialogue.

But before they had gotten beyond hand on breast and thigh, and mouth on mouth, the van slowed. "We're coming into town," Faience called back.

"Damn!" Tourette muttered.

But Bry was half-relieved. He desired her, but caution told him that sex at this time could be disastrous. There had to be a way to make their association legitimate.

They got themselves back in order and got out when the van stopped. Faience joined them, and they went to the movie. In the dark theater, Bry put his arm around Tourette's shoulders, and she rested her head against him and touched his knee with hers. It was sheer bliss.

When they returned to the van, the front seat was full of supplies, so Faience had to rejoin them in the back. "Sorry," she said.

"It's okay," Bry said. "You introduced us."

"I can face away and stop up my ears."

They both laughed. "You're curious what happened on the trip down," Tourette said.

"Yeah," the girl admitted, abashed.

"Well, first we kissed like this." Tourette kneeled, hugged Bry's upper torso and pulled him in for a very solid kiss. Actually it had been the other way around, but it hardly mattered. He loved kissing her regardless. "Then he put his hand on my blouse, like this." She guided his open hand and mashed it into her breast.

"No, first I touched your thigh," Bry said, with mixed emotions: amazement, desire, and laughter. The more he discovered about Tourette, the better he liked her. Once her genie had been uncorked, she had poured out a whole lot of personality.

"Oh, that's right." She moved his hand down, and up under her skirt. "Or did I put my hand into your pants? I forget."

"Damn, I wish I had a boyfriend!" Faience exclaimed.

"We're teasing you," Bry said. "That's as far as it went."

"Oh. Still. It must be nice."

"It *is* nice," Tourette said. "I love him, just as you surmised, and I think he's halfway hot for me."

"Three-quarters of the way," Bry said, kissing her again. "Going on four-fifths." Then she sat on his lap and they embraced and kissed some more, just to make Faience jealous, they said.

But after a bit they disengaged, because both were aware that if they didn't ease off, they would soon get into full sex in Faience's presence, and that was beyond what they could handle.

The rest of the ride back was routine. For Bry, for now, that was enough. But he worried about the future.

"I love you," Tourette repeated, kissing him one last time before she disappeared into the forest.

"I never saw her so hot and happy, before," Faience said. "And desperate. It's as if she thinks the end of the world is coming."

"She does." He hesitated. "Faience, if she doesn't come

next week, will you show me exactly where the Bones layout is?''

"Are you thinking of doing something romantic and stupid?''

"If I have to. Her dad may not let her come.''

"It's just down the road, that way. They've got a bunker and guardhouse. You have to go in the front way, because the rest is surrounded by mines and barbed wire.''

"Mines?''

"That's what Tourette said, once. They've got a siege mentality. Automatic guns that track you, that sort of thing. They're not nice people, Bry.''

"Except for Tourette.''

"Except for Tourette,'' she agreed. "Did she show you her knife?''

"Right by her breast.''

"Yeah.'' She looked momentarily thoughtful. "I wonder if I should wear a knife there? When I'm off-campus, I mean.''

"First get a boyfriend to show it to, or to let him feel for.''

She laughed. "Yeah.''

During the week, between projects, he talked with Jes. "I have a problem, maybe. Something you should maybe talk me out of.''

She was nursing her baby. Her breasts had grown enormously with pregnancy and childbirth. She caught him looking. "Yes, I hope they stay this way, after. I'm tired of being mistaken for a man.''

"You mean the pacifism is getting to you? You want to be soft like a woman?''

"When I want to be. But I'm no pacifist. I think that part of Dreams philosophy is unrealistic. Come the crash, how will they stop the crazies from overrunning them for their food and supplies?''

"I don't know. How's Ittai feel about it?''

"He loves it here, but he doubts, too. I think our family

is split about evenly between believers and doubters. That may be a problem."

"Well, maybe my problem relates. I have to tell you something private."

She nodded. "Tell."

"I've been seeing a Bones girl."

Her eyebrows elevated in mock shock. "Consorting with the enemy?"

"I think I love her."

"Think?"

"Actually, I'm pretty sure I love her. And she loves me. And her dad maybe won't let her out any more. Which mean's I'll maybe have to do something stupid."

"Like going over there and demanding to see her?"

"Yeah."

"And you could use a backstop."

"Yeah."

"Why do you think I'd be more help than, say, Sam?"

"They all go armed, all the time. Even the women and children. You might relate better."

She laughed. "I might indeed. Very well, little brother; I'll go with you. I'm starting to go stir crazy here anyway."

"Thanks," he said, relieved. "Maybe it won't be necessary."

But Saturday morning, Tourette was not there. "Uh-oh," Faience said. "She was right. 'Cause I know she'd come here if she could."

"I guess I'll have to beg off the movies, this time," he said. "You go on in alone. I've got business here."

"And miss the show? I'll go with you."

"Thee will not," her mother said sternly. "I can't stop the visitors from being suicidal, but thee is mine."

"It's no democracy here, either," Faience grumbled. But she joined Fay in the van. "But if thee gets thyself stupidly killed, Bry, I'll never speak to thee again."

He had to laugh, and not just because of her humor. Her mother had used the plain talk, and that had triggered Faience's switch to it. But he was distinctly nervous. He knew he was going to make what could be a bad scene.

He went back to Jes, who, evidently anticipating this, had just finished nursing her baby and had turned her over to Snow. She was wearing a jacket and skirt, and carried a bow and arrows. "If they want to see Diana the Huntress, so they shall," she said.

They drove their own van to the Bones entry. It was indeed closed, with a guard who came alert as they parked and came forward. He carried a rifle at port arms. "What's your business?" he demanded.

"I'm Bry, and this is my sister Jes," Bry said. "We're from the Dreams community, trial new members."

"They don't carry weapons."

"Maybe I'll flunk my trial," Jes said.

"We don't have anything to do with them."

"Well, I do," Bry said. "I have come to see the chief's daughter."

"Petition denied. Go back where you came from."

"I call her Tourette."

The man jumped, his rifle swinging around. But Jes was faster. Her knife was in her hand, the tip of the blade pointing at his face. "At ease, soldier," she said.

He hesitated, so she did her trick with the knife, flipping it and catching it an inch from his nose.

The guard shrugged, then looked at Bry. "Describe her."

"Age sixteen. Shoulder-length brown hair. Brown eyes. About yea tall." He held his hand at the level of the top of her head. "Very nice figure. Very nice person."

"What's your business with her?"

"I love her."

The guard whistled. "You're in trouble."

"Just take me to her."

The guard lifted a walkie-talkie. "Two from Dreams being admitted on temporary passes to see the chief's daughter."

The gate cranked open. Another guard appeared "This way," he said curtly.

He brought them to a Jeep, and drove them along a winding drive to a massive building that had the aspect of a fortress. A device on its roof moved to track them, just as Faience had said.

They parked near an armored door. "I must search you before you enter," the guard said.

"Like hell," Jes snapped.

"Electronic."

She shrugged. "Okay. But where I go, I go armed."

"Understood. This way."

They passed through a frame similar to that of an airline inspection station. There was no buzzer, but Bry saw the guard look at a computer screen. Then he spoke into a mike. "Man, unarmed. Woman, with bow, ten arrows, three knives, and a club."

"Do they come in truce?" a woman's voice asked from a speaker.

"Yes," Bry said. Jes hesitated, then nodded. Evidently that was good enough, because the metal door slid open.

"You will be met inside," the guard said.

They entered. A woman in a clerical uniform rose from a desk just inside. She wore a gun, and looked vaguely familiar. "What is your business here?"

"You already know it," Jes said tersely.

The woman smiled. "So you understand the situation."

"No."

"The boy made illicit contact with one of our members. Further contact is denied."

"Let *her* tell me that," Bry said.

The woman lifted one hand to make a small beckoning signal. A door opened behind her, and Tourette emerged. She was in a black uniform: military cap, close jacket, trousers, boots. And a wide belt supporting a holster with a gun at her right hip, and a sheath with a knife at the left hip.

"So you came," she said to Bry.

"I love thee."

She glanced at him, startled, and he realized that he had used the plain talk. Fay to Faience to him: it seemed to be contagious. But he realized that it was also because he now identified with Dreams, and did want to be a part of it. Well, so be it.

After a strained pause, Tourette spoke. "Please leave."

"Thee knows I can't."

"Bry, I told you. It can't be. Please."

"Tell me thee doesn't love me."

"I—" Then her face crumbled. "Mom—"

Mom? But there was indeed a family resemblance. That was why the woman had looked vaguely familiar.

The woman shook her head. "My daughter does love you, Bry. But she may not associate with you at this time." She lifted a hand, forestalling Bry's objection. "It is not just her father's disapproval. Were you to qualify to join this community, it would be possible. But there is illness, and we do not wish to spread it to you. Separation is a kindness at this point."

"Illness?" Jes asked.

"It seems to be the flu, a deadly form. We fear that secondary infections will be resistant to treatment. My husband caught it in Africa, but it did not manifest until he arrived here. Otherwise he would not have returned. The least we can do is confine it."

Bry exchanged a glance with Jes, knowing she was as surprised as he was. "Maybe—maybe we could help. I mean, the Dreams community. They have herbal medicines—"

"I doubt it. Now please go. You may be at risk here."

Bry looked at Tourette, and saw tears streaming down her face. Surely what they said was true. The sensible course was to leave immediately.

But he wasn't sensible. "Come with me," he said to Tourette.

She didn't move. "I've been exposed." Then she started

to twitch. She must have been controlling it, but she was
under such tension that it was getting away from her. Her
shoulders jerked and her head tossed wildly.

Something buzzed in his mind. He stepped across, so
quickly she did not react, and took her in his arms. Her
body relaxed. He kissed her, steadying her face with his
own. She returned the kiss, avidly. He tasted the salt of her
tears.

He lifted his head and looked around. The woman was
standing with her hand on her pistol, and Jes was standing
with a knife drawn. Threat and counter-threat.

"Now I have been exposed too," Bry said.

"You have done a foolish thing," the woman said, and
Jes nodded agreement.

"Whatever Tourette suffers, I want to suffer too. If you
won't let me in, let her out. Maybe she doesn't have it.
Maybe she'll be safer in Dreams."

"They will not speak to an armed person," the woman
said.

"They speak to me," Jes said.

The women studied her, appraisingly. "Will you join
Dreams?"

"I don't know. As I see it, there are occasions when pacifism simply doesn't work. I would have to give up my
weapons if I joined, and I'm not sure that's wise."

"You might be more comfortable here in Bones."

They called it Bones too? No, probably that was just a
facetious acceptance of the term, leaving the real community
anonymous. Just as was the case with Tourette.

Jes stared at her. "You are inviting me to make a trial
visit here?"

"With your husband, of course. We have need of organ-
izers of his caliber. We would also be interested in your
closest brother, as we are a high-tech community."

Jes seemed intrigued. So was Bry. How could the woman
know so much about their family? "What of his wife?"

"We are an equal opportunity employer. We do not discriminate on the basis of color or past condition of royalty.''

''But you do on the basis of ideology,'' Bry said.

''And Dreams does not?''

''Touché,'' Jes said. ''I will think about it. But our family is unified. We won't split between hostile groups. We'll all go to one, or to another. And there are those of us who would not come here.''

''I know. You will have a difficult decision.''

''What of us?'' Bry asked. ''Tourette and me?''

''You must stay, or she must go. If you stay, you risk the illness. If she goes, she risks spreading it.''

''If she has it,'' he said. ''If she doesn't, she can escape it.''

''It is a serious gamble, either way. I take it upon myself to make that decision. She may go.'' Her mouth quirked. ''With thee.''

''Oh, Mom!'' Tourette cried.

''It is a rational decision. May God forgive me if I am mistaken.'' She touched a button on her desk, and the door slid open. ''Go quickly.''

They went quickly. The guard was waiting outside. They got into the Jeep, and rode back to the front gate. Then on out to their van.

''She let me go,'' Tourette said in awe. ''I never thought she would.''

''She loves you,'' Jes said. ''She wants to spare you the plague.''

''Yes. But what if I have it already?''

''We must warn the Dreams.''

Something bothered Bry. ''When I kissed thee, and thy mother started to draw her pistol, and Jes warned her off with her knife—doesn't Bones have better protection than that?''

Tourette laughed. ''Mom could have had the room flooded with nerve gas, knocking us all out in an instant. But she liked your sister's look. She got downright friendly after that.''

"And she knew about us, about our family," Jes said. "Did you tell her?"

"No. I said nothing at all. But we have personnel who research in the computer data bases and on the Internet. They must have made files on you. Knowledge is the best defense. I didn't know they had it in mind to recruit you."

"Then why didn't they want me to see you?" Bry asked.

"I think Mom thought you were just using me. But when you kissed me in the middle of a twitch, she changed her mind. Maybe she saw that you had committed to Dreams, and to me too, because you addressed me with the plain talk. And she does like your sister." She snuggled against him. "But if I carry the plague out—"

"We'll warn them," Jes said as she pulled into the parking lot.

But Marc shrugged it off. "We have people going in and out all the time. We are constantly exposed. We'll handle it."

"But this is really bad," Tourette said. "A killer flu."

"We are equipped. If the malady is in Africa, with a several day lag time, it is elsewhere too. We'll be exposed to it from some other source, sooner or later."

"I'm not sure it's smart for Dreams to be isolated from Bones," Jes said. "We need to talk with the Dreams community elders."

"To what point? We have no common ground with them."

"Please," Tourette said. "I wish I could talk to the elders. There are things that need to be understood."

Marc looked at her. "As long as thee evinces thy lack of sympathy with our philosophy, by bearing weapons, there is no point. I think thee will encounter a similar attitude wherever thee inquires."

"But it wouldn't be honest for me to disarm myself," Tourette said. "I am as I am, and I don't care to hide it."

"Then perhaps thee should return to thy community."

They let it go. The elders might be pacifists, but that

didn't mean they weren't tough-minded. They had their standards, and would not abridge them. "You can stay with us," Jes told Tourette. "With Bry."

"But the propriety—"

"We have seen it all. You do as you choose."

Tourette clutched Bry's hand. "This is so unexpected. I hardly know what to feel."

"Neither do I," he confessed. "Except for love."

That afternoon Bry spoke to Flo. "I brought Tourette home. I think she needs to meet the family."

Flo always knew what was serious. "Half an hour hence?"

"Okay."

They were all there. "Some of you already know Tourette," he said. "That's not her real name, but it will do. I love her, and want to be with her. But she's from Bones, and there's plague there. She's afraid she has been exposed."

"We know about illness," Ittai said. "We'll cross that bridge if it comes."

"And—she has Tourette's syndrome," Bry continued. "That's an involuntary twitching and grunting. It comes and goes. It's okay just to ignore it."

They nodded.

Then Tourette spoke. "I love Bry, but I'm a militant and I think he's a pacifist. He's using the plain talk now, anyway. I don't know if this can work."

"Join the throng," Snow said. "Several of our couples split along those lines. We can't decide whether to join Dreams. We may have to return to the big city."

"But that's where the trouble is," Tourette said. "We built Bones to escape all that."

"Which is exactly what Dreams is doing," Flo said. "Similar solutions to a similar problem—and the two communities don't speak to each other."

"And one set of leaders is as stiff-necked as the other," Ned said. "It is an irony."

"Isn't there any way to get them together?" Tourette asked. "I don't think either community can survive alone. Oh, they think they can, but can they really? I mean, if civilization collapses?"

"I think they can't," Jes said. "Dreams will be overrun by the first wave of teenage thugs looking for drugs. Bones may never run out of bullets, but what about fuel for its generators, and food? Stored supplies won't last forever, after the crunch comes."

"We plan to survive the bad times on supplies, then to emerge to re-colonize the country after it has cleared," Tourette said. "We have supplies for a decade. We have trucks that will run on natural gas."

"And if illness takes out half your personnel?"

"That makes me nervous," Tourette admitted.

That was all. The family had been introduced to Tourette, and now knew her place: with Bry. He was the last to find his opposite number.

They joined in the folk singing in the evening, and Bry introduced Tourette to anyone who was interested, but did not explain the name unless asked. She was accepted as an addition to the visiting family, though she did not conceal her origin. The weapons she wore made it clear enough.

"I think it's great," Faience said. "You went in there and got her out."

"Thee gives me more credit than is due," Bry said.

"Bry! Thee has joined us!" She hugged him.

"Well, not without my family," he said. "But I guess it's true, for me; my vote is to join. But I've got to be with Tourette, too."

"So are you changing sides?" Faience asked Tourette.

"No. I can't turn my back on my family, on my community, or on my nature. I will return to Bones soon. When the threat of plague is gone, if I don't have it already. I'm really only on temporary leave from there."

Faience shook her head. "I think it's great that you two are together. But you know, Romeo/Juliet romances don't work out so well in real life. There are some awful differences to work out.''

"We know," Bry agreed.

They shared a chamber that night, and a bed. But now Tourette was diffident. "Anything you want," she said, but there was some reservation.

"What is it?"

"I've never been away from home like this, before. I miss Mom, and Dad, and everything. And I don't know what's going to happen. I can't relax."

"Then let's just be together, until we're sure."

She turned to him. "Thanks, Bry." She kissed him. He was gratified simply to be with her.

In the night he felt her motion and heard her grunt. He found her hand, and squeezed it reassuringly, and she settled down. He wasn't sure she was even awake. He knew that he could touch her anywhere, and she wouldn't object, but her hand was enough.

As daylight came, he woke and gazed at her. Her hair was messed across her face, and she was snoring. He liked that too. She was a real girl.

Sunday morning the family prepared to go to Meeting. "We don't have to go," Bry said. "We're still trying to get the feel of Dreams, to know whether it's really for us."

"If you go, I'll go," Tourette said. "We have church services too."

"We just sit quietly, and anyone who is moved to gives a message. It's sort of nice."

Several people glanced at Tourette as they approached the meeting house. She was wearing one of Wildflower's dresses, but over it wore the belt with the pistol and knife in plain view. She was refusing to pretend to be anything other than what she was. Jes, also armed, came to join them, lending tacit moral support. They picked a pew and sat, Tourette flanked by Bry and Jes.

The first message was a prayer: "Lord, we thank Thee for Thy beneficence. Lead us down the path of righteousness and mercy. May we stand before Thee without affectation. May we remember that he who is noble needs not a weapon, needs no man to guard him; virtue defends him.'' The last sentence was a quote from one of the songs they had sung the evening before, but the reference seemed rather pointed to Bry.

There were other messages. Tourette seemed uneasy. Then, to Bry's astonishment, she stood and spoke.

''I am not of this community. I apologize for not knowing the proper forms of expression, and I regret that my presence here makes some of you uneasy. But there is something I must say. It is said that we are made of dreams and bones. You are of Dreams, and I am of Bones, and I think that it is a mistake to separate the two. I think that the two communities are not as far apart as they may think. Both seek to survive, when human civilization and culture collapse. We merely have different ways to achieve a similar objective. You are trying to build a self-sustaining community; so are we. You want peace. So do we. You want to see a better future. So do we. So we differ only in the means, not the ends. You believe in nonviolence. We believe that there are occasions when violence is necessary. We do not seek it, we don't desire it, but we prepare for it in the hope that preparedness will make it unnecessary. But even here, we do not necessarily differ from you beyond the possibility of compromise. There is a martial art known as Aikido. An Aikidoka will not attack; indeed, he has no means to attack. But if another person attacks him, he will quickly immobilize that person. He doesn't have to hurt the other, he merely makes it impossible for that person to hurt him. I think this is a form of violence some of you could accept. We would teach it to you, if you wished. It does seem better than standing helplessly by while others who are not pacifists come to kill your men, rape your women, steal your children, take your goods, burn your houses, and destroy your dreams.''

She paused, and her body began to jerk. She grunted. ''No!'' she cried, and it seemed to be a protest to her in-

capacity, not a denial of her message. Bry didn't know what
to do, so he followed his own advice: he did nothing, ignoring her seizure. No one else moved or spoke. What a
scene to make in the midst of a worship service!

Bry sat frozen. Tourette had spoken well, amazingly well,
surprising him in more than one respect. He knew that she
was rehearsing, to a degree, a philosophy to which she had
had a lifelong exposure. Still, he had not before appreciated
how well she could express herself when she tried. His love
for her swelled in his chest as if his heart were a furnace.
Yet there was nothing he could do to help her in this situation. She had to finish in her own way.

Then the siege passed, and she resumed talking. She was
blushing, but pursued her message doggedly. "I am, as you
can see, not a normal person. This is part of what I am. But
I am other things too. I am not a pacifist. I carry a gun and
a knife, and I will use them to defend myself or some other
person in need of defense. I will not conceal my nature; I
will not pretend to be something I am not. That would be
hypocrisy. All my people carry weapons, and are trained in
them. None of us are hypocrites. We do not seek quarrels,
we only stand ready to defend ourselves when this is necessary. We are satisfied with our philosophy, and do not
intend to change it, or to ask anyone else to change theirs.
We are not roughnecks; we are educated and civilized, as
you are. But we are also realists, as we fear you are not.
We are preparing for a future that may be ugly beyond belief, because the alternative is to risk suffering calamity beyond belief. Even now the first wave of it is coming; my
father is dying of a plague we can't fight, and the rest of us
may fall too. It is my hope, my prayer, my fervent wish that
I have not brought this terror among you also. If I have,
then how can my shame ever be abated?

"But that isn't all. I find that my life is incomplete. I
have been protected—too much, perhaps. Now I have found
love, outside my community, outside my philosophy. I never
knew love before; maybe my inexperience makes me fool-

ish. But it is the greatest passion I have experienced, a mountain when I have known only foothills. I would do anything to preserve and consummate that love. But I can't change what I am, and do not seek to change what he is. I love him as he is. I love him without reservation or limit. He is my sun, my moon, and all between. But our communities do not approve of our association, and we do belong to our communities. How can we be together, when our people are at odds? I know only that if there is not some way to bridge across the social and philosophical gulf that separates us, I may lose that love, just as I may lose my father, and then I will die of despair, and perhaps my friend will too. We need each other, and I think our communities need each other, or both will perish. The world is not bound by a single creed; there are many creeds, and it is right that there be these differences, for what works in one situation may not work in another. Maybe no one way can save the world. Maybe no two ways can do it. But two are surely better than one. Can we not accept each other as we are? We differ much as man differs from woman, yet we must act together if we are to survive. I beg of you, I beg of the world: is there not some way to do it? Isn't there some way?''

Then, abruptly, she was done, unable to speak further. She sat, and Bry saw that she was crying. The hell with protocol! He put his arm around her, and she wept silently into his shoulder. She had tried so hard, speaking so brilliantly, baring her soul, suffering such humiliation—and for what? ''I love you,'' he whispered into her hair. ''I love you, I love you, no matter what.''

There was a pause of several minutes. Bry glanced across at Jes, and saw her sitting stone-faced. The embarrassment of the good people of the Meeting was almost tangible. Surely there had never before been a message like this!

Then at last an elder rose to speak. ''We stand rebuked. We were perhaps too hasty to judge by appearance. There must be a way.''

In a moment another stood. "With due respect, I beg to disagree. I suspect that 'rebuked' may be too moderate a word. We stand shamed. We have walked the path of isolation, instead of reaching out to help those in need. May the Lord forgive us that error, and see that we never repeat it."

Bry knew, with sudden revelation, that the embarrassment of the people of the Meeting had not been for Tourette, but for themselves. *She had gotten through.*

Then a third: "I believe there are those among us who would like to inquire about Aikido."

And another: "Perhaps we have seen it already." There was a general chuckle.

Soon the eldest elder turned to shake hands with the adjacent elder, and the Meeting was over. But the group did not disperse. Attention was centering on Tourette.

An elder approached her. "We know something of antibiotic-resistant diseases. We have alternative techniques that are not generally known to medicine. We may be able to treat thy father, and others who fall ill. What is the telephone number by which we can reach a responsible person in thy community?"

Then Bry knew it was going to be all right. The God of the Quakers—the God of all people—had answered.

In the 1990s antibiotic-resistant strains of disease increased dramatically. For example, Streptococcus pneumoniae, *causing pneumonia, meningitis, and some deadly bloodstream infections, evolved variants that could not be cured with penicillin or other common antibiotics. Diseases that had seemed to be on the way to extinction returned with renewed force. This was a sinister indication of the future.*

Chapter 20

SYMBIOSIS

*One of the most significant trends in the later history
of mankind was the formation and expansion of cities.
These brought the advantages of safety from assorted
predators, convenience for trade and association, and
comfort. Civilization was largely built around great cities. But cities also put a strain on the local productivity
of the land, reaching far out into the countryside for
their sustenance. Their garbage—solid, liquid, and
gaseous—polluted earth, water, and air. Their increasingly crowded conditions made them prime reservoirs*

of disease. Infectious agents prosper best when there are many targets within easy range. Thus the large predators of the early years were replaced by the invisibly small predators of the later years.

In the twentieth century the growth of cities accelerated, a function of the growth of global human population and its increasing concentration in metropolitan areas. By the end of the millennium there were perhaps twenty cities with populations greater than ten million people. As the climate changed, food became scant, pollution got worse, and treatment-resistant diseases evolved, such cities were increasingly ravaged by modern plagues ranging from flu to AIDS. As in ancient times, such as during the plague of Athens, civilized restraints broke down, so that plagues of human ferocity amplified the effects. Life continued for some, but the quality of it was drastically reduced.

A few had acted on their awareness of the mischief they saw coming, establishing enclaves of civilization and relative affluence in remote districts. But in time these, too, became prey for the brutish remnant of the larger societies. It required a very special combination of qualities to survive such onslaughts.

The time is circa A.D. 2025; the place is the Andean mountain range of Chile, South America. It is midsummer: December.

FLO LOOKED UP FROM HER work as Wilda dashed in. "What is it, dear?"

"Bad men!" the child gasped. "Up on the fog ridge!"

This was probably mischief. "How do you know?"

"Flint and I were up there picking berries, and we saw them. We didn't know they were bad, but we didn't trust them, so we watched. They took down the baffles."

That made the diagnosis almost certain. "Dirk," Flo called.

Dirk came from the other room. "Something's up?"

"The children saw strangers taking down the baffles."

"I'll go inquire."

Flo felt a chill. "Alone?"

He paused. "Maybe put in a call to Tourette's father. We can go together."

She picked up the phone and touched the key for Tourette's address. In a moment the young woman answered. "Yes, Flo?"

"Strangers are taking down the baffles. Dirk thought your dad might want to go with him to inquire."

"I know he will. Meet at the fork in half an hour?"

"That will do."

Flo hung up. "Fork in half an hour."

"On my way." Dirk went out.

Flo continued working on her bread, but she was uneasy. The baffles were vital to the well-being of both the Dreams and Bones enclaves. They were large vertical frameworks covered with fine nylon mesh that collected condensing water from the high mountain fog. Though the effect was diffuse, enough water dripped down to not only provide for the needs of the two enclaves, but to run a generator on the way down. This supplemented the current generated by the Solar Stirling engines, especially on cloudy days. But the water was the essential element; without it they would soon be in trouble.

In fact water was the main problem, here in the Andes. Immediately inland from the Pacific coast was the Desierto de Atacama, perhaps the longest and thinnest desert in the world, paralleling the great Andes range. It very seldom rained in this locale, and few rivers made their way down from the mountains. That was why it was a largely barren region. Which was in turn why the enclaves had been established here: to be well away from any big city. But even here they were not entirely safe.

It had been coincidence that two enclaves had set up so close together. Neither had been aware of the plans of the others until preparations were well under way. At first relations between the two had been tacitly hostile. Then the plague had come to Bones. The medics of Dreams had gone to help, using their array of special therapies. They had brought Tourette's father to the heated greenhouse, to isolate him, and plied him with derivatives from rare medicinal herbs salvaged from the declining rain forests. It was a difficult search, but in time they found an antibiotic to which the disease was not resistant, and then he mended. Just in time, for by then others were coming down with it. They had used the treatment on those others, and stopped the plague before it was fairly started. It was clear that they had thereby managed to save a number of lives that would otherwise very likely have been lost.

After that, relations between the two communities had thawed considerably. The folk of Bones wanted to repay the favor, in money or in kind, but the folk of Dreams would accept no payment for doing what was right to do. The matter faded without resolution. Now it was six months after the onset of the illness, and all were recovered, and both communities were doing well. They still existed apart, with different philosophies, but visiting occurred between them, and Bry and Tourette were not the only young folk dating across community lines. When anything important came up, of mutual interest, the communities kept each other advised. Hence her call to Tourette, because both communities depended on the cloud harvest for water.

In due course Dirk returned. "Remember Bub?" he asked. "He's the leader of a band of raiders. They demand that we send two female liaison personnel within the hour, one from each enclave, to stay with them and negotiate terms."

"Terms?" Flo asked sharply.

"In general, they want to take a hefty chunk of our supplies: food, blankets, clothing—" He broke off, looking uncomfortable.

"Women?" she prompted.

"They want girls, yes. They promise to return them after they are through with them."

Flo grimaced. That would mean barefoot, pregnant, diseased, and dead in spirit. "And what is their threat?"

"The baffles will not be allowed up until they are satisfied with the deal."

"What is their strength?"

"We don't know, but it is clear that they have a sufficient force to maintain possession of the baffles. They showed us just enough snipers dug in around the area to satisfy us that it is not an empty threat. We will have no water until we deal with them."

"They mean to bleed us dry," Flo said angrily. "In more than one sense. And they may destroy us after that anyway."

"Yes. This is a bad situation. They demand that two more people, one from each enclave, come within the following hour to serve as runners, arranging for the goods to be delivered. The first batch they want by dusk today. Now I must report to the elders."

"The elders are not going to agree to any of the demands. Neither are the folk of Bones."

"I know," he said heavily. "But if we don't get those liaison people out there within the hour, the raiders will burn the baffles. Then they'll shoot us down as we run out of water and come out."

"It's hostages they want. Women they can use or torture while they wait. To goose us into prompt capitulation."

"Yes. They have figured it out. Apparently that is their business: preying on isolated communities. When they have squeezed one for all it's worth, and the pickings diminish, they move on to the next. They are experienced in what they do, and make few mistakes. They don't just charge in, because some communities have mines and traps for the unwary. They force representatives to bring the goods out to the raiders, on a regular schedule. It is all very organized."

"I'll go," Flo said.

"What?"

"I'll be the hostage from Dreams. That fits their demand, and they won't be much interested in raping me."

"Flo—"

"Who else should be sent out?"

Dirk shook his head ruefully. "I'll tell the elders." He kissed her and departed.

Flo prepared herself, then walked out on the trail to the fork. She had tried to make it seem routine, pre-empting the decision of the elders, but she was afraid. She knew the elders would not readily agree to bring out their goods, and would absolutely balk at sending out any young women. The community of Bones, with a more militant attitude, would angrily refuse. That meant that the hostages would be in trouble. If Bones even sent a hostage.

But there at the fork stood a young woman: a slender beauty with lustrous black hair, in a skirt and blouse as if going on a picnic. She wore a knife at her hip, in the Bones manner. No, not a woman, but a girl of nine or ten, not yet grown. "Oh, honey," Flo said, hurrying to meet her. "You must not be the one. Those raiders—"

The girl turned great dark eyes on her. "Do you not know me?"

"Dear, I don't. But I must warn you that this is no polite encounter. You must go back and have them send out—" She hesitated, not wishing to affront the girl. "An older, unattractive woman."

"I am Minne. Adopted daughter of Hugh and Anne. We met once, a while ago."

Flo remembered Hugh and Anne, the musician and dancer. They had met seven years ago on the coast. They had had a darling little girl. The age was consistent. And that child had been—could it possibly be? "And you—how could you be—?"

"Your natural daughter? I am, you know. That is why I chose to come here. I knew I would be needed." She glanced up the path. "We must go, or they will become impatient."

"But Minne, you don't understand. This is no innocent picnic. Those men—"

"Please, Flo. We will have time to talk. Then I will show you the mark between my toes. Now we must reach the baffles in time." She walked on up the trail, forcing Flo to hurry to catch up. The girl simply would not listen to Flo's real concern, and Flo was reluctant to spell it out. What would a child of nine know of rape and torture and killing?

They moved up the mountain, and in due course reached the ledge below the baffles. There were now just the frames, because the nylon nets had been furled. When spread, the nets were huge, six meters high and twice as wide, though they looked small from this distance. Ten million droplets of fog had to coalesce to form a single drop of water, but on a heavy fog day, thousands of gallons of water dripped off the nets into the main collection pipe. This was one of the driest regions on earth; this was the only significant source of water for the two communities. Which was what made it so vital. Without the spread nets, they could not survive here.

And the baffles were now in the hands of a ruthless enemy. Several rough men were standing around the ledge, looking up at the empty frames, holding rifles at the ready.

A man strode down to meet them. "Well now: one winner and one loser. Have your groups agreed to the terms?"

"No," Flo said tightly. Obviously she was the loser— which meant that Minne was the winner. That was not good news for either of them. Obviously these brutes would stop at nothing.

"No," Minne echoed, seeming undaunted.

He nodded. "Sometimes it takes time for them to see the light. If they do not come to their senses by dusk today, they will hear your screams." He looked meaningfully at Flo.

Minne stepped between them. "My father will not harm my mother."

He stared. "What?"

Flo decided to let the improbabilities of the girl's attitude go for now. This was Bub; she had no trouble recognizing him, even after so many years. "You raped me, ten years ago. This is our daughter."

"It's not possible!" But he looked shaken. Obviously such a thing had never occurred to him.

"As you wish," Minne said. She took a seat on a rock. "We will be here for the day. Because I know you, Father, I will give you this advice: if you value your life, flee at dusk, and never return." She looked away, dismissing him.

Disgruntled, Bub went to consult with the other men. Flo looked at Minne. "I do not like him," the girl said. "But he is my blood father, so I had to come to warn him."

Flo struggled again with the weirdness of the girl's manner. She still wasn't sure that this *was* her natural daughter, though it seemed likely. But that made Minne the very worst possible hostage, as far as Flo personally was concerned. How could she allow such a child to be abused? "Maybe figuratively," she suggested. "You identify with someone."

The girl turned a disconcerting gaze on her. "Someone 33,000 years ago," she said.

Flo could not fathom this, so let it go. "Maybe you can slip away at dusk. It is not wise for a girl like you to be here among these brute men."

"I came to protect you. I shall see that you are not harmed."

The strangeness would not let go. "Within an hour, the community representatives will arrive. After that, the mood will turn ugly."

"I will divert the men."

Apparently nothing she could say would get through to Minne. Could the girl be simple, or out of touch with reality? That would explain a lot. But she seemed neither stu-

pid nor out of touch. Rather, she had an eerie awareness of
reality that Flo was beginning to envy.

After a time, Minne spoke again. "I came here also because I wanted to be with you, one time. To love you." She
removed her shoe and showed her left foot. There was the
mark between the first and second toes.

Something melted in Flo. Suddenly she accepted everything, regardless of the confusion. "Oh, honey, I have been
looking for you all my life! I'm glad you found a good
family, and I'd never want to deprive you of it, but how I
have missed you!"

The girl hugged her, crying. "Mother."

"Baby." Flo was crying too. This was a fulfillment of a
kind she had longed for, but never expected to experience.
Reunion with her lost child.

In due course the emissaries appeared—and Flo was surprised and dismayed. Bry and Tourette! Whatever had possessed them to volunteer for this dreadful danger? The girl
was even dressed in a foolish skirt and blouse, similar to
Minne's outfit, showing too much of her legs and bosom as
she walked. Sheer folly!

Bub walked out to meet them. Flo couldn't hear what was
said, but she didn't need to: the two enclaves were not ac-
ceding to the terms. But what would that mean for the water
supply?

Bub turned angrily and signaled to his men. Four dashed
up and grabbed Bry and Tourette by the arms. Bub was
taking them hostage! Because they hadn't brought him the
capitulation he demanded. Flo started to get up, to protest
this violation of the normal procedures of truce, but Minne
drew back on her arm. "Accept it," she murmured.

What did she know, that Flo didn't? The raiders could
hardly have better hostages than these. Tourette was the
daughter of the leader of the Bones enclave, and beloved by
the Dreams enclave too. Bry, too, was respected by both
groups, and not just because he was so plainly in love with
Tourette. Any threat to one would devastate the other.

Bub searched Bry, running his hands efficiently over body and clothing. Bry was unarmed. Then he searched Tourette, taking the trouble to squeeze her breasts and bottom in the process, and found a small pistol and a knife. Flo realized that Minne had so disconcerted the man that he had forgotten to take her knife from her; she still wore it.

The men hauled the two of them across to join Flo and Minne. "Those idiots are going to get two of you tortured," Bub said darkly. "And two of you will do for entertainment until more girls are delivered. By dusk. You had better hope that your enclaves see the light by then."

"Flee at dusk," Minne repeated to him. "Don't tell your men."

"My presence is all that keeps my men from raping you right now," Bub replied contemptuously. "You think you're too young, but you're not. They get a special thrill from youth. After dusk, if the goods aren't here, I'll let them." He paused, reconsidering. "In fact, maybe it's best to encourage your folk now. Sound carries well, up here. Let's see what it takes to get a good scream." He turned to Tourette. "You first. Take off your clothes, or we will tear them off you. We encourage you to scream. There's no point in hurting you more than necessary. But scream you will, repeatedly."

"Have your men gather," Minne said. Then she stood, assumed a pose, and began to dance.

Bub stared. So did Flo. What was the girl up to? She was well formed for a child, and had good motions, but she *was* a child. Yet her dance was fascinating in its suggestive expertise. In a moment she had the attention of every man in the vicinity, and probably of the hidden snipers too. Flo was appalled; too many of the men obviously did have perverted interests. This was an excellent way to get herself raped before Tourette.

But the men, restrained by the glowers of their leader, merely watched. Bub might not believe what Minne had told him, but it surely made him hesitate before abusing her.

Minne danced with increasing flair, her skirt and hair flaring out. It wasn't just her slender body; there was something about the way she moved that was captivating. The way her mother Anne had danced, years ago. Flo had not before realized how much of the appeal of a dance was from the motions, rather than just the body. Minne had unparalleled grace. For the moment she was actually distracting them from Tourette, who merely stood watching.

Dusk was approaching. But the girl did not stop. She danced indefatigably, and the men watched, unable to draw themselves away. When at last their interest seemed about to flag, Tourette joined her in the dance. Tourette's motions were not as smooth, but her body was quite well formed, and her blouse was tight, showing the motions of her breasts, which were not tightly bound. Her skirt spread out and up often, showing glimpses of her well fleshed thighs. If she suffered any twitches, they were masked by the energy of the dance. This was more than enough to renew spectator interest. The girl had been the appetizer; the woman was the main event. The two circled each other, moving in tandem, as if they had rehearsed this number. As surely they had.

"What on earth are they doing?" Flo asked Bry. "This is just getting those brutes more excited."

"Dusk is the key," he replied enigmatically. "It will not be long now."

Minne whirled, then faced outward and looked directly at Bub, warningly. *What did she know?*

Bub looked around. "Someone's missing," he muttered. He walked into the closing darkness, looking.

Minne finally ceased her dancing, and returned to join Flo. "It keeps me warm," she confided.

"Come close to me; I'm warm," Flo said. The girl agreed, and snuggled close.

Tourette continued a little longer, then also stopped. "Now it is dusk," she said. She and Bry joined Flo and Minne against the rock.

"Party time!" one of the men said.

"Not till Bub says," another warned him. "He wants that second gal first."

"Well, we'd better set up anyway."

The men brought wood to make a fire. There wasn't much, but they did find enough to make a small one. The chill fell quickly, even in summer, this high on the mountain. Several grouped around it, warming their hands. They did not offer the hostages a place by it.

Flo had a dark suspicion that made sense of certain mysteries. But she didn't dare ask any of the three young folk about it.

"Hey, where's our cook?" a man asked. "It's time for dinner."

"He was sleeping in the hollow over there."

"I'll go wake the lazy bastard." The man walked into the shadow.

After a time, another looked into the darkness. "Hey, what's keeping you?" There was no answer. Disgruntled, he went out himself.

In time, the remaining three men began to get nervous. "Something's wrong," one muttered. "Where's Bub?"

Flo looked around. The flickering light of the fire illuminated the rock close to it, while the one against which they sat was mostly in shadow. She realized that this was not the best place to be, if her suspicion was correct. "We should move," she said, and hoisted her bulk up. She and the others walked to the other rock, closer to the brightness of the fire, and settled down against it. The girl rejoined her, while Bry and Tourette sat close beside them. The three men seemed not to notice; they were peering nervously out into the darkness. Flo wondered whether the four of them could simply walk out of there. But that would accomplish nothing; without hostages, the raiders would simply burn the baffles. In any event, this was probably the best place to be, and not just because it was a bit warmer than the other. They were fully visible here.

"Where the hell are they?" one man demanded. "No one's supposed to sneak off like this."

"I'll check the cook myself," another said. "Probably somebody's stupid idea of a joke." He walked into the night.

"Keep in touch," one of the others said nervously.

"Okay, I'll whistle." He did so, and the sound of his halfway tuneless melody floated back as he walked.

Then it stopped.

"Hey, whistle!" a man by the fire called. But there was no sound.

"Damn it, now I *know* there's trouble," the other said. He lifted his rifle. "And these bitches are probably in on it." He whirled and fired. The bullet struck the rock where Flo had been until recently.

Flo flinched. This made her look prescient. If they had stayed there, they might have been hit. But that wasn't why she had made them move. It was only for the light.

"Stop that," the other man shouted. "They're our hostages. And I think maybe we need them."

"For sure." The first man reoriented his rifle. "Come here, bitches."

"Close your eyes," Minne said. Bry and Tourette did.

"But—" Flo protested.

"Now." The girl put her hand across Flo's face.

Not knowing what to make of this, Flo obeyed. There was a minute or so of silence.

"Okay, now you can look."

Flo opened her eyes. The men were gone.

Flo looked at Minne. "What happened?"

"We can go home now. We can use brands from the fire to see our way."

"But the men—the snipers—"

"Tell them what you saw, when you return to Dreams."

"But I didn't see anything! The men were there, then they weren't."

"Yes."

"But what am I to make of that? They wouldn't just go away on their own." But she already had a notion. She had chosen a bright spot to sit, so that anyone firing a rifle would be able to see exactly who the four of them were, and where. So as not to shoot them by accident. She had been caught by surprise by the deadly silence of it.

Minne looked at her. The girl's eyes reflected the fire eerily. "Remember the plague?"

"Yes, but—"

"It's payback time," Tourette said.

That was confirmation. It did make sense. The pacifists of Dreams had done the folk of Bones a significant favor, when a problem had come that the survivalists couldn't handle. Dreams had not accepted payment. But there had been a debt. Now that debt had been paid, in a way the pacifists could never acknowledge. Maybe they would elect simply not to question where the raiders had gone.

The two girls from Bones had distracted the raiders, including any nearby snipers, so that they would not be alert for the developing siege. So that they would not realize that the hunters had become the hunted. Until too late. They had deliberately risked getting raped, showing the kind of discipline for which they had been trained.

Probably the bodies would never be found. Trust the survivalists to know their business. If they could take out armed raiders one by one without a sound, they could surely handle the rest of it. And with luck, no other raiders would come, for they would have warning that this region was dangerous. Because of the surprising symbiosis of communities with fundamentally opposing philosophies.

"Apparently they just went away," Flo said as they all picked brands from the fire. "That is all we need to know."

Minne nodded. That was the proper answer.

Thus humanity survived both the diseases and the crazed remnants of the population. Isolation and special cooperation were the keys to such success. In time, with the greatly diminished prospects that such a limited, widespread population provided, the major diseases died out, and the world was safe for human re-colonization. This was the hope of Earth. Perhaps this time it would be done with more care for the future.

AUTHOR'S NOTE

THEORETICALLY, THE AUTHOR IS GOD of his creation, having everything in his story exactly the way he wants it. But in practice it often works out otherwise. It wasn't just complications of scheduling, which caused the writing of this novel to stretch out a year beyond my original completion date. It wasn't the fact that I started it on the Sprint word processor in DOS, and finished it on Microsoft Word 7 in Windows 95, with aspects of my formatting changing accordingly. The material itself developed its own will. This volume has a number of examples. Like the preceding two volumes, *Isle of Woman* and *Shame of Man*, this one samples the whole of human history and geography, from *Australopithecus* of five million years ago to Modern mankind of the recent future. As with the prior volumes, I had a number of definite notions to explore. As before, much of the work of research was done by my researcher Alan Riggs, whose own first story was published in the interim in *Tales from the Great Turtle*, and with the help of the library of the University of South Florida, which freely lent us arcane references. But several of my favorites turned out quite differently than anticipated.

I worked out special character traits for each major character, especially their curses: Sam was afraid he would marry an ugly woman, Flo would lose what was most precious to her, Ned was doomed to be betrayed, Jes would be unmasked, Bry would have misfortune, and Lin would be disfigured. But it was hard to follow though; the story line preferred to follow its own complications. Oh, those curses did manifest, but after a time they faded out or were resolved. After that I focused more on the story lines rather than trying to hold my characters to particular molds. So you might say I stopped trying to be God, and yielded to the imperatives of the novel.

The names were a separate challenge. I needed to keep the names the same or very similar throughout the novel, so that readers would know the basic identities, but names that will do for a cave man and his mate, such as Ugh and Oola, don't work as well for contemporary times. In the first novel, I gave my main characters descriptive names, like Blaze and Ember, and stayed with them throughout. In the second novel, I started with simple sounds, like Hu and An, and embellished them as human society became more sophisticated. This time I used simple modern names, ignoring seeming anachronism. Of the three approaches, I think the first works best, so for the next novel I may try descriptive names again. I learn from each novel. The time passing for the main characters varies too. The first novel covered three generations, the second one generation, and this novel covered about half a generation. I think the second approach works best: one year between chapters. It gets complicated when several years pass in a single chapter, as is the case in Chapters 10 and 15, but I still had the other characters age only six months per chapter, overall. This is apart from the way the characters are illustrating global history spanning millions of years, and a simple fixed personal rate per chapter seems best.

Normally I try to space out the regions and times of the settings, so that the story line constantly traverses the globe and doesn't stay long in any particular time or place. But early man was mostly in Africa, so the first settings cluster there. This time the middle settings tended to cluster around Europe, and sometimes it was not possible to space them out without losing the variety of experience I was also trying for. For example, Chapters 14 and 15 were both in western Asia, set only forty years apart. One related to the terrible bubonic plague, and the other to a special event in Mongol history; who would have thought they overlapped in space/time? But they did, so I played it through as it was. Chapters 17 and 18 both occur in France, though almost 300 years apart; I wanted the minuet and the Maginot Line, and could not escape France, though I tried.

I was going to show how ancient the making of cloth must be. But there is no record of truly primitive cloth; I believe it existed, but without proof, my case is weak. So I had to hedge. However, after I completed the novel, evidence of 27,000 year old weaving at a site in the Czech Republic was published in *Discover* magazine, and its evident sophistication suggested that it had developed a long time before that. So I think my thesis is on the way to being documented. I was going to show my character Sam always doing construction, on roads, walls, buildings, fortifications, and the like, but so much of the novel is before any real building was done that I had to find other employments for him. By the time there was real building, the complications of scheduling other characters prevented me from having Sam as the protagonist. So while things did not fall apart, they did get somewhat muddled in terms of my original notions. I could manipulate history only so far, to fit the needs of my characters.

More and more evidence has been appearing to indicate that mankind came to the western hemisphere long before the traditional date of 12,000 years ago. In the prior novels, I deemed the evidence insufficient, but this time I scheduled a major chapter showing how it could have been. But after I wrote that chapter, more evidence appeared on the other side, invalidating some of my basis. The early stone arrow and spear points—that it was thought only man's hand could have chipped—turn out to have been chipped by falling off a cliff onto a particular surface. The chipping may indeed date from 35,000 years ago, but required no hand of man. So were there really people in the Americas 33,000 years ago? There could have been, but I fear there were not.

For Chapter 8 I had something really special in mind: the Sphinx. I got a video that indicated that the Sphinx in Egypt was actually far older than the pyramids. The reasoning was that the Sphinx showed patterns of weathering that had to have been caused by water erosion. How could that be, in the dry desert? Well, 10,000 years ago the Sahara was a good deal wetter than it is today; in fact there were several major rivers through it. So the Sphinx must have been made back then. The video was persuasive, so I had my re-searcher, Alan, view it. But he was a real spoilsport, uncon-vinced. He pointed out reasons that it wasn't so. The problem with Alan is that he's usually right; he has messed up any number of my bright notions, so that I have had to stick with reality. Since this series is history, not fantasy, regardless what the publisher may put on the cover, that's just as well. So my setting of the carving of the Sphinx 10,000 years ago, with all that implied for the true nature of early Egyptian history, had to be ditched. Ned was going to be a designer, getting that great figure right. Wona was going to be attracted to him because of that importance. What was there left to write about, in that region then, with the Sphinx gone? Well, as it turned out, there were artistic works of mankind dating from the Sahara region at that time. So it was a much less dramatic setting, but historical, as it seems the early Sphinx was not.

Next the Ice Man, in Chapter 9. Ah, the Ice Man! I tracked him from his discovery in the mountain glacier, knowing I would write about him, waiting eagerly for the book about him to be published, reading articles about him. And he came through nicely. He was named Otzi in Europe, so I went along with that. Ongoing research required me to substantially revise the chapter, after the first draft; I was unable to have the story line I first tried, because it wouldn't have made sense in terms of what was known of the times. Again, history was pushing me around. After I finished the revised story, more was discovered and published, starting to invalidate some of the bases of my setting. Too bad; I can't endlessly rewrite as interpretations change. I worked from the best available evidence and theory at the time. Later indications suggest that he was not a mere shepherd, perhaps instead being a metal-smith, but the final verdict is not yet in. So did he have a nice daughter named Snow? Who can say? He was surely a family man of some kind, and could have been as I portray him. I couldn't spare him his fate, but at least I could save his daughter.

In each of the GEODYSSEY novels I have tried to have significant chapters at the one-quarter, one-half, and three-quarter marks, with the major one in the center. Thus Catal Huyuk in the first one, one of the world's earliest cities, likely origin of the later Sumerian culture of Mesopotamia. Thus the Philistines from the Greek culture in the second one, giving the primitive wandering Hebrews a hand up toward civilization and receiving no gratitude in return. And the Greeks themselves in this volume. I resisted getting into the standard classical cultures, because of my aversion to the ignorant standard view of civilization, wherein it starts with Egypt, flowers in Greece, and was spread by Rome and then lost before being revived by modern western Europe. What of Asia, Africa, early America? There was a hell of a lot more going on in the world than the standard texts knew of, and I have tried to show it in these volumes. But though classical history was by no means all there was, neither was it insignificant. So, reluctantly, I have come to it in this volume, and discovered lo! it is interesting too. But what dragged me into it was not my sense of fairness, but rather my fascination with the trireme or trieres, the triple-decker rowing ships. When I was in school, they didn't know how these were managed. Now they have figured it out, though no actual vessel has been recovered. There were even four-and five-decker ships. So could a tomboy girl have found work on a trieres? Who can say she did not, in that position of pipeman, that required a sense of beat and music rather than heavy muscle? Especially when the ship is captained by Ittai, a good seafarer from the prior volume, and guarded by Kettle, a simple but honest former slave from the first volume? And so, from my childhood curiosity about a three-tiered ship came the longest story of the first three volumes, a 48,000 word short novel in itself, featuring travel, battle, conscience, work, plague, challenge, and love. I made my fortune on funny fantasy, but this historical adventure is closer to my heart. Even so, there was more to be known than I could compass. Everything from the nature of threshing grain to weaving tapestry. So I slid by some things without going into much detail, keeping the story moving. It is too easy to get lost in the marvelous detail, and lose the living animation of the cultures which is my main purpose. And naturally, after I had carefully structured and written the chapter, my researcher discovered that I had an error in the sequencing; the Spartan siege and the onset of the plague came not in the fall, as I originally had it, but in the spring. So I had to make significant adjustments, hoping that my narrative still made sense.

Chapter 11, with Petra, I wanted to show in the prior

volume. But I already had too many settings around the Mediterranean Sea, so substituted a Japanese setting. So Petra is in this volume—which is even more concentrated on the Eurasian theater. I had to juggle chapters to make it fit, even so, which made my ongoing family relations tricky. But what a grand vision Petra turned out to be, with its temples carved into the faces of cliffs. I couldn't show all of them, because some had not yet been constructed at the time of this setting, but it was still impressive. I had expected it to follow the British Boudica, but the dates didn't quite mesh. I had no idea that it would overlap the Biblical King Herod, or how intriguing that intrigue would be. The fact is, anywhere in history is fascinating; it has just to be sampled, and the glory and skullduggery appear. What a louse Herod is! He gets into the sack with his niece, and decides to kill his wife, not to mention that business with the plattered head of a critic named John, and execution by torture of a mystic named Jesus.

And Queen Boudica, in Chapter 12, spelled as our research indicates is authentic. I had read about her decades ago, but was reminded of it by an ad for silver coins dating from that period. So I did what I love: I got into the actual guts of it, and learned what had actually happened. The supposedly civilized Romans acted with stunning barbarism, publicly stripping and flogging the queen and raping her young daughters. Exactly how young is not known, but they could have been children. Rome was lucky not to have lost Britain as a result of that caper. But if there was anything the Romans could do well, it was fight battles; they had discipline like none seen before. So they kept Britain. But what was I to do with Wildflower, the queen's younger daughter? She disappeared, nameless, in history, after her awful experience. So I rescued her, and she became a worthy continuing character following in the steps of the Ice Man's daughter. I hadn't seen that coming.

Chapter 13 was a surprise. I wanted to explore the matter of the word ''slave'' deriving from ''Slav.'' It turned out to be an uncertain connection, and difficult to illustrate fictively. But my researcher discovered the Kingdom of Samo, unlisted in most references, and since my lead character for that chapter was Sam, I couldn't resist. So once again the novel went in a different direction, and perhaps not a consequential one. Yet I wonder: *could* there have been a Sam? It is also tempting to conjecture that the word "avarice," meaning extreme greed, derives from "Avar," the people who raided Europe for its booty. Of course the Avars were only doing what every conqueror does, including especially the Europeans when they invaded the rest of the world. Reputation sometimes depends on whose ox is gored.

Then the Mongols. I have been fascinated with them since college. In fact, since high school, when I discovered Coleridge's poem "Kubla Khan" and was entranced. Conventional history largely ignores them, except when they threatened Europe, but they were a major factor in Asian history. They were the ultimate conservatives: they solved the crime and welfare problems the old-fashioned way, by slaughtering anyone who was into mischief or who would not or could not work. It was said that after the Mongol conquest, a beautiful virgin could travel alone with a bag of gold from Asia to Europe without being molested. That may have been an exaggeration, but suggests the way of it. Those in the path of the Mongols learned fear in a hurry, or they died. But I, being of liberal bent, would not have cared to live in that society. I study it from afar. I remembered an episode from a book I read in 1970, of a prince who just couldn't hold on to his territory, until about the third or fourth time after Tamerlane rescued him, he turned suddenly competent. What could account for that? In that quarter-century curiosity of mine was the genesis of a 32,000 word novella, wherein Wildflower finally gets her man. I found that the later Mongols were just as shifty and treacherous as anyone else in history. So was there an aphrodisiac herb of the type Sahara described? That is doubtful. My earlier researches in the Arabian Nights tales acquainted me with the rich folklore of the Moslem region, and the hyperbole used. For example, there was the fabulous "bhang," a sleep-inducing narcotic, a strong dose of which was said to be such that if an elephant merely sniffed it, the creature would sleep from year to year. In that spirit I conjecture a love potion whose potency would be mainly in the belief folk had of its nature.

Meanwhile there was the Great Chinese Wall. I sent Alan into that research, expecting to have a setting around 221 B.C. He returned with a verdict similar to that on the Sphinx: no can do. There was no such unified wall. What? But all of history says—but all of history was wrong. Again. It did not impede the Mongol conquest of China, because it wasn't there. Most of that wall was built in the Ming dynasty, in the sixteenth century, *after* the Mongols had been expelled from China, the setting for my Chapter 16. There is not now, and never was, a unified three thousand mile long stone wall. Only disconnected local walls, most of which were of packed earth rather than stone. So I learned what did not entirely please me, and now you know it too. Is it true that the Chinese Wall is the only man-made artifact that shows from space? No—because it isn't there, and if it were there, it would be too thin to be seen from such a distance. Another illusion of history bites the dust.

Chapter 17 derives from a cute little melody I heard on the radio that started a chain of thought: Suppose there is a meeting of enemies, the men just about ready to fight, the women afraid the truce will come apart before it starts, with great mutual harm. Then a child brings a scribbled bit of music, and the musician plays it, and the women start dancing and hauling the men in, and instead of battle there is harmony after all. Because of that new little dance, the minuet. I remembered the minuet from the time I was hauled in to see a first-grade presentation in which my daughter Cheryl participated. You know the type; you have to watch and applaud so as to support your child and the school, no matter how amateurish the production is. But when my daughter's class performed, it was the minuet, in period costume, and I was entranced; it was the most darling thing I had seen in years, and Cheryl was just perfect. Those stately, mannered steps and turns—my boredom was transformed to wonder and delight. So, close to twenty years later, I told Alan, "Find me that setting." We had too much of Europe, and not enough of the New World, in this volume, so he looked in America—and couldn't find it. America of those days was rough frontier country; there were no fancy balls with costumed women, and certainly not with armed men present. So we had to go back to Europe, to the court of King Louis XIV, one of those foppish settings I have avoided all my life. And lo, Louis turned out to be much more interesting than I had thought, and a master of the dance and great supporter of the arts. Later in life he was to become spoiled by power, but this was his beginning, and he was a remarkably apt and appealing figure. So I couldn't have my original notion, again, but found one perhaps as worthy. So what was the cute little tune that had set me off? It turned out to be from the movie *The Piano*, a creature of quite a different nature.

Chapter 18, about the Maginot Line of France, had a similarly devious derivation. In the 1980s I asked my literary agent of the time, Kirby McCauley, what genres were hot, and he said High Fantasy and World War II. Well, my fantasy might better be called low, and why should I want to mess with World War II? After all, I was there, and my family barely got out of Europe in time, after my father was arrested without cause by the fascist government of Spain at the time Hitler met with Franco; Poland and France had fallen, and England was seemingly next. We came across on the last regular passenger boat, the *Excalibur*, on the same trip that the one-time king of England, Edward VIII, took, in 1940, and I had my sixth birthday on that ship, with a cake made of sawdust because supplies were short. What interest did I have in World War II? Right; the question brought the answer, and in due course I wrote my World

War II novel *Volk*. But one of the things I had planned to explore therein got squeezed out, by processes similar to those described here, so I had no section featuring the Maginot Line. So I decided to show it here. Which put me right back into France. Again.

For Chapter 19 I had in mind the Solar Stirling engine, one of a number of intriguing developments in the arena of sustainable power. I first read of the original Stirling engine in *Scientific American* decades ago, and was never quite able to figure out how it worked, but I saw the potential in its external combustion. When I learned of the solar variant, I went after it. The material I got related to Sunpower Inc., a small company designing and producing such engines. It turned out to be mind-bendingly complicated to grasp in detail. I read the book *The Next Great Thing*, which was interesting in its coverage of Sunpower's desperate efforts to make the engine work, but not very clear on technical detail. My son in law John read it and contacted Sunpower and got more material. Researcher Alan read it and consulted with John, and discussed it with me. But when I presented it in the novel, I had to simplify so drastically for clarity that most of that research was wasted. This is the nature of research novels; some of the best material has to be left out. But the Solar Stirling engine exists, and may indeed be a significant aspect of the future. Of course my planned community uses proven old technology like the hydraulic ram too, and is getting into the useful plants hemp and kenaf, which truly do represent two of the world's best hopes for the future production of useful fibers. The existing timber and pulp industries managed to suppress such alternatives in the past, but as the trees run out and the need becomes more pressing, significant changes will occur. For the setting I chose a type of planned community that intrigued my elder daughter Penny and me as we listened to a tape of Pete Seeger's song "The Garden." For the sponsoring religion I used the Quakers, because I was raised as a Quaker and profoundly respect its principles, though I

elected not to join that religion as an adult. Quakers tend to
be good businessmen and socially conscious citizens, and
many are concentrated in the state of Pennsylvania, so well
could be associated with a project of this type. This is not
the first time I have had reference to the former Quaker use
of "thee"; it occurs in my unpublished World War II novel
Volk and a variant is in my ADEPT fantasy series of novels.

The cloud harvesting shown in Chapter 20 is already being done today, in the area described; it solved the water
problems of local villages in the Andes.

So there was a good deal of misadventure, or at least
changed direction, in the course of the writing of this novel,
and much of it did not go at all the way I had anticipated.
But that's the thing about writing, especially historical fiction: the author can indeed not have it all his own way.
Perhaps that is the way it should be. The settings and the
characters should have some say in their presentation.

I didn't have that kind of problem in the early chapters,
because there there is no recorded history to align with; the
social aspect is mine to invent. And while I find the whole
of history interesting, my greatest interest is in the early
aspects. I saw the significance of the lockable knees in a
public service TV program, and locked on to it immediately:
such a seemingly small thing, with such a significant effect.
To be able to stride without fatiguing the legs—a subtle but
crucial change that enabled human beings to travel erect
longer with less energy, and less heating, than other hominids. Scavenging for bone marrow was in the same program,
and similarly critical; it gave mankind a good food source
where for most creatures there was nothing, because they
lacked the ability to crack open the bones. Provided he could
not only get there, but get it away from other animals: encouragement to develop effective weapons.

But for me, the most important change was how mankind
handled heat. I was satisfied that human beings lost much
of their body fur during an aquatic phase, as shown in the
two prior novels, but Alan dug up two obscure articles that

showed another theory. None of the books seemed to have it, which is odd, because it is the most compelling argument I have seen in this particular arena. Lose the fur, dissipate the heat that your burgeoning brain generates—and suddenly mankind is the naked ape. Forget the Aquatic hypothesis; this makes sense on the open plain, where mankind was striding. It all fits together. Alan also found evidence that there are a number of (small) holes in the human skull that allow veinous blood to pass between the brain and the skin. Normally it flows from the brain to the skin, but when the body is under heat stress, it reverses, and the cooler blood of the skin flows to the brain. The fossil record shows that the number of these channels has increased steadily as the brain expanded.

Then the triple ploy, which is my own conjecture, based on research that showed me scattered parts of it. Sex, love, attachment, used in sequence to capture and hold a man who would rather be sowing his oats far more broadly. The change of the female breasts to become not merely to feed the baby, but to make her continuously appealing to the man. Thus the foundation of monogamy, because now it was possible for a single woman to satisfy the continual passion of a single man; and better for him to stay close to her than to wander too far afield, because otherwise she could breed at any time with someone else. In battle of the sexes, the man became larger and stronger and possessed of more physical ambition, but the woman became the major ongoing object of his desire. The downside was that this led also to prostitution and rape, because the woman could not readily turn off her sex appeal. But overall, it seems likely that even today a woman would rather live without a man, were she otherwise provided for, than a man without a woman. She has what he wants. Even the most intelligent, independent, or least scrupulous men still fall for the triple ploy.

There is also my answer to the reason for mankind's burgeoning brain, the largest known in the animal kingdom, relative to body size. He had already established his niche in the world, and was no longer in danger of extinction because of starvation or predation by panthers. It seems likely that the development of vocabulary and language was the engine that powered that expansion—but why was it necessary? That monstrous brain was a phenomenally expensive burden, forcing significant changes in all the rest of his body and life; why balance such a delicate albatross on the top of his precariously erect body? Because mankind's main competition now was either his own kind, or a near relative. He was in a mental arms race, and he who was slightly stupid lost out. This race continued until modern man developed linguistic tools as potent in their fashion as locked knees and hand weapons had been in theirs: syntax and high-velocity speech. These enabled modern man to accomplish more, verbally, with less actual brain, than *Homo erectus* could manage. That translated into better planning and organization, superior tools and weapons, and coordinated drives to achieve long-range objectives. Neither *Homo erectus* nor his offshoot Neandertal man could compete. But though the modern brain is not the largest ever, it remains a giant compared to that of any other creature.

And art, that enabled mankind to form larger and thus more powerful groups without as much internal dissent. If there is anything that defines mankind, aside from his intelligence, it is art. No other creature we know of even cares about it. Every human culture has its art, and many past cultures have left dramatic artistic monuments.

So the things that I hope made an impression in this volume are locked knees, bone marrow scavenging, the brain/heat/fur-loss/clothing connection, the triple ploy, the arms race, and the art/numbers connection. Thereafter it's mostly history, wherein the nuances of the creature's vast potentials are constantly played out. I hope you have found that worthwhile too.

And where is this history leading? To disaster, as I see it. Mankind's burgeoning brain enabled him to conquer the world, and his continuing interest in reproduction enabled him to overpopulate it. Panthers may have limited his population in the early days, but they have long since been nullified. No natural limit seems to exist. Now it seems that only mankind can limit mankind's population, and that isn't happening. Except—one of the seemingly conquered predators is returning. Disease. It is taking the place of the panthers. Through history it was always formidable. The plagues of Athens and other cities, and the bubonic plague, are only samples of an ongoing and deadly threat. There is also war, wherein the human creature's most formidable enemy is other human beings. Over the millennia various ways have been tried to protect communities from attack by other communities, without perfect success. Isolation and defense did not save the Ice Man's village from destruction, and might not have saved the community of Dreams, but for a special circumstance. Massive linear walls and defenses saved neither the Chinese nor the French. As long as there are too many people for the available resources, neither isolation nor defense lines can suffice. Mankind's refusal to take reasonable precautions, to discipline itself, is leading to an infinitely more brutal discipline by nature, and by mankind itself.

Because GEODYSSEY is a series, I try to have characters from prior novels appear in later novels, though each book has its own primary cast. Did you recognize them? Bub from *Shame of Man* raped Flo in Chapter 1. This time Blaze from *Isle of Woman* appeared in Chapter 4. Ember appeared in Chapter 5, with her husband Scorch and baby Crystal. I try to show such prior characters at the age they were in the historical time of the particular setting, but this can be tricky, because Blaze and Ember aged four years per chapter, while Hugh and Anne from *Shame of Man* aged only one year per chapter. Thus Blaze and Ember aged about seventy years in the course of human history, while Hugh and Anne aged only about twenty years. Sam, Flo, and the other siblings of *Hope of Earth* aged only about six months between chapters, or about a decade in the full novel. Thus when the characters of different novels interact, they do so at different ages. Blaze was ten in Chapter 4, while Ember, who paralleled him, was fourteen in Chapter 5. This is especially tricky in the case of Mina, the foundling who turns out to be Flo's lost baby; she aligns with this novel here, and ages at a different rate in the prior one. As I tried to clarify in the Introduction, the people are not really the same, nor are they strictly the descendants of those in earlier chapters; they are essentially similar types that appear throughout all human history. At any rate, Crockson, who is mentioned in Chapter 9 and appears in Chapter 10, is from *Woman*, and Ittai as already mentioned is from *Man*, while Kettle is from *Woman*. Guillaume, Jacques's commanding officer in Chapter 18, is the French version of Bill (William) from *Man*, the intelligent one, whose son Bille will later meet and love Mina. "Bil" actually first appeared in Chapter 3, along with his band leader Joe, also from *Man*. He appears again in Chapter 19, with his wife Fay and daughter Faience. Min appears again in Chapter 20, as Minne, with a problem of age because of the different time lines. But because all the characters live their full lives in each of their settings, Min can be nine years old in this novel though she was closer to fourteen at this time in the prior novel. Bub also appears again. How can he be a leader of raiders here, when he had other roles in the prior novel? Because these characters are actually representations of types, appearing all over the world all through human history, doing different things in different situations. The real unity in the series is its background: the phenomenally rich course of human experience.

So will the real human history lead to cannibalism, as in *Woman*, or in exhaustion of resources, as in *Man*, or in disease, as in *Earth*? I fear that if it does not, it still will be supremely unpleasant. If we don't take warning and do something to change course very soon. I hope we do. Our knowledge and intelligence and plain common sense should enable us to avoid destruction and become the true hope of Earth—if we choose to apply them.

TOR
BOOKS The Best in Fantasy

CROWN OF SWORDS • Robert Jordan
Book Seven in Robert Jordan's epic *Wheel of Time* series. "Robert Jordan has come to dominate the world Tolkien began to reveal."—*The New York Times*

BLOOD OF THE FOLD • Terry Goodkind
The third volume in the bestselling *Sword of Truth* series.

SPEAR OF HEAVEN • Judith Tarr
"The kind of accomplished fantasy—featuring sound characterization, superior world-building, and more than competent prose—that has won Tarr a large audience."—*Booklist*

MEMORY AND DREAM • Charles de Lint
A major novel of art, magic, and transformation, by the modern master of urban fantasy.

NEVERNEVER • Will Shetterly
The sequel to *Elsewhere*. "With a single book, Will Shetterly has redrawn the boundaries of young adult fantasy. This is a remarkable work."—Bruce Coville

TALES FROM THE GREAT TURTLE • Edited by Piers Anthony and Richard Gilliam
"A tribute to the wealth of pre-Columbian history and lore."—*Library Journal*

Call toll-free 1-800-288-2131 to use your major credit card or clip and mail this form below to order by mail

- ✂

Send to: Publishers Book and Audio Mailing Service
PO Box 120159, Staten Island, NY 10312-0004

❏ 550285	Crown of Swords	$6.99/$8.99	❏ 534077	Memory and Dream	$5.99/$6.99
❏ 551478	Blood of the Fold	$6.99/$8.99	❏ 551516	Nevernever	$5.99/$6.99
❏ 530349	Spear of Heaven	$5.99/$6.99	❏ 534905	Tales from the Great Turtle	$5.99/$6.99

Please send me the following books checked above. I am enclosing $_____. (Please add $1.50 for the first book, and 50¢ for each additional book to cover postage and handling. Send check or money order only—no CODs).

Name _____

Address _____ City _____ State _____ Zip_____

TOR
BOOKS The Best in Fantasy

ELVENBANE • Andre Norton and Mercedes Lackey
"A richly detailed, complex fantasy collaboration."—Marion Zimmer Bradley

SUMMER KING, WINTER FOOL • Lisa Goldstein
"Possesses all of Goldstein's virtues to the highest degree."—*Chicago Sun-Times*

JACK OF KINROWAN • Charles de Lint
Jack the Giant Killer and *Drink Down the Moon* reprinted in one volume.

THE MAGIC ENGINEER • L.E. Modesitt, Jr.
The tale of Dorrin the blacksmith in the enormously popular continuing saga of Recluce.

SISTER LIGHT, SISTER DARK • Jane Yolen
"The Hans Christian Andersen of America."—*Newsweek*

THE GIRL WHO HEARD DRAGONS • Anne McCaffrey
"A treat for McCaffrey fans."—*Locus*

GEIS OF THE GARGOYLE • Piers Anthony
Join Gary Gar, a guileless young gargoyle disguised as a human, on a perilous pilgrimage in pursuit of a philter to rescue the magical land of Xanth from an ancient evil.